ML
F

W9-CFQ-573

PRINCE

OF
FIRE AND ASHES

Tor Books by Katya Reimann

The Tielmaran Chronicles

Wind from a Foreign Sky
A Tremor in the Bitter Earth
Prince of Fire and Ashes

PRINCE

OF
FIRE AND ASHES

▼

Katya Reimann

TOR®

A Tom Doherty Associates Book
New York

PRINCE OF FIRE AND ASHES

Copyright © 2002 by Katya Reimann

Edited by James Frenkel

This book is printed on acid-free paper.

A Tor Book
Published by Tom Doherty Associates, LLC
175 Fifth Avenue
New York, NY 10010

www.tor.com

Tor® is a registered trademark of Tom Doherty Associates, LLC.

Library of Congress Cataloging-in-Publication Data

Reimann, Katya.
    Prince of fire and ashes / Katya Reimann.—1st ed.
        p. cm.—(Tielmaran chronicles)
    "A Tom Doherty Associates book."
    Sequel to: A tremor in the bitter earth.
    ISBN 0-312-86009-9 (acid-free paper)
        I. Title.

    PS3568.E4858 P75 2002
    813'.54—dc21
                                                    2002022558

First Edition: July 2002

Printed in the United States of America

0 9 8 7 6 5 4 3 2 1

To Sovigne and Grace
in spite of, because of, with love.

Acknowledgments

Thanks dearly to the members of my writing groups, Pengames and Tech Noir, for all the work and help they gave me and this book; to my agent, Shawna McCarthy, and my editor, Jim Frenkel, for having the faith that made this possible. Thanks also to my assorted daycare providers (sequentially credited): Aryn Eaton, Gerri Lynch, and Amanda Haldy, each entrusted with keeping the girls safe and amused during all those hours when my study door is shut.

On a metaphysical note, I have to thank the landscapes of Spain's Picos de Europa, Yorkshire's Dales, and Turgenev's Bezhin Lea. These places all took me farther than I ever expected when first I found my way to them.

Closer to home, thanks go to Tim Gardner, for laundry and other associated chores at the key moments—and beyond this, for steady love and support.

MONTEVIA ROAD

BISSANTY EMPIRE

LAKES COUNTRY

North

Great River Bas

AVERIOS

River Potomia

Bassorah

Feeder

Dunsanius Ford

Fructibus Arbis

THE NEEDLES

GREAT MA CRE

Murver Sopra

Locatus River

Batlik Sirti

High Plateau

Sanai Valley

Clarins Seat

Arciers

HIGH ROAD

Ilara's Kettle

Haute-Tielmark

BISSANTY FINGERLAND

La Ma

Pontoeil

TIELMARK

BOOK I

▼

MIDSUMMER'S MOON

Prologue

▼

THE RED PATH

*"The Path of the Prince of Tielmark will run red with
the blood of the Common Brood."*

—**Lousielle's Prophecy**

The rough-hewn stones of the wall behind the altar smoked, etched
with the ashy outline of two giant figures. In the great hall of Tielmark,
the Twin Goddesses had descended to bless a marriage.

But now They were gone. The chaos that had been suspended for
the short time They had remained broke free.

The Bissanty plot to destroy the Tielmaran God-pledge lay in ruins.

The young princess and her new consort huddled against the altar.
Shielded from the fighting in the Great Hall by the flashing wall of the
Common Brood's spell, they devoted themselves utterly to prayer. In the
glittering aftermath of the Great Twins' departure, the young couple bent
their heads and prayed, blessed with the certitude that they had seen their
gods—and pleased them.

Whatever the attending crowd chose to believe.

Gabrielle Lourdes, the young Duchess of Melaudiere, looked beyond
the fading brilliance of the spell-wall and frowned. Tielmark was saved—
yet those loyal to the Princess and the land remained scattered. Regrouping their power would require more even than a visitation from the gods.

It would require facing down an enemy who had become as intimate
as brother, as friend.

Outside the spell, Bissanty-loving traitors, clumsy in their finest and most elaborate court garb, fought hand and fist with similarly encumbered Tielmaran loyalists. A handful of conspirators, refusing to acknowledge defeat, were still struggling to reach the closed circle of the altar's dais. The flashing spell-wall blocked them, spinning them aside so they roared with pain and frustration.

They were so entrenched in power, so sure of the controls they had exerted over the young Tielmaran Princess. This wall of spell that had severed their control—even with failure staring them in the face, they did not want to believe it could exist.

Gabrielle took a shaky breath and rubbed the old scars on her wrists. The traitors weren't the only surprised ones. Ironically, despite her strong skills as a diviner, she had joined the Common Brood without foreseeing this victory. It had been duty, not belief, that had made her pledge to old Princess Lousielle's secret coven. Now she—along with everyone else in Tielmark, loyal or otherwise—would have to adapt herself to the sudden change of circumstances.

Lousielle's seven witches, robed in Tielmark's princely blue and white, had penetrated the Bissanty defenses and taken control of the altar at the crucial moment. Raising the spell-wall that had severed the young Princess's sorcerous bonds, they had thrown aside her usurper Bissanty consort and married her to her secret Tielmaran lover.

What had happened next had been a thing of legend and history: The Goddess-Twins Elianté and Emiera had made themselves manifest to approve Corinne's match, and this was no feeble matter of a priest mouthing pieties. It was a horror of God-flesh incarnate, of the eyes of the Great Twins flashing as they strode upon the altar, passing judgment. Even the most pious among those crowding the Great Hall had not really understood that the gods would come to earth for Corinne as they had for her forebears every cycle past. Human memory was so fleeting, so easily changed and reformed. The fifty-year passage over which the God-pledge cycled—it was too many years for those who had witnessed it as children to believe it would come again in their old age—

"It was a trick!" a man beyond the spell-wall called, furiously disbelieving. "It was not the Goddess-Twins. It was those foul bitches' spells! We are befuddled—believe not what your eyes have seen!" He threw himself wildly at the translucent silver shield. Gabrielle, safe behind the spell, was close enough almost to smell his panic as the pain of contact sent him reeling back. "Believe not what your eyes have seen!" he screamed. "This marriage is a perversion!"

Gabrielle recoiled. The more dedicated traitors had too much at stake to concede that the Great Twins had truly descended, that Tielmark's God-pledge remained unbroken. So many who had sought to break the pledge were crowded into the Great Hall tonight, disappointed in their expectations of triumph. Even as the great spell faded, she could not tell whether the loyalists or the traitors would prevail. The goddesses' blessing aside, Tielmark was weak, and the Bissanty traitors were strong.

Who would consolidate Tielmark's power and lead the land forward out of chaos? One of those outside the circle? One of those trapped within it?

There were ten of them inside the great spell. Ten who breathed the hot air, the deep stink of magic. The seven witches of the Common Brood, young Princess Corinne and her consort, and, lastly, the Bissanty Prince who had been fool enough to imagine that Tielmark would not rise to protect its own. He cowered now at the edge of the altar's dais, a sick expression on his face as full realization of his danger seeped through him. Her gaze flickering past him, Gabrielle found herself staring from face to face, her six partners in the making of the great spell doing likewise, seeking direction or focus. The others, Gabrielle realized, were just as stunned as she was by their victory.

And Princess Corinne still remained prostrate on the altar, god-struck by this unexpected joy and freedom, allowing precious moments to slip away in lieu of rising to command.

Gabrielle frowned. Easy for Corinne to leave the aftermath to those who had fought so hard, and at such great cost, to unite her with her shepherd-boy lover. Was it for this that the young duchess had suffered so many losses, so many privations? Exhausted and strained from the effort she'd exerted to perform her part of the spell, Gabrielle fought back self-pity. It was no easy struggle. She was two years younger than Corinne, and when she herself had married, there had been a great scandal, with no one there to protect her from the consequences. With her own father a Bissanty traitor, Gabrielle had suffered under Bissanty domination all her life.

Now, with the chance of freedom before her, she was uncertain of her authority to act. No one had expected the old Princess, the founder of the Common Brood, to be dead when they faced this moment. They had thought that Lousielle would be there to make the choices, to guide her sheltered daughter, to decide everything—

"We don't have much time," Richielle said. The herder-witch, the oldest of the Common Brood, reached up and touched the spell's apex with the tip of her herder's crook, a height already visibly fallen. "The wall won't hold much longer. We have to act, or the chance is lost for another fifty years."

Though Richielle was the oldest of the Brood, Gabrielle mistrusted her leadership. The herder stank of unwashed goats and grease and slaughter. There was something impetuous about her, something disordered. Despite Richielle's age and her wide experience, Gabrielle did not believe that the old princess had ever intended for the herder to lead them.

Yet Richielle was brave enough to face the big question. The terrible question. Gabrielle could only wish that she had found the courage to speak first. The Brood had only a short time before their spell fell to pieces—would they have resolve enough to free Tielmark, for once and for always, from the ongoing Bissanty incursions? More troubling: should they? Gabrielle did not believe she was the only member of the Brood with doubts.

"We know what we have to do," Delcora High Priestess said, echoing Richielle. "We have to free Tielmark from Bissanty. For now and ever after." Tielmark's most powerful religious sorceress, a spare, excitable woman, was visibly heady with the spell's success. The green magic of the Goddess-Twins flowed through her with incredible potency, and it was Delcora's strength which had provided the river of power from which the others had formed the great spell. Delcora should have been tired, but the close contact with her gods had left her flushed with energy. Her face shone with self-importance as she pulled a flag of shining silk from beneath her robe: Tielmark's princely blue quarters replaced by the crimson color of a king's red. "Elianté-bold and Emiera-fair will witness this!" she said. "We will make Corinne Queen!"

"We haven't agreed to any such thing," Gabrielle said sharply, alarmed that Richielle and Delcora seemed to have secretly colluded, preparing for this moment. "Tielmark has lived free of Bissanty for two hundred and fifty years. We bought it fifty more years of freedom with this night's work. Just because we've worked this spell doesn't mean we have the right to make more decisions for our Princess."

"Altering the very nature of Tielmark's rule requires rewriting her God-pledge," Tamsanne broke in. She was a south-border witch, a strange, usually unobtrusive woman, whose magic was tied closely to the raw power of the soil. Until Delcora declared herself, Tamsanne, the first member Lousielle had initiated into the Brood, had stood aloof. "Our Princes sweated blood to make that pledge, and we have only just renewed it. Even if Tielmark really is ready to make such a change as you are suggesting—tonight's stars certainly are not right for it. This seeming urgency will pass." The slender witch gestured to the chaos beyond the spell-wall. "It is no weakness to pause and consider what we are doing before we act."

Gabrielle rolled a thankful glance in the border witch's direction, grateful for her tone of moderation. Tamsanne was a little older than the four court sorceresses—herself, Dervla, Melaney Sevenage, and the warrior countess Marie Laconte. Despite her reserve, she was easier to talk to than the old harridan Richielle, or tiny prepubescent Julie, whom Princess Lousielle had dragged up from the gutter to fill the coven's seventh place. Gabrielle trusted and respected Tamsanne's judgment.

"We need to act *now*." Richielle pushed forward, shoving Tamsanne aside—for all her bluster, a liberty she would not have attempted with any of the court women. The herder's yellow eyes shone with a ruthless light. "Look at those sheep out there!" She gestured beyond the spell-wall. "They're already trying to convince themselves that none of this has happened. Denying the evidence of their own senses. This happens every fifty years—every cycle of rule since free Tielmark was founded. It will go on happening again and again. Tielmark's freedom jeopardized unless we do something today. Think of the tragedy of Berowne. The horrors that befell Princess Ann. Will our heirs face easier circumstances? We need to act. This moment is why Lousielle took our pledges."

"The old Princess trusted us to protect Tielmark's future," Gabrielle said stoutly.

"Lousielle bound us to protect her heirs," Richielle sneered. "But we can do more than that. We can make Tielmark great. We can make Tielmark free."

"Lousielle wanted more than that," Gabrielle protested. "She wanted Tielmark to be a productive and just land for her people, whatever sacrifices she had to make herself."

"Then why bind us to prophecy?" Richielle said. "*The path of the Prince of Tielmark will run red with the blood of the Common Brood.* Do you imagine that that bond is unraveled by the strength merely of this night's work?" Emboldened, the herder-witch stepped near to the young duchess, so close that Gabrielle could smell her stink of grain and blood. *Allegrios Mine!* the young woman swore, fighting to conceal how the older woman unnerved her.

Tamsanne, with more poise than Gabrielle expected, slipped in between them, breaking the two women apart. "Perhaps Lousielle bound us to prophecy because she knew Tielmark's problems could not be resolved by a single night of magic." Her voice was mild, but something in her eyes made Richielle step away. "The Brood-pledge ties our blood to Tielmark's future, whether or not we chose tonight to paint the Princess's path the red color of Kingship."

The future. Before this night, young Gabrielle had scarcely been able to imagine that there would *be* a future. "I don't claim to understand all that the prophecy entails," she said aloud, meeting Richielle's eyes as calmly as she was able. "But I was willing to pledge my life to protect Tielmark from Bissanty when Lousielle called for it."

"You don't believe that the running red is the crimson blood of kingship, or you don't want to believe it? Which is it?" Richielle asked. "The prophecy is a dangling sword. We *ourselves* are the blood of the Brood. We have the power to turn Tielmark's path from princely blue to kingship red. If we don't, our lives will be sacrificed—"

"Don't use that tone with me," Gabrielle said angrily. "I won't stand for it." Richielle's glance of contempt made the younger woman squirm. As though she had tried to pull rank on the herder, and the herder had ignored it! As though she were a sheltered court lackey, fool enough to attempt hauteur as a shield against this horrible woman! As though—

"What exactly is it that you are proposing, goat-herder?" Tamsanne said dryly, rescuing Gabrielle from her confusion. "Blue, red, purple. A prince, a king, an emperor. We all know that red can signify kingship as well as blood. You say you want to act tonight. What exactly would you have us do?"

"Commit that one's life to the gods." Richielle nodded at the Bissanty Prince, the sick-faced young man who stood hunched almost against the wall of spell, trying to avoid the witches, the young princess bent in prayer—and everything else within the spell's confines. "Let his blood feed our earth. Let Corinne rise over him as our Queen. In Bissanty, they call that man the orphan Prince of Tielmark, and claim he is bonded to our soil." The herder grinned, showing her bad teeth. "Let us make acknowledgment of that bond. Let the gods take his life in pledge, freeing our land forever and after from Bissanty." As she spoke, Richielle unsheathed a knife she had held hidden in her skirts.

The Prince turned ashen. One hand reached to touch the whirling barrier of spell—then he snatched it back, wringing burnt fingers. Delcora laughed, but many among the other witches shifted uneasily.

"What kind of a kingship would that make?" Tamsanne asked softly. "An unwilling sacrifice. Tielmark's throne baptized by blood tyrannically shed. What sort of king would rule us then?"

"A King—a line of Kings—never again beholden to Bissanty's cruelties."

Tamsanne shook her head, but several of the other witches looked uncertain.

"A vote," Gabrielle broke in. "We'll take a vote. That at least will show our thinking."

"All right." Richielle nodded forcefully. "Who stands with me, for Tielmark's lasting freedom? For *Queen Corinne* ruling over us?" Delcora was already at her side, vibrating with excitement.

Marie Laconte, the Countess of Tierce, shot Gabrielle a resigned, almost apologetic look, and stepped up to Richielle's other shoulder. "We can't fight Bissanty forever," Marie said. "Not with these odds. Sooner or later, one of Bissanty's plots will succeed. Our ruler will marry wrongly and the Great Twins will return our land to Bissanty and our people to oppression." Proud warrior Marie bent her knee to no one but the Princess, and her expression clearly showed her dislike for following old Richielle's lead. But when it came to measuring strategic odds, she had a pragmatic turn of mind. Gabrielle could not be surprised by her choice.

"And those against?" Tamsanne ignored Marie and looked directly at the young duchess. Little Julie was already at the border witch's shoulder.

Which left only two votes uncast.

Gabrielle glanced over to Melaney. Melaney returned her glance, her expression somber. The two women had been friends since childhood. Children of privilege, born to high Tielmaran houses, both had suffered much under the reign of the Bissanty traitors.

"Well?" Melaney asked.

"We have to leave some choices for our children, and we have to trust that they will make good choices," Gabrielle said. "Fifty years from now this choice will come again. We have to trust that Tielmark will be stronger then, that there will be better choices." She stepped to take the place at Tamsanne's other shoulder. "I don't want to take this man's life," she said. "Not if he won't offer it freely."

Richielle let peal a mocking laugh. "Looking for the easy answer, highborn missy?"

Gabrielle felt her cheeks flame, but she refused to rise to the bait. "It's down to you, Melaney," she said. "Choose wisely."

Melaney hesitated between the two little groups. She was a passionately beautiful woman, and her heart was a match for her beauty. When she made her decisions, she seldom changed them, but she was wise as well as passionate, and careful in her choices. Even knowing that the spell that protected them from the Great Hall's mêlée was fading, she did not want to rush her vote. Gabrielle wished she could say something—anything—to sway her.

Melaney turned to study the Bissanty Prince. "Ighion Pallidonius," she said, almost mockingly, tasting the outlandish name as if it coded its own answer. "How would you advise me now?"

Fear was plain on the Prince's face. His lips worked, but no sound came out. He had assaulted Melaney rudely more than once in the week leading up to this moment, when she had been powerless to speak against him. His lack of nerve now that the tables were turned made Melaney shake her head.

"You are worse than a coward," she told him, disgusted. "Your father sent you—the choice you made to come here was not even your own. Can you be surprised that the price for your actions may be your own blood, when you have meddled in our God-pledge so cravenly, so destructively?"

The prince dropped his eyes before her passion, her beauty. He had no answer.

Richielle, smelling triumph, cackled.

But the herder's very glee made Melaney shake her head. "The Bissanties choked us with the bitter taste of tyranny," she said. "I can't believe oppressiveness on our own side will taste any sweeter. It is beneath us to slaughter a helpless enemy, however craven." She paused, trying to follow her own logic, her own duty, through. "And yet my own life is pledged to sacrifice. I could live with the personal dishonor of killing an unwilling victim, if it would make Tielmark free."

Tamsanne shook her head. "Lady," she said. "You would sacrifice your honor vainly, if keeping Tielmark stainless were your hope. By our pledge to the old Princess, we are tied to the land. Our dishonor would rebound through the soil—"

Whatever Tamsanne intended to say, no one would ever know. Richielle, seeing Melaney nodding, darted toward the Bissanty prince and slashed downward with her knife.

In the general start of horror, Melaney alone moved to act. She obstructed the herder-witch with her own body and scrambled, fearless, for the blade. The old witch tried to sweep her out of the way, but Melaney refused to back down. By the time Richielle understood this and turned her weapon against Melaney, the others had acted. Marie Laconte seized the old woman in a powerful headlock and wrestled her to the floor. "Gods' honor!" Marie said, her warrior's sensibilities shocked. She twisted the dagger out of Richielle's hand and flung it away. "Not that way."

Melaney was bleeding, her hands and arms cut in many places. Tamsanne rushed to swaddle her wounds, while Gabrielle, recovering herself, moved to assist her. Delcora, moving as if in a dream, picked up the fallen dagger and tucked it within her robes, where Richielle could not hope to reclaim it.

"We won't be shedding this man's blood." Melaney gasped, pale but decisive, the cloth that swathed her hands crimsoning. "That's my vote."

"Melaney!" the young Princess called, the scuffle drawing her at last from her reverie by the altar. "Goddess-Twins! You're hurt! What have they done?" She leapt up and ran to the woman's side, almost slipping and falling in the smear of Melaney's blood.

The Princess's path was running red, Gabrielle thought grimly. Would it be for the last time?

She rather fancied not.

Fifty Years Later

As twilight dropped over the mountains, the mist lifted, revealing a shattered landscape of white stone. Day faded quickly in the high Lanai massif, but there could be no rest for the Dramaya. Their pursuers had pushed them away from the watchtowers' trail onto this rocky side-path; now all that was left was this insane retreat, ever higher up the hardscrabble into the mountains, following the line of the thin—and in some places nonexistent—trail.

After so many hours of climbing, Vidryas had come to accept that this retreat could end only at the edge of an impossibly high cliff, or huddled at the back of a blind canyon. Either way, there would be no escape.

Listless with fatigue, the young warrior stumbled on, near the back of the war party. More than a quarter of the Dramaya were dead or abandoned, picked off by their Lanai pursuers during the first hours of climbing. It had been dawn when they'd left the safety of the main Bissanty camp. Now, at twilight, they were adrift in this desolate limestone valley. There was no question that even the small glory of finding—let alone destroying—the Ocula-Koinae watchtowers had eluded them. They were too high now, too lost.

For hours, the nothingness of cloud had enclosed them. How Ochsan had managed to keep them moving through the featureless mountain limbo no one knew; whether he had truly managed to keep to any trail no man dared question. All anyone knew was that retreat, which had begun miles down the valley, had to continue. If the Lanai tribesmen caught them, they would mercilessly cut them down to their last man.

This was Vidryas's first campaign, his first chance to prove himself. But he could no longer conceal his tiredness, no longer hide his fear. He was going to die, and die badly, every man around him recognizing his cowardice, his weakness.

The man in front stumbled, then pulled to a halt. Vidryas, distracted, walked into him.

"Llara's Eyes!" the aggrieved man snapped. "Do you want to kill us both?"

"Sorry," Vidryas muttered, craning even as he spoke to see what called this halt.

" 'S all right. Just watch yourself," the man muttered back. Then, "What can you see?" somewhat more politely.

Vidryas, half-Bissanty, half-Dramaya, was tall enough to see over every man's head to the front of the line. The deference the man gave him for it a little revived him. "Ochsan's stopped. He's looking for the way on."

Up ahead, the Dramaya leaders stood with their heads together, shuffling sheepskin scrips and arguing in soft voices. Vidryas despised his uncle. If not for Ochsan, Vidryas would not have been assigned to the Dramaya detachment. He would have been back at the Bissanty camp, readying himself to fight in a real war, with proper lines of men and battle and glory. Not running up an empty mountain, his hopes of honor crushed.

"What else?"

"Markal is with him." Markal-the-daggerman was Ochsan's wizened second. "They're taking readings from their scrips."

The man nodded, satisfied. "They'll see us through," he said confidently. "The gods smile on Ochsan, and he'll take us to glory with him. Don't you worry, first-timer."

Vidryas, staring up to the head of the line, pretended not to hear. To the Bissanty, the Dramaya were barely human figures of ridicule. The rich Dramcampagna land supplied the Empire with huge reserves of grain and fat beef cattle, but it had been ruled for so long as a subservient Princeship, its people had lost their pride along with their independence. Melancholy swept through him, thinking on the ill-fortune his birth had dealt him, forced to plod with cattlemen when he could have marched with real soldiers.

Livening wind touched the boy's upturned face, and with it fresh rain. Ahead, beyond Ochsan, the mist continued to dissipate, exposing more bald rock and an ominous ceiling of storm cloud. The way onward was a horrible traverse on slick, rain-wet stone. Where Ochsan and Markal stood, the track dwindled to a crack that cut at a rising angle across a massive, tilted slab of limestone.

Vidryas leaned against a boulder, easing the weight of his pack. He closed his eyes, just for a moment, trying to remember what it was to feel safe.

A slap to the ribs shocked his eyes open. Advey, Ochsan's point man for the end of the Dramaya line, had come up behind him. Vidryas remembered him cheering Ochsan the night previous, back when they were all happy and drunk, nested in the safety of the Bissanty camp. Unlike Vidryas, who could have passed for pure Bissanty, this man looked every inch full-blood Dramaya, and unlike Vidryas, he had volunteered for this detachment. He was short and bull-throated, with wiry, close-cropped hair and a muscular barrel of a chest. His temperament, equal parts stoicism and hardheaded zeal, was also typically Dramaya.

"They've moved," he told the boy. "Push on."

"The fog won't cover us much longer," Vidryas said, doleful. "Why don't we make our stand here? We're finished, either way."

Advey laughed. "Finished? Not while Ochsan lives. The Lanaya missed their chance in the lower vale." Vidryas could not help but notice that Advey called the enemy by their old name, as if Dramcampagna was still a free nation, and their equal. "If they didn't catch us below, they'll never reach us here. There's not a commander alive who can marshal numbers across terrain like this, and Achavell will take their arrows in this wind. The sky's shifting. Can't you feel it? There's a big storm coming up."

"Is that what's making the mist rise?"

"The mist isn't rising. It's running. Can't you smell it? Llara Storm-Queen has followed us into the valley."

"A storm?" Vidryas's heart dropped.

"They're moving!" someone interrupted. "Twelve alive! Don't stand there as if night and Llara weren't coming!" Ochsan and Markal were already across the limestone slab. Now they were urging the others over, almost at a run.

Too soon, it was Vidryas's turn. The rock he faced was sheeted with running water. He hated the slick limestone, so alien, so harsh, with its rain-carved funnels and treacherous surface.

Ochsan waited at the far edge, his jowls set in an expression that he might have intended as encouraging. "Move faster, Viddy," he called. "Don't leave time to fall."

Vidryas took a tentative step. Then another and he slipped. Both hands windmilled against the rock before he caught his balance.

A flash of lightning lit the valley walls, followed by a crack of thunder. Then a second flash came, almost on its heels, the crack of thunder almost on top of it. The Storm-goddess, Llara Thunderbringer, strode below them in truth, hurling her white-fire spears. Boxed between the towering limestone cliffs, the lightning clashed off one wall and then bounced back again off the other.

"Move, boy!" Ochsan shouted. "You're not the last one!"

Hating his uncle more than ever, Vidryas forced another reluctant step. The rain was falling hard now, creating thin waves of water on the slab's surface. It pooled in the trail-crack, then washed on downward. Where the crack was deepest, the water took on a faint whiteness. His heart leapt at the discovery—those whitenesses would show him where to put his feet. He took one step forward, then another. It was better if he did not look up, better if he did not do anything but focus on the white.

He stumbled off the stone and fell against Ochsan's burly chest before he even knew he had reached safety.

"Go on then," the war-leader said gruffly, pulling the boy past with a pat of approval. "Make room for Advey."

Advey was quick. Ochsan gave him a short nod, then pushed along to the front of the party. There he scrambled onto a plinth of rock and turned to make an address.

"Llara will be with us soon," he said solemnly. The rain had lumped his hair into odd-looking knobs on his temples, but his dark gaze was intense, even compelling, as it settled on the exhausted men. "If we meet her tonight, we will surely die." A flash of lightning momentarily illuminated his stocky figure.

"But for the green hills of Dramcampagna, I swear on Llara's great name, I have not brought you here for death.

"There will be shelter ahead. Where vale meets crag, there will be shelter. We must reach it before the storm catches us. The Bissanty sent us here to find our deaths—but we will show ourselves men, and return safely to camp with unexpected glory. We must move to shelter—at a faster pace than any we have yet put forward in all today's toil. But follow me, and we will persevere. Dramcampagna lives in our bravery!"

A single man dared groan.

But to the last man, at Markal's whistle, they clapped fist to chest, and shouted Ochsan's name. Vidryas, fear almost gagging him, joined them.

Ochsan jumped down from the stone plinth, and then there was no time for thinking. He set a new, brutal, reckless pace, jumping forward from stone to slippery stone, almost at a run. Vidryas, riven with fright, tears mingled with the rain on his cheeks, had no choice but to hare after him, along with the others. The pace—it was faster than the wind that swept around them.

Turning a hairpin corner, Vidryas glanced downward. The cloud parted and he caught sight of the great limestone slab, gleaming whitely, already far below.

In the split second of his hesitation, a spear of lightning jabbed to earth, shattering the stone to a thousand pieces, destroying the trail's thread. The wind howled, a great horrible howl like laughter, and once again the cloud closed in.

Vidryas ducked his head, pretending he had not seen the death of their last hope of retreat.

In his terror, he almost wished for the Lanai archers and a swift end.

Flash upon flash of lightning, clash upon clash of thunder, shook the tall trap of the valley below her. The old woman, standing at the cliff edge, studied the Dramaya soldiers in their scrambling flight: the squat, bullock-bodied leader and his men, spread behind like frightened sheep.

Her features were impassive, but her eyes were ablaze with triumph. Fifty years of wandering had passed and gone. At long last the stars were near aligned to reform the future; at long last, Tielmark would be free of Bissanty chains. In a final cruel justice, it would be the Bissanty themselves who supplied the tools and means for doing it.

She had planted five men with the vision, knowing that only one would be destined to fulfill it. She had never expected it would be the

Dramaya-man. When she had last seen the Dramaya leader, he had been a dark and ornery calf, troubled by dreams of rebellion, barely capable of comprehending the vision of crushing victory she set before him. But perhaps—perhaps where wiser men had questioned her augury, he had lowered his head and stuck it eagerly in her noose.

Far below, the bullock leader glanced skyward—was he canny enough to sense her? No—he was gauging the storm clouds, judging where Llara Thunderbringer would next strike.

She allowed herself to smile. It would not have been surprising if he had sensed her. The cattleman had surprised her in so many ways, following the path she had laid for him.

A crack of lightning crumbled a stone just below the scattered warriors.

"Quickly now," Richielle murmured. "Quickly, or Llara will have you." She glanced tensely at the thunderclouds. So many things could still go wrong. Perhaps, if little black bull and his men did not run, the Grey Goddess would shatter them, and with them her plotting. There were branches still in the prophecy, despite all she'd done to close them. In just one month it would be Midsummer, and God-King Andion would rise in the sky over Tielmark. She had to be ready, and she had to ensure that Tielmark would be ready. If these soldiers did not crush the Lanai here, driving the tribesmen to retreat into Tielmark for a season of war, the seat of Tielmark's power would remain in the midlands, where Richielle's power to act would be limited. No—she needed this war in Tielmark's western outlands, drawing the Prince himself away from the center. She had followed the omens, the cards, the auguries. Surely even Llara could not stop her now! Staring down at the men, she willed them to run faster.

The Dramaya leader, bless him, redoubled his pace and crested the last rocky saddle. From there he would be able to see the black line where the cave mouth lay, promising safety—

The storm, ruthless and unmerciful, swept upward, obscuring the rest.

The woman stepped back from the edge of the cliff, satisfied. Though fog-blinded, her footsteps were secure and steady—she had prepared the path before the vigil began.

The Dramaya bull at least would reach the cave, and perhaps some of his men with him. In the morning, whatever were left would rise and follow the path she had laid to the edge of the great gorge.

There she would meet them, and offer the choice.

For decades, she had prepared for this moment: the beginning of the end for Bissanty. No longer would it be an Empire of five bound Princes, five subject peoples. Tielmark would be free. Great fruit had grown of little seeds, great changes would be wrought by these ignoble Dramaya cattlemen, subject for so long to Bissanty's rule. Perhaps their own freedom would follow.

By the Rhasan cards of prophecy, by the ruling Gods, by the Dramaya-man's own bellicose nature, she was certain that Ochsan's choice would be the right one.

Vidryas hardly slept. Last night, just barely, they had outrun the thunderclouds. Ochsan had brought them to the protection of a shallow inclined cleft, moments before the lightning came stabbing up the valley. The last yards of running, of slipping on the wet rock, had been sheer panic.

Ochsan had them up before sunrise. There was a queer restlessness to him. Though their mission lay completely in ruins, Ochsan behaved not at all like a beaten man. But neither did he address his troops, and this odd aloofness much demoralized them. They had rallied to him the night before—and they needed him once again to rouse them.

Morning stretched into a misery of wet equipment, harsh sun, and a relentless march, ever upward. They crossed a broad, empty bowl of limestone, heat rising off the white stone with eyestraining intensity.

At noon, they came to the edge of a vast gorge, a breathtaking chasm between two towering mountain massifs. Down below—far, far down below—a thread of green marked a river's course, cascading along the gorge's bottom, giving the harsh land brief, vivid life. Through the heat, across the vast descending distance, the land seemed to shiver, the river to twist.

Vidryas and Advey were trailing at the back of the line, when Ochsan called a halt. Half the men threw off their packs and went for a closer look at the chasm.

"Look." Advey pointed. Within the gorge, toward the horizon, the mountain river from the gorge's floor ascended a series of cascades, like giant's steps of running water. At the top was a jeweled **V** of green. "Llara in me, who could have dreamed it! There's Ochsan's plan! Viddy—do you see it? That's the Lanaya High Pastures."

Vidryas's stomach almost turned over.

The entire Imperial army dreamed of the Lanai's mountain strong-hold, the hidden pastures where the tribesmen's cattle were kept safe while their warriors descended to war. The High Pastures lay at the top of the great Fini-Koina valley, with Lanai tribesman dug in all the way down to the piedmont, and the Bissanty battle camps. The pastures them-selves were unguarded. With such natural protections, there was no need.

"Imagine us, up there," Advey said. "Forty Dramaya cattlemen, and a thousand head of Lanaya cattle. What do you suppose we could do?"

His eyes lit with enthusiasm. Vidryas could see what he was thinking: Cattlemen knew how to start a stampede. Starting it would be simple. Keeping it going, simpler still. Animals, especially in panic, instinctively move for the easiest course. Vidryas could not help but picture it: The cattle, moving slowly at first, would gain speed—and increase in panic—as they descended onto the steep slopes of the Fini-Koina. They would reach the first Lanai outpost. They would flatten it. And then the next, and the next, all the way down to the rear guard of the main Lanai force.

The Lanai warriors would not know whether to kill their own cattle or to run onto the waiting Bissanty spears.

Vidryas took a step back from the sheer cliff. "Imagine it—certainly. Do it—never. We're not birds," he said bitterly. "How would Ochsan propose we get over there? It's impossible." Taking another step back, he looked to see what the others were doing.

Ochsan had scrambled out onto a spur of rock and pulled out his surveying scrips.

"I don't see why he's bothering." Vidryas picked up his pack and readjusted its laces. "What's the point? We're above the Lanai watchtow-ers, and we'd never make it across to those pastures."

"What would you have him do?" Advey asked dryly. "Sit down and die in the sun?"

"What can we do?" Vidryas said bitterly. "There's nothing we can bring the Guarda now."

Advey shot him a curious look. "You think your uncle brought us all this way for some skinny Bissanty Guarda's sake?"

"If we want to bring Bissanty glory—"

"Screw Bissanty." Advey spat. "We're Dramaya cattlemen. Do you imagine Ochsan's putting us through this for Empire's glory? Not likely, by Llara's grace. And as for you—if Bissanty had ever truly wanted you, half-breed, they would have had you long before now."

Vidryas glanced around, half-frightened, to see who had been near enough to overhear Advey's treason. "What do you mean, Ochsan brought us here? The Guarda sent us."

Advey laughed. "I'm sure that's what the Guarda thinks."

Vidryas's mind reeled. "Ochsan wanted this? Wanted us to lose ourselves in the mountains? You knew that, and you volunteered?"

Advey shook his head. "I'd like to be at home with my stock," he said, "in my own mountains. But when Ochsan spoke, I knew I would go with him."

"I don't understand."

"What's to understand?" Advey said. "Bissanty holds Dramcampagna for her riches, but what does it offer in return? We've suffered a Bissanty Prince on the Dramaya throne too long, with too little care returned to us. Ochsan's going to remind the Bissanty what Dramaya men are made of."

"But—but the Emperor is Llara's Heart-on-Earth," Vidryas protested. "Gracious Sciuttarus's line traces to her directly. His Princes on our throne—that puts Llara over us."

"He's an Emperor, not a god," Advey said, amused. "And not even Sciuttarus takes the Princely thrones seriously. Look how he plays with them, popping one man on, then pulling him off again. No one even pretends Llara's hand is in that."

Vidryas went silent. He knew the matter to which Advey referred—at just the last hustings, the Emperor had deposed his half-wit brother and raised an upstart cousin in his place. Rumor had it that the new prince, Tullirius Caviedo, had not even been formally presented at the Imperial court. "It's a game, then?" he asked, his voice almost quivering.

Advey shook his head. "For them it's a game. For us it's our lives."

" 'Ware!" a man called. "Something's coming."

On the spur of rock, Ochsan bundled the survey scrip back in his pack.

"Close up," Markal hissed. "Advance to me and follow Ochsan."

The uneven terrain made it impossible to form ranks. Vidryas, near the back, had to reach the spur's crest before he could see anything.

Ahead lay more shattered white stone, leading away to a short white peak. Between the spur and the peak, on a craggy dome of rock, a single figure emerged from the waves of heat.

It was a woman. It was, Vidryas had no doubt, a witch.

A tall, lean witch, with ragged grey robes that streamed down her lank body. Her face was weathered teak. "Little black bull!" she greeted Ochsan, raising wide her hands. "How far you have come to find me!"

Around her, the rocky dome shimmered with movement. Hairy shapes, at first invisibly merged to the color of the rock, gaining form as cloven hooves struck stone. "A goat-herder," Vidryas whispered.

All around him, men sketched Llara's god-sign for protection.

Ochsan pushed forward, his hand at his hilt. "Woman!" he called boldly. "What is your business here?"

The woman smiled. Her teeth were a grim bridge of yellow ivory in the sun-dark skin of her face. "I think you already know, my little black bull. You have seen it in your dreams. What do you think my business might be?"

"We have come far to find this place." Ochsan pointed across the impossible distance of air to the cascades that led down from the green notch. "There lie the Lanaya Pastures. But the passage over to them—it is closed to us. We need the key to open it."

Vidryas shivered. It would never happen. The cascades—perhaps they were climbable, but there was no possible way to reach the valley floor. This back door, if such it was, was bolted and locked.

"A key?" her tone mocked him. "Perhaps better a sacrifice to the gods, that they should show you the way forward."

"I sacrifice only to Llara," Ochsan answered.

"Very well," the old woman replied, as if that had been what she'd expected. "Then my business here today must be to provide you with a sacrifice." Darting down among her goats, she kicked them aside in her impatience. No definable stiffness or fragility betrayed her age, but watching her, Vidryas could not help but think she was very old.

Passing many animals, she paused before a black nanny, a lean old thing with a bulging milk bag that sagged below its scabby knees. Trapped under the woman's scrutiny, the nanny bleated and tried to back away, but the old witch, swooping down, was too quick. When she turned back to Ochsan, she clutched a pair of tiny goatlings, one to each hand.

"Choose, black bull," the witch said. "Choose your sacrifice, and make your future."

One of the kids was pale orange, the other mottled black and grey. Both were tiny, perhaps prematurely delivered. Behind the witch, the old nanny bleated in protest.

"Will you have Beleaguer?" the witch asked. She held up the orange-furred kid. It fought her, tiny hooves dancing in the air. "Or will you have Demstar?" The black and grey was gentle, even passive. Its bulging yellow eyes were mournful, as if it had accepted the inevitability of fate.

Ochsan made Llara's sign. "I will not choose for my men," he said. "My choice is only for myself."

The witch let out a harsh laugh. "Then you are more stupid than I believed. A man who leads soldiers to battle never chooses for himself only."

"I am no fool," Ochsan said coolly. "Whether I die or live, I see that the choice with which you tempt me will far outlast this battle. I know those names, witch; they call upon an ancient magic, and dangerous. Beleaguer and glory, or Demstar and peace. What if I won't choose, woman? You are here alone, and I see others in your flock that might please Llara better."

One old woman, thin enough for the winds to dash into the gorge, against two score men. She should have been more frightened, but she was not.

"If you are no fool," she said dryly, "you will gladly seize on that which will be offered to you but once."

"Beleaguer, then," Ochsan said, casting aside hesitation. "For Dramaya's glory, and for mine."

"He is yours—if you can catch him."

Before Ochsan could prevent her, she flung the orange-colored kid away, down the dome of rock. It landed, in a sprawl of legs, at the top of a rocky chute. By some miracle, it was uninjured. Recovering, it gave an angry bleat.

Markal cursed and raised his bow to drop it, but Ochsan called him to hold. "Not that way," he said. "Llara will not accept a sacrifice cut down like hunter's quarry. I must kill it with my own hands. Fetch it to me, and we will light the goddess fire together."

Ochsan's daggerman glanced doubtfully toward the little goat, perched so precariously at the top of the rocky chute, and then at his master.

Firming his mouth, he made Llara's sign and started after it.

The kid, suspicious, would not let Markal approach. Emboldened by its distrust, it darted downward onto the skree. The breath of every Dramaya caught as it slid, bleating, toward the brink, but it gave a scrambling hop at the very limit of the edge and scampered sideways, its delicate feet finding footholds on an unlikely slanted ledge. Markal, once again making the goddess's sign, gave a last unhappy glance at the impossible gulf of the chasm, then stepped after in pursuit.

When he had almost reached it, it once again skipped beyond him.

Already Markal was forty feet below the edge of the cliff, trending downward on a previously invisible line of footholds across an otherwise featureless stone wall. The goat was another twenty feet below, safe—for the moment—on a small flat place on the rock.

Markal, unnerved, turned back to Ochsan. "I'll never catch it," he said. "One step more, and I'll not be able to come back, either."

Ochsan stroked his beard. He surveyed his men. Then he looked again at the witch.

"It is a long way to the bottom." Doubt colored his voice.

She laughed. "Where is your faith, black bull? You seek the key, and that animal will be your sacrifice to lead you to it. Have you not planned all your life for this moment? You want success—but what are you willing to risk to attain it?"

"I am willing," Ochsan said fiercely. He rounded on his troops. "Glory on the head of the man whose hand first holds that kidling!" He loosed a cry that echoed out into the gulf.

The little goat, already agitated, fled. Miraculously, it ran, but did not fall, trending always downward. Markal, clinging to a narrow rock edge, shouted in dismay, cut short as Ochsan descended the skree chute and aggressively pushed past him.

For a moment, no one but Ochsan and the goat moved. Then Advey, breaking the stillness, pushed his way to the front. "Glory on my head!" he cried, striding to the chute. "I call to Llara for it!" Scarcely minding where he put his feet, he flung himself downward.

Vidryas could barely contain his horror. His uncle intended to chase the little kid until he caught it, or until he lost his footing and fell to his death. Already Ochsan had passed the safe flat where the kid had stood to look back. He was traversing an even unlikelier thread, down and across the rock, the kid always keeping a little ahead of him. Advey, above him, was fast closing on Markal's narrow perch.

"The trail will close!" Markal shouted urgently to those who remained safely above. It was clear he meant to move on rather than risk letting Advey pass him. "Swear yourselves to Llara and follow! This madness will not stay to help us long!" His face a picture of frightened concentration, he turned to follow Ochsan's line, out onto the pure white rock.

Ochsan's warriors, doubtful but resolute, began to move for the edge.

If Vidryas did not join them, he would be stranded alone in the high massif. He started to cry, first single tears, and then a blinding torrent.

Somehow the witch was near him. "Tears!" she cackled, reveling in his humiliation. "A fine soldier boy you are!"

Driven by blind, terrified passion, he put up a hand to push her away. Her arm was surprisingly hard and strong, and he could not move her. Mistaking him, or choosing to mistake him, she seized him by the wrist and turned his palm upward.

"Shall I make a future for you, boy?" Her grip was like a human vise. Her breath smelled sickly sweet like fermented grain, the flap of her robes against his arms like the harsh brush of a goose's wing. "I can read it into you, if you will let me. I did it for your master, you know, when he was a boy not much older than yourself. And see how finely it has served him!"

Goaded beyond fear, he hit her. She had not expected that. She dropped his wrist, freeing him.

"This is not war!" he cried. "This is not the glory I wanted!" Running, he reached the chute as the last man disappeared into the precipice.

The goat-herder strode to the edge. The men's retreating backs were already far below her, the strange Bissanty boy laboring at the rear.

"This *is* war, boy!" she shouted after him, laughing crazily. "Believe it! Bissanty and Tielmark will be forever changed!"

The boy ran like a rabbit—the last in the straggling line of the descent. More fool he. The terror that possessed him would make him clumsy. She doubted he would reach the gorge's bottom whole.

But the others—the Dramaya cattlemen would gain the High Pastures, and they would decimate the Lanai herds. The mountain tribesmen would be forced into Tielmark to recoup their losses, and Tielmark would once again know strife and war and change. She would be there, in the middle of it, seeing that the Prince of Tielmark too, like Ochsan, made the right choice—or had it made for him, if that was how the cards played.

She glanced back at the domed rock. Her goats were scattered—the black nanny, the oldest fertile female, was in a foul mood for having one of her twins stolen. With her grey and black kid safely returned, she had charged back in among the younger nannies, separating them from their own in reprisal. Cursing, the old woman turned to round them together.

A god had prevented her from reading the young Bissanty's hand. What god, she did not know. She was old enough not to care. But she had read the young man well enough for her own purposes. If there was hidden mettle in him, it would not rise in time to affect the outcome of his uncle's campaign, or, more importantly, any part of her own plot.

For the first time since he had begun his wild descent, Vidryas turned his face outward. Wild elation swept through him.

The sparkling river was still far below, but they had descended beneath the most perilous of the cliffs. Upriver—Vidryas was low enough now that there was an upriver—he could see where the cascades began their ascent, a secret, water-covered stair. In the far distance, on the high horizon, the Lanai High Pastures lay silhouetted against the sky.

How Ochsan must have laughed beneath his stolid façade as the soft Bissanty Guarda had sent him to decimate his warriors beneath the walls of an impregnable Lanai watchtower. He had accepted the miserable, hopeless mission because it had given him a chance to impose a real defeat. To gain glory. A real soldier's glory.

It would be the greatest triumph in decades of summer campaigning. A decisive Dramaya victory over the Lanai would change everything— not least Bissanty attitudes toward his homeland. Bissanty would be forever changed, and perhaps Dramcampagna too.

Vidryas hastened onward, suddenly eager to join with his uncle.

In his excitement, he did not think of the witch, did not wonder, did not query why her last words had been of Tielmark, the rebellious lands that lay just over the other side of these mountains.

▼

chapter 1

Gaultry Blas, the huntress-witch of Arleon forest, had at last arrived home to Tielmaran soil.

Overhead, the sun shone brightly, lighting the land's handsome rolling fields and groves of willow and ash trees. Evidently Tielmark's twin goddesses, bold Huntress Elianté and graceful Emiera, had smiled on Tielmark in all the time of Gaultry's absence. Farmers and travelers of every description choked the High Road as far as the young woman's eye could see, loaded with proofs of the Goddess-Twins' bounty. Strings of fat geese jostled panniers of brightly colored chickens; pretty grey-faced donkeys, overloaded with bags of green-cut hay and early barley, pressed against healthy-looking sheep. The prosperous crowd, headed in both directions along the road—west for a horse market at a place called Fairfields, east for the great Midsummer fair at Soiscroix market-town—offered every evidence that Tielmark's gods were happy, and all was well in the land.

But to Gaultry, who had spent the last weeks in flight from homicidal imperial soldiers, this bounty simply presented a new series of hardships. She had journeyed for more than a month in the Prince of Tielmark's service—even if against his wishes and knowledge—risking body and mind against one of the most powerful sorcerers ever raised by the Bissanty Emperor to destroy Tielmark's independence. Somehow she had envisioned her return to her home soil would have a more glorious aspect. . . .

"Pigs!" she snapped aloud, startling her companions, along with everyone else within earshot. "Whoever thought tying a pig to a lead was a good idea?" And yet there they were, blocking the way, a nursing-thin mother and her eight robust progeny tied on leather tethers in the hands of a corpulent farmwoman. The two most active piglets had tangled their leads in the wheels of a tinker's rickety handcart. All traffic had ground to a halt as the farmwoman's son attempted to extract the young pigs without destroying the wheel's age-weakened spoke-work.

Like a slowly erupting volcano, the farmwoman lumbered around to face the young woman on her fee-rented horse. Her embarrassment at the obstruction she had caused was obvious; obvious too was the fact that Gaultry's outspoken complaint marked her as a convenient target on which to vent this feeling as anger. "What's your hurry?" she snapped. "Danton will soon have them free. You'll have time enough to set up your sideshow once you reach Soiscroix. Dirty players." She spat on the road in front of Gaultry's horse.

"Players?" Gaultry replied, at first not understanding what the woman meant.

"Spongers, more like. What's your hurry? People won't be paying you 'til they've settled themselves, to my way of thinking."

Gaultry cast an uncomfortable glance at the little group that had accompanied her home from Bissanty. For one guilty moment, she could see what the pig-woman was thinking: She had mistaken them for itinerant performers.

Everyone, herself included, looked miserably road-filthy, hollow-eyed, and hungry, the inevitable wages of too much travel too fast, on insufficient food and sleep. They were out of place on this happy road, a pass point between prosperous towns where the three days of the Midsummer Festival would be celebrated with all good feeling.

Firstly, there were the animals: the rented horses, too fine for their scruffy riders; the skinny, half-grown dog with its nervous eyes and frightened air; and worst of all the pair of exotics that clung to Gaultry's saddle crupper: a delicate grey monkey and a striped tamarin with a pointed muzzle—the latter of which bore more than a passing resemblance to anyone's idea of a small, if beautifully furred, demon.

She could only guess what the farmwoman would think if she saw the enormous desert panther that was also traveling with them—shadowing the little party some ways off the road, in an attempt to avoid casual confrontations with cattle and livestock. Picturing Aneitha-cat's probable reaction to the pigs, Gaultry would have cracked a smile, had the pig-woman not been glaring. She had to consider herself lucky that the animal contingent ended with Aneitha. The soul-breaking sorcerer whose magic they had defeated to escape Bissanty had maintained an enormous, varied menagerie to bolster his magical strength. If their departure from his stronghold had not been so precipitous, no doubt her party would have been lumbered along accompanied by something like an entire zoo!

Then, of course, there were the people, two of them obvious outlanders. The Sharif, a respected war-leader in her own land, looked dangerously foreign and possibly contagious, her long frame emaciated by ill health and her hair cropped short and strange. Young Tullier, riding with the skinny pup at his heels, had the unfriendly face of a boy trained too long, too young, and too hard as a warrior. It could not be denied that he looked like some sort of half-criminal delinquent—an appearance that was only partly deceiving! Of course, Tullier was much more than that. Indeed, Tullier was most of the reason Gaultry was hurrying to make report to Tielmark's Prince. The boy's travel-stained clothes gave no outward indication of the bizarre, magically influenced destiny that had left him heir to the Goddess-blood normally reserved for the sons of the Bissanty Emperor. If they could just get him safely to the Prince's court, and arrange for the Prince to put him under a pledge of protection, Tielmark would have leverage against the Bissanty empire for the first time in decades—if only they could convince the Prince of the veracity of Tullier's bloodlines.

Gaultry suspected that none of this hidden information would suffice to placate the farmwoman.

Finally, there was the Tielmaran half of the group, which was only a little more savory in appearance than the foreigners. Gaultry's accent gave instant evidence of her modest south-border origins, and her threadbare garb betrayed nothing of the power or importance she had earned since she had left that simple upbringing behind her.

Only Martin, confident astride his big gelding, managed to appear anything approaching respectable. Handsome dark-haired warrior Martin, for whose sake Gaultry had risked all the peril of journeying deep into Bissanty. Riding at the back of the group, he watched with a half-amused expression as Gaultry struggled for the right words to rebuff the farmwoman's bad manners. If it had been Martin who had challenged the pig-woman, not Gaultry, she had no doubt but that the woman would have stammered and moved hastily out of his way.

Blood rushed in her cheeks. This situation felt exactly like old times.

Before she had traveled; before she had learned the true strength of her magical powers or of the prophecy she had inherited, binding her to the Prince of Tielmark's service. Old times, before she learned that she had been born to the Common Brood, the coven of witches blood-sworn to protect Tielmark's Prince.

On this crowded summer road, it little mattered if she had challenged the gods, or if she had risked the things dearest to her heart to keep her country free. Those things were a part of an invisible past. Here was only the lamentably disreputable present: rough clothes, shady companions—and her lack of a quick tongue in the face of a direct challenge. A reprisal against this woman with magic—that would cause more problems than it would solve. A reprisal with quick and clever words—worse!

Complaining aloud had been a mistake. The things she had done in Bissanty—she could not do them here at home.

Bissanty was not like her native Tielmark. Bissanty's loathsome hierarchy slaved the field-workers and the serving class both with god-bonds and with fear. In Bissanty, for simple survival, she had exploited every incidental advantage the empire's own customs offered: the passivity of the field-workers, the pathetic cringing of the slaves. But she was back in Tielmark now, and in Tielmark any tough-minded beggar had the right to argue his case when he felt ill-used.

Let alone so substantial a woman as a farm-mistress off to market with an entire litter of pigs.

"Good-woman, please. Allow us room to go by you." Gaultry gamely attempted to moderate her tone, though from the pig-woman's expression, the time for that had come and gone already. "Our business is in Princeport, not in Soiscroix, and it is important."

The woman was not appeased. "If you want to move, tell your boy to get down and help me," she said gruffly. "Or your man. Or—" Despite being encumbered by the pigs, the woman reached with surprising agility and caught hold of Gaultry's bridle. "You could come down off your high horse and help me yourself."

"Let go and get out of my way," Gaultry said coldly. She was not so fine a rider that this woman's sudden grab did not threaten to unseat her. "You've been foolish and greedy. Nine pigs on the road is not my problem."

It was sheer bad luck that her tone and her horse's little jump together startled the woman's boy. He made a sharp movement, sawed on one of the trapped pig's leads, and snapped one of the tinker-cart's wheel-spokes. A piglet squealed, jabbed by a fragment of wood. As it struggled, a second spoke fractured.

"What have you done?" the tinker shrilled, his voice a fair match for the piglet's. His cart listed slowly on one side as the wheel began to fold.

"Not me!" The farmwoman shouted back. "It's these outlanders, making trouble for all of us!"

Martin, seeing the situation moving out of control, stopped smiling and kicked his horse forward. The pigs bolted, sawing on their leads. The farmwoman was forced to relinquish Gaultry's bridle strap.

"If it's trouble you're having, we'll gladly stop to help." The big soldier grinned unpleasantly, his teeth a wolfish flash of white in his handsome, sun-darkened face. "Unless, of course, you already have the situation under control."

The woman's bluster faded. Gaultry she might mistake for a sideshow-sponger, but not this man, however dirty his clothes. "My apologies, Sieur." She backed away, moving the pigs with her. "My boy Danton ought to have kept the little ones in order. But we will have them back in hand soon enough." She sketched the Goddess-Twins' sign, seething but respectful.

"Very good. Perhaps the two of you can better sort this from the road's side." Martin, sliding his horse past without waiting for an answer, reached down from the saddle and seized the cart's sideboard. Straining, he raised it up off its collapsed wheel and held it upright until the boy and the tinker pushed it off onto the grass.

The crowd around gave a rough cheer, amused by the display of muscle and will. Martin, smiling more broadly, whipped off his hat and gave something like a bow, drawing an even larger salute.

The woman—forgetting Gaultry, and eyeing daggers at Martin—was obliged to follow, chivying her pigs out of the traffic's flow. She made up for this surrender by initiating a noisy quarrel with the tinker. But the tinker was sharper than his mournful appearance suggested. He seemed likely to gain one piglet at least for his repairs.

Thus, Gaultry thought grimly, hastening her horse on by, thus was concluded the defeat of the pigs.

Behind her, the Sharif and Tullier exchanged a private laugh, no doubt, Gaultry guessed from their glances, making light of her mishandling of the affair. She scowled, and set herself to ignoring them.

Passing two heavily laden hay carts and a small herd of bawling cattle, she urged her horse up to Martin's.

"This is like damnation to Achavell," she complained. "And it's my fault that we're stuck here. If I hadn't insisted we rest that extra night in Truit, we'd be through Soiscroix by now and out of this crush."

Martin shook his head. "We couldn't have pushed on earlier. Everyone needed to rest. Who could predict that the Midsummer crowds would be so plentiful this year? It's not anyone's fault."

"We have a duty to Tielmark," she said. "Bringing our news to Prince Benet should have driven us forward."

"We were dead on our feet," Martin replied flatly. "There is only so much fatigue a body can withstand. Of course we need to reach Princeport as quickly as possible. But you arguing with every farm-mistress between here and there isn't going to help us accomplish that faster."

"She was in the wrong."

Martin drew an impatient breath. "If you want to fight with me, go ahead. But you know you should have left well enough alone. Bissanty is behind us."

"I know." Gaultry sighed. "But it's so hard—and these people! None of them know what we've been through, yet everything we've done has been for them! Yet here they are, blocking our way, delaying us further."

"Perhaps they should open a path on bended knees," Martin said sardonically. "Would that better suit your taste?"

"Our business is more important than bringing pigs to market."

"Yes, well, and you'd have proof of that in hand if Benet had actually sanctioned you to follow me to Bissanty." If Martin had not been so tired, she would not have been able to draw him like this. His capture and transport to Bissanty was not something he often referred to, and particularly not during their periodic quarrels. "Next time, wait 'til the Prince hands you his sigil before you skip town."

She was tired too, or she would not have answered angrily in turn. "You'd be dead today if I had waited. You, and the Sharif too—and certainly Tullier as well." Even as she spoke, she regretted it. She knew she had gone too far as soon as the words left her mouth. "Martin," she said, immediately contrite. "I don't mean that. Or at least—I don't mean it angrily."

He smiled, tiredly, glancing over his shoulder, perhaps to see how close the Sharif and Tullier were riding. "You have accomplished amazing things, my love. For everyone around you. I can grant you a little shortness of temper." As she gave him a wan smile, he urged his horse against hers, and gently bumped her leg with his own. "But unfortunately," he continued more seriously, "the events to which we are bound range far beyond our own desires. You will have to keep your temper better if you want to make any headway at court."

Gaultry sighed. "I know. Huntress help me! I can only trust that Benet will forgive my small trespasses in return for my larger services. Or that his court around him will have persuaded him to do so. Your grandmother has his ear, of course, but so as well does Dervla." The High Priestess of Tielmark was a jealous, somewhat spiteful woman, with whom Gaultry had clashed too often for comfort in the past. "And then there is the rest of the ducal council. Will they follow your grandmother's lead, or Dervla's? The Prince's courtiers—"

"Not to mention the other members of the Common Brood." Martin frowned. "Or all the people Tullier alienated, with his attack upon the Prince, before you whisked him out of Tielmark from under their ravening noses."

"What we've learned since about Tullier's heritage makes him more valuable to Tielmark alive than dead."

"That is so," Martin conceded, "and all the more reason that you must speak to the Prince before tangling with the others." He brought his horse against hers once again. "It's all going to unfold too quickly. After we arrive in Princeport, we will no longer be our own masters. With the summer campaign against the Lanai started, it won't be long before I'm sent west to fight at the border. It does not please me to know that I will have to leave you to fight for the boy alone."

She looked hastily away from him, off ahead down the road. Half a mile away and a short climb up a hill, a tall tree marked a boundary into more rugged territory. Arriving in Princeport only to have to be parted from Martin was not something she wanted to think about. "Perhaps it will not be so bad," she said. "The very fact that Tullier was born puts the Bissanty succession in doubt. Tielmark could become free of Bissanty by simple merit of the Imperial line's collapse."

Martin shook his head. "Tielmark has to make its own freedom. Bissanty has been collapsing on itself for centuries. The fact that the line of Imperial succession is in disarray is more threatening, not less so. Since we crossed Tielmark's border, we've been hearing time and time again about the battles to our west. It's not the usual summer campaign. The Bissanty raised a huge force against the Lanai this year. Come disarray, an empire wants its citizens looking outward, not inward toward a shaking throne."

She shivered. "Sciuttarus is still Emperor. Tullier being here doesn't affect that."

Martin shrugged. "If Sciuttarus has lost the Goddess's blessing, everything is affected."

He was right. They had skirted riots throughout the last days of their flight from Bissanty. The scraps of song they'd heard, the rumors, the terrible omens: crops sickening, calves dying—and the unspoken awe with which the Bissanty land-bonded regarded Tullier—all pointed to a profound disruption to the order which had held the Empire together for so many centuries.

"That said," Martin continued, "You're right. Sciuttarus hasn't lost any of his practical power. As sitting Emperor, he has much in his hands to ensure that power will remain with him while breath is still in his body. The campaign against the Lanai confirms it. He wants a distraction—and he doesn't want the army at home in Bassorah to rise against him—while he sorts out family business."

"He wants Tielmark too," Gaultry said.

"Two birds with one stone."

Tullier's pony jogged up to Gaultry's stirrup. The boy whose birth threatened the Imperial succession was short, with a deceptively light build, black hair, and intense slanted eyes the color of green ice. When Gaultry had first met him, those eyes had shone with constant rage and pain. Now, after weeks under Gaultry's protection, his expressions, if not softening, were at least becoming more varied.

Gaultry sighed. Of course, most of the boy's emotions were still problematic, not least among them his ill-concealed jealousy of her feelings toward Martin. He hated to see Gaultry with Martin—and hated it even more when the pair of them discussed his future outside his presence.

"What are you talking about?" he demanded.

Gaultry gave him a falsely bright smile. "If we reach Soiscroix tonight, we should be able to make it to Princeport by tomorrow evening. We've just been talking about what we can expect when we reach the city."

"Nothing good for me." Tullier raised his brows. He was sensitive enough to know when she was humoring him, and to dislike it. "Did you see the look that awful pig-woman gave me? She hated me—without even knowing who I was. That's how everyone in Tielmark will feel, once they know who I am."

"I'll protect you," said Gaultry, nettled. It exhausted her, constantly having to reassure him, though sadly there was no doubt that he needed any comfort she could give him.

Tullier had been a Sha Muira apprentice when she first met him, a member of the Bissanty assassin cult where his father, the sitting Emperor's uncle, had hidden him from the time Tullier was a newborn. He had been trained to commit atrocities without questioning, to expect death at any moment—indeed, to accept death as a blessed event, uniting him with Grey Llara, the mother-goddess of Bissanty. That upbringing continued to haunt him, not least with the reflexive certainty that mercy would not be offered where he himself had never expected it.

"They'll want to string me up for what happened to those boys my old master killed," Tullier said. "I don't see how you'll protect me from that."

Gaultry did not know how to answer him. In his last act as a Sha Muira, Tullier had been involved in a brutal attempt to compromise the right to rule of Tielmark's reigning Prince. There had been five murders, not just two. From hints Tullier had dropped, she knew that he had been responsible for the death of at least one of the boys' guards.

"You're privy to a blood tie that devastates the sitting Emperor's right to succession," she said. "That will be more important to Tielmark than what you did while the Sha Muira ruled you."

"Only if you manage to explain before the mob seizes me."

"They'll have to get past my own dead body first," Gaultry replied grimly. "That at least I can promise you." She kicked her horse into a trot, taking advantage of a gap between two wagons to slip out of conversational range.

She hoped the things she was telling Tullier were true, or that she would have the power to make them true.

It was hard, riding on this easy road and pretending that the gods and death weren't riding with them. Gaultry would have preferred almost any open confrontation to that hidden specter of doom.

What help was it to acknowledge that Tullier and Martin were at each other's throats; that the Sharif was growing thin with longing for her desert home; that the animals she had rescued from the Bissanty inferno were languishing? All she could do was ride on, hoping that the journey would end before any of these problems reached crisis.

Her own inadequacies were worst of all. The events that had brought them to this road had wakened Gaultry's long dormant magical powers: the blazing golden fire of her Glamour-magic. That magic had the capacity to give her a power akin to the greatest strength that could be called down from the Twelve Highest Gods—and without the necessity of prayers, of bowing and scraping to distant, mysterious, and oft-distracted deities.

But what help was this if she was still frustrated by pig farmers, still set to confusion by the complexity of her country's fate, and still incapable of using her magic to help herself or her friends? Her magical power was like a golden sun, but she could not control its power—when she came close enough even to touch it, it burned her, with immolating strength. Those few times she had called upon it—in extremity, when no other course opened itself—the consequences were terrible and harsh. It took her body days to recover from the aftereffects.

Her sense of inadequacy rose like bile in her throat. She rode on, struggling to ignore her many anxieties.

By mid-afternoon the road began to descend over a series of granite ridges to the wooded edge of a river bluff. Though the day had become seasonably warm, a cooling breeze fanned up from the river. Overhead, the screen of leafy branches sheltered the riders from the bright summer sun.

Under the green ceiling of leaves, the crowd thinned as it stretched along the road. Gaultry finally found herself relaxing. She loved the scents of birch and oak, of pineberry and redleaf-rustin and even the darker smells: the moss and decaying leaf mold. Leaving her horse to find its own footing, she stared dreamily out over the drop to the river. The tannin-dark water rushed mysteriously over jumbled stones, making little falls and pools, overhung with ferns and wisps of pink flower.

This was the Tielmark she loved. Its wild loneliness, its beauty.

The riverbank opposite was a solid ridge of granite topped with young pine volunteers, trending gradually toward the near bank, forcing the water fast and high as the stream channel narrowed. It reminded Gaultry of a place near her home on the south border where a limestone-bedded creek made narrow, slippery slides down into deeper, river-dark pools. The fast water was a little dangerous, but Gaultry and her twin sister, Mervion, had spent many summer days lazing there, alternately sunning on the rocks and cooling themselves with laughing rides down the wildly slippery water chutes.

The memory of that cool water made her feel acutely how long it had been since her last full bath. Two weeks, and longer. Not since before their flight began from Bissanty. Counting the days back did nothing to improve the suddenly itchy feel of her skin.

"There's a bridge ahead." Martin, who had been riding in front, slowed his horse to ride with her. "Warn the Sharif that her 'shadow' will have to find its own place to make a crossing. There's some kind of gathering at the bridge."

Tullier was once again at Martin's shoulder, edgy and unwilling to let them speak privately.

"I wish there was a place where we could climb down to the water to cool off." Gaultry stood up in her stirrups to relieve the heat that had gathered on her seat. "Or even swim across, or ford, rather than going over with everyone else. I don't like the idea of yet another crowd."

"If there were a place to ford, there wouldn't be a bridge," Martin said thinly. "Can't you trust your temper for two minutes together?"

"What's wrong with Gaultry looking to find her own way?" As Tullier spoke, he moved his pony, subtly, so Martin's horse was forced to break its pace. "If Gaultry wants to swim, why not? There must be a place where we can make our way down. It's not as though we're laden with market-goods and a cart."

Gaultry shot Tullier a wary look. She had become so accustomed to the boy challenging her that his support was unsettling. He often backed her now, even in her smallest caprices—much to Martin's displeasure.

Still—she did want her swim. "Why not?" she asked. "A short break would give Aneitha a chance to find her way over."

Aneitha-cat was aggressive, constantly hungry, and her narrow, rangy body challenged the size of Tullier's pony. Only her intelligence, enhanced by the soul-bond she had briefly shared with the Sharif, made it possible for her to stay with them, on the hazy understanding that the journey would return her to her natural home. Since they had crossed into Tielmark, the great cat had been forced to range the countryside as their shadow. There had been a number of awkward moments, even guessing that the Sharif had kept the worst from her.

The sooner Aneitha and the Sharif were shipborne and homeward bound for far Ardain, the better. Both were fast losing flesh and condition in this unfamiliar damp country.

"Aneitha has to take care of herself. If she can't keep up, that can't be our problem." Martin scowled at Tullier, a rare show of irritation, then turned back to Gaultry. "We're not stopping and taking off our clothes to go swimming. We all need to reach Princeport. We both need to explain ourselves to Benet—you more than I." He reached for a lock of her horse's mane and twined it loosely around his fingers. "Don't ask for what I can't give you."

The curl of yellow horsehair looked gold against Martin's sun-darkened skin. Gold, like a marriage ring. An unfortunate coincidence, considering that Martin *was* married, however honestly estranged from his wife. They both saw it at the same moment. Gaultry jerked her reins, making the horse start so it twisted the lock of mane free.

"I'd give you anything " Martin said, suddenly intense.

"I try not to ask for impossible things." She patted her horse's neck, at once apologizing to it and comforting herself. "We have a bridge to cross. That's clear enough." Ignoring Tullier's look of glee—though clearly he did not have the least idea what they were arguing about, or what they were trying not to argue about—she swung away, looking for the Sharif, and female comfort.

The Ardanae war-leader had dropped to the back of the party. Her eyes met Gaultry's. The woman shrugged. *Arguing again?* she asked. *They're proud men. They both want your first loyalty.* Despite brutal fatigue that made her slump in the saddle, the Sharif's mind-voice pierced Gaultry through, clear as ever. The woman had suffered tremendous hardships: as a casualty of war, as a slave chained to an oar, and then in her flight with Gaultry across half of Southern Bissanty. Gaultry wished she had served the woman better—but there had never been adequate time to rest and recoup their strength.

The Sharif could share the voice of her mind—a voice that was deeper than language—only with those she trusted. Sometimes it amazed Gaultry that the woman could still communicate with her so, after all they had endured, after all her bad choices as the little party's nominal leader.

Tell Aneitha she must find a place to cross the river. The bridge is too crowded.

The Sharif sat up in her saddle and straightened her shoulders, the desert yellow of her eyes focusing inward. For a moment, she looked strong and handsome, in command of her body and her mount. Then a deep shudder wracked her chest, as even what should have been for her the simple effort of reaching out exhausted her. *It's done.* The proud shoulders slumped and she rolled tiredly in her saddle.

Even so, when Gaultry shot the woman an anxious glance, she answered with a good-humored smile. *Far better Aneitha to make such a crossing than me.* The desert-woman could not swim, and her adventures with Gaultry had not made her love water any better. *At least this time I get a bridge.*

Never fear! Gaultry said, hoping to be cheering. *There's a bridge for every crossing from here all the way to Princeport. We're a civilized people, in Tielmark.*

I believe what I see with my own eyes, Gautri. The Sharif smiled, and rubbed the base of her neck. The thick black hair she had lost to the lice of the slaver's hold grew longest there, and she had gotten into a habit of tugging at those short strands.

We'll show you we're civilized, Gaultry assured her.

I believe what I see, the Sharif answered, a little more seriously. *More now than ever.*

▼

chapter 2

The crossing bridged the narrowest point between hard granite banks. As they neared, the reason for the gathered crowd became obvious. The bridge was narrow and much-repaired, so overgrown with vines that it was difficult even to see the age-whitened boards from which it had been constructed. The center of its three short spans sagged dangerously. The bridgekeeper, a stout, dark-haired man with an enormous belly, collected two-penny tolls and directed the marketgoers into ragged lines on both the banks, ensuring that the bridge never bore the weight of more than a handful of travelers and their livestock, or the mass of a single cart or wagon.

From a distance, Gaultry conceived a fanciful impression that the entire structure was held together only by the unusual wealth of ivy that swarmed up over its sides and supports. Coming closer, she was appalled to discover imagined whimsy was actual fact. A spindly, vine-covered arch had been erected on the bridge where it went onto the first piling. As she approached, she saw that it was marked with the hex-signature of an Emiera Priestess who had grafted the vines to the bridge to keep it from collapsing. From the hex-signature, she read that the work was dated for new attention—as of three years prior.

"This is Tielmark's High Road!" Gaultry said, shocked. "Who would allow this bridge to get to this state?"

Martin loosed his reins and rubbed his neck. "Who do you think? The late Chancellor of Tielmark was also the Master of its High Road and bridges."

The late Chancellor of Tielmark had been a Bissanty loyalist. Gaultry, who had been personally responsible for his death, paled with shock as her poor understanding of the far-reaching consequences of a disloyal chancellor came freshly home to her. "How could Tielmark trust something so important to a man up to his elbows in paper and court protocol? Even if he wasn't a Bissanty snake? And why send a Priestess instead of a builder to fix it?"

"Benet has been a long time coming into his power." Martin sounded tired. He slid out of his saddle, pulling his reins over his horse's head so he could better control the animal in the crowd. "Years of regency after his father died, then a traitor chancellor. He's actually held the throne of Tielmark for almost eight years now—yet with the regency and the ill-counsel of his chancellor considered, his marriage this spring can be counted his first entirely self-ruled act as Tielmark's ruler. Do you wonder that his bridges are rotten?"

Gaultry stared, first at the bridge, then at the marketgoers who waited, patient but increasingly surly, on both riverbanks. "This bridge has been collapsing for more than eight years," she observed. "Was Benet's father ineffective too?" Martin was old enough to remember, even if Gaultry was not.

Martin shrugged. "Ginvers was a soldier, like his brother Roualt before him. You'd have to go back to Corinne for a ruler who took the time to care about her roads. Besides, the lands that border the High Road are a patchwork of small estates, each owing allegiance to different power-holders. There must be some local dispute."

Following Martin's example, Gaultry and the others dismounted, leading their horses to the back of the queue that twined round on their side of the bank.

Gaultry was dismayed at the numbers—and the volume of the produce—that lay ahead of them. "We'll be here hours. Maybe it would have been faster to find a place to wade."

Tullier smirked.

"Not necessarily." Martin, catching Tullier's expression, eyed him with a look of serious displeasure. "I'll not argue with every pig farmer, but this—obviously we can't waste the rest of the day standing here." He slapped his reins into Gaultry's hand and pushed through the crowd to speak with the bridgekeeper.

"Talk about choosing one's battles unwisely!" Gaultry said between her teeth. "Just watch. This will prove worse than me with the pig-woman. Tielmaran farmers won't stand for queue-jumping."

Sure enough, as Martin finished speaking to the bridgekeeper and beckoned them to the front, calls of complaint rose from both banks. The monkey and the tamarin particularly drew the crowd's ire—as if the creatures were proof that the travelers were performers or players, greedy for a chance to set up a stall early.

"Get back in line!" one man behind them shrieked. To judge by his dress, he and his companions actually *were* actors or minstrels. "We'll all reach Soiscroix in good time, if no one pushes forward unfairly!"

"Quiet! Quiet! They're on the Prince's business," the bridgekeeper protested, his breathy, soft-toned voice scarcely audible above the tumult. "Their business gives them right of passage—"

No one listened. Martin, ignoring the catcalls, stepped onto the bridge and beckoned. Gaultry tossed her reins to the Sharif and hurried up to him. "Martin—this isn't a good idea."

"Hurry up. There's going to be a surge if we don't make this quick." He manhandled Gaultry past him. "Come along you two!" he called to the Sharif and Tullier. "Prince's business!"

Gaultry, reluctant, took two paces along the bridge. A man at the bridge's far end stared back across the heads of the people who would be the last to cross before them, a furious expression on his face. "Who are you to push ahead?" he yelled. "Elianté's Spear! Wait your turn!"

Gaultry set her face and stepped forward. Whether Martin was wise to have leapt the queue or not, he wasn't in the wrong to have done it. Ahead of her, the angry man's eyes bulged with affront.

Then she realized the reaction was more than simple offense. Something was happening in the crowd behind him: There was a sharp spike in the crowd's movement, and the man fell, or was dragged, out of sight.

A short, slope-shouldered man took his place. At his back, another; then a third man and a fourth. At first Gaultry did not recognize what she was seeing.

Tullier grabbed at her sleeve. "Bissanty-men! What are they doing in Tielmark?"

The man in front swung his sword clear from his belt. "For Llara!" he called. "For Llara's Heart-on-Earth!" Sword upheld, he loped forward to close with them. Marketgoers scattered to either side, clearing a path.

"Stop them!" Gaultry shouted. "They'll kill us!"

But the crowd thought the men were only giving them a fright for their audacity—they seemed deaf to the invocation of the Bissanty goddess, the imperial title. Some even cheered the swordsmen forward. For a crucial moment, Gaultry, half taking her cue from the crowd's reaction, could not decide whether she should press forward or turn back, unable believe the attack was really happening. She darted a quick look at the bridgekeeper, and saw him standing to one side, obviously wanting to be out of it. Martin was still behind her.

"I am Gaultry Blas!" she shouted, as the swordsmen almost came up on her. "Glamour-witch, and protector of this realm!" But of course the men must already know who she was, if they were Bissanty and attacking! Still—she could bluff—"Don't test me, if you choose to live!" As the men kept coming, she remembered at last that she did not have to bluff. Touching the vine that encircled the rail at her side, she opened a channel toward the signature of the priestess who had bound it to the bridge, calling on the strength left dormant there. As she touched it, her own power surged up. "Know my power!" For a moment, her heart leapt with hope: She would turn the spell, and use the magicked vine to trap the attackers before they reached her. All it needed was a little extra call of power—

An unfamiliar countersurge slapped against her as she reached the signature board. The first sweet shock of her own power staggered, lurched and dropped, with an angry recoil that was as painful as it was unexpected. Some other witch, unnamed, had left her mark on the boarded archway, along with a fresh, aggressive spell. Gaultry jerked her hand back from the vine, swearing, not sure what had gone wrong, and turned with angry fear to face the descending sword.

But as she turned, the vines all along the bridge made a violent, flexing motion. Beneath her feet, the bridge ties shifted and shrieked in protest, and awareness pierced her of the nasty drop from the bridge to the swift-running, rock-strewn waters that ran beneath it. The panicked marketgoers still remaining on the bridge, ignoring even the men with the swords, scrambled for the safety of solid ground. The sallow-skinned face of the first of the Bissanty attackers paled. "Llara on me—" he cried, lurching as the bridge shifted beneath him.

The vine unfurled from the spot where Gaultry had touched it and reared back away from the bridge, twisting like a serpent, made all from leaves. And not just in that place. All along the bridge, fronds of ivy writhed like a many-armed creature waking from sleep, breaking up parts of the bridge as it tore itself free.

"What have you done?" Tullier shouted. He was the closest of her companions.

"It's not me!" Gaultry shouted back. "I swear by Elianté, Huntress-god, it wasn't me! Jump clear!"

Instead he snatched at her hand.

The flailing, many-armed mass of ivy arched over the bridge behind them, blocking retreat.

A frighteningly strong frond grabbed at her arm, then ripped Tullier's hand away. A plank shifted and fell away from beneath her. When she tried to make a dash for stable ground, a mantle of green swept over her head, a living robe of leaf and vine that blocked her sight as it engulfed her. As she drew her knife a vine-tendril looped three times around her arm, then contracted, hard enough to tear her skin. She screeched with pain, but clung to the knife, knowing she would never be able to retrieve it if it dropped.

She heard Tullier call out again, his voice pitched high with anger, but she could not distinguish his words. The vines extended and coiled like leafed snakes, lashing her knife arm against her chest. She threw herself against the bridge's rail, trying to break free. "Martin!" she called. "Anyone! Help!"

The bridge rocked sharply. With a harsh chorus of cracking and splintering, it began to come apart. A board dropped out right beneath her feet, and then, as she struggled to hold the rail, another still was wrenched away. Gaultry fell, clutched at a broken piece of rail to brake herself, and knocked her chin against something hard. She fell again, a terrible slipping fall, twice and more again the height of a standing man, punctuated with a bruising crash against what remained of one of the bridge supports.

Then she was in the water, forced by the current against the edge of a half-submerged rock.

The vine loosened as she dropped, deprived either of its purchase or of the magic that grounded it. Gaultry got a confused partial view, through whipping snakes of vine, of the remnants of the bridge above her. Martin was still aloft, facing at least one Bissanty man. Tullier—she could not see Tullier. He had to be down with her in the water. And the Sharif—the Sharif had been holding the horses—

The Sharif was in the water not far from her, pressed against one of the bridge's pilings, strung between two of their mounts. The chestnut that Martin had been riding lunged furiously, striking with all its strength against a closing noose of vine. Gaultry's horse had broken bones in the fall. Shrieking in pain, it plunged wildly, trying to right itself. The Sharif was strung between the two panicked animals, bound in a tangled snarl of bridle straps and vine.

Let them go! Gaultry called, not understanding at first how seriously the woman was entangled.

Oh yes. And then the river takes me and I drown, the woman shot back.

The exchange between the women roused the vine. It moved sluggishly in the water, fronds extending, slow to regroup. Snaky masses of leaf noosed once more around Gaultry's chest, tentative at first, then gaining strength enough to constrict her breathing. Somehow she had managed to keep hold of the knife. She was torn between trying to make use of it and continuing to paddle and keep her head above water.

At last the vine had power and purchase enough to make the decision for her. It wrenched her away from the protection of the half-submerged rock and dashed her into the current. A rush of white foam blinded Gaultry briefly, disorienting her as she twirled into the main stream. Water forced its way up her nose and into her foolishly open mouth. It was only when the vine whipped her against another ridge of stone that she was able—just for a moment—to orient herself. She thrashed out, trying to reach a stone that jutted up from the water a bare yard from her head, and cracked her foot against a hidden ledge of stone in the water beneath her.

Gaining a precarious life-hold on that unexpected rock, she tried to take a normal breath and gather for a counterattack. Touching a cluster of leaves, she probed outward with her magic, this time covertly, trying to determine what had set the plant in action against her. Her Bissanty-attacker had appeared shocked when the vine had come to life—but Gaultry had been running from enemies for too long to believe that simultaneous attacks could be coincidental.

The source, when she found it, was a palpable, angry thing. It hated with a vitriolic personal strength that Gaultry could feel like a physical force, even just thrusting a thread of power toward it. Rather than risk testing it further, she settled back into the water. If that magic sensed she had found her feet, it would sweep her back into the depths.

She forced herself to concentrate, to push her fear aside. She stared at the vine, trying to understand its violent animation. It was not the old priestess's spell that had bound the vine to the bridge in the first place. She could sense that woman's touch, still in the vine, gently binding the

vines to the worn-out boards. This was something new. Something op-
portunistic. Dimly, she became aware of a green nimbus where the new
magic had bound itself over the old. As she focused, the nimbus deepened
in color to a green so dark as to be almost black. Angry green, hate-
spawned and curdling black. Recognition of a sort tore her: Goddess
Elianté wore that color, when she tore through the forest in her aspect
as Huntress-avenger.

Gaultry had no breath to cry out at the betrayal: her own goddess,
called to power against her. What was it that she had done, that this
violence had come crashing down upon her? What could she have done,
to draw this hate?

Pushing these thoughts away, she focused on the vine itself, searching
for weakness, then almost crying in relief when she found it: as the black-
green magic used the vine to mete destruction, it consumed it, withering
the leaves and breaking the bark.

Above, on the bridge, a man cried out. A body with a fluttering grey
cloak dropped into the water. A Bissanty body. Martin, she thought with
a stab of relief. Making quick work of their attackers. She wrenched
around, fighting the vines, trying to see what else was happening. Then
she saw Tullier.

He was struggling in a cluster of greenery overhead, hanging more
than a man's body length above the water, like a fly caught in a web.
Moving toward him on the remains of the bridge's framework were two
of the men who had first accosted them.

"Tullier!" she screamed. He turned to her, even bound amid the entrapping vine, just as the first man reached him. "Tullier!" she screamed
again. The first man's sword flashed and caught the sun as it descended.
Crimson stained the vine that sheathed both Tullier and his attacker.

Her rage erupted in a flood of strength and heat. With it, her
Glamour-magic leapt to power. Like golden heart-fire, it burst forth, driving in gleaming channels through the wrathful green of the magic that
engulfed her. The dark-green magic was potent, but unnamed. Whoever
had cast the spell had not been a master-planter, so the spell had not
become a part of the vines, using some part of the plant's inherent nature
to enact itself.

Which was lucky for Gaultry, because the vines, already weakened,
became vegetively inanimate and fell away, just as soon as the spell was
diverted into direct engagement with Gaultry's power. She hardly noticed, she was so riveted on Tullier's fate.

The river coursed back from her body, repulsed by the force streaming from her body, and left her standing on a naked slab of stone as the current rushed breast-level in dark walls past her. She screamed out, throwing the channels of her power wider, and drank in the rank green magic, letting it distend the channels of her power with the volume of its sick, potent might. The vines that had wrapped her chest, still in the grip of the river's current but freed now of the spell, were whipped away by the water's force. Above her, she was vaguely aware as the ivy mass on Tullier's body abruptly unraveled, plunging his limp form into the merciless current.

Black-green power fought against gold. Gaultry braced herself on the bare rock, walls of water hissing past her, her body buckling as she scrambled to overwhelm the spell. Beyond those walls, under the bridge, she sensed rather than saw Tullier's body turn in the current and strike a rock. The sickening sound of meat striking stone carried to her over the rushing sound of the water.

That sound gave her the will to shatter the green magic. She screamed, triumphant, and it exploded from her in a cloud of infinitely small speckles of light, singing vitriol to the air.

Then—then it was just gone.

The river walls collapsed. Gaultry, taken by surprise, bobbed to the surface and began to paddle wildly, clutching at the jutting stone. She stared down the river, searching for Tullier. His dog, trapped somewhere up on the bridge, howled in despair.

Gautri. The Sharif's voice pierced her, the slur of her foreign pronunciation unusually enhanced. *Gautri, I need you.*

The young woman unwillingly broke her search for Tullier and turned back toward the Sharif. What she saw made her gasp in horror, newly appalled. As the spell had broken, the vines entrapping Martin's chestnut horse had dropped away. Panicked, it plunged for the shore. The Sharif, still tangled in the reins of both horses, the first broken-legged and half-insane with pain, the other lunging, determined to regain dry land, was pinned between them against one of the bridge pilings. The tendons of the war-leader's arms were stretched in agonized cords down across her chest.

Not long. Somehow, even in the face of the water, the woman had regained her nerve. *Not long now.* Her words held an eerie calm. *Sun-god, Andion-King, if ever you loved me—*

From the corner of her eye, Gaultry spotted the black crown of Tullier's head, downriver now and moving swiftly away. She looked at the horses, at the Sharif, unable to come to a decision. The Sharif, for certain, needed help right now, but Tullier—

"Go for the boy!" Martin, his sword a red slash of gore, appeared atop the bridge's wreckage. Even as he spoke, he threw himself recklessly across the broken gap, sloshing down crazily amidst the torn hulks of wood and vine. One of the horses reared in terror. The Sharif howled, her arms newly wrenched. But at least Martin was there—

Gaultry flung herself loose into the stream, heading toward the point where she had last seen Tullier's head.

Rocks and debris snarled the river's course. At its present midsummer volume, the current was not swollen to the top of its strength, but it was powerful enough to be frightening. Under good conditions, Gaultry could swim like an otter, but she was badly winded and her desperation to reach Tullier served against her. Her position, low in the water, had her terrified that she would lose him in a swirling eddy, or in the lee of a half-submerged log or stone.

She crested a mossy ridge of rock, tearing her knuckles against it, and, wallowing for a moment against that edge, once more caught sight of him. Somehow he had managed to escape the main current and pull himself over to the edge of a shallow, bankside pool.

"Tullier!" Gaultry screamed. "Tullier!"

Above him stood a man with sloping shoulders and sallow skin. One of the bridge attackers. He had escaped the wreckage of vine and wood and run along the bank to intercept them. As Gaultry watched, he raised his sword.

Tullier was too weak to protect himself. He stared up, his ice-green eyes steady, ready for what was about to happen.

The man hesitated. Something in Tullier's expression slowed him. Looking down at the boy, his lips moved. Gaultry was not close enough to hear the words, but Tullier made no effort to answer. She scrambled forward in a frenzy, desperate to reach the bank before the sword descended.

The man, seemingly unaware of her approach, cast the god-sign for Llara, a jerking lightning bolt slash at the air, and touched his hand to the edge of his blade. He was the fast man, the one who had clambered across the chaotic tangle of collapsing bridge and vine to reach Tullier. His fingers caressed his blade's edge—the blade that was still slick with the boy's blood. As Gaultry watched, he deliberately sliced the honed edge into his palm, then clenched his fist. Blood started from between his fingers, mingling with Tullier's. The Bissanty man stiffened.

"Llara-born!" he said softly. This time Gaultry was near enough to hear. The man stared at Tullier with fascinated horror. "I have struck the Llara-born." Eyes widening in agony, the man drew his blade up.

Tullier, hunkering down just a little beneath him, shut his eyes.

The man let out an indescribable cry. His blade flashed down, un-erring.

Gaultry screamed again, this time in pity.

The Bissanty-man was a soldier of Great Llara, and he was very quick. His cry was cut short as the force of his own blow disemboweled him, and his body struck the water, the sword falling from his dying hand. A wave washed past Gaultry's body, and she felt a horrible cooling around her in the water. Icy certainty pierced her: As punishment for striking a boy who was his own goddess's kin, the man's soul had died with his body.

Gaultry, stumbling out of the water at Tullier's side, pulled him up by his shoulder, dazed by what she had witnessed. She had not understood this implication of the boy's Imperial god-blood, had not understood the threat Tullier posed to the Emperor's will that his own sons should suc-ceed him. From what she had just witnessed, so long as Goddess Llara reigned as Bissanty's patron, no citizen of all the Imperial lands could draw a drop of the boy's blood and hope to claim the Grey Goddess's blessing—and what man could live, knowing the punishment his Goddess would wreak upon him?

This power of death over life, this was the prize the Emperors of Bissanty fought so jealously to possess.

Tullier's shirt was dark with blood. He rolled listlessly onto his side as she lugged him out of the water, revealing a deep, water-leached gut wound.

Frantic, she pulled him against her own body, trying to warm him. He was conscious enough to cling to her, throwing his arms around her neck and pressing his head against her as she stumbled up the bank. She tried to lay him down on a bed of moss, but he refused to let her go.

"It doesn't hurt," he said, his voice faint. "But this leaving you—"

"Tullier." She would not let him slip away like this. "It's not your time yet."

"I had a month of living," the boy gasped. "That was better than never being alive."

His uncharacteristic passivity frightened her. Wadding up the tail of her tunic, she pressed it against his wound, desperate to stanch the flowing blood.

"Gaultry," he pleaded. "Let me go."

"Shut up, Tullier," she said harshly. "We'll get a healer for you and you'll be fine. I won't let you die. Mervion—" Tullier held half her sister's Glamour-soul, and Mervion was a great healer. Perhaps if she could reach out to that part of her sister in him—

He clutched at her reflexively, a shudder of disappointment running through him. "Of course," he said. "If I die, I'll take part of Mervion. Just take it," he groaned. "Take it and let me die—"

"Shut up, Tullier," she said. "That's not my point." Though as she spoke, the possibility that he might really die—and take half Mervion's Glamour-soul with him—was like a dagger in her heart. She could not let that happen, any more than she could let Tullier die, here, while he was under her protection. "Elianté's Spear! What I mean is that I'll try reaching to Mervion's power in you to help you. Mervion's the healer, not me. If you relax, I'll try to reach out to her soul in you and buy us some time."

"Yes!" he croaked, suddenly eager. "Do it!"

She stared at him, doubtful. What had she suggested that made him so suddenly change his mind?

"Open yourself to me." She stroked his cheek, trying to calm him. "Relax. Let my magic move through you." His water-softened hair felt cold under her fingers. "Remember how it was when we were together in Bissanty. Purple and gold—our magic twined together. Goddess-Twins! That alone should be strength enough to keep you here."

"I want you—" Tullier started to say, then coughed, and did not finish. His grip tightened around her fingers with surprising strength. "Just do it," he finally managed, his voice weak.

She held him tightly against her. His flesh was river-cold, as though the stream had taken his warmth as well as his blood. For a moment, she was afraid that he was too far gone, his soul already retreated to the house of the Gods, past recalling. The overloaded channels of her power felt weak and shrunken, depleted by the effort it had taken to disperse the wrathful black-green magic, but she ignored that, and once again reached out.

Just as she was sure she could attempt her push no longer, waves of imperial purple swept across her vision. She redoubled her efforts, recognizing the great mass of power and soul that was Tullier's god-blood. Veined with blood red streaks and pulsing like a heart's beat, it curdled backward, drawing her inward to a plane where the senses beyond vision slipped away. Distantly, Gaultry felt Tullier's body spasm against her, his nails digging into her skin as he clutched at her neck, an almost sexual embrace. But none of those things felt real. Only the edge of his wound was real, the edge of the wound and the blood that still flowed from it.

The shroud of purple dallied, ripe like grapes ready for harvest. Gaultry's urgency had not communicated itself. The golden edges of her Glamour touched the Blood-Imperial and it responded languorously, cleaving a supple fold in its center to form a cradle for her. Warmth flushed through her at the contact, and Gaultry's sense of pain fell away.

"Death wish," Gaultry muttered, wishing Tullier would concentrate harder on saving himself. If she allowed him to keep the pace so slow, surely she would lose him—and with him, perhaps, herself. This in mind, she fought with renewed vigor against the rising lassitude, her rising sense of comfort, and forced herself to focus on the horror of Tullier's wound.

She did not know how long she remained there, fixed in contemplation, but suddenly, shining like a beacon, Mervion's golden half-soul rose up above her, radiating soothing balm. Gaultry felt pure closeness with her sister—the beloved twin whom power had parted from her.

Abruptly, that moment passed. Mervion's power shrank. Gaultry saw suddenly how it could be used as a tool to cauterize and close the big breached vessel in Tullier's gut. She reached out, confident now, halfway between the spirit plane and the riverbank where the boy's bleeding body lay. In this place, she could twist Mervion's power into place, almost like a bandage, as purple waves of strength caressed her, interfusing her with fresh strength. It was heady, this sense of Tullier's god-blood, intermixing with her own Glamour.

With a last twist of strength, she finished binding the wound and withdrew. The riverbank came coldly back into focus. For a moment her body trembled, as if a fever had taken her.

Tullier's head had rolled back, exposing his throat. Gaultry tilted his face to a more natural angle. Though he was deeply unconscious, his lips were twisted in a disturbing smile, as though he was very far from his earlier pain.

"How is he?" Martin stumbled down the bank, Tullier's dog at his heels.

"He'll live." Gaultry covered the boy's face with her palm, hiding his expression from Martin, and shakily laid him on the ground. The edges of his wound bulged with inheld blood, but she knew he would not die. Not this time. The dog whined and pressed its body against Tullier's legs. "Who did this?" she asked angrily. "Who set those men on us?"

"I don't know," Martin said. "But every man of them was Bissanty born."

"The spell on the bridge was Tielmaran magic," Gaultry told him. "Why Bissanty men if it was Tielmaran magic?"

"I don't know," Martin said. "But the Bissanties at least were waiting for us. It wasn't chance that launched that attack—they knew you and me both. That from a man before I had to kill him."

"Elianté in me!" Gaultry invoked the Huntress and made her sign, peevish and frightened together. "I thought we were supposed to be safe now we were home in Tielmark." She was crying now, delayed reaction from all the danger. "You don't know what I had to do to keep Tullier alive. They almost killed him. I had to raise my Glamour, and he the Goddess-blood!"

Martin, disconcerted, yanked Gaultry up and away from the boy's unconscious form. "This can't go on," he said angrily, shielding her for a moment against the warmth of his body. "You must stop sharing your power with him. You're forgetting what he is, and who you are. His fate lies in Bissanty—yours is here in Tielmark."

Gaultry struggled free of him, feeling obscurely guilty. "Don't you think I know that? What would you have me do? He would have died without me."

"A habit he seems unwilling to break," Martin replied hotly. "For all it brings you close to him."

"He's just a boy!"

Martin raised his hand to the smooth curve of her cheek. "With this magic, he has trespassed too far inside you. Gaultry—consider what you have shared with him already."

She thrust his hand away. "Don't touch me. Not right now."

The expression on Martin's face shifted from anger to ice. He withdrew, and gave her a mock salute. "As my lady pleases. As I myself have trespassed, I am sorry. But my rudeness doesn't alter what I've said. You must stop sharing your power with him. For Tielmark's sake, if not for mine."

"I don't know what you mean." She sounded childish now—she knew it, and he knew it too.

"You got your swim," he said, derisive, as he stood away from her. "I hope getting your way is enough to make you happy."

chapter 3

In the confusion after the wounded and the bodies had been dragged out of the water, the sentiment among the marketgoers left stranded on the river's banks was not weighted in the travelers' favor. Martin had killed three men, and the fourth man had taken his own life. With one side slaughtered, unable to be questioned for their side of the story, no one could agree what had precipitated the violence.

As the corpses were laid on the bank, the mood of the crowd grew ugly. The market crowd knew nothing of Bissanty conspiracies; all they had seen was four men attempt to stop some queue-jumpers, an act for which they had paid with their lives.

One woman had broken her ankle escaping the bridge's collapse; others suffered bruises. Many of those trapped on both banks carried perishable goods. A few responded constructively. Three carpenters who had been traveling to Soiscroix went down into the water to salvage the scrap lumber, and, with many hands helping, it was not long before they had rigged up a narrow plank bridge. But anyone who had goods in a cart or wagon was seriously out of luck.

As much as the chaos and violence, the animated vine had frightened them. As work progressed on making the temporary bridge secure, some men began to systematically destroy what remained of the vine, building a fire and laying bedraggled garlands of leaves upon it. The garlands steamed as the flames touched them, casting off foul-smelling smoke.

Others still turned to mete justice on the queue-jumpers.

The bridgekeeper, who should have been able to vouch for them, was too timid to take charge and quell the mob's rage. Fierce questions revealed he'd been approached, days before, by one of the dead men, and asked questions regarding certain travelers—travelers who matched Gaultry, Martin, and Tullier's description. But the bridgekeeper was so slow-witted—or unwilling to risk the ire of the crowd—that he could not name the day the exchange occurred, or other useful information.

The crowd was mutinously angry, and Tullier and the Sharif were in no state to be quickly moved. Gaultry, still fussing over Tullier's wound, did not want to leave his side. "Martin." She cast him an apologetic look, in the hope that he would temporarily put aside their argument. "Please do something."

Martin, who had recovered two of their horses and then gone into the water to dispatch the unfortunate animal with the broken leg, shot her a tired look.

"They'll listen to you," she said, encouraging. "You know if I try they'll only get angrier."

He almost smiled. "I can't argue with you there." A man bumped him aggressively as he spoke. Martin answered with a hard shove. "Stand away." He loosened his sword in its scabbard. "Stand away, in the Prince's name, or you'll meet more trouble than you'll know how to answer."

Before the man could recoup, Martin pushed past and sprang up into his saddle, a movement shocking in its trained grace and speed. He deftly used the animal's body to open up ground in front of the wounded, forcing the crowd back. "Quiet down!" he called. "In the name of Benet and Tielmark, be quiet! Settle this matter by Benet's laws, and we will gladly yield to you! We have wounded to be tended and bodies lie here, un-shriven and begging consecration to the gods; we recognize that we cannot leave until these matters are well-shifted. I hear angry voices raised against us. But if the dead have no voice to speak their case, no one here can speak for them either. This matter must be referred to the local justice for fair hearing." He swung around to the bridgekeeper. "Who is the Justice for this shire?"

The bridgekeeper, cowed, did not answer, but Martin's appeal to the right of law swayed some in the crowd toward him. "It's Jumery Ingoleur," one of the men tending the vine fire offered. "Aye, bring them to Sieur Jumery!" another man called out. "He'll see justice done!"

The justice's name was an invocation that distinctly changed the crowd's mood. For an odd moment it was almost as though Sieur Jumery's name had frightened them. Martin, unsettled by the reaction, glared and touched again the hilt of his sword. "Where does this Jumery Ingoleur reside?"

"A matter of two miles hence," the fire tender said, throwing a fresh heap of vines on the flames.

"Organize a cart for the dead and the wounded." Martin settled his gaze on the fire tender, who squared his shoulders, then nodded assent. "And we must have an escort, to ensure that we arrive in good time and health for this man's judgment."

To Gaultry's astonishment, the crowd complied. They were not over-joyed to assign their spare hands to form the escort—a carter's extra handler, the husband of a woman bringing woven goods to market, and four others. A farmer headed westward was particularly aggrieved when one of his carts was appropriated, even when it was pointed out that he would not be able to pass on until the bridge was more stoutly rebuilt. But taken as a whole, relief that Martin had laid down a palatable course of action was the strongest sentiment. Muttering surrounded them as the corpses were loaded, but the crowd's impulse for rough judgment had faded.

Tullier's limp form was laid by the corpse of the man who had taken his own life. Those two shuttered faces were unpleasantly alike. Only the boy's lips, flushed a seemingly unnatural crimson against his pallid skin, separated his color from that of the dead.

The Sharif climbed up next, assisted by two women. Where Tullier was pale, the Sharif's face was unhealthily flushed. The horses had dis-located both her shoulders. One of her arms had been rotated back into place by those who had pulled her from the water, but the other, after several crude tries to right it, had been left to dangle. The women who made a place for her among the corpses propped her body so that the still-dislocated arm was supported against one of the dead.

Tullier's pup whined at the back of the cart until he too was lifted in. Then, just as they were setting forward, the tamarin ran up, soaking wet, and vaulted into the cart. The little creature settled into the Sharif's lap, chittering to itself and combing its wet fur. A rumbling from the crowd suggested that they did not like the look of its strange pointed snout and brightly striped fur.

The graceful grey monkey which had traveled with them all the way from Bissanty had been lost to the river. Gaultry was almost too deep in shock at her companions' injuries to miss it.

"What are you doing?" Martin asked, as she reached for the cart's back rail and put one foot on its wooden step-up bar.

"I'm going to ride with Tullier and the Sharif."

"Not a chance," Martin said. "You're able-bodied and you'll ride at my side."

"They need me."

"I need you more," Martin hissed. "Don't imagine that we've been forgiven for this fracas yet. You're going to ride with me and put on a good face and show them we're not guilty of breaking their damn bridge. So swing yourself up into that saddle and try to look a little less tragic."

"Tullier was almost killed!" Gaultry seethed back at him. "He needs someone close by him."

"Allegrios mine, I just slaughtered three men. Do you think what I did was nothing to me? You can't do anything for him now—he's stable. I'm the one who needs you, so get moving!" His tone made the words a command, not a supplication.

Gaultry swung mechanically up on the Sharif's horse, somewhere between numb and furious—at what, she hardly knew. Martin Stalker had renounced his name, his title, and the property, rights, and even the family that went with it. But he could never strip himself of the authority he had earned in more than a decade of leading men into battle. Sitting high on his horse, he only needed to scowl and give orders for anyone—herself included—to follow.

"Sorceress!" The ugly wrath in that shout turned her head. A black-haired man raised his fist, far at the back of the crowd. He pointed toward the bodies in the cart. "That man killed himself for you! Do you really believe the gods will forgive such a trespass?"

She stared back, astonished by the man's vehemence. Could he really believe she had the power to force a man to cut out his own guts? Beneath her flat, expressionless gaze, the man silenced and withdrew.

After that, she raised her chin, dug her heels into the horse's sides, and pushed her way to the place at Martin's side.

"I'm here for you," she told him. He was so strong, so able to maintain a steady face, that sometimes it was difficult to know when he really needed her. "You're right. Tullier will keep, and this crowd will not."

Their watchful escort circled, and got them moving.

"Don't look back," Martin warned her, as she half-turned her head to a last catcall.

She risked a glance at him instead. "Do you think this Sieur Jumery will give us a fair hearing?"

"He should. With luck, I'll know him from my court days, and that will go a long way to explaining." He paused. "The name sounds familiar. Did I fight a summer campaign, along with one of his sons? I can't quite place it."

"We'll know soon enough."

He nodded.

The disagreeable, hemmed-in ride ended at an ancient, half-ramshackle manor a few miles out of Soiscroix, tucked back from the road behind overgrown hedges. It had once been a beautiful building, with two gracious stuccoed wings flanking the ancient stone keep at its center. Now, the building's western wing was shuttered, its roof dangerously bowed, and even the inhabited wing was overrun with wisteria that had run riot and cracked the stucco cladding.

Gaultry, exhausted from the backlash of the energy she had used to disperse the green magic, had fallen into a torpor. She roused only as her horse passed the manor's gate. Half of the men who had accompanied them reined up at the cut in the hedge rather than crowding into the manor's shabby court. Despite the estate's obvious decline, it was evident that their escort regarded its owner with great deference. Agitated murmurs revealed that interrupting the justice at home was beginning to concern them more than presenting him with supposed bridge-breakers.

The cart creaked to a halt outside the faded grandeur of the manor's entry. A boy was sent to bring notice of their arrival.

"Why is everyone nervous?" Gaultry whispered to Martin.

"I don't know," he whispered back. "It could be anything. Just hope that whatever it is isn't bad news for us."

They and their escort had a long awkward wait before the house's master shuffled into view. At first glance, Gaultry could not help but wonder what it was in him that their escort so feared.

Sieur Jumery Ingoleur was old. Old and decrepit, with a frail-looking neck and staring, nearsighted eyes. His justice's robe trailed duskily behind him, giving the appearance that he had lost height since the garment was first cut. The Prince's orb, a polished blue sphere with silver inlay, bobbled in his hand, as though its weight was uncomfortable in his aged

fingers, an impression confirmed when, immediately following his acknowledgment of the little crowd, the old man pressed this heavy stone
symbol into the hands of the attentive body-servant who accompanied
him. "I trust that there is a good reason for this disturbance?" his old
man's voice quavered. "Why aren't you all headed to market? Isn't Midsummer busy enough without bringing me into it?"

"Sieur Ingoleur." The foreman of their escort, coming forward to
catch the Justice's attention, made a respectful bow. "We bring frightful
news from Sizor's Bridge. Men have died, Sieur, and the bridge itself is
broken in pieces. These people here are the cause of it."

"We claim otherwise," Martin interjected. "But we will cede first
telling to this gentleman."

The foreman gave Martin an unhappy glance, sensing that the tall
warrior's courteous words dampened the dramatic effect of his own. But
when Sieur Jumery indicated that he should go on, he rallied, and briefly
outlined his version. It started out more fairly than Gaultry expected,
though she winced as the man described Martin's short but brutal dispatch
of their attackers, an action which she had been too busy in the water to
witness.

What she had not expected was his perception of her own role in
the affray. "She was a terror," the man said, casting her a nervous glance.
"She controlled wind, water, and a man's own hand. Elianté and Emiera
both! This I swear is true: She shattered the bridge with one touch of her
hand, and the one poor man who tried to stand against her drew his sword
and killed himself, the moment she touched him with her gaze."

"That's not true!" Gaultry protested, then realized that she did not
want to explain what really had happened—at least, she did not want to
explain about Tullier's blood-heritage. "Someone had set an offensive
spell on that bridge before ever I set foot upon it. It collapsed around me
when the men attacked! Besides—by your own account, it flung me helpless into the water. Why would I have brought the bridge down under
my own feet, even if I had the power to do it?"

The old man turned to Gaultry. She was still on her horse, a little
back from Martin and the foreman. It was as if he was seeing her for the
first time. His nearsighted gaze focused, and a look of something like
recognition flickered over his features. His pale eyes went unfriendly. "You
are a sorceress," he said. "Or is that too something you deny?"

His expression, so inexplicably hostile, chilled her. "I have some power," she admitted. "But it is pledged to my sworn sovereign, Benet, and I did not use it to attack anyone today."

Sieur Jumery, something flickering and unsettling moving in him, returned his attention abruptly to the foreman. "Tell me the rest."

When the man finished, Sieur Jumery eased forward, put his hand on Martin's bridle, then moved close to his stirrup. "You," he said. "You who are traveling with this sorcerer-woman. Do I know you? Should I know you?"

Martin shifted his foot, turning his toe so it did not point at the man's face. "I think I know you, old man," he said softly. Then, louder, "My name is Martin Stalker, good Sieur. I may once have been known to you as Martin Montgarret, heir to Seafrieg County."

Gaultry stiffened. Martin only identified himself by the name and title he had forsworn in circumstances where he felt dangerously threatened; further, his personal connections to the titled classes meant he seldom bothered himself with punctilious regard for the titles of lords and ministers. What had he recollected of the man's history to make him respond in this way?

"Of course," the justice said. "The Duchess of Melandiere's grandson. It has been a decade—more—since I heard the name. You fought at Pontocil with my sons—that terrible summer the Lanai raided east and burnt half the old town. Fergaunt's son has taken his spurs, you know. Just this past spring. He's already left for the border."

"I remember Fergaunt," Martin said. "He was a bold man."

"Then there was that ugly business with your wife and your father's title. . . ." Sieur Jumery's gaze drifted from Martin to Gaultry, and he did not complete the thought. "Who is this woman?"

"This is Lady Gaultry Blas." Martin did not look at Gaultry as he made the introduction. Something in his tone made Gaultry guess that he was willing her to keep her mouth shut. "If you have recent news from Princeport, you will recognize the name."

The old man nodded, his eyes unpleasant and intense. A measured pause went by, as he digested Martin's information. Then he left Martin's stirrup and came to Gaultry's. He held up a frail, blue-veined hand, as if to assist her down from the saddle.

"Thank you, Sieur, but I will not trouble you." Something intangibly threatening in him made her slide out of her saddle without touching him. She made a little bob, curtsying, to cover her refusal of his touch.

The watery blue eyes studied her. The justice was a tall man, for all the height he had lost to age, and he looked a little down at her. Under his scrutiny, the skin tingled at her scalp. Then Sieur Jumery smiled, revealing age-yellowed teeth. "You did great service to our country this past Prince's night. I must say, I never thought to meet the woman who brought our blessed Prince to his full power. I am too old now to have thought of traveling to see her, and I never dreamed she would come to me."

"We're on the Prince's business now," Martin interjected, coming to stand by Gaultry. "We want to see justice done for what happened at the bridge, but Benet has called us to return to Princeport and we are not at liberty to linger." Strictly speaking, this was true: The Prince had ordered all members of the Common Brood to make haste to Princeport—six weeks before, at a time when they had been no more than two miles beyond the capital's boundary stones. Martin, of course, omitted mention of their extensive divergence from strict regard for Benet's edict. "We must be judged here for what we have or have not done, and then we will be on our way."

"On your way?" Sieur Jumery said. His gaze shifted past Gaultry to the cart. "Only if what you would have me believe is true. Beyond that—I was told that you have wounded. And I see for myself you've brought me some bodies. That does not argue for any swift leave-taking."

"I doubt anyone will claim those men," Martin replied. "They are foreigners—Bissanties. Whoever set them to ambush us won't want their name known."

"Fergaunt's son has been sent to the Valle de Brai." Sieur Jumery abruptly changed the subject as he reached to touch a foot that protruded stiffly over the cart's back rail. "He writes me that it is cold land, and hard. Have you been there, Martin Stalker?"

"I have, Sieur."

"You must tell me something of the ground there." The old justice stood up on his toes and looked into the cart. "This one alive here—is she your woman? Can you talk?" he asked the Sharif, sitting grimly wedged between two bodies, her proud face full of pain and tauter than ever.

"She does not have our language."

"But she is yours?"

Martin nodded. "She is a war-leader from the far south. We hope to reward her service by returning her to Ardain."

"And the boy?" The watery gaze took in Tullier. "Yours too? These people are not fit to travel."

Their escort's foreman, troubled by the justice's air of placid curiosity, could no longer hold his peace. "Sieur Ingoleur, you can see for yourself that these people have conspired with foreigners and demons. They used that power to destroy Sizor's Bridge. Look! See their demon-familiar, straight up from Achavell!"

The tamarin, as if on cue, raised its head from the Sharif's lap. It regarded the old man with its luminous, smoke-colored eyes. With its slitted crimson-red pupils and fierce pointed snout, the little creature did indeed look somewhat demonic. Sieur Jumery gave it a curious look but did not overtly startle.

"This woman cast a spell at the bridge," the foreman insisted. "She tore it to tinder with the very vine that had been set by the Great Twins' magic to mend it. How anyone will get to market now—"

"Do you know who this woman is?" Sieur Jumery pointed at Gaultry. The foreman shook his head. "She is the Prince's Glamour-witch, Gaultry Blas. If you don't know the name, you'll have heard at least how she and her twin sister called the gods to earth to bless our Prince's wedding?"

The foreman goggled. "But Sieur, the bridge—"

"Enough," Sieur Jumery said. "Look here. Have none of you the wits to see?" He turned back to the cart. "These corpses bear clear witness that you have misunderstood what you saw. These men are wearing Bissanty soldiers' boots." Gripping the cart's rail for balance, the justice pushed up the puttee worn by the nearest corpse. Embossed in the leather, near the top of the boot, was a square with a cross drawn in from its corners, the sign of Imperial Bissanty. "What honest Bissanty men would lie waiting for travelers at Sizor's?"

"I do not know," the foreman said, rattled. A bluff farmer, he obviously had heard only in its vaguest outlines an account of recent doings at court, but he recognized the imperial mark. "We did not look at their boots when we laid them in the cart." His manner shifting, he cast Gaultry a glance trending toward a friendly reverence. "Truly, this is the Prince's Glamour-witch? The strong one, who remade the God-pledge? We have been very wrong, good Sieur. Were these men Imperial spies? And to think, they would have harmed our Prince's guardian." The man seemed genuinely upset.

Sieur Jumery repossessed his orb of office from his servant. "We will lay these men in the stable," he pronounced, holding up the shiny sphere.

"Their bodies will be searched for further signs as to who might have plotted this attack. I will question this man Martin Stalker and Lady Blas, looking thoroughly into this matter before I dismiss it, but I suspect it will be swiftly proved that they acted in their own defense."

He raised the orb over his head, steadying it in both hands. His tone took on an incantatory cadence, the tremor of age momentarily ceasing. "So say I, Sieur Jumery Ingoleur, Prince's Justice, speaking by my right as the voice of Benet, Prince of Tielmark; vesting this last day of Rios Sword-god's moon with my authority and Benet's. For verily, the young hay lies cut in rows upon the meadows, and Midsummer Days are on us, come next morning's dawn." Lowering the orb, he met the foreman's eyes. "As Rios and all the Great Twelve are in me, do you accept my ruling?"

The foreman drew a long breath. "Sieur, as the Great Twins rule me and Tielmark together, it is not mine to oppose you." The other men of their escort, once so keen to administer justice on their own account, nervously nodded in agreement.

Gaultry, although relieved, could not herself quell a pang of apprehension at the invocation Sieur Jumery had chosen.

Rios Sword-god, First Harvester, the Shining Blade of Justice, was not a deity to call upon lightly. He was a cold god, and seldom moved by mercy or forgiveness. If the old justice made a practice of calling Rios to witness his judgments, it was little wonder that the locals hesitated to air their complaints before him.

"Now, is there anything more you would have of me?" Sieur Jumery waggled a finger. "Speak now, the gods are watching. Tomorrow is Midsummer Market. Have you no business there?"

"Sieur—that's my cart those men are laid in." The farmer at the foreman's side would have said more, but the old man quelled him with a sharp gesture.

"Very well. Unload the dead in my stable. Then you can take your cart away with you." Sieur Jumery addressed his serving man, "Girian, go quickly and bring Hesbain and Gisella to the guest quarters. No, better still, tell Hesbain to come directly here to tend to the wounded.

"Your people will need a night at least to recover." The justice turned to Martin. "You'll serve our Prince best by allowing them their rest."

Martin swung down from his horse. "Good Sieur, we are in your hands."

"Martin," Gaultry whispered, as they jostled together between their horses' bodies, tying up stirrups and securing reins. "What's going on? Why is everyone so timorous as they defer to him?"

"Rios aside?"

She nodded.

"The Ingoleurs used to be a very influential family," Martin whispered back. "Until Corinne was made Princess, fifty years past. I haven't heard the name for years—but I should have known it immediately. The family is older than the hills. Rumor would have it that their land ties were once tremendously strong. That makes for strange loyalties—beyond Benet, deep to Tielmark's very earth. So keep your distance. We're going to be trapped here for the night at best, longer if your Tullier won't wake up." As the servants took charge of their horses, he took her arm. "Try to help the Sharif, and take some rest. I'll keep with the good justice and find out what can be learned from the bodies." He bowed to the old man as he drew Gaultry onto the manor's front step. "My lady Blas is tired, Sieur. As you heard, she took a tumble in the water when the bridge went down. But she will see our wounded settled before she takes her own rest."

"That is as I would expect," the old man said. Once more Gaultry had a sense of something intangible, unsettled, rising from him. "I hear tale that you are Tamsanne of Arleon Forest's blood," he added softly, coming near her.

"She is my grandmother," Gaultry replied, before she remembered Martin's advice to keep her mouth shut.

"So it is true," the old man breathed. "When you were up on the horse I thought I saw the likeness. At first I thought my old eyes must have deceived me—" He shook himself, and then, rather awfully, he smiled. "Forgive me. I am an old man. My memories have become confused. It pleasures me, in Rios's name, to offer you my hospitality."

Once again, that curious invocation of the Sword-god—appropriate to the day and season, but a little perilous to call down, outside ritual. Gaultry guessed that the old man took his role as justice almost too seriously—that was enough to make any man fear him. Fairness and justice were not always the same.

But—he had known Tamsanne. That was interesting. Her grandmother had not been a public figure for fifty years. Gaultry had met no one outside of those very close to the center of the Prince's power who had any memory of her, and she herself knew little about Tamsanne's life as a young woman. "You knew Tamsanne?"

"I was there when she and the others of the Brood helped Princess Corinne fulfill the Tielmaran God-pledge." The old man made a self-deprecatory gesture. "Myself, along with the rest of Tielmark's court. I was not at the heart of the action on that blessed day, but at least I was there to serve witness."

The arrival of Sieur Jumery's healer, accompanied by a handful of other servants and a stretcher, interrupted the chance for further questions. The rail at the back of the cart was unhooked, and Tullier's body gently slid out. Gaultry, exhaustion tugging at her, leaned against Martin and watched as they settled the boy on the stretcher. The Sharif managed to stagger out under her own strength, on the verge of collapse. The tamarin, losing the lap, leapt lightly down and into Gaultry's arms. She stroked its soft fur, grateful for the comfort of its warm body. Tullier's half-grown puppy, still in the cart, whimpered at the jump and had to be dragged down.

"Take them inside," Sieur Jumery said. "Call Didion if you need some muscle to help with the woman's shoulder."

"Go on." Martin fairly pushed her toward the door in the stretcher's wake. "Go with them."

The front door let into a tall but modest-sized entry clad with old-hewn stone. A massive, richly carved staircase of dark-colored wood curled up to the second floor. As with the manor's exterior, everything was grand but worn. Sieur Jumery's servants maneuvered the stretcher up the somewhat narrow and constricted steps and along a hallway to a plain white-washed chamber. There they laid Tullier on the bed, comatose but steadily breathing, and shut his pup in to watch him.

Gaultry and the Sharif were brought next door, to a room that boasted a massive bed with elaborate hangings and a dusty cover. The tamarin, chittering, jumped down from Gaultry's arms and darted across to a comfortable spot on one of the pillows. A sweet rush was set to burn in a jar by the window, clearing the chamber's air.

"We haven't had guests since autumn last." Hesbain, the healer-woman, sat the Sharif on the edge of the bed. "Sieur Jumery's sons had good hunting here then.

"And now," she said. "This patient. That tunic must come off. And the shirt under it." She took a fold of the Sharif's sleeve in her fingers and began to feel for the seam.

"I have a knife." Gaultry unsheathed it.

The woman shook her head. "We'll slit the threads." She sent the other woman, Gisella, downstairs for a sewing hook. Gaultry, noting the faded bed linens and the women's modest dress, did not argue the delay. If the tunic could not be replaced here, it would have to be retained in a fixable condition.

We're going to strip you, Gaultry told the Sharif. *Get ready.*

The Sharif gave a scarcely perceptible nod and pressed her eyes shut.

Gisella returned with the sewing hook, a little breathless for having hurried. With elaborate gentleness, Hesbain peeled away the layers of the Sharif's clothing: tunic, shirt, and last the thin cotton undergarment beneath. The old woman's eyebrows raised as the Sharif's lean body was revealed. Her skin was dark all over, not just on her hands and face; more notable, the war-leader's back was a tortured expanse of overlapping, poorly healed whipping scars and branding burns. Even Gaultry, who knew what to expect, felt the gall rise in her throat. The Sharif, who had been wounded in battle before being taken prisoner and sold to the Bissanties, had endured flogging and branding and hardships that had never given her the time to recoup. Now, the knob of her left arm pushed grotesquely at the skin next to her shoulder blade. "Call Didion," old Hesbain said hoarsely. "We won't fix this without another pair of hands."

"Can't we do it ourselves?" Gaultry asked.

"Not now that it's swollen up. Fixing it will hurt. If she hasn't fainted already, we'll need Didion to help keep her still."

Hesbain was right. It took four of them to twist and coax the arm's knob back into its socket. Gaultry, feeling light-headed, was not sure in the end how it was managed, but it evidently took as much guesswork as skill. The Sharif came close to blacking out as they worked on her, her body chilling and her skin becoming worrisomely clammy as she withdrew dangerously deep into herself.

"Can't you give her something for the pain?" Gaultry asked, concerned.

"Best to finish first," Hesbain panted, focusing on the task at hand. "I'll give her something then."

Afterward, Gaultry could not have said which was the greater relief: the moment when the Sharif's arm went back into its socket or after, when the Sharif took a mouthful of Hesbain's draught and lapsed into deep, heavy-breathing slumber.

"She looks better already," Gaultry said gratefully, soothing the sleeping woman's brow. "Now for the boy."

Hesbain shook her head. "I saw him in the cart. There's naught I can do. With a deep wound like that, all we can do is pray to Allegrios Rex that the river won't poison his system."

"Nothing can poison that boy," Gaultry said fiercely. "The Water-god wouldn't dare harm him. But his wound needs to be stitched up and he must get some rest. Both of which you can help him with."

The healer raised her brows at her vehemence, but acquiesced without further argument.

Under Gaultry's watchful eye, the healer sewed up Tullier's wound, an unpleasant business that involved putting sinew-stitches into several different layers of the boy's flesh. The sword had slipped past two ribs before cutting downward into his abdomen. Hesbain glanced doubtfully at the swollen blueness that distended the boy's belly along its right side. Gaultry, doing her best to ignore the woman's incredulity that her attentions were helping anything, held Tullier's head in her lap while the old woman worked. At long last, when the healer had done all she could with his wound, she gave the boy a few gulps of her sleeping draught, stroking his throat to force him to swallow. "I can't do anything more for him," Hesbain said, shaking her head as the boy began to cough and spit. She wiped his mouth with a rag and stood away from the bed. "The rest is prayer."

Gaultry leaned over and listened to Tullier's breath. Though his face seemed no less pale, the color of his lips no longer looked so unnatural against his skin. "You've helped tremendously," she said. "The gods watch him. He will be fine."

"The river's poisons—" Hesbain began.

"Pray for him," Gaultry interrupted. "That should be all he will need." If the first shock to the boy's body had not killed him, his Blood-Imperial would certainly keep him alive. Or so she hoped. She bent to tuck the bedclothes around the chilled body, doubt stabbing her anew now that there was nothing left to do.

"Put his dog with him," Hesbain suggested. "That should warm him." The puppy cowered near the door, afraid of everything. Gaultry caught it by the scruff of its neck and hoisted it onto the bed. "Lie still," she told it, patting its head to encourage it to settle. "Bark if anyone disturbs him," she added hopefully. The puppy, happier by Tullier than it had been by the door, pressed its back to Tullier's side, folded its gangly legs, and closed its eyes, shutting the world out.

Hesbain led Gaultry back to the other room and made her sit on the bed, on the far side from the Sharif. She knelt to pull off the young woman's boots. "The blow broke two of his ribs," she said, massaging Gaultry's feet. "The swordstroke cut the vessels that feed the stomach wall. He bled into his gut. He should be dead."

"The gods be thanked, it will take more to kill Tullier than that." Gaultry felt tremendously tired, along with a returning sense of worry. She hoped Martin was having an interesting time with Sieur Jumery. It seemed like the old man had some understanding of their situation. She herself was still too rattled to puzzle through the implications of the attack that had taken place at the bridge. Their assailants had been Bissanty men, but the black-green magic that had attacked them . . . that had been Tielmaran. Of that she was certain.

But who in Tielmark would serve them such a turn, and who had been the target? Herself? Tullier? Martin? All of them together?

"A spell saved him," Hesbain hazarded, bringing her back from her thoughts.

Gaultry shook her feet gently free of the woman's hands. "Glamour magic saved him." It was not for her to share Tullier's secrets, and the fact of Gaultry's power—Sieur Jumery already knew of that. "From what your master said, I'm guessing you know what I did for Tielmark on Prince's night." She had not touched a mouthful of the woman's draught, but she felt suddenly as though she had swallowed an entire sackful. "Me and my sister both." She lay back on the bed and curled up her legs. It was too warm for covers.

Hesbain stood, a hesitant expression on her homely old face. "We celebrated here when we learned of the Prince's renewed God-pledge. Was it true that you saw the Goddess-Twins?" The old woman looked down, too humble suddenly to meet Gaultry's eye. "There's some who claim that part never happened."

"We saw them," Gaultry said seriously, wishing that she were less tired, more able to think. "Elianté-Huntress and Lady Emiera together. It seems almost beyond belief as I lie here now, but I saw it with my own eyes. The Great Twins make themselves incarnate for us at the end of every cycle, whatever the naysayers may tell you. What a gift to Tielmark." She snuggled sleepily down, even as memory of facing her gods swept her, terrifying and reassuring both. "It was more than awesome," she murmured. "They were so beautiful." A sleepy thought came to her. "But what am I saying? You must have heard what it was like—last time, your master was there to see."

"The Twins are Great," Hesbain answered, reverent.

Gaultry, sighing, closed her eyes. "The Twins are Great."

The touch of Hesbain's hand on her own faded. Gaultry pulled up the faded bedclothes and slipped into a deep, dreamless sleep.

chapter 4

▼

W hen she awoke, she lay stretched at the Sharif's side with her covers kicked down to her ankles. The room, lit only by the thin stripes of moonlight that had found their way through the shutters, seemed stuffy and overly hot.

At her side the Sharif was breathing heavily, the tamarin curled against the woman's cheek like a fur-covered pillow. But it was not the Sharif's noise that had woken her. Gaultry swung her feet over the edge of the bed and lurched upright, stumbling as she groped for her boots. "Ilesbain," she mumbled, toeing at the floor with her naked feet. "Where did you put them?"

Disturbed by her movements, the tamarin opened its luminous eyes and raised its head.

"I wish I had your eyes," she told it. The creature had excellent night vision, and she was tempted to spirit-take from it to heighten her own sense of sight, but now was not the time for such a spell, however falsely comforting it might have felt, invoking that familiar part of her magic, after such a long day of enigmatic puzzles.

She stood quietly for a moment, listening. Identifying no immediate threat that could have caused a noise to wake her, she decided to explore. "Where have my boots gone?" she asked the tamarin. The little creature sat up, indifferent to her plight, and began to groom itself. Gaultry leaned over and touched its brightly striped fur. It was such an odd animal. When she had first seen it, clinging to the bars of the cage in which Lukas Soul-breaker had imprisoned it, those curiously expressive eyes had been filled with pain and rage that had been almost humanly intelligent.

Like Gaultry, the tamarin too had been a pawn in a political game. The Soul-breaker had used the little creature in his magical experiments as he sought the secrets of power.

The Soul-breaker. In a quiet moment like this, it was difficult not to shiver at his memory. She had fought him to a standstill of a sort, but without Tullier, she would never have had the power to defeat him. The cruel master-mage had torn animal spirits and human souls alike, binding them together like exchangeable puzzle pieces. Each new success had further augmented his power, and Gaultry had engaged with him at a moment when it had almost been too late to counter his force.

Gaultry picked up the tamarin and held its warmth close to her, remembering the incandescent light that had shone in the Soul-breaker's face as he had declared himself the reincarnation of Tarrin, White Soldier-god. What drove such a man even to conceive that he might achieve such power? In the rush to free Martin, and then to escape themselves, there had not been time to learn much about the forces that had compelled Lukas Caviedo to strive for such power, and once the Soul-breaker was dead, there had seemed to be little value in pursuing the question. From Lukas's twin sister Columba, Gaultry had learned that a wandering fortune-teller had unleashed Lukas's fledgling ambitions, and even aided him in taking his first step toward power: the seizure of Columba's Blood-Imperial. But his own mad force of character seemed to have been all he'd needed to propel himself forward to imagined apotheosis from there.

She could only wonder what the fortune-teller might have received in return for creating such a monster, a man who could only be killed within a roiling inferno of literal and magical flame. It seemed such a misuse of power—

She cuddled the tamarin once more, and set it on the bed. The tamarin and the little grey monkey had been among the few creatures who had followed their rescuers out of that inferno. Now, after all they'd been through to reach Tielmark, the monkey was dead. She wondered if the tamarin missed its companionship.

"Go back to sleep," she told the little creature. "You're safe here tonight, and I'll make do without my boots."

Next door, Tullier was asleep, lying on his good side, with the puppy—also sound asleep and doing poor duty as a guardian—clutched in his arms. Gaultry, gladdened to see both of them resting peacefully, eased the door shut.

She padded, barefoot, along the darkened hallway, wondering whether Martin was asleep, or still awake and conversing with old Sieur Jumery. Awake, she guessed, sharing stories of battle and glory on the western border. For all his doddering, the old man had seemed keen to press him for information about the land where his grandson was performing service.

At the top of the stairs, she looked down the dark well of the steps and paused to listen to the house. She was grateful for the old man's hospitality, even if he made her feel uneasy. She did not like to think how Tullier and the Sharif would have fared in rough beds culled from some hayrack in Soiscroix—or, worse, inside a cold lock-house, if the justice seekers from the bridge had had their way.

Tomorrow they might reach Soiscroix. And maybe Princeport the day after. Then she would be back in the Prince's court, where she did not understand the private battles and alliances among those in power, and where she must, somehow, learn to serve her Prince, lest she see him struck from power.

Outside a night bird called. She padded down a few steps to the landing. The hall beneath her, the house around her, were comfortably quiet. After the day's turmoil, the quietness of the ancient house was refreshing. She took a deep breath, taking in the odors of the sweet rushes strewn on the floor below, the waxy smell of the well-rubbed paneling, the hint of used leather and dog and sweat that lay beneath the more pleasant scents. Moonlight streamed down through a single glassed-in window over the landing. She stood in an island of milky light, dappled with blue and red diamonds from the colored patterns in the mullions.

Outside the moon was heavy, full with the ending of the month, the promise of the moon days ahead and then the new month. The moon of Rios Sword-god, in his aspect as Early Harvester.

It pleasures me, the old man had said, *in Rios's name, to offer you my hospitality.*

What did he mean by that? Rios was a god more commonly invoked by those with a grievance than by those offering hospitality. Staring at the glowing whiteness of the moon, Gaultry reviewed all that had passed since she'd entered Sieur Jumery's domains. If the Ingoleurs had fallen from influence after old Princess Corinne's wedding, it was likely that they, or the lord they were sworn to, had made some dealings with the Bissanties—though the fact that they had not been stripped of their estate argued that these dealings had not risen to the level of treason.

Further, Sir Jumery had offered this welcome to her alone, and not to their party generally. What did that mean? He had spoken of knowing Tamsanne, but what grievance could he have there? Tamsanne had returned to Arleon Forest immediately after Princess Corinne's wedding— that much, at least, Gaultry knew of her grandmother's history. What grievance could the man nurse against Tamsanne so strong that in his dotage he would invoke the Sword-god on her granddaughter?

Unable to answer her own question, Gaultry descended the last of the stairs, anxious to find Martin and learn of all that had gone forward as she slept.

The passage beneath the stairs led deep into the house. The rushes strewn on the floor crushed softly underfoot. Gaultry passed two doors, and then a third, with the weak light of a single candle shining from behind it. A woman's voice reached her, then a child's. Ahead, impressively carved double doors barred her way. A bright crack of light shone between them, feebly lighting the passage. As she raised her hand to the knob, a loud laugh broke out from its other side, startling her, followed by a voice she seemed to recognize.

"You've got the Great Twelve's luck, Stalkerman. The mob will lynch you one day, I'm sure. I could hardly credit the wild stories I heard, riding into Soiscroix—I had to come and see for myself. What possessed you? They've no love of wolves like yourself in this neck of the country, man."

"If it please you," their host's voice interrupted, sounding firmer than Gaultry would have expected in the shadow of that booming, confident laugh. "Your Grace will address my guest with respect. He has had a very long day."

"A long day?" The other laughed. "Mine has been a long day. Him— he's had a long month, more like, and then some. Where did the Sha Muira men take you, Martin? What did you have to pledge them to break free? Imagine—all those quarreling toads, falling over themselves in Princeport for recent news, and here I am, the first to find you."

"You're looking well, Haute-Tielmark," Martin's voice broke in. "Not that I like your news. And what you're doing here instead of marshaling men on your own border, you've yet to tell me."

Gaultry sank against the wooden panel, completely astonished. Of all the people she would have expected or desired to meet on the road between here and Princeport, Victor Clement, Duke of Haute-Tielmark, was far down the list. A gigantic, gold-bearded bear of a man, he controlled the western province of Tielmark with firm, capable hands. Too firm, some whispered. If it were not for the fact that the duke's lands lay on Tielmark's most vulnerable border, that he needed constant support from the rest of Tielmark to hold the Lanai at bay, many questioned whether he would continue to pay Benet the tithes he owed him. Many more still wondered about his constant conferences and meetings with Bissanty bordermen. Haute-Tielmark claimed to be Benet's man, but he had worked closely with Lord Edan Heiratikus, the Prince's late and unlamented Chancellor, and his actions, whether inadvertently or not, could have prevented the renewal of Benet's God-pledge.

She did not know what could have brought the Duke here—unless he had been the force behind the attack at the bridge, a disturbing thought indeed. In the dark of the hallway, staring at the door, Gaultry considered that bleak possibility. The attack had combined Bissanty and Tielmaran elements, and Haute-Tielmark was a man who stood, in a very real way, poised between those powers. She did not like their prospects for reaching Princeport if these suspicions had foundation in truth. Haute-Tielmark was a seasoned campaigner. If he intended to prevent them from reaching Princeport, he would have arrived at Sieur Ingoleur's with a force sufficient to successfully execute his plan.

"You'll not believe what the border is like this year," the Duke said. A creaking noise suggested some poor stick of furniture had been subjected to his massive bulk. "It's not just a few wild boys come tearing down from the mountains on donkeys, looking to steal a few cattle because they're piss poor and young and hot to meet a bride price. It's whole tribes, led by seasoned war-leaders. After the defeat the Bissanties wreaked on them in their summer pastures, they're desperate to rebuild their herds. The right word is that the King of Far Mountain crossed the four massifs to direct the campaign, eager to redress the family dishonor his son-in-law brought, in the Bissanty defeat in the High Pastures. This isn't like last summer, when Tielmark's finest could while away half their summer in wine-houses, traveling west, and it made no difference to those at the front whether they arrived or not.

"And speaking on that, Stalkingman, after all I've told you tonight, I'm expecting you to clear business in Princeport and haul your tail out west as soon as Benet will release you. There's nothing for you in Prince-port—just a passel of fools who've played games with words for so long they've forgotten they have the power to act."

"What do you mean?"

The Duke's chair squeaked under another abrupt movement. "The Prince's court is too busy fighting itself to bother themselves with the war, and this is not the summer to play that game. One half accuses the other of conspiring with the Bissanties—the other makes the same accusations back. Both sides whisper that there's a new plan alive to drive the Prince from his throne.

"All they care about is raising their own stature with Benet. What does it matter to them if the western woods are being overrun, if my people are being savaged? There's so much strife in Princeport that Benet's even delayed sending his knights west." The Duke snorted. "He needs to whip his peers in line. Not half the dukes and counts have provided their full levy of men. Great Twins! We need Benet in the west himself, and not just his men. It's his border, as much as mine. I came east to tell him so, for all the good it did me. Can't hold it by myself, and I've lost patience with risking my sons' blood—and my own—trying. More fool I. That bitch Dervla tried to get me served a writ as traitor for petitioning the Prince to lead the army himself. As if his father and every Prince before him hasn't done just that!"

Gaultry pricked up her ears. In her own experience, Dervla of Prince-port had never seemed satisfied with her position as High Priestess. Gaul-try and her sister both, south-border girls without court connections, had often felt the edge of her resentment. But the High Priestess had always shown respect to the most powerful among the court's inner circle. Some-thing must have changed for her to dare to go after such a powerful man so openly.

"Dervla has convinced Benet that the Bissanties are fixed on breaking his rule by corrupting the Common Brood prophecy," the Duke went on. "As evidenced by their abduction of you, Martin Stalker, and by what they sent their Sha Muira men to do to that other Brood-woman and her children. For all I know, it's true—they certainly went to enough trouble to grab you. But even if she's right, that doesn't mean that the fighting in the west is of no significance! 'Briern-bold settled the matter of holding our borders by force of arms two hundred years past,' Dervla-bitch told me. 'The Bissanties won't get at us that way again.' How that helps us when we have Lanai tribesmen raiding as far east as Arciers she wouldn't tell me!

"Prophecy!" The Duke snorted again. "The Bissanties may be plotting to break Tielmark by twisting our prophecies, but it's not stopping them from trying to break us with the Lanai as well."

"Prophecy and the gods rule Tielmark." That was Sieur Jumery.

The duke paused. When he spoke again, his tone was more measured, his rising temper damped. "I'm a pious man," he said. "I believe that Elianté and Emiera watch my actions. The Goddess-Twins stand at my border as well as in Princeport's halls, and I am beholden to Benet and all of Prince Clarin's line who have maintained the link that holds them there. But a strong Prince must have the confidence to ride out to protect his outlands, not just his center. Instead, Benet has called all the Brood-blood to Princeport, and now they're strutting his halls, arguing about the meaning of power. All well and good, if you don't have a country to run and a border war!"

"My grandmère is of the Brood," Martin said dryly. "As am I."

"You're a fighting man," the Duke said impatiently. "And your grandma Melaudiere I can respect. But some of those court spiders . . . They want the power of ruling Benet, and the rest is excuses to justify their encroachments."

"Perhaps the Brood thinks Benet needs help rebuilding his power," Martin said. "There has been talk that it is time to raise Tielmark from a mere Principality to a Kingship. Indeed, that is the very heart of the Brood-prophecy that has ruled myself and my kin since Princess Corinne's days."

"Benet has to make his own power!" the Duke shouted. "Gabbling old women can't stop Lanai tribesmen from burning my villages."

If he had more to say, he did not get the chance to say it. The door opened, so unexpectedly that Gaultry, who by now was tightly pressed against it, almost fell inside. Recovering awkwardly, she found herself staring into Jumery Ingoleur's watery blue eyes. He stood unpleasantly close to her, his breath a little heavy, his hand a skinny claw on the door's handle. The stillness in his eyes unnerved her. He had known she would be there when he pulled the door open. "Good evening, demoiselle," he greeted her. "Why don't you join us?"

"I fell asleep," she blurted, trying to explain herself. "Then I thought I heard something—"

"That would have been me and my horsemen," Victor of Haute-Tielmark cut in. He was sitting in one of a pair of delicately carved chairs, a goblet of wine in his hand, his great legs sprawled out before him like fallen tree trunks. Though he was every inch the confident bear of a man that Gaultry remembered, he was also, even to her frequently fashion-blind eye, oddly dressed, somewhere between silk court equipage and leather riding gear, his gold hair and thick beard half elaborately pressed into chevalier's locks, half disheveled by the rigors of a hard ride. The metal edge of the military baldric he wore strapped across his chest had torn the silk threads of the finely embroidered stag head on the front of his tunic. He heaved himself to his feet and made a half-bow. "Uncouth of me to have woken you. Brought you down in bare feet, I see." He grinned at her, not unpleasantly, revealing his crooked canines.

"Good evening, Your Grace," Gaultry acknowledged the Duke with an awkward curtsy. She curled her naked toes into the rushes, embarrassed. "I could not find my boots."

Martin, standing at the back of the room, came forward and reached for her hand. Behind his impassive expression, she sensed he was ill at ease.

"The Duke heard rumors in Soiscroix that piqued his interest," he said mordantly. His voice betrayed little of the nervous tension she could feel running in his body. "The number of men who died at Sizor's Bridge has grown tenfold. Rumor has a mile of road buckling as well as the bridge. Haute-Tielmark rode out here to discover for himself what part of the talk was truth."

"How many men did he bring?" Gaultry asked. Wishing she had the Sharif's ability to communicate without speech, she let Martin tuck her hand under his arm and draw her into the room. Whatever her argument had been with him this afternoon, just at this moment, his presence at her side was deeply comforting.

"He said six."

"Six and two boys to rub the horses down. They're in the stables now," the Duke offered, "admiring the Stalkingman's corpses. It's late, and my men are not known for their restraint. My apologies if their clatter woke you."

Sieur Jumery's meeting room was lined with time-scarred oak paneling. Its large hearth had been swept and scrubbed clean for the summer. The mantelpiece decoration showed the motif of a sword with scales balanced to either side. A well-used room, if a little spare and empty. A folding traveling desk stood upended beside a sagging sofa. Two delicately carved wooden chairs—one of the pair creaked plaintively as the Duke retook his seat—had been arranged next to a small table. The men had been drinking wine before her arrival, from silver-chased goblet cups and a matching decanter. Though everything in the room was expensively made and had once been very fine, now it was threadbare and a little shabby. The mood within the room seemed even less friendly than Gaultry had been able to intuit from the passage. A trio of massive dogs lay on the hearthstones of the empty fireplace, quiescent but alert. One raised its head as she entered, studying her with suspicious eyes. Sieur Jumery, leaving Gaultry's side, crossed to the hearth and touched the animal with his foot. The dog laid its head back on its paws and pretended it had not moved. Even from across the room Gaultry could sense its fear-based loyalty.

Without waiting for permission she sat on the sofa, touching Martin's arm so he would sit at her side. "I suppose you've had a look in the stable yourself?"

"After what I heard in Soiscroix, I had no choice but to see for myself." The Duke stroked his beard with a red-skinned, hamlike hand. "According to the word in town, a fire-haired witch rose up and broke the bridge into tinder, then turned and set her spells on the unfortunate man who had tried to stop her. It sounded most spectacular. And the witch's henchman—something in his style made me think of a man I'd seen in battle myself."

"Those men's deaths are not on our heads," Gaultry said. She thought back to the awful moment when her fear for Tullier had changed into dreadful recognition of what the man was about to do. "Someone sent those men to ambush us."

"I was told that one man turned his blade and slit his own belly," the Duke said. "Something must have made him do that."

"Believe what you like," Gaultry said. The secret of Tullier's imperial blood was not for casual sharing—and certainly, not with a man of dubious loyalties like Haute-Tielmark.

"Sieur Ingoleur." She turned to their host. "I have not yet had a chance to thank you for all the help you've given us."

"Dear lady," the old man replied courteously. "It is no more than my duty thus to serve you. Allow me to pour you some wine. Your friends—they are safely resting? I trust they are comfortable?"

"As much as can be expected."

"Let me pour for you." His old hands trembled on the decanter as he set a fresh goblet before her. He watched as she took her first sip. The wine tasted a little past its prime, a metallic savor dominating. She tried not to look at the old man, standing near enough that she could smell the musty odor of his robes. "Red wine for a red lady," he murmured, topping up her goblet before she could demur. "Tamsanne drank this very wine when she came to this house."

"I'm empty here." Haute-Tielmark banged his goblet down, startling the old man so he drew a little back. "Lady Blas can drink after she's finished answering my questions. I want to know who she thinks set up the attack."

Gaultry took a long sip of the metallic wine, annoyed at the interruption. Her mind was in a whirl. Tamsanne had been in this very house? "The rumors you heard in Soiscroix were exaggerated, but it was a serious and well-laid trap. I think whoever set those Bissanty soldiers on us planned for me to use my own magic, thus triggering the spell that was laid upon the bridge-binding vine. Now, if you want to talk about powerful magic, there was a serious spell."

Victor of Haute-Tielmark held his cup up to Sieur Jumery to be refilled. Raising it to his lips, he threw it at one gulp into his throat, and held up the cup again. When Gaultry had first met the Duke, he had been downing mugs of raw ale in the noisy public room of an inn on the Bissanty border. There he had been among his own men, in his own land. The power and confidence that had radiated from him had filled the room—at the time it was rather intimidating to Gaultry, for whom he had been searching, with orders to take her prisoner.

"Bissanty men, a Bissanty plan," he said, swirling the fresh wine in the cup. "There's an easy line to follow."

Gaultry shook her head. "I must differ. The magic that shattered the bridge came from Elianté. It wasn't Bissanty—or mine either," she added, remembering belatedly that she had offered no explicit denial of the charge of bridge-breaking.

"This is hardly your business," Martin broke in. "We've answered to Sieur Ingoleur for our actions. You can ride up in the middle of the night and pound on his door demanding to see Bissanty corpses, but you have no right to question us."

The Duke laughed. "I'm not questioning you. I rode here to discover who was fool enough to have the nerve to try to stop you. They're more hot for your return at court than either of you seem to imagine."

"What do you mean?" Gaultry asked.

"Court games rot the mind for real business." The Duke's manner grew abruptly serious. "I've no appetite myself to play the fool. If immortal Elianté and Emiera became incarnate to bless Benet and his marriage, I'm a man to honor their wishes.

"My grandfather bore witness to the Great Twins' descent to earth, and my father with him. I've been fool enough already, thank you, letting politics stand between me and that blessing at this turn of the cycle." The Duke turned his face to stare into the fire, hiding his expression. When he spoke again, something in him had hardened. "I could have looked into the faces of my gods," he said. "Instead I listened to the wiles of an unrighteous man, and I missed my chance.

"This summer will be a turning point for Tielmark—the troubles on my own borders tell me that. But the court players want only to interpret the omens in a way that will enhance their own power. They won't accept that Benet must be a power unto himself."

He was standing now, staring down at Gaultry, solemnly watching the candlelight play on her face. "Too many of them at court hate you," he growled. "They hate you because you were the one to stand on the Prince's altar and talk to the gods, and then when you descended from that altar, you didn't pretend that the Great Twins had annointed you as his sole trusted advisor. You would have been better served at court if you'd lied and told Benet that the gods spoke only through you, and now you alone knew what it was they wanted. They would have understood that."

Gaultry shook her head helplessly. "The Goddess-Twins were there that day for one thing only: to witness the marriage of the Prince. It was chance, almost, that I was the one to stand before them to announce the Prince's bride."

Sieur Jumery made a soft sound, deep in his throat.

"I want you to understand me clearly." The Duke rose to his feet, and laid his hand over the stag's head on his breast. "My greatest grand-sire was the first lord to vow himself to Clarin, when Tielmark was first struggling to free itself from Bissanty. In this day, I have given my vows to Benet. I have lived outside of court long enough that I can recognize you for what you are: a weapon in my Prince's hand. The man who tries to break you tries also to break my Prince."

Incredulity swept giddily through her body, stronger than the wine. The most powerful of the Prince's dukes, Victor of Haute-Tielmark, had come riding through the night, soiling his silks and spoiling his freshly coifed hair, because—

"You're here to protect me?" she said faintly, setting down her cup. "I'm not Benet's only weapon. Martin is too. So are all the Brood-blood."

The Duke snorted. "They haven't proved it by me. Why should the Brood be trusted? Their fate may be bound to the Prince's, but that does not make them love him—or each other. Dervla would have had you tried in absentia for treason if the Prince had permitted it."

Gaultry's mind, already flustered, now staggered. She had known that the High Priestess disliked her. But an accusation of treason? "Great Twins! What's the base for such a charge?" Her eyes flickered to Sieur Jumery. Was this why he had treated her with such wary reserve?

"You protected the assassin who sought the Prince's death."

"Tullier was never supposed to kill the Prince," Gaultry said hotly. "The Emperor planned for Tullier himself to die—"

Martin elbowed her in the side. The Duke shot him an ominous look, but Martin only shook his head, not at all intimidated. "The truth is more complex than Dervla will allow, and all will be explained in its due time and place. Gaultry protected the boy. We are confident Benet will thank her for that. But that is for Benet to decide, not Dervla."

The duke smiled, his crooked canines fierce above his golden beard. "Indeed. And after six weeks of Dervla's working at him, I'm sure Benet is in a happy frame of mind to receive your lady's explanations in good faith."

"By your own words, we must trust Benet will make the right decision," Martin replied. "If you truly believe in Benet, you must believe also that Dervla will not prevail."

"She will be punished for the evil she has brought forth," Sieur Jumery said, setting down the decanter. "Justice will out."

For a swift moment, Gaultry was unclear who he was consigning to retribution—herself or Dervla.

Haute-Tielmark caught the same inflection. "Words of truth, good Sieur Justice. Where they be aptly applied." Antagonism charged the air between the two men: the harsh, towering master of the western lands and the frail old man with his sly manners. As a contest of wills, it was decidedly unequal. In no more than a moment, the old man dropped his gaze. "A High Priestess set against her own Prince's will." His wrinkled hands arranged, and then rearranged, the decanter and two cups that were left on the table. "A melancholy day, when Tielmark comes to that."

Sensing capitulation, the Duke's smile deepened. "Words of truth," he repeated. "The gods watch us, and justice will out. Great Twins protect us, that we bear no sin we might hesitate to present them."

The old man would not look at him. "As Your Grace pleases."

"Your guests have traveled a great distance," the Duke said. "Tonight, however high Rios's moon stands in the sky, they might be spared the bleak judgment of the Sword-god's ways." Plucking the decanter from the old man's fingers, Haute-Tielmark sloshed himself a final refill. "These people must return safely to Princeport, and the sooner the better. The girl owes duty to Prince Benet—and her man is dire needed on my border. Tonight my men will guard their doors; tomorrow I will outfit them for travel and see them swiftly on their way.

"I would spare them more words tonight. By Benet High Prince's name, be kind, good Sieur. I would beg that you accommodate myself and my own men this night, that I may more briskly complete my arrangements come morning."

The old man's shoulders slumped deeper. "My house is humble," he said. "It has been many moons since we have supported so large a party of guests. But all will be done as you require." Some deep strain had moved between the men—some deep warning. Gaultry could not conceive what battle they had played. She knew only that Sieur Jumery had been bested.

The Duke swung back his wine and set his goblet down, his hand steady despite the massive volume of alcohol he'd consumed. "I would have my men called to me."

"So it please your Grace." Sieur Jumery tugged at the bell pull by the mantel. Deep in the house, an answering bell resounded. The Duke's men soon came tramping in from the stable. Like their master, they wore an odd assortment of riding leathers buckled on over finery. They shot Gaultry and Martin many curious looks as they accompanied them upstairs, through the moonlight of the window over the landing, and along the quiet upstairs halls to the rooms the old man had assigned them. Sieur Jumery, stony-faced, led the way, carrying the lantern.

"If it so pleases your Grace," he said, "I would have you share the grand chamber over the court, along with the Stalkingman. My women have not had time to air another room."

"I would not have you put out," the Duke answered smoothly. As Gaultry opened the door to her room and stepped in alone, he arched a brow and smiled. "Not bedding together?" He turned to Martin and grinned, "See, now I'll have all your news before it arrives at court."

"Good night, Your Grace." Gaultry pulled the door hastily to, her cheeks burning. What good were the chaste relations that Martin and she had so carefully maintained, if everyone already believed they were keeping consort?

Outside the door, the Duke's guard noisily settled himself.

Across the room, the Sharif's eyes were open, brimming with questions. Gaultry shook her head. *Go to sleep*, she told the woman. *Go back to sleep if you can. We have a surprise ally, and all is well.* She touched the Sharif gently on her bandaged shoulder. *I'll try to explain in the morning.*

In the morning, when they were out from under this harsh judging moon, and out of this strange house.

▼

chapter 5

Gautri." The call invaded her dreams, once, twice; then again, more urgently. *Wake up, Gautri.*

Humid air filled the bedchamber's predawn darkness, dampening the sheets and the covers. Gaultry rolled on her side, uncomfortable, and pushed the tamarin's tail out of her face. She thought she had been having a bad dream—she was sure she'd been having a bad dream. The Sharif's exhortation had broken its hold.

"What is it?" she groused, pushing sweaty tangles of hair from her face.

Aneitha.

"Great Twins." Gaultry, unpleasantly, came fully awake. She had not given the big panther a moment's thought since the debacle at the bridge. "What's wrong?"

The Sharif understood Gaultry's tone better than her words. *She fell into a black place, full of sharp sticks. She can't climb out. She is giving herself to panic. Gautri, if you could hear her cries . . .*

"Wonderful," Gaultry said wearily. From the strained look on the woman's face, there was only one thing to be done. *I'll go and get her out myself. Just tell me where she is.*

Her call is loud. Carefully moving her arm, the Sharif pointed: westward, and a little north. *That's where I hear her. She must be close. I couldn't hear her otherwise.*

Inside the old man's hedges? Gaultry asked.

The Sharif didn't have an answer.

Tell her not to hurt herself while I look for her.
She will not listen to reason for long.

Which meant Gaultry had to hurry. She rose and splashed some water from the sideboard's basin on her face. Behind her, the tamarin chirped. He was sitting on the chest at the foot of the bed, next to Gaultry's neatly laid out boots and short-stockings.

"I'm glad one of us watched where Hesbain put these." She shushed the little animal out of the way and picked up her stockings, which she had no memory of the woman having removed. "Now stay here while I attempt not to volunteer for the meat that breaks Aneitha's fast." The tamarin chittered and ran back to the Sharif's pillow.

Be careful, the Sharif told her, as Gaultry sheathed her knife in her belt. *The pit that trapped Aneitha is big enough to catch you too.*

Gods in me, I'll try, Gaultry answered. She sketched the goddesses' sign, and made for the door.

The duke's sentry, a young soldier with rumpled, wheat-colored hair, was awake, and even something approaching alert, the moment she opened the door. He scrambled up, anxiously blinking. He looked tired and disheveled. "Lady Blas. Where are you going?" He fumbled with the ties on the front of his tunic, conscientiously attempting to tidy himself.

"Stay here," Gaultry said. "Guard my companions. I'll return shortly." She walked hastily past and on down the hall. Company was the last thing she needed on her hunt for Aneitha.

Outside, the humid summer landscape was saturated with mist-filled light. The full moon, in descent but still well above the horizon, looked very small. It had lost its luminescence to the fast greying light of the dawn sky. Smoke from the kitchen chimney indicated that someone had risen to stoke the kitchen fires, but between the early hour and the midsummer holiday, the fields were unusually empty. Gaultry crossed a vacant, close-cropped paddock, heading in the direction the Sharif had indicated, then skirted a small orchard. At the far side of the first field beyond that she paused and took bearings.

From under its veil of morning dew, the heady moisture-rich scent of the soil rose all around her, refreshed and promise-filled. The field had been recently cut and the hay raked in. The hay stubble had a dense and healthy look, already with pale green shoots rising amid the darker, scythe-cut growth. This field at least would have yielded an excellent harvest of green-cut hay for the midsummer fair. If Sieur Jumery's house was slowly sinking into ruin, it was not because his land had failed.

The old man's holdings were expansive. Gentle rolling hills, some wooded, some tilled, stretched far away to the blue horizon. The nearest outbuilding was more than a mile away, obscured by mist and indeterminate as either cottage or cowshed. Gaultry could not see any obvious hedge or marker that might indicate the limit of the old man's holdings.

As dawn quickened, birds rose from their nests, creating a rousing cacophony. The sheer volume of happy waking songs made Gaultry doubt that Aneitha could be anywhere nearby, but she had to trust the Sharif's judgment. Determined to relax and focus, to fall into the rhythm of the hunt, she made herself stand and listen.

Weeks had passed since she'd last hunted alone. So far from her home in Arleon Forest, many of the bird cries were unknown to her, and at first all she could hear was confused chattering. Then, in a pleasingly familiar outfolding, she began to recognize distinctive voices. A jay. A bevy of hedge-sparrows. Mixed in with the unknown bird cries were the songs she had heard in the deep of the forest since before she had learned to speak.

A vital warmth spread through Gaultry's limbs, as though the dawn sun had already crested the horizon and touched her. Her ear began searching for harsh or disparate notes, something apart from the happy waking chatter. Her indecision and her concerns for her companions seemed suddenly far away. The land pressed on her, filling her lungs, her ears, her throat. She felt herself merging into her own element, as if the land spoke to her through all of her senses, pulling her ever deeper.

She bent and seized a clump of dirt. "Huntress Elianté," she intoned, crumbling it, "I commit this hunt to you."

The smells of the earth and the trees flooded her, and she listened ever more deeply. There was something there, something . . . Before she knew what had caught her attention, she'd turned toward a tall line of poplars. The trailing row of trees beckoned, three fields away, slightly over to her left, farther than she had imagined from the Sharif's brief description. She fell into an even-paced jog, hurrying toward it.

High in the poplars' branches, three crows perched. Beaks agape, their wings were unfolded in stiff black-feathered mantles.

Gaultry broke into a run.

After two fields, a thin mewling sound reached her and she knew she had guessed aright. She ran faster, stumbling over unkempt tussocks of grass. She topped a mounded earth work, softened by years of scraping by plows, and came into one final field. The ground here was fallow and dense, unseeded and unplowed for two years or longer.

Beyond the poplars, an overgrown hedgerow blocked Gaultry's way forward. From the twists of the land, it would not be the High Road that lay beyond it. It had the appearance of an ancient property line, long since overrun. Aneitha was trapped somewhere on the far side. The panther's cries sounded bewildered and strained. "Shut up!" Gaultry called, searching for a gap. "I'll be right through, so shut up!"

The cat, whether it heard her or not, continued to cry.

Gaultry stopped to catch her breath and gazed up at the crows. "Where's the break in the hedge?" The hedgerow was heavily barbed with hawthorn and sloe, both shrubs densely-boughed, ancient, and bristling with inch-long spines. It would not be possible to force a way through. Craning in both directions along the hedge, she could not see a gap in either direction, or even a thin spot through which Aneitha might have squeezed her narrow feline body. She stared at the crows again. If only one would come near to her! Crows were possessed of a native curiosity that made them easy to ensnare with magic. If she trapped a crow and borrowed its spirit, she was sure it could lead her to a break in the hedge.

Sadly, Aneitha's cries kept the birds wary.

She stared once again around the field, absorbing the possibilities. If the hedge was overgrown, the field was similarly wild. It had grown rife with sweet summer plants, still heavily laden with a veil of shining dew. A broad dark trail, the mark of her own passage, broke the silvered surface across the field's center. She studied the field more closely. As well as her clumsy, obviously marked course, there was a multitude of more delicate trails. Places where rabbits had passed, or other small animals.

Thinking on the rabbits, she moved closer to the hedge. Rabbits would likely have created a hole somewhere. She wouldn't need a spell to find that. She scanned the field for the most obvious tracks, and it was not long before the patterns revealed themselves. The most trafficked trails led to scattered burrows on the east edge of the field, but in two places those tracks crossed to the hedge for cover.

Gaultry found gaps at the hedgerow end of both of those trails. The first was hopelessly tiny. She was not even sure that it reached all the way through. The second tunneled through to an unwelcomingly small window of turf. If she was willing to crawl on her belly, it gave every appearance that it would take her through.

"Gods in me, Aneitha, how did you get yourself into this?" She studied the ground for signs that the cat might have used this hole itself. "You've been howling to the Sharif this whole damn time—why don't you tell me what's going on?"

She lay down on her stomach, securing her dagger so she would not lose it somewhere in the hedge. The hole was so low she had to press her cheek to the earth start her entry, and it narrowed down so quickly that she had to back out and try again, this time with only one arm extended. She thrust herself unenthusiastically forward, more hemmed in and trapped with every inch. Twigs and thorns snarled in her hair and dragged painfully at her exposed ear. The hedge was little more than two yards wide, but it felt much broader. When her extended hand finally clawed at open air rather than thorns she could not help but release a small moan of relief.

Then, as she wriggled sufficiently free of the hedge to get a good look at what lay beyond, the sound died in her throat.

The hedge surrounded a narrow strip of land, far longer than it was wide. Unlike the fallow field outside the hedge, it was meticulously tended, the turf as smooth as the bowling field she had once seen in the palace gardens in Princeport. Before her stood two rough pillars of stone, between them, a bleached white table-stone with a bowl-like cavity carved into its surface.

Beyond the stones rose the long, gentle curve of an earthwork barrow, taking up most of the enclosed strip.

Gaultry scrambled the rest of the way out of the hedge. Brushing herself down, she nervously eyed the velvety green hump of the barrow. She had encountered such things often enough in the south, though seldom shrouded with the secrecy of this site. They were ancient remnants of the wandering tribes, the people who had inhabited Tielmark from before the time the land had yielded to Bissanty rule, deep in the mists of history. The tribes had worshipped all the Great Twelve, and spoken to them directly through Rhasan magic—the ancient mystical symbols that bound past to present, present to future, man to god, man to animal. Although the wanderers had lived without fixed borders, they had built massive earthworks and erected crude stone temples to the gods' honor, testament to their strength. Gaultry, who had been touched three times in her life by true Rhasan magery, could not quite comprehend why a people who had commanded such strong magical powers had ever yielded to Bissanty rule, but that they had done so was a proven matter of history.

Some of the barrows and temples had been abandoned for centuries, others overbuilt. A few, places of great power, were still in use, their connection to the past unbroken. The temple of Emiera in Paddleways, the village nearest Gaultry's home in Arleon Forest, had a crypt that dated to back to the wanderers. Other sites still were scoured and cleaned according to ancient cycles: seven years, twelve, twenty, fifty. Some even longer.

When she was a small child, a stone near her grandmother's cottage had reached the summer of its ritual scouring. She had a hazy recollection of Tamsanne's displeasure at the local farmwives' intrusion on her forest demesnes. Her memory of the scouring itself was clearer: dirty water running down the rough sides of the stone as it emerged, coal-black, incised with a network of scarlike lines, from beneath two score years' of forest debris.

Unlike that stone singleton, the stones before her had obviously been recently treated. The center stone was bleached and pale, the outriders bare of staining vegetation. The cavity in the center stone brimmed with dark reddish liquid. Gaultry recognized it: treated blood, mixed with herbs so it would not clot and thicken.

She would have to free Aneitha and retreat as quickly as possible. These places were not often sacrally interdicted, but casual visitors were seldom welcome.

Aneitha's noise made her easy to find, along with the logic of the pit into which she had fallen. There was only one break in the hedge, on the far side from where Gaultry had entered. The pit had been positioned a little inside that entrance, where anyone who did not know it was there would blunder in. Gaultry moved cautiously closer. Dense turf covered the network of branches and straw that had been laid to cover the pit. From the state of the turf, it was evident that this trap had been constructed many years past. The point where the grass made the transition from pit-cover to solid ground was indistinguishable. She was not surprised Aneitha had been caught.

As she neared, the edge crumbed beneath her feet, demonstrating exactly how well concealed it remained. Scrambling energetically, her heart in her mouth, she threw herself backward. From below, the panther howled as the new sheet of falling earth landed. Gaultry inched forward with heightened vigilance and peered warily over the edge. All she could see of Aneitha was a dark, earth-covered shape with wild, fear-maddened eyes. Spying Gaultry, the panther snarled ferociously, newly frightened by the apparent assault. Gaultry, drawing back from the edge, took a deep gulp of air.

The pit had been built to kill or mangle. Gaultry could not imagine how Aneitha had survived the initial fall. The "sharp sticks" of the Sharif's description were barbed spears with murderous rusting heads, pointing skyward. A god's luck had been with Aneitha that she had managed to drop in among them without being fatally impaled. As it was—one hind leg was wedged and trapped between a pair of closely seated spears. Gaultry swore. To release that leg, she was going to have to actually go down into the pit. The drop was not so far—little more than twice a tall man's height. If the panther's leg had not been wedged, it would have been well capable of gathering itself and jumping out.

"Why didn't we leave you in Bissanty?" Gaultry's fright intensified as she dithered at the pit's head. "Damn you to Achavell for getting into this mess."

The cat had calmed a little at her withdrawal. Now it was meowing, simultaneously pathetic and terrifying. "The Sharif better be telling you not to bite me," Gaultry told it anxiously. "You'd better not bite me if I come down there."

One side of the pit had partially fallen in when the cat had broken through the pit's cover. Gaultry circled to that side and swung her legs over the half-collapsed lip of earth.

Then, praying to all the Great Twelve, she released the edge, and slid downward.

At the bottom, when she tried to stand, she discovered that the loose earth on the pit's floor made it almost impossible to balance. She cut open her hand against one of the spear shafts when she stupidly used it to support herself. The cat was a body length away, its eyes unfriendly. "Aneitha," she called raggedly. "Good cat. Just keep calm—" She touched the tawny fur with a tentative dart of magic, trying to guess how it would react when she approached. "Keep calm, good cat—" Aneitha turned wild yellow eyes toward the young woman, and snarled.

"Gentle, gentle—" Gaultry crawled a little closer. "Just keep calm, gentle, and I'll get that leg free. . . ."

The cat shivered, and put its head on its front paws. Gaultry struggled not to cough as the scent of its strong musk hit her. At last, the creature was close enough to touch—or to bite. It mewled again. Its claws were sheathed, fangs covered. Gaultry cautiously buried one hand in the fur at the crest of its spine, trying to avoid its head. With the floor so treacherous, freeing the animal would not be enough. She would have to spirit-take, subsume its strength, and then drag its comatose body out. All without giving it a chance to tear her throat out.

She didn't want to threaten the animal, but she needed a firm grip for the spell. She drew her other arm around Aneitha's forequarters, trembling as she felt the muscular body quiver and bunch. *Ah, Elianté, protect me!* she prayed.

Then she summoned the spirit-taking.

At the first tickle of magic, Aneitha panicked and reared. Gaultry, completely terrified, threw open a channel and brutally vacuumed the great cat's spirit inward, abandoning any effort to soothe it in the desperate need to subdue it before it impaled either her or itself on the barbed spears. For one agonizing moment, she clung like a half-unseated rider to the great animal's shoulders, not sure that she could take the creature's spirit fast enough to save them both. One of the spears trapping the cat's leg came unseated, and Aneitha, throwing her body forward, almost impaled them on another spear. Then the spell licked open, like fire consuming tinder. She wrenched the cat-spirit deeper. The great muscles slackened. As the balance of power shifted between then, Gaultry gained enough strength to push the animal's body down into the loose earth, subduing it. *Oh quiet, Aneitha, quiet,* she told it. *Everything's fine, everything's right.*

The panther-spirit twisted in the narrow space she opened for it in her body, too panicked for the moment to try to be clever. Gaultry, who had some familiarity with spirit-taking from house cats, stood up with the appalling realization that this animal was exponentially more clever, more powerful, more keen to break free. She was not confident that she had either the strength or the wiles to hold it, once it stopped panicking and began to scheme for freedom. *Good cat, Aneitha,* she told it. She only had to keep control for as long as it took to crawl out of the pit. *I'm not stopping your strength, I'm just borrowing—*

She tried to make the big cat feel the fur of its own body, the warmth of its own flesh, through her fingertips; tried to reassure it that its body was still there, still softly breathing.

None of which strengthened Gaultry's hold on the creature, but at least Aneitha's spirit, a little preoccupied, did not attempt an awkward break for freedom. Disconcertingly, her senses dropped and rose as the cat's spirit shifted. Allowing it her eyes, she found she could see every grain of sand as it settled down the pit's steep sides, every tiny motion, but the colors were dulled and dreary. Her hearing had sharpened. Outside, somewhere overhead, the trio of crows had begun to caw and chatter, perhaps encouraged by the silence from the pit.

Time to move. With the cat's great strength and powerful balance, she set her back against the pit wall and drew the animal's weight into her arms. Aneitha's spirit-response was to settle. A note of interest rose above the animal's panic. Gaultry, unsure of how much control she could assert, concentrated for a moment on reassuring thoughts rather than action.

A long moment passed. Then the panther's spirit gave her a little nudge, helping her gain her balance in the sliding dirt. Gaultry could feel that it had cognizance that she wanted to escape the pit, and it was ready to join her.

That's right, she told it. *Take a look at that dawn sky overhead. That's where we're going.* She maneuvered the creature's dead weight toward the fall of earth where she had slid down. She wanted to call on all her Glamour-magic to power the Huntress-born spell, wanted to own the cat, not to be bargaining with it, she was afraid. . . .

The legs, she urged, fighting her own panic. She braced her feet against the earth. *I want your strength there.*

At least for the climb out, the cat submitted. Feline energy pulsed through Gaultry's spine, through her hips, through her haunches. She took hold of Aneitha's body by its neck-scruff, as a mother cat might carry its young, as a panther might drag its kill. With one hand free she ripped deep into the crumbling earth, gaining enough of a hold to shove herself upward. She imagined great claws on each of her fingers, cutting deep into the soil. Aneitha sent her an image, perhaps to encourage her: a tall rock, a strange pale deer with short horns, the taste of blood in her mouth as she dragged it upward. Something Aneitha had known back in her homeland.

Then at last she lay sprawled on the grass, free of the pit, Aneitha's hot, cat-rank body clutched against her own, and the image dissipated. Yet she could feel the desert warmth on her body still, in her legs; the confidence—

"You should never have come here." The voice cut through the heat like a splash of icy water. "The taint is in you, you should not have come."

Gaultry, arms still buried in Aneitha's fur, opened her eyes.

Sieur Jumery Ingoleur stood not ten feet away, his thin arms folded. He wore diaphanous grey robes. A sword with an age-pitted blade was belted at his waist, held in place by a silver chain.

"This creature is not a demon," she told him, not sure what he meant by his accusation. *Quiet, you,* she told Aneitha. *Be quiet!* "It's just a foreign animal, like the funny monkey in the cart. We've been trying to keep her off the road so she won't frighten the marketers. But she lost us after the bridge crossing yesterday. I had to come find her—"

"Your grandmother kept more secrets than she told lies," the old man said, reproving. "Her line has fallen since."

Gaultry sat up, wary, and cradled the big cat's head. If this was not about Aneitha's trespass . . . "Fifty years is a long time to nurse a resentment," she said cautiously. "What did Tamsanne do to you, that you should offer me insult today?"

"You're a fool, I see," the old man said. Her words had increased his agitation, rather than lessened it. "Fifty years is *nothing.*" He stepped toward her, his fingers fluttering on the hilt of his sword. "Tamsanne at least knew that."

"Don't come any closer." Gaultry scrambled up and stepped protectively in front of the panther's body, her movements fluid with its borrowed feline grace. "If you have something to tell me, say it from where you stand." She glanced skyward at the descending disc of Rios's moon: still above the horizon, still the vengeance-moon of early summer. "You have no quarrel with me," she added, hoping to defuse the man's ill-suppressed rage. "I and mine have brought before you nothing but truth. We travel in service of the Prince, and it could only harm him to delay us. If you harbor unfinished business with Tamsanne it has naught to do with me."

"It has everything to do with you." His fingers flexed on his sword-hilt. "To keep her own unclean get safe, she robbed my sons of their blood-heritage!"

Aneitha's spirit, not liking the man's hostility, flooded forward like water. Gaultry, mentally catching both herself and the cat-spirit, could not follow the leaps of the old man's accusations. "Tell me your quarrel," she said. "By Elianté's Spear!" She paused, again suppressing the cat. "If Tamsanne truly has wronged you, perhaps I can offer amends."

Sieur Jumery raised his hands, his gauzy sleeves drifting back to expose his bone-thin arms. "Tell me what you see."

Rows of scars braceleted every inch of the old man's arm-skin. Shallow scars; evenly, ritualistically, placed. Gaultry's mouth went dry. A holy man's bleeder-scars, not wounds taken in battle. She glanced uneasily over to the table-stone. "It is your blood that fills that stone basin," she guessed. She stepped back and touched Aneitha's body with her foot, needing the assurance that the cat's strength remained at her command.

"Mine." The old man's watery blue eyes were lit from within with baneful fire. "Correct—if by mine, you mean my own, mingled with that of all the generations of my fathers before me. The Ingoleurs have been here longer than Tielmark. Longer than empire. The blood-link, father to son, was never broken in all those years. The past lives of my fathers whisper through me," he said. "The earth has no secrets from me."

Gaultry stared at the blood in the carved basin on the ancient stone, at last understanding what she was seeing. The first Ingoleur ancestor must have cut and filled that basin, and his sons ever afterward had maintained it with their own blood. Charged by magic or prayer, such a blood-link could offer those who shared it tremendous power, access to the land's most arcane secrets. But—

But the man was old and tired, and his house was falling down as he waited for his sons to return home. "I don't believe you. What you say cannot be true. If ever such sweeping powers of knowledge were in your possession, you certainly don't hold them today."

"Exactly." The old man's eyes glittered with hate. "The link has been severed, and fifty years of trying has not mended it."

"Tamsanne broke it!" His reaction, a narrowing of his eyes and another step forward, confirmed the guess. "She must have had her reasons. Did you use your power to rifle Tamsanne's secrets?"

The old justice unsheathed his age-pitted sword. Its tip quivered as he raised it. "The forfeit was Tamsanne's honor, not mine," he said. "The sacrilege was hers, but in her guilt, she broke my power."

"Someone must have set you to rob Tamsanne's secrets," Gaultry said. "Why not hate them instead of Tamsanne?"

Deaf to reasoning, he leapt at her. Gaultry easily escaped his attack, feinting away from him and whirling. He was an old man, stiff with arthritis. She was young, lithe, and full of a large panther's strength. Her bond to the great cat, her need to protect its body, was her greatest weakness against such a frail opponent—its body was too large to protect easily, and any blow the panther took, she would feel, amplified, in her own flesh—but Sieur Jumery was too overwrought to realize this. He threw himself at her—fruitlessly—and she dallied with him, up and down the barrow hill, letting him exhaust his strength in stroke after useless stroke against her. One small part of her guiltily recognized that this terrible game was Aneitha's spirit, its animal cruelty, exercising itself through her senses. Another part cried vengeance against this man who had exploited his ancestral powers to steal from Tamsanne—especially something she held so precious as her own secrets.

After a terrible, humiliating interval of this cat-and-mouse game, they stood, facing each other across the white altar of stone. Between them, the basin of blood looked very dark, very fresh. The old man panted for breath, miserable, at the limit of his physical strength. He could not pretend to himself he had the stamina necessary to keep after her.

But he still had the strength to hate. "Of course you can outrun me," he said. "The very corpses of the ground rise to renew you."

"Insult me as you like," she sneered in answer, feline cruel. He still had not intuited her connection to Aneitha, did not suspect why the great cat lay sleeping on the grass, while she feinted and dodged before him with graceful animal power. "It is not Tamsanne's heirs whom the earth here has rejected."

"It was one question only," the old man said hoarsely. "Fergaunt and Jerry did not deserve to lose their grounding for that. The answer revealed her sin—no transgression of mine."

Gaultry stared, puzzled. Her grandmother was not a vengeful woman. Snapping a man's ancient link with his ancestral past, destroying that link for even his sons after him . . . What secret could Tamsanne have possessed that could have been so important? Her puzzlement swung her into the old man's trap. "What did you learn?"

A look of ugly triumph lit the old man's face. "Your grandfather was a dead man when Tamsanne used him to get with child." Which fact, if true, would mean that Gaultry and Mervion's mother was necromantic spawn, and unclean.

In the shock of her surprise, Gaultry lost control of the panther. The next instant was a blur. With Aneitha in full control, she felt her body lunging over the altar, one heel slipping and spattering ancient blood. Then the old man was beneath her, and her fingers and teeth were on his throat.

Without intervention, she would certainly have killed him. The old man gasped beneath her, half-strangled and already in pain at his loss of breath. Thankfully, intervention came, in the form of a pair of massive hands which grabbed her by the shoulders and peeled her away. Still kicking and struggling, she was hoisted up in the air.

Victor Haute-Tielmark, expressionless, held her until she regained control. "Are you all right?" he asked, concerned, as she slowly stopped fighting him.

She lashed Aneitha's spirit in place with angry bolts of power. *Enough!* she told it. *Try that again and you will regret it.* "No," she panted aloud. "I'm not all right."

The old man was flat on his back before her, his face patchy white and pink with his fear, yet full of his ugly triumph. Gaultry stared at him, defeated. He had vented his poison, there was nothing that could roll the foul knowledge back. Her own grandfather could not have been a dead man. Such a thing was not possible. If it was—Tamsanne would not have, could not have "Kill him, Elianté!" Tears ran freely down her cheeks. "Send him down to Achavell!" She wished it were in her to stab out and kill the man. But the Duke had cut short Aneitha's attempt to vent that murderous rage, and now it was too late.

Haute-Tielmark, looking down at the old man's trembling and pathetic body, shook his head. "Whatever he said to you, death cannot be the punishment. You'll have to settle for the knowledge that you held his life in your hands—and let it go."

"You stopped me!" she spat.

The big duke released her shoulders. "Go ahead," he said.

Gaultry stared down at the old man, hating him. What he had said about her grandmother could not be true! Yet even as her mind cried denial, doubts assailed her.

Gaultry had never known her mother, Tamsanne's daughter. Severine had died in childbirth, birthing prophecy as she had borne her magical twins, Gaultry and Mervion. *Your grandfather was a dead man.* No, it was not possible that Severine's father had been a corpse. Of course, Glamour-power such as she and her sister possessed was not possible either—not in this age. It was the magic of the heroes and war-leaders of the distant past—not of the living. *Your grandfather was a dead man.* Her grandmother's magic was powerfully of the earth. Oh, she could not believe that Tamsanne would commit an act so unclean—yet could this be the source of Severine's powers? And through Severine, of Gaultry's?

Breaking free of this inward spiral, she gave the Duke an angry glare. "You know I cannot do it now."

He shrugged. "That is what makes it a choice."

The Duke had arrived at the barrow-ground accompanied by a pair of embarrassed-looking soldiers, one the sentry who had guarded her door.

They stood over Aneitha's prone body, prodding curiously at the creature to spare themselves from watching the scene before them.

Gaultry felt the prods like cudgels against her own back. "Leave her alone!" she snapped. She would have to consider the fears the old man had raised in her later. "Goddess-Twins, what do you think you're doing?"

It was past time for Aneitha to make herself scarce. Twisting in the big duke's grip, Gaultry spread her hands and opened a channel, flinging the big cat's spirit outward. It twisted back toward her with surprising determination, unready to return to its own body. She slapped it roughly with a flash of magic. *What, are you having too much fun?* she berated it. *Get out of here! Take back your body and make yourself scarce.*

Across the green, the soldiers drew back as the panther rose, a quiver running along its tawny body as its spirit resettled within. "Get out of here," Gaultry shrieked aloud. The cat's eyes met Gaultry's with a brief, inscrutable flicker. With a disdainful twitch of its tail, it turned, made for the hedge-gap beyond the pit, and vanished.

Sieur Jumery stared after it, transfixed. "The panther—it was in her. She was using its power. . . ."

Haute-Tielmark cleared his throat. "Well, Sieur, you have learned this morning what you ought to have known before time: Gaultry Blas is not a woman to be dealt with lightly." He gestured to his soldiers. "Rolf, Piers. Escort the good justice to the house. I do not think he can walk alone."

Sieur Jumery opened his lips in protest, but no words issued forth. After a moment, one of the young soldiers reached out a solicitous hand and helped the old man to his feet. He supported Sieur Jumery as the old man shook out his robes, then dusted the grass off his back. The other soldier fetched the pitted sword from where Sieur Jumery had dropped it on the turf. Thrusting it naked into his own belt, he offered the old man his elbow.

"Your Grace." The old man turned back to where Haute-Tielmark stood, holding Gaultry's elbow. "I will expect an accounting in this matter." His voice was very weak.

Haute-Tielmark nodded solemnly. "You will have it, Sieur." He and Gaultry watched the soldiers walk Sieur Jumery around the fallen pit and out through the hedge. "Whether you'll have satisfaction of it is another matter altogether," he muttered, out of the old man's earshot.

"He has nursed a great evil for many years," Gaultry said, still feeling revolted. "Now maybe he feels he's purged it." The Duke was holding her painfully tightly, as though she might yet reconsider her decision not to attack. "You can let go," she told him.

Haute-Tielmark released her. "He is a very old man, and he was raised in different times. He doesn't know where to direct his hate."

She looked at the altar. The bleached stone looked clean as ever, the dark basin of blood undisturbed. Yet when she looked down at her boot, the leather was blood-soaked where her foot had gone into the basin. She shuddered. That blood, periodically intermingled with new sacrifice and renewed, had stood beneath the sky for more than a thousand years, whispering the land's secrets to the family that had been tied to it.

She would have to get new boots and burn the old.

She shivered, and stared up at the Duke. "I feel ill."

"I'm not surprised."

"Should I try to mend the Ingoleurs' broken land-tie?"

The Duke shook his head, his expression grave above the golden beard. He sketched the Goddess-Twins' sign. "That's the old man's burden, not yours. This is not your land."

She saw then that he understood something of what had transpired. "But it was my grandmother who broke the blood-link—"

He shook his head again, more vehemently. "I've no doubt Tamsanne had the power to do so. But she could not have accomplished it here on his own land if the ground itself had not conspired to break with him."

"You don't know Tamsanne," Gaultry said. "Even if the land had screamed in protest, she could have done it."

"Perhaps." She read in the Duke's eyes that he did not agree.

"What makes you think the land turned against him?"

"Perhaps he asked for knowledge that threatened the land. This must have been just before the close of the last cycle of rule," the Duke reminded her. "Lousielle was Princess, but Bissanty-backed courtiers ruled Tielmark. Even the loyalty of a man with an ancient bond to Tielmaran soil could have been set to doubt."

"Someone set him to discover my grandmother's secrets," Gaultry admitted. "He as much as told me so—or at least did not deny it."

"And now he's shared Tamsanne's secrets with you. Was there something in them that might threaten Tielmark's freedom?"

"I don't think so." Doubt curdled through her. *Tainted*, Sieur Jumery had called her. "But who could have the power to make a man like Sieur Jumery seek such things?"

"His liege lord could have commanded him." The Duke frowned.

"Fifty years back that would have been Roger Climens of Vaux-Torres. Or perhaps his father. It was before my time. Not that the Climenses have ever been particularly zealous in their loyalties, their current duchess included." He looked at Gaultry. "Did you not wonder why I came to you so fast last night when I discovered where you were lodged, and the strange circumstances that had brought you there?"

"I noticed you had hurried." The Duke still wore the tunic with the torn embroidery he had arrived in the night before. He had not, it seemed, even paused to have his servants pack an extra shirt.

"Sieur Jumery owes allegiance to Argat Climens—old Roger's granddaughter. The Dukes of Vaux-Torres have always been slippery in their promises to Tielmark's Prince. Argat Climens has taken at least one Bissanty lover. I couldn't leave you in the house of one of Vaux-Torres's knights unprotected—with good cause, it would seem, though Sieur Jumery's personal animus here was not quite what I expected."

Gaultry looked again at the basin. "Do you really think that what he learned of Tamsanne threatened Tielmark?" A thousand-year link, a thousand years of ancestry cast adrift. She shivered. *Your grandfather was a dead man.* Could those words be a lie?

Would Tamsanne have severed an ancient ancestral link merely to punish a lie?

"I don't know," the Duke said. "But anything concerning a member of the Common Brood could also concern Tielmark."

"I want to go back to the house," she said, shivering. "I can't bear to be in this place another moment."

"I would speak with you of another matter first."

"What more could you want of me?" she spat.

The Duke did not immediately answer. She thought it was because she had spoken rudely. Flushing, she forced out prettier words. "Your Grace, as you are at my Prince's service, so am I."

He smiled. A surprisingly gentle smile, showing his crooked teeth. "You are only two years older than my son Hoy." He seemed a little amused. "Sometimes I forget."

"I am no child," she protested.

"Neither is my Hoy." The Duke vented a fond snort. "But he is still young enough to be unsure of his powers. Of course, there are many, even among those granted the highest powers, who refuse to learn their duties. It is of that which what we must speak."

As he spoke, he opened his hand. An ornamental piece of silver lay on his palm. It looked like a ring, but the large hammered flower at its front would make it impractical to wear on one's finger for any duration. "What is it?" she asked.

"It's a gift." Taking her hand, he closed her fingers around it. "A gift to keep private to yourself."

Gaultry pulled away and opened her hand, examining the object more closely. There was a pin-sized insertion hole in one side of the hammered flower, as though the ring was intended to be display-mounted. More curiously still, a sliding prong had been constructed within the ring-band, designed to press outward and prick its wearer when the display-pin was pushed into the insertion hole.

"I believe that it is a sort of key," the Duke told her. "I found it in Chancellor Heiratikus's private chambers."

"How is that possible?" she asked. "The Chancellor's chambers were cleared immediately following the Prince's marriage, and you did not arrive in Princeport for another week. There would have been nothing left."

The Duke sighed. "This goes back to the lunacy of my old politics. I was close enough to Heiratikus to know where he kept his private hiding-hole. But believe me, by the time I reached Princeport I had come to peace with the fact that I'd allowed myself to be blinded, almost to the end of treason. It pleased me very little to know that Benet bore me no trust—and that I'd earned his suspicion. It was the Goddess-Twins' own mercy that I even got the chance to abase myself before him."

Though Gaultry had been at the Prince's palace at the time, she had not been privy to the particulars of Haute-Tielmark's interview with Benet, except for knowing that the outcome, against the expectations of court, had been in his favor. Despite colluding with Heiratikus, Victor Clement had not only been reinstated to power, he had held on to everything in Haute-Tielmark. "So what did you do then?" she asked, unwillingly curious.

"Heiratikus had been Bissanty's highest man in Tielmark. But Bissanty always has more plots going against Tielmark than a single man can manage. It stood to reason that Heiratikus must have had knowledge of those plots. It came to me that he might have left clues behind that would expose other spiders. I wanted to bring those traitors to light—in my own time, and in a manner that would bring me back to Benet's favor."

As he spoke, the sun finally made its appearance. They were within the shadow of the barrow-ground's hedge. By mutual unspoken agreement, they moved outside of the shadow and started walking toward the field with the rabbit-trails. The touch of light caught in the Duke's beard and hair, revealing grey strands which Gaultry had not noticed earlier.

"But I could not move quickly," the Duke continued. "I had withheld my knowledge of Heiratikus's private cache. An unfriendly mind could read fresh treason in that. But then came the attack against the Common Brood at Emiera's feast. I was sure Heiratikus must have known something at least of the early arrangements that were made for that, and decided it was time to find out, and see what I could do to stop it.

"Dervla High Priestess has appropriated Heiratikus's old rooms to couch four of her tiresome acolytes. I sought an interview of Dervla's highest acolyte in those quarters. Once I was inside, my men created a distraction. Heiratikus's hiding-hole is built into a panel—I thought I knew the trick to opening it." The Duke shook his head. "I had too good an opinion of my own plotting. It took longer to open than I expected. There were papers inside, along with this trinket. I had time only to seize the ring and a single packet of letters. Then, barely, I got the panel closed and stepped away, just as the rabbit-faced girl I had come to treat with returned.

"Two days later, Dervla announced her discovery of Heiratikus's cache. My clumsiness, and a report from her acolyte, had led her to it. By virtue of the information she found there, two men were hung and seven young knights were sent from court in shame. The letters I found were of little use. Somehow Heiratikus had got hold of correspondence written between Argat Climens and an old Bissanty lover, but there was nothing in what was written beyond what any court lovers might have set to paper. Unless the High Priestess has become newly subtle, that must have been the only evidence against the good Duchess of Vaux-Torres, because she was not one of those charged in Dervla's first round of accusations.

"But it seems that what Dervla wanted most of all from that cache is the object you now hold in your hands. Whatever it is, the other papers in the hiding-hole must have revealed that it had been stored there. I mentioned last night that she trumped up a warrant against me, accusing me of treason? Truly I think she was driving for the excuse to search my quarters, hoping to find that very piece of silver you hold in your hands. She knew that I had been to Heiratikus's hiding-hole first, and she seemed to want, desperately, something that I had taken. The search revealed nothing—I had already burnt Vaux-Torres's letters.

"But Dervla was not satisfied. She called me out before half the court, where she so lost her sense of fitness that she insisted my own person be searched—an outrage no duke has suffered in three hundred years of Tielmaran history."

"What did you do?" Gaultry asked, fascinated. "Did you have the ring with you?"

"I was very proud," the Duke said. "Righteously so." His eyes gleamed mischievously. "I am sure Dervla imagined I would beg my rights to a private search, and in private she might have had her merry way with me—I know the power of her spells. But I called her bluff. I declared the entire accusation an affront to my honor. Charging every able body of my house to step forward, I called for all among us, men and women together, to strip naked for the court's pleasure, that our High Priestess and anyone else might satisfy themselves that none of Haute-Tielmark's house had anything to hide. Dervla was shocked to see herself mocked; my Prince, I am pleased to say, comported himself nobly throughout the farce. When Dervla, filled with fury, had finished her ransack of our belongings, he invited us to dress, and asked our pardon."

"Where was the key?" Gaultry asked.

"I had swallowed it." Haute-Tielmark grinned, unrepentant. Seeing Gaultry's disbelieving expression, he patted his immense girth. "It took an inordinate amount of sour whiskey to bring it forth again."

"But why hold it back? After all, she is High Priestess."

"She called me a traitor, and sought to rob me of my land." The coldness in the man's voice left no doubt of his feelings. "I had committed myself, body and soul, to the Goddess-Twins, yet still she wished to see me brought low. I will render nothing to her. Traitor? She doesn't know the meaning of the word. She imagines it is anything that goes against her own plots. As if Benet need bow to her. She would set herself up as a new Heiratikus, to rule him."

They had reached the fallow field. Ahead, the roofline of Sieur Jumery's manor hove into view. "But you don't even know what you're denying her." Gaultry fingered the silver ring. "It could even be something to make Benet strong."

The Duke kicked at a tussock of grass, sending clumps of dirt flying. "Dervla's obsession is not to make Benet strong. Whatever that key opens, it will not help with that."

"Then why put it in my hands?"

The Duke shrugged. "The gods guided me to you. Until the Lanai go and crawl back into their mountains, I'll be stuck riding the western border. It is better with you. You can return it to the High Priestess if you so choose—or discover for yourself what it unlocks."

As they crossed the field, she held the key up to the light. The silver caught the sun, and dazzled Gaultry's eye. She flinched. How could she set herself against Tielmark's High Priestess?

The Duke caught her wrist. "The Goddess-Twins' power may be strong in Dervla, but it's also strong in you. There is space between any priest, however pious, and any of the Great Twelve. To defy Dervla's whims does not set you against *them*."

She pushed his hand away. "I have taken your key," she said sharply. "I have listened to your words. Do not mistake that for cooperation. I am Benet's servant, not yours."

The Duke grinned again. "I'm counting on that. Without true servants, the court games will overwhelm him."

Unknowingly, he touched her deepest fear. How would it be possible for her to serve Benet rightly, through all the intricacies of the court intrigues? Fifty years of bitterness—more—governed the alliances in Benet's court. Who could expect her to navigate that maze successfully?

"Leave me alone," Gaultry said. She hastened her steps toward the manor, not caring how he responded.

She did not look back to see that the Duke had stopped to watch her progress, a satisfied expression on his bearded face.

chapter 6

▼

Ictor Haute-Tielmark had secured them places on the Soiscroix fish wagon. They spent the day traveling with tubs of live lake fish and barrels of gutted trout and perch packed in rotten, straw-smeared ice. The fish were destined for the Prince's table in the capital. Evidently the fighting on the western border had not meant the cessation of midsummer banquets at the Prince's court.

The swift-moving wagon jolted its passengers constantly, limiting talk. By noontime, a light rain began to fall. As the day wore on, the drizzle saturated the wagon's canvas cover and began to drip inside. Much of the ice had melted by sundown. Damp penetrated everywhere, and the smell of fish permeated everything traveling in the wagon's bed. For a time, Gaultry managed to nap uneasily. She spent the remainder of the hours brooding over all she had learned at Sieur Jumery's manor. Tamsanne's secrets, Dervla's pride—the Common Brood seemed poised more to bring about Benet's downfall than to consolidate his power.

Tullier, wavering between consciousness and fainting, had the best place in the wagon. He slept fitfully on a narrow cot wedged between fish tubs, the dog curled at his feet. Gaultry and the Sharif had settled one on either side of a tall barrel, a little away from Tullier, cold and rather uncomfortable. Martin was riding on the front seat with the driver. But it was Aneitha who traveled the most malcontent. They had taken her into the wagon in a field outside of Soiscroix and penned her in a makeshift cage—a calf-box purchased from a Soiscroix marketgoer. The animal, none the worse for her adventure at the barrow-ground, found her time in the calf-box not the less miserable for being stowed under one of the more persistent drips in the wagon's canvas ceiling.

She was not born to caging, the Sharif told Gaultry. The Ardana's arms were folded into loose slings. From her posture, it was clear that she was still in pain. The tamarin, on the Sharif's lap, groomed its damp fur with restless fingers, a picture of dissatisfaction.

Aneitha endured a cage when traders brought her to Bissanty, Gaultry answered gruffly. *If she wants to see her home desert, she'll have to put up with it for now. The driver wouldn't have taken her on without the box.*

It was a little after the late midsummer twilight hour when the wagon's wheels finally clattered into Princeport's streets. Gaultry climbed over a barrel to the wagon's side for an unobstructed view. Princeport, a large town of tall houses with blue slate roofs, was situated on two low hills which flanked the town's ample harbor. Beyond, the distinctive silhouette of the Prince's palace rose up on the craggy headland north of the lower of the two town-hills. By daylight Princeport was a pleasant town, too small to support sprawling slums or crumbling tenements. But this night, under thin drizzle and gloomy clouds, it seemed dreary and empty, dampened by more than rain.

When Gaultry had first come to Princeport, she had found the cobbled streets and stone-slated houses grand and fine. Until Princeport, she had never been to a village of more than two score houses, and the sheer number of buildings had been a revelation. The thatched cottages and rutted village lanes that characterized the hamlets of Arleon Forest were nothing, compared to Tielmark's capital. Before Princeport, Gaultry had never understood that it was possible to travel out of sight of field or forest.

She had traveled a long way since those first innocent observations.

Now, as the fish wagon rattled along the town's cobbled but deserted High Street, Gaultry found herself mentally comparing the narrow houses and streets to those she had seen in Bassorah, Bissanty's foremost city. Bassorah, a true metropolis, boasted numerous thoroughfares and squares, many of them beautifully laid out and paved, built as monuments to emperors, army commanders, and highly placed noblemen. Tielmark's capital, by contrast, was a working seaport, devoid of large-scale architectural splendors.

The dynamic thread of commerce that energized Bassorah's streets, as citizens from every quarter of the empire converged upon the great city to vie for favor from one or another of the ancient Bissanty houses or of its powerful ministers, was conspicuously absent.

The Midsummer celebrations had one more day to run before the new month opened. Traditionally, the biggest feasts were held on the final day of celebrations, after two feverish days of market fairs. Staring down from the wagon at the quiet streets, Gaultry could not quite suppress a niggling sense that Tielmark, with its shuttered houses, had failed to honor the festival's spirit. A holy day in Bassorah would see the streets unruly until well after the midnight hour, the citizens overwrought with their extravagant displays of wealth, locked in fiscal competition to pay reverence.

This was not, she knew, a just comparison. Tielmark's citizens, if anything, were more zealous than the Bissanties in their prayers. Indeed, without a class of slaves to worship for them, they had little choice but to be more active in their devotions. When it came to public displays of that devotion, they simply did not have the coin to make a costly show.

"Bassorah city sucked the land around it dry," Gaultry reminded herself sternly. "The liveliness of its business was paid for by the thin lives of its people." Her need to voice the thought aloud disturbed her. If she could feel this emptiness so strongly, could it be any wonder that Tielmaran courtiers, who lived in far greater expectation of luxury than she, felt similarly? Might not some of them then conspire to betray their Prince in order to achieve that distant, luxurious life?

She turned away from the wagon's side, something in her deeply uneasy. Tielmark's simple farming life had little in it to satisfy the worldly and ambitious.

"Martin," she called, clambering forward to look into the wagon's front seat. Martin, sitting in for the usual guard, was slumped next to Saucir, the driver. "How much longer?"

Even over the rattle of the wheels, he heard and responded at once, stretching his hand out to her. "Soon now." Over the height of the bar that separated them he could just reach to brush her fingertips with his own. "Left turn here," he said to Saucir. "And on to the corner."

She remained pressed against the wagon's front, spying on him through the cover of darkness with greedy intensity. The business at Sieur Jumery's house had somewhat papered over the argument they had had over Tullier at the bridge, but she knew he had not quite let it go yet. As ever, he was so close to her—and so distant. Tantalizingly, it had been like that since the night she and the others had rescued him, more than three weeks back. She could only hope that now they'd returned to Princeport, now they were safe from the hazards of Bissanty and the road, she and he would finally find a chance to speak of matters other than their own immediate safety. Unless—unless the Prince gave them a grim welcome, and sent Gaultry and her foreign companions to a cell and Martin, a valued war-leader, riding off to Haute-Tielmark's war.

Yet despite the rain and her many worries, she found that her mood was lifting. The damp night air, plucking at her hair as it funneled in via the wagon's hood, felt suddenly pleasant and fresh.

"Left again as you come into the square." Martin pointed toward the dim façade of a house that stood near the center of the row across from them. "It's the house with the stone fish over its door. Pull up next to the white steps."

Princeport's main square had been laid out by Bissanty engineers centuries past. It faced the sea on a gently sloping piece of land. Tall houses had long since been built up to screen much of the sea view, but the area's proportions remained gracious and pleasant, reminiscent of similar piazzas in Bassorah. On the seaward side, an irregularly paved avenue led down to the harbor, the much-modified incarnation of an earlier Bissanty terrace. That avenue, with its slate steps, was too steep for horses, but each of those stone steps was wide enough to hold a small stall or market stand, making it an excellent place for an outdoor market. Here, finally, was some of the activity that Gaultry had missed elsewhere in the city. In honor of the Midsummer trading, the shallow terraces were crowded with stalls, many with their lessees still awake, finalizing transactions and securing their wares from the relentless drizzle. Their activity lent the square an attractive liveliness. A few steps down the avenue, the lighted door of a tavern beckoned, its open doors spilling laughter and music into the street. The publican had set up sputtering candles and a leaky awning to attract trade. In her fragile, changeable mood, Gaultry found it oddly cheering.

By contrast, the house to which Martin directed the driver had a distinctly forbidding aspect. Shuttered and barred, it had evidently been left closed and empty for weeks, if not months.

The driver reined the tired team of horses up outside the door. Martin leapt from his seat and disappeared into a narrow passage at the house's side. After a long interval, the door under the carved fish creaked in protest and opened. Martin, fumbling with a jingling ring of keys, stepped out.

"We're here," he called, coming around to the back of the cart. "Let's unload our things, then I'll ride on to help Saucir with these barrels."

Gaultry clambered past Tullier's cot and jumped stiffly onto the hard paving stones. "I'm cold," she told him, as the first drops of rain struck her. "Leaning against those damn ice barrels all day would make anyone cold."

"You can light a fire in the salon when you get settled," he said, not unsympathetically.

The dark house was four stories high, fronted with tall, shuttered windows, three to each level. Though the fish over the door's lintel was the only carving, the building could scarcely be called plain. Its tall plastered front was beautifully painted with trompe l'oeil framing in blue and grey. "You own this house?" she asked, unable to hide her surprise.

"Are you asking how I can afford to keep it?" he said frostily.

"I expected it to be plainer." She matched his tone. "Last I'd heard, you'd surrendered all your wealth to become a soldier."

"A profession in which I have achieved not a little success." He scowled. "If it doesn't kill him, a decade of fighting should bring a man some rewards."

Imagining the painted house as the fruit of battle made her feel even colder.

Martin, watching her expression, relented. "It's not all blood purchase," he said. "Besides, I wanted to maintain something apart from my doting grandmère."

That, Gaultry understood. The Duchess of Melaudiere did not shy from using people to her own purposes. It was easy to understand Martin wanting to live out from under her roof.

"Elianté's eyes!" Gaultry changed the subject. "Isn't it strange to be back in Princeport? After Bassorah, everything seems so grey and small."

Martin nodded. "Unfortunately not so small that Bissanty will leave us alone." He frowned. "It's late. Let's unload. I still need to get up to the palace tonight."

"Are you sure I shouldn't come with you?" Gaultry asked.

"And leave them alone?" Martin gestured into the back of the wagon.

"It's not a matter of wanting to leave anyone." Gaultry sighed, knowing that she could not abandon Tullier and the Sharif to the cold house while she gallivanted up to the palace and the relief of homecoming. "I'm concerned as to how they'll receive you."

"Someone has to talk to Grandmère before we risk presenting the boy to Benet. It makes best sense for that someone to be me." He wiped the rain off his face with an impatient gesture. "Grandmère will have a good guess as to how Benet will react to his erstwhile assassin, now we know about his heritage. She'll also be able to tell me what's gone on at court since Haute-Tielmark took off for the west border. What's to argue? Confronting her and Benet simultaneously won't give her a chance to marshal arguments to support you."

"I know all that," Gaultry said crossly.

"So help me get our friends settled so Saucir can get some sleep tonight. And me, too," he added. "I'm not looking forward to shifting those barrels."

"All right." *Climb down*, she called to the Sharif. *It looks like we'll get to sleep in a warm bed tonight after all.*

I don't need a bed, the Sharif answered, shivering. *Just to escape from this horrible cold.*

Martin and Gaultry carried Tullier's cot upstairs to the handsome salon at the front of the house. "I could have walked," the boy said weakly, as they set him down near the ample tile-fronted fireplace.

"Not while I'm here," Gaultry said. She brushed her fingers comfortingly in his hair, trying to believe that the swelling in his belly had subsided. "Give yourself another day to recover."

When Martin asked him how his stomach felt, the boy turned his face to the wall and would not answer. Giving Gaultry a quick glance to gauge her reaction, the tall warrior shrugged, then turned to dump a bucket of coal into the grate. "Let's go and bring that damn cat in," he said.

They left the Sharif with Tullier and directions to start the fire, and returned outside for Aneitha's box. It was an unpleasant chore. They had to unload four barrels and two loosely covered fish tubs before they could ease the cage out.

With Aneitha inside, the weight of the calf-box was perilously close to the limit of what Gaultry could carry without hurting herself, even with Martin shouldering more than his fair share of the burden. "Stop rushing," she snapped, first terrified that the weight was too much for her to control, and then frightened that if they went too slowly she would sprain her back. Amazingly, they got the box into the hallway and set it safely down without incident. Aneitha growled, soft and anxious, as they leveled the box.

"Don't complain," Gaultry chided. "You're the luckiest of any of us. You didn't even have to face the wet."

After that they had to go back to reload the wagon.

"Is it my imagination, or has the rain picked up again?" Gaultry flicked back damp-curled ringlets of hair from her face and stooped to grab one side of the first fish-barrel. "I wish Saucir would come round and help." Saucir was hiding on his seat at the front of the wagon, doing his best not to mind their business.

"It's picked up." Martin said, anxious to get going. "Let's just get this finished."

They heaved the barrels up, and then the first of the tubs. The second tub was slimy with fish scales. Reluctant to get that on her hands, Gaultry rushed and hefted her end a little before Martin was ready.

A wave of odiferous tub-water slopped over him. "Allegrios Rex," he swore, disgusted. "Watch what you're doing! Gods in me, it's vile!"

"Is it very bad?" She swallowed a nervous laugh, the strain of the day cracking her reserve. "I didn't do it on purpose. Oh Flianré, I can smell you from here!"

They shoved the tub deep onto the wagon bed and pulled its cover straight. Martin put up the bar. "Saucir will love my company now," he grumbled, wiping his front with his hands. "He's been complaining about the stench all day."

Gaultry reached to brush off his tunic. "It's certainly pungent," she admitted. "I am sorry."

He trapped her hand in his before she could pull away. "Your fingers are cold." His grey eyes looked almost black in the falling light. Rather than annoying him, her laughter had released another emotion. "All that ice. We should have changed over during the ride."

"I'm not cold now."

"Neither I." Pulling her to him, he cradled her hand against his mouth.

The sudden open heat between them filled her with joy. She cupped his jaw, feeling its strength, the warmth of his flesh. Traveling with the Sharif and Tullier had kept them so distant and formal.

"Haven't you done there yet?" Saucir called from the front of the cart, impatient. "Didn't I hear the wagon bar fall?"

"Everything's loaded," Martin called back. "We're just saying our good-byes."

"In the rain?" Saucir sounded disbelieving. "Hurry up."

In the shadow of the wagon, Martin drew Gaultry against his body.

"You've been avoiding me," she told him.

"Saving our own skins has had to take some precedence."

She shook her head. "It's been more than that. You've been angry."

"Not with you," he said warmly. "Never with you. More with this tangle of powers that seems set on pushing us apart." He hesitated, then, drawing himself up, continued. "You know, everything changed, the day I broke my father's sword." That had been the day the Emperor's Sha Muira envoys had taken Martin prisoner and forcibly transported him to Bissanty. "And now there's this business with Tullier—that foolish boy wants you, and it seems like the only way to keep his skin whole is for you to share yourself with him—magically, if not otherwise. Don't imagine that's pleasant for me."

Gaultry sucked in a long breath. "I couldn't have let him die."

"I know." Martin smoothed her hair. "It's not you I doubt; it's him. Right now he doesn't know what he is, and you are his only stability. That's a huge responsibility, considering who he is."

"We have many responsibilities," Gaultry said softly. "They shouldn't hold us apart in those few moments we manage to find together."

Martin nodded. "I know. We share a love-bond that will never lessen. What remains to be determined is whether we will be granted the space and time to derive any joy from it. Or whether the life to which I have been formed since my brother's death—since I earned my father's sword— will wither it." He looked Gaultry deeply in the eyes. "I meant what I said about everything changing when I broke my father's sword. Something happened in my body when Dinevar was shattered—something involving sorcery. Dinevar had me under a spell, and I still don't know why. It's important that I speak with Grandmère as soon as possible—on top of all this business with Tullier and the Prince."

"Why didn't you tell me?" she asked, alarmed.

"Trust me," he said. "I need to talk to Grandmère first."

"I see." She grimaced, then stroked his face. "Martin, I am sure we both have secrets. We can't let them keep us apart."

He lowered his mouth to hers. Their shared touch was anxious, and despite the fragrance of fish that surrounded them, very sweet, the heat and the saturating rain drawing them together, making the moment more private, more intense.

"Go on," she said, finally pulling away. She felt happy enough to concede him anything. "Go wake Melaudiere and tell her we've brought her a hostage instead of an assassin."

"I'll return soon," Martin answered. He glanced, with an expression of distaste, into the back of the wagon. "If only it doesn't take too long to unload all these damn fish."

She woke cuddled under a white dustcloth on a heavily brocaded divan. It was already morning. Shafts of bright light filtered in through the shuttered windows of the pleasantly appointed salon where they had set up a temporary camp. From her comfortable bed, she stared around, taking stock. Tullier was asleep on his cot, close enough that she could hear his soft breath. The Sharif, snoring, was a little farther away, stretched flat on her back on the coarse bearskin rug in front of the grate. Gaultry sat up, and wrinkled her nose. Something in the room still smelled strongly of fish. She hoped it was not her.

Yawning, she sat up taller on the divan and discovered that they were not alone in the room. She almost bit her tongue clicking her jaw shut.

In an overstuffed chair beside the door, a thin girl, tidily dressed in Melaudiere's green and grey livery, had folded her legs and curled into a ball. She too was dozing.

Gaultry hurried over and shook her urgently awake.

"When did you come in?" she demanded. "Where's Martin?"

"Oh!" The girl jumped, and fell out of the chair. "Please excuse me!" She scrambled up and bowed, a little clumsily, but only because she was stiff from sleep. A court upbringing was stamped on her bearing, along with the rudiments of a swordswoman's grace. Gaultry looked her over, assessing. Her equipage was very fine: a handsome tunic with full sleeves, leggings with finely sewn leather inners, and an empty swordbelt. Her rough, curling brown hair, somewhat in need of combing after her unsettled night, was tied back from her round face in a single thick braid that reached almost to her hips. Tullier's age, or perhaps a year younger. "Lady Blas! I've brought a message from the Stalkerman."

"Why didn't you wake me when you came in?" Gaultry said angrily, though furious with herself rather than with the youngster. She should have woken. Someone should have woken. If the girl had been sent to harm Tullier—

"He told me to let you sleep." The girl, probably accustomed to Melaudiere and her progeny's bossy manners, ignored Gaultry's tone. "Of course, if you had been awake when I arrived . . ."

"Do you have a message for me or not?" Gaultry said. "I want to see it."

The girl pulled a wax-sealed scrip out of her wallet. "It's here," she said, "and there's a purse for you as well."

"Please sit," Gaultry took the letter and gestured the girl back into her chair. "I may have some questions."

The writing was rushed, almost illegible. The ink had not been properly blotted before the page had been closed and sealed.

Gaultry—
I send this letter with my sister's squire Melaney. She is a good girl, and discreet. She will tend to your immediate needs in my absence.

The fighting in Haute-Tielmark is worse even than the Duke told us. I may be called west sooner than I had hoped.

Gaultry looked up from the letter. "What has happened in Haute-Tielmark?" she asked.

"Duke Ranault's war-leader was killed," Melaney said gravely. "We got news of that just yesterday. Also two of Basse-Demaine's sons. Lots of others too. It's horrible. They say that the tribesmen took their heads for prizes instead of their swords."

"Nice news for a Midsummer day," Gaultry said. She turned back to the letter.

Grandmère is dangerously fatigued. She has cast spells too precipitately for a woman of her years and health. My appearance excited her overmuch—still more, our news. She fell ill as we spoke. It is not possible for me to leave her tonight to rejoin you.

Benet is aship, with half the summer court. His timing could not be worse. The best of the court's physicians sail with him, your sister included. The ship will return at noon tomorrow; we will not be able to speak with him before then.

Rest, and prepare for that meeting. Melaney informs me that Julie of Basse-Demaine—Dame Julie, the youngest of the original

Brood coven—will perform for the court tonight. Meet me by the Prince's stair before the concert. We will go up and submit ourselves together to Benet's mercy.

Melaney carries a long purse. Apply to her for anything you require.

Martin

Gaultry gave the girl a sharp look. "How long has Melaudiere been unwell? Is her condition dangerous?"

Melaney answered haltingly, as though loathe to betray her mistress's secrets. "Her Grace had been well—but the battle news took her poorly. It became serious when the news of the Latial in Haute Tielmark turned bad. Before the Ides of Rios. The tribesmen raided the Valle de Brai and burnt the manor where her Grace was fostered, so many years back. The news hit her hard—all the family who once sheltered her are dead, down through the great-grandchildren." The young squire blinked, a little too young to cover her feelings. "It cuts her Grace sorely to see her juniors go to the grave before her."

The Sharif, awakened by their talk, rose from her place on the bear skin. Her condition seemed greatly improved by the night's sleep. Standing, she stretched up to her full height and gently rotated her long arms. The way she moved, so controlled and certain, even these simple gestures looked like trained martial forms. Watching her, Melaney's eyes widened.

"Who's that?" she asked softly.

Gaultry, engrossed as she reread the letter, did not answer.

Crossing to the nearest of the room's long windows, the desert woman threw open the shutters. The flash of bright sunlight brought Gaultry's head up, and lightened all the room. "Andion Vesa," the Sharif intoned, stepping into that morning brightness. "Andion Vesa y Iryas!" She stiffly raised her palms, her hard horsewoman's fingers reaching upward to catch the rays. As Gaultry and the young girl watched, her body seemed to draw in the light, her height to swell.

"What's she saying?" Melaney asked. "Is she praying?"

"She's an Ardanae war-leader," Gaultry explained. "Come with me from Bissanty. The Ardanae worship Andion, the Sun King—so, yes, she's praying." Gaultry was more interested in the serious news in Martin's letter—and in the questions it did not answer—than in the Sharif's morning devotions. "Martin writes that you are his sister's squire. Where is your master?" Mariette was a good ally.

"My Lady is in Haute-Tielmark, marshaling Melaudiere's troops. She's serving as Melaudiere's war-leader. Goddess-Twins bless me that I were there with her." Melaney swung her legs over the edge of the chair. "My mother begged Lady Mariette to wait another year before she took me into battle." She wrinkled her face, obviously disgusted by her parent's interference. "So I've had to stay home with all the sour summer court, running errands for old Melaudiere."

"Sour?"

"Her Grace says everyone who loves Tielmark has either ridden west to fight or they're at home tending their own land," Melaney answered. "Why summer in Princeport when there's so much work to be done elsewhere in Tielmark?"

"The Duchess herself is still in Princeport." Gaultry smiled.

"Melaudiere had to stay," the girl said. "The Prince ordered all the Common Brood to court."

The illogic of old Melaudiere staying in Princeport while her Brood-blood granddaughter went off to the front had evidently not occurred to the girl.

Gaultry sat down, trying to sort her thoughts. If Melaudiere was too ill to back her, who would help her find her way at court? Even if she had not always agreed with the dictatorial old woman, Gaultry had always been able to trust her for support—if not for partially disinterested guidance.

Who is this? The Sharif, finished with her prayers, came to tower over young Melaney.

Martin sent her. Gaultry explained Melaudiere's sudden illness and the Prince's brief absence from court on his ill-timed Midsummer voyage. Why the prince would go pleasure cruising when he had an army to prepare and a court to rule was an unpleasant, unanswerable riddle. *She's pledged to serve Martin's sister. Her parents must have the funds to train her for a knight, but not a lady.*

The Sharif nodded, her desert eyes narrowing speculatively. Then she grinned, her teeth very white against her dark skin, and lightly brushed her hand against Melaney's hair. *A pretty girl, freshly blooming, born to privilege. Your grey wolf must have sent her to keep Tullier busy. Men! They are less subtle than they like to think.*

Gaultry glared, caught by surprise. *That's ridiculous,* she snapped. *She's a baby, come to run errands for us. This is not about pairing.*

Melaney smiled up at them both, unaware of their interplay. The

Sharif, in massive good humor, flexed her fingers and rotated the shoulder Sieur Jumery's woman had fixed. It was giving her less pain than the one which had been popped back by the marketgoers at the bridge. *Of course not. You are a civilized people, with water and bridges. Coupling is the last thing on your minds.* She laughed, a broad open laugh, like the whinny of a horse.

Melaney cast Gaultry a doubtful look, understanding that some sort of a joke had been made, and sensing that it was at her expense. "Are the two of you speaking?"

"Oh yes," Gaultry said dryly. "That's Father Andion's blessing on the Ardanae Sharifs—speech without words. Watch what you say before her—she has only a little of our language but she understands more words than she can speak. Worse, if she comes to trust you, she'll be able to half-pick the thoughts from your brain."

The girl made a tentative bow, obviously thrilling to the woman's outlandish powers. "Melaney Caris at your service, my lady."

The Ardana, her laughter settling, bowed formally back, respecting the girl's air of innocent seriousness. "I am Sharif of the Ardain," she said, "and of Gautri Blas. No other title, mine."

"Has she no name?" Melaney asked.

Gaultry shook her head. "It went when she fell in battle. That's the way of her people. They never capitulate, not even involuntarily. Warriors who surrender become paraiyar—outcasts. Our Sharif had what she considers the bad luck not to have bled to death on the battlefield. The enemy took her prisoner while she was unconscious—but that makes no difference to her people.

"She is still a Sharif—the title recognizes her ability to mind-tie, and that's not gone. But her name—she can't reclaim her name until she returns to Ardain and fulfills her obligations to the families of the warriors she failed to lead to victory."

Gaultry could tell from the girl's reverent expression that she already worshipped the woman and her proud warrior traditions. It made her obscurely jealous—which, much to her embarrassment, she knew that the Sharif would sense, and all too easily at that.

The rest of the morning passed quickly. Melaney had brought them a huge hamper of food from the Duchess's pantry, complete with chops of greasy uncooked meat for Aneitha and Tullier's dog. Gaultry, after checking Tullier, who was sleeping peacefully and not ready to wake up, left the girl alone with the Sharif to set about the business of feeding the big panther. With all that lay ahead for her at court, mediating between her companions was too exhausting.

By midday, Gaultry's spirits had risen. She had new clothes on her back— a blue dress with braided cord decoration that she was able to purchase, already made up, from a tailor's stall. A visit to the laundrystones had left her with a wet but fish-free bundle of clothing.

Under the light of a new day, Princeport had taken on a more prosperous air. Everywhere the young huntress looked, she saw children wearing grass and cornflower wreaths, familiar from her own village's Midsummer customs. It was evident now that much trading had been completed in Princeport during the past two days, and that full-hearted celebrations for a successful Midsummer Market were to follow. The perfectly clear sky and gentle heat made it easy to relax.

Down on the harbor quay, fishermen's children clamored for coins from a good-humored crowd. By now everyone knew the story of their own Prince of Tielmark's introduction to his bride: years past, Lily had been one of these screaming children, leaping boldly off the dock to retrieve thrown coins from the water. Benet, after watching her swim for a time, had intervened to protect her from some bullies who had tried to half-drown her before taking the coins she had retrieved.

Manners had improved somewhat since those days. With Benet's example before them, the coin-throwers no longer publicly incited fights among the children.

Though of course today there was no scarcity of coins to fight over.

Gaultry was amused to observe that since her last visit to the harbor, older girls had begun to join the young in the water. The quixotic interest Lily's story inspired among the court's fashionable young gentlemen probably had made that inevitable.

Two sisters, clad in near-transparent shifts with strings of blue and white flowers in their hair, were receiving the most attention. As Gaultry—and the rest of the crowd—watched, a hopeful young gallant pressed one of the pair for a kiss instead of a dive. Fixing her eye on the coin in another man's hand, she laughed and brushed the offer away. "I'm the Sea King's bride today, not your'n!" The silver coin, flashing in the sun, cut a bright arc in the air. In a splash of foam and wave, the girl disappeared into the water to retrieve it, leaving the young man, a little abashed, to be heckled by the crowd.

Gaultry had come down to the docks to look for the sails of the Prince's ship. The crowds made that impractical from the main quay, so she walked out onto one of the long piers that extended into the harbor. At first the glare off the water was so strong she couldn't distinguish any shapes, then her eyes adjusted and she made out the tops of the distant buoys which marked the harbor's entrance. The carved, brightly painted sea-sprites warned sailors of the rocky shoals.

Beyond them, far out past Murciel's Point, a tiny point of azure, deeper than the sky, paler than the sea, trended toward the shore. "Excuse me." Gaultry stopped a passing sailor. "How long do you make it for that ship to come in?" She pointed.

The burly, sun-reddened man raised his hands to shield his eyes. "That's Benet's ship," he said, and made the Great Twins' sign. "They'll bring it in to Little Harbor, not here."

"How long?"

"She has a good sail-master." The sailor grinned, tracing the ship's course with an outstretched finger. "Look how tight to the wind she's moving. Shouldn't be long."

Gaultry nodded—although, even if she had been able to see the trim of the sails from where she stood, she would have been no more the wiser as to how well they were managed. "How long?"

"This offshore wind will hold them back a time, but they'll touch quickly once the sea breeze rises."

Gaultry thanked him, and began to turn away. A thought struck her. "Who is the Prince's sail-master?"

The sailor waggled his beard, disgusted by her ignorance. "It's Benet himself," he said, "and who better?"

Gaultry stared at the speck of color. The news that Benet enjoyed sailing had passed her before, but she had not understood the extent of his interest. So far as she knew, Tielmark had never had a seafaring prince. "I wonder if they like that at court," she said softly.

The sailor cast her a strange look. "That's not for them to say, is it?"

"No," she said. "It's not for them to say." Thanking him, she hurried on.

The foot of the terraced avenue was even more crowded than the docks around the divers. Unlike the dock crowd, which had been mixed working folk and gentlemen, many of the people here wore their best clothes, finished already with their day's business and set to enjoy the holiday. Gaultry, needing to pass up the steps and also curious, pushed her way to the crowd's front.

A troop of itinerant puppeteers had erected their traveling theater on the avenue's bottom step, where there was a widening of the street. From the intensity of the crowd's attention, the entertainment was something beyond the ordinary.

The boards of the gaudily decorated front of the theater had been painted and repainted for many seasons. Worn shadows of past years' figures were still evident beneath the fresh coat of this year's paint—a parade of horsemen marching toward the purple outline of a mountain.

She had missed the show's opening. At first she could not follow the action's meaning. The talent of the puppeteers seemed more important than the plot—if it could be called a plot.

A mouse-prince danced with his lady, the two figures set twirling in an energetic caper. Their strings tangled and snarled, wound and unwound, constantly threatening to render the wooden figures immobile, but always the puppeteers above kept the strings loose enough that the figures could continue hopping, skipping, and waving their arms. It was astonishing to see, even without the dialogue.

"I love you to distraction!" squeaked the Prince. He dropped onto one knee and threw wide his little hands. By magic or the highest skill, the Princess puppet ended up posed on his lap in a lover's embrace.

"Darling!" she cooed.

"You will always be with me," he said, touching the painted ring on her finger. "What the gods bring together, no man will part."

It was not until this moment that Gaultry realized that the mouse-prince was meant for Benet. She drew in a half-angry breath. A mouse was not how Gaultry imagined Tielmark's tall, serious Prince. The crowd, however, seemed to find it hilarious.

"No man will part us?" The Princess mouse inclined her head, coquettish. "Is it a woman you fear then? Just wait until the cat comes home. Ah me! Come that you'll love your hidey-hole more than you'll love me!"

The crowd laughed, completely captivated. "Answer your lady!" a sailor crowed.

"Sieur!" The mouse-prince lurched up to confront his heckler, carelessly dropping his lady off his lap. "Think you I am in a tangle? Pshaw!" He gestured into the wings with a flick of his miniature hand. "I have advisors enough to free me from worse than this!"

With a drumroll and a noisy crash, a wooden green tabby cat thumped down from the theater's ceiling. It landed on top of the mice, sending them sprawling. "Did somebody call for an advisor?" the cat asked. It had a purring woman's voice, comically dispassionate as the mice struggled to untangle their strings and stand up. "Here I am, ever ready to provide assistance!" Even without the goddess-green paint, the animal was an obvious parody of Dervla.

"Haven't you done enough?" the mouse-prince asked. He staggered backward as the puppeteer above twisted his arm strings into those of his legs, tripping him up.

"Enough?" purred the cat. "Just look, you can't stand even without my help!" She turned to the audience. "Who but I can make the Prince stand free? Who but I, indeed!"

Wooden claws extended from the puppet's paws, and it sashayed over to the mice. Waggling its claws, it made the appearance of untangling them.

"No knotting, no untying!" The hinge of the cat's jaw opened, giving it a toothy smile. "Are you so sure, my Prince, that you were ever bound together?" The wooden claws made a last flicker and retracted, and the two mice flew apart. The mouse-prince's puppeteer made him land inelegantly on his wooden rear.

"Princess!" The puppet-prince sprang to his feet, arms reaching for her.

"Husband!"

The cat moved, almost lazily, between the smaller puppets. It batted the princess-mouse with its tail, as if inadvertently, sending her tumbling toward the wings. To Gaultry's dismay, the crowd's reaction to cat-Dervla's manipulations was mere nodding, amused recognition. If this puppet-show was to be regarded as a true mirror of the Prince's court, she did not understand why people were not more upset. "Oh me!" the little princess squeaked feebly. "Who'll rise to protect me now?"

The next scene offered little more to encourage her. A pair of dog-puppets with silly painted smiles marched on, clomping their wooden feet. They helped the little Princess up—terrifying her with their clumsiness, and making imbecile comments. These puppets were crudely carved, painted a sort of gingery-orange. Once they had the Princess on her feet, they sat back on their haunches, an obscurely vulgar posture, somehow out of place with the other figures, and settled to watch the remainder of the show passively.

Gaultry's cheeks reddened. She did not need to hear the strong southern accents to understand that these figures were intended to represent her sister and herself. But she and her sister were not alone in being satirized. She watched, with mounting indignation, as more wooden animals still were trooped on stage. Most disturbing was a bed-bound crow, squawking doom, that could be meant for none other than the Duchess of Melaudiere. The old woman's illness must be serious indeed, for news of it to have spread into this puppet entertainment.

After a while she could not tell if the other animals had been introduced merely to heighten the ridicule, or if they symbolized specific court figures. The reactions of the crowd supported the latter guess. A bleating nanny goat, blundering onstage and knocking into the cat, was greeted with a hearty cheer; an aggressive weasel, noisy boos. There were many buck-toothed courtier rabbits. One in particular, to the crowd's amusement, birthed a bewildering succession of baby rabbits—simple carved blocks, painted in bright colors, each jerked along on a single string—out of a small hatch in its belly. That rabbit trailed miserably across the stage in the mouse-princess's wake, begging her weepily to maintain the "economical management" of her household. A songbird, overshadowed by a piebald cuckoo three times its size, came next, chirruping of chains and lost freedom.

Soon the stage was so full of jostling figures that it was beyond comprehension how the puppeteers were able to keep them all moving. Yet the wild motion continued, the figures at one moment appearing hopelessly tangled, the next wildly isolated.

The movement peaked when a gaudy vulture, painted imperial purple, flapped creakily across the top of the stage, suspended on a very obvious wire. "Doom! Doom!" it squalled, clacking its beak. Below, the animal puppets cowered.

The mouse-prince, dramatically wrenching free from the twining strings of two rabbits, the cat, and the weasel, leaped to his little wooden feet, and pulled a ludicrously tiny sword from his belt.

"Follow me!" he squeaked boldly. "He's at a run already! Victory rides with us!" He clattered off stage, waving his sword. Soon after, sounds—more like those of desperation than success—echoed forth.

The effect of these noises on the beasts of his court was more comical than rousing. A handful moved to follow him, including the mouse-princess. But rather than making progress to join him, they tangled into each other's strings. The action degenerated into a fight, each puppet struggling selfishly to untangle itself, unmindful of the expense to those around them. The result was a finale that fabulously displayed the puppeteers' talents, as the puppets both continued to move with animated purpose and determination, and were jerked about, crazily random, as other puppets tugged at their strings.

At last, in time with the beating of an offstage drum, the puppets dropped to the stage, one by one, feigning exhaustion.

The green tabby was sprawled to one side, one limb tied by its string to the elbow joint of a rabbit. Only the strings that controlled its skinny tail were free to move. Its tail wagged vigorously, in time to the fading drum. As the audience watched, even with the string to its jaw hung slack, that jaw began to move—either magic or a hidden spring, triggered at the last moment. "We helped him!" the cat said. "Goddess-Twins as our witness, we helped him!"

With a loud chorus of barnyard noises, the curtain dropped.

"What artistry!" A plump boy emerged from behind the theater, holding out a greasy black hat. "What a show! Your appreciation, gentle companions! Show your appreciation!"

Still laughing, the crowd began to disperse.

"The mousie marriage!" A woman passing near Gaultry giggled, and dug a hand into her purse. The boy was instantly at her side, proffering the hat. "They should appoint you to show your play at court. That would learn them!"

Gaultry, seething, pushed past and made for the stairs.

She had not risked her life in Bissanty so that she could appear in a puppeteer's play as a stupidly grinning lapdog.

▼

chapter 7

The tamarin wrestled in Gaultry's arms, unsettled by the bright lights and noise. Gaultry, uneasy herself, could do little to comfort it. "It isn't always like this," she murmured. Her plan to bring the tamarin and gift it to the Princess seemed, at least for the moment, a foolish and untimely indulgence. The palace's lower court was packed with bodies, many of them already half soused. "Usually it's quiet—and pleasant."

Her intention had been to arrive early for the Prince's concert, but she had not allowed for the crush of Midsummer celebrators. In the steep, narrowing streets that led to the palace headland, the throng had been so thick that even moving forward had been a challenge. The gates to the palace's lower court were thrown open to honor the holiday, and anyone was welcome to enter. Two bonfires blazed in the center of the yard, bristling with clay-capped ironwork tubes, and a great hogshead of wine broached to provide refreshment. As Gaultry wrestled toward the stairs that led up to the inner palace, the tubes, reaching peak heat, began to pop their caps, showering the crowd with foil, confetti, and toasted beans—as well as occasional slivers of hot clay. In the scuffle to capture these favors and amid a chorus of swearing as the victors singed their fingers, Gaultry was much jostled and almost lost her hold on the tamarin.

The deserted half-battlement of the upper palace was a relief after the wine-heated crowd. The full Midsummer moon had just topped the palace walls, luminescent silver in the deepening marine-purple of the sky. Gaultry picked up her pace. A draft of warm air touched her face, wafting up from a small garden court. After the overwhelming human crush below, the breeze was a pleasure, rich with night plant aromas and an undertone of burnt wood. The fires in the lower court would not be the only offering to the changing of the gods tonight.

At the bottom of the next staircase, she came to a manned guard point. One of the sentinels sketched the goddesses' sign as she approached. Gaultry, who had a poor memory for faces, was pleased to recognize the man making the greeting.

"Ciersy," she smiled. "You're looking well."

"You're late," he told her.

"Is that news?"

"The Prince will welcome your return, my lady." He ushered her on.

Mounting the steps, she patted the tamarin's fur, obscurely comforted. She had not imagined that her entry to the palace would feel so much like a homecoming.

"Behave," she told the tamarin, hefting its weight higher on her shoulder. "Martin will meet us where he said."

Tielmark's palace had been built in stages over more than three centuries, progressively overtaking the craggy headland, surrounded on three sides by the sea. Its inner buildings had been altered and reconstructed numerous times to conform to successive rulers' tastes, rendering it a motley collection of architectural styles, some humble, some grand.

The oldest part of the palace, predating Tielmark's freedom from Bissanty by more than a century, was the armory block, a solid, squat building of roughly dressed stone. Next oldest was Clarin's great hall, the massive building raised over the holy stone where the first Free Prince of Tielmark had stood to declare his land's liberty. Both of these buildings were on the west side of the palace grounds, where the land was steep and rocky, discouraging new construction.

To the east, the ground was more gently contoured. There, where construction was less of a challenge, the buildings had been demolished and reconstructed completely since Clarin's days, according to his heirs' whims. The principal buildings were twinned, arcaded palaces with gracious proportions, arched galleries, and ranks of glass windows facing the garden courtyard between them. Their construction had been overseen by Berowne-the-Builder—the troubled monarch who had lived out the last two decades of his reign in an involuntary regency as Berowne-the-Mad. Most of the formal business of court went forward in these palaces. There rigid protocols were observed: When the Prince passed their doors he was no longer a man, but a symbol who represented Tielmark.

Gaultry was not very familiar with this part of the complex. In the days immediately following his marriage, Benet had granted her and her sister a suite of rooms in the Summer Palace. This palazzo, a smaller, less stylish building, tucked away behind the palace offices, was a remnant of older times and a less distinguished building style. Except for its situation, perched on massive arched foundations above the headland's steep north cliffs, it would have been razed and replaced decades past. Gaultry had passed what little time she had spent at court in that building and its grounds: a lovely deer park that overlooked the sea on one side. She thought of the coziness of her own rooms and sighed.

Tonight she was headed for considerably grander chambers.

The smell of burning wood hung heavily in the air. An open archway gave her an unexpected view into the palace's largest court, half a story below. At the court's center, a great bonfire burned. Unlike the fires of the lower court, here there was little gaiety. The wood had been stacked in a towering pile, with wedges of faster burning branches spread throughout so sections of the pile would burn at different speeds. This was a ritual fire, not a part of the citizenry's madscrabble celebrations.

The wooden figure of the god at the bonfire's top had already caught fire. Rios Sword-god, his wicker sword raised above his head, saluted the passing of his moon. The god's wooden skeleton flickered black and crimson through the flames. The fire's tenders, their faces shining red with the fire's light, were intense and joyless. A single figure, a thin rail of a woman with flowing unbound hair, danced wildly at the edge of the flame, whipping the fire's edges with a blazing branch.

Gaultry drew away, and touched guiltily at the hidden ring-key that Victor Haute-Tielmark had given her, now tied on a string around her neck. She had witnessed Dervla making her devotions more than once, and the bleak quality of the dance and the flame were an uncomfortable reminder of the sheer power the woman wielded. A stab of fear touched her. She must not meet with this woman—not at least until after she had seen the Prince, and assured him of her loyalty.

And yet—the ceremony had a hypnotic quality that made her hesitate to turn away. As High Priestess, part of Dervla's role was to align earth and sky. Here, her dance guided Tielmark through the rites that honored the gods' passage in the night sky. "The new month will start when Rios falls," Gaultry whispered to the tamarin. If the figure fell before the warm orange star, Andion's lamp, crested the horizon, it would be an unlucky sign, one god usurping another's prerogative. "Dervla's power has to hold it up until just the right moment."

She hurried on, hefting the tamarin onto her other side. She had been carrying it so long the creature's light weight had begun to get heavy. "They'll read an omen in the way the god falls, and all who are watching will share in its portent." Witnessing the figure fall, if it went down in one piece, was lucky, but Gaultry wanted no share of the bad luck if the figure broke in pieces.

Ascending a last covered staircase, she emerged into the lovely ordered gardens of the arcaded court between Berowne's palaces. Prince Berowne, more than a century past, had planted the fruit trees and named it Adnam's court after his son, but that name had proved unlucky. Now it was called glass court, for its beautiful windows.

Although the sky overhead was still vivid, the towering walls of the palaces had already thrown the garden into the deep shadows of night. In prettily trimmed rows, its lush fruit trees sparkled with the intense silver light thrown down from the moon, their shadows inky black. Overhead, the colored windows of the palaces' grand salons blazed with light. Elaborate colored pictures had been worked into the leading, depicting the events that had closed Tielmark's second cycle, two hundred years back. Gaultry, standing in the silver and black quiet beneath one of the peach trees, felt momentarily suspended between two worlds: the first shadowed and serene, heady with the scents of plant and fire; the second static and poised, yet ablaze with fiery colors and acts of heroism.

Berowne had been Briern-bold's son—Briern, the great war-leader Prince who crushed the Bissantics in open battle on Tielmark's marches in the North. The row of windows depicted Briern's heroic exploits, following his life from the wild days of his foolhardy boyhood through to his great victory against the Bissanty army. Gaultry stared up, her eyes tracing the stories she had known from her earliest childhood, so superbly rendered in the glass panes.

On every level, the work was a masterpiece. The jewel-bright windows were one of Tielmark's most glorious treasures. Tonight was the first time she'd had opportunity to see the picture cycle entirely backlit, and the breath caught in her throat at the beauty of the colors and the grand scale of the work. Some scenes—that of Briern's future wife, Arcana, beating her plowshare into a sword (the window of a small corner room which did not see much public service) and a large picture of knights spurring their horses toward a battlefield—were entirely new to her. The big image of Briern, smiting Bissanty soldiers from the saddle of his great dappled stallion, shone so brightly she could almost imagine that the great Prince was ready to charge free from the window and leap toward the night sky. Nothing had caught her imagination so strongly in Bissanty, and for a moment enthusiasm and pride leapt in her.

The tamarin, pulling her hair as it climbed onto her shoulder to reach for a half-ripe peach, brought her back to earth.

"Of course Berowne brought in Bissanty craftsmen to do the finish work." She sighed, reaching up to twist down a plump fruit. Would Bissanty and Tielmark ever be truly separate? In this, as in so much else in Tielmark, the ties to Bissanty were still strong, however many years Tielmark had been a free state.

The tamarin bit wetly into the peach's riper side, giving Gaultry an anxious moment for the front of her dress. "Be careful!" she scolded. It was already well past time to go in. A few more steps, and she would reach the entry to the foyer where the grand state staircase led up to the Prince's public rooms.

"I hope Martin's there," she said, throwing the peach pit into a bush and smoothing her dress with her clean hand.

A pair of muscular footmen in Tielmark's blue-and-white livery rose as Gaultry entered. "You've missed the first movement," the first man said helpfully, as his partner resettled restfully into his niche in the wall. "They're tuning for the second now. You may go up to the landing, if you'd like." He knew who she was! The warmth, the feeling of homecoming, swelled.

"Have you seen Martin Stalker tonight?" she asked. "He's supposed to be waiting for me."

The man shook his head.

The staircase was built on an intentionally intimidating scale, with tiles glazed in gilt and silver, and painted inlays on the banister. Engrossed by her thoughts, Gaultry took little notice of the party of men and women who clustered on the first landing, their attire neatly brushed, their faces a mingling of pleasure and nerves. Then an elegant, patrician-lean gentleman, coated in formal black, emerged from among them and stepped into her path.

"Lady Blas." The man spread his hands in a courtly gesture, gracious, yet effectively broad to block her. "What a delight that you have chosen to join us tonight."

Paré Ronsars was the Prince's warder. A man whom Gaultry, in her short time at court, had already crossed too many times, with her many accidental lapses from convention.

"Sieur Ronsars," she blurted, pulling up in an ungainly half-curtsy. "I wasn't expecting to see you."

"Nor I you, my lady." Ronsars returned her greeting with a shallow bow. "You can imagine how many here tonight have begged to hear Dame Julie's performance. It's not often she comes out of her retirement to perform. Sadly, I have not seen your sponsor tonight. If you would be so kind as to wait for your call—"

"Sponsor?" Gaultry stiffened. "I am not here with a sponsor." Surely he did not mean to prevent her from seeing the Prince? "My duty is to Prince Benet—"

"As is mine," Ronsars answered smoothly, making no move to get out of her way. "My humblest apologies, my lady, but if you have no sponsor you must wait here until you are called."

This landing was one of the places the Prince's petitioners had to stand, if they had business they wished to bring before him out of turn and had not been granted a public hearing—unless they could bribe Ronsars or one of his toadies and get leave to approach the Prince more closely. Gaultry glanced at the beautifully tiled steps, twelve in number, that led up from the landing to the double doors of the long salon, each one decorated with a god's mark. The long salon, she recollected with a twinge of acrimony, was yet another place where the ministers of protocol could delay petitioners. Then, if they wanted to be completely punctilious, they would also stall them in the crimson-painted corridor that opened into the grand salon.

The subtly downcast faces of those crowding the landing observed her interchange with Ronsars with ill-concealed interest. Who was she, the faces seemed to ask, to think that she could push ahead of them? These, she belatedly realized, would all be people who wished to air some plaint to Benet before the next assizes. They were not here to listen to the music. They were here hoping that the Prince would stop a moment and listen to their troubles as he descended from his night's entertainment. Small wonder stress marked their faces. With a war to plan and a household full of powerful witches, she doubted Benet would have time for them tonight.

"I don't need a sponsor," Gaultry said firmly. "I am not a petitioner."

Ronsars had no right to delay her, but she did not, after a six-week absence, wish to greet her Prince with an aggrieved warder dogging her. The court maze was complicated by slyly opened and closed doors of access. If she openly challenged Ronsars in front of these petitioners, certain other doors would quietly close to her. "I must apologize, Sieur. But there has been a misunderstanding." It was a struggle to keep her voice cool. "I have an urgent presentment to make to their royal Highnesses, and the only delay here tonight can be for me to wait upon their pleasure in the concert chamber."

Ronsars tucked his hands into his ornate belt, momentarily concealing his expressive fingers. "I was not given to understand that the Prince had called you." Someone had bribed him—or ordered him, if they had sufficient authority—to hold her there. The patrician face, as always, communicated nothing, but the hiding of his hands—hands so eloquent in covertly offering a desperate petitioner hope, or denying for once and for all the possibility of passage, told Gaultry he was suddenly uncertain. He could not tell if he would best protect his prestige by continuing to hold her there, or by allowing her through.

Heat rose to her cheeks. Under the cover of the tamarin's fur, her own hands flexed angrily. "Goddess-Twins! However the Prince chooses to reward my actions, I can guarantee to you in all the Twelve's names that he will want to see me. If your understanding is otherwise you are sadly misinformed."

Ronsars's face revealed nothing of his feelings as he digested this little outburst; then, coming to a quick decision, he swung his hands free and saluted her. "I will escort you in personally." He offered her his elbow.

Gaultry tried to smile as she shifted the tamarin into the crook of one arm. "Elianté will bless your courtesy," she said, laying her freed hand on the warder's sleeve.

A thin man lounging dispiritedly at the side of the landing snorted. "A better coin than mine, it seems."

Ronsars, on firmer ground here, answered him with a dismissive cast of his fingers. The man, taking the warning, melted back into the crowd.

"You are fortunate," the warder told her, as the footmen opened the door at the top of the steps. Bright candlelight spilled down into the light-colored tile of the dimly lit stair. "The Prince himself was late tonight, so you have missed only the first movement of Dame Julie's piece."

"Was his Highness's ship late reaching harbor?"

"The Princess was indisposed," he said dryly. "Even Dame Julie must wait on the Princess's will."

The long salon, with its pale blue tapestries and iron chandeliers, was as empty as Gaultry had ever seen it. War and summer farming had thinned the court's ranks. Clusters of young, uncomfortable-looking men and women, dressed in ill-tailored livery, stood beneath the rings of lighted candles. The more polished courtiers Gaultry had come to recognize were away from Princeport, conducting the serious work of the summer months. One boy refilled his partner's glass from the carafe on a server's plate before the server could move and do it for him. Ronsars, seeing where Gaultry's eye had fallen, allowed himself a subtle shudder.

"One of Ranault's boys," he said. "There are six sons there, this one the youngest. He'll become accustomed to accepting service before the summer's out."

Gaultry bit her tongue, having seen nothing out of order in the boy's comportment.

Beyond the crimson corridor, the grand salon blazed with candles, brilliantly colored raiment, and rising voices—the core of the court that surrounded the Prince and his ministers. Glowering over the crowd was the battlefield window showing Briern on his horse. From inside, with oncoming darkness behind it, the colored glass gave the appearance of flat black panels. The window leading had been gilded so the outline of Briern on his horse was the only visible part of the image. But that simple gold outline, Briern with one arm upraised, the horse with its churning hooves, was in its own way as impressive as the bright colors seen from outside.

The Prince and his young Princess sat on tall chairs far across the room. Benet, a smooth-featured man with straight dark brows and flowing, wheat-colored hair, was surrounded by courtiers, a carefully neutral look on his face. Lily, seated closely by his side, showed little more expression. A cowl of white lace covered her dark hair, casting her face in shadow. The young Princess looked sad and tired, not at all as though she had been enjoying the night's performance. Gaultry's gut lurched. At their root, every struggle and hardship she had endured had been for the sake of this young couple, for her faith that Tielmark's fate lay bound with theirs.

"How are their Highnesses enjoying Dame Julie's music?" Gaultry asked, hoping Ronsars would miss the depth of her feelings if she kept him talking.

"It does not please them." For some reason, the warder seemed gratified. "They wanted songs to lighten their mood. But there's no looking to Dame Julie for lighthearted music."

The Prince had been out in the sun much since Gaultry had last seen him. His wheat-blond hair was streaked with sun-silver, heightening the severity of his straight dark brows. For a moment, Gaultry thought his eyes were on her, then he turned to the man at his shoulder and she decided that he could not have seen her after all.

The crowd surged, and she momentarily lost sight of him.

"Where is old Melaudiere's cortege?" Gaultry asked, failing to spy either Martin, her sister, or any of her few court acquaintances. She wondered if the Duchess's health could have taken another turn for the worse. Where else could Martin be? "If they're not here, I'd like to stand where I could speak to the Prince when the music is done."

"I have already escorted you further than you deserve," Ronsars answered, his manner abruptly hostile. He circled her around to a cluster of young people, in a position oblique to the Prince's line of sight.

Gaultry answered him with a blank stare. Her obvious innocence of whatever breach of protocol she had just committed only stoked his hostility.

"We will teach you manners," he muttered. "Just as we taught your sister."

He turned abruptly and would have left her, but Gaultry closed her fingers on his arm. "What did you just say?" she asked sharply. "What lesson has my sister learned?" In her worries for Martin, in her worries for herself, Gaultry had not been thinking of her sister. But Mervion was never clumsy in matters of protocol. If Ronsars and his cronies had interfered with her, it would not have been for benign purposes.

Ronsars, trapped, stood stock-still, disbelief drawn across his features. He could not pull free without attracting attention to his effectively helpless position. Gaultry herself could hardly believe her effrontery—restraining the Prince's own warder before the core of his court!

But she would not allow a threat which touched Mervion to pass unchallenged.

"I don't know what your words mean," she said softly, "but if I discover that you have pursued any course of action tending to my sister's discredit, you will come to regret it deeply. I swear this on Elianté and Emiera together, no lower than my duty to Tielmark and my Prince."

"Benet is my master as he is yours," Ronsars stammered.

The tamarin, responding to Gaultry's upset, let out a fierce sound and made as if to bite. Gaultry loosed the warder's arm to prevent it from succeeding.

Ronsars clicked his heels primly, the gesture allowing him to step back without overt retreat. "Your servant, Lady Blas." His eyes shone with dislike in the closed mask of his face. "I will remember your words."

"Your servant, Sieur." Gaultry curtsied politely, equally cool. "Know you well, my words promise action. Keep that in mind, if you would meddle with my family again." If the man had done anything to harm Mervion, he was already her enemy.

The warder turned sharply and retreated toward the long salon.

"Filthy spider," Gaultry muttered. "Go tie someone else in your webs."

"You gave him quite a shock," a soft voice said, almost in her ear. "Perhaps he's finished for the night." Gaultry glared as she swung to face this new assailant, then forced herself to soften her expression. The voice's owner was a slender girl with jet-black hair, pale skin, and a sumptuous yellow dress. She had eyes like dark topazes and hard, even features, chiseled to a beauty that would have seemed arrogant but for her mild expression. She was staring now at the tamarin, obviously intrigued. "What a beautiful animal," she said. "What is it? Would it really have bitten him?"

Gaultry, mollified by the compliment, ruffled the tamarin's fur. "He's harmless, if you don't provoke him. You can touch him if you like."

The girl let the tamarin sniff her fingers. "His fur is beautiful," she said. "So soft. Would you like me to hold him for a moment? You see, there's a piece of foil in your hair, and it will spoil if you don't pull it out carefully—"

Gaultry hastily handed the tamarin over. Her hair was tied up simply, with a single cluster of flowers, and her fingers soon discovered the object to which the girl was referring—a disk of gold foil, stamped with the face of a grinning sun. "I came in through the lower court," she explained. "These things were exploding out of the bonfires. Perhaps you would like to have it?" She reached and took the tamarin back. The little animal was getting heavier by the moment, but she didn't think she should take advantage of the girl's good nature by leaving him too long with her.

The girl accepted the piece of foil, and smoothed it out. "Benet ordered these to be put in the fire for luck," she said. "He had a sun-priest come to bless them. Thank you."

"You're welcome," Gaultry said. "I hope it brings you good fortune." Her own experience with Andion Sun-King's priests was limited to a single unsettling episode, some months back. Andion-priests invoked a power that was raw and fiery.

"Were you here for the first part of the music?" Gaultry asked. "Was it good?" She did not recognize any of the instruments on the musicians' dais. Two were oversize fiddles, a third a stringed instrument so large the performer would have to sit and clutch it between her legs.

"It was wonderful." The girl sighed. "When they play they share a single mind and soul. Dame Julie trained them in Home Hall. That's her manor in Basse-Demaine."

"Which one is Dame Julie?"

The girl pointed to a tiny woman dressed in robes of a supple, faintly shimmery blue material. Dame Julie had been barely fifteen when she had led the song that had focused the spell at the cycle's last closing. That made her threescore and five now, but there were few clues in her appearance to hint at her advanced age. Her pale face was delicate and unwrinkled, youthful blondness lingered in the mass of her softly curled white hair. She was exquisitely dressed. Gaultry's heart sank. "She looks very well kept." She had not expected Dame Julie, who she knew had not been born to a title, to look the part of the consummate court lady.

The girl missed the inflection of Gaultry's doubt. She nodded enthusiastically. "She's wonderful. Wait 'til you hear. I would have given my eye teeth to have trained with her!"

Gaultry, a little astonished at the girl's eagerness, gave her a closer look. There was something mismatched in the girl. Even in a callow summer court, her open eagerness for animals and music made her too young, too unguarded. Her sumptuous yellow dress only served to emphasize the discrepancy. Certainly she was beautiful in it: cut by a master tailor, the dress made a sophisticated display of her body, from the smocking of velvet ribbons at the waist to the gauzy half-cape that framed her pretty shoulders. But the girl inside the dress was too raw for the sophistication; whoever had put her in it hadn't bothered to match it to her girlish manner.

It occurred to Gaultry suddenly that Ronsars must have had some reason to leave her at this innocent's side. "We have not been properly introduced," she said, trying to brake the girl's enthusiasm.

"But I know who you are," the girl said. "Everybody knows. You're one of the Brood-blood twins from Arleon Forest. The one who got Prince Benet to marry Lily. You look like your sister—thinner, I think, but you have the same face. I am Elisabeth Climens. I was not at court when you were here before. That is my mother, standing at the Prince's side."

Gaultry's eyes narrowed. Climens. She did not have to see where the girl pointed to recognize that name. Haute-Tielmark had given her that name, the morning she attacked Sieur Jumery. The girl's mother was the Duchess of Vaux-Torres, Jumery Ingoleur's liege-lord.

"I do apologize," the girl rattled on, looking faintly guilty. "I assumed you would know. . . . Perhaps you won't want to speak to me now." A strain of loneliness underlaid the girl's candor. "At the moment, not many here will give me their company, for all my mother's power. Dervla is investigating my family, you see, and the Prince himself views us unfavorably. I would not have taken the liberty to speak, you see, but after you cut Sieur Ronsars . . ."

"I had not heard of your family troubles," Gaultry said. Haute-Tielmark had said that the letters he'd found concerning the Duchess of Vaux-Torres had been suggestive, but not compromising. Had Dervla discovered a more damaging correspondence? "Elianté in me, I trust the investigation is unfounded."

"The Climenses are loyal to Tielmark," Elisabeth said stoutly, though her eyes, as she met Gaultry's, revealed ill-shuttered doubts. "My mother called me to court to manage her affairs while she builds her defense. I was supposed to have another year at home, so I am a little unready. I can only hope that I stand for her as loyally as—as you have just done for your sister."

Gaultry shrugged, disconcerted by the girl's effusive praise. "As I presume you have already learned, Ronsars does nothing without a motive. I'm sure he left me by you intentionally, guessing we would speak."

The girl patted the tamarin again, avoiding Gaultry's eyes. "I see. It does you no credit to be seen talking to me, I suppose."

"None at all," Gaultry said tiredly. "If being mistaken for a Bissanty traitor concerned me, I'd distance myself from you right now, and give you as nasty a leave-taking as I'm able." She knew as she spoke that she would not be able to muster the energy for that leave-taking, branding the girl, as so many others must already have done, as confirmed in her mother's guilt. "Prince Benet is right to hate the Bissanties and their collaborators," was all she could think to say in consolation.

"The High Priestess cannot prove that my mother has done wrong," the girl said loyally. "I will stay here at court until our name is cleared."

"Well spoken," Gaultry said. If she spoke truly, Elisabeth was braver than she looked. Gaultry did not think she herself could bear to linger at court while under a cloud of suspicion.

Around them, the room shuffled and resettled. On the dais, the musicians were taking up their instruments, plucking at the strings to adjust the fine-tuning. Through the crowd, Gaultry caught a fleeting view of the Princess, her head turned as she spoke to one of her attendants. "Who is that woman at Princess Lily's shoulder?"

"Which one?"

"She's talking to her just now." The attendant, a pretty, stressed-looking woman with protuberant teeth, was very obviously with child. The rabbit, Gaultry thought. The pregnant rabbit from the puppet show. The flash of recognition dismayed her. She knew less of this diminished court than the crowd in Princeport's busy streets. She could scarcely remember the parade of puppet-figures, let alone match them with the people in front of her now.

"There was a weasel," Gaultry said aloud, trying to think through the cast of puppets. "And a song-bird with a cuckoo-child—was that Julie?"

As the girl started to ask her what she meant, the Majordomo called for quiet.

Dame Julie nodded from the front of the dais. The music began.

There were five musicians: three players and two singers. From the first note it was clear that Julie not only led the others, she controlled them. She stood to the left of the stage, her posture stiff, like a sibyl offering prophecy, though the notes that emerged from her mouth were sweet and harmonious. As the music progressed, her voice rose above the string instruments like a gathering wave, sweeping the other players with her. The sounds crossed, countercrossed, harmonized, broke harmony. Dame Julie's voice was beautiful, but hidden within the beauty, like a fast approaching storm, was curling, lashing rage.

Gaultry, sucked into the swell of sound with the rest of the audience, found herself accepting that her first judgment had been woefully lacking. Although Julie covered her power with the polish of a courtier, beneath that surface something deeper surged.

Each of the seven original Brood-members had possessed magical strength which manifested as a creative force. Old Melaudiere was the artist, touching and forming metal, glass, and clay. With Tamsanne it was the deep forest magic, the opening flowers of spring, the sharp closing of harvest. With Julie—

With Julie it was the seductive power of her music.

Elisabeth had said in innocence that the musicians shared one soul and mind. She'd been partly right: Julie, as she sang, projected her magic outward into the other musicians, amplifying the message of her song. Gaultry glanced around the attentive crowd, gauging the reaction. The music was not a dynamic spell. Julie was making no attempt to coerce or influence her audiences' feelings. But despite this, as she sang, everyone in the room leaned in, entranced. They experienced the pain of the Common Brood's blood-bond. They felt, in the music, the pain of abandonment, of power lost and gained, of tragic bonds and unfulfilled promises.

The last movement was bright and sprightly, an unexpected dawning of hope. The youngest player, a too-thin girl with fragile wrists, was suddenly thrust to the lead, and Julie's voice fell to a whisper, then dropped away entirely. This child, playing the second big fiddle, was so intent on her own music that she did not appear to notice as the other musicians stilled and fell quiet around her. Her music was the stuff of air, untouched by pain. A rebirth. Gaultry stared at the girl's pale hair, a silver white like Dame Julie's, with only a hint of blondness.

When the child laid her bow aside at last, there was utter silence. The beauty of her music, after Dame Julie's song, was somehow even more painful.

"That's Dame Julie's granddaughter," Elisabeth whispered. "Rumor has it she will be a greater musician even than Julie one day."

Gaultry stared at the blond girl. Julie Basse-Demaine had a reason to be angry. Fifty years past, when she had been a scrappy gutter-urchin, barely aware of the burgeoning power of her own voice, she would have had no idea that her blood would birth this prodigy, this musician of pure talent.

It would be a crime against the gods to taint such a child with bloodlust, with the politics of protecting a Prince and his realm.

But Julie, like all the other members of the Common Brood, like Gaultry's own grandmother, had forged a prophecy that could not be broken merely by will.

The path of the Prince of Tielmark will run red with the blood of the Common Brood.

Unless the Brood-blood found some way to paint the Prince's path crimson with the sweet power of independence, of Kingship, the red that ran so freely on the Prince's path would continue to be that of the Brood and its children.

▼

chapter 8

The Prince had seen her after all, but the concert had ended and the crowd was breaking up before he sent someone to find her. Gaultry had reached the head of the screening stairs and almost given up hope of an interview when an impassive footman with a soldier's cast to his features tapped her shoulder.

"The Prince will see you now, Lady."

He ushered her back into the inner chambers and brought her to a paneled door, leading into a cramped, austere salon. The royal couple, along with Dame Julie, were already ensconced within, the Prince and his wife seated in tall wooden chairs, Dame Julie on a high-backed bench beneath the room's single window. A single branching candelabra illuminated the room; even with only that small collection of flames, the space felt uncomfortably heated.

The room was silent as Gaultry entered. Princess Lily's lips were set in an angry line; Benet and Dame Julie studiously ignored each other. The footman, breaking his air of detachment just long enough to cast the young huntress a speculative look, made a shallow bow in the prince's direction and withdrew.

Prince Benet's voice cracked the silence as the door shut. "I asked you to give me one night of entertainment," he said sharply. "Was that so onerous a request, from a prince to a player?"

Gaultry hovered by the door, tempted to retreat. She had anticipated that the Prince would greet her with some form of reprimand, but nothing had prepared her to expect it to fall on Dame Julie's shoulders. The singer was an elderly woman of great power and dignity. Why would Benet have called Gaultry to witness this rebuke?

"Answer me!" Prince Benet said. "I won't have your silence!"

"Others would say the music was appropriate to the occasion," the old woman said crisply. "I am too old to chirp unthinking of pleasures, during time of war." Dame Julie sat half-cloaked in the darkness. From outside, the rising moon touched her profile with silver light, hiding her expression in shadow. "I have been at court for more than a month, my daughter and granddaughter with me. We are wasted here—and your request that I fill my time entertaining your court with light-hearted caroling is little more than an insult. Let us serve Tielmark where we are best suited. My daughter is a soldier. She should be at the front. My granddaughter—Joia's too young for court. She should be at home. As for myself—I'm ready to go home too. I'm an old woman and I miss my hearth." Away from public performance, Dame Julie looked tired and faded, but also angry and more willing to show the strong character that lay beneath her composed performer's bearing.

"I need you in Princeport," Benet said through his teeth, "and if you have been here so long, it is in part because Tielmark suffered unexpected departures." His eyes swept the shadows where Gaultry waited, and a faint frown passed over his face. "Your impatience is no greater than what I myself have suffered these past weeks, and with less foundation. If I asked you to help speed that passage of time with entertainment, surely it was not beneath you, as my sworn servant. Surely it cannot have escaped you that with my High Priestess charging treason against the highest of the land and the lowest alike, I have not been free to ride with my knights for the border, even as every Tielmaran with soldiers there has been clamoring for me to go."

"It has not escaped me, my Prince," said Dame Julie, infinitesimally less brusquely.

Benet smoothed the front of his silver-threaded tunic. "Tielmark needs to leave off the witch-hunt for anyone who ever took coin from a Bissanty-man and concentrate on ousting the Lanai. In this, my High Priestess stands against my will. I need respected counselors at my side to balance her. You dislike Dervla. I would have thought that you of all people would support me against her prosecutions."

"Save for this last month," Dame Julie said dryly, "I've been absent from this court for nigh on fifty years. My songs have gathered magic enough to build me a seating of power in Basse-Demaine, but here in your capital, a different warp and weft make power's cloth. If you want to rein in your High Priestess, you must look to someone whose magic meshes more closely with the power that dwells within these walls."

"There is no one else," Benet said. "Dervla is using the Great Twins' magic to bully cooperation from even those most loyal to my wishes. She's abusing the powers the goddesses gave her, using them as a weapon, not a gift. I need the other witches of the Common Brood to balance her excesses. My duchess Melaudiere has played that role for thirty years. But she is fading now and I need someone to fill her seat."

"That won't be me," Dame Julie said. She self-consciously touched the papery skin of her throat, where age had loosened her flesh. "Please understand, my Prince. I mean no disrespect. But Gabrielle of Melaudiere cut her teeth on political meat from her cradle days. When old Princess Lousielle formed the Brood Coven, there was never any doubt but that the original circle of seven would include the young Duchess of Melaudiere. She knew the ins and outs of court even then—it had been necessary for her survival.

"As for me—I was not even a woman when my music's magic elevated me from ragged wharf-urchin to the old Princess's notice. My power would prove as strong as that of any Brood member—but Lousielle had no expectation that the members of the Brood would be interchangeable. I was not chosen to join them because Lousielle mistook me for a leader."

"I can't offer you a choice here," Benet said. Once again, his gaze flickered over Gaultry. "Someone must draw the Brood back together. Your fate is tied to Tielmark's. Split in factions, you are at once too vulnerable and too powerful. I can't risk Tielmark's fate for your squabbles. Look what happened to Destra Vanderive and her young family. Look what happened even to Martin Stalker. Bissanty has taken notice of the Brood's powers, and you can be sure, they'll happily pick you off one by one if I allow it."

"Do you propose some exalted mission, then, to draw us back together?" Half-hidden by shadows, a grim smile flickered on Dame Julie's lips. "One might be forgiven for imagining that the protection of Tielmark's God-pledge should have been enough to focus any Tielmaran's loyalties, yet factional politics split the Brood from the day the old Princess called us to serve. You can hardly expect things to be different now."

"The Brood has yet to fulfill its pledge," Benet said harshly. He rose from his seat, candlefire sending glints flickering from his silver tunic, as though a deeper fire had touched him. "It's stalking you even now. Do you think you can avoid it forever, burying yourself out in Basse-Demaine? The Brood-prophecy offers two choices: your own blood shed for my line's protection, or Tielmark raised to a Kingship. Even if you have forgotten your duty, rest assured, the Bissanty have not. What do you imagine Marie Laconte's great-grandchildren were thinking, when the Bissanty assassins came to cut them down? Would you consign your own granddaughter to such a fate?"

There was an awkward pause. The candles flared.

When Dame Julie spoke again, her voice was subdued. "Your Highness, Kingship is a high cause indeed, but the price is higher still. Perhaps it would be better for all the Brood to lie buried beneath the ground than for Tielmark to risk crying to the gods for the red of Kingship. That attempt could mean dangerous new God-pledges, your own body made one with the land—or it could utterly fail, taking your life with it in a vain sacrifice. In the old days, when the gods were close, a brave man such as yourself could freely pledge himself to the land, and the gods could be depended to bestow either him or his heirs with the red crown of a King. Now—the Great Twelve do not confer Kingship so easily."

"To rise from Principality to Kingdom would sunder Tielmark for once and always from Bissanty's imperial claims," Benet said stubbornly. "What we—what I—have suffered from Bissanty in these past months—I would not see that repeated, nor wish it on my heirs."

"The price for Kingship is high," Dame Julie said grimly. "The gods will never make it lower."

Gaultry, still standing in the shadows by the door, shivered. Throughout her childhood she had been told and retold the old stories of Kingship. Every tale was bloodier than the next. Kingship was like old Sieur Jumery's land-tie, only deeper.

"Tielmark's soil is more than my wife," the Prince said. "I would die for her." His dispassionate calm was more compelling than if he had blustered. "What I have experienced in the past months has shown me how mercilessly the Bissanty pursue us. Fifty years from now, I don't want my grandchild or my son to sit upon Tielmark's throne, facing some new Bissanty cruelty, sent to bind and destroy all he cares for. Prince to Emperor is ever as child to father. A King—before the gods, a King holds his land freely, to rule as he will. I want that freedom for my land—and for my people, my grandchildren among them. If my life need be offered in sacrifice—so be it."

At his side, Princess Lily, his young common-blood wife, the living symbol of Benet's land-tie, paled but remained silent. If she thought her Prince spoke madness, apparently it was a madness they had agreed to share.

"Would it be enough?" Dame Julie laughed, a sad cackle with no humor in it. "A man can offer his body to the earth for the King's pledge just once, but who can say if the gods will accept it? Your own father died in battle while protecting his borders—and his brother before him. But they died Princes, not Kings, as did their mother and all their line back to Clarin before them. The gods took no notice. The secrets of making the Kingship sacrifice are long buried."

"Old Lousielle believed that the Common Brood could recover the kingmaking secrets," Benet said urgently.

"Those were desperate times, my Prince." Dame Julie shook her head. "Bissanty sympathizers controlled Tielmark's court. Lousielle knew that the Bissanties meant to see her out of the way before the cycle of rule closed, ensuring that they could have their way freely with her young daughter. Rather than raise their suspicions that she intended to defy them, she let them murder her—do you understand? All to ensure a better chance of the Brood's success.

"On Prince's night, the Common Brood crushed the Bissanty spells, and Corinne renewed the God-pledge. Kingmaking—it was discussed among us, but Corinne herself was not ready. After that, it was too late. The portents were not with us for making it happen."

"You know the Brood should have done more," Benet insisted. "It is not right that Tielmark remains bound to short cycles of rule, to an Empire that wishes to reclaim our land. The Goddess-Twins themselves blessed you that night, you were powerful—"

The old woman shook her head. "We were powerful, my Prince, but we were sworn to Lousielle, not to each other. Once we helped young Corinne meet the God-pledge, there was nothing more we could accomplish. Lousielle was dead. Without her strong hand, we could not work together as a united coven." A shudder ran through Dame Julie's body. "I cannot lie to you, my Prince. As that cycle closed, as Prince's Night waned, an abortive attempt was made. We all wanted to make Tielmark stronger for young Corinne. But the path from Prince to King was not a clear one, Corinne was clearly unready, and we voted for inaction."

"But you could have done it," the Prince urged. "If not then, why not now? Andion God-King's month is upon us. If ever the stars align to make a King—now must be the moment."

Julie shook her head. "The Kingmaking secrets are long-lost, but it remains plain at least that it takes a great gathering of power to catch the gods' attention. Some claim the Kingship sacrifice must be made with a certain ceremonial dagger. Others, that no forfeit of life is necessary, only a show of matchless bravery. How else, those believers say, can a man perform the Kingship 'sacrifice,' and yet live on to wear a crown?

"It is darkly spoken that a ceremonial substitute must be offered, and Tielmark, of course, has two princes to choose from—yourself, the ruler of Free Tielmark, and the shadow-prince Bissanty has raised to its land-empty throne. But no one truly knows.

"As for myself—there have been many songs about the King's red. Perhaps I could have discovered something there. Perhaps Delcora, Dervla's mother, could have delved into her archives, and found the key to it. She was clever that way. But we could not agree to act, and we lost our moment.

"My Prince—I am sorry to tell you this, but your eagerness to walk the red path has come too late. The prophecy has run to the path of the Brood's ruin for too long. We are powerless to change that."

Gaultry had listened to the old woman's story, completely rapt. Her grandmother, Tamsanne, had hidden everything from her about her own role in the Brood's business, and it was fascinating to be hearing at least a part of the tale from another Brood-member's lips. But this resignation—she could not allow that to pass unremarked. "The Brood-prophecy affects more that its original members," she said angrily, breaking into the conversation. "You have a daughter, and a granddaughter. How can you think to leave the Brood-prophecy to run its own course? When you accepted the Brood-pledge, you as good as slaved yourselves to the pursuit of Kingship. Not just yourselves, but your families too." She stepped forward from the shadows, forgetting that she should be patient, should wait until Benet called for her.

"Tielmark broke from Bissanty to free itself of slave-bonds. Before I traveled to Bissanty, the urgency of that fight meant little to me. But in Bissanty—" Dark memories flooded her, and she could hardly speak. "In Bissanty, I saw a man cut off his hand to protect a friend from slavery. I saw innumerable hopeless people who would have killed themselves, save that the very slave-bond that held them forbid it. Yet you sit here, so comfortable, the key to your chains within your grasp, and you do nothing to make yourself or the heirs to your body free. I never thought to believe a Tielmaran so craven, nor a Bissanty so stalwart—"

Benet cut her outbreak short. "Lady Gaultry. How opportune that you have rejoined us." She could not tell from his expression if her interruption had pleased or annoyed him. He held out his hand, Tielmark's blue-and-white shield shining on his signet. Trying to school her expression, she offered him her hand in return, then bent and pressed her lips to the ring.

"My Prince," she said. "I am yours to command." Her anger against Dame Julie was his to control, if that was what he wanted. Was this why he had called her here?

He presented her formally to the singer, his pressure on her fingers making her bend her knees and offer the old woman a clumsy bow. "I'm sure you will have recognized your old coven-member Tamsanne's granddaughter. You must forgive her abrupt address. She has just returned from Bissanty, where I sent her to rescue Martin Stalker, Melaudiere's grandson, from Tarrin's altar. The subject of slavery is perhaps too fresh in her memory."

"Dame Julie," Gaultry said awkwardly, torn between anger and fresh confusion at the Prince's words. If he wished to rewrite history, she was not going to protest—but her journey to Bissanty had certainly never received Benet's prior consent, let alone his permission. "Please excuse my hasty words. I'm honored—"

"Indeed," Dame Julie said stonily. A glimmer of unidentifiable emotion flickered across her face. "Come into the light where I can see you. It would seem you have inherited something of your grandmother's looks, if nothing of her patience."

Gaultry bridled. She knew almost nothing of Tamsanne's early relations with this woman, but she sensed from the woman's tone that she was enjoying some private joke at her family's expense. "I inherited Tamsanne's blood," she said stiffly, the impulse to placate this old woman dissipating as quickly as it had risen. "And with it the prophecy of the Common Brood. I know little of my grandmother's life, but now, having witnessed the Bissanty slave-bonds in action, I do not imagine Tamsanne would have intended any such thing for me. I am surprised to learn that you view your own bond so differently."

Dame Julie shot Gaultry a second sharp look. "I have not seen a slave for fifty years. How happy that our Prince has you on hand to so vividly refresh my memory." She rubbed the small of her back, as though sitting had made her stiff, and glanced away from Gaultry to Benet. "So this is the one Dervla wants to string up in court? Good luck to her. I suspect this one'll prove harder to pin down than even her grandmother was—as if anyone ever took joy in standing against Tamsanne."

The Prince raised his brows. "Lady Gaultry understands her place at court," he said blandly. "She has learned to respect the gods."

"Respect the gods?" Dame Julie shook her head. "How Dervla must hate her." She shot Benet an amused look. "You've grown sly, my Prince. It's too late at night for an old woman like myself to think of crossing swords with such an upstart."

Benet allowed himself a thin smile. "Then you'll agree to help?"

"Yes, but not with Dervla." Dame Julie loosed a half-resigned sigh and shook her head. "I'm not the woman to split hairs and ferret out where her accusations have merit. Besides, Bissanty traitors should have a reason to be afraid. Who knows? Perhaps she'll get past personal vendetta and move on to uncover the real turncoats." She shifted, a little arthritic in her movement.

"However," she continued, "the Kingship songs—there I may be able to help. I'll delve into the old lore. The old ballads are not all prettiness and light. Your own court bards could help me there. They are possessive of the history songs, but perhaps if you would charter them to perform for me I could learn something."

"My bards?" the Prince said, more than a little surprised. "They are relicts of a past age. Under my father's rule, much of what they were required to learn was set to parchment by younger hands. I do not know what they could tell you."

"Exactly so," said Dame Julie. "And all the more reason to question them."

"It has been long since they were called to active performance," the Prince said doubtfully. "But do as you see fit. I'll command them to obey."

"I'm an old woman." Dame Julie rose and made a stiff curtsy, obviously satisfied by this concession. "You've had your way with me. Now give me leave to get some rest."

"You are free to go," the Prince said. "I would not hold you past your comfort."

Dame Julie made a sound that was suspiciously like a snort, and curtsied again.

She collected her shawl from the bench, along with a leather-bound songbook. Turning to the door, she stopped for a last look at Gaultry.

The young huntress shuffled her feet under the old woman's scrutiny. The tamarin, quiet all the time that they had been talking, shifted restlessly, and she almost dropped it on the tiled floor. Dame Julie watched as she juggled to hold it.

"You have served to turn my mind tonight, but you have no understanding of what the Prince is asking. Asking of us, of the Brood." Her dark hazel eyes were cold, even angry. "With half the old witches gone, it will take much to uncover that answer."

"You're still alive," Gaultry said uneasily. "And Gabrielle of Melaudiere, and Tamsanne. Rumor has it that Richielle may be too. Perhaps she knows something." Richielle, the seventh member of the original coven, was a mysterious figure reputed to have been old even at the closing of the last cycle.

The old woman thumbed the edge of her songbook and drew a heavy breath. "Richielle—if the gods favor us, the goat-herder's safely dead and in the ground with all her secrets. Rediscovering the Kingmaking secrets should prove terrible enough without her." She pushed abruptly past the young huntress and was gone.

The Prince sank onto the bench Dame Julie had abandoned, and pulled his wife down beside him. Though the Princess's face was carefully expressionless, her fingers sought his for comfort. Looking down at his young bride with tender concern, he drew her hand close to his heart, unconsciously revealing as he did so how much had been at stake in this interview.

"She seems afraid," Gaultry said softly. She averted her gaze and studied the door, giving her rulers a moment to compose themselves. "Why did my talk of slaves alter her so?"

"She wanted to change her mind," the Prince said. Giving Lily's hand a last caress, he rose from the bench and returned to the princely chair near the candelabra. As he took his place, he assumed a cool expression, the straight dark brows quirking sternly. Gaultry's heart sank. The cramped space of the room, which had grown increasingly warm throughout Dame Julie's interview, seemed suddenly stifling. The time had come for her own scolding.

"I crossed paths with the Stalkingman in Melaudiere's sick-chamber," the Prince began, as if conversationally. "Somewhat reluctantly, he informed me of the circumstances of your arrival in Princeport, as well as the number of your present company." He shook his head. "Your unsanctioned abscousion from my court, as a murder enquiry opened, would have been insult enough to my authority—even if you had not carried the prime suspect away with you. What am I to do? Your return now,

with that selfsame murdering boy in your train, only flaunts your diso-
bedience."

Gaultry dropped to her knees. "Your Highness," she said hastily.
"Disloyalty *to you* was never my intention. But a life was at stake.
Martin—"

"If you were speaking only of the Stalkingman, I could commend
you," the Prince said dryly. "I owe the man my life. The least I would
have done was send you in his train, and I certainly would have done
more, given the opportunity. But your flight was only partly to rescue
Martin. Against prudent council, you decided to protect the boy—the
young monster who killed innocent members of your own Common
Brood."

"Martin's safety was foremost," Gaultry protested. "And Tullier—the
boy was never more than a pawn. On great Elianté's honor, I swear with
clear conscience that he did not commit the murders of Destra Vanderive
and her children. That was his Sha Muira master. A man Tullier himself
killed in his turn."

Benet shook his head. "The boy was Sha Muira-trained. The murdering taint was in him. But this is by-the-by. How do you think the facts
appeared to my court? Even if the boy did not kill the Vanderive family,
my entire court bears witness that he is guilty of a greater sacrilege. On
Emleia's Feast Day, he sought to defile the love that the Goddess-Twins
bear me. I could have despoiled the harvest of an entire summer that day.
Can you wonder that my High Priestess calls you traitor?"

"No, my liege."

"Well then—explain yourself!"

"My Prince," Gaultry said softly. "The plot to which the boy was
party on that day was certainly a sin against the gods. But I was the first
to call warning. If you can but believe me—"

Benet cut her short. "The boy drew a knife on me before all my
assembled nobles. How can he be forgiven?"

"I don't ask that you forgive him," Gaultry said, panicking a little as
she tried to keep pace with the rapid questions. This was leading toward
Tullier's worst fear—return, and a summary trial and execution. "But I
would beg you pardon him. Tullier was Bissanty's tool. You can wound
Bissanty severely by wresting that tool from them—"

"You risk your own reputation by protecting him," Benet said, unrelenting. "My own restoration to power is fresh, and we have not done
with hunting Bissanty traitors. Yet here you are, back at court, the boy

still under your protection, and what is your first public action? Cozying up to the Vaux-Torres girl right where I cannot possibly ignore you?"

Gaultry stared up, appalled. "What does Elisabeth Climens have to do with this?"

"She is the Duchess of Vaux-Torres's daughter. Vaux-Torres, the woman at the center of Dervla's accusations—"

Fortunately for Gaultry, the Princess intervened. "You can't blame Lady Gaultry if Sieur Ronsars escorted her to the Climens girl's side," she said. Taking the seat by her husband's side, she fussed with the fine cloth of her gown, smoothing it over her belly with a delicate pat. "And as Lady Gaultry is newly returned to Princeport, she couldn't have known about the High Priestess's newest denunciations."

The Prince glanced at Gaultry. "Well?"

She took a deep breath. She would have to speak without heat to convince him. "My Prince, I truly believe Tullier has earned your clemency. But beyond that, when you have heard all that I have to report from Bissanty, I am sure that you will see it would be politic for you to treat him with mercy. I can only ask that you hear me out before you decide his fate.

"As for Elisabeth Climens—without evidence, she cannot be held responsible for her family's alliances, whatever they may be. I'm not ashamed that I spoke with her. If you want my opinion, I'd say she has a loyal Tielmaran's sense of justice. What has she to gain by staying at court if the rumors are true?"

The prince smiled wanly, looking suddenly careworn. "Elisabeth is a good girl," he said. "It remains to be seen if the same can be said of her mother."

He waved for her to rise and take Dame Julie's old seat on the bench. "Get off your knees, Lady Gaultry, and make yourself comfortable. If Dame Julie is right in her gloomy forecasts, in the coming days you will need your strength."

The Prince took his wife's slender hand in his own, gathering strength from her nearness. When he returned his attention to Gaultry, his eyes gleamed in the candlelight. "Now," he said, "I want you to tell me everything that you learned in Bissanty."

▼

chapter 9

The corridors of the summer palace were cool relief after the heat and activity of the twin palaces. No guards here, no petitioners, no loitering courtiers. Just Gaultry and the flickering oil lamp she'd picked up in the building's spare, stone-paneled foyer. She walked quickly, her steps loud and purposeful on the time-worn stone tile, the light casting weak shadows on the pale plastered walls. Her arms felt empty with the weight of the tamarin gone. The Princess, she'd been relieved to discover, had been delighted to accept the animal as a gift—or, more properly presented than Gaultry had managed, as a tribute to her stature.

The interview with the Prince had gone better than Gaultry had dared hope. Her disobediences had been pardoned. Even more unexpectedly, Benet had entrusted her with his sigil, a small blue-and-white leather shield embossed with his personal seal and her marker, to allow her free passage within Tielmark, in case she should again need it. "I'll not be leaving this in your hands indefinitely," he had told her, sternly. "But for now, if you should need to go hieing off again without warning, I don't want the trouble of explaining to my ministers." Gaultry was grateful for this physical evidence of his trust.

Most importantly, for now Tullier was safe. There had been an unusual note of dissention on this count from Lily, who took a hard line against anything Bissanty, but Benet had not been blind to the political advantages of offering the protection of his court to a runaway Bissanty heir. He agreed to withhold judgment on the boy, at least until he had a chance to give Tullier a personal hearing. For now—the boy was safe.

Gaultry passed through a stone archway and bobbed briefly to the little shrine there, a fresh double-twist of the Goddess-Twins' oak and ash. *Once again, for delivering me,* she intoned. *And for delivering those I love.* The Prince had commended her for freeing Martin from Bissanty chains. Her cheeks warmed. The image of the Prince, so sober and calm, superimposed itself on the memory of Martin as she had found him, chained in the darkness of the Bissanty temple, the grey wolf bound in shadows at his side. The Prince had spoken of her mission so solemnly, but the Princess—Lily's dark eyes had stared into hers knowingly. *You have served your Master well,* those eyes had told her. *But you can't pretend to me it was for Benet that you chased after the Stalkingman.*

Gaultry squirmed, embarrassed that the Princess found her feelings so obvious. But the Princess, she knew, was timid and bold together. She could hope that the shy part of Lily's nature would prevent further discussion with her husband of her own and Martin's sorry case.

She turned a last corner, approaching her own rooms. In front of her, the red glow of a torchère left to burn itself dry sparked up, sudden and fierce, startling her. "What idiot—?" she exclaimed, darting to tamp the flames down before the wall behind it scorched. She crushed the flames with the base of her lamp, near burning her fingers. The red coals winked evilly, then died back.

Staring at the deadened torch, she began to tremble, the significance of her recent interview with Benet finally coming home to her. "It's madness," she muttered. "Midsummer madness."

An alteration of rule such as Prince to King was a task for the gods. The Prince's sights were set high, if this was his goal. She belatedly realized that the lucky gold foil suns being dispersed to the Midsummer celebrants were a discreet hint that Benet's ambitions lay with attracting the Andion God-King's notice. Would this have been equally obvious to everyone at court who had a shrewd understanding of religious politics? Perhaps the hint had not been so discreet. "Urging so great a woman as Dame Julie to play Kingmaker. Imagining that I could serve my Prince, and play the game myself . . . Dame Julie said it herself. I don't know what I'm doing." An image came to her of Benet crowned King, the red sun of Andion risen over him. It was at once delightful—and a terror.

She crushed out the last ember in the torchère and turned for her own door.

It was easy to nod obediently when a fierce old woman like the Duchess of Melaudiere told her Benet must be made King. It was easy, in another way, to journey to Bissanty, and see with her own eyes the cruel fate that would overwhelm all Tielmark if Imperial power regained possession.

But to hear Benet declare himself to Kingship's bloody path, to learn that he considered her, and the Brood, so pivotal to aiding him on that journey—that was not a charge to accede to carelessly. It was not a charge that she had expected him to set upon her so privately.

She had expected—had dreaded—being questioned before his council of ministers. This private audience suggested a desire that these plans not be revealed, a trust in Gaultry herself that she was not confident she merited.

By the time she reached her own familiar door, these thoughts had deeply fatigued her. She was grateful to spy the reassuring green copper of the Great Twins' double spiral hung from the latch of her own room's door. The salon beyond was warm and tidy, a banked fire in the grate, a red robe laid welcomingly across the somewhat threadbare divan. A large copper tub, sealed over with a warming towel, had been prepared on the tiles in front of the fireplace, evidence of current occupation. Gaultry's heart leapt. Only one other person would use this space so familiarly.

"Mervion?" she called. "Mervion, I'm home!"

There was no response to greet her. The door that led to the private bedchamber the sisters shared was closed and locked, the door to the workroom a little ajar, but the room beyond unlit. Puzzled, Gaultry crossed the main salon to the room's long terrace doors and stepped through to the shallow terrace that overlooked the deer park. "Mervion?" she called again.

The moon, now in descent, cast the landscape into deep shadow. A flash of movement caught her peripheral vision—a doe, darting behind a row of trees. Beyond the rough curve of the park wall, far, far below, the gleam of the night sea beckoned. She stood quietly on the terrace, assessing. The distant crash of the surf, at the base of the cliff below the wall, did not obscure the soft noises of a park ground at rest under the moon. Crickets and the gentle suggestive sounds of deer grazing were carried on the gentle breeze.

Nothing to intimate that Mervion was anywhere out there beneath the trees.

Leaving the door open to the night, she turned back inside. It was too late to return to Martin's town house. She'd sleep here, and perhaps meet Martin in the duchess's chambers the next morning before she rejoined the others.

Unraveling her hair from its dressing, she kicked out of her slippers and threw herself full-length on the divan.

Her sister's perfume clung to the folds of the discarded robe. A chill of loneliness touched her, and she drew it over her own clothes as a makeshift blanket. It seemed such a very long time since she had seen her sister.

Mervion could not be far. She would not have ordered a bath—an indulgent luxury on a night when the castle staff would be mostly engaged in their own celebrations—and then abandoned it. It would not be long before their reunion.

Gaultry covered her face with her palms. She did not know what role her sister might play in the Prince's plans. Benet had mentioned nothing of it, so she did not even know—had not even asked—if he had a role for Mervion. That thought bit her, like a new betrayal.

She had always depended on Mervion. As the younger twin, she had imagined herself always a step behind.

Her self-knowledge was greater now, and nothing was so simple.

As children, Gaultry had been shy, Mervion outgoing—and thus Gaultry had avoided many tasks she regarded as unpleasant. On Market Days in Arleon Forest, when the young twins had emerged from the protection of the greenwood, Gaultry, too shy even to speak, had clung to old Tamsanne's skirts. Those days, Mervion, by default, had ended up doing most of the real work.

Gaultry had imagined herself the grateful recipient of Mervion's support, but she had little considered how she had grown to expect it, grown to rely upon it.

Now, her recent escapade with Tullier revealed how she had come to demand it, irrespective of Mervion's own will.

The Prince might credit her with saving Tullier, and it had indeed been Gaultry who had been seized by the impulse to save his life.

But in the end it had been Mervion who had supplied both the power and the means.

Looking back, Gaultry could see that her sister had not wanted to save Tullier's life. Where Gaultry had seen a suffering child, Mervion had seen a Sha Muira assassin, so dedicated to his craft that he had poisoned himself before entering battle to prevent any chance of himself falling alive into enemy hands on his mission's completion. Mervion, unlike Gaultry, had been willing to let that poison run its course.

That poison was the Goddess Llara's gift to the Sha Muira: a toxin so baneful that even the strength of her Glamour-soul was not enough to stop it. But with Mervion helping her—with the power of two Glamour-souls combined, there had been a chance.

She had not given Mervion much choice about helping.

The fact that together they *had* had the power to stop the poison in him, but that this success had demanded more of both their powers than Gaultry had predicted . . . that only made what Gaultry had done worse.

Request or demand—whichever it had been, gaining Mervion's support to help Tullier had been a coercive act.

Gaultry stared into the banked fire, wishing Mervion would return.

In Bissanty, she had watched Tullier's half brother and sister—twins, like herself and Mervion—scrap for the power that they could have shared, and in so doing, destroy themselves. In appropriating Mervion's power so heedlessly, she feared she had taken the first steps along the same track.

She needed to speak to Mervion soon—if only to apologize.

The warm salon was comfortable and familiar. Gaultry drifted on the edge of sleep, nightmare images from the past weeks flowing before her: Martin bound to the enormous wolf; the white twin Columba, angry passion in her dark eyes as she accused Gaultry of sucking strength from her own twin; the long empty stretches of marsh they had traversed, struggling to reach Tielmaran shores; the marsh slaves of Bissanty, up to their thighs in black water as they harvested the rice. . . .

A hand touched her shoulder, and a man's lips brushed her cheek, gentle yet insistent. "You should use that bath," a voice whispered affectionately against her ear. "Or I'll have to apologize to Helène and Jene for calling it for you."

Gaultry, snatching her hand up to protect her face, shot fully awake, and recoiled along the couch. "Coyal!" she blurted. "Elianté's Spear! What are you doing here?"

To his credit, the young knight recoiled almost faster than Gaultry. He was also quicker to recover his composure. "Lady Gaultry." He backed away, a forced smile on his face. "I beg a thousand pardons. When did you get back to Tielmark?"

Coyal Memorant. Gaultry had last seen him on Emiera's Feast Day, before and during Tullier's attack. First he had strutted like a golden gamecock—and then he had fought like a lion. She remembered now, he had saved her life, taking on his face the dagger thrust Tullier had intended for her back. The scar, a neatly healed red line, ran from his brow to his ear, catching at the corner of his left eye. It hadn't spoiled his looks, Gaultry noticed, with odd resentment. On another man, it might have looked rakish. On Coyal's boyish face, beneath his mop of curling golden hair—it made him look vulnerable and kind.

Quite a transformation for a man who had sided with the Bissanty enemy in the recent conflict.

She sucked in her lips, mind spinning, trying to think what to say.

Repeating herself was all she could manage. "What are you doing here? Why didn't you knock?" Besides the obvious. Balling up Mervion's robe, she threw it behind the tub. "Where's my sister?"

Coyal gave her another forced smile. "I take it you got past Ronsars to attend Dame Julie's command performance. The rest of us outsiders were not so lucky."

"Mervion wasn't invited?" she asked, stunned. Then she was stunned again—at herself. In her preoccupation with her report to the Prince, she had failed to attribute any such significance to her sister's absence. "What's going on?" she said. "Martin told me she was with Benet on his ship. You're telling me she has to beg for invitations? Gods in me, who'd dare cast Mervion as outsider?" Then she remembered Ronsars, and frowned.

Coyal gave her an unfriendly look. "She has had no easy time here at court since you abandoned her. Don't pretend you didn't think of that. You have the Prince's ear. Your sister—she does not."

"That's not so. Without our magic, he and Lily would never have married. Benet trusts us—" In a horrible moment of clarity, she understood that this was not true: Though both twins' powers had been engaged to form the magic at the wedding, Gaultry had withstood the traitor Chancellor's spells; Mervion had not. To Gaultry's mind, that was a matter of small importance—after all, Benet himself had fallen thrall to those same sorceries, and it was only Gaultry's love for her sister that had girded her with the power to resist them. But from Benet's view, perhaps with court folk such as Dervla and Ronsars at work on him, Mervion's failure had not been so easily excused.

"I don't need to talk to you about these things," Gaultry said hotly. "I need to talk to my sister."

"To me?"

Gaultry swung to the door, tremendously relieved, but what she saw there wiped the smile from her face, replacing it with uncertainty. Yes, it was Mervion who stood at the door, but she was not alone. By her side was a short, birdlike wren of a woman, wizened, with powerful hands and intense dark eyes. "Tamsanne!" Gaultry had not known that her grand-mother had arrived in the capital—certainly Benet had not told her. A belated wariness overtook her. Why had the Prince not mentioned Tam-sanne's arrival?

She wanted to throw herself into Mervion's arms, but with Tamsanne present as well as Coyal, she hesitated. Should she make introductions? No, she could see from the way Tamsanne nodded to Coyal as she entered the room that the two had already met.

Tamsanne offered Gaultry a dry cheek to kiss. This, at least, was familiar. Despite her strong love for her granddaughters, the old woman was seldom physically affectionate.

Gaultry paused. She wanted very much to kiss her grandmother's cheek, but so much had passed since they had last seen each other. "Grandmother," she said hesitantly. That, not least, was a part of her hesitation. The last time she had seen Tamsanne, she had believed that the old woman—her sole guardian and Mervion's, through all their child-hood—was only her great-aunt. Tamsanne had concealed so much, trying to protect them from the dangling sword of the Brood-heritage.

Tamsanne, hesitating in her turn, took Gaultry's hands in her own. Her eyes flickered to Coyal, as if reminding Gaultry that they were not alone. "My beautiful granddaughter." Her strong fingers clasped Gaultry's hands, a little hungrily. "You have grown and gained in every way since I last laid eyes upon you."

Gaultry kissed her warmly, wishing Coyal would sink into the floor. She had so many questions—not all of them pleasant.

"Gaultry. We heard that you had arrived. We were wondering when you would make your appearance." Mervion came forward and gave her a light hug. She smelled smoky and aromatic, as if she had just come from attending a fire. Gaultry hugged her back, burying her face for a moment in her sister's hair. They were exactly of a height, the hug close enough that Gaultry could feel the accelerated pounding of her sister's heart. Had Mervion been as nervous of this meeting as herself? Of course. When her sister had vested half her Glamour-soul in Tullier, she must have imagined the gift would only be temporary. She could never have imagined that Gaultry would take him and run off to Bissanty for nigh on six weeks.

What had it been like to wait in court, through the waxing and the waning of the past moons, wondering if Gaultry would even realize the sacrifice she had made?

"I—I came as soon as I'd cleared the dust of the road," Gaultry said. "Tullier—the Sha Muira boy—is with me." She loosed her sister and looked fiercely into her eyes, willing Mervion to understand the depths of her feelings, her regrets. "I know that you and he have unfinished business."

From the relief that passed across Mervion's features, Gaultry could tell that at least some of her message had made it through to her.

"I know you were not sure whether it was right that we should save him," Gaultry continued awkwardly. She glanced again at Coyal, wondering how deeply Mervion had taken him into her confidence. She herself certainly wasn't ready to trust him with Tullier's secrets, let alone her own. But what to say to Mervion, here, now—Mervion, to whom she owed an explanation? "But Tullier is more important than he first seemed. I've just made my report to Benet, and he's given me—us—his blessing for what we did." There—that was adequately discreet.

"He did?" Mervion looked surprised, then suspicious. "What exactly did you tell him?"

Gaultry would have given almost anything to have been alone with Mervion then, sharing all that she had been thinking since the day she had discovered what Mervion had risked—the loss of half her magical strength—to keep the young assassin alive. "Everything that was important." She flushed. She had hardly thought of Mervion throughout that interview, and certainly the idea that she might need to put in a good word for her sister had not passed her mind.

"Did my name even come up?"

Gaultry did not know how to answer. An awkward pause grew between them. Her sister's cool face hid whatever it was she was thinking. She looked, as always, beautiful and composed. None of the distresses Coyal claimed for her showed on her face. Yet Gaultry, for all she disliked the young knight, could not imagine why he would lie to her. "Mostly Benet spoke to me of the future, not the past."

Mervion took a step backward. "I have missed you, Gaultry." The sentiment would have felt sweeter if she had not taken another step away, and reached for Coyal's hand. "Now that you are here, I'll move my things, so you will have your privacy."

"You're not leaving?" With him, Gaultry wanted to add, but she was shy of saying such a thing in front of Tamsanne.

"You take over a space." Smiling to lighten the criticism, Mervion stooped behind the forgotten tub, and picked up her crumpled robe, straightening it across her arm. "You will feel better for having more room."

"Where's Tamsanne staying? Won't you all be staying here?" Gaultry turned to the old woman, beseeching. She had imagined that her family would share the same small suite of rooms—just as they had shared Tamsanne's tiny cottage for so many years, in the borderlands of Arleon Forest.

"I have found a place in the palace grounds that better suits me," Tamsanne replied. She would have continued, but a light knock at the door interrupted.

"Come in," said Gaultry unwelcomingly.

It was Martin. The number of people greeted him unprepared. "I see I've come at a bad time," he said, lingering outside. "I'll come back later."

"Twins' blessing on your safe return to Princeport," Mervion said. "Please do come in. We were just going out ourselves."

"I'd rather not disturb you. I know how Gaultry has been longing for this reunion. I'm interrupting."

Everyone was interrupting. Gaultry did not know whether to shout or cry. These people—Coyal excepted—were all the people she most dearly wanted close to her. But privately, not en masse. What she needed to say to each of them, to ask—these were matters that needed to be teased over confidentially before being shared, even with each other.

"I missed you at the concert tonight," she told Martin.

"My grandmère is very unwell," he said. "So unwell—I know I should not have disturbed you so late, but it could not wait. You must come to see her." He glanced uncomfortably at the chamberful of her relations. "First thing in the morning. You must not delay."

"Does she have something she needs to tell me? Is it about Tullier?"

Martin cast an unfriendly look at Coyal. "No," he said. "It's not about the boy. Look, Gaultry, you're busy, and this is important. I'll talk to you tomorrow."

With that, disappointingly, he was gone. Worse, on his heels Tamsanne and Mervion made their departure, accompanied by the detestable Coyal. She realized then that Mervion and Tamsanne both must share her wish to speak only privately, but could not control the stab of disappointment at this abandonment. "Mervion," Gaultry whispered in her sister's ear, giving her a final hug before Coyal reclaimed her. "You must come and meet with Tullier and me privately. As soon as possible. Tomorrow, no later. Can you slip away and find us at Martin's townhouse?"

"So soon? It will be hard to arrange. In the evening?"

That would get Mervion there after the Prince's visit. Gaultry shook her head. "Earlier? I have an appointment at sundown. And I want . . ." She wanted Mervion's Glamour-soul out of the boy and safely back inside Mervion where it was supposed to be, before Tullier had his interview with Benet. "Mervion—Tullier wants you to have what is yours. What could be more important than that?"

An inscrutable look flickered on Mervion's face. "Earlier then. I will see what I can do." Turning from her sister, she once again took Coyal's hand, and went away with him, Tamsanne on her other side, carrying a large cloth bag stuffed with her things.

Gaultry slept restlessly in her own bed, miserable and lonely. Thoughts of Kingship scarcely impinged upon her. She dreamed of her family, of the deep woods in Arleon Forest, of the days she had spent alone with her sister, through long snowy closed-in winters and bright joyous summers.

When she woke, the first thing she thought of was Coyal. Of the way Mervion's eyes had lit when he had touched her.

Those days of togetherness with her sister were over. A door had been shut between them. She desperately wanted it reopened.

T he Melaudieres' ducal chambers overlooked the sea from the roof
of the manse that flanked the west wall of the palace complex. The
enormous suite was a little palace unto itself, built onto the roof of the
older building, with its own narrow staircase leading up from north court.
Even with one and a half stories taken off the climb by the height of the
yard in the north court, Gaultry arrived a little breathless, wondering how
the old woman had managed the stairs for so many years. A solemn-faced
Martin met her in the antechamber.

"It won't be long," he greeted her, exhausted. Daylight revealed stress
lines in his face. He almost reached to touch her, then thrust his hands
into his pockets, as if touching her right now would be a mistake. "Come
in. The vultures are hovering. But she'll be glad to see you. Gavin should
be here," he blurted. "And Mariette." Between the Lanai summer wars
and the Brood-pledge, Martin's cousin and his sister were the only other
surviving members of the family. "Damn Haute-Tielmark's border for being so far away. They won't even know for weeks!" The swift changes in
his tone alarmed her, but, even seeing her reaction, he turned away without explaining.

The room beyond was airy, full of astonishing light reflected up from
the sea, so far below. The effect was ethereal, oddly illuminating the
downturned faces of those crowded within.

Indeed, the room was so crowded that at first Gaultry could not even
see the figure on the bed. There were almost as many clerks with papers

as there were nurses and priests. A duchess in illness was not granted privacy.

Someone moved, clearing Gaultry's view to the bed, and giving her a terrible shock.

She knew at once that she had come too late. The air left her lungs, and for a moment her sight darkened, the force of her reaction was so strong. She had been expecting—she had been expecting the Duchess, lying limp and weak, but offering wisdom and considered words, offering stern yet tender counsel.

But the body that lay before her on the bed would not be issuing any counsel. Not today—or ever again. Gabrielle of Melaudiere was shriveled and small, reduced almost to nothing beneath the sheets. Her color was already gone. A smell struck Gaultry's nostrils unpleasantly as she moved closer—the appalling smell of a body lost to life, yet not gone from among the living.

Something clenched inside her. When Martin had told her the Duchess was ill, she had not understood. Because he had spoken in front of Coyal, he had inadequately explained—or perhaps he himself had been unready to face the truth.

Gaultry took another step forward, then hesitated. The old woman was surrounded by busy and important-looking people, most of them carefully not looking at the bed and its pitiable contents. If Martin had not been at her side, she certainly would have retreated. In one small mercy, Dervla was not present, though, almost as bad, one of her acolytes was there to fill her place—Palamar Laconte, heir to the warrior-countess Marie Laconte, one of the original brood seven. Gaultry shifted uncomfortably at the sight of Palamar, and nodded an uneasy welcome, which Palamar politely, if uneagerly, returned.

The acolyte was a plump, helpless-looking woman, with protuberant front teeth. It had been Palamar's sister, and her sister's sons, whom Tullier's Sha Muira master had murdered. A wave of guilt by proxy swept her, and Gaultry was relieved when Palamar herself found some excuse to turn away. Gaultry very much did not want to talk to Palamar—she wanted to see Melaudiere.

The great Duchess lay silently, staring at the carved white plaster of the ceiling.

"Go to her," Martin said hoarsely. "Never mind the others. She asked to see you last night. The verger made her rest. I thought there would be more time, but this morning she can barely speak."

Gaultry went shakily forward. The serving woman sitting near the Duchess's head, a bowl of water in her lap, motioned for Gaultry to take the empty stool at her side. With the rag in her hand she gently moistened the old woman's lips, and, more horribly, the unblinking eyes.

"Lean over her face," the woman said. "She'll see you if you lean over."

The old woman's hand protruded limply from the bedclothes. As she leaned in, Gaultry took that hand gently in her own, terrified by the papery feel of the skin, the brittle delicacy of the bones. "Your Grace," she said, bending close to the old woman's face, "I'm here."

The hand contracted feebly in her own. With a tremendous effort, the head turned a few degrees toward her. Melaudiere's eyes were like sunken marbles—bright still, and startlingly alive in the pallor of her face. This was not a woman who was ready to be dead.

"Gaul-try," she managed. But that was all. She was too far gone for more.

"She can hear you," the serving woman unnecessarily assured her. "She knows you're here."

A impracticable, desperate thought rushed to her: She would send a runner to bring the Sharif, and then she would force the desert woman to mind-speak. With the Sharif, the Duchess's physical weakness, her inability to talk, could be bypassed. Gaultry could get the answers she needed—

As quickly as the idea had come, it receded. The complexities of state were behind the old woman now. Ahead lay only the business of dying, and of trying to manage that well.

She dashed back tears. It was Martin's place to cry here, not hers. She must do nothing to intensify this woman's last painful moments, nothing to give her grief. Her mind was a horrible blank as she ran through the many things she had intended to say, to ask. Which of them were worth voicing? Which of them could be said in a crowded room, where undoubtedly there were unfriendly ears listening? What could she say to ease the woman's passing?

Gaultry glanced down the old woman's body; what she saw there made the pain in her heart stab clear down to her knees. Martin, taking a stool by his grandmother's feet, had removed one of the old woman's bed slippers and was massaging one shriveled foot, as though trying to keep her circulation moving. The expression on his face—she was torn between retaining her hold of the old woman's hand, and rushing dramatically to his side to comfort him.

One day I'll marry your grandson, she wanted to say. She wanted to shout it, to tell not just the old woman, but the whole room. *When his wife finally lets him go, and he is free to have me*. But Gaultry had little idea if this revelation would make the Duchess glad or angered. For fear of the latter, she would have to hold her peace.

Instead she would try to assure Melaudiere that her life's efforts would not die with her, and hope that she would be right.

"The Prince asked me to help him follow the red path," she whispered, her face hovering just above the old woman's. "I agreed. Julie too. Now—if we can just get everyone else on our side, Gods willing, Benet will be king."

The Duchess rolled her eyes to look at the serving woman, who took the cue and obediently daubed her cracked lips. The meager body strained beneath the covers, though all that effort was hardly enough to register as a flutter in her hand. "Don't," she managed at last, "hurt anyone. Too high, the price—"

"She strained herself last night," the serving woman said apologetically. Briefly, Gaultry was angered at the interruption; then she realized that Melaudiere had already stopped.

"Who let her do this?" Gaultry said. "Didn't they know she was ill?"

The woman shook her head. "She would not be stopped. She insisted on finishing the gift."

Gaultry looked to where the woman pointed. A cluster of men with the Prince's blue-and-white livery stood by one of the room's large windows, bending over a cradle. She did not at first understand what she was seeing. The cradle was empty, even of bedclothes.

"Her last work," the woman said. "She finished it at the midnight hour, when Midsummer was over."

Gaultry realized then that she was supposed to be looking at the cradle, not the men. The former—as soon as she focused on it, she could see it was the Duchess's own work, forged with the woman's fabulous creating magic, her artistry.

Carved from a single piece of burl wood, the exterior was the likeness of a great foaming wave, the bubbles cunningly carved to match the grain of the burl beneath. Silver inlay traced the edges of the bubbles and also the scaly backs of two serpentine fishes that rode the edge of the wave, forming the cradle's rails. During her past sojourn at the duchess's grand mansion, Gaultry had seen works in metal, clay, and glass—all mediums that could be flowed, molded, and mixed with a sorceress's magic. This piece had been painstakingly carved. Without thinking, Gaultry thumbed the duchess's lax hand. Even the calluses on the old woman's hand seemed to have thinned and faded. How had she managed to hold the chisel? The serving woman, reading Gaultry's thought, shook her head.

"The carving was done months past. It's the spell she cast into the completed work that finished her."

"But why?—" Gaultry looked again at the cradle, and its significance became suddenly obvious. She should have seen this the previous night: Princess Lily was pregnant. Newly pregnant. Which was why the heavily expecting court lady attended her—an old custom for luck—why Ronsars had said the Princess was indisposed, and why Lily had patted the curve of her belly as she had spoken of the future.

It also explained, to some degree, why Benet was focusing his vision so determinedly on his own legacy.

She turned back to meet the old Duchess's eyes. "I understand," she said, hoping that this was true. "But you don't need to worry. I'll protect the child too." The mounting tears in her throat made it difficult to speak clearly.

With a sudden fierce pulse, the old woman's fingers tightened in her own, exhorting her without words.

Gaultry kissed the withered cheek and floundered her way out of the room before she completely lost her composure.

It was simple bad luck that Gaultry met Dervla as the High Priestess mounted the stairs outside, and simply Dervla's character that she could not let the young huntress pass unchallenged.

Gaultry was in no fit mood to talk. She had parted painfully from Martin, two minutes alone in a cramped side chamber, both of them with tears streaming uncontrolled down their faces. After that, she was not near ready to carry on conversation. Compared to Dervla, sleek, composed, her silver priestess's chain looped over carefully brushed robes, she must appear a new-released lunatic inmate.

Unfortunately, her grief was so fresh and strong, the thought that Dervla probably preferred approaching her in this moment of vulnerability went only a little way to helping her pull together.

"She is going quickly, isn't she?" the High Priestess said, unsparing.

"That is so, your Veneracy," Gaultry managed. She was a step or so above the older woman, and could not help but use this to position herself to advantage.

"I trust you will support me not to let her dreams of Kingship die with her," said Dervla, nettled, and coming up another step.

Gaultry glanced up to the open porch outside Melaudiere's door. This was not a private place, and she was not sure how Benet would want her to answer. "Of course, your Veneracy," she said apologetically. "But I have just now been in to say my good-byes to my Lady Melaudiere. It quite upset me. Perhaps we can speak of this another time?"

Dervla moved another step up still, putting the level of Gaultry's head beneath her. "I want to know I can depend on you," she said, an unfriendly glitter in her eyes.

Sensing a verbal trap, Gaultry shrugged, but did not answer. She would wait for a question.

"Much has changed since you departed Princeport."

Again, Gaultry kept her peace. This was hideous—Gabrielle of Melaudiere had been so fragile, so near the edge. The young huntress had never seen an old person so close to death's dark portal—and still so unwilling to let go. She was not ready to cross swords with Dervla, and wished she would go away.

But the woman persisted. "You may not know this, but in your absence Melaudiere and I stopped two more Bissanty attempts against the Brood. We recovered Destra Vanderive's infant daughter before she could be sent into Bissanty, and prevented another attack here in the city."

"That is happy news," Gaultry said. She had not known that poor murdered Destra had children other than her slain sons. She hesitated. From Haute-Tielmark, she knew Dervla was pursuing real traitors. But still she could not quite trust her. If what the Prince said was true, Dervla was also using her powers as inquisitor to compromise those who would merely challenge her authority—Gaultry and her sister included. It was safer, she reckoned, to change the subject, than to answer the woman's plea for her support. "It must pain you deeply, to be losing such a longtime ally as Gabrielle of Melaudiere. My own grief is sharp indeed, and I have known her only a short time."

"Of course," Dervla said. "My grief is deep." Her hand went to her chain of office, turning the links over in her fingers. "But just at this moment, seeing you returned in such a timely wise, my hopes for Tielmark have become much stronger." She ascended another step, then another, increasing the disparity of height between them. "We will speak soon, Lady Gaultry, when we have both better collected ourselves."

With that, she was gone.

Gaultry had an uncomfortable feeling about Dervla's words. She could not believe the woman had meant her last words as a pure compliment—there had to be a hidden meaning. There always was, with Dervla. The thought of her own actions meshing well with anything related to the High Priestess . . . Could that be good for anyone beyond Dervla?

But Dervla had been defending the Brood in her absence, and seemed determined, in her own right, to seek the Kingship path. That, Gaultry hoped, descending the stairs and heading back toward her own rooms, could well be something to build upon.

▼

chapter 11

The bell at the kitchen gate rang again, unmuffled here as it had been in the salon, and insistent. Gaultry, hurrying through the unfamiliar territory of Martin's townhouse kitchen to answer it, jumped at the noise and knocked her hip hard against the trestle table. "That has to be Mervion," she muttered, fumbling open the kitchen door and crossing the few steps of neglected garden to the back gate. Her sister's impatience was uncharacteristic. "Benet isn't due for hours yet."

But there were two figures, not one, waiting when Gaultry opened the battered green gate into the dusty alley. For one moment, Gaultry thought the cloaked figure at Mervion's side must be Coyal, and she drew in her breath in disappointment. Then the deep cowl turned to face her, and Benet's eyes flashed upon her.

"Am I early?" he said levelly, a touch of iron in his voice. "I trust I have not inconvenienced you."

"My liege!" She bowed, then shot a glance at her sister. "Mervion. Please come in."

Her sister's pale features were set in a rigid expression, revealing—to Gaultry's sisterly eye—carefully suppressed anxiety. The Prince, heated and sweaty in his unseasonable long cloak, was likewise distressed and openly impatient. His hand lingered on the bell-pull, as if pulling it again would have made her come faster.

"What took you so long?" he demanded, glancing along the alley as Gaultry struggled with the gate's archaic latch.

"My liege," Gaultry greeted him again, a little recovered from her surprise. "The house is half-closed, and there was no one in the kitchen. We didn't immediately hear the bell." She peered into the rubbish-filled alley. "Where's your escort?"

Mervion, standing behind the Prince, made a small gesture of bafflement, expressing that the particulars of their arrival had been entirely outside her control. "We're alone," she said. "The Prince left them at the palace."

Benet, propelling Gaultry backward in his haste to be out of the alley, stepped inside the gate, drawing Mervion with him. "They would have been a hindrance to our business," he said shortly. His expression grew downhearted. "Melaudiere has gone. If I had not come now, there would be no chance for me to escape the minutiae of her funerary arrangements. So let us complete the business of this boy of yours. My time will not be my own again until after Melaudiere is in the ground."

Gaultry sucked in a sorrowful breath. Benet gave her a sharp look. "I know," he said. "It's hard to believe. But it makes it all the more important that we settle the business with your boy. She would have been your strongest voice on the ducal council. I want this resolved before it moves to the quagmire of arguments and a cabinet vote."

"I understand." She nodded. "You will not regret that you have come. Tullier is still recovering from his wound, but he should be able to assure you that his intentions in Tielmark are honorable."

Gaultry fumbled to close the gate's latch. Her hands were shaking, and the gate hung awry. Benet watched her, making her clumsiness worse.

"I spoke with Lady Mervion as we came," he said abruptly. "She told me of her own business here with you this evening. A fascinating revelation. I understand at last how the pair of you conspired to overmatch the power of Llara-Thunderbringer's Sha Muira poison."

Gaultry's fingers stilled on the latch, hope dying that she and Mervion alone could settle the not insignificant matter of the Glamour-soul business between Mervion and Tullier before Benet even learned of it. "There was no conspiracy," she said, as levelly as she was able. She closed the latch, her fingers dexterous and certain at last, in her need to prove that his discovery did not daunt her. "Merely the need—and the act—to save a life."

"The very echo of your sister's words." Benet's expression was impenetrable, which usually meant he was displeased. "I will be most interested," he said, "to see how willingly your boy gives up the power that Lady Mervion so graciously shared with him."

"He is willing," Gaultry said fervently. "No question there." She had wanted so badly to talk to her sister—alone—before Benet came to speak with Tullier. But from the way Mervion kept to Benet's far side as they crossed the little yard and entered the house, Gaultry could see that her sister did not intend to exchange even a few words privately. "My liege," she added politely, trying to cover the quandary she felt she was in with Mervion. "Our dinner was delayed—we were eating when you rang. I must apologize for what little hospitality we can offer." An understatement that neatly bypassed description of the fire young Melaney had started in the kitchen chimney while attempting to heat their evening meal on the long-cold range.

"I have already supped," Benet said. "I wish only to see your boy."

They swept into the salon without warning. The scene that greeted their arrival was thus predictably informal. Tullier lay propped on the chaise by the window, disheveled. Aneitha, thankfully, was out of sight somewhere up on the floor above, probably making a greasy mess of Martin's fencing gallery. The Sharif and Melaney were at the small table where Gaultry had left them, finishing their meal. The young squire, recognizing the Prince, scrambled up and dropped an appropriately respectful bow. The Sharif, taking her cue from Melaney, made a slow courteous nod in the door's general direction. Setting aside her bowl, she unfolded her long frame from behind the table and rose to her feet. *Your Emir?* she asked, bowing her head to Benet in a outlandish but obviously formal obeisance.

My Prince. Gaultry paused. *Blessed of the Goddess-Twins Elianté and Emiera to rule Tielmark.* She glanced around the room, sensitive to its worn, musty, and overheated aspects. Martin's roughly kept soldier's lodgings, well-used and faded, seemed suddenly insufficient to the occasion. Benet was accustomed to grander surroundings, and to court-regulated exchanges—save, perhaps, for the time he spent at sea on his own ship. It was for her to play host, but she had a poor idea of who she was supposed to introduce to whom, and in what order of precedence. "His Royal Highness, Prince Benet of Tielmark," she announced aloud. A quick glance at Benet's blank expression told her that could not have been right. "And Mervion Blas, my sister." If she could not be correct, she would at least be clear. "Please be welcome to our lodgings. This is the Sharif, late of Ardain, a valiant comrade who joined my company in Bissanty."

Benet gave the Sharif a curious glance. "Lady Gaultry speaks highly of you," he said graciously. The Sharif, responding to his tone, acknowledged him with a solemn inclination of her head.

"And Tullier—you've met Tullier before, but not as Tullirius Caviedo, son of Siri Caviedo, Bissanty's Sea Prince and the Emperor's own uncle."

Benet shed his cloak and handed it ceremoniously to Mervion. Beneath he wore a blue-and-silver coat, very formal and grand, making a clear statement that official business was his intention. "Nothing else?" he asked, unexpectedly curt. "Nothing you would care to add, by way of setting all allegiances clearly upon the table?"

"I don't think so," Gaultry said, puzzled by his tone. He was formidable in his shining coat, moreso amidst the salon's faded furniture. "My liege, I am not familiar with the courtly forms. If I have offended—"

"Perhaps I need offer assistance with your introductions," the Prince said grimly. "As matters stand in Bissanty today, your young friend is considerably more than the Sea Prince's son." His wrist brushed against the hilt of the beautifully ornamented sword that hung from his belt, an involuntary hint at dampered animosity. "He is Caviedo the Fifteenth, Bissanty's newly designated Prince of Tielmark, fifth in line to the Imperial throne. Recognized of the Goddess-blood, in direct descent from divine Llara, the great imperial forerunner. Making him, not incidentally, the Bissanty counterpart to my own power," Benet finished sharply, in case Gaultry had missed this point.

"How can that be!" Gaultry reached for the nearest chair and sat, or rather collapsed, into the time-softened canes. Utter shock washed over her. It could not be true. The Bissanty Emperor wanted Tullier dead, not elevated as a potential rival. Surely this could only be a fresh ploy to flush the boy out, to make him vulnerable. Yet Benet seemed so certain!

"Tullier is a fugitive," she protested. "Not an honored Prince. They hunted us for him all through our flight from Bissanty. We saw the bounty postings—a price had been set on his head. Alive or dead. The Emperor didn't care which." Tullier had gone utterly stiff on his sofa, his ice green eyes bright with—disappointment? Defeat? She had promised him safe haven here in Tielmark, thinking that, at least, was a promise she could see completed. "I would not have brought him to Tielmark if he could have remained safely in Bissanty," she said. "Matters in Tielmark are complex enough without this!"

"She did not know." Mervion's voice cut like hot steel on ice through

Gaultry's confusion. "Your Highness, I would swear to you by Elianté and Emiera together that she did not know."

"But did he?" the Prince asked sharply. "He could have deceived her."

"Tullier would never—" Gaultry said.

"I could not say—" Mervion said, both at exactly the same moment.

Gaultry stared at Mervion, finally understanding the distance her sister had maintained since her arrival. "He asked you to judge if I'm telling the truth," she said furiously. "And you agreed."

Mervion stared back calmly, as if from across a great gulf. "We are not at cross purposes," she said. "We both are sworn to serve Tielmark. You have nothing to fear from me."

"It's not you I fear," Gaultry snapped. She had forgotten how angry her sister could make her. Since that moment in Bissanty when she had discovered that coercing Mervion to save Tullier's life had necessitated Mervion risking half the strength of her Glamour-soul, Gaultry had been lost in guilt. Columba, Lukas Soul-breaker's subordinate twin sister, had accused Gaultry of dominating her twin, of echoing Lukas in her propensity to use her sister's powers as if they were her own. The grain of truth in Columba's words had been more than Gaultry wanted to accept.

Now, as she looked into her sister's face, it came flooding back, the huge number of reasons why she had been able to reject Columba's judgment. Where the stakes were high, Gaultry's impetuous nature could compel Mervion to premature action, but Mervion, given time to reflect, could almost invariably outtalk her.

"I'm not afraid," Gaultry said again. But if Tullier really had been invested as one of Bissanty's Imperial Princes, what did that mean to his plea for sanctuary here in Tielmark? He was no longer a thorn in the imperial side—he was an Imperial insider, set up as a rival claimant to Benet's throne. "Though it does wound me to discover myself so thoroughly untrusted."

"We lent our power to a foreign Prince," Mervion said. "However unknowingly. Our Prince is wise to consider carefully our motivations." She crossed the room to Tullier, and touched the yoke of the boy's shirt. The recent sweat of his fever had dampened the cloth, but not discolored it. "It's hardly believable that it's true," Mervion marveled. "But you really *are* no longer Sha Muira. The poison has run its course." The Sha Muira Goddess-poison was so pervasive and strong that it permeated even the cult members' body fluids, tainting them black, making it poisonous to touch them—and denying them physical contact with anyone outside of the sect. As her sister touched Tullier's collar, Gaultry remembered the moment the boy had first cried clear tears. Those tears, miraculously, had washed clean tracks on the dark sweat on his face.

It had been at least a day after that before she had first been able to touch him.

"Was it our power, finally, that saved you?" Mervion asked the boy softly, "or your Goddess's will to relent?"

"Great Llara does not know mercy," Tullier answered, defiant. "That is her strength. It most certainly was your power."

Mervion, shaking her head, stood back from the boy and turned to Benet.

"My sister's loyalty is yours, my liege. I do not need to read her face to tell you that. As for this boy—if he is faithful to the Bissanty Emperor, that is now a matter of choice, not physical necessity."

Tullier and the Prince regarded each other across the length of the salon with distinct displeasure.

"By all the Twelve, then," Benet said. "Are you Empire's man?"

"I owe you no answers." Tullier bristled, arrogant even in his supine state.

"I could have come here with soldiers," Benet said equitably, pacing across the salon toward him. As he passed the unshuttered windows, a flash of light from the setting sun momentarily lit his face, "I chose to come alone, on the security only of Lady Gaultry's word. If you choose not to parlay with me directly, I can retire and call soldiers in to question you."

Tullier squirmed. "What does my answer matter to you? If my glorious father—" he stopped, too late to swallow the Sha Muira epithet for Emperor which rolled so naturally off his tongue. "—If my Imperial cousin has politicked to raise me as your rival, what choice do you have but to expel me?"

"I certainly won't be sending you home with half of one of my Glamour-witches' power," Benet responded. "I am here tonight, as I have belatedly discovered," he shot Gaultry a quick critical glare, "to ensure at least that. But you have not answered my question."

Tell Tullier to give him a straight answer. Gaultry glanced at the Sharif, willing her to pass on the direction. Tullier, with his odd upbringing, did not understand how to ask for kindness, for compassion. The Prince would offer it, she was certain, if only Tullier would give him an opening. *Tell Tullier to answer him straight so the Prince can offer him mercy.*

The Sharif, glancing back, raised one dark brow and frowned. She had not followed the exchange in its entirety, but she had its gist. She gave Gaultry a single rebuking shake of her head.

"Gaultry's sister can have her Glamour-soul." Tullier spat. "I did not cry for it. By Llara, I asked for nothing—"

"As a Sha Muira soldier, there was nothing you *could* ask for," Benet pointed out. "You existed only to feed the poison in your blood, to worship Storm-mother Llara with your kills. As a Bissanty Prince, the range of your ambitions is considerably broader. Now: on Lady Gaultry's word, answer my question. Whose man are you?"

Tullier vented an angry breath. "For her—" he gestured at Gaultry. "For her word, I will tell you the duty I owe to Bissanty now—which is nothing!" He heaved himself up, painfully, and choppily sketched Llara's storm-bolt sign. "Llara as my witness, here is truth: My father murdered my mother the day I was born, and condemned me to living death among the Sha Muira from the first day of my life. He did not care what we suffered, he cared only to revenge himself on his Imperial nephew Sciuttarus, who now reigns as Emperor.

"Why should I love him? Either him, or my Imperial cousin, Sciuttarus-the-cruel, whose actions set my father on this brutal course? I disown them—all of them. My family's machinations are nothing to me. I will not be a pawn in their games."

Benet listened to this outburst with saddening eyes. When he finally responded, his voice was both more gentle and more firm. "Poor Tullier," he said. "You speak more than you are intending. You can be a pawn, or a power-broker, but you cannot so lightly escape this game. Llara's blood cannot be so easily foresworn. Only one member of the Imperial house has been known to do it." A shadow of pride flickered on Benet's face. "That was my own greatest grandsire, Clarin, who convinced the gods to accept his Blood-Imperial as payment for a measure of this land's freedom. What would you aspire to, to be rid of the god-blood within you?"

Tullier let himself fall back on the couch, an exhausted expression on his face. He made no other answer.

Benet made the Goddess-Twins' spiral-sign, as if to clear the air between them. "We could ponder these questions through the night, but I have other business." He gave Tullier a serious look. "First, I want to see the power returned from you to my Glamour-witch."

"I have already said I am amenable," Tullier replied, a little pale. "I will do whatever is required."

Benet turned to Mervion. "So—the boy has agreed to return what is yours. Before I will decide the matter of offering him my court's protection, I want your power reclaimed." He glanced around the room. "We can clear the room, if you need privacy."

The Sharif and Melaney, who had been standing by uncomfortably for some time, the one not following all the conversation, the other not sure she should be there to listen, took this as their cue, and made for the door. From his expression, Benet had no intention to join them.

"What can I do?" Gaultry asked Mervion. She held out her hand, an offer of the power of her own magic, her own Glamour-soul.

Mervion shook her head. "I'm ready. I prepared before I came." Her gaze was downcast to Tullier's chaise, her expression hidden.

Gaultry, surprised by her sister's rebuff, however gentle, tried again. "We brought a soul-figure with us back from Bissanty," she volunteered. "One of Lukas Soul-breaker's creations. It can hold your Glamour-soul until you are ready to receive it. Shall I go unpack it?" The horrible silver figurine, with its stubby vestigial arms and merged legs, was still in her pack, nestled among layers of wadding.

"Destroy it." Mervion shuddered. She loosened the laces of Tullier's tunic and settled her hand inside, her slender fingers spread on Tullier's bony chest. "I won't use it. I don't even want to see it."

"Then how—" As she spoke, Gaultry realized that Mervion had already begun. She stared, the discovery that her sister did not need her fearful and bewildering.

The human soul was a wellspring of power, its manipulations best left to the gods alone. Gaultry had learned that as one of the deepest laws of magic and life, as something immutable and changeless. Besides, to manipulate a human soul required power beyond anything a normal person could command—even the most powerful sorcerer. The only exceptions were those who were double-souled themselves—like those born to an Imperial house, or to Glamour. Even then, their ability to touch or affect the human soul was insignificant. It took someone like Lukas Soul-breaker, who had commanded the power of three souls—his own, his Blood-Imperial, and the Blood-Imperial of his sister Columba, to reduce the human soul to something like an animal's spirit: something that could be twisted, controlled, used as a tool.

But even Lukas had been forced to augment his power during the soul transference, using the silver soul-figures to aid him. Indeed, Gaultry had retained the soul-figure in the belief that Mervion would need it to reclaim her power.

Evidently Mervion did not need it. A shimmer of gold emanated from her as she stood over Tullier's sofa and touched her hand to his wound. Tullier shivered, his eyes opening wide, his pupils dilating. The room filled with a shock of power, a pulse of strength that popped Gaultry's ears and sent her reeling. Benet grabbed for the back of Gaultry's cane-seated chair.

"I am done," Mervion said simply. She rose from Tullier's bedside and shook out her hands. Then, with more open satisfaction, "I have done it." For one moment, triumph lit her, then, just as quickly, she hid it away.

Tullier's face flushed with a healthier color than Gaultry had seen in him since his wounding. Fresh sweat trickled from beneath his hair. He pressed his palms to his cheeks. "What did you do?" he said shakily. "What have you left me?"

"You should feel better now." Mervion smiled. "My sister is a butcher, not a healer. I have what is mine now, but with what I did, you should find your wound much soothed."

"I feel so empty—" A sudden sound of a scuffle rose from the street below, cutting him short. Everyone glanced inquiringly toward the open window.

"What was that?" Benet said sharply. He stepped to the window and glanced down into the street. "Men. Wearing palace uniforms. Someone's letting them into the house." He cast Gaultry a suspicious look. "I did not call for them. Did you?"

Several things happened very quickly. A scream rang through the house, terror and alarm combined. The sound of rushing feet clattered on the stairs, and, in seemingly the same instant, the salon's door burst open. Three swordsmen propelled themselves inside, the first stumbling, recovering awkwardly from the kick that had driven the doors inward.

"Stand back." Their leader, a thin man with a swordmaster's scars on his sunken cheeks, kicked a chair out of his way as he advanced. "We are here for the boy. The rest of you—" His eyes swept the room. Shock crossed his lean face as he spotted Benet, his blue-and-silver coat gleaming in the last light of the window. Then he regained his resolution. "The rest of you just stay out of our way."

There were more men behind him, crowding the landing, ready to follow the three swordsmen into the room.

"You have no business here." With two steps, Benet took a stance in front of Tullier's sofa and unsheathed his sword.

Gaultry scrambled up to join him, glancing around for a weapon, and seeing none. In expectation of company, their equipment had been tidied away upstairs.

"Nor do you, Sire. Let us take the boy and leave, and no one will be hurt." The swordmaster flicked the tip of his sword, and his pair of arms-men spread out, the man who had kicked in the door moving a little clumsily, as though he had bruised his foot.

"Siànne," the clumsy man addressed his leader in obvious bewilderment. "What is *he* doing here?"

The swordmaster shook his head. "Twins in me, that is not for us to ask." As he spoke, he touched the silver gorget at his throat, and sketched a ceremonial gesture with his free hand.

"Don't cast it." Mervion, who had not moved from her place by Tullier's side, spoke directly to the swordmaster. She was the first to recognize a calling of magic in his gesture. "Leave here before worse than this threat to your honor befalls you." Her voice was sweet, almost dreamy, in contrast to her words. But there was something dangerous in her eyes. Dangerous, and intense.

It was not enough. The swordmaster bit his lower lip, concerned, but he advanced another step, ignoring the warning. He touched the backs of his knuckles to his throat, another ceremonial gesture, then flashed the flat of his blade outward.

"Elianté blessed me with good hunting," he intoned. "To her alone, I am pledged. I have found my quarry, I will take it—"

Green fire struck out from his sword, driving Benet, foremost of those arrayed against him, to his knees. This was not an effect the lean swordmaster had anticipated. Horror blossomed on his face, twisting fearfully with fear and helplessness, but the spell had him now, and he was in its thrall. He moved forward, jerkily, like an animated doll, the smoothness of his swordsman's stride disrupted, transformed into something hideous and intent.

His armsmen closed in nervously behind him, overtly dubious, but obedient to whatever orders had set them to this course.

Gaultry held wide her hands, even as she attempted to shield her fallen Prince. "This is treason, but stop now, and you can redeem yourselves!"

The swordmaster kept coming. The green fire spread off his blade, sheathing his body like armor as the spell reached its full effect. He bore down on them, his blade windmilling almost aimlessly, more like a farmer's scythe than a weapon. It seemed he was fighting the spell—and losing.

A clash of arms rang out from the landing. A bloodcurdling scream, half woman's cry, half feline's yowl, was followed by a man's shriek of terror. The Sharif, and Aneitha too, coming to their rescue.

With no weapons to hand, Gaultry snatched up the cane-seated chair, hoping to hold the swordmaster off, at least until the Sharif and the cat could reach the salon. Another flash of magic from the sword took her, this time spreading its enveloping green flame. She fell back against Benet, and the flame spread to take him too, slapping them both with alternating waves of fear, cold, and wrath.

As her own magic surged to repel it, recognition shot through her. Black-green. This magic was an angry black avenger-green, indistinguishable from the power that had struck at them on Sizor's Bridge. But this time the spell was not bound to a physical focus, like the vines that had sheathed the bridge. It was free to jump from one object—or person—to another, wreaking havoc in its trail. She felt like she had been struck by a thunderbolt.

Behind her, a wave of magic smacked Benet down, then flared to a new peak of power. Gaultry threw the chair at the swordmaster, and retreated, stumbling back against the sofa.

At the edge of her vision, she had a confused impression of Mervion, emerging at last from her dreamy torpor, rising from the sofa and opening out her arms with an unfamiliar, slow-paced deliberation.

As Mervion opened her arms, Gaultry sensed, rather than heard, the word of power she invoked. It thundered and grew, pounding in the air, rising as Mervion stretched wide her hands and flattened her palms toward the ceiling.

One of the swordmaster's armsmen staggered, drew in his hands, and covered his ears, an action exactly counterpoised to her sister's outward motion.

Mervion spoke again, challenging and loud. "For Benet!" she cried.

The man cried out too, his words and tone parroting Mervion's. "For Benet!"

"For Tielmark!" Mervion screamed.

"For Tielmark!" the man echoed her. He thrust with his sword, cutting the swordmaster from behind. "For Tielmark, and for my Prince!"

As the armsman's blade took him, the swordmaster let out an ago-nized cry. But he fell toward Benet, his sword clutched in his outflung hand, even this intervention failing to deter him. The Prince, writhing under the nimbus of green magic, barely raised his own blade in time. Gaultry threw herself into the scrum, trying to separate them, just as the armsman Mervion had suborned struck again. By a miracle, his blade again pierced the swordmaster, missing Benet and Gaultry.

The green magic hissed and flared, even as the swordmaster weak-ened. It seemed, weirdly, to be gaining power from the body to body contact of the Prince and his assailant. The swordmaster, still horribly animated, pressed Benet backward so they crumpled together across Tul-lier's couch.

"It's Tielmaran magic!" Gaultry yelled, as Tullier was knocked over the back of the couch. "It's taking strength from the Prince!"

Frightened cries rang in from the landing. Gaultry caught a glimpse of the Sharif, and then of the great cat Aneitha, tearing open a man's throat in a roil of feline savagery. Someone else was fighting there—fighting on their side. Melaney? The girl had not been armed that Gaultry could remember. Their attackers were in total disarray, uncertain whether they should be fighting at all, unable to retreat without orders, and un-willing to enter the salon to join the attack on the Prince. If it had not been for the green spell's rising power, there would have been no question who would win this fight.

"It is *you* who must control the magic!" Mervion called to Benet. "It will serve you   it is yours!"

Benet, grappling with the dying swordmaster, got his hand over the man's sword hand, still clasped over his sword's hilt, and tried to press it backward. "I can't!" he panted. "It is too much!" Yet even as he spoke, his action belied his words, and the swordmaster's blade fell back.

Odd light glimmered in the Prince's eyes. The doomed swordmaster continued to fight despite his horrific wounds, but Benet had him in retreat. The angry magic sheathed them in vivid, pulsing green, slapping Gaultry free and knocking her against the wall as it sought to focus and sustain itself. "Gods in me!" Benet screamed, his voice unnaturally high, full, unearthly. "This is my land! I am master!"

A fresh shock of power rocked the room. The green fire shattered into a thousand bearded sparks, fizzled, and vanished.

Benet knelt, alone, over the dead body of his opponent, breathing heavily. The armsman who had killed the swordmaster threw down his blade, cursing and crying together. "Siànne! Why did you bring us here! Oh Siànne!"

The other armsman threw down his weapon as well, his face as pale as death. "Stop the fighting!" he shouted, turning back toward the landing. "Stop, oh stop! Benet himself is here!" Darting to the door, he almost met his death on the tip of the Sharif's sword, as she appeared, soaked in blood, in the doorway.

"Is over," she said, jerking her blade aside to avoid running the man through. "Is over." The armsman dropped to his knees and covered his face with his hands.

Behind the Sharif, another face. Coyal. The young knight was kitted in half-armor, his bloody sword held at rest. "Mervion!" Relief spread on his face as he spied her, safe, backed behind the sofa at the far end of the room. "I saw them pushing their way in. Gods in me—I wasn't sure if I should go after them, but I knew Benet was with you. . . ." Catching sight of the Prince, his words dribbled away.

The Sharif stepped into the room. Before any of the Tielmarans could forestall her, she ran quickly across to Benet, and helped him up.

"Tielmark's Prince," she said, in her strong accent, her honey-gold desert voice. Then, more strangely, in her mind voice, crashing through Gaultry's senses so sharply that it was painful: *This is my land! I am master!* Her words—they were in Benet's voice, just as he had spoken them before banishing the magic. There was something reverent in the Sherif's demeanor, and she held her hand out to him. *Sun-marked, for certain*—that in her own more familiar voice.

Gaultry, not sure what the war-leader meant by this mysterious invocation, started toward her—then realized that the Sharif's mind-speak had not been intended for her. Benet's face was turned upward and he stared at the tall war-leader with a look of spreading wonder. At first Gaultry did not understand what she was seeing—she had never seen the Sharif accord trust instantly to another, never seen her make the leap of mental communication without delay.

Benet, dazed, stared deep into the woman's eyes. Gaultry was certain that the Sharif once again spoke to him. Did Benet reply? The Sharif put her hands on his shoulders, and raised him up. "Andion Vesa!" she cried aloud. "Andion Vesa!" Something passed between them—a communication, or magic, Gaultry could not determine which.

"Let me be," Benet said raggedly, all at once pushing the Sharif's hands away. "This is too much, too quickly. Great Twins in me—who is this woman, to touch me so?"

Gaultry dragged over a chair, wishing she were privy to their interplay. From the landing, Coyal pushed a pair of frightened men into the room and made them stand by the hearth. Then he lined up the two armsmen beside them. "There are two injured men out on the landing, and three dead," he reported. He gestured to the Sharif. "That one's cat is watching them." He shook his head. "I've never seen anything like it—and hope I won't again."

Gaultry looked at the armsman who had avoided the worst of the fighting—the man who had called for its end. His lined face was set in the expression of one who expected the worst—and fervently believed he had earned it. "Who sent you?" she demanded.

He shook his head. "Siànne knew." He sighed. "Siànne only. We are loyal men, all of us, what could we do but obey? I don't know why the gods would punish us, sending us here."

Gaultry turned to the Prince. "Who knew you were coming here?" she asked. "Whoever sent these men didn't know you would be here."

The Prince roused a little. "Not many," he said. "My day-warder, Sieur Jardine. He keeps the day's appointments. Also Jardine's servants. I came here in private—but not in secret."

"Melaudiere's people?" Gaultry asked. "Did you tell them why you would have to be late to her service?"

Benet shook his head. "No. Jardine gave them only the message that I would be delayed. Who else? High Priestess Dervla knew. She and Dame Julie were with me when the news of Melaudiere's death arrived. Their servants knew, and mine, of course."

Gaultry looked down at the body of the dead swordmaster, at the silver gorget that lay exposed at his throat, repository of the green magic that had moved him. A pang of unexpected disappointment stung her. Some part of her had been certain that Dervla's hand had been in this. The strength of the green magic that possessed the man had been well beyond what an ordinary priest or village sorcerer could call. But the attack, however powerful, had fallen into shambles the moment Benet's presence had been discovered. If Dervla had been behind the attack, that did not make sense. Gaultry did not believe the High Priestess was so subtle that she would plan an attack which she intended would fail.

"So with this man dead, we cannot know who sent you."

"On my life I swear to you, that is the truth of it." The man paled. "But we are palace soldiers, lady, drawn from the morning watch of the sea gate. Siànne would not have taken orders from anyone outside the court."

"You *were* palace soldiers," Benet said. Glum silence answered him. For a moment, a suspended quiet filled the room, as everyone took stock.

Then, as the last light of day faded, the deep, far-off sounding of bells awakened them.

"Sunset tolls the palace bells," the Prince said. "For Melaudiere. I must get back to the palace." He glanced around the darkening room and grimaced. "Though not before matters are set in order here. Perhaps I should have brought Jardine with me after all." Jardine, Gaultry knew, was a counselor as well as an appointment-keeper.

But it seemed to Gaultry that Benet managed well enough without him. First, with an expression of bemusement, he ordered Coyal to round up the former castle soldiers and chivy them back up to the palace, where they would be more thoroughly questioned and the matter of their punishment sorted. An ironic arrangement, considering that Coyal was supposed to be in disgrace, tarred with the brush of his Bissanty collaboration. But the young knight's well-timed appearance, the unrestrained way he'd thrown himself into the battle, supporting the Prince's side, had at least temporarily restored his name to the roster of the trusted—Gaultry's narrowed eyes watched him, as he organized the melancholy little troop.

The disgraced knight's arrival might have appeared a little too convenient for his self-reconstruction as a true Prince's man had it not been for the fact that Mervion had requested he shadow her and wait outside the house for her protection. The thought that her sister looked to him in this way made her stomach twist. She did her best to conceal her jealousy when he stooped to kiss Mervion's hand before he took his leave—even with the Prince and the rest of them watching.

Benet appointed the Sharif and Aneitha to return with him to the palace as a sort of an honor guard—a surprise to Gaultry, but she presumed that the Sharif must privately have agreed to it. *Where did this trust come from?* she asked the war-leader, bewildered.

The Ardana only shook her head. *Later. Your Prince and I will talk first.*

Gaultry had no idea what to make of that!

Then it was her turn, and Mervion's. "Ladies," Benet said, "I'm assigning you the less than pleasant task of staying here to see to the corpses.

I'll send someone down from the palace to help you. And *you*," he said, finally addressing Tullier. "You will stay out of trouble until we find time to speak again. I am hereby appointing Lady Gaultry your guardian, and extending you the full mantle of my protection. I will have Jardine enter this order in the rolls as soon as I reach the palace." He turned to Gaultry. "Do you have any objections to this responsibility? Consider carefully: To accept Bissanty's Orphan Prince of Tielmark as your ward is not a casual thing. I will expect you to keep *my* interests foremost, even as your obligation will be to keep *him* safe."

"My Prince—" After all the suspicions Benet had aired against Tullier, Gaultry had not expected this generosity. "Are you sure this is wise?"

"Is this wise?" Benet shook his head. "Only the gods can answer. But whoever sent these soldiers today intended to abscond with the boy before I had the opportunity even to extend such an offer. I will not see my choices thus usurped."

Gaultry knelt and made the vows that formally invested her as Tullier's guardian.

Gaultry found Melaney lying crumpled in the area just inside the front door. The young page was stone dead. Her neck was broken, her clothes disarrayed. Gaultry guessed she had been picked up and thrown. From the looks of things, Gaultry doubted Melaney had even had a chance to wound her attackers, let alone to worry or slow them.

"Who did this?" Gaultry whispered. The bodies on the landing had been terrible enough, particularly the two killed by Aneitha. But those men had been soldiers, committing treason against their Prince. Melaney had been sent to run errands, to answer doors; to stay safely at home another season, away from the battles in the west.

Gaultry smoothed the glossy hair back from the young face, unmarked save for dark, wounded-looking circles beneath the closed eyelids. She did not relish the prospect of reporting this disaster to Martin as he was struggling with the fresh grief of his grandmother's death. "I'll kill them for you," she whispered. "Whoever planned this raid, I'll kill them for you. This should never have happened."

When Tullier and Mervion came back from the garden, where they had dragged the last of the attackers' corpses, Gaultry was still kneeling over Melaney's body, her eyes closed in prayer.

"What are you doing?" Tullier said. He held a bucket of soapy water and some rags. "Is she too heavy to carry out?"

"You're looking better," Gaultry said. A little hunched, but it was clear Mervion's magic had somehow improved him. "But do you really think you should be up?"

"I can help you with that one," Tullier said, "if you just want her put with the others."

"We're not dumping her in the alleyway," Gaultry explained wearily. "We'll clean her up and wait for Melaudiere's people to come for her. She can go into one of the upstairs bedchambers while we're waiting." It was a little too much for her at the moment that Tullier was short on understanding burial customs. Fortunately for her temper, he caught her meaning, and did not insist on the imagined practicalities of piling all the dead together in the dry little court.

"I'll help," Mervion said. "He can scrub the landing clean while we cleanse her."

The air of the long-closed bedchamber where they laid out the young squire's corpse was cool and stale. Mervion removed the covers from the wardrobe and chest to make a protective pad for the bed before they set her down. They took Melaney out of her ruined tunic, then stripped the remainder of her clothes when it became obvious that she had fouled herself. Gaultry left the room to find something clean to cover her while Mervion sponged down the body.

"You made that man attack the swordmaster, didn't you?" Gaultry asked, returning with an unsoiled sheet.

Mervion nodded. She was brushing out Melaney's lovely thick hair. As Gaultry unfolded the sheet, she began to rebraid it.

"And you took back your Glamour-soul from Tullier, without even needing the soul-figure."

Mervion, working intently with her fingers, nodded again. "Only half my Glamour-soul," she corrected.

"It makes no difference," Gaultry said. Her sister's renewed appearance of calm was infuriating. "Not even Lukas Soul-breaker could coax a soul free without spells and magical apparatus. Without preparing, and making a big fuss, and imagining that the gods walked on earth in his body."

"I knew you would come back," Mervion said evenly. "I did prepare myself and make a fuss. And you are wrong. There is a great difference between moving half or all of a soul from its seat—or returning it there."

"That's not my point," Gaultry said. "Your power—the things you can do—"

"Leave me alone, Gaultry." Mervion abruptly set aside the brush and went to wash her hands in the newly filled basin on the bedstand.

"You could use it," Gaultry said. "You could use it to help the Prince."

"How?" Mervion asked, a little shakily. She lathered her hands, then plunged them in the water. "Tell me how. As a courtier? I have chosen an acknowledged traitor as my lover. Benet's inner court will never accept me. As a bodyguard? I am not fit. Look what I did today, bringing death to the one man who could have explained what we witnessed."

"Your loyalty will prove its own vindication," Gaultry said, swallowing at Mervion's unexpected honesty regarding her relations with Coyal. "As to the other—killing the point man who attacked Benet—that wasn't your mistake."

With a sudden violent sweep with her hand, Mervion sent the basin crashing to the floor.

"Whose was it then?" she asked coldly, across the wreckage of pottery and spilled water.

Gaultry stared back, completely taken by surprise. Her sister never lost her calm like this—never! "That man's death was no mistake." Mervion needed her calm now, that much was clear. "And if it needs to be someone's fault, it is the fault of the sorcerer who set him against the Prince."

"Look at me, Gaultry," Mervion shrilled. "Have I ever used my magic to hurt anyone? No!—not once in all of my life. There is no desire in me to see my powers used in this way."

Gaultry, shaken, bent and picked up the largest basin shard. She wanted to offer Mervion her comfort, but something in her sister's stance warned that she would reject any such overture. "Benet could have been killed today," she said. "Whoever set that spell did not expect to find Benet standing between that man Siànne and Tullier. What you did was right. If Siànne had not been wounded, he would have killed Benet."

"So what if I was right this time?" Mervion said, watching Gaultry gather the basin shards, her hands clenching the drying-towel. She had only partly regained her composure. "I do not want there to be another."

Gaultry frowned. "We are Brood-blood," she said. "There will be another. And another. Until we all are dead, or Benet is King."

BOOK II

▼

THE MONTH OF ANDION SUN-KING

Prologue:

▼

THE DARKEST HOURS

Palamar Laconte, Brood-heir, acolyte to Dervla, High Priestess of Tielmark, had stood attendance in the funerary chapel for hours. Her feet ached. Her back was tired. The strain of standing so long without relief had exacted its physical price.

The oppressive, low-ceilinged space, with its single slitted window, its heavy stone trusses and smoke-stained carvings, made her feel entombed, forgotten. The incense of the altar's funerary flame was making her itch, worsened by the ugly funerary costume, with its stifling long sleeves and tar-stiffened skirts. The muffled sounds of the temple bells, which she had heard ringing high above her in the temple's campanile through two complete changes, had long since ceased tolling. She longed to sit, but her obligation to the ritual would not allow that.

Dervla was overdue to relieve her, but Palamar would outlast her impatience. Everyone imagined that Palamar was weak, that she was ineffectual, that she was the fallen descendent of a great warrior-sorceress— but she would prove everyone wrong soon enough.

Too much had gone forward this day for Dervla not to come. The sacral chamber that lay hidden below the altar would call her. Dervla would come, needing to renew herself.

Palamar would be waiting.

As flame-watcher, Palamar had scoured the altar, had tended the funerary flame, had meticulously trimmed the bouquets of deathbed lilies that jammed every hopper on the arched beams of the little chapel's sides. She had done everything.

Of course, it would never be enough.

She drew a weary breath, puckering her cheeks. Dervla was a most excellent finder of faults. After the strength of her goddess-magic and the fortune of her birth, it was the trait that most enhanced her power as High Priestess. Palamar was not alone among Dervla's twelve acolytes in suffering it, though the High Priestess singled her out often enough that it sometimes seemed that way.

She had once thought this was simply the contrast of her own character with that of Elsbet, who had preceded her in Dervla's service. Palamar's oldest sister had been like Dervla: talented, superior, confident of her strength. When the call had come for Elsbet Laconte to report to Princeport to pledge herself as acolyte, Elsbet had welcomed it as an expected entitlement.

Palamar's call had arrived under less auspicious circumstances. After Tielmark's traitor-chancellor had seen her older sister murdered, Palamar had been brought to court to take Elsbet's place.

Initially the knowledge that Dervla's cruelty rose from her mourning of the talented Elsbet's death had provided Palamar a meager but sufficient comfort. As granddaughter to Marie Laconte, Countess of Tierce, "the proudest woman of her generation," a sworn member of the original seven Brood-members, Palamar had been bred to know the meaning of duty. Mantled with the weight of her grandmother's reputation, Palamar had dutifully accepted Dervla's harsh treatment as her lot.

But that was before Dervla had broken her promises. In the heat of feeling after Elsbet's death, Dervla had sworn to protect the remaining Lacontes—and then reneged, allowing Palamar's sole surviving sister Destra, along with Destra's young family, to be slaughtered by the Sha Muira.

It was not Dervla's fault—everyone told her it was not Dervla's fault, Dervla included. Palamar accepted that. It had been hard, but she'd accepted it. The gods did not allow all human promises to be fulfilled.

But she had also learned from what had happened. If the Lacontes were to have protection or vengeance in this world, Palamar would have to do it herself.

She suffered now—oh, certainly, she continued to suffer—but it was no longer because Dervla burned her with the acid of her tongue. She suffered because she had to wait and bow her head; had to hold strong her shaking patience; had to wait until Dervla, all unawares, allowed her to get close enough to her sisters' murderers that she could act and finish, for once and ever, this family business.

Palamar plucked up a handful of white lily buds. Her fingers were shaking, ill-controlled, as she placed the furls of petal on top of the embers in the altar-brazier. The bright fire sheathed the slim white forms, like miniature winding-sheets on a cremation bed.

Death images like these followed her constantly now. Her own turn must be fast approaching, she was sure, treading the red path of the Prince. But she would see her vengeance completed first.

The buds, thick and moist, resisted their impromptu cremation. After the first flare, the licks of flame curled back. Palamar, not liking that, touched the brazier with her magic. With this push, a line of fire flared at the stem-base of first one bud, then another.

A single fallen bud, streaked with immature green and protected by the brazier's metal edge, continued to resist destruction, defying even magical flame. Watching that lone brave survivor fight the inevitable, tears dampened Palamar's cheeks.

The funeral rites for the old duchess would be spectacular. The terrible old woman who had lived a full life, who had made her own choices, who had used the people around her more ruthlessly than even the High Priestess.

The traitor-chancellor's plot against the throne had killed not only Elsbet, but also Dervla's niece, sweet young Lady D'Arbey.

But neither of those young women would have been put at risk if the old duchess's arrogance had not sent them to their dooms, careless of their lives as she tried to force out Heiratikus's secrets. More would have followed in their footsteps if Melaudiere had considered it necessary. Yet for wicked old Gabrielle of Melaudiere, even the Prince would come to kneel at her coffin.

By contrast, Palamar's sisters, first Elsbet, then Destra, had been laid into cold earth with little fanfare. "The kin of my acolytes never truly die. They'll live on inside of you," Dervla had said to reassure her, in a rare offering of pity, as she burned a single votive branch following Destra's simple funeral. "As my acolyte, as one who may one day even rise to be High Priestess, the smallest tincture of power that Elianté and Emiera vested in your sisters has passed to you—and that at least will not be lost to the grave."

As if that news should mend Palamar's grief. The thought that her sister was dead—that both her sisters were dead—yet that some ghostly shadow of the strength that had lived so brightly within them was forced to linger, forced to feed her power—this made the young acolyte feel the opposite of powerful.

This was something that Dervla could neither understand nor acknowledge. Indeed, the High Priestess's eyes had gleamed with an emotion opposite to grief as she contemplated her acolyte's newly fortified potential—fortified by her family's tragedies. "Your power descends from such a strong line, and just think—with the deaths of your sister's children, all your granddam's power has come to empower you. There is no one else left." The High Priestess, staring into the fire of Destra's funerary offering, had seemed satisfied rather than mournful. "It has been your fortune to earn your power early. I was fair middle-aged before my mother died, and none of my immediate family preceded her. The title High Priestess was mine before any of my family's power came to me—as it inevitably did, whether they lived or no, on my ascension."

Afterward, when it transpired that Destra's baby girl, Marina, had somehow escaped the Sha Muira slaughter, Dervla viewed this almost as a setback. "How can I use your power when you have yet to claim it?"

What lingering loyalty Palamar had felt for Dervla had died the day she'd said that. The young acolyte continued to work with the High Priestess, dutiful to her vows—how else to gain the chance to set her traps for those who had destroyed her family? She continued to observe all her duties and offices—more punctiliously even than the other acolytes, so that Dervla increasingly looked to her for assistance. Her vows and pledges—she kept them and respected them, but her loyalty to Dervla was gone.

At the young acolyte's back, the chapel's door creaked on ancient hinges. Behind her, she heard the distinctive rustle of Dervla's robes, the signature clink of the silver chain the High Priestess wore at her waist.

Before Dervla could step forward and see what she was doing, Palamar forced her anger to a peak. The glow on the last bud flared black-green with magic, and collapsed into flame. Then—so quickly—the bud was crumbled ash, and the green fire winked out. Turning to Dervla, Palamar tucked her hands, no longer trembling, out of sight behind her back, and curtsied.

"What are you doing here?" Dervla greeted her sharply. "Didn't Ilary come to relieve you?" There was something in her tone. Grief, anger, and fear. Palamar's heart raced. She dared for a moment to hope. Someone was dead. Someone—

She stepped away from the altar, giving Dervla a glimpse of the funerary flame, flaring ordinary white-yellow and orange in the ornamental brazier. "Veneracy," she said aloud, a tremor in her voice. The little tremble would distract the old woman, and Dervla would not look closely at the altar, would not see the marks of Palamar's angry strength. "The flame is almost done and I am very tired. No one came to relieve me, and I could not desert the flame. Isn't Ilary watching at Her Grace's body?"

The High Priestess jerked the bronze-strapped door shut, granting herself privacy to loosen her temper. Without further ceremony, she strode briskly across to the young acolyte and slapped her face. "You stupid child." Her fingers caught a handful of Palamar's soft hair, tearing it. "You can't do anything right. Not even a simple task."

"The flame—"

"I am not talking of the flame. I am talking of Siànne. All I asked was that you convey a simple message, stopping him. Why couldn't you get even that right?"

"He had taken his men and gone," Palamar said softly—in the quiet, faintly bewildered tone that best stoked the High Priestess's impatience. "You told me I was not to draw attention, not to inquire—"

Dervla slapped her again. "Stupid, stupid," she raged. "Benet might have been killed. Siànne almost killed him! Twins in me! I charged you most particularly to stop them."

Palamar ducked her head, and made herself whimper. A hand raised to fend the blows completed the picture of submission.

Yet elation pounded in her heart. Someone had died in Siànne's attack. Dervla would not be so angry or alarmed if no one had been killed. It was not Benet, of course. Dervla would be in sackcloth, if her beloved Prince was dead. Who then? Whose death could have made Dervla so upset? The assassin-boy? The dart of hope that ran through her was almost enough to ruin her cover of fear. "What has gone wrong?" she asked. "I did as I was told. You charged me to speak only to Siànne—"

"They killed one of the Stalkingman's house servants. A noble girl, scion to the Caris family. Worse, they got themselves butchered, and failed utterly in the abduction." Dervla wrung her hands. "Twins in me, more fool I, trusting to your competency."

Disappointment flooded her. "Mistress," Palamar said, smoothing the disorder of her hair. "From what little you say, it is your purpose that has gone astray, not mine." Oh, she should not have said anything so provoking as that—but the disappointment! For a moment, it was too strong even for the iron of her control.

"You don't understand anything about purpose!" Dervla spat back. Oblivious to Palamar's slip, she seized a stalk of lilies from the nearest hopper and flung it onto the brazier, still dripping wet. "Burn for Gabrielle," she told it, passing her hand in the Twins' sign. "I at least honor the ceremonies. Honor *all* for Benet. Burn!" For a single searing moment the blossoms shone red with fire, a shocking burst of light that brightened the chapel's darkest corners before dying back. "I do it all." Dervla struck the hot edge of the brazier with the palm of her hand. "No one can match me for the sheer power from the Twins!"

Watching Dervla play with the fire, her attention half to her call of power, half to the impression she was creating, emotion twisted angrily within the younger woman. The efforts Palamar took to conceal the full extent of her powers—they were hardly needed, with one so self-absorbed as Dervla.

Palamar arranged her features in an appropriate expression of respect. "What happened, Veneracy? Please tell me."

Dervla hesitated. Then anger outpaced the impulse to secrecy. "Benet got between Siànne and the boy who killed your sister. Then Siànne attacked the Prince like one possessed, trying to reach the Sha Muira." Dervla frowned. "Attacked him. Did you put something in the spell to make him go after the boy's protectors?"

Too close to the truth. Where Dervla wanted to make the boy her secret prisoner, Palamar just wanted him dead. She pressed her hands to cheeks still hot from Dervla's blows. "The men had gone before I reached their quarters," she said tearfully, returning Dervla's attention to this other fault. "You told me not to call attention, going after them. You should have told me Benet had gone. I would have followed them."

"But why did Benet even go there?" Dervla muttered, dismissing Palamar's explanations as tedium. "What did the Glamour-bitch say to draw him?" She sketched the spiral sign of the Great Twins over the altar and threw a pinch of fresh incense into the brazier. "We will go below, to discover the answer."

Palamar, recognizing the preliminaries of the spell that opened the vault beneath the altar, moved obediently to face her across the stone plinth.

When Dervla had first revealed the chapel's secret, initiating Palamar to the fellowship of three who guarded the High Priestess's deepest secrets, the young acolyte had felt thrilled and awed. Now she watched Dervla posture with a sense of growing disdain. Was this power? This prancing, this posing, this elaborate coiling and calling of earth and the gods' forces?

Whatever it was, it was not power as the Lacontes taught it. Great Marie of old had described the strength of her magic as a burning lance, fit to pierce and destroy her enemies in the Prince's name. *My power is a sword unto my hand,* the old Countess had written, in the scanty archive of neatly preserved scrolls that was all the record Tierce stronghold boasted of her life and accomplishments. *It served me well, as I served Princess Lousielle, and the pledge to which I had so willingly sworn myself.*

A rush of cold air, as though the ground had taken a ragged breath, announced the completion of the ritual, as Dervla pierced her finger for the few drops of blood that unsealed the hidden door. Squinting, Palamar glimpsed the shadow of steep steps concealed beneath the altar stone. All that was truly needed here was a drop or two of blood, along with the call to Elianté and Emiera. The rest—the rest made a pretty show of power, but it was no more than posturing.

"Shall I stand and watch the flame?"

"It will keep." For the spell's duration, the altar stone was a mere specter, allowing access to the staircase. Dervla's foot was already on the top step. "Come with me. You will serve witness for me as I read the scrolls."

Palamar gave Dervla a little bow of acquiescence. *Serving witness.* The words of a High Priestess to one in training beneath her. In Dervla's mind, everything concerning the High Priestess's power was an honor to beg for. It was how Dervla herself had learned from her own mother, who had served as High Priestess before her. She could not see that her own acolyte, lacking the feelings of child to mother, could not accept it in the same wise.

Palamar stepped down through the spectral altar of stone, cold like the passing of a shadow, into the tight coil of steps. She ducked as she passed the brazier, avoiding its substance and heat. Once, this all had seemed a wonder. The widening spiral of the steps had seemed a perfect mirror of the Great Twins' power, a cord, a corridor, leading her to the past, to ancient wisdom.

With her knowledge now of the travesty that lay beneath, that surety had long since departed.

She descended, calmly, in memorized steps through the blind realm of the staircase. Dervla's chain clinked, magnified in the small space of the steps to a sound like dropping water. This space was unnaturally dry, parched sere by centuries of magic.

At the spiral's end, a beautiful green light awaited. Goddess-light, from the spiral vault of the sacral chamber. Palamar stooped to enter the narrow crevice of its door. Dervla was already across the room, hunting in a rack of well-thumbed scrolls. The circular room, lined with beautifully dressed stone cobbles from the center of the floor to the apex of its vault, had been built to a design of masterful simplicity—a simplicity that had long since been obscured by a chaos of scroll racks, of boxes and cases burgeoning with parchment, of paper, bound books, clumsy sheaves of vellum and ill-cured rolls of animal skin.

Marie Laconte had left her heirs a tiny archive of her life, and a forbidding creed of unwritten principles. Delcora, Dervla's mother, had created something far more terrible and complex.

Palamar, bile rising in her throat, could not make herself look at the high racks, the massive clutter. Dervla had told her once, and proudly, that all this massive accumulation of paper had been brought here by her mother. So familiar was she to the room's stink of her mother's rank, stale power, trapped overlong in this mass of paper, that she could not see that this was a matter for shame, not satisfaction.

Of the original Brood Coven, Marie Laconte's warrior strength had been at the center of her magic; just as it had been artistry for corrupt old Melaudiere; or music for Dame Julie. Delcora's special ability had been to capture power in words. But something in that talent had turned her mind when she'd begun to set those words to paper. In the morass between record, history, and capture, the old High Priestess had lost her bearings.

When she'd inherited her mother's High Priestess's chain, Dervla had done nothing to clean house. Steeped and stewed in Delcora's histories, she insisted that every word her mother had written was truth akin to prophecy.

By now, Palamar had read enough of Delcora's bitter ravings that she no longer believed this was possible. The old High Priestess had recorded countless visions along with her histories and interpretations of worship, court, her enemies and her friends.

But even if she did not believe in Delcora's strength of prophecy, it could not be denied that there was power in what the old woman had committed to paper. The words, whether read or spoken aloud, held a curious, augmenting power. To read them enhanced one's own strength with a certain thick, curdled energy. Palamar did not care for the feeling herself, but she could understand why it drew Dervla here so often. Sometimes the power the High Priestess received from the scrolls was so strong, it gave her a nimbus of pale green goddess-light.

Old Delcora's writings had power, that was certain, but whether they held truth—that was a different question.

Across the room, Dervla scrambled to her feet, completely blind to her acolyte's secret musings. She clutched a half-unrolled scroll of parchment, the dun color of the sheets on which her mother had recorded her most treasured foreseeings. Impatient, she swept a lectern clear of its cluttered paper and weighted the scroll open with a pair of velvet sandbags.

"It is Andion's Moon," Dervla read aloud, her voice low, incantatory.

It is Andion's Moon, and the Great Twins came and danced in my dreams. Fair Emiera, with a gown of stars and moonbeam. Elianté, the huntress lady, clothed only in her ragged hair. They laughed unto me, and set a mirror in my hand.

—Why come to me this night?— I asked them, all despairing. —Corinne is dead, her son unfit to rule. Why come to me?—

Their laughter burned me. In the mirror, I saw a blaze of light, a new sun rising, the hope of Kingship reborn. My heart burst, for I saw then that Rouault-the-fool would not live long as Tielmark's Prince. Another, not yet born, would arise in his place, rise and fulfill the prophecy to which old Lousielle bound us.

I dreamed this in the richness of a summer that has brought us Corinne's last child and our sweet Princess's death. But I see a future, a summer, when all I have seen this night shall come to pass. Midsummer and the Sword God's moon will pass away with a great betrayal of trust and faith. Only then, under the God-King's Moon, Tielmark's Prince will wax to King.

All this I did foresee, as the Goddess Twins moved within me, beyond my poor mortal strength.

Dervla's voice trailed away.

"A betrayal," she said grimly, still standing at the lectern. "Foreseen for the very night of the passing of the Sword-god's moon." She closed the scroll with an abrupt gesture.

"Benet must have made a pact to protect the assassin-boy." As always,

Dervla had a ready interpretation for her mother's vaguest promises—however often her prior interpretations had come to nothing. "I insisted that he not offer the boy Tielmark's protection, and he has betrayed that trust. The gods watch closely now—perhaps the Goddess-Twins drove Siànne against him as a warning."

Palamar remained silent. If the High Priestess could imagine no other betrayals had gone forward this night, it was not for a lowly acolyte to correct her.

The High Priestess loosed a melancholy sigh. "If only this were not a necessary passage, a fall through which our dear Prince must pass, learning to humble himself before his blood becomes one with the land as King. If only he would listen! Instead, all must be done secretly to prepare him."

She turned to Palamar. "We have come at last to Andion God-King's Moon, and it is time to share my mother's deepest secret."

Palamar held herself very still, startled.

Dervla crossed to the center of the room. She levered up the center cobble, revealing a secret cache that Palamar had not known existed. The High Priestess called a spell, and the object within levitated to her like a falcon to its master's fist.

It was a knife. A short, narrow blade, inscribed with runes. The metal was dull colored and dingy, as though it had been intended for use centuries past, but missed its purpose, lingering on into this age, full of thwarted, darkening power.

"What is that?"

"It is the *Ein Raku*, the Kingmaker blade. My mother bested the goat-herder for this weapon," Dervla said, holding up the blade, her eyes alight, eager. "With that victory, she earned the right and duty to play Kingmaker herself, a right she passed to me, for the closing of all Tielmark's cycles."

Palamar recognized the blade from family stories, though the Laconte version had run a little differently. It had been Marie who had seized the blade from the goat-herder's hand, not Delcora.

"What are you going to do?"

"Use it to complete what is foretold: Under the God-King's Moon, I will use it to make Benet King."

A coldness touched Palamar's neck. A shadow of apprehension swept her. For a moment, she almost believed in Delcora's prophecy.

"But what does that mean?" she asked. "What are you going to do?"

"The Bissanty Envoy had a meeting with the Prince today—just before Benet met with Gaultry. I was present when he shared the news: Sciuttarus has confirmed the rumors. It's official now. The killer-boy has been raised to Bissanty's Tielmaran throne."

"Confirmed the rumors?" Palamar had heard no rumors.

"Why else have we been chasing him?" Dervla said impatiently. "Do you attend to *nothing* that I share with you? Why else have I been so pleased with Gaultry Blas's return, so set upon bringing her boy in?"

Dervla had told Palamar only that the Brood would be best protected with the boy in her secret custody. She seemed to have forgotten that in this rush to a new plan.

"You were going to kill him?" Palamar said, fever heat coursing through her. If so, all her secret planning had been for nothing. If she had just known, she would have put the weight of her magic behind Dervla's plan's *success*. "You were going to strike him through the heart with the Kingmaker blade?"

"At the appropriate time and hour." Dervla nodded. "But it won't happen that way now. Not with Benet having sworn him Tielmark's protection." She flourished the *Ein Raku*. "But while we have this knife, and the boy remains close by, all is not lost. We only need to find some way to get around Benet's pledge without dishonoring it."

Palamar stared at the *Ein Raku*, fascinated by its promise of power. Small wonder the metal looked old and tired: The power trapped within that blade screamed strong enough to call the gods' attention. She found herself thinking of the prophecy: *The Path of the Prince of Tielmark will run red with the blood of the Common Brood.* The Brood-prophecy Marie had sworn to set her heirs on the path to make the Prince a King, or die trying. This was the blade that could complete that prophecy.

She watched as Dervla flashed the blade, focused only on herself, holding it possessively to her. The woman was blind if she imagined Palamar would let the chance slip past for vengeance and Tielmark's Kingship both.

But then, Palamar already knew she was blind.

Dervla had stood helplessly, watching the old Duchess slip away, her heart's-blood-energy syphoning into the unborn Princeling's cradle. "Gabrielle, Gabrielle!" she had cried. "You must not go so far! The protections for the child are strong enough already! Keep something for yourself!" The High Priestess had never suspected that it was her own charm on the old Melaudiere's neck that forced the old sorceress to push beyond her strength's limits, had no idea she was witnessing the righteous punishment of Elsbet Laconte's murderer. Palamar's secret thread of power within the High Priestess's charm had spent itself completely undetected, breaking the old woman's vigor, sending her to her death completely in secret.

A public hanging would have been preferable, but Palamar had accepted that she would never get that. She had a pragmatic turn of mind; as the warrior-countess Marie's granddaughter, she had been trained to live within the limits of her strength and influence.

The young heir to great Marie Laconte stared at her mistress, and willed herself to be patient.

She would have the *Ein Raku*, and the killer-boy, and she would be the Kingmaker who completed the Brood-prophecy. Nothing, she would let nothing get in her way.

They all thought she was weak.

She would prove them wrong.

chapter **12**

▼

It rained the entire day the Duchess's body lay burning in the priests' oven. Midsummer days, with the Sword-god's harvest moon, were over, and with them had gone the fine hot weather. With dawn a storm had moved in, bringing a dark sky that loosed driving lashes of rain. Combined with the attack on the Prince the night before and the Duchess of Melaudiere's passing, it seemed an inauspicious opening for the first day of the Sun-King's month.

The preceding night's events had advanced with bewildering suddenness. While Gaultry, Mervion, and Tullier had closed the townhouse and moved up to the palace—including the sad business of icing Melaney's body and turning it over to Melaudiere's servants for its final journey to her family's manor—the Prince had met privately with Martin and Sharif, a meeting that extended for unexpected hours.

There had not been much left to the night when Martin delivered the Sharif to Gaultry's suite of rooms and asked Gaultry—muzzy after dropping off to sleep while waiting for them—to join him in the vigil of the Duchess's cremation.

Now a full day had passed, and the grassy slope of the graveyard, which led all the way down the back of the palace headland to a partially sheltered bay with sandy beaches, was cloaked in twilight's darkening shadows. The rain muffled the sound of the sea, increasing the prospect's melancholy.

Gaultry stood in the darkness of the crematorium's porch, listening to the rain and the sounds of those working in the crematorium. It had

been a long day; a long uncomfortable day. A long night lay ahead, promising no improvements. Martin, sworn as the Duchess's chief mourner,
could not leave the crematorium until the ash-dividing ceremony at
dawn, and she had taken a mourner's oath with him, intending to keep
him company throughout his sad vigil. She smiled, a little grimly, con-
templating the day's events. The custom of burning the dead was little
practiced in the dense greenwood area where she had been raised. If she
had fully understood the complexities of the cremation burial of a high-
ranking peer, she might have hesitated before promising to join him.

After an entire day of prayer while the body lay burning, prayer, and
the cremation, would continue through the night. Tomorrow, with the
ash-dividing ceremony at dawn and the formal interment of a portion of
the ashes in the Prince's funerary chapel at noontime, the rest of the day
would be filled with speeches and services as the remainder of Melaudiere's ashes were dispersed by special messengers to the Duchess's numerous
land holdings.

After threescore and more years of service to Tielmark and its Princes,
the Duchess's lands were large and widely spread. It was sobering, how
broadly the old woman's ashes would lie scattered. To Gaultry, it felt
quite unnatural.

This lull of relative inactivity—it would give way, soon enough, to
fresh action. From the arrangements that Martin had made with various
servants who came to him throughout the day, Gaultry understood that
not only had Benet persuaded Martin to ready himself to ride west the
very next morning to the Lanai battlefront, but that Benet intended to
ride with him, accompanied by the knights of his inner circle.

The Prince's change of mind had been sparked, to everyone at court's
surprise, by the unexpected mind-communication he shared with the Sharif. Gaultry did not know the particulars, other than the fact that something in that exchange had profoundly emboldened and transformed him.
After a brief, flurried debate with his counselors, he had determined to
leave politics behind and ride for war, and the west.

Separation from Martin loomed, sooner than either of them had anticipated.

None of these matters had yet been discussed between them.

If the day of mourning had felt constrained and tedious, the hours just after the light faded made up for it. Just as the sun dipped behind the palace

ridge, the wind and rain breached the lower oven of the crematorium. For almost two hours, the ceremonies were abandoned as the crematorium's caretakers called Gaultry, Martin, and the three acolyte flame-tenders to stanch the leak while they worked hastily, and with no little fright, to shore up the spell-embrittled stone at the oven's back. As night settled in, the physical labor of running for sandbags and aiding in the stone work degenerated into a squalid and even dangerous task. The steadiness of the head caretaker's nerves, as he drove wedge after wedge of cold flint into the scorching hot stones, was admirable and even impressive. But it was after midnight by the time the last sandbag had been packed and the job completed to his satisfaction.

Then there was a second rush of activity as the acolytes—and Martin with them as chief mourner—hurried to catch up with their prayers.

From that last, at least, Gaultry was thankfully exempt.

A slight noise from the crematorium made her look up.

"There you are," Martin said, coming out to join her. His eyes looked puffy and tired, the hours of prayer clearly weighing on him. "Have you managed to get yourself clean?"

Gaultry shook her head. "I'll wait until morning. It's dark, and I don't have the energy."

"They've finally caught up on the prayers. Happily, this little fiasco we've been through didn't slow the actual cremation." He managed a grin. "I think Grandmère would have enjoyed the spectacle of all this dirty work going on so frantically around her. It's a fitting completion— her death serving to expose a hidden weakness in a destabilized form. Maybe I should pledge my part of her legacy to rebuilding this place."

They took refuge together in a protected niche at the side of the porch. The bench there was cold and hard, but utterly welcome. Gaultry tiredly pressed her head against his damp shoulder, grateful for the cover of darkness that allowed them this intimacy.

The day had been trying and hard, with the sadness of loss intensified by the foul weather, but there had also been fine moments too. To stand by Martin's side, close so that the cuff of his sleeve touched the cloth at her hip, circumspect in display of their shared feelings, yet openly unified in their grief . . . something in that was stronger than Gaultry's feelings of loss, and the ambivalent silence she'd chosen to maintain regarding Martin's imminent departure.

They had been granted one day away from affairs of state. Even as she had hauled hot, ashy, slippery stones out of the collapsing back of the crematorium oven, one part of her had known this would be a time she would come to cherish in the days ahead. Time with Martin, effectively alone.

She drowsed off leaning against Martin's side, and fell into a sleep so comfortable and still she did not notice when he gently eased away to perform another round of prayers.

Martin roused her a little after dawn. She rose from the scratchy folded blanket wedged under her head, and stepped out of the porch niche. The wind had settled, but the rain continued, a dull drizzle. The somber light of the clouded dawn freshly revealed her own filth and Martin's. Crustings of ash and earth from their work in the foundations covered their skin and clothing.

"Dervla's here to divide the ash," Martin said, pulling on his boots and raking his hair into order. "She must want to get this part of the ceremony over and done with before she breaks her fast."

The High Priestess was dressed in simple funerary regalia, grey to hide the ashes that would inevitably find their way onto her clothes. The beautiful silver-wrought chain of her office hung at her waist, her head was uncovered and her long hair, a thick mass of brown shot lightly through with silver, worn loose as a sign of mourning and respect. Her immaculate appearance contrasted sharply with that of those who awaited her on the porch, though the fatigued tension in her face suggested that she too had spent the night uneasily. She did not acknowledge the mourners as she passed into the crematorium's antechamber and opened the upper oven's doors, even as the trio of her acolytes gathered around her, whispering the particulars of the accident with the foundations.

As she listened, standing in the burnishing light of the opened oven, Dervla seemed emaciated and spare, as though a long fasting had brutally reduced her flesh. When they were finished, she nodded curtly and directed them to their places. She leaned a little way into the oven, her stern carriage proof against the blistering heat, singing in a low voice and casting signs. The stiff line of her back reflected an angry or ill-satisfied temper.

"Does she seem unwell?" Gaultry whispered.

"She has not been happy," Martin said. "And she must be even less happy, given Benet's resolve to ride west to the battle lines this very

noonday. She will be trapped at the palace completing the funeral ceremonies while he mounts up to ride west."

Noon. The very hour when Dervla would be preoccupied with the
Duchess's last rites. "I don't understand," Gaultry said. "Doesn't he want
to take the High Priestess's blessing with him to battle?"

"He already has it," Martin said shortly. "He obliged her to give it to
him last night, in private, against her strongest inclinations. She wanted
a public consecration, and he refused her. Lily will perform the Prince's
functions at Grandmère's funeral, while Benet and his war-party ride
west."

Benet's outmaneuvering of Dervla should have been heartening, but
all Gaultry could hear in Martin's words was that Benet had taken Martin
into his full confidence, moving him one step closer to accepting a formal
post among the ranks of his military commanders— a move the Prince
had long wanted, and Martin, disillusioned with titles, had long resisted.
Gaultry, disturbed, fixed her eyes on the glowing interior of the crematorium. Atop the fire-table, just visible in the oven beyond Dervla, a long
mound of ash glittered orange and black in the reflected light of the oven's
walls.

Gabrielle of Melaudiere had always known that Martin must serve
his Prince. With his military talent, it was inevitable that at least a part
of that service would be to support Tielmark on the battlefield. But the
old woman had confided to Gaultry more than once the fears that had
risen in her following the death of Martin's older brother Morse, in service
as field commander to Prince Ginvers—Benet's father. Before Morse, she
had lost both her sons in this same way, in this same posting. She had
wanted to prevent—or at least delay—Martin's rendezvous with a similar
fate, and she had urged him never to ride at Benet's side into battle.

"Will you be riding west with Benet at noontime?" Gaultry asked.
She spoke the words as neutrally as she was able, but she was too tired to
fully hide her pain when Martin reluctantly nodded.

"I will. I had hoped that you would perform in my place at the noon
ceremony. Grandmère would have wanted that."

It was too soon. She had watched him send for servants, watched
him make the preparations for his departure. But it was still too soon.

"The Prince and I agreed on the timing the night Grandmère died,"
Martin said. "Allegrios Rex! It was as much as I could do to dissuade him
from mounting up that very night. Your Ardana—are you sure she hasn't

bewitched him? I would say yes, save for the matter that she agreed when I tried to tell Benet that giving his knights at least a full day to prepare and gather their equipage and men was a better course than forcing them to ride out on a whim in their nightshirts."

"I know the Prince is needed at the front," Gaultry said. "But I wish he would leave it a while longer."

Martin sighed. "Then you should not have introduced our Prince to the Ardana. Whatever *sun-marked* entails, Benet has taken it as the sign he's been waiting for, telling him there's no time to delay his departure."

Sun-marked. The Sharif had managed only a garbled explanation in the few moments they'd had before the war-leader collapsed into her makeshift bed, and Gaultry left with Martin for the crematorium.

The Sharif could share her mind with those she trusted, but that trust was something earned, rather than voluntarily granted. Yet during the confusion of the mêlée at the townhouse, the Prince had called out to the Sharif and imposed that connection. She claimed he had called her and invested her with a berserker power—though Gaultry privately thought that the horror of fighting at the side of a monstrous cat would be sufficient to drive most anyone into a killing terror. Whatever the case, the Sharif had held firm to her story.

The power to call me, to invest me with such strength—only those destined to become great and powerful rulers can own it. The Sharif believed what had happened between her and Benet proved the presence of her god. *Andion Sun-King rules in Ardain, where we give him primacy among all the Great Twelve. I never thought to see the Sun's touch on your white-faced Prince. Be assured, Andion's eye is watching him.*

"Sun-marked means the Sharif believes Benet has the strength to be King," Gaultry said dryly. "I'm sure Benet was very ready to hear that."

Inside the crematorium, Dervla accepted a tray of clay reliquary vessels from one of her acolytes. She cast the Twins' spiral sign with one hand, then set the little pots to warm in the dying embers beneath the fire-table.

"If it wasn't the Sharif, I'd say it was flummery," Martin said. "But you're right. It's what Benet wanted to hear, and it came just at the time he wanted to hear it—in the moment he was flushed with the heat of battle, after the long chill of court." He passed his hand tiredly through the thick of his hair, then smiled thinly. "If it's upsetting the court's political calculations, it has to be a good thing. I would have liked to see Dervla's face when she discovered that Benet had requisitioned a ship to return the Sharif and her big cat to Ardain. It's not an honor that has been awarded a foreigner in my lifetime."

Dervla had not been the only one surprised by Benet's arrangements. "The Prince's generosity has helped me fulfill the oath I swore to see her safely homeward bound," Gaultry said. She left silent her secret dismay that the Sharif too would be leaving her. "But I will miss her counsel."

"As I will miss Grandmère's, departed on a longer journey."

They fell silent for a time, Gaultry considering the curious bond the Prince and the wild desert Sharif had formed, Martin lost in grief.

Inside the crematorium, Dervla started separating the Duchess's ashes into the reliquaries. When she was partway done one of her acolytes came out to them, bearing a pair of the little clay pots. He was the youngest, a short youth with a crown of chestnut-colored hair. Gaultry bobbed him welcome, not knowing him by name; Martin simply inclined his head. The boy handed the thickly glazed pots to Martin, bowing and casting the Twins' sign. "Goodman Stalker," he said respectfully. "I understand from my Mistress that you won't be attending the final ceremony. Nor the wake, up at the palace, neither. So—by my hand as intermediary, Flianté and Emiera held in faith, her Veneracy offers here the relicts for yourself and Melaudiere's heir. Swear to me that you will dispose of them with due respect for the gods and their creations."

"I so swear," Martin said. "By the Goddess-Twins, Allegrios Rex, and all the Great Twelve after."

The acolyte frowned at the invocation of the Water-god, but he did not allow the unexpected response to distract him from the proper form. "By my troth, by Elianté and Emiera together, I dismiss you from your mourning service with their divine blessing." He cast the Twins' sign again and returned inside the crematorium.

"Let's get out of here," Martin said gruffly, casting a last glance inward to the oven. "Help me with these, would you?" He handed Gaultry one of the vessels. Its surface was almost burning hot from the embers' heat, or from the heat of the ash inside. Gaultry cupped one hand over the brim to protect the contents as Martin led her out from under the sheltered porch into the rain.

Below them the cemetery spread across a broad slope that descended gently toward the sea, studded in places by pitted outcrops of rock. The most important buildings and monuments were at the top of the incline where the land was most sheltered. Gaultry glanced longingly toward the outline of the palace on the ridge above, and pulled her hood up over her hair. She was tired and chilled. She wanted—she had earned—a hot bath and a warm bed. But if Martin and the Prince planned to ride for the border this very noontime, those matters would have to wait.

The wind beating in from the sea had almost completely diminished. The rainbank of cloud passed magisterially across the sky, shedding its solemn cloak of moisture. A seabird's shrill call sounded distantly over the water, though none were visible on wing.

Martin pointed to their destination, a spit of sand that jutted into the rain-washed waters of the sea, down past the bottommost precincts of the cemetery. Gaultry was not keen to descend a long slope only to have to reclimb it later, but willing for now to follow Martin's lead, she left the thought unspoken.

He chose a line that took them straight down the hill. Gaultry matched his long strides, falling into a rhythm of movement at his side. It was a relief to be away from the sickly burning smells of the crematorium. Their boots crushed the long summer grass underfoot and sent up a sweet grain smell that combined with the sea-tang in the air to raise her spirits. Passing quickly out of the more densely used area of the cemetery, they were soon deep into uncut sea grass. The graves at their feet here were older, lower to the ground, and the ground was more uneven. When she stumbled over one low scoured rock, almost hidden in the grass, Martin paused to let her catch her breath.

Four lichen-covered reliquaries, tucked securely into the rock's crevices, were visible between the straggling grass stalks. One was anciently broken, tipped on its side, spilling moss rather than ash.

"These are the oldest graves," Martin commented, clearing the grass back from the rock with the toe of his boot to reveal the god-marks scratched onto its surface. "Anything higher up the hill will have been reused many times over. Anything lower will have been obliterated over the centuries by the high winter storms."

Gaultry, drawing her hands into her cuffs for warmth, looked down toward the water. This grave was still high above the obvious tideline, on the last grassy plateau before the final descent to the beach. As an inlander who had never witnessed the sea under storm conditions, she found it hard to picture the force that could sweep waves this high. "It's so calm today," she said. The pellucid, rain-dimpled blue of the water had turned an extraordinary turquoise color under the morning's low slanted light.

"I think the folk who had their ashes left here must have been sea-worshippers," Martin said, staring across the little bay to the open sea. "They would have known the surf would take their dust."

Gaultry shrugged. She had wanted to support Martin through the rites of death that were familiar to him, but she was not entirely comfortable with the necromantic touch she detected in the elaborate dispersion of the ashes. If there was power in the sad remains of the dead, she wanted to know nothing of it. "Are you going to put your share of the ashes in the sea?" she asked.

Martin nodded. "I'll save my cousin Gavin's until I meet with him. But my own—this war with the Lanai is a serious thing, and I want to dispose of things properly before I ride. I know Grandmère would prefer going into the water off the cliffs of Seafrieg, but the sea is one land before the gods, and this will have to serve her."

"I wish I were going to Haute-Tielmark with you," Gaultry said.

Martin took the vessel he had given her to hold and nestled it safely into the grass by the funerary stone's side. "We share that desire," he said. "But this is not a good year to introduce you to the field of battle. If this summer's campaign were limited to the traditional ground at Llara's Kettle, I would want you to travel with me. The lake there, and the great waterfall—they're so beautiful, I would love for you to see them. But this year the war has three fronts. The hills of western Haute-Tielmark are in dangerous upheaval. The Lanai skirmishers aren't limited to the usual war parties. They've been reinforced by Far Mountain's warriors, men who've earned their living as raiders and mercenaries. Those warriors live a motto more complex than guts and glory—though this summer their honor is at stake too, considering the disgrace their king has shouldered. He has sworn to rebuild the herds his son-in-law saw slaughtered in what should have been safe pastures."

Martin took Gaultry's hand. His flesh was warm from the clay pot. "There is also the no small matter of the role that may be played by the Bissanty genius who orchestrated the Lanai defeat in the High Mountains. Report has him as a military prodigy, half Bissanty, half Dramaya, and combining the best of both those ancient tribes. He's barely the age of your boy Tullier, and already he's showing brilliance. He and his men have been recalled to Bassorah City. Who knows what could happen if the Emperor sends him to march on us from the north?"

Gaultry cast the goddess-sign worriedly. "The border in the north is God-pledged. Elianté and Emiera will protect us."

"That's true," Martin said. "For all the good it will do us, if our warriors were engaged there while the Lanai were still tearing into our backs from the west." He shook his head. "Let's not speak of this now. I have other matters I wish to share instead."

He had retained his hold of her hand. The heat of his palm—

Gaultry realized abruptly that something more than the pot's fire had warmed him. Her cheeks reddened, and she would have pulled away, but he gently tightened his grip. "Gaultry. Before we journeyed to Bissanty, you and I spoke plainly once of the ties that bind us. Magic fueled our passion from our first meeting, but the bonds we share go far beyond enchantment. Before I leave you today, I need to tell you what happened to me in Bissanty."

"It changed you," Gaultry said. "You are wilder now. Do I need to know more than that?"

He nodded. "You do. Before Bissanty, I warned you that something in me was withdrawing its ability to feel emotion. The spell-fire of the geas your father laid on me to protect you had burned away more than a decade of numbness. But once the geas ran its course, I could feel myself freezing up, returning to that numb state. Without the power of magic to heat me, I feared that the years I'd spent serving as a soldier had extinguished my capacity to love."

"You told me that just before Tullier made his appearance at the Prince's Feast," Gaultry said. Martin had come to her then in a strange fever of emotion—a fever that had not touched the calm beat of his heart. "You scared me, but I didn't see what I could do."

Martin nodded. "My head and my body seemed separated by a wall of ice. I did not understand then what was happening, only that it felt so unreal, and yet so strong. But then the feast was interrupted, and we learned of the Sha Muira's orders to kill the Brood-members. I broke my father's sword that day, releasing the magic that would whisk me away to protect Helena and her son."

He cast Gaultry an apprehensive look, hesitating. "That was when everything changed for me—when I broke Dinevar and released the magic. There was more in that release than I had bargained for."

Gaultry closed her eyes. She saw again the flowing magic, the scintillating shards of metal as the great sword disintegrated, releasing the full force of its magic on Martin's body. Her own father had died on that sword, taking his escape from the noose of magic in which the traitor-chancellor had bound him. Who could tell what powers had been constrained within its metal? "Is this what you needed to ask Melaudiere about, the night we returned to Princeport?" she asked.

Nodding, he released her hand. "After Morse died, Grandmère took certain measures, as she thought, to protect me," he said. "Perhaps they did, but she should have asked me first if it was what I wanted. She bound me with shielding oaths the day she buckled Dinevar to my belt—but those oaths shielded more than my body. They also froze my ability to love and feel. Shattering the sword set me free. Perhaps to meet my death, but also once again to love those in the world around me." He threw his cloak down next to the stone and shucked off his boots. "I am free now," he said. "Nothing can keep me from reaching for the things that I desire.

"Come with me." The grey eyes bore into hers, lit from within by a sudden fiery gladness. "I'm going to return my part of Grandmère to the sea, and I want you with me."

Gaultry, unsure what he intended, doffed her cloak and boots and put them neatly beside his, her movements a little exacting, compensating for her uncertainty.

"Are we going to get wet? I'm a little chilled already—"

"You won't be cold," he said. He pulled his tunic up over his head. At the open collar of his shirt beneath, he wore a blue glass amulet, cut with the sign of the water-god. "The water here will not be cold like the harbor's. The whole bay is shallow—you'll see."

With his reliquary vessel cupped in one hand, his fingers protectively covering its mouth, he turned and sprinted, impetuous, for the beach.

What would Dervla think? Gaultry removed her tunic more slowly, glancing self-consciously up toward the roof of the crematorium, just visible over the curve of the land above her. From the beach, there would be a clear view to the crematorium's porch. Was this a known ritual Martin intended to perform, or something more intimate?

She was wearing the strange silver ring the Duke of Haute-Tielmark had given her at Sieur Jumery's manor, still hidden on a string that she wore around her neck. She held it in her hand for a moment, trying to decide if she should wear it into the surf. The Duke had said he thought it was a key—would she ever find the lock? The hammered silver flower of its decoration was distinctive, but she had yet to see anything that came close to matching it—not that she had any time to actively look. She nestled it safely into the toe of one of her boots, giving a guilty glance up the hill toward the crematorium. What would Dervla do if she discovered it in Gaultry's possession?

By the time she reached the beach, Martin had already run ahead to the end of the spit of sand. She followed, a little diffidently, keeping above the waves' sweep. The sand was surprisingly warm under her feet, and the water, when one wave curled to slap her ankles, was positively comfortable, compared with the chill drizzle that sprinkled her arms and face. She realized then what Martin had known from his seaside upbringing— the heat of the past days had remained in this shallow water even as the rain chilled the air that flowed above it.

Martin knelt in the shallows at the farthest reach of the sandy bar, the vessel held between his palms, the foam of the surf lashing at his knees. He began to pray in a low, shifting language with which Gaultry was unfamiliar. The words started susurrating and gentle, then began to rise. Soon, no longer echoing the sound of the surf, his prayer began to lead it. It rose, with a gentle, rippling power until, to Gaultry's astonishment, the waves began to curl away from Martin's body.

A path extended outward from the shallow spit into the water, a sandy, wave-rippled path with walls of seawater inclining in from both sides. Martin, chanting, fixed his gaze and concentration on this path as it spread open before him. The strength in his voice pounded back the surf, pushing the narrow sandy line out almost a field's length, until, at its end, the waves swept back and revealed a grey, deeply pitted rock. Beneath its mantle of seaweed, the stone was cut in many places by the sea's force—and by human hands.

The prayer peaked. Martin rose from his knees and walked swiftly forward, bearing the reliquary pot.

Behind him, Gaultry hesitated at the brink. What fueled the magic here? A power in Martin, long dormant, now loosened? The death-strength of his grandmother? Something Dervla had ceremonially invested in the vessel's ash? Martin had appealed to the land's old god— Allegrios, who ruled the coast before the Goddess-Twins, before Mother Llara, before the Bissanty had swept south to rule. She accepted the ancient trinity of Llara, Andion, and Allegrios—the oldest gods, the sky, earth, and sea come together to form the world at time's dawning. But she had not thought to see some aspect of this triad's power vested through Martin.

Martin had reached the stone. He scraped the seaweed aside, searching for a place to leave the pot. As she watched, he found a cranny and wedged it in with a handful of seaweed.

Then he turned to her, still singing, and opened wide his arms.

She stared at the sandy path, at the turquoise waves beaten back to either side, unnerved. Holding her gaze in his own, he began to walk back toward her.

She saw the predator's strength in him then, the strong ripple of his arms, his body. She saw the wolf's eyes, measuring her, assessing her fear. Ash from the crematorium foundations still streaked his face, emphasizing the high hard bones of his cheeks. She saw the danger in him, the death that stalked him, the turbulence of war that threatened his life.

And she saw also the desire that ran all through him, the strength he yearned to share. Within the body of the warrior, she saw the vulnerable fire of his love.

"Gaultry," he said, incorporating her name into his song, calling her.

"Martin!" His name escaped her in broken return as she ran to meet him. His prayer ended against her mouth as his arms enfolded her.

The sea path held for only a heartbeat longer. Gaultry had a crazy final glimpse over Martin's shoulder of the rock where he had buried his grandmother's ashes, and then the sea reclaimed it. The waves crashed in from either side, closing in up to Martin's shoulders. Martin snatched her off her feet, safeguarding her from a ducking.

The surge of the water was not rough, as Gaultry had imagined. They were out in the water beyond the turbulence of the surf. As Martin had promised, the water was warm, luxuriously so. She felt weightless, buoyant, the wash of warm water caressing her clothes against her skin. He cradled her body against his own, holding her head clear above the water. Her legs clasped naturally around his hips, helping him to hold her up, and, clutching him to her, she pressed her mouth against his hair.

"I love you," she whispered. Despite the brine, the rain was falling hard enough to keep the water sweet in her mouth. "Even without all the power of the sea in you."

"And I you," he answered solemnly. "From here forward, our separations will only be temporary."

They remained in the water a long time together, lost in the motion of the waves. When they finally left the water and went back up into the cemetery to collect their rain-soaked outer garments and their boots, it was Martin, not Gaultry, who was overcome with shyness at the audacity of their act. However chaste, it had not been innocent.

"I want to make you a more substantial pledge," he said. "Before I ride today, I will petition Benet to allow me to send word to Helena."

Gaultry, lacing the front of her tunic, stilled. When it came to his wife, Helena, there was only one matter on which Martin would be petitioning the Prince. A request for the dissolution of marriage.

"Now?" she asked.

"There will be obstacles," he admitted reluctantly. "Even if Benet agrees, he will have to petition Dervla as High Priestess for approval. Benet I think I can sway to my side. Dervla—that's another matter entirely."

Separation between peers of the realm—and Martin's wife held his father's old title—was a serious business. For Martin to legally separate from Helena—the woman with whom he had not shared a household for more than a decade—he would have to enter a complaint against her conduct. Gaultry could think of only one complaint he could offer: the illegitimacy of his putative son. Young Martin Montgarret, the boy Martin had left in place as his heir when he had separated from Helena and renounced his rights to the family name, title, and property. "Are you sure?" she asked. "In Arleon Forest, common law would legitimize any commitment you and I agreed to follow."

Martin shook his head. "I owe you more."

She would have laughed—debt was not the description she would have used for her feelings—but it was clear from his expression that he would not welcome levity. "You and I own no titles or land," she reminded him gently. "Helena's son—you have allowed him to grow to the threshold of manhood with expectations. After all this time, it would be cruel to destroy his hopes—unless reclaiming the lands of Seafrieg is your real intention here."

"This is not about property," Martin said stubbornly. "When I married Helena, I made a pledge before the gods. Until I am released from that, she will continue to have a claim on me."

"Certain ties must be acknowledged," Gaultry said. "On your honor, I would not have it otherwise. But a public dissolution of a peer's marriage? That is a matter of property, not of love."

"Women like Helena are supported through great accumulation of property." Martin could not meet her gaze. "Allegrios mine, the matter is more complex even than I have told you. I would have mentioned this long before, but there was neither time nor place. My sister has threatened to challenge Helena for the title and all of Seafrieg's holdings. Mariette told Grandmère she could no longer sit idly by, leaving Seafrieg unrighteously in Helena's hands. If I did not want Seafrieg—she feels it should be hers."

"She has a point."

Martin sighed. "Mariette was not even ten years old when Helena and I separated, and Morse was yet living. In my own pain, I did not foresee the time when she might have a serious claim to the title."

"And if Mariette successfully challenges young Martin's legitimacy before you divorce Helena, she and her son will be left with nothing. You don't want that." Disappointed, Gaultry, her outer clothes in place, picked up her cloak and wrapped it tightly around her body. "Weren't you just saying dissolution of the marriage was something you owed *me?*"

"What would you have me do, Gaultry?" Martin's tone echoed her own frustrations. "Allegrios mine! This was the past. My heart was caged and wounded. I did not know then that it could ever heal, ever come bursting free."

Gaultry shook her head. "I love you, Martin, and I will not live to see that fire dampened. But better I had loved a simple forest man, and not be confused by property matters that lie beyond my interest."

Martin reached for her and took her in a hard, enveloping hug. "It feels almost insane to be thinking of such things," he admitted. "In scant hours, I will ride with my Prince for the battlefield. This time, I can feel the doom that hangs over me: The Brood-prophecy will dog me at every step. With every engagement, I will be thinking 'Here is the moment I will spill my blood, like so many members of my family before me.' Yet the stakes here are higher than my single life, so I must go."

Though he spoke calmly, there was hidden tension in him. "Gaultry," he said. "The tide of battle has swept me up. But you will be here, and there is much you can do. Uncover the secret that will paint Benet's path with the red that is not Brood-blood. That is all that can save you—can save us—from the prophecy. Uncover the Kingship secret. Gaultry—I'm depending on you."

"You mustn't go," Gaultry said sharply, the sudden clear horror of Martin's danger washing through her. "Remind Benet of the risks. Does he want more of the Brood-kin killed? Tell him you can't go."

"And leave Mariette to face the red path's dangers without me? As Grandmère's military commander, she had no choice but to remain at the front. Should I leave her there to support Benet alone?"

Gaultry clenched him in a tight embrace, burying her face in the front of his tunic. But the cloth was swiftly dampening from the wet shirt beneath, and there was little comfort to be found there.

"I will get the Brood to parley," she said, her resolve hardening as she spoke the words. "Elianté and Emiera in me, I will get them to parley. Dervla and Tamsanne and Julie. Marie Laconte's heir too. Everyone. We will know what it will take to make Benet King before the ripening of the new moon—this I pledge. Then I'll ride out to you—to Benet—to meet you with the answer."

"That's a dangerous oath." Martin pressed his cheek against the top of her head. "But it may well be all that makes the sacrifice of our own lives a worthwhile cause."

"I will not lose my life in this," Gaultry vowed. "Neither my life, nor yours. And Benet will be King, and the Brood-prophecy will be complete."

"The power is in you to make your oaths come true." Martin brushed a strand of her wet hair from her face. "But the gods are cruel. They may even give you what you think you want."

Clasped in the circle of his arms, Gaultry shivered. Martin was right. Despite her brave words, she doubted there would be an easy release for any of the Brood. The gods, having granted great power, would see a price exacted in return.

"If life and honor were the same, the gods would have less power," she said.

Martin, releasing her, stooped to retrieve his cousin's funerary vessel from its temporary resting place by the stone. "And men greater. From what I've seen, that would improve nothing."

They held each other in a mutual gaze, Gaultry drinking in the mental and physical longing for rest that already lined his face. It would be weeks, if not months, before they saw one another again. Unwilling tears pressed at her eyes. She choked them back. She did not want to cry, did not want to make this parting more difficult than it was already.

A gull, calling from the sea, broke the moment.

They began the long trek back up the slope to the palace.

chapter 13

▼

After Gaultry's intense experience of the cremation and her time with Martin, the Duchess's funeral felt anticlimactic. The actual ceremony, attended only by the Princess, Gaultry, one of Melaudiere's aides, and representatives of the other six ducal houses, was conducted in the chapel below the palace's main temple. It was a low, unpleasantly crypt-like room. Arranging the witnesses in a circle around the stone altar took longer than the actual interment ceremony.

Speechifying from the temple steps followed, in which Gaultry played no active role. The lawn was crowded with mourners from both palace and city. In consideration to the rain, Dervla, Melaudiere's personal priest, and the other speakers kept their commentary brief. Even with brevity, the odd combination of eulogy, legal jargon, and land law made much of the content impenetrable.

To Gaultry, standing on the temple steps and looking out across the turreted landscape of the palace, it seemed that the Prince's court had passed momentarily into another world, a darker, greyer world, where peoples' faces were closed and sad regardless of whether or not they were in true mourning. On the battlements that faced the city, the normally gay flutter of the flags and banners of the noble houses, regiments, and services had been suppressed. Today Melaudiere's flag flew alone beside the Prince's, the former with a mourning pennant raised on the flagpole above it. For the first time, Gaultry saw plainly the impact the Prince's edicts could have on those around him: Before mounting up and riding west, Benet had declared for three days of mourning, and his court, given a direct command, had made a zealous response. The results were at once heartening for their display of unity and depressing for the atmosphere they created of a world plagued by loss.

The Duchess had made generous provision for memorial banquets. As the speeches ended, the crowd dispersed dutifully to the palace refectories. Gaultry, as befitted Melaudiere's representative and a member of the Common Brood, had a place in the Princess's inner dining chamber. Being allowed one guest, she had chosen the Sharif, who, on Benet's personal order, would be sailing the next day with the morning tide.

The Sharif saluted her somberly in the quiet of the corridor outside the beautifully painted doors of the dining chamber. The tall Ardana owned no mourning clothes in the Tielmaran style, but the Prince had afforded her coin to clothe herself in the manner of her native land, and she appeared wearing flowing dun-colored robes that fastened at the shoulders and left her arms bare. A brazen amulet formed like a rising sun was pinned to the front of her robes, centered on her chest. In acknowledgment of the official mourning, she wore a meticulously pleated scarf of black cloth draped loosely across her throat and back over her shoulders.

How did it go? she asked.

Fine, Gaultry replied. *Though I spent more time staring at the altar-brazier than anything else. Dervla hardly pretended she was interested—she just wanted the ashes interred and the ceremony done with.* That was harsh, she thought, but fair. The High Priestess's thoughts had seemed far away throughout.

This should be interesting, Gaultry added, as the Princess's pregnant lady-in-waiting, the rabbity Duchess of Ranault, pushed past them. *Ourselves aside, this crowd marks those who will form the Princess's inner court in Benet's absence—friends and those whom she must acknowledge together.*

You are in that circle.

Gaultry shrugged, knowing the Sharif was right, but uncomfortable with the distinction. Her status could only do her harm if she did not soon find some way to satisfy the Brood-pledge. But she did not want to voice this to the Sharif. *It was good of you to agree to come,* she said. *You have much to accomplish before tomorrow's sailing.* Almost the entire day, as Gaultry had stood witness to the Duchess's cremation, the Sharif had worked with the Prince's sewermen—Tullier at her side to translate for her—obtaining the knowledge of water pumps and valves that she intended to bring with her to her water-poor desert home.

Or at least that was how she had filled those hours in which she had not been closeted in private conference with the Prince. The desert woman's unanticipated effect upon Benet had seeded turmoil in the palace corridors, as the Prince had sent his calendar-man scurrying from the room with fresh orders and thrown his military outfitters into upheaval with the declaration of his imminent departure. Gaultry was glad her day of mourning had spared her from that.

I am glad for this final chance to observe your Prince's chieftains and their clans, the Sharif told her. *Ardain is a land that has not seen a month of peace the course of my entire life, nor neither the life of my mother before. To see how those who do not live constantly in war comport themselves—this is a matter of interest to my people as well as myself.* She paused, and there was a flicker of humor in her eyes. *Almost as important as your valves and pumps.*

Peace was a relative term, Gaultry found herself thinking, as a footman approached and ushered them onward.

The inner dining chamber was a narrow, white-washed room with windows along one of its long walls to its own private court and terrace. The wall behind the head of the table was decorated with a tapestry depicting one of Tielmark's lady Princes, possibly Corinne, eating a feast in a fruiting orchard, a man in a humble farmer's smock, obviously intended for her consort, accompanying her. The room had a musician's alcove as well, curtained today with brocade drapes. Gaultry and the Sharif were among the last arrivals.

Princess Lily had already taken her place at the head of the magnificent walnut table, the top of which was hewn from the trunk of a single tree, heartwood included. The fiery color of the table's surface, the dazzling meal laid before her, and the bright tapestry at her back made the already diminutive woman seem smaller still, and without inner luster. Her pretty features looked tired. She fiddled disconsolately with her marriage ring as she waited for her guests to take their places.

Gaultry hoped she was doing a better job at concealing her loneliness for Martin than Lily was managing for Benet.

In Benet's absence, the Princess wore a silver tiara, a formal reminder of her authority as Tielmark's ruler in his place. The Duchess of Ranault, seated to Lily's left where she could best be attentive, kept jumping up and touching at the Princess's hair, as though nervous that the little bridge of silver would slip. Whether the Princess found Ranault's attentions irritating or an assurance was not obvious from her expression.

The room hummed with respectfully quiet talk. All members of the ducal families in residence at the palace were making an appearance. Judging from their dry silks, the rain had deterred them from the lawn outside of the temple. These peers were a mixed group of elderly relatives, ducal spouses and their young children. The dukes themselves, save for the disgraced Argat Climens, were all away at the front.

Adele Chevrier, the crippled daughter of Michael of Arleon, who held the ducal border lands where Gaultry had been born, was one of the few faces that Gaultry could identify—and Adele she recognized only by her cripple's chair and attendants. Back in Arleon Forest, these were folk she had barely known existed, except by their heraldic signatures: crosses and garlands and brightly colored animals. She wondered what the Sharif made of them. Except for Adele, they were a handsome, hard-looking lot, very much a healthier breed than the effete nobles Gaultry had been exposed to in Bissanty.

Sitting amongst them, the young Princess's slim figure appeared even tinier. Lily's folk, fishermen from Princeport's harbor, were not a people bred for the rigors of war fought astride large horses urged forward in body-crushing charges.

Around the room servitors were chivying guests so the meal could begin. Gaultry and the Sharif had been accorded seats at the walnut table, two out of twenty-four places, each with its own plate and table setting as well as an individual chair rather than the more customary trestle bench. Many more than twenty-four crowded the room. Those guests who had not been assigned seats were expected to help themselves from the sideboards.

Inner circle of the inner circle, the Sharif commented dryly, running her fingers along the polished wood of her chair-arm.

For today at least. Gaultry shrugged. *By the accident of timing that makes me old Melaudiere's chief mourner.*

Converging forces of influence had determined both guest list and guest placement. The land's highest peers and ministers were complemented by the Duchess's close personal servants and friends, along with a scattering of the Brood-blood. At the table, the traditional landed hierarchy dominated. Ducal kin and a few highborn ministers with whom Gaultry was passingly familiar crowded the seats closest to the Princess. Dervla, in her place as High Priestess, had a seat at the Princess's left hand. She was the only Brood-member seated above the nobles.

Lower down the table, the hierarchical allocations became less obvious as Brood-blood mixed with members of Melaudiere's household. Tamsanne and Dame Julie sat across from each other on opposite sides of the table, their venerable stature fitting them to mark the invisible border between titled blood and the rest. Tamsanne, wearing an ancient black dress—like all the old woman's clothes, well used and carefully greased at the seams to repel further wear—looked like a visitation from another realm. She circled the golden rim of her place setting with one wrinkled, work-thickened finger, face down-bent, focused. The dignity of her comportment just barely rendered this tic a mysterious, meditative gesture rather than bad manners. Gaultry had not crossed paths with Tamsanne since their brief meeting the night before Melaudiere's death. She wondered what Mervion had told her about the attack on Tullier—and the Prince—in Martin's townhouse, and their own argument after it.

To her great relief Mervion was seated below her grandmother on the far side of the table, in a seat between Palamar Laconte and a sweet-faced blond woman. The old duchess at least had ranked Mervion as an insider, Gaultry was warmed to see. Melaudiere's priest, next to Palamar, had been assigned that side of the table's last chair.

It took Gaultry a moment to realize that the blond woman talking animatedly to her sister could only be Dervla's niece Jacqual, sister to the girl who had killed herself after being tortured by the Prince's traitorous ex-Chancellor. The familial resemblance was obvious—indeed, Jacqual was enough like Dervla to be her daughter, but the young woman's expression, free from the stress of the responsibilities that Dervla wore as High Priestess, bore innocent notice of the older woman's unhappy mental frame.

Below Dame Julie, on Gaultry's side of the table, were Melaudiere's steward, the Sharif, Gaultry—and, filling the last chair on her side of the table, Argat Climens, the Duchess of Vaux-Torres.

Argat was the last seated, ushered to her chair by an apologetic servant.

"What an interesting summer it has been," the Duchess said. She sank gracefully into her chair, the silk layers of her dress rustling expensively. "You have no idea, the arguments that went on behind closed doors, to secure me even this place. How embarrassing," she sniffed, surveying the table with amused, sardonic eyes. "Any lower and I'd have had to scramble for Benet's chair." At the bottom of the table was an empty chair, unclaimed by custom in honor of the traveling Prince. "What would Dervla have made of that?"

Gaultry picked up her napkin and preoccupied herself with unfolding it. Her cheeks warmed as Vaux-Torres, still waiting an answer, turned to study her from behind long, curled lashes, an ironic smile curving on the smooth ivory of her face. For a woman who was supposed to be in disgrace as a suspected traitor, the Duchess created an entirely successful impression that she was enjoying herself, however bittersweet her pleasures.

Who is it? the Sharif asked, as she nodded politely to Melaudiere's steward, seated on her other side, and somehow managed a gracious gesture to indicate her lack of language.

The Duchess of Vaux-Torres, Gaultry told her. She covered her internal talk with less suavity than the Sharif. Catching the unspoken interplay, the Duchess's eyes infinitesimally narrowed.

"This must be the infamous Ardana Sharif," she said silkily. "Do introduce us, Lady Gaultry. I am most eager to meet the woman who has set the order of our realm tumbling on its heels."

Sensing that she was out of her league, Gaultry made clumsy introductions. That sense was confirmed as Vaux-Torres acknowledged the introduction with a short salute in the Ardana's own language, followed by rapid, fluent speech, first in a languid tongue, then in a tongue more guttural. Evidently Argat Climens, unlike Gaultry, had given the seating arrangements due consideration before making her appearance.

The Sharif, raising her brows in surprise, started to answer in the guttural tongue, then broke off, frowning, and shook her head. "I won't use the talk of my enemies," she said, speaking slowly to ensure she would be understood.

The Duchess, with a placating gesture, spoke once more in the guttural language. The Sharif laughed, won over, and then answered back. *Clever!* she told Gaultry, laughing still, although she did not go so far as to share the joke. *This one has a dangerous humor.*

The Duchess, satisfied by the Sharif's reaction, turned to greet Melaudiere's priest, seated across from her at the bottom seat on the table's other side.

It was a fascinating performance. In conversation, Vaux-Torres made no secret of the charges that had sent her plummeting from her rightful place at the top of the table. By taking the charges so lightly, she made them seem littler.

But even such a performance could not make the circumstances of her disgrace entirely vanish. Gaultry caught her once in an unguarded look, staring hungrily up to where her daughter Elisabeth was holding the Vaux-Torres seat between dowagers who represented Haute-Tielmark and Basse-Demaine. Was there pain in her face in that brief moment?

Gaultry could not be sure. Vaux-Torres carried herself throughout four courses with a detached, ironic humor, managing to embarrass Gaultry twice with some dry comment that made her laugh into her food, the first a sly observation about Dervla, the second a comment on Tamsanne, who was, Gaultry realized after Vaux-Torres pointed it out, doing a very poor job of appearing absorbed in the comments of the minister who sat next to her. "And why indeed should she attend him?" Vaux-Torres said mockingly, as Gaultry dabbed her napkin to her face, trying to recover. "He'll be out of his seat in a year or two, while your grandmother endures."

Gaultry could see why the Duchess's daughter Elisabeth floundered about court with an air of being over her head in uncharted waters. With such a mother providing running commentary, young Elisabeth must constantly be wondering at the levels of intrigue or communion she was missing. No untutored neophyte could hope to match the sophistication and complexity of Argat Climens's grasp of court affairs. But then, perhaps the Duchess had been too clever, had tried to play her advantages against her pledge to the Prince—and her judgment had failed her. Perhaps Dervla was right to charge her with Bissanty collaboration—

"She charged Haute-Tielmark too," the Duchess interjected. Even as she had turned for a moment to exchange a bon esprit with Melaudiere's priest, she had followed the play of Gaultry's eyes and expression. "And she would have charged you as well, if not for that old woman whose ashes went in the ground today. On that happy note, a toast to Gabrielle Lourdes, and all she's done for us and Tielmark together! May her ashes rest in peace, in all their scattered corners." The Duchess picked up her chalice, and Gaultry found herself doing the same. What could be the harm, indeed, of drinking to the honor of the woman who had mentored her at court?

"And now we have the moment Gabrielle herself would have been eager for," the Duchess said. She gestured with her cup toward the top of the table, where a pair of house servants were tidily folding back the drapes that had concealed the musician's alcove. "The moment when she gets to play good fairy and bad at her own funeral."

As the servants stepped aside, an enormous fat man in a black wool jacket, his outsize head surmounted by a very obvious horsehair wig, came to stand at the center of the alcove. Portentously, he unrolled a scroll. He identified himself as the Duchess of Melaudiere's solicitor. This was to be a public reading of the Duchess's last will and testament.

Like the speeches on the lawn, a great part of the document was

devoted to a precise description of Melaudiere's lands and ducal proper-
ties, and of Gabrielle Lourdes's absolute acknowledgment that her own-
ership of the same was held in stewardship for the blood heirs of her long
dead husband, Hugh, including but not exclusive to those of her own
body. Indeed, a long part of the text was devoted to a recitation of Hugh's
nephews, cousins, and other potential heirs, in the event that Gabrielle's
grandchildren did not survive her long enough to reproduce.

As a sweet was served, peaches in syrup, the solicitor came to a short
passage regretting Hugh's early passing, "for that you preserved me of the
Bissanty scourge, and protected my body with your own, in a time when
even a title could not offer me safe haven." It was an odd juxtaposition,
the dessert served by smiling servants in that comfortable room and the
deceased woman's evocation of the past horrors that had swept Tielmark's
court. Why were all these people here? Gaultry found herself wondering,
staring around the room. To mourn the dead? For what they might gain?
To appear well in the young Princess's eyes?

"It's started," Vaux-Torres said. "Look at them flocking up to receive
their gifts. And remember, those are the ones who truly care that she has
left us." The servitors formed a queue of those who had been eating from
the sideboards and began moving them toward the alcove. Gaultry recognized a number of faces from Melaudiere's retinue: a squire here, a
knight there, a young serving woman. As the solicitor read their names,
they came forward and some small legacy or memento, or both combined,
was awarded. The Duchess was a generous woman, even in death. Gaultry
felt a fresh pang of grief, thinking that young Melaney should have been
among these sad-faced, flustered, and yet quietly joyous people, learning
that their mistress's death had come with the gift of their own independence. "She doesn't seem to have forgotten anybody," Gaultry said softly,
as one serving lady broke out with a mournful, crying laugh. Her legacy
was a pension from Melaudiere's household, payable in quarters, and certainly enough to live on.

"It takes work," Vaux-Torres commented. "And Gabrielle's steward
and bailiff both are renowned for their soft-heartedness. But wait for her
man to start reading the gifts to those at the table. The Princess will have
intervened to soften a few blows here—the duchess will have left her a
long purse to compensate for unintentional omissions, and some of it will
go to keeping the peace among those whom old Melaudiere wanted to
slight—but you can be sure Melaudiere will be left with at least some of
her fun. Indeed," the dark eyes sparkled dangerously, "I'm sure my own

gift will be pointed. Melaudiere could be lacking in humor."

"The whole table of us will be getting presents?" Gaultry asked. "But these aren't the Duchess's friends."

"My point precisely," Vaux-Torres answered, spearing a peach with her fork. "But they have to be honored with legacies for form's sake. Some of those old biddies," she gestured to the ducal dowagers at the top of the table, "are safe enough. And I'm sure Elisabeth will receive a nice mourning ring. I hear the Princess selected the design herself—poor Gabrielle didn't have the opportunity, once her last illness came on her. But others . . ." She paused, and took a mouthful of peach. "With others Gabrielle will have made a pointed gift, and Lily throwing a gold ring in on the side won't soften that."

Melaudiere's priest was the first called up from the table. He went up slowly and respectfully, not, like some of the earlier recipients, at all in a hurry. Unlike the sideboard guests, his legacy was not read aloud. The solicitor privately showed him the place where his name and legacy appeared on the will, and one of the solicitor's aides took a scroll out of a little bag and handed it to him. His fingers trembled a little as he reached to take it.

"It's a good one," Vaux-Torres said. "Look at the way his back has straightened." Gaultry had not noticed the minute squaring of the man's shoulders, the slight puffing of his chest. "But prepare yourself," the Duchess continued, her lips pressed in a cool smile. "There's something in this last bag of gifts that is going to make someone very unhappy. They'd read everything out, if it was all going to be harmless."

The priest returned to his seat, a properly somber expression on his face. Yet underneath, Gaultry could see that he was excited and pleased. She wondered what Melaudiere could have bequeathed him, to make him so happy.

Vaux-Torres was next, as those seated at the great table were called from lowest to highest. A server came to escort her. "Forgive me," she said lightly, "if I have somewhat lost my humor on my return." Her manner was loftily disdainful as she rounded the table, heading toward the waiting giant with his ill-fitting wig.

Gaultry took the moment to explain what was happening to the Sharif.

The Ardana nodded comprehension. *We have the same in my country when a leader dies. Also many pledges, in memory of the dead one's name.*

Across the table, Palamar Laconte, whose turn for a gift would come next, stood prematurely. Vaux-Torres sidestepped to avoid a collision, but Palamar, lurching the wrong way, contrived somehow to stand on the train of the Duchess's skirt. There was a flutter of movement as their respective footmen untangled them, then the Duchess, with an acid look at the younger woman, glided onward. Palamar, whose turn with the solicitor came next, remained awkwardly on her feet.

The plump acolyte could not get even a simple matter of timing right with a footman to lead her. Gaultry wished she could sympathize. Poor Palamar had suffered such great losses. Moreover, it could not be pleasant to play run and fetch in her ongoing role as Dervla's lackey. Still, something in the silly woman drew irritation rather than compassion. Her awkwardness seemed so unnecessary—if she had just waited in her seat, the clumsiness with Vaux-Torres at least would have been avoided.

The Duchess returned from her visit to the alcove a little breathless, two spots of color high on her cheeks that no degree of self-control could conceal. Cautious of the woman's temper, Gaultry took another peach, and busied herself with cutting it open.

"You can look," the Duchess said. "Indeed, I will show you. It's nothing so terrible—and yet so ingenious. She must have known I would not be able to resist it."

Nevertheless, when Gaultry looked, Vaux-Torres had her hands cupped beneath the edge of the table so none of those seated nearby could share the view.

Nestled in the Duchess's hands was a beautiful golden egg, its surface intricately enameled with crimson curlicues and flowers. At the touch of a hidden catch, the egg sprang into two halves, and a mechanical bird unfolded glittering wings of a surprising, delicate span and raised a tiny crest. "Cuckoo!" it tweeted, from within tiny bellows inside its chest. "Cuckoo!" The little bird was enameled all over in red and gold. There were four tiny eggs at its feet, each a different color: red and gold, golden-brown, diamanté blue, and lastly one elaborately swirled in blood red crimson. The first three were constructed with tiny crested heads protruding, the last—the swirled crimson—with only a small beak broken out. "Cuckoo!" the mother bird chimed a third time, then folded its wings and closed up. The egg-halves snapped back together with a distinctive click.

"It's beautiful," the Duchess said, rubbing a finger along the fine enamelwork. "And so obviously Gabrielle's own handiwork. So intricate. Imagine. She took all this trouble just for me," Vaux-Torres's tone changed and hardened, "who quite frankly she despised in her later life, knowing full well that the feeling was mutual. A cuckoo-bird. How unsubtle. Yet she made it a thing of beauty. Where's the insult in that?"

Gaultry looked across the room to where Palamar was receiving her gift from the big solicitor. From a distance it appeared to be a simple ring, though suddenly Gaultry wasn't so certain. If the old Duchess had expended such energy composing a message for this woman, surely she would have left a message for poor Palamar too. "Your bird has a pretty song," she said hesitantly, turning back to Vaux-Torres.

"I hold Vaux-Torres in my own right," Argat Climens said audaciously. "I cannot cuckold the title. Old Gabrielle always resented that, having married a title only a man can truehold from the Prince. I suppose her independence must have felt threatened by that, after Hugh was gone." She snapped the egg open again and let it replay its brief song, this time interrupting its cycle before the shell snapped closed, and stroking the tiny eggs. "The real cleverness here is in these eggs. This one—" she touched the red and gold egg, "this one is my Remy, heir one day to my title. Here is Anna, and Beaumorreau, and this one—" she touched the closed egg with the crimson swirls "—this one is my Elisabeth. All quite obvious, to my closest friends, which Gabrielle never claimed to be. Imagine, that she found my every peccadillo so intriguing."

Gaultry gulped. She was vaguely aware that Vaux-Torres had four children, but she was not so close at court to have heard that doubts had circulated as to their parentage. The Duchess, sensing her confusion, gave her a feline smile as her glance slid past to the footman at her shoulder. "It's your turn," Vaux-Torres said. "I will be most interested to see your gift, if you care to show me."

Grateful for even a momentary escape from the woman's overpowering presence, Gaultry went quickly around to the black-coated giant. His broad face was benign and friendly, his manner as he greeted her surprisingly intimate. "She didn't have time to make you a gift," he said regretfully, as he reached into the velvet chambered box proffered by one of his assistants. "I'm sure that would have been her wish. So there is only this ring, and the message of her undying respect." With an ink-stained thumb, he pointed to Gaultry's name where it fell on the rolls, marked in near the bottom with a scratchy hand. "Initialed H. L. & G. M.," read the ring's description, as if that was all that had been needed to make an identification.

The ring was not gold, as Palamar's had been, seen briefly glinting in the room's subdued light. Set with a small sapphire cabochon surrounded by tiny oak leaves, it was silver, and small for any but Gaultry's most slender finger. She glanced down at the inscription before slipping it onto her hand. H. L. & G. M. Hugh Lourdes and Gabrielle Montgarret. A gift given a young woman by her future husband before the marriage that had made her Duchess of Melaudiere.

"You're smiling," Vaux-Torres said, welcoming Gaultry back. "Let's see your ring." Of course, she had watched Gaultry receive it from across the room, just as Gaultry herself had watched Palamar. "How inexpensive," she said, taking Gaultry's hand and turning it so the little sapphire caught the light. "The value clearly cannot be in its price. Now what might that mean?" Gaultry found her smile had widened reflexively at the imp of mischief in the Duchess's expression. "Gabrielle wouldn't have slighted you after all you'd done for her. So obviously it is an important gift, whatever its appearance. It's initialed." She shot Gaultry a mocking glance. Clearly, Vaux-Torres had looked for more than her own name on the rolls when the solicitor had shown her the written confirmation of her gift. "Gabrielle's courting ring, at a guess. At the time, Hugh couldn't risk giving her anything better, or her father would have discovered his suit. The oak must have signified the pledge of his strength to protect her." The Duchess released Gaultry's hand. "Quite a piece of history, if I'm right."

Gaultry looked again at the stone. Sea-blue, almost the color of the old Duchess's eyes, surrounded by silver oak. "You could be right," she admitted, inwardly glowing. "The rolls did not record any story."

"You have to read past that," Vaux-Torres said. "Gabrielle would have been careful of what she chose to commit to text. Words written in a will can so easily become outdated. Printing out the name of her grandson and offering him over to you would certainly have been an indiscretion."

Gaultry choked on a mouthful of peach. The Duchess smiled sweetly. "But that is how you read it, no? I see you smiling."

"Martin Stalker is a married man," Gaultry said, her heart pounding with stupid joy as she swallowed down the peach. If that truly had been what the Duchess had intended! "This ring has nothing to do with him," was all she said aloud.

"Of course," the Duchess agreed demurely. "I understand. And after all you had done for her, you are even a little angry with Gabrielle that she was not more generous. Perhaps you'd like to trade me for my egg?"

Gaultry covered her gift with a protective hand, and Vaux-Torres laughed. "I thought not. Though trust me, with her own artistry put into it, my gift has the greater intrinsic worth."

The Sharif went up and returned with a gold mourning ring—heavy, hammered gold, with the broad, crosslike sword of the Melaudieres raised across its face. Similar-looking rings were given out up the table, as well as several uniquely crafted sculptures like Vaux-Torres's egg, and scrolls to two of the Princess's ministers, the contents of which left one man puffed with outrage. When Dervla went up, she received something small and golden—but if it was a ring, she did not choose to wear it after she returned to her seat.

Finally everyone but the Princess had been served their turn. The solicitor stepped aside and handed off the will to one of his assistants. A low cart covered with tapestry cloth was wheeled forward. The shape of the cloth's folds told Gaultry that this last gift must be the cradle she had seen in Melaudiere's death chamber.

Lily rose to her feet. A hush fell, followed by an indrawn breath. Though the Princess wore a traditional black mourning coat, beneath this top coat she was dressed in blue and white, long skirts that fell away from her waist like foam-chased water, threaded in places with silver to catch the light.

"I wish to see my gift," she said loudly. "My Benet would have done Gabrielle Lourdes the honor of seeing it given here, and not in private."

The solicitor's wig wagged worriedly. "Your Highness—"

"Great Twelve above, I will see it now. I understand it is Melaudiere's gift to the future. Let us all see what she thought the future might hold."

An awkward silence hung throughout the room. Clearly some protocol had been determined, and the Princess had chosen to flout it. By Gaultry's side, Vaux-Torres shifted, her eyes gleaming in anticipation.

"Your wish commands," the solicitor said. At his signal, two footmen drew the tapestry cloth back.

The cradle was more beautiful than Gaultry remembered, and also more sinister. In the brilliant reflected light of the Duchess's chambers, she had not noticed that the serpentine fishes that formed the cradle's rails had a fiercesome aspect. Here, in the shadows of the alcove, they appeared almost menacing, silver-traced guardians coiled atop the cresting foam.

Lily pushed back from the table and passed around to the alcove. She knelt, her skirts spreading. Her child-small hands caressed the smooth wood of the cradle's interior, then touched the serpentine heads and gave it a tentative push. It rocked smoothly. The silver inlay flickered in the light. For an odd moment, the silver threads in the Princess's skirts and the glitter of the silver trace merged, and Gaultry felt she was seeing Lily as the Prince himself must first have seen her—merged with the sea in her dark sea-folk's coat, her legs lost in the foam below, the delicate triangle of her face intense.

"This is beautiful," Lily said, emerging from her reverie. "It will rock Tielmark's heir many a long day." She stared out at the crowd, defiant. "Melaudiere has done us a great honor here, and I will honor her sacrifices in my turn. The tide of life ebbs and flows. A life has ended, but another begins.

"You have come today to mourn the death of my most faithful Duchess. You leave today with the new pledge of the life that grows within my body. Pray to all the Great Twelve to fulfill their promise, and you will see a child in this crib before Elianté shoots her green arrows in the spring."

The uproar that greeted her announcement was fervid, but not entirely joyous. The upper ranks of the table were noticeably restrained. As those standing in the room's corners clapped and cheered—one woman falling to her knees at the Princess's feet and reaching up to kiss her hand—the ducal representatives could be seen casting nervous glances Dervla's way.

In the midst of impending disorder, Tamsanne rose to her feet from her place near the table's center. "Silence!" she called, her dry, cackling voice breaking across the room's noise. "Silence, all of you! Where have your manners gone?"

It was not Tamsanne's place to call for quiet, but somehow everyone obeyed her. She was like a black angry crow in their midst, and somehow everyone feared her. "Fill the cups," she told the footmen, her black eyes snapping fiercely. She turned to Dervla. "Make the toast. Say the prayers and make the toast. Your Princess has made her announcement. Don't pretend that you have forgotten your duty."

Dervla, glaring daggers, did not respond. The footmen moved nervously in the room, sloshing every cup full. Tamsanne, waiting for them to finish, did not move. But finally, when they were done, she spoke again. "Dervla of Princeport. Make the prayer. Your Princess has called."

This time, Gaultry felt it. A reverberation of power shook the table. Tamsanne was readying herself to speak words of power—ancient words, with the strength of unmaking. Power that Tamsanne had reached back through the ancient trees to find, the first rootings of magic that the gods had lain under the earth—

Dervla could feel it too. Dervla and Mervion and Palamar. Gaultry could see the fear, the awareness, on all the faces she could see where magic lived. For a moment it seemed Dervla would resist Tamsanne's challenge—

Then the High Priestess reached for her cup, and raised it. "New Life in the Prince of Tielmark's line," she said. "Let us all praise it."

The toast was drunk, the prayer said. Tamsanne lapsed back in her seat and lowered her head. Dervla whispered something to a footman. He passed word to his fellows, and they quickly moved the guests into a queue, lining them past the alcove to kneel and kiss the Princess's hand. The wake had been transformed into the public celebration of the Princess's conception.

After another moment, it seemed Tamsanne had never spoken, never risen to interrupt.

"It may be that we will not talk again soon." Argat Climens rose from her chair and gave Gaultry a little courtesy, responding to some invisible signal that had half the titled guests risen from their seats. "But how pleasing that we had a chance to open this discussion. Your grandmother is quite remarkable. What do you think? Yourself and your sister aside, was there some power vested in the original brood that can never be recaptured?" She glanced up to the top of the table. "Dervla certainly doesn't want to think that."

With a whisper of silk, she was gone.

She never waited for any of my answers, Gaultry told the Sharif bitterly. *She never even gave me a chance to show I could match her wit.*

The Sharif, fingering her new ring, cast a soothing look Gaultry's way. *That one doesn't need your answers,* she said. *She's looking to make you ask questions. All you need to do is decide if they are questions that would be useful to you, or no.*

I don't need to involve myself in Vaux-Torres's power moves to establish her innocence, Gaultry answered. *If she colluded with the Bissanties, that's her problem, not mine.*

That one would never be happy with a single plot running, the Sharif said, watching Vaux-Torres's back as she moved to join the line of those stooping to congratulate the Princess. *She spoke nothing to you of her Bissanty affairs, am I right?*

Well yes—

She wants your help on another matter, the Sharif told her. *She is too proud to ask, but she would steer you in that direction.*

I'm not going to help her, Gaultry replied heatedly. *She must help herself.*

The Sharif smiled. "Gautri," she said aloud. "You tell me the same thing, the day you took me from the slaver."

It was time to take their places in the line that led to the Princess.

▼

chapter 14

After two days of rain the sky was cloudless, the air perfect and clear. A breeze coming in off the water contained the heat. It felt good to be outside, to feel the air in her hair. With the Midsummer festival over, the docks and quays were almost deserted—everyone was busy elsewhere or out on the ships. Gaultry stood with Tullier at the tip of the Prince's personal dock and watched the Sharif's ship, a deep-bellied vessel with a high deck and weathered once wine-colored sails, as it drew in its sails and picked up speed. Though a Chlamanscher ship from the distant south, it flew Tielmark's blue-and-white pennant beneath its own colors, per order of the Prince.

As the ship receded, the Sharif stood tall in the stern, Aneitha, bound by a collar and chain, frisking at her side. The war-leader's robes fluttered in the breeze, and her gaze rested on them, smiling, until they could no longer distinguish her proud figure from the woodwork of the ship. She had finished her good-byes. There was no last mind-call as the ship rounded the headland and passed out of sight beneath the glistening walls of the palace, heading to the east and the south.

"I will miss her." Gaultry scuffed her foot against the boards of the dock and turned her back to the sea. Another companion leaving. Princeport's skyline was bright and shining under the morning sun, the crisp angles of the roofs rising along the spine of the headland toward the palace. A pleasing view, though not enough to quell the sadness that rose in her throat. "But I suppose I'm also relieved. After what happened to Melaney, I'm glad she's safely away."

Tullier, still facing the sea, hesitated before answering. His health was much improved. Mervion's attentions and two days of rest while the Tielmarans performed Melaudiere's funeral ceremonies had served him well. He could stand without pain and he'd recovered much of his cockiness, although the episode had left him with an inward pensiveness that had been previously lacking.

"Whoever sent those men to the townhouse won't strike in that way again," he said. "They wanted to get me before your Prince gave me a place at the palace. The attack wasn't so personal that it wasn't constrained by political proprieties. But whoever planned it—he or she is admirably focused." His voice was infuriatingly admiring. "They don't care what they destroy en route to achieving their objective. I had that focus once."

"Stop regretting that it's gone," Gaultry said testily. "There are things to admire besides the willingness to kill, you know."

He turned to face her, grinning.

Realizing that he was teasing her, if blackly, she boxed his shoulder. "Let's explore the tide-line a ways before we go back up to the palace. Supposedly a path runs somewhere along the bank." She looked along the shore toward the intriguing tangle of small warehouses, drying fishnets, and cottages. "I'm not in the mood just now to run into Dervla or Ronsars in the halls, and have to play wary to their intrigues."

He nodded acquiescence. The Prince's warder had visited Tullier in Gaultry's quarters to explain the more abstruse aspects of the terms of the boy's protection. In the three hundred years of Tielmark's history as a free state, a wealth of precedents had been established to govern every circumstance concerning the sojourn of a Bissanty Prince in residence at the free Tielmaran court, though to Ronsars the fact that Tullier had not yet reached his majority was an opportunity to tease out further intricacies. The boy had not been grateful to the warder for bringing his attention to these stultifying implications of his unasked-for status as Bissanty's Fifth Prince.

After the last dock they came to the narrow, ill-kempt footbridge that spanned Glassmouth, the broad, lazy river that drained into Princeport's harbor. The far bank was dotted with fishermen's cottages. On the near side, a path led inland along the river's rising sandstone bank, crowded on both sides by artisans' shops and odd little fences that demarcated their yards. The crooked path looked more interesting than the bridge.

As they walked, Gaultry considered what Tullier had said about the townhouse attack. Part of his assessment felt right. She thought, with grief, of young Melaney's crumpled body. Yet until the raw green magic had possessed the swordmaster, kidnapping had been Siànne's stated intention, not murder, and even once the spell had been invoked, she was not sure whether its intention had been merely to kill Tullier's protectors, or the boy as well.

"Why would a Tielmaran want to kidnap you?" she asked. "The magic that took Siànne—its source was certainly Tielmaran."

The boy shook his head. "It doesn't make sense. I could see why Bissanty might want to reclaim me that way, but Tielmark? No."

Gaultry kicked a stone on the path, hard, and watched it skitter down the embankment toward the water. "I'd think it was Dervla behind this," she said, "if I could just find a way for that to make sense."

A little way along the path, they came to the first of the glasswork factories which gave Glassmouth River its name and reputation. These were small, family affairs operated out of home-workshops at the top of the river crag, beneath which lay the seam of pure sand from which they crafted their stock. The smell of hot molten glass hung in the air as they approached. Gaultry herself had not yet had a chance to explore this corner of Princeport, and she found herself sharing Tullier's curiosity as they craned to see into the yards where the master craftsmen worked.

"The Bissanties built one of their first encampments in Tielmark here because of this sand," Gaultry told him. "Melaudierc told me that there are some ancient pieces in the Prince's palace, beads and cups and amulets and things, that date back even to the wanderers' time. And the farmers hereabouts still sometimes dig up odd fragments of glass and clay when they're plowing their fields."

"Bissanty can make its own glass now," Tullier said. "They have quarries almost as good as this in Dramcampagna, and even as near to Bassorah as Polonna Major."

"Yet another reason your Empire shouldn't need us." Gaultry sighed. "Not that it makes Tielmark any richer that you've lost your need to trade for raw materials."

The path broadened onto a muddy square. A handful of makeshift shops crowded the front rooms of the houses at the square's sides, a few with glass-carvers seated outside, taking advantage of the bright morning sun for finishwork on small pieces. Tullier was curious enough to ask one woman to show him her wares. She called her son to bring out a padded leather tray of carved pendants and multicolored beads. The work was surprisingly fine.

"That one's very nice," Gaultry said, pointing out a fused cameo of a white bird with a topaz-colored back.

"It's almost like a dove." Tullier shook his head. "It reminds me of my sister." He picked up the smooth piece of glass by its edges, avoiding contact with the white of the cameo bird. "I wonder what she's doing now." He set it down, with an air of putting Columba too away from him. "Really I'd prefer not to know." Columba had attempted to betray them, back in Bissanty. Gaultry didn't blame him for not wanting to think of her. His hand moved over the tray. "This one," he said. "This one is more to my liking."

It was a dark green glass pendant. The carving was a dense spiny tree with spreading branches. "An acacia," the woman said, picking it up and polishing it with a piece of leather. "For eternal remembrance. And affection."

"Very nice." Gaultry reached for her purse. "Everyone who went to the Duchess's wake yesterday received tokens of her regard." She turned to Tullier. The boy had never known the grand old woman, but her advice had been so pivotal in Gaultry's life, she wanted suddenly to include him in the ceremonies of her passing. "I'd like you to have something as well. Do you want it?"

He touched it with one finger, and she knew the answer was yes.

The woman sold it to them with a cord. He would not immediately put it on. He held it in his hand as they wended their way through quiet back streets, and finally turned toward the palace. The boy seemed tired. Gaultry hoped the walk had not overtaxed him.

"You're going to lose it that way," she warned him, watching him play with the cord.

"I won't," he said. "I'll be careful. It's just—I haven't worn anything on my neck for more than a month. And my last necklace was not exactly something I wore by choice."

Gaultry realized then that the last necklace Tullier had worn had been his Sha Muira poison beads—the antidote pearls he had ingested daily to counteract the Goddess poison that had permeated his flesh.

She wondered if it had been a mistake to give him the pendant. With Tullier, it was so hard to know where one was making a misstep.

· · ·

An aggressively toned message from Princess Lily awaited them on their return to the palace. She wanted an immediate audience, and had sent a footman to wait at the palace gate, with orders to bring them directly on their return from giving the Sharif their farewells.

"I never get a chance to properly tidy myself for these meetings," Gaultry muttered, as they paused by a small mirror in the anteroom of the Princess's chambers, and the footman gave them a brief opportunity to brush the street dust off their clothes. "I'm so tired of walking in, and finding everyone else perfectly groomed."

"You look fine," Tullier snorted. "No one expects you to look the part of a titled lady. That's not why you hold people's respect."

"When I'm Tamsanne's age, I'll believe that." She shot him a sour look. "Don't forget. Unless the Princess asks you something directly, let me do the talking. She's suspicious of anything that comes from Bissanty—with good reason, given her experience. It's better if you and she don't have words."

"Are you saying you're a more proficient diplomat than I?"

"Neither of us were born to be diplomats," Gaultry said. "But Lily doesn't like you. So try to keep quiet, and do your best to look like a good boy."

The footman led them down a tiled corridor and out to the Princess's private garden, a high terrace that overlooked the eastern flank of the palace, away from the city. Beyond the palace orchards lay the shining expanse of the sea. Despite the broad vista and feel of exposure given by the panoramic view, the curve of the battlements sheltered the garden's terraces. Under the noonday sun, its promenades felt overbright and overheated.

Lily's omnipresent Duchess of Ranault sat collapsed nearby under a shade tree, two maidservants fanning her as she languished with the obvious discomforts of her heavily advanced pregnancy. Beyond her, several other ladies played cards at a covered table on the terraced battlements, close by the cooling spray of a little fountain. The Princess herself sat alone on a cushioned chair, an embroidery hoop in her lap, on an elevated deck with stone balustrades.

At a little distance, standing watch over the tamarin as it investigated an aromatic bed of flowers, was Elisabeth Climens, Argat's daughter. The girl wore her usual sumptuous attire, paired today with a brocaded mourning cloak that looked uncomfortable in the terrace's heat. She had the closed expression of a well-mannered child who yearned to be down on her knees at play with the clever creature, rather than just obediently standing back to watch it.

Princess Lily saw where Gaultry was looking as she and Tullier approached. "Elisabeth seems to like my new pet," she said, after she greeted them and had been formally reintroduced to Tullier. "I've appointed her its warder. I thought she needed something to keep her occupied."

"Very good, your Highness," Gaultry said. "I'm sure she is grateful."

"It might not seem like much." The Princess shifted her embroidery hoop and fussily adjusted the tension of a thread with her needle. "But when one's heart is sore, an animal or even a basket of laundry can offer a blessed, if brief, distraction." Gaultry guessed Lily was thinking of her own experience, of the bleak, lonely days when her future husband had languished under his chancellor's thrall, and the young laundrymaid had believed herself abandoned. "I would not see Elisabeth stand idle until her mother's case is heard."

"Her mother's case. Will it be tried soon?"

"In two weeks. During the assizes at Andion's Ides. Dervla says she needs the days to gather her last evidences." Lily shrugged. "More likely, she wants the sacramental aspect of the day to give weight to her own testimony. The evidence, as I understand it, is quite extensive, but more circumstantial than otherwise."

Gaultry nodded. On the Ides of the month, when the moon was waned, the High Priestess's power would be at its peak. It would be a good day for Dervla to question witnesses—no one would want to lie to the High Priestess on the day she was nearest to the gods.

Lily shifted restlessly. For all her pose as the great Lady of Tielmark calmly receiving underlings, Gaultry could see that she was uncomfortably aware of her inexperience.

It had been just two months since Lily had served as laundress to some of her card-playing ladies. Now she ruled them—not just as the Prince's consort, but in his absence as their ruler. Small surprise that Lily had chosen to raise herself on the little deck rather than take her ease amongst them. Gaultry shifted uneasily. Lily's lack of confidence made dealing with her a matter of considerable delicacy and tact. Benet's young wife could not always distinguish between those who did not jump to follow her orders out of disrespect and those who questioned her for justifiable reasons.

"Is there something you'd like me to tell Elisabeth?" Gaultry asked, when Lily did not immediately volunteer the reason she had called them.

"Did she have some questions about the tamarin's keep?"

"Not that." For one moment, Lily continued to hesitate. Then her chin went up and her expression chilled. "I've brought you here for another reason. Caius Lepulio, the Bissanty Envoy, has petitioned to be granted an audience with your ward. I can think of no reason to deny him."

At her side, Tullier stiffened.

"What does the Envoy want?" Gaultry asked, doing her best to hide her dismay.

"His intention is to inform Tullirius Caviedo, the publicly acknowledged son of Siri Caviedo, Bissanty's Sea Prince, that Emperor Sciuttarus commands his presence in Bissanty. Imperial Sciuttarus wants your boy to begin taking on the duties that devolve from the throne of Bissanty's Fifth Prince." Lily added two stitches to her embroidery, then paused to thread a needle with a new color. "If the boy wishes to go, I will see that nothing hinders him. My dear Benet believed that he should remain in Tielmark where we could keep an eye on him. But Benet bonded the boy as your ward rather than indenturing him as a court-bound hostage. If Tullirius agrees to leave Tielmark, I will dissolve the ward-bond."

"Tullier's not ready to go back to Bissanty." Gaultry avoided looking at him, even as she wondered what he made of the news that his father had at last publicly acknowledged him as his son, perhaps the final link in the chain that would lead him back to Bissanty.

"I would like young Tullirius to meet with the Envoy," Lily said stolidly, tellingly avoiding anything that might sound like a familiar address. "The circumstances under which the boy left Bissanty have changed. His life is no longer in danger. The Emperor has recognized his claims to the imperial throne, rather than seeking to eradicate them."

Gaultry was quite sure that was not what Emperor Sciuttarus had done, but she could think of no polite way to suggest this. The stubborn tilt of Lily's chin warned that she had already decided that Tullier must meet the Envoy. It was, no doubt, why the Princess had called them to her in such a public place, where any argument would appear as a public challenge to Lily's authority.

"We are yours to command, my Princess." Gaultry made a half bow— not perfect, but certainly much improved from her first efforts in that area. If she did not respect the Princess's orders, how could she expect the ladies of the court to do so in their turn? She risked a glance at Lily's pale young face, touched a little by the fierce sun on the terrace. With

Benet absent, Gaultry had no doubt that many invisible forces at court had begun to home in, exerting invisible pressures, probing the young princess for her weaknesses—and finding her strengths. It was a position Gaultry did not envy, even as she had to plead her own suit. "Of course, in my capacity as the boy's guardian, I must be present to hear what the Envoy proposes. Tullier will agree to nothing without my approval."

"Very well." The Princess gestured for the footman who had escorted them in to approach. "But I'm charging you to consider seriously what the Envoy has to offer."

"I'll consider it," Gaultry answered grimly.

"So there it is." The Princess plucked again at her stitchery. "I am glad you see sense. My man Savin will take you to the Envoy's quarters directly." Her young face hardened. She addressed Tullier for the first time. "I have not forgotten the day we first met. The smell of those poor boys you murdered will stay with me always, the sight of you clutching that bloody knife as you fought before my husband's table. Benet is merciful. He has offered you sanctuary at our court, and I will honor his wishes. But you are dangerous to him, and I would far rather see you gone."

"Princess—" Gaultry began.

Lily cut her short. "Don't defend him," she said sharply. "I won't believe it if you tell me he wasn't at fault. Do you think it matters whether it was this boy or his masters who cut the Laconte boys' throats? Who mutilated poor Lady Destra's corpse? He stood by and let it happen. Why should he be forgiven that?"

"Because he *is* a boy—" Gaultry hissed through her teeth, glancing at the footman, Savin, who was standing by ready to hustle them out, in the event that they offered the Princess undue disturbance.

"I'm hardly younger than she is," Tullier interrupted furiously, voiding her efforts to coddle the Princess's feelings. "Your Prince stole this silly doll from its cradle. If you expect her to know her own business, I have certainly earned the same. Don't use my youth to defend me—I am man enough to hear her charges, if she is woman enough to make them."

Lily flushed pink to the roots of her hair. Her embroidery hoop dropped from her hand, forgotten, and rolled away along the terrace. "You dare—"

"When I find you sitting in a less comfortable chair, I will countenance your insults." Tullier did not make the mistake of stepping toward her. His naked anger was insult enough. "What can you know of the day those boys were killed? How can you guess what I thought or did?"

Gaultry could only stand awkwardly by, wishing she could unsay his words. Tullier was too right about their ages. It was unlikely that Lily had been born more than a year or two his senior. But where Lily's hardships had matured her early, exposing her first to the thin, hardworking life of the dock folk, and then to the backstairs life of court, Tullier's austere life as a Sha Muira novice, for all the bloodthirstiness of his cult, had sheltered him from the intricacies of human relations. Between them, there would never be understanding.

And with Lily's husband's life in the balance, there would certainly never be sympathy.

Ranault's duchess anxiously puttered over, her heavy body making her ungraceful. "You are unwell, my Lady." She recovered the errant embroidery hoop, and laid a comforting hand on the Princess's arm. "The sun and heat have drained you. If your audience is completed, perhaps we should go inside."

"Savin will take you to Envoy Lepulio's quarters," Lily said curtly. The young Duchess's deferential fussing had allowed her to regain her poise. "I follow my husband's will. Think well on what I have said as you meet Lepulio and treat with him."

Fisher-troll!" Tullier spoke loudly enough for Savin to glance back disapprovingly. "If she didn't want to be insulted, she should not have cast the first stone!"

"Go on ahead," Gaultry told the big footman. "We need a moment to confer before you bring us to the Envoy." They were in glass court garden, a little distance from where Gaultry had fed the tamarin the peach the night of Dame Julie's concert.

"There's nothing to discuss," Tullier said. "I'll accept his offer and ship myself out of here. It's clear no one wants me."

"Forget it," she told him. "And if I were you, I wouldn't embarrass myself by trying to tell this Envoy that's what you're planning. If I have to stick half my own Glamour-soul back in you, I'm not going to let you go."

"You can't do that without asking Mervion to help," Tullier said, sounding suspiciously snively. "Don't even say you'll try."

Gaultry closed her eyes, trying to collect her wits. How to reassure him that he was wanted? Wanted enough that she would face down his wounded pride to keep him? Of course he was right—she could not imagine herself going to Mervion and asking such a favor. Not after those hateful words that Coyal had spoken! She did not—she did *not*—take her sister's support for granted. "Ask Mervion? I wouldn't hesitate," she lied. "But you won't push me to that. Lily upsetting you is no good reason to slave yourself to Sciuttarus's call. Elianté in me—can't you admit even that?"

Tullier looked away. "Gaultry," he said faintly. "I never told you about the spell Corbulo made that day we killed the family and their guards."

Gaultry could not look at him—not even at his back. A perfect, ripe peach was hanging by their side, just by her shoulder. She reached out and twisted its stem, letting it fall into the cup of her hand. The peach fuzz was soft, its flesh warm, the color a perfect balance of pinkish yellow and red. "You never told me," she agreed levelly. If she had asked, he certainly would not have told her.

Even now, she was not sure she wanted to know, but the boy was determined to tell her. "The spell didn't come out right. Something happened, and Corbulo couldn't finish it the way he wanted."

"You interfered?" Gaultry said. She tried not to be disappointed when the boy shook his head.

"The mother did. It killed her, but it also stopped Corbulo from completing the part of the spell that was intended to cloak him. That was why he cut her body so—the frustration. Llara in me! Her sacrifice was brave, but it seemed so pointless. Her boys were already dead. Why should she even have *tried* to be anything other than a pawn to our plans?

"But if she had not ruined the last part of the spell, it would have been Corbulo, not myself, who stood in front of the Prince's table that day the Princess remembers. Unlike me, Corbulo had enough experience that he would have seen the mission successfully completed. Your Prince would have desecrated himself and the festival, and then Corbulo would have finished our triumph by taking Benet's life. Who knows how many my master would have brought down, before your Prince's court overwhelmed him? Myself, cast adrift by Corbulo's death, I certainly would have died, in some stinking ditch or gully, as the Sha Muira poison in my blood rose up and consumed my flesh."

Gaultry inhaled the scent of the peach's sweetness. Destra Vanderive had been Palamar Laconte's sister. Thinking of Palamar, of all the woman's awkward foolishness, it was difficult to imagine she had once had a sister who possessed courage enough to outface a pair of Sha Muira killers.

"Tullier," she said. "Running back to Bissanty because you're feeling pangs of conscience isn't the act of a brave man. This *should* be hard on you. The thing you and your master did—the gods can be cruel, but that's no reason for men to follow their example."

"Llara blessed our act," Tullier said doggedly. "She gave it her direct sanction. That is what it means to be Sha Muira."

"You can both believe that and acknowledge that what you did was disgusting."

"Am I disgusting?" Tullier asked. "For what I did?" He glanced up at her with wounded eyes. "I won't pretend that anyone forced me. Back then, my faith was not so weak as that. But when I remember that woman's courage—"

"Tullier," Gaultry said. "The very fact that you regret what your Sha Muira masters trained you to do means you can't go back to Bissanty yet. I won't lie to you. One day you will have to return to Bissanty. It's in your blood; you won't be able to deny it forever. But now is not the time."

"How do you know?"

Gaultry pressed the warm peach into his hand. "It's summer," she said. "Give yourself a taste of life before thinking of going back to those soul-suckers."

He stared down, as if trying to read a message on the peach's velvety skin. When he looked up, his eyes were bright with unshed tears. "If that woman hadn't died, I wouldn't be alive today. I don't regret that."

She had no answer for him.

"Let's go and see the Envoy," she said. "What Sciuttarus wants us to think he has planned for you should make for an interesting discussion."

Caius Lepulio was a hard-faced man with a grey cast to his skin—the pallor associated with the highest born Bissanty noblemen. Above the hard features, the dome of his skull was closely shaved, making it difficult to guess his age. Anywhere between forty and sixty. He might have been a self-indulgent man during an earlier age of life—there were marks of dissipation in his face—but clearly he had toughened with age—toughened and grown dangerous. From the instant she first saw him, Gaultry disliked him, an impression immediately confirmed by his patronizing greeting. When he saw Tullier, he fell into an overelaborate genuflection, the crimson velvet of his cape fluttering behind him like rippling fire. Yet his expression throughout remained cool and distant. *I bow to you,* that expression said, *but I am in control. Watch as you learn to heed me.* "Most Serene Highness," he addressed Tullier. "I delight to find my-self in the gracious frame of your presence. Llara's Heart-on-Earth sends you fair greeting."

"Talk to me," Gaultry cut brusquely across the obsequities. He did not like that, and his face briefly showed it, despite his polish. In Bissanty only a few women—widows with titles or those who held religious of-fice—could speak with a legal voice. "I am the boy's guardian. You must speak through me if you wish to talk."

There was a pause. The Envoy rose and adjusted his clothes. "Lady Gaultry Blas," he said, tidying his cuffs. His tone spun her name and title into an insult. "I have been instructed to commend you for your loyalty in preserving our young Prince's person, but Bissanty no longer requires your services. Gracious Sciuttarus has welcomed a lost cousin back to the House Imperial. All Bissanty rejoices in the investiture of their newest Prince. As I am sure you already know, I have been sent to Tielmark to complete the stages of the accession and to return him to his homeland. There is nothing left for you to do."

Gaultry's eyes narrowed. "In helping Tullier, I have never served Bissanty. I take orders only from my own Prince. And as far as I'm con-cerned, only Benet of Tielmark can dissolve the guardianship I've been granted. Prince Benet, or the Princess speaking in his voice. I admit—I am most curious as to your offer for Tullier. But if you imagine I will allow you to return with him to Bissanty solely on your master's command, you are sorely mistaken. So perhaps you will explain to me exactly what it is that you have come all this way to offer?"

"What is your interest here?" Lepulio asked smoothly. The Envoy's quarters, on the main floor of one of the newer palace buildings, faced the harbor. In this room, the only furnishings were a single massive chair and a heavy table with a leather top, with three velvet-wrapped packages laid out on its surface, along with a pair of yellowed parchment scrolls. As he spoke, the Envoy retreated behind the table. "I must admit I am personally curious to know your motives for interfering here, besides Imperial Sciuttarus having commanded me most particularly to ask you." His voice was silky, poisonous. "Are you seeking some further guarantee of Tielmark's borders? The personal security of a title or land? A blood-tie to the House Imperial? Come now, you must have some stake. Tell me so we may reach a satisfactory agreement."

Tullier, who had been peering intently into the man's face, suddenly stepped forward. "I know you," he said. "You served as quaestor the year the Sha Muira charter was renewed." Then, to Gaultry, "This man oversaw the Sha Muira finances the year the Emperor ordered their review. He lives and breathes Sciuttarus's most interior court." Despite himself, the boy flushed with excitement. "There are only five such men in all Bissanty—and Llara's Heart-on-Earth has sent him here to treat with me!"

"Indeed." Lepulio flicked the leather surface of the table with a finger. The gesture was like the rest of him, complex. It conveyed so much: a sense that he found the table, the room, his quarters—even Tielmark!—unclean and beneath his dealings; but he would complete his charge, on sufferance, because it was what his emperor required. "You may regard my presence as a register of the solemnity of the Emperor's concerns."

"Tell me what you have come here to offer," Gaultry said, determined not to let him unnerve her.

"Security," Lepulio said smugly. "I have been instructed to remove young Tullirius from his current perils and bring him safely home."

"Don't make me laugh," Gaultry said.

"There have been two attacks upon Tullirius in the last week alone, from what my sources have told me. Why shouldn't I be serious?"

"Discounting for a moment the manhunt that pursued us through all Bissanty," Gaultry said coolly, "here in Tielmark, there were Bissanty soldiers at the first attack. Indeed, the man responsible for wounding my ward at Sizor's Bridge was a Bissanty soldier. Who knows what hand the Emperor might have had in the second?" It had still not been discovered who had sent Siànne and the other palace soldiers, but the possibility of a high-ranked Bissanty-sympathizing Tielmaran could not be ruled out.

Lepulio set down the scroll, caressed the dark gem on the centerpiece of his chain of office, and assumed a pensive look. "If there were soldiers, they could not have been the Emperor's men. The Emperor is fully cognizant of the futility of sending soldiers against the boy. Tullirius has inherited great Llara's blood. To raise a hand against him invites her fury, and offers only damnation.

"By Llara's own laws, the boy should never have earned this blessing. Two Imperial Brothers cannot pass their Great Mother's blood to their children. When Sciuttarus earned it from his father, his uncle's opportunity to pass it to his progeny should have been forever closed. And yet—and yet there is no denying that this is just what the Emperor's uncle has accomplished."

Lepulio smiled, a smile more of bitterness than humor. "You cannot imagine the bleating flocks of priests the Emperor has assigned to study the problem. But the fact remains—there is not a soldier in Bissanty who can stand against the boy, unless he acts in ignorance. And now that my blessed master has raised the boy to an Imperial throne—what soldier can claim such bliss?"

"Both attacks came before Benet had officially welcomed Tullier to a place at his court," Gaultry said. "Until then, we were traveling privately, without an order of protection. There was room enough for Bissanty to try for him, before he came under Benet's shield."

"The same could be said for anyone in Tielmark who had motive against him," the Envoy said. "Which could be anyone, ranging from the ill-starred Destra Vanderive's family to everyone who believes him a danger to your Prince—regardless of whether they believe him a murderous Sha Muira or an upstart set up to challenge your Prince's sovereignty. So you see," he was untying the largest of the velvet-wrapped parcels as he spoke, his fingers stroking in the lush nap of the cloth as he unfolded it, "Bissanty should be Tullirius's home. If he has enemies there, at least he will be able to count them on one hand's fingers."

The cloth parted, revealing a fabulous chain of office. Heavy overlapping plates of gold were overlain with alternating bands of wirework and inlaid rubies. He laid it beside the parchment scrolls, which he next picked up. "This scroll is young Tullirius's deed of lands." He tapped its edge. "The other, his deed of property. In your own land," he looked at Tullier, who looked not quite scruffy in the secondhand tunic and trousers Gaultry had procured for him, but certainly not pristine, "you are a rich man, with great resources and power. You own houses, rich fields, slaves— even a levy on your brother Princes' lands to pay the expenses of raising a regiment, should you desire to prove yourself in war. The lands of Tielmark are not yours to command, it is true, but Bissanty's Orphan Prince of Tielmark is far from a pauper."

The second package contained a jeweled dagger. The third, an enameled orb. "You see my Imperial Master's condescension. Not one of these emblems of power has traveled beyond the gates of Bassorah city for six hundred years, and yet he has sent me here with the entire collection. So great is the Emperor's trust, I have been instructed to pass them to your stewardship."

The gleaming treasures had the effect of flame to moth. Gaultry unconsciously shifted forward for a closer look. The bands of golden wirework on the chain of office depicted Tielmark's history of origin, the battles that the Bissanty had undertaken to claim it, so long ago now that time had all but swallowed them. Crude but intricate, the tiny pictures showed the clashes of mounted knights, fields and houses in flames, tall stone idols tipped and broken.

"How did Prince Costin respond to his deposal?" Tullier asked. Unlike Gaultry, he had not approached the table. If anything, he'd retreated. He touched the collar of his tunic—as though reassuring himself that the glass charm Gaultry had bought him earlier still lay safely there beneath the cloth.

"Costin?" A flicker of perturbation fluttered on the Envoy's face, quickly smoothed.

"Sciuttarus was unmarried when he rose to the Imperial throne," Tullier told Gaultry. "His brothers—and my father, and a cousin—filled the five Princely thrones beneath him, until he could get sons on his wives to take their places. To this day, he is two sons short. Costin Aggripinelus is Sciuttarus's youngest brother, by almost thirty years. In Bissanty, he has sat on the throne of Tielmark for twenty years, since the time he was a young boy. I am sure it could not have pleased him to have been deposed for my sake."

Gaultry, not being Bissanty, had not been able to spy the obvious flaw in Sciuttarus's apparently princely offer. What the Emperor chose to render unto others, he could also reclaim. "How interesting," she said to Tullier. "How long do you think it would be before the Emperor decides to remove you in your turn?"

"The case is different here," Lepulio interjected. "Tullirius, once raised up to the throne, cannot be removed by earthly powers. Llara's blood runs in him, and the Great Mother jealously guards her mortal heirs. He could never be deposed for a man who lacked that blood."

"Which is something Sciuttarus is still trying for gain for his sons, hmm?" Gaultry said. Llara's Imperial Blood did not descend to an emperor's heirs until he had sired five boy children. While a rival line— Tullier's father—seemed to have claimed it, it was not obvious how the Emperor could ever earn it back—though it was certain he would try. "All those priests at work on the paradox—how can Sciuttarus's heirs even hope to mount the Imperial throne if a rival cousin has somehow already climbed up to that seat?"

"If that is so," Lepulio said, "the priests have yet to prove it. Do not mistake this overture: The Emperor is offering the boy real honor and power." He reached down and picked up the great chain of office. The mass of its gold was obviously heavy in his hands, the rubies winked with bright fire as he turned it in the light. "If he can't make anything of that power, that is not blessed Sciuttarus's burden to bear. Llara's Heart-on-Earth would not offer you an empty promise. He knows what it means to rouse Great Llara's ire, even for one so powerful as he. He would not risk it twice in his life. My word on it, and his through me. For Tullirius, the throne of Tielmark will be a life appointment. Llara's Blood flows in him. It is his right that we acknowledge that."

Tullier laughed bitterly. "As quaestor, you traveled to Sha Muira island," he said. "You inspected the cells, the training grounds, the jobi-rooms where the slaves are killed. They even allowed you to the inner sanctum of Llara's temple. Before your master sent you here, I'm sure you reviewed every detail of my life. My former masters will have provided you with every particular, on the Emperor's orders. What did you make of my performance in the Muir Reic passage? My endurance while facing the Khai Sha?"

Lepulio put the necklace down and covered it carefully with a fold of velvet, realizing belatedly that the sight of it had served only to fan the boy's temper. "I am the lone member of the inner circle who has direct experience of the Sha Muira," he admitted. "The Emperor felt I was best qualified to negotiate with you so you could take your throne."

"But I am not Sha Muira," Tullier said coldly. "You will not find the key to owning me by looking into my past." He turned to Gaultry. "We are finished here. This fawner was sent to offer me an empty plate. I will not treat with him for barren favors."

"Sciuttarus wants you in Bissanty," Lepulio called, as Tullier threw open the door. "He is willing even to pledge—"

Tullier did not stay to listen. He stalked angrily out through the antechamber and on into the corridor. Gaultry followed behind, proud of his spirited rejection, though curious to discover what she'd missed in the exchanges. Sha Muira island was a closed sanctum, outside visitors a rare occurrence. She was hungry to understand the advantage the Emperor thought to gain by sending a man who had seen the island to talk Tullier over to him.

She reached the domed entrance hall of the outlander dignitaries' quarters just in time to see Tullier disappearing out to the yard. "Hothead," she said concernedly.

"He could be Emperor of Bissanty one day," a voice said from her side. "With that in mind, doesn't it offer a thrill to think you own him?" Gaultry whirled around. Argat Climens rose from the hard seat of the bench where she had sat waiting, and flared her skirts. Heavy red linen today, with stiffened insets of cream-colored lace. "My turn next," she said. "More's the pity. I don't imagine you've left him in any good temper."

"You!" Gaultry said, startled. "What are you doing here? Don't you have charges enough standing against you without private meetings in the enemy's quarters?" She was in no mood for the Duchess of Vaux-Torres's sly thrusts.

"Private meetings," Vaux-Torres said. She issued an annoying soft laugh. "If I truly had private meetings with the Envoy planned, perhaps I would not find myself in such trouble."

"You should think of your daughter," Gaultry snapped. "Don't you want to protect her?" She cast a quick glance at the woman. The Duchess of Vaux-Torres looked beautiful today—too beautiful to have garbed herself merely for a business parley with the envoy of an enemy state. Ivory shoulders gleamed above the cream-colored lace, the rich ebony of her hair was artfully curled in a waterfall of tresses against her neck. Beneath the fabulous dress, her sensual, assured humor showed in every lush line of her body, every detail of her mature beauty revealed.

The red of the dress reminded Gaultry of old Melaudiere's gift, of the cuckoo egg's red enamel. "Think of Elisabeth," she found herself saying. "Think of your family's honor." She swept past the Duchess and made for the door, following Tullier.

"What makes you think I am not?"

In her impatience to catch Tullier, Gaultry scarcely heard those words.

▼

chapter 15

Gaultry blinked against the sun as she emerged into the gravel court outside the Envoy's quarters. She raised her hand to block the glare and looked around, but Tullier was nowhere in sight. Numerous archways and three stone staircases led away from the narrow, irregularly shaped yard. Unfamiliar with this precinct of the palace and unclear even of the most direct way to return to her quarters in the Summer Palace, Gaultry had no way to guess which way her ward had gone.

"Terrific," she groused, unwilling to question one of the lounging footmen or palace servants, lest rumors rise that she was failing to keep the boy under control. "Fine. Lick your own wounds. I hope you feel the better for it." She loosed a weary sigh, and headed for the stone stairway at the far side of the court.

A wave of loneliness swept her as she ascended. The exhaustion of tending corpses and making so many good-byes weighed heavily, as did the pressure of appearing so constantly in public among unfamiliar faces, so many of whom might be concealing ill will. Court life was more cloistered, more claustrophobic, and more confusing even than she had remembered.

The clipped grass of the palace lawns and the artificiality of the planted flowerbeds were suddenly oppressive. She longed for an unpaved path, a planting wild and grown untended. Without presuming on the raw power of her magic, she did not know how long she could maintain even the appearance of being able to keep up with the twists of court politics looping around her, all of them subtly moving her attention further away from addressing the real problem that faced Tielmark here: solving the Kingship riddle. Yet if she were to stoop to using her magical powers . . . That would be tantamount to admission that court ways were too much for her. Everyone certainly would rise against her then, like wolves on a foundering deer. Her freedom to move within court without restraint would be curtailed—and how then would she be able to reach those she must influence to her purpose? How then would she be able to save Martin, her family, Tullier or herself?

Gaultry leaned against the cool shadowed stone of the wall at the staircase's side and closed her eyes, for a moment imagining that she was back in Arleon's ancient forest: the massive moss-hung trees, the rolling hills, the wildness and the familiar dangers of the borderlands. She pictured herself moving beneath those trees, fluid and confident, tracking a deer or a hare, or just resting on a jutting overlook, the purple-blue waters of the River Rush, with its alluring taint of magic, curling deep below her on its long languid journey to the sea.

Feeling a little recentered, she began once more to climb the steps.

Martin and the Prince had probably passed the rebuilt Sizor's Bridge by now, pushing their horses and men west. On the High Road, which ran like a spine all along the northern edge of Tielmark, through the Bissanty Fingerland, and then on into Haute-Tielmark, it would take them more than a week of hard riding to reach the western border. She wondered what their war party would find there. The ducal armies, amassed for a final push against the Lanai? A fragmented battlefield, with pervasive death and chaos? An unexpected early victory, with the Lanai tribesmen forced to retreat? From what Victor Haute-Tielmark had described, she doubted the ducal armies had yet been so lucky as to consummate the latter.

Memory of the towering bearlike duke chivying them into the cart the morning they departed Sieur Jumery's flashed on her. Gaultry found herself grinning.

She had dismissed the man as an enemy, possibly as a traitor, yet somehow he had convinced her that she had been overhasty in her judgment. The moment the balance of her opinion had turned to his favor had probably been his mischievous description of thwarting Dervla and her plan to publicly disgrace him. What traitor would so freely admit to working to tweak the nose of the High Priestess? Besides, Gaultry could too well understand the apparent contradiction of desiring to frustrate the High Priestess while remaining loyal to Tielmark itself.

She touched at the silver ring Haute-Tielmark had given her, still concealed after all this time on its leather string under her clothes. She would have to hunt for its secret soon or find a safer place to keep it hidden. Now that Dervla had completed the ceremonies of Midsummer and the unexpected and time-consuming business of Melaudiere's funeral rites, she would be free again to snoop for those who might defy her will. Carrying this ring on her person was a risk, knowing that it had come from the traitor Heiratikus's secret cache—and not knowing why Heiratikus had secreted it there, or why Dervla believed it important.

As she reached the top of the steps, the roof of Tielmark's great hall hove into view, and beyond it the domed white temple where Dervla held sway. Gaultry shook her head. She did not understand the High Priestess's insecurities. It was as though Dervla needed attention always to be centered on herself as a source of power. To Gaultry, this did not make sense. The magical gifts of the Goddess-Twins were so obvious in the older woman. They were a seething reservoir of power, tangible evidence of the Great Twins' favor. If the gods recognized her merits, rewarded her with such strength, why did Dervla behave so threatened by anyone who attempted to support the Prince, independent of her own plans?

Thinking on Dervla brought Gaultry inevitably to the Common Brood. She had told Martin she would try to unite them, but she did not even know what had driven them apart to begin with.

Egotism, combined with conflicting ideas of the best route to Tielmark's future, must surely have played its part. Without a powerful and experienced ruler to quash their individual ambitions and to focus their vision on a single goal, the coven had simply fragmented. She sighed. On the surface, that was not so different than the same challenge that faced them today.

Gaultry, reaching the head of another staircase, paused before taking the first step down. It was time to learn the real reasons for the Brood's split. It was time to confront Tamsanne.

In all the years Gaultry had lived with her grandmother, the old woman had been uncommunicative about her life before her retreat to Arleon Forest. Knowing what she knew now, Gaultry could see that Tamsanne had concealed so much to give her granddaughters the gift of an innocent childhood. The burdens that they had assumed as adults were grounded on the strength of that upbringing, the simplicity of its truths.

It came to Gaultry suddenly that she had been avoiding Tamsanne.

Her upbringing had taught her to avoid confronting her grandmother with questions. But now there were certain things she needed to know—certain questions that she *had* to ask for the sake of all the Brood, not just for herself and Martin—she had to have answers about the Brood's past decisions, about Kingship. But where her grandmother's private affairs intersected with these public queries . . . there were questions that she wanted to avoid.

Your grandfather was a dead man when Tamsanne used him to get with child. What grain of truth informed the harsh words Sieur Jumery had spoken? Gaultry knew so little of her family's past. Her mother Severine had been fey, unstable. Tamsanne had mentioned more than once that her match to the steady stableman-turned-warrior Thomas Blas had been a good one, a balance to her fundamental wildness. But the source of Severine's instability had never been discussed. Nor the possibility of how it might ultimately manifest itself in her daughters.

When Gaultry had first left Tamsanne's with Martin, the old woman had spoken nothing regarding the heritage her granddaughter had been on the verge of discovering. She had not told Gaultry of her true lineage, she had not hinted at the magical power that was so soon to rise in her.

And yet Tamsanne had cast a Rhasan card for her, had performed a reading. The Rhasan deck Tamsanne used had passed through her family for generations, accumulating power, becoming increasingly dangerous and strong, increasingly direct in its predictions. Gaultry's card had been the Orchid—the card that symbolized the power of Glamour. Seeing that card, Tamsanne must have guessed at least something of the power that was about to manifest itself in her granddaughters. Gaultry could only wonder what else Tamsanne had sensed in that reading, what else she had kept concealed.

There had to be a connection between all these events: her mother's feyness, which had taken her so early from the world, the Glamour power that had manifested itself in both of Severine's daughters, and Sieur Jumery's words. *Your grandfather was a dead man.* Tamsanne had always spoken strictly, passionately, against the use of necromantic magic. Was this because she had used it once herself, in getting herself with child? The horror that her beautiful Glamour power might have its roots in death magic—Gaultry did not want to face that. *The very corpses of the ground rise to renew you,* Sieur Jumery had said. Perhaps this was why her Glamour was so painful, even dangerous to use. The thought filled her with revulsion.

But she could depend on her grandmother's reticence. The Kingship problem could delay, for a time, investigation of these more private fears.

If she asked her questions cautiously, perhaps Tamsanne would reveal the information Gaultry wanted, yet leave the rest unsaid. A dubious hope at best—Tamsanne had been pregnant with Severine at the time the Brood cast the spell to protect young Corinne. These events—somehow everything was linked.

Crossing another yard, she made for a stair that led up to the palace battlements, the sea breeze on her face refreshing her a little as she worked her way around to the eastern side of the palace, helping her drive the worst of her fears back. Sieur Jumery had been a bitter man. It could be that her grandmother would have some more innocent explanation for what he thought he had learned. In time—in time she would be brave, and ask Tamsanne what the accusation really meant.

For now, she would focus on deciphering the Kingship riddle. Tamsanne would know what had soured the Brood on acting in concord. She would know why the Brood had failed to play Kingmaker, failed to crown Corinne as Queen, and why the matter of transforming the nature of Tielmark's rule been left to another generation to settle.

The other questions Gaultry hoped could wait on a less warlike season.

Tamsanne was quartered in the palace's orchards, below the outlook where Gaultry and Tullier had met with the Princess.

As Gaultry reached the orchard grounds, someone—several some-ones—were playing lutes and harmonizing. She stifled a groan of impatience. Instead of finding Tamsanne alone, she had managed to run smack into Dame Julie's cortege. A scattering of court folk she vaguely recognized were dispersed among the trees; clustered ahead in a green clearing, she recognized the musicians from Julie's concert.

Gaining a private conference with anyone within palace precincts seemed an unattainable goal. She was beginning to understand why court was a maze of circles nested within circles. Who ever found the time to talk to anyone without someone else listening?

"Elisabeth," she said, hardly surprised as the girl, tamarin in tow, came into view from behind one of the plum trees that bordered the tiny field where the musicians had assembled. The girl seemed destined to pop up wherever Gaultry made an appearance. "What are you doing here?"

"I came to listen to Dame Julie." Elisabeth picked up the tamarin and came to join her. "She played a suite with her granddaughter." She gestured at the young viol player, now seated beneath a leafy plum tree, concentrating on a complex tuning as her pale blond hair, cut short and sleek, fell over her face. "Everyone was dancing, just before you arrived. Now Dame Julie's resting in the orchard-cot with your grandmother." She nodded over her shoulder. The orchard-cot, a modest cottage with mossy thatching, was just visible through a screen of trees. "But the rest of her musicians continued playing, so I stayed on."

"I've just seen your mother," Gaultry said. Despite the girl's candidness, it was hard not to be wary, considering her mother's questionable connections. Circles within circles. If Gaultry's own appearance in the orchard had been any less spontaneous, she would have had to wonder about the coincidence of Elisabeth's. "She's looking well. All dressed up for her appointment with the Bissanty Envoy."

Elisabeth's face fell. "Coltro Lepulio." Gaultry had not been told that the man had a title—or in her confusion as she received his other news, she had not absorbed the information. A Coltro was the Bissanty equivalent of a Tielmaran Count, though in Bissanty, Coltros had more influence. They possessed some of the army-raising rights of Dukes, a rank for which there was no comparable title in Bissanty—that role being reserved for the Imperial Princes.

Elisabeth's concerns about the man, however, were more personal. "He keeps calling her to see him," she said dejectedly. "I don't know why she even agrees. Why doesn't she find some reason to defer until her business with the High Priestess is complete?"

Gaultry found it curious too. "Doesn't your mother have other business to keep her occupied until the Ides?"

"Loads." Elisabeth nodded. "Even though I'm standing for her in all her public roles, she still has to treat with all our tithemen. It's cumbersome and inconvenient that they have to come up to court during summer rather than her visiting them, but so far they've accommodated. They come themselves, or else send messengers." She smoothed the tamarin's fur, and pulled a dark-purple plum from her pocket for it. "You should see some of the people they send!" A smile warmed her earlier dejection. "They've never been away from their master's fields, and Mama is rather overwhelming—let alone court, and the city!" Because Elisabeth seemed to be laughing with her mother's country bumpkins rather than at them, Gaultry smiled too. Argat Climens was certainly overwhelming, no question there.

"This morning we had a man from one of our country justices. His livery was so decrepit that Mother had him newly outfitted at her own expense." Elisabeth smiled again. "Now that's her own weakness. She cannot bear for anyone to look anything other than immaculate. She claims it improves performance all around—though I'm quite sure that's not true of me." She patted the tamarin's nose, and it playfully snapped at her fingers, eager for more plum. Juice had run on to the material of her sleeve, but Elisabeth seemed not to notice. "But perhaps she's right— the man was certainly grateful for his new outfitting. He seemed quite taken with it all—the clothes, the glitter of court, the liveliness. It's more than he is used to, back at Sieur Jumery's."

Gaultry stiffened. The tamarin caught it immediately, focusing in with bright, inquisitive eyes. Elisabeth, intent on her story, did not. "You would think the old man's estate is falling down, the way his servant talked. But I think it must just be the contrast with the splendors of Princeport. What do you think? Do you find Princeport impressive? I did, when I first came up at summer's start. Now, of course, I've had to become a little more acclimated."

"It's a matter of comparison," Gaultry said evenly, trying to conceal her perturbation. The arrival of Sieur Jumery's man, so soon after her own, could be no coincidence. "And also, I suppose, of whether or not one is accustomed to making comparisons. When I first came to Princeport I had never been to a village that served as a market center, let alone to a large town or city. Now I've seen Bissanty's capital as well as Tielmark's. The sheer busyness of so many people in one place still overwhelms me, but at least when I'm in a crowd now I have something to compare it against." She was babbling, but she needed to say something to cover her confused dread. If Sieur Jumery had sent a man to report to Vaux-Torres, what information had he brought with him? Harmless details of the attack at Sizor's Bridge? An angry account of their own fight at the burial ground? The bitter charge the old man had made against her grandmother? *Your grandfather was a dead man.* "This man you're describing—did he have anything interesting to report? Or was it all talk of the fields and the early harvest?"

Elisabeth shook her head. "I don't get to hear any of that. My mother doesn't mind me standing as the Vaux-Torres figurehead, but Beaumorreau is the one with whom she shares the real business. If my brother wasn't leading the army in Haute-Tielmark this summer, he'd be standing in my shoes at this very moment." She cuddled the tamarin, then set it down to explore the bole of a nearby tree. "Sometimes I wish she trusted me more, but that is the burden of being the youngest. I suppose a part of me must be grateful for the Lanai wars and for my mother's problems for giving me this season at court—though I hope that is not true!"

"You seem to be managing well enough," Gaultry said encouragingly. She liked the girl's self-deprecatory humor. "Now, if you will pardon me, I have some business with my grandmother."

"Oh I—you are busy, and I have kept you." The girl's cheeks flushed with quick embarrassment. "Please excuse me—"

"Elisabeth," Gaultry stopped her. "Don't chide yourself. It's pleasant for me too, to find a friendly face among these busy courtiers." Damning Dervla's petty games, which had left the girl so isolated, she gave the tamarin a last pat, and found her way around the musicians and through the trees to the orchard-cot.

The little cottage was built low to the ground, with thick walls and an over-heavy wadding of thatch on its roof. She hesitated at the front door, which had been wedged fully open with a time-smoothed triangle of wood. The doorway breathed coolness from the building's interior. Looking within from the brightness of the sun, everything was dark. Gaultry smiled to herself. Tamsanne had occupied the one building in all the palace grounds that had the smell, the feel, the ancient earthiness, of her own cottage in Arleon Forest. The scent of herb-fragrant air that emanated from the cottage sent her spiraling back to her childhood, to all familiar things. To the person she thought of as her true self: a woman who could touch lightly her magic powers, but fully engage them only under duress; a woman who was bashful and reserved, save for the moment she played point on a hunt; certainly a woman too shy to trouble her elders with questions they did not wish to answer.

All qualities she could ill afford today.

"Tamsanne?" she called. "Are you busy?"

"Gaultry," Tamsanne answered. "Please come in. I was wondering when you'd find the time to come and see me."

Gaultry stepped into the cot's darkness, taking a moment to adjust her eyes. The little building had a scrubbed floor of wide, pale-colored boards. The hearth had a wooden mantel and a tiny cooking range, with a sleeping niche beside it instead of in the loft. Save for these details,

Tamsanne had everything set up exactly as it would have been in her own home, from the herbs hung to dry in the rafters, to the untidily piled boxes and bags, and down to Bellows, her ancient black dog, asleep on a blanket in front of the hearth. No doubt some part of the things she was looking at belonged to the orchard-cot's temporarily ousted crofter. Notwithstanding this, it felt comfortably familiar.

But that feeling was brought short by the subtly perfumed presence of Dame Julie, who sat with Tamsanne at the rough lime-wood table, pushing finely polished wooden pieces across a checkered gameboard. The two old women were a contrast of styles: Tamsanne wrinkled and birdlike, wearing her fusty black mourning clothes, Dame Julie slender and tidy in muted grey robes, the white tresses of her softly curled hair beautifully dressed.

"You have met," Tamsanne said briefly, taking a turn at the game and removing one of Dame Julie's pieces.

"Benet introduced us," Julie said. She made a quick countermove.

"Should I come back later?" Gaultry asked. "I have some questions that need answering."

Tamsanne rubbed the thickened knuckles of her hands, focusing on the gameboard instead of directly answering. "It's been years since I've played," she complained. "An advantage I see you've learned to fully exploit."

Gaultry approached the table. Whatever the game, it looked more complicated than checkers. There were carved horsemen on both sides, a king-piece, and a pair of sorcerers. Not knowing the rules, she could not tell at first glance if one side or another was dominating.

"You're up on me two games already," Julie said dryly. "It would not appear that the intervening years have hurt your play." She looked up at Gaultry. "It's been fifty years since Tamsanne and I sat at this gameboard together, and still she makes me feel an untutored girl, giving her all the advantage." Under these apparently innocent words, Dame Julie's tone was mocking. It showed in the ill-concealed amusement of her eyes.

"My grandmother has always had the confidence of her power," Gaultry said. It galled her that her hesitancy seemed to be as obvious to the two old women as it was to herself. "Age has little to do with her advantage." As she spoke, Gaultry realized the truth behind the defiance of her words. "I may not possess such confidence myself, but my sister already has it."

At the board, Tamsanne nodded. "Mervion does not need to use her strength to know that she has power."

"See?" said Julie, only half amused. "She doesn't waste breath boasting that she can beat me. She needs only imply it, and my play is thrown."

Gaultry looked down at the board, reconstructing the course of the game—Tamsanne, she could now see, had Julie in retreat. Watching her grandmother capture another horseman, Gaultry's mind darted to the moment when Mervion had reclaimed her Glamour-soul: her perfect composure as she had bent over Tullier, seemingly aloof to the possibility that she might need outside aid; her ease as she'd invoked the power to perform the spell; her steadiness as she'd performed it. In these things, her sister's performance echoed Tamsanne's. In others—such as her sister's tortured disclaimer of her will to perform—it did not.

She stared at her grandmother's bent head. An unpleasant idea came to her, that perhaps Tamsanne's façade of strength, like Mervion's, might conceal hidden doubts.

These were not matters to air in front of Dame Julie.

"I came here to speak with Tamsanne, but I have a question for you both. Why exactly was it that the Brood didn't make Tielmark a Kingdom at the last cycle's close?" A stillness grew in the old women as she spoke, a forbidding stillness, discouraging further questions. Gaultry, determined, ignored it and stumbled onward. "I have a right to know. The Brood-pledge ties me too. Given the prophecy's wording, you must have known what Lousielle intended you to do, beyond rescuing Corinne. You must have understood the threat that lay in wait for your heirs, as well as the promise of release if you raised the Princess to the red throne of Kingship. Between all the members of the Brood, you must have had the power and knowledge to do it. Dame Julie said you took a vote—but why really didn't you try?"

"What makes you think we didn't?" Julie asked. "Do you think we were so simple as to not have seen the trap that lay ahead?"

"I don't know," Gaultry said doggedly. "That's what I need you to tell me."

"Lousielle made the Brood from seven women who had never had children," Tamsanne interjected. Her voice was dry as paper. "And only one who was married—Gabrielle Lourdes, then newly wed. Did any of us then possess deep wisdom concerning time and fate?"

"So you did try," Gaultry said. "What happened?"

Julie leaned back from the board and put her hands against the table's edge. In contrast to Tamsanne's, her fingers were long, thin, nails carefully kept. "Kingmaking means sacrifices," she said. "How else can one man earn the right to stand in power over others? Would Tielmark's farmers be any happier, any the richer, for having a King rather than a Prince on the throne?"

"We went through this the other night," said Gaultry impatiently. "I already know you agree that Tielmark's farmers would be better off ruled by a King than slaved to the Emperor of Bissanty. Do you have a plan to topple the Emperor's throne? To end Bissanty's constant plots to repossess our land? I'd be glad to hear it. That would save us the trouble of changing the fundamental nature of Tielmark's rule."

"What sacrifices would you agree to make to reach that end?" Julie countered. "Your own history of personal sacrifice is not so steady there. What were you willing to sacrifice to confirm Benet as Prince, just this last Prince's Night?"

Gaultry swallowed. On that terrible night, Mervion's life had been put in her hands, set in balance against the Prince's. Even with Tielmark's fate in the balance, she had wavered. Only Elianté and Emiera's grace had preserved her from that terrible choice. By looking directly into the Goddess-Twins' faces, Gaultry had found the faith to deliver Mervion into their hands.

Putting her sister's life in the hands of her own gods was not quite the same as offering her as a sacrifice for Tielmark's freedom.

"What could I personally sacrifice?" Gaultry asked. "I can offer no more than my own life." Her own death. She shuddered. As if such an offering would come easily! Images of possible futures flashed through her mind. "I could only hope that the moment of choice would come on me quickly."

"What if you needed to sacrifice more than your own life?" Julie pressed forward. "What if the gods demanded Mervion? Or Melaudiere's soldier grandson? Would you sacrifice them, could you sacrifice them, if you knew they were not willing?"

"The gods would despise such an offering," Gaultry said. She was sweating, the cool dark of the cottage suddenly choked, claustrophobic. "Tielmark would have a King, but the nature of the sacrifice would poison the temper of his rule. The sacrifice would not be worth the price paid in return."

Julie nodded, lapsing back in her seat. "Your grandmother made exactly the same argument, fifty years past."

Tamsanne picked up her king-piece and closely examined its miniature carved features. "Some among us were willing to sacrifice our scruples to make Corinne Queen. Others were more squeamish. And Corinne simply was not ready to choose for herself. At that time, for her, the immensity of fulfilling the God-pledge seemed a great enough gift."

Gaultry could not read her grandmother's expression. Despite the oblique phrasing of her response, Gaultry knew that Tamsanne would not have been one of the number who had foregone their scruples. "Tell me what happened," she said. "I need to know."

"As I told you before, we took a vote," Dame Julie said. "It was me, Tamsanne, and Melaudiere against Richielle, Delcora, and Marie Laconte."

"And Melaney Sevenage took your side," Gaultry guessed.

"It took some convincing." Julie glanced at Tamsanne. "It was not your grandmother's arguments that brought her to our side."

"But you won," Gaultry insisted.

"Maybe." Dame Julie took the king-piece from Tamsanne and set it back in its square on the board. "Except for the problem that failing to overcome our scruples meant that our lives and those of our families would be evermore bonded to the lives of our princes."

"Did it really have to be that way?" Gaultry asked. "You could have chosen against having children. You must have guessed the fate to which you had doomed us."

"That would have been one solution," Dame Julie agreed, her voice like ice. "Unfortunately for some of us, choice did not operate in the decision to become a mother. Aha!" She moved a sorcerer from the back of a line of horsemen and placed it next to Tamsanne's king. "I win at last!" She glanced at the older witch. "You weren't concentrating."

Tamsanne tipped her king on its side in concession, her face void of expression. "The nature of the vote left great bitterness. The Broodmembers who sided against us—I don't include Marie Laconte in that number, she came round after Melaney cast with us—saw that we paid for our decision."

"It was never proved." Dame Julie glanced toward the door. "Mind what you say. Bad things might have happened, even without what they did."

Tamsanne laughed, a dry-leaves crackle of a laugh that made Gaultry shiver. She looked directly at her granddaughter for the first time since Gaultry had entered. "Great treachery occurred, and it was all in the name of supporting the Princess. As punishment for holding the swing vote, Melaney was transported to Bissanty. She died there, under the most horrible circumstances. But that was not the end of it. Julie was betrayed and given to a party of Bissanty soldiers, to play with like a bonded slave-woman. Those were not pretty times. Bissanty sympathizers maintained great strength in Tielmark, even after the spell that set Corinne free. I—if I had remained at court I would have lost my child—the babe I had chosen to carry at great cost to my personal honor. Only Gabrielle they could not touch, by virtue of her title. It would be pleasant to believe that Richielle and Delcora were behind none of these incidents. Unfortunately, it would not be truth. If those two had not fallen to squabbling between themselves, who knows what would have happened next?"

The babe I had chosen to carry at great cost to my personal honor. That would have been Gaultry's mother Severine, held within Tamsanne's womb through the maelstrom of magic that had confirmed Corinne as Princess. Had that magic touched the baby in the womb, marking her for her short life, or had the seed of Severine's wildness been planted earlier still?

"Grandmother," she said. "You were pregnant with my mother when Lousielle asked you to pledge to the Brood. Help me understand. You at least must have had some sense of the long pledge that Lousielle demanded of you. Why did you take the pledge? And once you'd committed to the pledge—why didn't you vote on the side of Kingship?"

"I may have been young," Tamsanne said flatly, "but I had already learned that ignoring a call to power is no route to avoiding pain. But Kingship—that call was not for me to make. That was for Corinne. Richielle and Delcora—they did not want the choice left to her. Their expectation was that they would be rewarded for presenting her with a fait accompli." She held her hands out, one hand closed as though she held a dagger, the other as though she touched its needle point.

"We had two Princes of Tielmark before us: Corinne of Tielmark praying to the ash left by the Great Twins' manifestation, and Pallidonius of Bissanty cringing on the dais beside her—Bissanty had sent their orphan Tielmaran Prince to marry Free Tielmark's Princess, the act that would have violated the God-pledge and returned our state to Bissanty's rule. Richielle had a dagger with her. An ancient dagger, called the *Ein Raku*. *Kingmaker*, in the wanderers' tongue. Even as we were tallying our votes, she would have buried it in Pallidonius's heart."

Tamsanne shook her head. "Perhaps if she had had more patience, she could have argued us to her side. Who knows? Perhaps we could even have convinced poor fat Pallidonius of the necessity of laying down his life. He was a weak man—and he liked Melaney very much. The power of her honor and her beauty would have moved many a man stronger than he. Her beauty might have swayed him to that one moment of noble selflessness that is all we would have needed to justify our kill." Tamsanne shrugged. "But that was not to be. Richielle's hurry for resolution in the face of Pallidonius's obvious defenselessness hardened us against her."

"Is that what Tielmark must do to make a King?" Gaultry said warily. "Killing one prince so the other can bathe in his blood? That is the sacrifice the gods demand?" Her heart caught in her throat. She saw now why Julie had spoken to her of difficult sacrifices. For the first time in fifty years, the two Princes of Tielmark stood together on Tielmaran soil. What had she done, bringing Tullier back with her to Tielmark?

"Richielle thought so," Tamsanne said. "With the *Ein Raku* in her hand, she was quite certain. Myself, I think it is the way to create a tyrant."

"Playing consort to a god is another route to Kingship," Dame Julie said, breaking the tension. "Or so the poets would have us believe. If it's true, the Great Twelve have grown circumspect in offering their favors."

She began to set up the game pieces for a new game. "I have begun to search the songs, as I told Benet. He has given me free rein to question the little guild of the court bards—the keepers of the histories. Questioning those bards—" Julie's mouth quirked in a wry expression. "They are not very used to unearthing their oral histories at another's bidding, but I have made some progress. There are ballads that tell of Kings made in love and war. If there's a precedent for ritual assassination, I have not discovered it, whatever Richielle had decided was the matter's truth."

"Is Tullier in danger?" Gaultry asked.

"He would be, if the goat-herder were to make her reappearance," Dame Julie said. "The matter that Benet has pledged the boy his protection wouldn't slow *her*."

"Richielle," Gaultry breathed. "Could she be behind the attacks on Tullier?"

"Oh yes," Dame Julie said. "If she were alive and in Princeport, she'd certainly be on his tail. There are rituals that she'd need to prepare, but she'd certainly be after him."

"If Richielle is alive, she's not in Princeport," Tamsanne said. Dame Julie shot her an inquiring look. Tamsanne shrugged and cast the goddesses' sign. "I have not been completely idle since my arrival. And Richielle—it is in me to worry more about Richielle than about Delcora's confused young daughter."

It was a stretch for Gaultry to imagine Dervla as either confused or young. "Do you think the High Priestess planned the attacks against Tullier?"

"It has to be someone well-connected," Tamsanne said. "But I would be quicker to suspect a Tielmaran with Bissanty sympathies, considering the soldiers involved with the first attack. Dervla herself has suggested that it might be Argat Climens." She smiled at Gaultry's reaction. "You had not heard that? It is true, Vaux-Torres has too many Bissanty connections for her own good."

Gaultry frowned. Somehow she did not want it to be the Duchess of Vaux-Torres. "Tell me more about the goat-herder," she said, seizing on that suspect in Argat's place. "Why do you fear her? Even if she's still alive, wouldn't she be so old now that she'd be weakened?"

Tamsanne shook her head. "Richielle was strong with the old wanderers' blood. A people who lived long and slow, accumulating power. It was not just goats that Richielle herded. She imagined that she could herd us too—otherwise she would never have sworn anything to Old Lousielle." She hesitated. "The goat-herder has an ancient Rhasan deck. Older even than mine, and stronger. And she was never so scrupulous as I, in offering readings from that deck."

Something in Tamsanne's description sounded familiar. "Did she predetermine the cards she drew?" Gaultry asked.

Tamsanne looked at her sharply. "She did. How did you guess?"

"There was someone I met in Bissanty," Gaultry said faintly. Past events wove together in her mind. "Tullier's half-sister Columba. A woman she called a marsh-witch did a reading for her one time. For Columba, and for her lover. The marsh-witch pulled three cards. The first two might have been ordinary readings. But the third—the third compelled them to a new future."

"That sounds like Richielle," Tamsanne said. "When was this?"

"I don't know. Ten years past? Five?" The night had been moonless and tempestuous when Gaultry visited the crumbling temple where that reading had taken place. She did not know how long the building had lain in ruin, only that after the taint of Rhasan magic had taken it, it had been abandoned.

"Then Richielle must be alive."

"Alive, and in Bissanty," Gaultry said. "What would she be doing there?"

"The wanderers never acknowledged the new borders," Tamsanne said. "To Richielle, our border with Bissanty is a political fiction that does not apply to her."

"I need to find Tullier," Gaultry said anxiously. "He'll need to know this."

"You should find some time to talk to your sister," Tamsanne said.

"I will. After I talk to Tullier."

As Gaultry left the cottage, Dame Julie picked up one of her horsemen. "I'll take you fairly this time," she said, and opened a new game.

She caught up with Tullier in the deer park outside her rooms. "I have bad news," she told him.

"Beyond what Lepulio had to offer?" Tullier kicked the turf underfoot. "You know, he still thinks I'm Sha Muira. Every offer he made was based on that. What could possibly be worse than that?"

Gaultry could tell he was still quite upset. She hesitated, not wanting to burden him with more.

"What could be worse?" Tullier repeated, contrarily eager for her to tell him now she had lost the desire to talk.

"You remember how your brother Lukas used a Rhasan reader to bind your sister?"

The boy nodded. "The Rhasan forced her to violate her pledge of chastity. As punishment for profaning herself, she had to cede Lukas her Blood-Imperial. How could I forget? It made him almost strong enough to kill us both."

"The Rhasan reader was a Tielmaran witch. Richielle of the Common Brood."

"Wouldn't she have been too old?" Tullier was dubious. "Gaultry, I know you like to think that Tielmark is strong—but it's a gnat that bites the Empire's side, no more. If you didn't have the God-pledge to protect your borders—"

"That's all true," Gaultry said impatiently. "Nevertheless, it was a Tielmaran witch who played fast and loose with your Blood-Imperial. Why would she do that? Neither Lukas nor Columba were positioned to inherit Imperial thrones, and Lukas gained prodigious power through what she did for him. What did she hope to accomplish? What did Lukas give her in return?"

"Are you sure it was this Tielmaran witch?"

"I am. The way the Rhasan deck was used, it could only have been Richielle."

Tullier refused to be worried. "So in the event that we meet her face to face, we'll have to take care not to accept any reading she offers."

"She may be able to force one on us." Gaultry frowned. "You should be taking this more seriously. Who knows what powers she's gained since she gave Lukas his strength?"

"If she's so set on upsetting the Imperial order, why are you worried? Isn't that what you want?"

"What I hope for in Tielmark is that we maintain the freedoms that set us apart from Bissanty." Gaultry looked at his narrow, boyish face. He had suffered so much in his short life, and now she had brought a new threat to loom over him. "This Kingship matter—there is so much more to it than I first understood.

"Tullier—something I learned today makes me want to send you away from Tielmark. Not to Bissanty. To the islands, or perhaps to the south, where you could meet with the Sharif."

"What has happened?" Tullier asked calmly. She almost smiled. He could be so dramatic, when he needed reassurance, yet when he felt doubt in her—he was solid as a rock.

"I think someone wants to make Benet king by killing you. As the Bissanty mirror of Benet's power, some think you the appropriate Kingship sacrifice."

He took the news more steadily even than she had expected. His reaction, a sort of level historical curiosity, should not have surprised her. He was even able to supplement what she told him with the garbled account that was the Bissanty version of those same events.

The Bissanty story mentioned nothing of the Brood, or even of magic. It told only that Prince Ighion Pallidonius had been unexpectedly spurned by the young Corinne, and sent home in humiliation—a scenario any thinking Bissanty should have found suspicious.

"The whole story just never sounded right to me," Tullier observed. "There was so obviously more to it. But from the Bissanty view, those events were overshadowed by what was happening at home. Ultimately, the Pallidon was lucky he spent that spring in Tielmark. There was a wave of Imperial fratricide while he was away—and Ighion P. was always a gentle man. He was far better out of that. He wouldn't have survived if he had stayed at home." He paused. "You know, this Pallidonius whom Corinne had rejected, he was my father's older brother. He reigned as Emperor in the end—he's Sciuttarus's father." The boy's eyes crinkled. "Now *there's* a contrast in ruling styles! Sciuttarus prides himself as a man of iron."

Gaultry would never have put these connections together herself. To Gaultry, the Princes before Benet were vague, almost mythological figures. Thirteen princes had reigned on Tielmark's throne from Clarin's time to Benet's, but only Briern-bold, who had ruled at Tielmark's centenary, and Berowne-the-mad, Briern's ill-fated son, had seemed like real people before she came to court. Tullier, by contrast, had been drilled in the personal idiosyncrasies of emperors dating back centuries. He could debate their motivations, argue on their policies and their victories and failures.

Lepulio must have taken this into account when he had offered Tullier the priceless implements of Bissanty's Tielmaran throne.

Tullier's response to Gaultry's story of the Brood disturbed her: his almost academic satisfaction at an Imperial mystery explained. Insofar as this revelation might relate to his own life or future, he was unnervingly serene.

In part, he was unconcerned because he did not believe in the goatherder Richielle, but mostly because he did not believe there was an easy recipe to catch the attention of the gods.

"Who knows what factors conspire to make a King?" he said. "Something that might have worked five decades back will almost certainly not reach the same result attempted under this year's sky."

"That doesn't mean some power-hungry lunatic isn't trying!" Gaultry wanted to shake him.

"If we know the plan, we can defeat it,"

"Let's hope that's true," Gaultry said. "In the meantime, we'll have to work harder to find another way to make Tielmark a Kingship."

chapter **16**

▼

If this was a dream, she should have been able to wake herself up.

She had been running a long time now. Around her, her surroundings had become progressively more intricate and confused. Here, an iridescent framework of glass towered overhead, impossibly delicate and complex. This chamber, a symphony of glass and sparking water fountains, was the most breathtaking so far, and at the same time the most debilitating. Jets of water rose from the floor, dampening her clothes, hampering her movement. Her body felt as stressed as if she truly had been running, her lungs dry and painful. *If this was a dream, the shuddering of overtaxed lungs would not be slowing her.*

Her pursuer—she knew she had a pursuer—stalked her with stubborn persistence, ever on her heels, ever unseen. She had tried to shake herself awake so many times now. Each attempt only served to open doors deeper into the enthralling labyrinth.

Her attempts to wake up had jolted her onto broken steps, dashed her over balconies, sent her falling down into new levels of tiled chambers. One attempt had sent her stumbling through a series of doors, endless until she had understood their rhythm, deliberately stumbled, and broken it. Once she'd found herself clinging to carved banister-supports, climbing the outside of a staircase. Always, a sense of her pursuer dogged her.

Now, standing beneath the towering roof of the glass water-hall, she was tiring. The search for egresses took such hard effort. One part of her wanted only to lie itself down to rest.

If she did not find sanctuary soon, her gut warned that her unseen pursuer would take her. That thought, and that thought only, kept her moving.

The water-jet hall was beautiful, a serene place, but she could not remain there. With a surge of will, she continued wading forward through the fountains until at last they parted, revealing the way on.

The next corridor loomed more surreal even than the water and glass chamber. Living flowers carpeted the floor underfoot, and the green and brown bark-covered walls were lined with portraits of men and women, their identities concealed behind beast-faced masks. Their hands and bodies had been painted to correspond with the masks: a bear-man, a weasel-woman, a sheep-man in a woolly judge's wig.

The last picture in the row, the only portrait left unmasked, was Benet's.

The Prince's expression was mournful, the set of his mouth determined and sad. Though dressed in a Prince's ceremonial regalia, a plain soldier's cowl covered his tawny hair. Clasped between his hands was a gold crown set with blood-colored rubies, surmounted by God-King Andion's sunburst emblem. The points of the brazen sun had cut Benet's fingers, drawing blood. As Gaultry stopped to study the portrait, the image quivered and began to transform.

Benet's features faded. From beneath, Tullier's green eyes emerged, his arrogant chin, his hungry expression. But Tullier too clasped the kingly crown, so tightly that his closed lips twisted with pain. The picture looked so real that Gaultry reached to soothe him, but even as her fingers touched the surface, the picture cycled again to show Benet. Gaultry withdrew her hand. The human melancholy visible in both men's eyes was the only constant, disturbing after the parade of inhuman animal masks.

She would have stood and waited for the picture to change again—oblivious now to her pursuer—but something shattered noisily, breaking the picture's hypnotic allure.

Bare paces away, a spiral stair ascended. It had not been there when she last looked. Unlike the glass hall and the portrait gallery, with their hyperreal intensity, their elaborate colors and carved doors that led her to nowhere, this stair was grey and misty, achromatic.

A sudden urgency, like a sending, came to her. *Quickly now: escape lies here—*

Entering that stair was like stepping into the land of vision. The stone was grey, the light diffuse. A numbness came over her laboring body as she ascended. After countless featureless turns of the spiral, a small window came into view. The glass had been shattered from its mullions, leaving only a framework of flimsy metal bars. Shards of glass crunched under her feet as she approached. Whatever had broken the window had forced itself inward.

A chill wind underlain with musk hit her face as she looked out onto the grey prospect of a distant, mist-shrouded hill. Within the mist, atop the hill's far crest, a figure waited, infinitely patient, malign.

I have the answers. Those words reverberated through the mist like the sound of falling gravel. Those words took up all the space outside the window, like thunder in a storm-filled sky. A voice hardened by age and power and arrogance. The words rode the wind, compulsive and fearful together. *Receive them of me.*

Gaultry grasped the mullions and heaved. There was no time to descend through the castle to reach the caller. The bright-colored maze of passages and stairs would enfold her, or she would run into the arms of her enemy. If only she could break the bars, she could transform herself into a bird—she could fly from the tower and reach the hill. This madness coursed through her like a stream rising in flood. Even as she understood the insanity, she could not keep from throwing herself once more into the attempt.

A strip of mullion-leading popped free, then the base of another. If only the mullions were not so close, so small! As she pried at a third bar, an eerie wail forestalled her.

She paused, struck still by that cry, trying to place it. When the cry came again, she knew. That cry was the flowers that carpeted the portrait hall. Someone passed along the corridor, crushing them underfoot. Someone who came for her.

The call from the far hill rose again, louder and more insistent. *Glamour-soul*, it cried. *Come to me! All answers are found in me.*

But despite the three broken window-leads, that way on remained closed. From below, the sounds of her pursuer on the stairs jarred her ears. She would not get the window open in time. Raw fear battled the compulsion of the hill-watcher's call and won. Gaultry fled onward up the tightening spiral.

I am dreaming, she told herself. *I am dreaming, and I will not stay in this dream.* As she ran, stumbling ever upward, she pressed her palms against her breastbone. Strengthened volition rose in her as she touched at her power there. She would not be the plaything of these forces who had invaded her night's sleep: her unseen pursuer; the watcher on the hill. She could—she would—fight them. *I will not stay in this dream.* Calling on her deepest will, she invoked the power within her breast. *I will not stay here.* Golden heat flared, enfolding her newfound resolution with stays of power. At the moment her Glamour blossomed, she met, running at full tilt, the face of an invisible wall.

It shattered as she smacked into it, the collision sending her reeling. Invisible spell-wreckage fluttered in the air, brushing, then prickling, her skin.

Half stunned, she stumbled on the stone-grey steps, struggling for more than mere physical balance. A spell. The wall had been a spell, trapping her in her own mind as she slept. She had broken it, but was she free? The coil of grey stairs that lay before her remained outwardly unchanged.

I want to be in my own bed.

To her immense relief, the stairs rounded a curve and revealed a familiar paneled door, painted with red birds and foliage. Gasping with relief, Gaultry thrust the door open and fell into a bedchamber—her own.

There was her bed, her nightstand, the age-beaten paneling of her room in the Summer Palace. Her thought, empowered by her magic, had taken the effect of a counterspell, bringing her to the place of her desire. There were her clothes, her hunting kit. All her familiar things—and something else.

Even within the dream, she flushed.

Her heart had conjured more than she'd intended.

Martin smiled to her from the room's shadows. Though fully dressed in soldier's garb, the texture of carelessly folded cloth was pressed on his cheek, as though he had been awoken from deep slumber.

What is wrong, my beloved? He rubbed his eyes and groggily moved toward her. *Why did you call me?*

Nothing is wrong. She slipped her arms around him. *I am having a bad dream.*

I cannot protect you from bad dreams.

You can. She kissed his throat. The true taste of his skin was there, the true smell. *Hold me. Fill my dream with all things of my desire.*

Gladly—the wolfish smile lit his whole face. His clothes opened and parted, and he pressed her against the warmth of his bare flesh. He raised her in his arms, as easily, as weightlessly, as he had done that morning in the sea, and settled with her on the bed.

O my love. In dream they could dissolve; in time-hung dream they could luxuriate in the embrace that circumstances of life would not allow them. This truth moved within the wild play of their spectral caress with a gentleness, with a water-smoothness detached from the texture and feel of life. But Gaultry, as she touched him, became slowly aware of something else: the solid drumbeat of Martin's heart, the strained pulsing of his blood. She could feel it under her fingers, she could hear it in her ears. That sound was not dream. It was—it was a warning that she could not ignore.

This presence—Martin—was not a harmless illusion, god-sent or otherwise, visiting only her mind. It was a magical fetch. Some physical part of her beloved lay with her within this room, even as his body, miles away, slept huddled in a cloak by the roadside. What stress, what strain, had she put on him, unthinkingly drawing a part of him to her across that great divide of space?

She bent and pressed her mouth to his ear—

Leave me now. As fleetingly fast as her escape on the grey stairs of dream, the words invoked her will. A gold flash spread beneath her. *I should not have brought you here. There's danger.*

Martin frowned as she spoke, an expression of worried revelation crossing his face. He reached for her—and then he was gone, leaving empty sheets.

She was alone. Alone in the bed, knowing that she was still lost in dream, that her enemy lurked not far outside her door. She lay stone-still. If she was quiet, if she was still, perhaps her enemy would not find her.

She lay immobile, trying to hold in even her breathing. She imagined that all might be well, until, horribly, a pulse of power crawled over her, a thousand tiny feelers spreading across her body in a wave. On the pillow by her cheek, she sensed a delicate movement.

I will not stay in this dream, she screamed, but in the wake of her tryst with Martin, that mantra had lost its strength. All she could do was remain still, very still, willing the motion to pass her by. It was not enough. At the edge of her vision, something long and thin rustled, growing swiftly toward her along the pillow. A creeper, black-green, with tiny, pointed, devil's foot leaves. Black-green. Avenger-green. The color of the angry magic that had snared her on the bridge, the angry magic that would have killed the Prince but for Mervion's intervention. The creeper, moving fast as a snake, wound itself into her hair where it lay fanned on the pillow.

Too late, she tried to fling herself from the bed. The vines dragged her back, tangling ever more insistently into her hair, along her limbs. Panic overcame her. The creepers that had seized her wrists lashed toward the bedposts, binding her so tightly that she could hardly move. The attack was so all-consuming, so fast and angry, she did not know where to begin to try to free herself.

As her struggles grew feebler the vines, crackling with power, began massing at her head. Like agitated maggots, the biparted leaves grubbed at her skin, pressing, rustling against the hollows of her ears.

The nightmare—not the nightmare, the spell—blossomed to full maturity with the vine. Something pricked at her scalp. The vines wreathing her skull put out long brittle thorns as they tightened. These pressed like tiny daggers at her scalp, her temples, drawing blood where she jerked her head against the pillow.

She could not collect her will. She could not break free. Panicked revelation filled her, a reservoir of hidden knowledge burst free: the enemy was outside her door, but she—the enemy—had not sent the killing-crown. If Gaultry could just call her, she would stop the attack. However much she hated Gaultry, she would not let the crown build, would not let the vines bear their killing fruit—

This is a dream, Gaultry screamed. *O help me! I cannot be killed this way! The horror—dying, helpless, in a dream!* A dazzling image of the Goddess-Twins, their impassive faces, their impossible beauty, flashed before her, even as her strength failed. *O Elianté*, she called. *Was it too late to pray, now her own strength was weakening? Emiera, the Great Lady. Have you come to watch me die?* Beautiful Emiera studied her with infinite calm. Impossibly graceful, she reached out her divine hand—

"Gaultry!" Someone shook her, hard, banishing the vision. "Gaultry, you're having a nightmare! O Llara—wake up!" Tullier, come into her room from his sleeping-place in the salon. Despite the interruption, the nightmare mantle that bound her did not release. A red veil of torment blinded her. She whimpered, succumbing—

A painful blow rocked her back into the mattress. With that cleansing shock of pain, she came abruptly awake.

"Gods save me," she gasped. Her eyes opened to blackness. For a moment she could not be sure she was truly awake, until she felt Tullier moving next to her on the bed, hesitating before hitting her a second time.

"Gaultry." His voice was a frightened whisper. "Are you awake?"

In the dark, she became gradually aware of her surroundings. Wetness sheeted her. Her bedclothes were wrapped around her body like winding sheets, an echo of the nightmare vines. Her room, except for the high dim squares of its pair of transom windows, was black as a pit, suffocatingly warm. Her body quivered with unreleased tension. The spectral press of thorns against her temples seemed to bite her still.

"Get a candle," she quavered, regretting she'd spoken for the fear her voice revealed.

"What happened?" Tullier blundered over something in the dark as he searched for the tinderbox. "I smell blood." He groped for her in the dark.

"I'm fine." She realized even as she spoke that this was true. Nothing was wrong save for the wet of the sheets. "You want to know what happened? I can barely guess myself."

All answers are found in me. The voice from the hill rang as clear in her mind as if she heard those words spoken afresh.

As she came more fully awake, splintered images intensified rather than faded. That distant, reverberating voice. Likewise the unseen stalker who had driven her up the stairs, the enemy who had waited outside her door as the vines strangled her in her own bed. Neither the moment when she had invoked her power to break free from the palace of dreams, nor the subsequent moment in her own bed when she had panicked and failed to invoke it, had been figments of her imagination. "Someone set a spell against me as I lay asleep. It tried to trap me in my dreams. Or, that failing, to leave me dead." Despite the room's heat, she shivered with reaction. The gods had been watching out for her. When her own efforts had failed, they had brought Tullier. . . .

She did not want to believe that. She could not believe that. The gods kept their own counsel. They would not have intervened. She could believe—she would believe—that Tullier had heard her calling to them, but nothing more. To imagine more—that begged divine rebuke.

"Wait," she said, as Tullier came near with the light. She fumbled for her shirt. "Now come."

Flickering candlelight touched the bed, revealing carnage. Her stomach heaved, and only an aggressive swallow saved her the humiliation of puking. Blood, not sweat, had caused the wetness all around her on the sheets. Tullier almost dropped the candle when he saw her. "You're soaked in blood. Where are you cut?"

In feverish moments, they determined that she was bodily unharmed.

Yet the blood on the sheets and her skin could only have been her own. Gaultry, harrowed, leaned against the bedstead. "This is ghastly. And now we've got laundry to clean. We can't leave it for the morning woman to find." For one hysterical moment, she imagined calling Lily to aid them. This was, after all, the area of her expertise. *Your Highness,* she could say. *Won't you help us, please, with our dirty bedclothes?*

Tullier set to work tearing the soiled sheets off the mattress. "How did you know it was a spell?" he demanded. "Even before I brought the light?"

"The thing holding me couldn't have been anything but magic," she answered. "I kept on breaking through parts of the spell, even if I couldn't wake myself up." Parts of the spell. That was not right. Spells. The dream had been in separate parts, with at least three distinct focuses of enmity. The fantastical pursuit, driving her deeper into the intricate palace-maze, had been clearly distinct from the grey encounter with the figure on the distant hill. The last part, the violent attack on her person—that had been something else again. The color signature of the vine, so dark green and angry, came to her once again. Three spells? Three attackers? She fought to suppress a second round of shivering.

"I did a conjuring to save myself," she said. "That I'm sure was real magic."

Tullier held a sheet in front of the candle. The light shone weakly through the coarse material. Backlit, the blotting where the material had touched Gaultry's body showed as a bright color, crimson red. "There's not a dangerous amount of blood here," he said analytically. "Despite how it appears."

You should know, Gaultry thought. *You've had plenty of training on the detail work of corpse disposal.* She said aloud only, "The last part of the spell was supposed to kill me."

The boy hesitated. "Maybe. But the blood here could be your body's own reaction, casting out the invader's spell, and you do not seem otherwise harmed." He stared for a moment into the darkness, then his face lit. "Llara in me, I've seen you bleed this way before. Your clothes were like this the day you reclaimed your Glamour-soul from my body. Were you calling your Glamour to escape the dream, or just your hunter's strength?"

"My Glamour," she said shortly, uneasily wondering if this child who had never been a child could be right. She had consciously owned her Glamour power for such a little time, and for so much of that time, that power had been inoperative, or split into weakened pieces. Having at long last fully reclaimed it, she was frightened to use its power. The physical cost of drawing on her Glamour-soul unnerved her. She could toy and play with the edges of her golden strength, but to attempt to use it in a serious way—no: its strength rushed like a storm to the point of her will, terrifying and dangerous. Would it continue always to overwhelm her when she reached to use it, or would she learn to master its full strength? "I used my Glamour, yes, but I'm still certain that at least part of the dream had the power to kill me." She shuddered. "In my sleep, I don't think I had power enough to turn it from me. If you hadn't woken me . . ."

Tullier's eyes looked large in the candlelight. Large, young, and full of sudden doubts. Concern mingled with pain spasmed on his face before he could turn away. "I don't know what woke me," he whispered. "I barely heard you. Gaultry, if you had died—"

Turning abruptly, he busied himself with the bed.

Watching him work, stripping the layers from the castle-made bed, she pictured the tendrils of creeper that had bound her, rustling against those sheets. The spell had been very strong. So strong—an idea came. Pushing Tullier aside, she grabbed the edge of the last bedsheet.

"That's clean," he protested, as she yanked it off the bed.

"We need to look inside the ticking."

The mattress cover fastened with coarse buttons. Clever interlayered lining contained even the sharpest points of the straw within. Another of the palace's luxuries to which one grew so easily accustomed. Opening the buttons, Gaultry began to pull out big handfuls of straw.

"Shouldn't we put down a sheet?" Tullier said, holding his end of the mattress closed to slow her. "Mix up this clean hay with the rushes on the floor and we'll have to get all new hay for the mattress."

Gaultry, starting to nod agreement, paused as something hidden within the mattress bag caught the candle's light. "Tullier," she breathed. "Please go stand by the door."

Protecting her fingers with a handy pillowcase, she reached to part the last cover of straw.

A crown of thorn-covered vines revealed itself, twisted and heavy with black-green magic, lodged just under where her head would have lain on the pillow. It was small, sized for a manikin or doll. Small but potent. Stinging prickles of power touched her through the material of the pillowcase as she teased it free.

"What is it?" Tullier asked. Ignoring him in her concentration, she slid the horrible thing into a fold of the pillowcase. It blacked the cloth where it touched it, a sort of heatless scorching. Holding it away from her body, she hurried through to the fireplace in the salon and shook it out on top of the firedogs. The little twist of vines glistened malevolently in the grate. It spat evilly and flared, as if consumed by flames of invisible hate.

Bile rose in her throat. "In my dream, that thing was large enough to fit on my head."

"What is it?" Tullier asked again. As they watched, fascinated, the circlet of leaves twitched angrily, almost turning itself over. Gaultry tentatively pinned it down with the fire shovel. To her great relief, the touch of cold iron stilled its movement. "Who put it into your mattress?"

"That I don't know. As for what it is—It's a fetish of some sort. Powered with the same magic that broke up Sizor's Bridge, the same that possessed that poor soldier Siànne that night at Martin's townhouse." She morosely prodded the circlet with the poker. So much for her hope that the magical attacks would cease after Benet formally extended them the protection of his court. "The question remains: Who was this spell sent to destroy? This crown was in my bed—did they imagine that was where you slept, or was I the intended target?"

Tullier set down the candle, hiding his expression. "The woman who takes care of the rooms knows where I sleep. It would have been a little thing to glean that from her."

"Just because you sleep there doesn't mean people don't think you spend time in my bed," Gaultry told him, embarrassed. "I'm sure your Bissanty Envoy thinks it, if no one else."

"Gaultry—" Tullier began shyly. "I know you and Martin—" He stopped.

The two of them stared at the fetish for a self-consciously long moment, pondering its intent.

"What are you going to do?" Tullier finally asked. "Burn it to ash?"

"Not yet." Gaultry stood and wiped her palms. "Tamsanne should see it first. Her magic—it runs to plants. She may be able to determine the vines' source. If whoever made this fetish was foolish enough to use material from their own garden, Tamsanne should be able to track that."

"Now, or tomorrow?"

"Now. This thing is so angry it may destroy itself by morning. Tullier, would you please run and find a servant who can fetch her? Tell whoever you find they should look for her in the orchard, not her cottage—she collects most of her plants by starlight. I'd go myself, but . . . I think I need to sit down." That was no exaggeration. The room seemed to wobble as she spoke.

He cast her a concerned glance. "Of course. You rest. I'll find someone."

Once he was gone, she weighed the fetish with the poker for good measure. Then, not wanting to linger alone with it, she escaped out onto the terrace.

The warmth of the night, the great bowl of stars overhead, the small gentle sounds of the crickets were as soothing as a familiar embrace. Trying to relax, she steadied herself against the metal terrace rail.

The confusion of spells and counterspells continued to whirl in her head. She had not been conscious enough to act fully rationally. Even now, she did not understand her own actions. What pathetic self-control did she possess, summoning Martin to her in the heat of her defense? Had it all seemed like a dream to him, or had her summoning brought him partly awake? Considering his response, she quirked a wavery smile. No, Martin had known it was more than a dream. But would he remember it when he awoke? Would what she had done have left him physically damaged? Remembering the vulnerable beat of his heart, so loud, so strong, so *present*, she could not help but be concerned for his fitness. A spell that pulled the mind across a distance, bringing in its wake a body's shadow—that was dangerous indeed. Would he recognize what she had done and be angry?

By the time Tullier returned, she had fallen into a dull reverie, considering the many faults of her actions.

"I found someone to go for Tamsanne." The boy joined her on the terrace. "He wasn't overeager when I woke him, but he went. I insisted that it was urgent."

"It *is* urgent." Gaultry's voice went shrill, but there was no help for that. Something more was needed to lay to rest the unease the spell had left in her. Something was required—a prayer, a sacrifice—to purge her heartsickness. "How can we stay here at court if we can't sleep safely in our own beds? And if we can't stay here, where can we go? Should we try to hide? Should we try to keep moving? I don't know what we should do. Tullier—I couldn't gather my own strength as I lay within that dream. I made so many mistakes—it should have killed me."

"That thing didn't get into your mattress by itself," Tullier said softly.

"And it didn't kill you, either. Whoever put it there was the one who made the mistake tonight. Whoever sent it tipped their hand. They used soldiers to do their dirty work earlier—now they're acting on their own account. We must be getting closer to the source. We should know who's behind this soon. That's dangerous—but also to the good."

"It doesn't feel good," Gaultry replied glumly. "It feels like I almost died in my own bed."

They stood, each buried in their own thoughts, and listened to the crickets. Beyond the outline of the palace towers, the rim of the moon showed itself: low, already in its descent toward the horizon. The pale twin-stars shone nearby, a little to the east, their triple diadems barely visible in the bright corona light of the moon. Looking at those stars, the special constellation of Tielmark's high deities, Gaultry felt a little steadied. "I wonder how long it'll take your man to find Tamsanne. I hope we haven't sent him chasing a wild goose."

"He'll find her," Tullier said. "I was explicit that he not return to quarters until he'd fulfilled his charge." The brief hardness of his face told her that the man would most certainly fulfill his errand.

"I think there's something I must do before she gets here." Gaultry raised her hand and put up two fingers, as though to touch the paired stars in the sky. "I need to offer Elianté and Emiera a prayer that I am alive to breathe this night air. Yes. I'm going to clean myself up and go over to the temple."

"Now?" Tullier said. "What about Tamsanne?"

"I owe it to the gods," Gaultry said, knowing her words for truth. The vision of Emiera's outstretched hand—how little it would have taken for Tullier not to hear her distress, for him not to have come to help her. "It can't wait."

"I'll not let you go alone," Tullier said. "Gaultry, if you could see your pale face—"

"I have to make the prayer," Gaultry said, increasingly certain.

"Then leave Tamsanne a message. Or go later."

Gaultry shook her head. "It has to be now. I don't know why—I just feel it. If you must come with me, could you please lock up while I find some fresh clothes? I'll leave Tamsanne a note." She glanced again at the stars, twinkling down to her, so bright and yet so distant, even with their diadems dulled by the moon. "She of all people will understand why."

chapter **17**

▼

Gaultry and Tullier slipped into the Goddess-Twins' temple through the small wicket door cut into one of the large, handsomely carved doors that fronted the temple's enormous central chamber. The scent of strong incense lingered, and the dark, warm space, with its hovering dome, greeted them with quiet serenity. Four oil lamps, suspended over the stone altar at the room's center, gave the room its only source of illumination. Their shuttered light cast a circle on the floor around the altar.

Gaultry handed their lantern to Tullier for safekeeping and strode for the altar. She had expected to find the temple guarded by some sleepy acolyte or priest, and was grateful for the unanticipated privacy.

The altar was an ancient chunk of stone, the Great Twins' double-spiral chiseled repeatedly onto its sides and top. Though she had visited the temple on several occasions since taking residence in Princeport, back before her travels in Bissanty, this was the first time she had the opportunity to view the altar alone, and closely. She tentatively traced a carved spiral's course. Hers were far from the first hands to have caressed the stone this way. The carvings were patinaed dark with the touch of many hands, polished smooth in testament to the many prayers spoken there.

In Arleon Forest she prayed comfortably enough beneath a canopy of leaves, but here, within palace precincts, it felt seemly and right to worship Tielmark's gods in their own house.

Breathing deeply the temple's heady incensed air, she moved her hands across the ugly grey stone's weather-beaten surface, searching to ground herself in its stolid form. The wear patterns told a story: The stone had stood outside under the open sky for centuries before being dragged in under this roof. Atop the stone, the modern altar-brazier was a practical pan and grating of hammered iron, large enough to receive branches of substantial size, aglow this night with carefully banked coals. She stared down at those coals, relishing the feeling of security that washed over her. Her nervousness, her horror at the trap of dreams—all of this slipped away.

Tullier, standing beyond the circle of light, could not conceal his impatience as she lingered. "Are you going to offer a prayer or not? If you want to get back for Tamsanne, we shouldn't delay."

She gave him a sharp look, not wanting to be rushed, then reminded herself that he had the right of it, and roused to look for appropriate prayer implements. The offering box next to the altar was tidily stacked with dry branches: ash for Emiera, oak for Elianté. Gaultry selected a pair of well-dried boughs and broke them up into the brazier.

"Great Lady Emiera," she prayed, stirring the embers. "Elianté, Valiant Huntress. For preserving me, I send to you my gratitude, my faith—" Leaping upward, the fire caught on a cluster of dried leaves, then started on its wood.

"I thank you," Gaultry intoned. "For my life and health this night, I thank you." The light of the fire grew momentarily so intense, she had to look away. She fixed on the brazier that contained the fire instead, seeing at first the dull reflection on its scoured surface, and then, past that, something elusive; something that faded the instant she tried to focus on it.

The brazier was a sturdy piece of metal, but worn. The edges were scoured and dented from constant use. An unexpected resonance rose: This was the second time in as many days that her attention had fixed on an altar-brazier. The first had been at the Duchess's last ceremony, down in the funerary chapel.

Branches for the gods this time, the last, white lilies for the dead. A fresh wave of sorrow swept her, and with it anger too. Neither Dervla nor Palamar had evidenced signs of mourning while conducting the final ritual of Melaudiere's funeral. Behavior appropriate to their ceremonial roles, of course, but Dervla at least had known the old Duchess well— had even depended on her support in the terrible months when the traitor-chancellor had held the Prince bound by treacherous magic. Gaultry could not believe it would have done the ceremony harm if Dervla had conducted it with a tincture of personal feeling.

Within the brazier, the oak branch caught flame. She shook her head, trying to clear it, trying to focus a prayer of gratitude. Compulsion had driven her here to give the Great Twins thanks, not to mourn for the manners of the High Priestess.

Yet something here nagged—something that would not let the meditative warmth of prayer rise and take her.

She found herself staring at the brazier again. *Something* about it had her attention, stronger even than the impulse to prayer. What? The pan was both larger and plainer than that of the altar down in the funerary chapel. Instead of hammered flower shapes and elaborate piercing, it matched the coarseness of the altar-stone.

The hammered flower shapes.

Through her tunic she clutched for Haute-Tielmark's ring, hidden so long on its leather string on her neck. As she touched its shape beneath the cloth, a picture of the brazier in the funerary chapel rose clearly before her, a picture of the hammered flowers that adorned the brazier's rim.

They matched those of the ring.

"Elianté-bold, Emiera-fair, I worship you." She pulled the ring free of her clothes and held it out to the sacrifice branches, reduced now to brittle dying ash. "I worship you for leading me. For answering the questions I did not know to ask." She quickly stirred and banked the embers.

"Tullier." She found his face in the shadows beyond the circle. "There's something we must look into before we rendezvous with Tamsanne. Gods in me, it can't wait until morning."

Seeing her expression, he did not argue. "I'm with you," was all he said.

The bronze-clad door that guarded the steps down to the funerary chapel was closed and locked. She set Tullier to open it. The lock was a simple, crude affair, intended only to discourage casual entry. He jimmied it open in less time than it had taken for her offering to burn. A cool draft rose from the well of pitch black that filled the descending steps.

"Lock it," Gaultry told him, as they stepped inside. Their small light did not penetrate very far down the steps. "I don't know exactly what we're looking for, or how important it will prove. I'd rather no one interrupt us until we have a better idea of what we're after."

Tullier nodded, and fumbled the lock shut.

The chapel, though darkened, was as she remembered it. The heavy low trusses, the patchwork of memorial tablets honoring the dead. Shadows concealed the carved grey cross of the Melaudiere panel, deep in its recess between two trusses. By now it would have been mortared in place, sealed until another Duke of Melaudiere was brought here. A melancholy thought.

Gaultry crossed the navy darkness to the room's single slitted window. Beyond, the only things visible were the flat sheet of the night sea and a sliver of the rugged cliff wall that faced the palace's northern prospect. In constructing the chapel and the temple, the builders had pressed the limits of their craft, sitting it precariously on the sheer edge. Their architectural feat meant light from this window could not be seen from the shore.

"You can open the light," she told Tullier. "It won't be seen, save for by those far to sea."

After the Duchess's funeral, the altar-brazier had been swept clean and scrubbed. A musty burned smell remained, but every trace of ash had been cleared. Gaultry paused to fumble for the ring.

"Where did you get that?" Tullier asked, as she drew it forth.

"The big duke who hired us that fishwagon. The first morning after the attack at Sizor's Bridge." At the accusing look in his eyes, she shrugged. "You were in no fit state to be told of it that morning, and afterwards, there was never a chance. He told me that he thought it was a sort of key—though he didn't know what it was intended to open."

Memory—or the gods—had served her well. The flowers of Haute-Tielmark's ring matched the brazier's design, and the gap where it fit into the brazier's rim was immediately obvious. A pin, designed to look like a tendril of plant, stuck up in the center of the gap, corresponding to the insertion hole in the hammered flower on the ring. "Look at this." She handed Tullier the ring and gestured to the brazier's rim. "These two are meant to join as one, don't you think?"

Tullier turned it over in his hand, studying first the pinhole in the hammered flower and then the hinged prong that was built into the ring's band. After a moment he held it up against the edge of the brazier, examining how the brazier pin would fit into the flower. "If you wear the ring when you push it onto the pin on the brazier," he said finally, "the prong will be forced inwards and cut your finger."

"That's right." Gaultry shivered. "The altar wants a taste of blood before it will reveal its secrets."

His eyes met hers across the altar, concerned. "If this were Bissanty, both your ring and the altar would be poisoned. Only those born to sufficient immunity to survive the poison would be able to make use of the key."

"Charming," Gaultry said, taking back the ring and putting it on her finger. Bissanty's rigid caste-sorting by personal poison immunity was one of the Empire's least attractive features. "Fortunately for me, this is not Bissanty."

Despite her bluster, her hand quivered as she positioned it on the brazier's edge. She wished Tullier had kept his mouth shut.

"Let me do it," Tullier urged, seeing her hesitation. "If it's poisoned, it won't hurt me."

She almost nodded. Tullier's Blood-Imperial, combined with the poisoning regimen of his Sha Muira training, had rendered him immune to all but the most God-potent toxins. But to show herself so craven, here in the temple of her own prince . . . "This altar is dedicated to *my* gods," Gaultry said, disliking that something so simple could be so quickly turned into an unreasonable risk. "To Tielmark, not to Bissanty. Whatever force is here, whatever magic, it will not be played by Bissanty rules. And Tielmarans are not poisoners."

He started to argue, but her expression shut him up.

This is faith—she told the Goddess-Twins, inserting the head of the pin into the ring's reception hole—*I hope you see fit to reward it.*

She pressed her hand downward. Flower met silver flower, completing the rim design. Forced by the insertion of the pin, the ring's prong snapped inward as she pressed down, biting her finger with a wasp-sharp sting. Startled by the unexpected intensity of the pain, she jerked away. A single drop of blood dropped and fell, quivering on the polished metal.

Nothing.

"Is that all?" Tullier said.

They'd both expected something more dramatic.

"Unless you have a constructive suggestion as to what I should do next, yes, that's all." Disappointment filled her. "Haute-Tielmark was so sure this ring was important. He risked his honor to keep it out of Dervla's hands. Well, we are here, and now we know what the ring is for. Why hasn't it done anything?"

"Try it again," Tullier offered. "Maybe something happened and we weren't watching closely enough to see."

Gaultry wrung her punctured hand. "You weren't so keen for me to do it the first time round. What happened to your misgivings?" The little wound stung. She was not eager for a repeat.

"You didn't keep your hand down on the rim very long. Maybe it needs more blood."

"Fine," she snapped. Of course that was what he would think. His damn training again. "I'll do it, then—" She stepped forward to brace one hand against the altar-stone, intending to get it over with quickly.

But the substance of the stone was not there. Her hands, instead of bracing her, slipped through the visible surface. She took an involuntary step forward in her effort to regain her balance and neither the substance of the ground nor the altar plinth was there to stop her from falling. Tullier grabbed for her. Together they did an awkward pirouette, lurching back from the concealed line of the brink. The lantern fell from Tullier's hand, hit the floor, and winked out.

"Gods!" Gaultry swore, at last finding her balance. "Stand still and let your eyes adjust. Who knows what else has gone to vapor?"

The slash of weak light from the window fell far short of the room's center, but it was enough to help them reorient. Tullier rummaged for his tinderbox. "I'll run upstairs for a light," he offered. "That may be faster than finding a patch—"

"Wait," said Gaultry. "I see something."

Her eyes at last had adjusted to the darkness, revealing a faint green image near the center of the room, just under where the altar stood. Had stood. As she stared, it became more focused. What she'd taken at first for the flat image of a shell, a creature of nautilus-like chambers, was in fact the faint outline of a descending spiral of stairs, positioned beneath the footprint of the altar-stone's base. She stepped cautiously forward. Her groping hands could not find the altar's edge. The dark had rendered it invisible as well as substanceless. "There's something underneath the altar!" Her voice skipped in her excitement. "Stairs. A hidden passage."

"Let me get a light going, and we'll explore."

Gaultry shook her head, then realized that he wouldn't be able to see the gesture. "It's goddess-light," she explained impatiently. "Can't you see it?" The eldritch color was the green of the Great Twins' power in its purest form. "I'm not sure I'll be able to see it myself if you make a light." She reached for his hand in the darkness. "Come stand by me. Can't you make it out?"

Tullier could not. "Llara is my god, not your pretty Twins." His voice cracked. "To this—I'm blind."

"I'm sorry, Tullier." Gaultry stared at the top steps, so dimly revealed by that warm green glow. Surely the gods would not have brought her to this place if they did not intend for her to explore it. "I've got to go down there, and it's the sort of place—if you need a light, that shows you should not be there. Will you wait, or accompany me?"

"I'll come." He paused. "Even blind."

"Good," she said approvingly, grateful for his nerve. "Take my hand." Her fingertips brushed his, then found a firmer grip. "It will be like that night you led me through the wall passages in your father's house," she added, trying to reassure him. The physical aspect of his Sha Muira training was so thorough, it was not often that she had him at a physical disadvantage. "Only this time you get to be the one playing blindman, and I won't play you to my advantage and bump you against walls."

Tullier didn't answer. She instantly regretted her forced levity. Back then the relationship between them had been very different. To remind him of it now must seem like pettiness rather than jest. "Come on," she sighed. "Forgive my words. I'll be careful of your skin—I want you with me. Even if it's not so nice for you. I'm not sure what we're going to find down there."

"Then let me bring a light," he said hoarsely.

"If we bring a light—" Gaultry was not sure how to explain. "The Twins would consider going down there with our own light to be an act against faith."

"Faith," he groused. "Tielmarans rely too much on it." Sanctimonious piffle coming from Tullier, who had dedicated the first fourteen years of his life to the service Llara-Thunderbringer.

"We'll take the lantern with us," she said, ignoring his words. "Just in case." The lantern, still doused from its fall, would surely comfort him, and she was sure that simply carrying it along unlit would invoke no harm to them. "And make sure that the tinderbox is ready in your pocket if the worst happens and the goddess-light melts away."

He freed his hand from hers briefly and fumbled in the darkness. "Got it," he said. "Let's go."

Still nothing," Tullier complained. After negotiating the confined spiral of the steps and a narrow cleft, they'd reached a terminus chamber. To Gaultry's eyes, the green goddess-light had grown ever brighter with every step they descended. In this final chamber, the light was as strong as day, though still tinted green. It was like the light on a windless day among trees in full summer canopy.

For Tullier there had been no change to the character of the darkness. "We're in a circular room." She paused, unsure how to describe it. Certain elements resonated with the Twin Goddesses' strength. Overhead, the beautiful dressed stone of the spiral vault palpably emanated the Great Twins' love and power, the source of all the bright green light. As she stepped toward the room's center, the focus was even stronger. An open sensation unfolded beneath her ribs—like the half-fearful feeling of standing on an exposed overlook, conscious of the dangerous edge, yet willing to risk it for the view. "This room must be a secret place for Tielmark's High Priestess to meditate. It's full of the Great Twins' power—not just the light, the stone of the room too."

"Should I even be here?" Tullier's brow was set with worry. In his blindness, his face showed nerves he would have hidden in full light.

"I think it's safe," Gaultry said cautiously. "But you mustn't try to light that lamp."

Back in Arleon Forest, Tamsanne had maintained a grotto with a similar feel—the stone parched by constant exposure to magic, the air crackling with power like a forest after a storm. "This place must have been used by Tielmark's High Priestesses since the time that Clarin freed the throne from Bissanty and built the first palace in Princeport. It's only old, not ancient." The room did not have the arcane resonances of a place like the Prince's cemetery by the sea, or Sieur Jumery's burial mound with its altar of blood—or even Tamsanne's grotto, though the godly power there was weaker. Rather than an old site subverted to a new purpose, it had been carved out of the matter of the cliff and dedicated with a single intent: the worship of Tielmark's Goddess-Twins. Gaultry could almost feel their comfortable presence, swathing her like a protective sheath.

And yet . . . Gaultry looked doubtfully around the chamber, absorbing the more peculiar elements of its contents. As the gracefully sculpted vault supports curved downward from the spiral dome, they disappeared behind piles of disordered clutter. Racks of scrolls, clumsy sheaves of folded vellum, and hoarded piles of leather-bound books, stacked haphazardly against the walls, covered much of the beautiful masonry. The effect was more squalid squirrel's nest than meditation chamber. At floor level, a palpable taint of human obsession overlay the Great Twins' presence. Gaultry had never seen so many books or so much paper, crowded all into one space. She had never imagined a repository of knowledge stored this way, all heaped in dusty piles and dirty.

Hairs quivered at the nape of Gaultry's neck. Something in this room was not a healthy reflection of the current High Priestess's mental state. "This place has a weird feel," Tullier said. "Are you sure it's not interdicted?" He was still by the room's entrance, one hand on the carved stone of the irregularly shaped doorway, the other half protectively raised in the air in front of his chest. Something in the way he held that loosely outstretched hand—thumb tucked away, fingers held together like a wedge—reminded her that part of his Sha Muira training had gone forward in the dark. Did that make him more or less wary of this place?

"There's some rather odd clutter," Gaultry said, "Papers and things. But the Great Twins wouldn't let me see their light if it was truly wrong for us to be here." She glanced once again around the rat's nest piles that filled the room, troubled. If Tullier too could sense the discord, surely she wasn't imagining it. "I don't know what it is that you're sensing, but I think maybe the paper has altered the resonance of the room. Dervla, or the Priestesses before her, seem to have filled up the floor with scrolls and books and things." She turned around, and then around again, trying to take it all in. The High Priestess, so far as Gaultry knew, was not required to keep accounts or records or other information regarding her tenure. Those were jobs for the Prince's clerks or historians. What business of the High Priestess's could possibly require these stacks of dusty parchment?

There was a lectern at the room's far side. Leaving Tullier by the door, Gaultry crossed over to it. Someone had stood there recently to write. Dry ink, a discarded quill, and trimming from a paper leaf cluttered the surface. The scroll rack at its side contained three scrolls, one so ancient and dry she dared not crack it open, and two of faded dun-colored parchment. Guessing that whoever used the lectern had reviewed these scrolls most recently, she spread one of the dun-colored scrolls open on the cluttered lectern.

It was stamped at its foot with a double-spiral surmounted by wings, the signature seal of Dervla's mother Delcora. The caption was a line of fastidiously ornamented script: *The PRINCE can have no truer protector than his HIGH PRIESTESS*. Beautiful ornaments in colored ink ran down both the vertical margins. The writing that filled up the space between was looser, less formal, as though the caption and margins and had been inked in well before the scroll's actual text.

The Power of the Great Twins is a river in HER body; through HER they speak, through HER the PRINCE is shown the windings of his fate. Tielmark's HIGH PRIESTESS leads the PRINCE in the eternal circle of the seasons' change. SHE holds the hidden mysteries that must be followed to maintain Tielmark's prosperity. The Gods, who give HER strength, bless HER wisdom.

A fortnight has slipped and gone since Corinne was confirmed Free Princess of Tielmark. We have reached Emiera's month, and already the Ides are upon us. More flowers have bloomed this year than ever I have seen in springtime, and the maying parties went forward with a wild abandon I trust I will not live to see matched. The Feast on Emiera's Ides was prepared with renewed joy and love, and the farmers came from every corner of the land to refresh their pledges to their Princess.

All was joy. When the time came for Corinne to sanctify her summer pledge, Great Lady Emiera accepted her offer with every evidence of divine delight. This season will bring a harvest Tielmark will remember for years to come.

I guided the Princess and her consort in the ceremony. Helpless and willing, they followed like children in all that I told. Fair Emiera rewarded their obedience with the most favorable portents I have yet lived to witness. Praise Her Glory and my strength for all that was accomplished here today!

Gaultry, realizing belatedly that the scroll was a narrative of the old High Priestess's daily affairs, closed her eyes and turned away.

"Where are you?" Tullier asked, after a long moment had passed. "What are you doing? I can't even hear you breathe."

She had not known she was holding her breath. She exhaled shakily and opened her eyes. Tullier had advanced a little away from the door, his hand tentatively brushing the edge of a wooden scroll rack in what was still, for him, the pitch dark. She could not blame him the edge of impatience in his voice. "I'm looking at the scroll I think Dervla was reading most recently," she told him. "Her mother, who was High Priestess before her, wrote it on the day of Emiera's Feast, fifty years back when the Brood made Benet's grandma Princess."

"What does it say?" His voice betrayed no feeling, but once again his expression twisted with dismay, as he forgot once more that she could see him. Emiera's Feast was the festival Tullier and his Sha Muira master had attempted to desecrate.

"So far just that Delcora takes credit for everything that went well during the festival. What else would you expect from Dervla's mother?" Gaultry smoothed the scroll guiltily with her hand. She hesitated to read on. Emiera's Feast celebrated the budding life of spring, the new life sown in the ground by Tielmark's farmers. Though the ritual that Prince and consort performed on Emiera's day was shrouded in mystery and discharged in secret, it was not entirely possible to conceal its substance. A disproportionate number of Tielmark's rulers were born nine months after Emiera's Day—in years that also brought harvest bounty rich enough to be fondly remembered from one generation to the next. Though Delcora's scroll detailed nothing of this, Gaultry, reading between the lines, sensed the old High Priestess's fevered excitement at her guiding role in this, the most intimate and secret of the Princely rituals, in a year and at a time when Princess Corinne, young and newly married, would have been ripe to bear her first child.

She could hardly begrudge the old High Priestess her excitement. Successfully leading Corinne in that ritual, the year Tielmark's freedom had been confirmed on the two-hundred-fiftieth anniversary of liberation from Bissanty, must have been the crowning moment of Delcora's tenure as High Priestess.

It was also not information to which Gaultry had any reason to be privy. She covered the scroll with her hand, uncertain whether she should read further.

It had never been her intention to intrude upon the sacred mysteries of the High Priesthood. She swore silently at Haute-Tielmark, cursing the mission on which he had unknowingly set her. Dervla had every right to hunger for the key traitor-Heiratikus must somehow have stolen. Every right, every reason, to seek zealously to repossess it. What was she doing, skulking with Tullier in this consecrated place, nosing in Delcora's private chronicle?

Flattening the scroll against the lectern, she began to roll it back into a tight cylinder, furious at her own meddling. Self-anger and the effort not to read further combined to make her clumsy, and she knocked over the jar of dried ink. The lid fell free, and she barely saved the contents from spilling. As she leveled the jar, the lid tumbled to a rest on the parchment, like a marker to a point below where she had stopped reading. Tamsanne's name leapt out, written in cramped and angry letters. *Tamsanne,* she read. *The changeling child of Tamsanne's womb.*

After that, there was nothing for it but to read the entire scroll through. She mechanically placed the lid back on the jar, riveted, as her eyes scanned back to where she had left off reading.

> . . . I guided the Princess and her consort in the sacrifice. Helpless and willing, they followed all I told. Fair Emiera rewarded their obedience with the most favorable portents I have ever seen. Praise Her Glory and my strength!

This, Gaultry realized, was the last of the description of the day's ceremonies. From there the narrative became more personal—and more damning.

> Today, even as I led my Princess through the joyous maze of all that is sacred, Melaney Sevenage set sail for Bassorah City. The ship sailed at noon, a great winged bird, flying swift and white to Llara's Heart before the wind. I had sworn two acolytes to bear witness, while I was occupied with Emiera's Feast. As they watched, Great Lady Emiera cast Her judgment: though Melaney called out most piteously, though she tore her hair and rent her clothing, even to the last moment when she was pulled beneath the decks, no one answered the fair Lady's cries for relief. She who sought to usurp my place in Corinne's heart is justly punished. The Gods are served.
>
> *The* PRINCE *can have no truer protector than his* HIGH PRIESTESS. I saw that pledge affirmed today.

Gaultry read this passage over twice, her heart pounding against her ribs. When Tamsanne and Julie had told her that Richielle and Delcora had threatened them, they had offered no specifics. She had thought they meant some nebulous menace, nothing like this deliberate plan and witness of one Brood member's destruction. As the Prince's sworn protector, Delcora had twisted her duty to take it as her right, if nothing more, to stand passive as Melaney was sent overseas to certain death.

This scroll—Gaultry stared down at it in horror—Dervla must have read it many times over. Did Delcora's daughter also believe that her rights as High Priestess extended to premeditated murder? Melaney delivered into the hands of the Bissanty . . . It was a thing spoken of with horror still, fifty years later. Surely Dervla could not countenance that! Following the passage about Melaney, there was another blank space. When the script began again, the writing was smaller, ragged, as though the author had written in the grasp of strong emotion:

A fever fell upon me as I recorded this day's acts. Emiera's cool hand swept my brow, Elianté lifted me. Empurpled clouds parted. I have seen a vision of things as they are meant to be.

Not all that comes of the Gods is made of sweetness. On the day we lifted Corinne to her Princely throne, my baby fell from my womb. This loss brought me pain beyond words—I, Delcora of Princeport, who have served the gods faithfully all my days. That child should have been my heir, the greatest Priest Tielmark has ever known. From within my womb, he witnessed Corinne's coronation. He felt the presence of the Gods. He knew their power. He would have borne that knowledge from the hour of his birth.

But I gave all my power to the spell that day, and nothing remained to hold him in my body. I must admit my frailty here: I questioned the Great Twins' wisdom on that day, even as I bowed to them. They, who upheld me through so many trials, seemed to have abandoned me in this.

But on this day, Emiera's Feast 250th, despite past puling, I see that the Goddess Twins have mercy, and that even myself, flawed servant to their mercies, will be rewarded. There was purpose to my loss: my body sacrifice will receive its reward, and that in greater measure. All that we of the Brood have earned with our acts will be requited. As Melaney Sevenage paid for her faithlessness, I too shall be requited in my due turn.

In today's fever, the balance scales of the Great Twins were revealed, and I glimpsed my reward openly. I tremble even to write here what I saw. The terrible symmetry is almost beyond my mind to fathom: if Tamsanne-bitch of Arleon Forest had only shared the secret that kept her own womb sealed, my son would have lived. In denying me this, Tamsanne killed my child, as surely as if her hands had twisted his neck.

Tonight the Great Ladies of Tielmark promised me the redemption of my loss. I will get another child. This very night I
saw her face as she grew from child to woman, her rise to power
like a meteor in its flight. Her name will be Dervla, and twinned
Goddess-power will run through her like a river swollen in spring.

The promise the Goddess-Twins offered me showed me more.
Lousielle's prophecy will follow unto my child, and all others of
the Brood, marking them for death until Tielmark has a King,
until Corinne or one of her children redeems kingship's red
throne. The fates of the Brood witches are ever laced together
until that throne is gained. Dervla must be made stronger even
than the Great Twins have shown me, if she is not to quickly
follow the Brood's fate.

I have decided what to do. The changeling child of Tamsanne's womb will serve to make my Dervla strong: all power
that is gathered in Tamsanne's child will pass to mine, the day
that I command it. I am High Priestess. I am the Prince's Highest
Protector. The border-witch will have to bow. When stars align,
when Andion's Moon rides the night sky, Tamsanne will cede
from her child all that is my due. From that day forward, Dervla's
power will shine forth like a star.

All this I foresee, and it will come to pass. I am Tielmark's
High Priestess, the true protector of the realm. I can see the
future.

Gaultry stepped back from the lectern.

"Some part of this happened," she said, disturbed. "But is any of it
truth?" Dame Julie and Tamsanne had not interpreted the punishments
inflicted on the dissenting Brood-members as divine retribution.

Gaultry seized the second dun-colored scroll and laid it open. It had
decorated margins like the first scroll, but lacked an ornamented caption.

I am finally dying. My daughter will take my place. She will close
my eyes, will don my chain of power. At last she will take into
herself the strength of my magical power. Despite my fears, she
has risen at last above the other acolytes, and the Goddess-Twins
have granted her the just reward: she *will* be the next High Priestess. But I am not content. Though her power is strong, Dervla
has yet to see the stars, lit from within by the Great Twins' power.

She has yet to hear their voices, whispering a thousand songs of beauty and despair. The fountain that is their strength does not yet run within her. What is holding her back?

Last night I felt Great Emiera's touch. I was too weak to receive the whole of the vision. One image remained to me only: a woman with auburn hair, dancing over a bonfire's coals. I thought long upon this vision, trying to discover its meaning. I strained to see the woman's face, but it was beyond my strength to bring her features into focus.

But if my vision is clouded, my mind remains clear. There is no doubt in me who the red woman must be: Tamsanne's cursed get, twin-child to my long dead first-born. The child the border-witch held within her womb the night the Brood confirmed Corinne's crown, and my first-born lost his life.

Tamsanne assured me her child was dead. Before we allowed her to disappear back into her forest, I examined her body and confirmed it. But somehow the border-witch deceived me. There was no miscarriage. I see now by this vision that she defied me. She defied the gods. All to preserve the monster in her womb.

Dervla will never have that child's power. The time for her to take it has passed. Knowing that she should have had it has lessened her. Giving my daughter the freedom of my archive has lessened her . . .

The remainder of the writing had been rubbed away, whether at the time of writing or long after, Gaultry could not tell.

She rocked back on her heels and glanced around the chamber. Was all the paper that she could see here old Delcora's records? Could one woman possibly have amassed so much paper and parchment in a single generation? She pulled a half dozen scrolls from a nearby rack and glanced at their contents: a description of a courtier's marriage, a list of the officiants; the record of a moonlit hunt for herbs; a list of the members of a Princely hunting party. The contents of another rack revealed more of the same. All dating to the years Delcora had reigned as High Priestess. The dun-colored scrolls were reserved for descriptions of state ceremonies and "fevers" that Delcora ascribed to visitations from the Great Twins.

A scattered survey confirmed her suspicion. All the papers—or at least all those she looked at—were Delcora's.

The room contained, unfiltered, the contents of a dead woman's mind. It was almost too much for Gaultry to take in. A dead woman, a powerful witch, who had sat for decades at the Prince of Tielmark's right hand, maintaining meticulous, if scatty, records of her service. Why had she preserved all this? Why had her daughter preserved it?

Gaultry looked again at the scrolls that Dervla had left by the lectern. Did Dervla use her mother's words as a touchstone, to defend or define her own actions? When had the High Priestess last viewed these two scrolls? What had been her purpose in doing so?

The third scroll, the fragile scroll, seemed to confirm that Dervla must have been the one who had most recently stood at this lectern as reader. It described the cremation preparations necessary to honor a peer of the realm—the same preparations that Dervla had performed the morning before Martin and the Prince had departed from Princeport.

The other two scrolls . . . had Dervla selected them after the funerary luncheon in Melaudiere's honor, following the moment when Tamsanne had challenged her authority at the Princess's table? Had that incident driven her to review this ancient enmity? Could Dervla possibly believe that Tamsanne had been responsible for her own mother's miscarriage? Could Dervla possibly share Delcora's belief that Tamsanne had been wrong to flee court in an attempt to protect her own unborn child?

Whatever the case, Gaultry did not like to think that her grandmother's affairs, let alone her own, were occupying Dervla's mind. *The* PRINCE *can have no truer protector than his* HIGH PRIESTESS! Did Dervla think that this axiom gave her the right to remove anyone who offered the prince the services of their own protection?

Did this mean that Dervla had been, indirectly, the hand guiding the attacks on her and Tullier? The signature of her power had not been there in the assault at Sizor's Bridge, or at Martin's house. The dark, rotted, vengeance green that had attacked her at the bridge, at Martin's townhouse, in her own dreams—that was not the power that she had touched in Dervla, those several times their spells had crossed. But perhaps that darker magic lay hidden behind the High Priestess's veil?

It was time to meet with Tamsanne and find out. There was nothing more for her here—a thorough investigation of the room's contents would take weeks. She and Tullier had been lucky to have learned even this much without being discovered. She did not want to press that luck.

Tullier turned his head as she approached, alert to the small sounds of her movement. "What have you found?" he asked.

"All the paper here records things old Delcora thought were significant. It's like a created world, all on paper, with everything slanted from Delcora's view." Gaultry paused, not sure what she should share with him of her discoveries. "The scroll Dervla left on the lectern described a grudge Delcora held against my grandmother. Maybe Dervla has held on to that feeling."

"Fifty years is not a long time to nurture a grudge."

"I know," Gaultry said wryly. "Where the gods stand watch, fifty years is nothing. But it feels strange: It's clear enough what old Delcora thought, but what does Dervla believe? She's a grown woman at the height of her powers. Delcora's been dead for decades, but her anger—the way she wrote about it—it seems so fresh. What does it seem like to Dervla?"

"Who knows?" Tullier looked stressed. Waiting for her in blind darkness was taking its toll. "But if she left that scroll out, obviously she's still interested."

"Let's go find Tamsanne," Gaultry said. "I don't know what else can be gleaned from this dumping ground."

Taking the lead, she once again helped him on the narrow steps. The goddess-light faded as they climbed. By the time they reached the funeral chapel, her eyes had adjusted so well to the lack of illumination that even the dim light from the window extinguished the last she was able to see of the faint green glow.

Tullier relit their lantern. When she tapped on the altar by the light of its flame, it had regained the substance of stone. The stairs below were once more blocked.

"I wonder how Heiratikus got hold of this ring," she said, pulling it from her finger, "or whether he ever discovered the secret it unlocked." She retied it to its string, and once again hid it under her shirt. "It seems unlikely. Surely he would have been blind to the goddess-light, and lighting a lamp—I think that would have invoked magic against an intruder. But Dervla must always have feared it."

Tullier shrugged. "What was there to fear? Her mother was long dead."

Gaultry shook her head. "Something is not right about the fact that Dervla's kept all that paper together in one place. As if something would be lost by dispersing it. I don't believe it's something Dervla would have wanted him to see, let alone to have had opportunity to rifle through at his leisure."

"Nor you neither."

"Let's get out of here then, before she finds out."

▼

chapter 18

O utside the temple, the sloped amphitheater lawn was wet with dew. From over the seaward wall, a gentle breeze lapped in off the water, though as yet the sky bore no sign of dawn. Elsewhere in the palace, movement had begun to stir. The quiet noises of people waking early to their morning's business drifted gently, distantly, in the predawn air.

"We were lucky no one caught us," Tullier said. "Someone will surely be up soon to tend the temple fire." Something unhappy in his tone made Gaultry glance his way.

The boy had been trained to follow a single bondmaster's orders unquestioningly, a master to whom he had pledged his life and trust. Though Gaultry had broken that bond, at times aspects of their own relationship unpleasantly mimicked that apprentice-master mold. She sensed a question behind his words, a question he didn't feel he could ask her directly. Surely he was not concerned about the danger of discovery. That sort of excitement was food to him. Was he angry because she had not detailed all she had discovered in the High Priestess's secret chamber?

"Tullier." She paused before they entered the Summer Palace's tiled foyer. "You have been a great support tonight. I wouldn't have been able to get past that first lock without you. But the information I found in that hidden room—it touches on my family history. On the forces that tore apart the Common Brood. It's information that could endanger you without offering you any real advantage."

"Gaultry, do you know what Sciuttarus's Envoy offered me at yesterday's meeting?"

Gaultry could hardly conceal her frustration that he should choose this moment to reopen that subject. Yesterday he had refused to discuss it entirely. "Beyond the offer I could see on the table?" An image of the great chain of office rose in her mind's eye, the time-burnished wirework images of Bissanty's long-past triumph over Tielmark's people. Envoy Lepulio's saturnine face, as he held the great chain out to Tullier, the golden links heavy on his palms, followed in another flash. She shook her head. "I don't pretend to understand the powers that Bissanty's Tielmaran crown confers. The Bissanty Prince of Tielmark is cut off from Tielmark's soil, so he can't take strength from that, as Benet does. What's left? Holding a symbolic seat at time-worn rituals? Ceremony?"

"It's far more than ceremony," Tullier said seriously. "Bissanty's Princes are the acknowledged sons of Llara. Those who die as Imperial Princes are worshipped alongside the gods. A minor cult, perhaps, but one which promises a modicum of immortality. So long as I held the Bissanty crown of Tielmark, Great Mother Llara would smile on me as her own son. If I died with that crown on my head, I could expect my soul to rise straight into her bosom. It would be guaranteed that I would receive her eternal blessing." He glanced back at the temple. "I spent my life as a Sha Muira fearing the fall from Llara's divine approval. Now, when her divine love is offered me unconditionally—I can't accept it, without conditions of my own in return.

"Lepulio said I should come home to Bissanty, where I could count my enemies on the fingers of one hand. Those enemies—he meant my family. Imperial Sciuttarus and his three sons. Maybe Siri Caviedo too— my father. That makes five, doesn't it?" He laughed, a miserable bubbling cough of a laugh. "I would have power in Bissanty, but I would never be loved there. My family would strike down anyone fool enough to stand by me. All I would be able to count on would be my land-tie—defunct, while Benet reigns as Tielmark's Prince—and Great Llara's blessing. For a real Sha Muira soldier, that would be enough." He brushed his brow tiredly.

"The Emperor wants me close by until he can find a means of removing me without provoking Llara's wrath—and once he finds the means, he *will* remove me. By this thinking, elevating me to Prince, guaranteeing me Llara's blessing, is all that is needed to bring me to heel. Why should I fear death, even at Sciuttarus's hands, knowing that Llara will love me in the after-realm? That was what I lived for as a Sha Muira.

"The Emperor sent Lepulio as Envoy because Lepulio knows the Sha

Muira. He doesn't understand—it must be beyond his comprehension—that the Glamour you and your sister wielded released me from that bondage. Llara is my goddess still, but I see now that there are many ways to please her."

Tullier's eyes were melancholy. "Once I would have welcomed the crown, and death—even if the land, held by Benet, did not acknowledge me. But—" the look in his eyes sharpened, "but to make that sacrifice of self, that my reward in this life should be the ties of a family who will always hate me . . ." Tullier made an angry gesture. "I don't want to do it. I am no longer a Sha Muira warrior. I won't court that pain."

"There's hate in what I discovered tonight," Gaultry said tentatively. She did not want to believe that hate was doomed to descend through the generations of a family, but it was hard to imagine another reason that the High Priestess would keep Delcora's bileful records so close to her heart.

"I'll protect you from it." Tullier was utterly serious. She could see in his eyes that he wanted to protect her—that he yearned for the right to do it.

"You can't. Everything I learned tonight could put you in danger too."

"You can't send me away to Bissanty right now, and keeping me in ignorance while I remain in Tielmark won't help me either. Your enemies are my enemies. You *must* tell me their names."

She sighed. She did not know how to manage the boyish passions that were awakening in him now that the painful shadow of the Sha Muira's poison had been purged. He was like dry tinder, eager for the touch of fire. Notwithstanding his many adult competencies, she did not trust the hot-headed boy in him not to overreact—possibly with killing rage. "I wish I knew who it was most important for me to protect you from," she sighed. "Your family is at the top of the list, of course. But who is your most dangerous enemy here in Princeport?"

"You know," Tullier insisted. "Those papers you read—"

"The papers didn't tell me who put the fetish crown in my bed this night. They didn't tell me who attacked us at Martin's town house. What I read in those papers . . . It was all Dervla's mother, nothing about Dervla. I have suspicions about the High Priestess's motives, but I don't have proof."

"I have suspicions too."

"Be patient a little longer. Tamsanne will give us some sort of definite answer about that crown."

"I want to know what you found out in those scrolls." He had reversed himself from doubtful reticence to stubborn obduracy. Less Sha Muira–apprenticelike, but equally annoying. She could not think how to answer him.

"Let's go back to my rooms," she said, after an uncomfortable pause. "We've been gone so long, we might even find Tamsanne waiting."

That thought, as much as the boy's frown, sped her on her way.

The scrap of paper bearing their message for Tamsanne was still attached to the knocker where Gaultry had tied it. Gaultry took it down, fumbled for her keys, and pushed the door open.

"Unshutter the lamp," she told Tullier, "and get the candles . . ." The words died in her throat as the light touched something that should not have been there—glistening white silk that trailed down from the thread-bare divan. For one light-headed moment, she thought Mervion had come to make peace, then she realized—"What in Elianté's name!"

It was Elisabeth Climens. She was bundled in a ridiculously luxuriant robe, too long for her body, huddled small on a corner of the sofa. Grass stains and pieces of leaf dirtied the robe's hem. She must have come, and in a hurry, through the deer park. There was nothing beneath the robe except a thin shift. Even her feet were naked. A delicate gold chain glinted against the bare skin at her throat, plunging downward. At her side, Gaultry sensed the flashing focus of Tullier's interest at the glimpse of the girl's uncovered shoulders, hastily suppressed.

"Please," Elisabeth said. Her hair was tied, night-fashion, in two loose plaits, in childish contrast to the shapely shoulders, the robe of silk. Her eyes looked huge and frightened in the whiteness of her face. "I didn't know where else to come."

"How did you get in?" Tullier said sharply.

She nodded toward the terrace doors. "The door was open there. I did not want to wait outside."

Gaultry and Tullier exchanged a glance. Tullier shook his head. He'd secured the room before they'd left it. Elisabeth should not have been able to walk in.

"Why are you here?" Gaultry asked, hard put to modulate her voice to an encouraging tone. She glanced at the grate, hurriedly concealing her relief when it appeared that the fetish-crown remained untouched. Gaultry had had enough confusion and interruptions for one night. Elisabeth was a nice girl—but what she was doing here in the stray hours of the morning was almost more than Gaultry wanted to face. She could only pray that she'd be able to resolve whatever silly urge had brought the girl and send her safely on her way before Tamsanne arrived. She glanced at Tullier, willing him to get out of the way so she could question Elisabeth more closely. The boy, nodding as he took her cue, went over to examine the terrace doors, taking himself away from Elisabeth's line of vision.

"It's an ungodly hour," Gaultry said. "What is it that you want?"

"My mother needs your help."

Argat Climens!? An image of the archly confident Duchess of Vaux-Torres flashed before her. Gaultry could hardly imagine another person less likely to need her assistance. Besides, why should Elisabeth imagine that Gaultry would want to entangle herself with the affairs of a reputed traitor? "Why would I want to help your mother?"

"She's in trouble."

"Is that news?" At the terrace doors, Tullier bent to examine the latch, then, tension running in him like a dog called to point, he slipped out onto the terrace. "Your mother seems perfectly capable of making all the trouble she needs for herself. And of getting herself out of it."

"That's all true," Elisabeth blurted. "I know how she must seem to you. But she is not a traitor. Not," the girl faltered, "never against the Prince. But all her past is rising to haunt her now. Without your help she's going to do something unforgivable."

Gaultry, itching to know what Tullier was after, instead sat wearily next to the girl on the divan. "Start from the beginning. Why are you here?"

Elisabeth fidgeted, twisting the edge of her robe. "Mama said you were the only one the Prince could trust."

Gaultry snorted, disbelieving.

"No!" Elisabeth said vehemently. "It's true! She told me that the very night you returned to Princeport, right after Dame Julie's concert. I had to report about everything I'd seen, and she thought it was funny when I told her about Ronsars putting us together. That's when she said what she did about the Prince being able to trust you. The way she said it—mocking—I could tell she really believed it was true. That," she faltered again, "that's why I'm here. Whatever you choose to do, after I have told you things—I know it will be right."

This, Gaultry thought grimly, staring at the frightened girl, was a predictably Climens-convoluted scenario. Should she believe that the Duchess of Vaux-Torres had complimented her genuinely, or did the Duchess think that Gaultry was an unworldly rustic who could be counted on to step the wrong way and obscure some more subtle treachery? She instinctively found herself trusting young Elisabeth—but what if Vaux-Torres had consciously contrived it that the girl would come here tonight to confide in her? The woman's feline smile rose before her, mocking and proud. Gaultry could not put it past Argat Climens to manipulate her daughter into singing some poignant song that Gaultry, in her own foolish soft-heartedness, would find impossible to resist. "Go on," she said to Elisabeth, with a sinking feeling. "Tell me what decided you to come here."

The girl's eyes flickered to the terrace doors.

"Is it about Tullier?"

"Partly," Elisabeth whispered.

"Then tell me the short version, and have done. It's been a long night, and I'd like to catch another hour's sleep before dawn."

"My mother does not know that I am here," Elisabeth started hesitantly. "That is the first thing that you should know." She would not look in Gaultry's eyes, but that seemed more a matter of protecting her own fragile pride than deceit or evasion. Her profile was set and hard, a glimpse of the woman she would become if she survived to stay on at court. She was like her mother, very like her mother, in her beauty and the swift, intelligent shifts of her thoughts. But there was something else in the girl's features too: a directness, a pragmatic, honest sort of boldness that surely had not come to her from her mother. It struck Gaultry suddenly that for all her faults, Argat Climens was an excellent parent. The woman could not help but overawe her children—along with most of Tielmark's population—but she had not raised them to be weaklings, either, once they spun free of her orbit. Elisabeth was a credit to her.

If, at this moment, a struggling credit, trying to tell in a straight manner a story whose convolutions she did not fully comprehend. "The things I found out tonight . . ." Elisabeth trailed off, looking regretful. "I suspected a little of it before, but I knew nothing for certain. If I had known—there are things I might have done differently." She folded her hands, which were fidgeting, in her lap.

"High Priestess Dervla came to visit my mother tonight. Very late. The servants came to wake her, and the commotion woke me in its turn—when there's a breeze, I can hear Mama's bell from my bed. My private stair lets into my mother's study. I heard voices, and I started down to find out who had come. Once I heard what they were saying, I could not reveal myself. I should have returned to bed, but what I heard—I couldn't make myself stop listening.

"My mother has close ties to Bissanty." Elisabeth glanced down, embarrassed, a touch of her girlishness returning. "You know, perhaps, about my sister Anna?"

Gaultry shook her head. "Should I?"

Elisabeth flushed. "They started out talking about Anna. Beaumorreau and I are the lucky ones. We were born with mother's face. Anna was not so fortunate. I'll show you—" From beneath her robe she slipped a tiny locket, appended to the gold chain, and snapped it open, revealing four tiny miniatures. Gaultry tipped it toward the light. There was little to see—how could portraits so tiny reveal details? One feature, however, was instantly evident. The artist had either been fastidious in accuracy, or most unkind. Anna Climens's face was set apart from those of her siblings by the unusual grey cast of her skin.

"Her father was a Bissanty man?" That grey was a pallor Gaultry had seen only in the highest born Bissanty nobles, men like Coltro Lepulio: well-connected, dangerous, and full of ambition.

"Mother was Tielmark's Envoy to Bissanty that year." Elisabeth said bitterly. "She could hardly have been less discreet."

"What does this have to do with tonight's business?" Disturbed, Gaultry let the locket swing free. The ties between the two countries were dangerous enough without such foolishness. She could not believe that Argat Climens would have got herself with child by a high-born Bissanty man for love. Elisabeth, perhaps sensing the unsympathetic trend of Gaultry's mind, hastily tucked the locket out of sight.

"The High Priestess had discovered the name of the man who fathered my sister. Also she had secured some of my mother's correspondence. Things she had written to men in Bissanty. Not just Anna's father. Others too. My mother's Bissanty friends are well placed—does she know any other kind? However it was, Dervla had their letters. There was nothing political about Tielmark in them, but they had furnished her with the names of the men my mother had known in Bissanty.

"My mother began to argue. At first, she didn't seem to care that Dervla had her letters. She said a woman's private affairs did not rise to treason, that she was willing to declare that openly before all the Prince's court. She said some ugly things," dark lashes fluttered on Elisabeth's cheeks, momentarily shuttering her expression, "but I suppose it was brave of her that she was willing to admit her indiscretions in a public forum. From what she said, Dervla had threatened her with this matter before, and my mother was holding firm that she had done nothing for which she could be condemned. 'Take me to trial tomorrow,' my mother challenged her. 'My reputation can weather it.'

"Dervla stopped arguing and laughed. She said that she couldn't be held accountable if my mother chose to throw prudence to the wind. 'Do you think I would be here tonight if my evidence didn't rise against more than your reputation? I've been talking to Envoy Lepulio,' she said. 'Do you imagine that he'll continue to shield you? Talk to him again, and you will find his song has shifted. In exchange for what I can give him, he's arranged that your past lovers will bear witness against you. You'll be crucified in court. Not just you, but your children too. The house of Vaux-Torres will lose everything. And perhaps Benet will even reward me by allowing me to appoint a successor for your lands.'

"Mama refused to believe her. She insisted that the Envoy would never collude in fabricating evidence against her, whatever he'd told Dervla. The High Priestess got angry, but still my mother wouldn't believe her. Finally the High Priestess lost patience, and she told my mother exactly what coin she'd offered to buy Lepulio's cooperation.

"Dervla has a weapon. An ancient blade, forged in the furnace of the past. It holds power enough to kill a god's own child—leaving the one who wields it untainted by that god's curse." Elisabeth stopped and glanced at Gaultry, who had startled and shifted.

A god's own child.

That was what Tullier was, now that Bissanty's Tielmaran crown had been acceded to him.

"Go on," Gaultry said. "You have my full attention."

"Dervla told Mama that if the Emperor wanted to keep his throne for his own heirs, killing the boy with this knife was the surest way to make that happen. She said it had been agreed that she would give the knife into Bissanty hands on their oath-bond that they would use it as she dictated. The silence that answered her told me that my mother believed her. Not only that, but that she believed that whatever hold she might have had upon the Envoy, this offer of Dervla's outweighed it. Finally she asked Dervla what she must do, and what guarantees Dervla would give her that her family would be protected.

" 'A small thing,' Dervla said. But that 'small thing' was for my mother to arrange for your assassin-boy to fall into Bissanty hands! Dervla did not want any connection to this action until after the Bissanties had completed their part. Then, once the boy was dead, Benet would be told the whole truth. "That made my mother angry. She said that if Benet knew the truth, she'd lose everything. 'The boy is under Benet's protection,' she told Dervla. 'If I were to arrange for him to fall to the Bissanties, Benet would skin me alive for betraying his word, whatever he personally earned by it.' "

"How did Dervla answer?" Gaultry asked. Her mouth tasted ashy, but she tried to keep her question calm. The knife Dervla wanted to give to the Bissanties—it could only be the *Eln Raku* blade, the Kingmaker knife Tamsanne had described to her in the orchard. Dervla, it seemed, wanted to take two birds with one stone. Raise Benet to King, and use the Bissanties to rid Tielmark of Tullier's presence.

"She called my mother a fool, and said that Benet would reward her for having the courage he lacked—that Benet should never have pledged his protection to the boy in the first place. My mother said one last thing to argue—she told Dervla that she didn't know Benet so well if she imagined he'd reward skullduggery. Then—then she agreed to do what Dervla wanted."

Elisabeth unclasped her hands and stood, flaring the hem of her robe nervously around her. "I hope all that's right. It's what I remember, even if I don't have every word correct. After that it seemed like it was just insults: My mother was defeated, and Dervla took her chance to rub that in." She touched her hands to her face, a tired gesture briefly covering her eyes. "For all her faults, mama is passionate for the Vaux-Torres's land, and she loves us, the children of her flesh. To protect that, I don't doubt that she'll do what Dervla told her."

Elisabeth paused. "I can't let that happen. I won't. After Dervla left, I went back to my bed and tried to decide what I ought to do. Finally it came to me—if you knew what was being planned, there was a chance you could prevent it. I thought maybe that if you heard it first from me, you could stop it in some way that did not touch my mother's honor."

Gaultry sat back, studying the girl's anxious face, her hunted air. Elisabeth had brought no proof for anything she was saying—nothing but the circumstances of her panicked arrival. She struggled to see the gain in anything Elisabeth said being lies. It didn't surprise her that Dervla wanted Tullier out of the way, that she might even treat with the Bissanties in order to get him out of Tielmark. But why choose the Duchess of Vaux-Torres for her tool? "Did Dervla say *when* she wanted your mother to turn Tullier over to the Bissanties?"

Elisabeth's brow furrowed. "I don't think so. She talked about the God-King's month and the alignment of the stars. When she talked about the right time to tell Benet what had been done, she said something about the Full Moon—as though she expected Benet to be back in Princeport before the end of the month. I don't know how that could be possible when he's just committed himself to battle on the Lanai front."

Gaultry glanced at the grate. From where she sat, the brittle strands of the fetish crown were just visible beneath the poker and shovel. "Did Dervla mention anything about why she came breaking in on your mother in the wee hours of the morning? What brought that on? Wouldn't it have been more discreet to wait until some more reasonable hour?"

"I don't know." Elisabeth seemed genuinely puzzled. "My mother didn't question it. Dervla might have told her before I started to listen."

"Maybe," Gaultry said. She looked again at the burnt strands of crown. She would willingly now stake odds that Dervla was connected to that attack. When the spell failed, Dervla must have sensed it—and rushed to string another arrow to her bow.

A soft knock at the door interrupted her train of thought. Elisabeth shot Gaultry a frightened look. "My mother—"

"We're expecting a caller," Gaultry reassured her. "You needn't be scared. But why don't you wait outside with Tullier while I answer it?" Elisabeth cast doubtful looks over her shoulder as Gaultry chivied her out onto the terrace, but did not argue openly, a small favor for which Gaultry was grateful.

Tamsanne's hand was raised to knock again as Gaultry opened the door. Looking up at her granddaughter, her head cocked inquisitively. She slowly lowered her hand.

"There you are. I almost thought—" Tamsanne's dark eyes, shadowed in the dim light of the hall, seemed uncharacteristically unsettled. "Well, never mind what I almost thought. Are you going to invite me in?" She was swathed in dark robes, a pouch bulging with leaves at her belt. Unlike Elisabeth, in her white beacon of a garment, Tamsanne was one with the shadows of the night. It must have taken the man Tullier had sent great effort to find her.

"We weren't sure when you would get here," Gaultry said. "I guessed you would be out."

Tamsanne nodded. "Your messenger roused half the garden staff trying to find me." She stepped inside. "So my visit here will be no secret, whatever prompted you to call me. I trust your need was truly urgent."

"Grandmother," Gaultry said, confused by this half-scolding greeting. It was still strange to think of this woman as her direct forebear, rather than as her great aunt. Tamsanne was so tiny, so dark and bird-delicate, where Gaultry and her sister were long-boned, fiery and robust. This woman had raised and nurtured them so tenderly, yet never once had she revealed their direct blood kinship. Her trust in this woman was so strong—and yet so fragile. "We've had an unexpected visitor. It's Elisabeth Climens. I'll need to get rid of her before we can talk."

Tamsanne raised her brows. "You are not alone? There is a woman here in your chambers?" A quiver of something like relief shook her voice.

"Yes, but it wasn't something I expected." Gaultry did not understand her grandmother's tone. "Because of what happened to make us call you, Tullier and I went to the temple to make prayer to the Twins. Elisabeth was here when we got back." Gaultry hastily sketched Elisabeth's account of Dervla's late-night visit to her mother. "The timing was a little odd. Elisabeth must have arrived here almost immediately after we left."

"So you have not in fact been here in this room in all the time since you sent for me?"

Gaultry could not see why her grandmother kept harkening to this point. Was she annoyed that Gaultry and Tullier had not waited in the room? "I tried to make sure we were back before you arrived," she said apologetically.

Tamsanne's reaction was not what Gaultry expected. She smiled, as if at an irresistible private joke. "So, you were not here at all then." She touched Gaultry's shoulder gently, almost as if she were welcoming her back after a surprise absence. "Yes, that makes better sense."

"Better sense than what?"

Tamsanne shook her head, her amusement passing. "Later. First we must consider these new threats. You say Dervla threatened Argat Climens through her children? How disappointing." Her expression darkened. "Our new High Priestess is truly old Delcora's child."

Gaultry hesitated, guessing that Tamsanne must have been remembering the threats Delcora had described in her notes, but the old woman added nothing further about either the High Priestess or her mother. "I need to speak to the girl." Tamsanne took a step toward the terrace. "Let me speak to the girl before you send her packing."

"Wait, Grandmother. The matter for which I called you—" Gaultry touched Tamsanne's shoulder and gestured toward the grate. She did not want her to talk to Elisabeth in ignorance of all that had preceded her arrival. "It lies there. Elisabeth was not my first visitor tonight."

The black sticks of crown lurked balefully, beneath the collection of fireplace implements Gaultry had set atop them. Tamsanne took a quick look and drew a hissing breath in between her teeth. "At least the iron stilled it. That was a clever thought. Has Elisabeth seen this?"

"I don't think so."

"Then call her in. We'll deal with her first."

Gaultry stuck her head out the terrace door. "Elisabeth," she called softly. The girl was a pale shape across the terrace, the dark shape that was Tullier close by her side. "My grandmother would speak with you."

Tamsanne, standing in front of the hearth, lit the mantel lamps as everyone trooped in. The room brightened, shadows fled. Gaultry was not sure if her grandmother had chosen that vantage point to conceal the contents of the grate or simply to brighten the room for her inquiry. Perhaps a little of both.

"Elisabeth Climens." The old woman gestured for the girl to sit. "I have seen you often enough at court these last few weeks. More often than one might have expected, now that I consider the facts. But no one thought to introduce us, so this will be our first true meeting."

Elisabeth curtsied deeply, and sat where she was told on the sofa. Somehow she managed to do it gracefully, even clutching the voluminous robe. Her cheeks were a little red, perhaps in the knowledge that no introductions had been made because she was a Duke's daughter, and Tamsanne, save for her appearance at Melaudiere's funeral, had presented herself at court from the marginalized position of a hedge-witch. "I'm honored—" she began, but Tamsanne, speaking over her, did not let her finish.

"You have attended many of Dame Julie's rehearsals. Along with that silly flower shearing the Prince commanded of me. I saw you at Melaudiere's last levee as well, before she became too ill to be seen in public."

"I have an interest," Elisabeth said.

"In the Common Brood, or in our magic?"

Elisabeth's posture went subtly wary. "I am my mother's fourth child," she said carefully. "The fourth child of a Duke is born to little purpose, saving several siblings' deaths. It pleased me to look upon women who have lived so long, knowing their life's purpose so fully."

Tamsanne smiled unkindly. "Yes," she said. "The burdens are indeed great, where one's birth is gentle." Turning her back on the girl, she crossed to the terrace doors. "Yet somehow, as I suspect you have begun to discover, every door is open to you." She pulled the doors closed and turned the latch, her wrinkled hand lingering on the metal.

Elisabeth cast Gaultry a doubtful glance, unsure what Tamsanne meant by these insults. Gaultry, confused herself by Tamsanne's unexpected unfriendliness, shrugged. Elisabeth raised her chin, defiant. Rather than responding to Tamsanne's cool tone, or trying to explain anything, everything—as Gaultry herself might have done—she chose to wait Tamsanne out, and see where she was leading. Gaultry did not know if she should admire the girl's mettle or fear for the girl in her ignorance. Outfacing Tamsanne was a tricky business at the best of times. Tamsanne almost always found some way to up the stakes for the other person without raising them for herself.

A charged moment of silence stretched, then the old woman resumed her questioning. "Tell me about the weapon. Describe the weapon Dervla spoke of to your mother."

Elisabeth looked surprised by the change of subject, and a little relieved. "I told Gaultry everything I heard."

"Did Dervla say she had passed it to the Envoy already, or did she hold it in reserve, for future exchange?"

"She still had it," Elisabeth said, then paused. "No. I'm not sure. The way she spoke . . . I can't be sure."

"Did the blade have a name?"

Elisabeth opened her hands helplessly. "She wouldn't have described the blade at all, but Mama would not believe Dervla had the upper hand on Lepulio without a compelling explanation."

"It is important," Tamsanne said patiently. "*Ein Raku?* Did she call it that?"

"I don't remember. She said only that it was old. Wanderer-old. Powerful enough to kill a god's child, and cursed with the strength to draw a god's vengeance from the hand of the one who wielded it."

Tullier had not overheard the blade's description as he stood outside on the terrace. His face went bleak. "No wonder Lepulio was so eager to assure me that I would hold the Bissanty Tielmaran throne for life."

Tamsanne gave him a sharp look for interrupting, then turned back to Elisabeth and nodded encouragingly. Gaultry shifted uneasily and glanced at her young visitor, who was visibly relaxing under her grandmother's now gentle questioning. When Tamsanne went mild and grand-motherly like this, it was not the time to lower one's guard. Poor Elisabeth was too inexperienced to suspect the trap. Tamsanne circled in—asking more questions about the knife, receiving the same answers. She rounded the sofa until she was almost in front of the girl.

When she struck, the transformation from grandmother to fury was irrationally alarming.

"Tell me, child." Tamsanne stepped so close that her fusty black robes almost touched Elisabeth's silk-swathed knees. "Do you know the name of the man your mother bedded to bear you?" Tamsanne grabbed Elisabeth's wrists, turning the girl's white palms upward. "Your mother bred herself like a pedigreed mare. Speculation is old and tired, trying to guess the web of power she sought to bring Vaux-Torres through these selective matings. Who do you think she chose to get you?"

Elisabeth did not know how to react. She would have taken refuge in shocked silence, but Tamsanne continued to push her back.

"I—I do not know." Elisabeth's eyes were wide with dismay. She tried to free herself from Tamsanne's grasp without struggling overtly, but the old woman's hold was like a vise. "My mother told me it was not yet my secret to learn."

"I could tell you," Tamsanne said, stark and cruel. She inscribed the goddesses' spiral on Elisabeth's palm. There was power in that simple gesture, power thick and strong enough to drain the candle's light, to thicken the room's air. Tamsanne drew in upon herself, frighteningly intense. The wrinkles deepened on her face. Gaultry could tell from Elisabeth's reaction that she felt a corresponding sharpening of power on her hand where the old woman had marked her. "You claim ignorance of your life's purpose, of the reason you were born. That may well be true. But a duchess has no obvious need of a fourth child, and your mother is legendarily vain of her body. Why would she welcome the burden of a fourth babe in her womb, if there was nothing to be gained by it?"

Gaultry, watching the girl's expression, was almost moved to inter-vene. She didn't understand why Tamsanne would taunt Elisabeth with her mother's infidelities, why she thought it mattered. Yet it must have been important, for Tamsanne to go to such pains to draw it out.

"I think my mother loved him," Elisabeth offered tremulously. "That is what she told me. She would not lie about that. After politics and war, she wanted a child for herself, for her love—"

"You know your mother best," Tamsanne said. "Perhaps it is even true that she would not lie to you. But think, child. When has she ever done anything important for a single purpose?"

Tears began to slip from Elisabeth's dark eyes. Embattled and silent, she made no move to brush them away.

"I could tell you your future," Tamsanne said, her tone once again gentling. She bent conspiratorially forward. "I could show you what your mother planned."

For a moment Elisabeth seemed hypnotized by the possibility. Then she jumped angrily to her feet, pulling even the train of her robes beyond Tamsanne's reach. "I don't need anything from you." She dashed away her tears. "I would far rather keep my mother's faith than owe anything to you." She wheeled on Gaultry. From the working of her mouth, the pulse at her temple, she was near an open display of grief, but she held it back. "Twins in me! I came here tonight with no expectation that you would help me. What I said will let you help yourself—at my mother's expense if you so desire it." She turned again to Tamsanne and threw back her head, an unconscious echo of her mother's arrogance. "Keep your prophecies. It is time for me to leave."

She crossed to the terrace doors, her composure slipping just as she reached them. "Elianté!" she whispered, barely loud enough to be audible. "Emiera! I have not deserved this." Hand on the latch, she bent forward and pressed her forehead against the cool glass panes, shoulders momentarily clenching as an unwilled sob escaped her.

Outside, the first grey light of morning touched the paving stones, the verdancy of the deer park. Today's bright dawn anticipated another beautiful scorcher of a day. The beautiful girl, with her sorrow, bent before it like the frozen embodiment of woe.

Then there was a whispery noise like an indrawn breath, and the moment was gone. Elisabeth opened the doors with an angry jerk, walked trippingly across the terrace, and disappeared among the trees.

When Gaultry moved to follow her, Tamsanne raised a restraining hand. "Let her find her own way home. Hinder her, and she may reconsider keeping this visit hidden."

"What was that about?" Gaultry said angrily. "Why were you so cruel? Elisabeth came here in good faith, whatever her mother's motives."

Tamsanne sighed. "She was your guest. You are right to resent me. Elisabeth is a good girl, and I am a foolish old woman. But the time for courtesies is fast passing. You called me here urgently. The messenger you sent stumbled across five meadows in the dark to find me. I have been waiting for something to happen. The Midsummer moon, the stars—everything in the sky this month points to the unfolding of grave events, with the Brood, yourself included, at its center. I thought your call meant those events had begun to move forward—and perhaps they have done so, in a manner I could not have predicted."

"What are you saying?" Gaultry asked. There was something in her grandmother's tone. Something conscience-stricken. Gaultry's heart jumped uneasily. Tamsanne, unlike old Melaudiere, had no inborn power of foreseeing. She had only her Rhasan deck. . . .

Tamsanne, reading Gaultry's expression correctly, allowed herself a weary nod. "I pulled a Rhasan card before I came here. It puzzled me—I thought at first it regarded you, my child, and that indeed was puzzling. But now that I have seen young Climens, I understand its true meaning."

"Did the Rhasan identify Elisabeth's father?" Gaultry blurted. What had prompted Tamsanne to open her deck? The magic there was so strong, so dangerous. What had Tamsanne expected to find? Why had she risked it?

"Her father?" Tamsanne shook her head. "Why ask the Rhasan that? The answer is obvious, just by looking at the girl. No, the cards revealed something of higher import."

"Obvious?" Gaultry muttered. "Only to someone as old as the hills." She could tell from the way Tamsanne spoke that she was not going to elucidate further.

"Behold." Tamsanne followed Elisabeth's steps and reached for the terrace latch. "Elisabeth's departure was more than it would seem." As she turned the metal handle, it broke off in her hand and crumbled into a palmful of grainy ash. "Magic-embrittled. I anchored this door with a powerful spell. Elisabeth should not have been able to open it so easily. And perhaps she would not have done so, if I had not riled her with insults and pushed her to show something of herself involuntarily." Tamsanne threw the ash outside on the paving stones and brushed her hands clean. "I'm sure she barely even knows what she's accomplished."

She pulled the terrace doors closed with an air of poorly suppressed excitement. "The girl who just walked out of this room will be Tielmark's next High Priestess. Isn't that astonishing? I'm sure it's not what Dervla expects, or she wouldn't be harassing the mother, setting her up to take the blame for her own covert actions."

"What?" Gaultry said, aghast. "Elisabeth will be High Priestess? Doesn't Dervla get to choose her own successor?"

Tamsanne shook her head. "It's in the Goddess-Twins' hands. It's true, a genuinely zealous priest usually knows who to anoint, but clearly that is not the case here, or Elisabeth, long since, would have been conscripted as one of Dervla's acolytes. Which informs me that Dervla and the girl's mother have made many mistakes, and compounded them, each orbiting alone in their own sphere. Knowing Argat Climens, who is not overfearful of the gods, I must doubt this was the intended outcome of her intriguing."

"Why didn't you tell Elisabeth?" Gaultry asked, angry and confused together. "Don't you think she should know?"

Tamsanne shook her head, still with that air of suppressed excitement. "Better she should hate me, than learn her fate out of its turn. She is clever, that one, and already knows this—look how she turned temptation aside when I offered it! Better I had done that myself, rather than opening my Rhasan deck tonight. The easy route is so often the wrong one.

"Poor Elisabeth!" Tamsanne's face twisting in an almost smile, the hidden, deeply amused expression Gaultry recognized from the moment the old woman had arrived and learned that her granddaughter was not the room's sole female occupant. "And what a relief it was to me to find her here. When I first saw the Rhasan's message, I imagined for an extremely confusing moment that the next High Priestess of Tielmark was going to be *you*."

chapter 19

A fragment of the fetish crown lay on the small round of paving stones at the foot of Gaultry's terrace. Tamsanne had surrounded it with figures scrawled in chalk. Small mounds of leaf and twig lay aligned within circles at the four cardinal points. Gaultry stood with Tullier on the terrace above, watching her grandmother work. Tamsanne made it seem like nothing, but Gaultry knew from past experience that each line, each placement, deepened the old woman's connection with the cluster of burnt twigs. The order was not predetermined. Tamsanne constantly adjusted, reacted, as she moved deeper into the spell.

To Gaultry, her grandmother's concentration was almost a tangible thing, as she wove an invisible basket of spell around the least corrupted twigs from the crown, working toward the moment when the first dawn light would touch the trees. Closing the spell just then would heighten its result.

To Gaultry's annoyance—no, to her anger—her grandmother had demonstrated no surprise when she had recounted the dream attack and explained exactly where she'd found the crown. Tamsanne had merely nodded and set to pulling the crown to pieces for the sample she'd need to trace its origin. If Tamsanne had known that such a thing could happen, she should have given warning.

If Tullier had not been standing by, Gaultry would have demanded an explanation. Judging when to share information, and what to do with that information once shared, was of course a delicate business. What, for example, was she to do with the information Elisabeth had brought her? Twist herself in circles, trying to prevent the Duchess of Vaux-Torres from doing a wrong thing? Set a trap, allowing the silly woman to act and hang herself? For all her anger and fear, she could see why Tamsanne might have hesitated to share her every suspicion. Still, if she had known something that might have protected Gaultry from the fetish-crown . . .

Tullier, at her side, was paying little attention to her grandmother's preparations. In the pale predawn light, she could almost imagine that he dozed, deaf to the rousing of her grandmother's power as he had been blind to the goddess-light in the hidden sanctuary.

Still, he wouldn't have been blind to the subtext of recent events. She wondered if he still wanted to remain in Tielmark on the heels of Elisabeth's revelation that Dervla claimed possession of an ancient, god-cursed blade. Even if Elisabeth had not been able to name it, there was no doubt that that blade was the *Ein Raku*, the Kingmaker blade Richielle had flourished on Princess Corinne's wedding day. Richielle must have given it to Delcora before she had departed from the Princess's court, and Dervla, as Delcora's heir, would have inherited the blade with the other accoutrements of the High Priestess's office.

When Tamsanne was done with her casting, she would once again remind the boy of his options.

Dawn's full color finally washed across the horizon, lighting the foliage of the trees and the rough masonry wall of the building at her back. Tamsanne, planted with her feet to either side of the crown's fragment, opened her palms outward to the morning like a tree with upraised branches. Gaultry, her hands on the terrace rail, felt her grandmother's grounding as the dawn colors melted and spread: a growing tremor in the earth, a frowning, unfriendly invocation of power. This was familiar— the course of Tamsanne's magic ran deep into the alien life of plants and their rootings, almost unfathomable in its breadth.

But there was something more here than merely the earth-bound, unwelcoming life of plants.

As the grounding deepened, something in Tamsanne's aspect altered. For a flickering moment, the roughness of bark, or husky fibers, swept across her skin. A suggestion only, as though the deep earth forces that were the root of Tamsanne's strength had momentarily revealed themselves. Then the suggestion of dark transformation was gone as if it had never been, and Tamsanne stepped away from the refuse of her casting.

For one moment, Gaultry thought she had imagined it.

Then, three steps away from the circle's center, Tamsanne stumbled and clutched at her throat.

Something had gone wrong.

Gaultry almost tripped down the stairs in her rush to catch her grandmother before she collapsed. "Tullier!" Her voice rose with fear. "Come and help me—we need to lay her on the grass."

He stared down, caught off guard. He had not felt the magical pulse, had not understood the significance of the old woman's stumble. Had not begun to react.

Alone, Gaultry dragged her grandmother off the chalk-marked paving stones onto the grass, pulling the cloth at Tamsanne's throat to loosen her collar. The old woman's face was suffused with blood, as though an apoplexy had overtaken her.

"Tullier!" She was in tears, chafing Tamsanne's wrists, hunting for a pulse. Belatedly, he sprinted down to help.

"Roll her on her side," he advised. "She'll choke on her tongue if you leave her like that."

"She needs to be touching the earth," Gaultry said, even as she followed his instructions and rolled Tamsanne off her back and onto one shoulder. She grabbed the arm on the upward side of Tamsanne's limp body, unfolded its fingers and raked them against the moss. "Feel that, Grandmother. Pull your strength from it!"

"What are you doing?" Tullier thumped his own palm against Tamsanne's narrow shoulders. "We need to get her lungs moving!"

"She has to touch the ground," Gaultry sputtered through rising tears. "She can only help herself if she's touching the ground!" Tullier rolled his eyes and let her continue, applying himself to a more mundane stimulation of Tamsanne's lungs and back. "Oh Goddess-Twins!" Gaultry prayed aloud. "Elianté Huntress! Do not take her! Please—not yet!"

Around them the trees brightened with sun. Tamsanne continued still and limp, defying their best efforts to recover her. "Keep going!" Gaultry cried.

The light reached the cap of the terrace rail, six feet or so above their heads, and something changed. Whether it was Tullier's ministrations, or Gaultry's, the old woman emitted a stuttering sigh. Her body stiffened, and she drew a short breath.

"Again," Gaultry demanded, frantic. "Do whatever you did again! Keep going!"

Tullier put his hand over hers, calming her. "Gentle! Don't you feel it? Whatever it was has peaked. She's coming back to us. Let her catch her breath."

They sat together by Tamsanne's side, watching the old woman fight to come to herself. Gaultry gently patted her shoulder, her dry, deeply wrinkled cheek. Beneath her intense relief, she found it frightening to see the unshuttered age of her grandmother's face, to realize the conscious will that kept the aged features animated with the appearance of vigor and strength. Looking into her grandmother's face, Gaultry was uncomfortably reminded of her last visit to old Melaudiere. The Duchess had commanded great magical power until almost the day of her death—indeed, it was the strength of the Duchess's final spell that had robbed her body of its last vital reserves.

The magic in the fetish-crown had been very strong. Had Gaultry unwittingly risked Tamsanne by similarly asking her to overextend herself?

Tamsanne's eyes slitted open. She glanced woozily upward, struggling for focus, her fingers reaching to touch Gaultry's face. "Listen to me—" she said haltingly.

"Put her on her back," Gaultry said. "Make her comfortable." She took Tamsanne's head into her lap. Her grandmother struggled to speak again, but no words came out. "Give yourself a moment," Gaultry soothed, smoothing her grandmother's hair. Then to Tullier, "She needs some water."

"I think she was poisoned." Tullier rose from his knees.

"Spell-poisoned," Gaultry answered. "I should never have let her near that thing, let alone asked her to spell it. I should have known it would be unsafe."

Tullier shrugged. "We needed answers. Whatever it was has peaked. She overcame it. The worst is past."

Gaultry inhaled a shuddering breath, biting back an angry response. He was too young to understand the real meaning of Tamsanne's greatly numbered years. Beneath her power, she was old and frail. It was a relief when he left to get the water. She did not want to be angry with him simply because he was too young to understand.

There was so much that Tamsanne knew. So much that Gaultry needed to screw up her courage and ask her.

Tamsanne, with a weak fluttering movement, indicated she wanted Gaultry's hand. Gaultry gave it to her eagerly, and then her heart spoke for her. "Draw strength from me. Draw strength from me to heal yourself." She bent her head and closed her eyes, picturing the flow of energy within her own body, vital and young, glowing with the green of the Goddess-Twins, the golden fire of Glamour. She pictured her grandmother's power, darker, more mature, maintained close to her body's core, only a weak thread extended outward to her fingers, connecting to her granddaughter's hand. As Gaultry gently traced that thread inward, Mervion's calm face, unbidden, came into view, Mervion back at the moment when she had bent over Tullier and recovered her power from him. Mervion had not needed elaborate incantations to pull back her strength; she had not needed incantations when she had, immediately afterward, wielded it outward like a weapon. All Mervion had needed was herself.

Gaultry pressed her grandmother's dry hand between her palms. *Have my strength, Grandmother, the way Tullier had Mervion's.* Even as she voiced the desire, she felt it coming true, felt power flowing from her young flesh into her grandmother's swollen old woman's hands. *Take it, Grandmother; take it and heal.* As her power funneled outward, something broke inside her, like a weakness in an old dam. For a breathless moment she felt giddy, weightless. Then her magic rose before her as it had never risen before, a thousand-faced beast, ready to twist and form as she willed it. She almost laughed, seeing in those faces old, constricted forms— herself puzzling to find the slenderest grasp upon power's form. In the swell of potential that awaited her command, she realized that all along, she had been asking questions outside herself, when she had needed only to look within. This was what Mervion had known so long; this was the knowledge that had given her sister so much power.

Now Gaultry had it too.

"Gaultry." Her grandmother's voice interrupted her wild mental career. "Gaultry, come back. You did what you set out to accomplish."

The colors spun, scintillating, obscuring her grandmother's words. Gaultry saw the spirits of animal after animal: a gull, an angry cat, a fierce wild boar. Images of every creature from which she had ever spirit-taken, trapped and mirrored within. As each rose in its turn, she cat-hissed, she mantled in crow-joy, she grunted—

Amid this chaos, a point of stillness emerged: a blossoming of color, a spot of purple. As she focused, she saw it was a purple orchid flower. It began to unfurl, to open, but instead of moving itself, it was as though all else around it was moving away. Gaultry, adrift in the sea of turbulence, reached for it, opening her hand to pluck it free. It was a struggle, but focusing her will, she seemed to slide forward . . . Her fingers brushed its stem.

All at once her eyes were open and the image of the flower dissipated. Above her was her grandmother's face, and beyond, the limitless blue of the morning sky. Somehow she was the one lying on the ground, her head in Tamsanne's lap, instead of the other way around.

"Grandmother." Her voice cracked in her throat. "What happened?"

Tamsanne brushed her cheek. "Your power broke loose when you gave me your strength, and you weren't quite prepared to control it. Twins be thanked, you revived me enough that I had the strength to guide you back to yourself. I sent you the image of the orchid flower—the emblem of Glamour's power. When you reached for the flower, pushing all else aside—you focused at last on your own magic, deep in your soul's center, and regained control."

She helped Gaultry sit up. Tullier, a tin cup in his hand, was standing by, pale with fright. "It's always been animals with you, my child. You've leaned on them, not trusting your own strength." Tamsanne's eyes burned down with an expression somewhere between pride and frustration. "I've watched you spirit-call to the beasts since you were a tiny child, never looking into yourself for that same strength. But you had to choose your own direction. What you chose gave you another kind of power. You learned that problems have many solutions if you do not rely merely on your own capacities and strengths. That is an important thing to remember, especially for one who is flushed with power. Tyrants seldom learn it." She took the cup from Tullier and made Gaultry drink. "Can you sit up? I want to tell you what I discovered, while it's still sharp in my head."

Gaultry tentatively lifted herself. A throbbing headache greeted the motion. "I'm listening," she said faintly. "But give me a moment before I move."

Tamsanne looked disapprovingly at Tullier. "I'd send you for more water," she said. "But this time I doubt you'd go."

"I have a right to know what you saw," Tullier said. "I'm not going to let you shut me out."

Tamsanne sighed, but did not persist. To Gaultry, she said, "Two sorcerers performed the spells of this fetish's making. The real question that yet needs answering—how much did each know of what the other intended? The magic was tightly woven, it's true, but contradiction lay beside contradiction as it would not have been if both practitioners were fully aware of each other's designs." She looked at Gaultry. "The fetish was intended for you, my dear. Its primary purpose was to drive you so deeply inside yourself that you would have been unable to wake up, unable to play a role in the games of power at court. Had its creators not been so secretive in their cross-purposes, it might have succeeded. But one merely desired you cataleptic. She secretly coded the time of your release. The other—the other one wanted you dead. Between these conflicting intentions, they unwittingly created multiple weak points in the spell. It was that, in part, which allowed you to escape."

Gaultry thought back to the intricate palace labyrinth in which her awareness of her dream had opened, the engaging pursuit that had driven her deeper into the maze. She remembered her delight, examining the animal-masked portraits, her fascination with the vivid carpet of living flowers. She had felt that hidden secrets were opening to her. She had wanted to see more. Yes, between the pursuit and the beauties, it was possible she might have remained, trapped within that realm. "What about the figure on the grey hill?" she asked. "The words she spoke? And what about the magic that almost killed you when you traced the spell?"

Tamsanne moved uneasily. "I cannot interpret everything. I can only tell you what the sorcerers who created the crown intended. As for the magic that attacked me—it was a simple enough spell. A syphon."

"A syphon?" Gaultry had never heard of such a thing, related to magic.

"A magical trap. It encouraged the success of my spell. Indeed, it heightened it beyond the limits of reason. My trace-spell was everything that I could have wanted, and more. The syphon drew so much of my strength into the spell that it would have killed me—either at the moment of its completion, or soon after. I learned much of what I wanted, but if you had not been standing by me, had not removed me from my grounding, forced my body to function—if you had not given me the strength of yourself—my life would have been ended."

Tamsanne frowned. She touched the black cloth of her sleeve, still stitched up in a mourning band, and made the goddess-sign. "One suspects, of course, that this is what must have happened to poor Gabrielle. She created a gift of incredible power for her Prince. When Benet's heir is born and laid within that cradle, the warding the child receives will be told in legend. But I find it hard to believe that it was Gabrielle's intention to pay for that casting with the vitality of her own life. I think she would have preferred a smaller spell, and the pleasure of being on hand to provide protection to the child in a more active and ongoing form."

"Who was it?" Gaultry said. "Who did this thing?"

Tamsanne shot a circumspect look at Tullier. "It is not so clear as I would like."

"You can talk in front of Tullier," Gaultry snapped. "If it wasn't for him, that damn crown might have killed me! He has earned the right at least to know who set it on me."

Tamsanne shrugged. "If you must have an answer, the base of the crown was certainly prepared by Dervla. The marking on the codes that would have released you was unmistakably hers. As for the sorcerer who wanted you dead—I don't know. A powerful talent, but secretive. My guess is one of Dervla's acolytes. Those people—they don't always share everything they know with their High Priestess. The competition to be the one the gods will choose to be her replacement is simply too intense."

Gaultry tried to picture the acolytes' faces. There was Palamar, of course. And Ilary, the acolytes' nominal head, a man near Dervla's generation in age. After that, the names and faces were less clear.

"Palamar must have a grudge against Tullier," Gaultry said dubiously. "And through Tullier, she might hate me. But it's hard for me to believe that Palamar would work against Dervla, even in secret. She always seems so obedient." Something else Tamsanne had said filtered through. "When did Dervla intend for me to wake?"

"The first night of the new Moon. After the end of the month, when the stars of the Sun-King's crown have spun down from their apex." Tamsanne offered a hand to help her up. Gaultry, rising shakily, noticed that while her grandmother appeared completely recovered from her ordeal, her own body was trembling and weak. "If she wants Vaux-Torres to deliver the boy into Bissanty hands, Dervla must be planning for the Bissanty to ritually slaughter your boy Tullier for her—thus getting around Benet's pledge of protection. Goddess grant me to know the logic of her thinking! What sort of ruler would Benet make, raised to the red throne of Kingship by a secret, oath-breaking murder? It would be a disaster for all of us." Tamsanne shook her head. "But at least we know when she will act. For the magic to take effect, the ritual must be aligned to the month's important astrological events, when the gods most closely watch our doings. Either the Ides, or the month's end, and the final waxing of the moon."

"The Ides," Gaultry guessed, shaken to hear Tamsanne so baldly state what she had feared. "Dervla told Argat that Benet would be back at court before the month's end. That's what Elisabeth heard her say. So

Dervla must expect her plot to be completed well before then, if she expects Benet to finish with the Lanai and return here from the border."

"The Ides are less than a fortnight away now," Tamsanne murmured. "That gives the Duchess of Vaux-Torres only a few days to organize Tullier's abduction. But in that space of days, Elisabeth's resolve to keep secrets from her mother might waver. That would return Argat the advantage of surprise."

"I don't think so. Elisabeth does not want to go against the Prince."

Tamsanne sighed. "I agree, to do so would not be her first intention. But you yourself have told me that the girl is not a liar, and her mother, as you well know, is a keen observer. Argat could have the information out of her before Elisabeth was aware she had given it."

"What should I do?" Gaultry said plaintively. "How can I protect Tullier? I'm being attacked even in my sleep. How can I guard against that?"

Tamsanne pressed her hand to her brow, a tired look overtaking her. She had not recovered so quickly as she made it seem. "You must remove the opportunity for Argat to take him. Leave Princeport. Take the boy with you and go. That would serve many purposes—not the least being to treat honorably with what young Elisabeth confided to you. Remove yourself and the boy, and Argat Climens will miss her chance to dishonor herself."

"The answer can't be that simple," Gaultry said. "Argat could follow. Or send men to pursue."

"Until Benet returns, the Duchess of Vaux-Torres is bound to Princeport on the word of her honor. Dervla can't ask her to break that, without breaking the very motive that might force Argat to obey her."

"I'm not supposed to be traveling either," Gaultry reminded her. "Benet ordered the Brood to Princeport for a reason."

"That didn't slow you the last time," Tamsanne said. "And didn't the Prince give you his sigil, allowing you to travel, in any case?"

The small leather shield she had received on the night of Julie's concert was in plain view on Gaultry's mantel. Tamsanne must have seen it when she'd lit the lamps. "Where would we go?" Gaultry asked. "Home to Arleon Forest? Out of Tielmark? I suppose we could take a ship and follow the Sharif south. I have been thinking of sending Tullier there in any case."

"Not that I'd agreed to go," the boy interjected. He had been following their talk with great interest. "But perhaps your grandmother is right.

I have no objection to putting some distance between myself and this *Ein Raku* knife."

Tamsanne considered the problem. "We do not know for certain that Dervla still holds the *Ein Raku*. She might have already passed it to the Bissanties, and any place that knife might be is not safe for you." She paused, thinking. "There is only one place you can go. You must bring the boy to Benet. That is the only place he will be truly protected."

"To Benet? Benet is riding hard for the western front," Gaultry said, dismayed. "And why would Tullier be safe with him?"

Tamsanne cast Gaultry an amused look. "Do you trust your Prince?"

"What are you suggesting?" Gaultry asked, insulted. "Of course."

"Then you must believe he would never agree to have this boy ritually slaughtered to advance his own claims to a King's crown. So on the Ides, or at the final waxing of Andion God-king's Moon, that is the only safe place for him. With Benet."

Martin had not wanted her at the western front. Not this year, he had said. The battle-lines are not clear. The chaos is too great. Stay at court, he had begged her, and discover there the Kingship answer that will end the Brood-curse. "What about finding another way to make Benet King?" she said. "One that doesn't demand a payment in blood? Someone needs to keep that in their mind's focus."

"Gaultry," Tamsanne said. "If I swear to you that I will work with Julie, that I will work with even Dervla—with all who remain of the Brood, will you agree to go?"

"Argat could still send her men after me. Or Dervla and her silent partner."

"Only if they think you have gone. Just think! Mervion could cover for you. Let everyone at court think you are still here—while you take the boy and go."

"And put Mervion at risk in my place? Why are you so eager to get rid of us?"

Tamsanne sat down on the first terrace step, suddenly deflated. "Because I am afraid," she said. "Because Dervla's accomplice, whoever that may be, works a magic that is tainted with dark and poisonous emotion, and his or her loyalty to Tielmark is so slender, he or she thinks nothing of murdering the Brood-members who could be Benet's strongest shield, if only they—we—could stop working at cross purposes. I believe Dervla's secret sharer murdered Gabrielle of Melaudiere. He or she—I think it was a she—must have feared Gabrielle's Kingship plans, or that she might have had the respect and power to unite us. Sadly, that suggests a Bissanty connection.

"Then there is the problem of the Kingmaker blade. I fear that an unwilling sacrifice to the *Ein Raku* would seal Tielmark to a brutal and ugly destiny. Dervla must think what she is doing is for the good—but she is wrong. A dark power is working by the High Priestess's side, turning her plans to its own purpose, and Dervla is too blinded by her own ambitions to see it."

Gaultry turned her grandmother's plan over in her mind. Somewhere within, she sensed the threat of a terrible, merciless logic. She wasn't sure what it could be, or who Tamsanne's plan would endanger. If not Tullier or herself, who?

"Even if I agree to go, I don't think Mervion will want to cover for me."

"You would deny her a chance to serve the Prince? Deny her the chance to come to your protection? It is no more than what you would do for her. Denying her is not a kindness, if that is what you think you are offering."

"You didn't suffer that fetish crown," Gaultry said coldly. "This is not about selfishness. I don't want Mervion at risk for something so serious as that."

Tamsanne shrugged, a little uneasily. "The Brood-blood runs equally in both of your veins. Mervion is at risk already. It will please her more than you understand, to turn that risk to a clear purpose. And if I am wrong—Mervion deserves at least the right of refusal."

"All right," Gaultry said. On that last point, she could not argue. "On condition that Mervion freely agrees, I will take Tullier west." She turned to Tullier. "We'll supply ourselves down in Princeport. No need to be obvious, heading into town with traveling packs. Go in and see what you can bundle together, without being too conspicuous."

He nodded and disappeared inside.

"We'll only go if Mervion agrees to cover for me," Gaultry reiterated. "And right now I hardly believe I'll be able to convince her to do that."

"We shall see." Tamsanne stared at her granddaughter as though trying to understand her hesitancy. "She loves you, you know. This new bond she has with Coyal has not ended that—any more than have your own feelings for the Stalkingman." Gaultry dropped her own gaze—until Tamsanne took a step to follow Tullier inside.

"Wait," Gaultry said. There was a last question she needed answered.

"Grandmother, young Elisabeth came here for help, but she went away with new questions. You told her you knew the name of her father."

Tamsanne frowned. "If Elisabeth herself was not ready to know, I'll not be the one to gossip. But the riddle is not a hard one. Argat Climens is an intelligent woman, but unbridled in vanity and ambition. Her children were born to be ornaments to her glory. It only takes a little thinking to know who she'd choose to father her children."

Gaultry shook her head. "I'm not asking to know about Elisabeth's father."

Tamsanne raised her brows.

"I want to know to about *my own* grandfather." The blood rushed in her ears at her effrontery. Tamsanne's air of detachment vanished, replaced for an flashing instant by an expression of naked pain. "I—you may not wish to tell me, but after what happened—Grandmother, I almost lost you this morning. When I was at Jumery Ingoleur's—something he said made me need to know. I know you destroyed the Ingoleurs' blood-link at the barrow at his manor. I do not believe that you would have broken his land-tie without good reason—you have taught me such things are infinitely precious, and as the years pass there are fewer such chains back into the past, unbroken. So I think—I think what he said about grandfather must be true."

A long moment passed between them. Tamsanne turned her back. Gaultry waited, terrified that Tullier would return too soon, interrupting them and giving Tamsanne an excuse not to answer.

"What did he say?" Tamsanne asked wearily. "What ugly thing did he tell you?"

It was Gaultry's turn to pause. *Your grandfather was a dead man when Tamsanne used him to get with child.* "He said—he said that grandfather was not alive when you—when he—when my mother. . . ."

"He thought I got your mother in my belly by riding on a corpse?" Tamsanne made a small sound, deep in her throat. A choked laugh. "What is it you have been thinking? Sieur Jumery's land-tie ran deep, but his imagination ran shallow, and he was predisposed to believe that anything he could find about me would be ugly. He could hardly have been more wrong. Your grandfather was a beautiful man. Tall and golden. Fiery like the sun. A huntsman in Gries Village, the place where I was born. His name was Jarret. He was not like the men you and your sister have chosen. Here at court, he would have been called simple. Jarret never left the woods. They were his home. His destiny." When she turned back to

Gaultry, somehow she had recovered her humor. "Did you *truly* imagine you were a child of necromantic origin? After all I have taught you to fear such things?"

"I did not know what to think," Gaultry said humbly, softened by her grandmother's smile. "However I turned it in my head, it did not make sense."

"You are like your grandfather in many ways," Tamsanne said softly. "You and your sister together. More ever than your mother was. She— she might have been a clever woman, but there was a wildness in her that kept her from so many things. I can tell you now, your likeness to my Jarret has given me much secret pleasure."

"I am like him?" Gaultry asked shyly.

"Like you, he was a hunter, and greatly skilled."

In her contentment at learning these things about her grandfather, Gaultry did not realize until much later that her grandmother had not said anything as to why Sir Jumery might have drawn the wrong conclusion about her mother's conception. Indeed, thinking on it, she realized that Tamsanne must have told her so much deliberately, to distract her from this line of thought.

She should have known better than to promise she would leave Prince-port if Mervion agreed to stand in for her. Mervion, when she found her in her city lodgings with Coyal, was more than ready, she was eager.

"I will stand for you," she said, her eyes agleam. "And Coyal—by my magic, Coyal will stand for the boy—look—the dog already likes him. Who will know the difference?"

Gaultry looked doubtfully at Coyal's slim but well-muscled figure, the gleaming wreath of his blond hair, the sturdy shape of his head and jaw. As he and Tullier bent together over the boy's thin, half-grown dog—it had gained weight in the palace kennels but still retained its woeful hungry look—Gaultry did not see how it could be possible to mistake the one for the other. The knight was not overtall, it was true, but he was nothing like Tullier. Most obviously, he had come fully into his man's figure, leaving gangly adolescence well behind him. "They are not much alike," she said aloud.

"No," said Mervion, "that is true. But no one will know the difference after I have disguised him. The boy's dog—that will be a nice touch. A further level of misdirection."

Already, her plans outpaced the things that Gaultry had thought of to make this work. If the dog was here—it was because she and Tullier had not finished the argument of whether to take or leave it.

At least trusting the dog to Mervion and Coyal would settle *that* small point.

"The dog should stay with us," Coyal volunteered, friendly and concerned. "The border will be no place for it, without proper training." A compelling logic that Gaultry had failed to present to the boy herself. He had been struck with an uncharacteristic boyish worry that the dog would be miserable without him.

"Why are you doing this?" Gaultry asked her sister. "I have told you about the most recent attack—it could be very dangerous. You may have to use your magic in ways you won't like."

Mervion critically held up Gaultry's new blue court dress, to see how it would fit her. "I need to," she said. "For Coyal and for myself. Coyal must prove his loyalty to Tielmark. I—" Mervion turned at last to look Gaultry in the face. "I was angry with you earlier. I can hardly describe how abandoned I felt, when you left me alone at court, and hied off in aid of Martin."

"It would not have been my first choice," Gaultry said defensively. "And it would not have been my choice at all, if you had only told me half your Glamour-soul was locked in Tullier's body."

"It was foolish not to tell you," Mervion admitted. "At first, you were so busy, I thought you did not need the distraction. Then later—it was too late."

"Mervion," Gaultry said. "I have made many mistakes too. I have demanded too much—"

Her sister shook her head, cutting her short. "I have felt that sometimes, but Coyal often reminds me, in these troubled times, it is not quite so. Our lives will not be our own, until the Brood-prophecy is over. That is why I must do this—why I want to play this charade."

Gaultry moved to embrace her. Mervion freely returned the hug. "Travel well," she whispered. "May the Twins ride with you."

"Take care of Tamsanne," Gaultry said. "She is weaker than she lets on."

The rest of the business was quickly settled. Coyal took Mervion's hand as Gaultry and Tullier descended the dark staircase down from their apartment into the cobbled yard below.

"Go safely," he told them, "and may the gods ride with you."

Gaultry, trying to set aside her dislike for him, tried to return this with a gracious farewell.

In the street outside, Gaultry glanced up the thoroughfare toward the palace. The far towers gleamed under the early morning sun, bright and clean and welcoming.

She sighed, and turned away. For now her road lay away to the west.

"Are you ready to ride, Tullier?"

He nodded, eager.

"We'll start out on hire horses," she told him. "I'll wait to use the Prince's sigil until we're farther out."

chapter 20

n the strength of the Prince's sigil, they were able to commandeer
horses all the way to the edge of the Bissanty Fingerland. Four days of
riding, a day of rest, and another day of riding. Gaultry was saddlesore at
the end of it, but beginning to believe they really would reach the battlegrounds at Llara's Kettle before the Ides were on them.

But when they reached the border, things did not go so smoothly
there as Gaultry had expected. The Tielmaran High Road ran through
the Bissanty Fingerland to reach Haute-Tielmark. The two-hundred-year-
old terms of the peace Briern-bold had secured against the Bissanty guaranteed it would remain open to free passage. Yet on the morning of their
arrival—the border was closed.

The Tielmaran border guards were philosophical about the closure.
"It shut the day Benet and his men went through," the senior man told
them. "The order came down from Bassorah just a few hours after the
Prince had already crossed over. I'm sure that wasn't what the Emperor's
officers intended!" When they showed him the Prince's sigil, he sent a
man to get them refreshment.

"It happens this way every summer," he assured them, in response to
Gaultry's expression of outrage. "The Emperor shuts it down—just for a
week or so—to keep us on our toes."

"We're supposed to be at Llara's Kettle for the Ides!"

The man counted the days on his fingers. "You might make it yet,"
he said, doubtful. "It's been over a week that the border's been shut. That's
unusually long. You could wait—and it could reopen tomorrow, or the

next day, or the day after. Otherwise, you'll have to travel the long way
round, skirting the Fingerland border."

"Or we could just cut across, at a place where there aren't Bissanty
guards." Gaultry had done that very thing, earlier in the spring. "I've done
it before, easily enough." Almost getting gored to death by the wildlife
didn't quite count as a difficulty; that ill fate had not, after all, actually
come to pass.

"In high summer?" the man scoffed. "You won't make it two miles
in. It's green-fly season. Those bastards haunt the low grounds, thick as
the air itself. During the day, they swarm heavy enough to carry a grown
man off. And at night, the air is choked with mosquitoes." He shrugged.
"Try it if you must, if your business is so important. But go south a fair
way before you do. The Bissanties keep an eye on things, at least for the
first couple of miles."

This was familiar, from her last visit to the Fingerland.

"How do the Bissanties avoid the flies?" she asked.

"Smudge-pots, burning all day and night. Makes the main postings
easy enough to see, but don't let that fool you. They do send some men
scouting, with mesh bags on their head and fly-bane rubbed all over.
When the Emperor sends word that the border is closed, they take the
order serious."

Gaultry thanked him. He ordered them fresh mounts from his stables
on the strength of the sigil, then watched rather dubiously as they
mounted up.

"If I see them coming back this way alone, it won't surprise me," he
warned them. "Those flies—they're something fierce, and a fine piece of
horse flesh—it only draws them worse."

"Then we'll send them back before we go over," Gaultry said. Later,
she would regret having been a trifle haughty. "Someone will reprovision
us on the other side."

"That'll do," the senior man nodded. "Loose the reins, and they'll try
to come running back here in any case. The land is thin out this way—
they know where to come when they want a full manger of feed."

The border guard had not exaggerated about the flies. At noon, Gaultry
decided they were far enough south to make a first attempt. She'd thought
they had found a good place to cross over: the last Bissanty military posting, clearly marked by the smoke of its smudge-pots, was far behind them,

and the ground across the border, though furrowed with low, muddy black trenches, did not look so different from the land on the Tielmaran side. The attempt with the horses was a complete failure. Almost immediately after they crossed into the Fingerland, a cloud of biting flies descended, bottle-green and golden-eyed, with wings that let off a teeth-grating whine. Though scarcely larger than the nail of Gaultry's smallest finger, they were fierce biters. They went for skin, for scalp, for the tender flesh at their mounts' noses and eyes. Gaultry had never experienced anything like the insect ferocity with which those flies assailed them—and she found it impossible both to keep control of her horse, and to protect herself.

They retreated in ignominy.

"We'll try again without the horses," Gaultry gasped, determined.

"I'm not eager," Tullier admitted.

"He said it was better without horses."

"No," Tullier said. "He only said it was *worse* with them. He didn't use the word better."

They rode on another couple of miles, looking for a ridge of higher land that might aid them in their passage. Then they repacked their equipment to be carried afoot. "We should tie up the horses," Tullier said. "We'll need them when we come back here."

"We aren't going to need them," Gaultry said stubbornly. "And we can't tie them up here if we aren't coming back."

"We will be."

"We won't. Elianté's Spear! Even if we do come back here, we'll still have the Prince's sigil. We can keep heading south, and beg fresh mounts from the farmers in the next village when we come to it."

"Will there be villages?" Tullier asked. "So close to the border?"

"It's not going to come to that," she said confidently. "We'll cross successfully here, and that will be the end of it."

I never realized the Bissanty border here was so well defended." Tullier had been right, and they were back where they started—only this time they had no horses, and they were half a day's walk or more from the High Road.

"I think you *wanted* to get rid of the horses," Tullier groused. She gave him a sharp look, then saw that he was only trying to make the best of the situation. He knew she hated riding.

"A small consolation has to be that no one from the capital is likely to follow us out this way." Gaultry looked around at the scanty country. The land by the Fingerland border was desolate and scruffy, with un-cleared growth under the trees—the mark of thin farming. "And we *will* reach Llara's Kettle going this route—eventually."

Tullier, his face red at the scalp with bites, nodded agreement. "From the map, we'll lose four days of travel if we have to march all the way around the low land," he said. "Maybe five. Less if we find remounts."

"Either way, we'll be on the road come Andion's Ides," Gaultry said worriedly. "Though I suppose there's no help for that, with the High Road closed." It was maddening. Traveling due west, crossing the Bissanty Fin-gerland took well short of a full day's ride. Going around the long way—Tullier was right. They'd lose the better part of a week.

But there was nothing for it. The road south toward Pontoeil along the Fingerland border was grassy and thin, trending toward high land well above the swamp. With the border so recently closed, they were among its first travelers this season—and most certainly they were the first with-out horses.

"We'll beg some food from the farmers in the next village when we find it." They were carrying provisions only for a few days, but this was a game-rich land. They wouldn't starve before they found fresh mounts.

Or so she continued to assure herself, for the first two dreary days of walking.

By the eve of the second day, they had yet to find a village. Worse, they had lost their way. What Gaultry had thought was a wood turned out to be a dark, round knoll. *Where on earth are we?* she wondered, stopping and staring at the fast-moving grey sky above. Night had overtaken them, and they had still found nowhere to rest. She did not like the featureless yet rolling land, with its dark trees and scraggy fields. And the road—she feared they'd lost the road a little after dark.

"We're lost," Tullier said at last, waiting for her to move.

"We're lost," she admitted. "But let's walk on a ways. I don't fancy making camp on this ground."

They circled the knoll and found themselves at the edge of a shallow hollow, long since plowed over, now abandoned. The cupped ground had the appearance of a cauldron with sloping sides. Several upright stones stood in its center, a collapsed head-piece lying between them, like an old burial mound where the earth had been cleared away, leaving only the stone supports. There seemed to be no choice but to cut across it, though the hollow itself was so still and silent, cut away from the winds that raced though the clouds above, that Gaultry felt deeply uneasy. It took them an unfathomably long time to descend, all the while the shadows slipping and sliding around them inexplicably, as fast-moving clouds above them swept high over head. It was almost airless in the shallow hollow's bottom where they had to walk, giving an unpleasant sensation as they looked up at that swift sky. The tall, thick grass on the hollow's floor was wet and lank; it felt clammy and horrible to walk through.

"This is too weird," Gaultry said, a pricking feeling rising at the back of her neck. The way the layers of clouds flew overhead seemed almost unearthly, unnatural. She supposed it must be a visual illusion, caused by the evenly sloping angles of the hollow's sides, but Tullier, from his expression, obviously agreed with her. "Let's climb to the top of that knoll," she suggested, "and take our bearings from there."

He readily assented.

The knoll was covered with rough tussocks of grass, making the climbing easy, though sweat had broken out under Gaultry's shirt by the time she reached the top, a little behind Tullier. It was a tremendous relief coming out in the open—coming out in the open and once again feeling the air moving against her face.

"What is it?" she asked, sensing something odd in his stance.

"Just look," he whispered.

The wind that had been surging above them since dark had at last swept back the edge of the cloud, revealing the great fathomless bowl of the night sky and all its rich splendor of stars.

"Elianté's Spear!" Gaultry swore as the sickle and dog star swept into view from under the clouds' canopy. "We've come totally out of our way. We should be heading west by now—and we've been walking due south."

But Tullier's eyes were not on the stars. The knoll sat at the edge of an enormous plain. A broad river skirted it, curving away in a wide semicircle along the plain's southern edge, otherwise the vast outlines could be distinguished only by their blackness from the blue emptiness of the air. After their long trek through the intimate snarl of hill and vale, all that emptiness was overwhelming.

"We're not alone," Tullier murmured. "Look there."

A little farther on, in the angle formed by a hill and the edge of the plain, a single fire flared, almost out of sight around the hill's edge. Figures clustered around it, too distant to be distinct. "Traveling folk?" Gaultry said. "Or maybe drovers." Some of the strangeness she'd felt in the cauldron hollow slipped from her. "We can camp with them, and move on in the morning. Maybe even bargain with them for mounts."

"Will it be safe?"

"Of course it will be safe," Gaultry said, annoyed. "This is Tielmark, not Bissanty. We just offer the traveler's sign, and they give us welcome. The least they'll provide will be the protection of their fire."

The boy hunched his shoulders, misliking the rebuke. If he had further concerns, he left them unspoken.

They made their descent safely, but had hardly advanced more than a few paces along the flat when a pair of ragged dogs came hurtling toward them, barking angrily. Shrill childish voices called out from the direction of the fire, and two or three short figures jumped to their feet.

Gaultry had been mistaken in assuming that the people by the fire were travelers. They were, she now saw, farm children from the local villages, keeping guard over the village horses. During the hot summer weather, the horses were driven out at night to graze, avoiding the daytime flies. She had seen the same thing in Paddleways, her home village, where driving the cows out before nightfall and back again at first light was considered a great treat among the younger children—a responsibility to be aspired to.

"Let me introduce us," she told Tullier. "You'll be a little strange to them." She made a warning sign to the dogs that quickly quieted them.

There were seven boys and two girls, all visibly relieved when Gaultry made the traveler's sign and shared her name and Tullier's. When they heard Gaultry's intended route, they were at once sympathetically, childishly dismayed. "You've come miles off your route," said Machen, the eldest of the boys and clearly the leader. "Perhaps the pine-witch fuddled you. If you want to reach Haute-Tielmark proper, you'll have to take the track west toward Pontoeil and turn north at the Brekker Crossing. But that's best left for the day." He glanced significantly into the darkness, and then back at Gaultry and Tullier. "Safer, you know?" He winked, as one elder to others, and gave a quick glance at the younger children. From his talk, Gaultry guessed that they had been telling each other ghost stories before she and Tullier had appeared. She could see Tullier looking them over as he opened out his pack and settled, barely able, at least to Gaultry's eye, to conceal his disbelief. It took her aback a little too, to see the children's relaxed and easy manners. Clearly the battles that raged through Haute-Tielmark did not touch them here.

Gaultry spread her cloak beside a well-cropped bush and tried to settle herself. It had been a long day, with many compounded mistakes. Her sense of how far they had traveled was very confused. The campfire, constructed mainly of grass, twigs, and dried manure, burned irregularly, casting rapid flashes of light beyond the circle of settled children and their dogs. Sometimes, there would suddenly emerge from the encroaching dark the face of a horse, bay or dun-colored or black, and one repeatedly seen mare with a single, inquisitively quirked eyebrow marked in black. After staring speculatively for a moment at the fire, each horse would snort, blink, and withdraw, returning to graze.

From the feel of the turf, Gaultry guessed that the plain had been experiencing a dry spell. The ground beneath her was pleasantly warm, and the air had a fine grainy summer smell. Tullier finished arranging things in his pack, and came to sit with her.

As the children resettled, one of the boys quickly finished a story about a water-sprite. Small wonder that their arrival had frighted them! Machon turned to a smaller boy named Phili as he made himself comfortable under his sheepskin.

"So you actually did see one of them little people, did you?"

"No, I didn't see him. You can't really see them," Phili protested. "That's not how it works. But I heard him. Really I did. He was in the holly tree. He made the green berries move, and he threw down a handful when I turned my back."

The others laughed at his insistence, disbelieving, and he turned a little pale, until Mechilde, an older girl with a little brother, interrupted their chatter. "I believe him," she said. "But you *can* see them. If they want you, they'll show themselves."

"What do you mean?" Tullier asked. Mechilde paused, considering whether or not she should answer this stranger. "Water-sprites and holly-tree goblins," Tullier scoffed. "You're making it all up."

"You're not from around here," the girl-child said softly. "How would you know?"

"The gods are all around us, and I have seen magic worked," Tullier said doggedly. "If there were ghosts and sprites and soul-weavers too, the world would be a crowded place."

A strange, sharp, sickening cry resounded twice in quick succession across the river. After a moment of chilled silence, it repeated, farther away.

Gaultry recognized it for what it was just as Machen said stoutly, "That was a heron." He met Gaultry's eyes across the campfire. "We're just a little too near the river here. The horses like it, and we won't go near the water until daylight. We're safe enough—but a little too close." He picked up a stick and stuck it into the fire, sending up sparks. Then he looked at Mechilde. "You've got to tell us now. What makes you think you can see them?"

Mechilde paused, and patted her brother's sleeping shape under the rough wool blanket that covered him. When she spoke, it was directly to Machen, as though Tullier, Gaultry, and the rest were nowhere near.

"You know the big stone by the slip where they water the horses?"

Machen nodded.

"I was there on Midsummer night. I'd been braiding crowns for the bonfire. Mama called for me and I left my cutting knife on the stone. I went back for it. It was dusk already but I went back for it anyway.

"I had found my knife, and I was just bending down to the water for a drink when I heard it. Like a woman's voice, calling my name. 'Mechilde, pretty Mechilde, wants a cleaner blade, a cleaner edge.' Then I looked out over the water and I saw it.

"You know how the lilies grow there? The white lilies in the shelter of the lee shore? I looked over there and a woman's face was rising out of the lilies. Her hair was all in coils and her fingers were white and narrow, like unopened buds. She held a slash of silver in one hand and her face was pale and calm.

"I didn't stop running until I saw the Goddesses' double-coil atop the Midsummer pile. Mama asked me what was wrong, but I wouldn't tell her." Mechilde's pretty face dropped. "Maybe I should have taken the knife. They say the fairy-blades make you a master crafter."

"Or maybe the water-lady would have pulled you under with those slim white hands!" Machen said, alarmed. "It's a good thing you ran."

"I know." Mechilde looked into Tullier's still doubting eyes, her expression adult and tired-looking. "But I think maybe I would have died happy. The drowned here always come to shore with a smile on their face."

"Drowned people are ugly." Tullier's voice was harsh. "There's nothing slim or nice about a water-dead corpse."

. . .

Gaultry awoke abruptly, finding herself swiftly, unwillingly awake. A current of fresh air brushed her face. Morning was beginning. She could feel it in the earth.

In the east it had begun to grow a little light. The surrounding scene had already become visible, if only dimly. The pale grey sky shone bright, tinged across with blue; stars winked their faint light or faded; the ground was damp and leaves were covered with crystal dewdrop sweat. The day ahead would be blazing hot and humid. Gaultry's body responded with a mild, joyful trembling, making her even more awake. She got briskly to her feet, trying not to disturb Tullier, who had cuddled his back up to hers sometime during the night.

The horse-children slept the profound sleep of the young and innocent about the dying fire's embers. The horses—including the inquisitive mare with the black eyebrow—were scattered, some grazing lazily, some standing guard above sleeping foals, some ranged away toward the brake of trees and scrub that marked the river's edge.

The river. Mechilde's story from the night before came back to her— the lily-white lady and the call of the water. Unlike Tullier, she had not dismissed the children's stories. Tielmark—in many ways Tielmark was less settled than Bissanty, less colonized by law and man. The local people knew what to fear; what stones to worship, what spirits to propitiate. If the children were chary of the river, they probably had good reason.

The river. A whim to see it for herself possessing her, Gaultry left the fireside quietly, and walked out toward the line of scrub. At first the going was easy, but then the summer growth became so thick and lush that she had to hunt for a place where the horses had broken through. A familiar tangle, she thought, pushing aside the last branches, the silver flash of water luring her on. The farmers near Paddleways left the river's edge similarly guarded to minimize the chance of coming up on it unexpectedly.

As she did now. Passing a clump of osiers, she broke through to a muddy bank, torn in many places by hoof marks. She caught her breath, realizing after a confused moment where she really was.

She and Tullier had come *very* far out of their way. She glanced at the stars. How could they be here? Afoot, denied the relief of horses? It simply was too far; it wasn't possible!

The edge of the water was normal enough. The torn mud bank gave way to a dense reed marsh; the reeds, to water. But beyond that—beyond that the broad stretch of the river itself was a glossier, more purple blue than the paling sky above could have created. The surface curled and dimpled, as if under irregular currents above and below its surface. Across the water—across the water the trees were writhing: slowly, sensuously, shifting colors fleeting among the foliage.

Somehow she and Tullier had traveled all the distance to Tielmark's southern border, and she was looking directly across the border river, the Great River Rush, into the Changing Lands.

Gaultry was familiar with the Changing Lands. She had spent her childhood in a cottage that overlooked that mysterious border, that magically haunted country. She cursed—she should have recognized the river they were describing as the Great Rush from the tenor of the children's stories. Should have guessed it from their fear of the night water, of the lily-woman. But that fear—that fear had been so familiar to her, she'd been unable to recognize it. Of course she felt comfortable with the horse children, at ease. They were border people like herself—they knew to fear and respect the boundary of the magical lands. No wonder they spoke of smiling corpses. Of fairy-blades, that made for master craftsmen. No wonder—no wonder Tullier had not been able to understand.

The river was narrow here. Tamsanne's cottage—Gaultry's true home—lay very far east, downriver, where the river widened and grew less turgid with the Changing Land's magic. The gloss of purple in the stream was so deep here, so intense.

She stared across at the far bank—a danger, she knew, but in this dark dawn hour, after so much travel, so much time spent from home, she could not resist. As always, as she stared, the far bank seemed to spin closer, to advance. She began to be able to make out the textured bark of the trees, the dappled color of the ground. What she had taken for a narrowness in the river was instead a sandy spit of land, overgrown with spindly trees, the river glinting beyond it. She could see the delicate shivering leaves, grown rangy from surviving repeated springtime floods. She could see the movement of the branches. . . .

And then—then she could see them. Pale shapes beneath the thin canopy of leaves, pale shapes among the branches. Attenuated figures, with flowing hair and naked skin. Her vision sharpened again, and she could see the tiny white and blue flowers snarled in their hair, men and women both, silent as they moved but somehow also laughing. Dryads.

She was up to her hips in the water before she even realized that she'd been drawn forward. The river bottom here was churned by the horses, half muck and sand, and very shallow. The water was a warm caress on her skin. She took another step forward, and another. The water did not deepen as she moved forward. She knew she should fear a drop, a hole underfoot. There were lilies and fleshy green pads around her, with curling stalks and spiky closed buds like white fingertips. But something was calling her now, something she had to see—

The spit of land loomed ever closer. Three dryad maids danced round a thin silver birch at its closest reach. Human once, they had fed their souls to the trees, and would never leave the Changing Lands. Gaultry did not wish to join them, and yet still something called, and she moved even closer.

Pink and golden dawn touched the far east of the sky. She did not have much time—time for what? The water was at her breast, her hands spread in fans on the surface as she steadied herself. The madness of what she was doing—she did not understand the impulse that was driving her. She thought of Mechilde, the water-sprite offering her the silver knife, the crafter's knife, her heart's desire. It was as though some high, distant music was calling her, as though something in her resounded to it. Once more she looked across to the spit of land, the pale water shining behind it through the trees, the transparent shifting figures.

A single figure broke from the dancing, and came, laughing, to join her in the water.

His hair was fiery red and golden—woven thickly with moss and flowers, but still fiery, mingled with the green. His face was turned to his dancing partners, he was almost off-balance as he slipped deeper into the stream—so shallow, no deeper than his supple hips. *Will you call for me?* Gaultry asked, as he waded closer toward her. *I have no need of a crafter's knife, and my heart's desire is far away, riding in battle on the western border. So what is it you think you can offer me?*

Then he turned, extending his hand toward her, and Gaultry found herself staring into something very like her own face.

The children were still huddled around the embers of the fire, deeply asleep. Mechilde and her little brother Alois had curled together against one furry dog's belly: the dog raised his head halfway and glanced at Gaultry intently as she approached.

I just want to look, she told the dog. Mechilde's pure young profile was silhouetted against his dark belly fur: the pretty, stubborn mouth half open, her uncombed hair in matted tangles. Her brother nestled tightly against her thin chest, asleep with his thumb in his mouth. Both children were utterly at peace. Gaultry, pierced by an emotion she did not understand, nodded at the dog, turned quietly, and went over to Tullier to pick up her pack.

"Let's go," she whispered. "Before they wake."

"Don't we want to ask them for their horses?"

She shook her head. "No. We just need to go. Don't ask me why."

The track Machen had told them of the night before headed off to the northwest, shrouded with smoky mist. Under their feet, the damp grass sent up a sweet scent. They had hardly gone a mile when the sun tipped up over the horizon in its full glory, painting the bushes and grasses of the broad meadow first brilliantly red, then glitteringly golden. At that first touch of sun, the birds all came awake at once, singing, chattering, quavering.

They heard a shout from their rear, and suddenly they were overtaken by the racing drove of horses, refreshed after the night. There was Machen, high on a black-faced mare, and Phili, on a dish-faced yearling at his side. Of Mechilde, Gaultry caught only a glimpse of her hair, and an impression of little Alois, his arms clamped tightly around his sister's waist. The children were laughing, making a last display, showing their youthful prowess as they cantered, bareback, across the meadow to the edge of vision. Tullier and Gaultry, side by side, watched them until they disappeared behind a tall line of trees.

"If the Lanai penetrate this far, that will be the end of their night camping," Tullier said.

"Tullier," Gaultry said. "There's something I need to tell you. Remember the children's story about the pine-witch?"

The boy nodded, his eyes lighting with scorn.

"They were telling the truth," she said. "We've come miles out of our way. That river we camped at last night was Tielmark's south border."

"That's not possible," Tullier said. "You must be mistaken."

Gaultry shook her head. "I'll admit, yesterday it did not seem I could have found my route along the High Road at noontime on a summer's day. But in this, I know I'm right. Something strange is going on. Something strange that's fuddling our route-finding."

Tullier looked suddenly grim. "Are you sure?"

"On my heart," she said.

"That's not good news. Tomorrow is the Ides. Weren't we supposed to find someplace safe to hole up, coming onto that day?"

"We were," Gaultry said. "Now . . . now I don't know."

Book III

▼

THE MOON IN ANDION'S SKY

Prologue:

▼

THE IDES AT THE LIGHT OF DAWN

Elisabeth **rapped on Princess Lily's door. "Your Highness?" she**
called. "My lady?" She exchanged a glance with the footman who had
escorted her to this inner sanctum from the public rooms of state. The
footman, a slender man with wispy red hair and an annoying complacent
manner, shrugged, indicating that she should knock again. Elisabeth
shook her head, refusing. She'd gain nothing by badgering the Princess
or her bed-servants, and from what little she'd observed of the young
Princess, she was not a woman who enjoyed being hurried by those born
her social superiors. Too many of the older noblewomen used this as a
subtle means of bolstering their own position.

Lily would not still be abed, requiring the summons of a door to wake
her. She would be in the garderobe or delayed by some detail of dressing—
or by some other likely inconvenience that occupied both herself and her
bed-servants. When she had worked as a laundry servant, Lily had risen
before dawn every morning to start her chores. This was not a habit she
had left behind after her marriage. Benet, after all, was an early riser too,
often for his sailing, but also for official business.

Elisabeth waited awkwardly, trying not to let the footman see her
anxiety. She briefly closed her eyes, screening out the footman's fidgets—
impatience, she was sure, he never would have dared express in front of
her mother.

Patience. Elisabeth almost shook her head. If even a footman was
free to jitter and prompt, why must she be compelled to patience?

The past days, the past week, had passed in a confused flurry of . . .

boredom. Whether or not her decision to take Gaultry Blas into her confidence had served to protect the Climenses' honor, there had certainly been a price. Elisabeth had had no suspicion of what it might entail, drawing herself to the attention of the Common Brood. First the horrible Tamsanne—and then the imperious Dame Julie.

Before the night she'd run to Gaultry's rooms, Elisabeth had been intrigued by the hushed whispers about the Brood's secretive contract with the Prince. The contract was said to give them power beyond that of the realm's highest peer, but little of this power had been in evidence. The old Duchess of Melaudiere; the High Priestess; Gaultry Blas with her Glamour-soul—of course these women had the Prince's ear. But as for the others . . . She had not suspected, until the horrible moment when the old witch Tamsanne pierced her with her eyes and asked her such terrible questions, that that power of the Brood might be turned to affect *herself*.

By noon of the day she'd run from Gaultry's chambers, the Princess called Elisabeth to her private chambers. For the first time Elisabeth had been escorted past the formal reception rooms into the privy chambers. Her first thought had been that Gaultry had betrayed her mother to the Princess, but she knew at once, looking into Lily's friendly but mildly puzzled face, that this could not be correct. "My dear tamarin-keeper," the Princess had welcomed her, smiling. "You have been reassigned. I am informed there is important work that needs you."

The Princess's gaze had flickered over Elisabeth's shoulder. Turning, Elisabeth saw that Dame Julie, the Common Brood musician, had come noiselessly into the room.

"I have been told you have a talent," Dame Julie observed curtly, coming up to her. Elisabeth had not realized that the old woman was so short. The top of her white head barely reached Elisabeth's shoulder. But for all that, her hazel eyes were fierce. "I have requisitioned your services to help me in a search."

"A search for what?" she asked, bewildered.

"A search for *how*," replied Dame Julie. "The Prince has set me a question. We are trying to understand the terms by which the gods might make a mortal man a King. Before month's end I must find the answer. You have been chosen to aid me because of your unique talents."

"What are these talents? And why does anyone think I hold them?"

"Tamsanne pointed me to you," Dame Julie said shortly. "As to the rest, you must discover it for yourself."

And that was all the explanation anyone had given her. Elisabeth did not see Tamsanne again and she was not sure she would have had the courage to question her if she had. *Every door is open to you*, the old woman had told her, those dark eyes burning so deeply into her own. What had she meant by that?

Elisabeth, rousing, knocked again on the Princess's door. She hoped that Lily would send someone to the door soon, as her mother's assizes-appearance was scheduled for noontime. Elisabeth knew she would need an hour at least to garb herself as befitted her mother's child. Already her morning had been broken up with this unexpected errand.

The week of her service to Dame Julie had otherwise passed so monotonously. . . .

Before this past week Elisabeth had been unaware—blissfully unaware—that Tielmark's history had been collectively entrusted to seven court bards who maintained a comprehensive archive of the nation's verbal histories and ballads. These bards were an earnest lot and they certainly knew their songs, but they were unused to working under pressure—indeed, with the bulk of their songs committed to memory decades past, Elisabeth might even have said that they were unused to *working*. They were also completely unaccustomed to taking orders or following anything like regulated procedure.

All of which was at odds with the project that Dame Julie, on the Prince's personal authority, now lay before them: Every song they had learned, every history, was to be repeated for Dame Julie.

Appallingly, much of this record had been preserved in oral form only. Four of the seven bards, assigned their posts during the latter part of Princess Corinne's reign and that of her oldest son Roualt, had made attempts to commit their songs to paper. Indeed, since the election of the fourth of these bards, a quorum had finally been reached declaring that written copies of the most modern songs were to be considered desirable. But the three senior bards, two hoary old women and one ancient man with a beard that cascaded below the greasy buckle of his belt, had received their training back in the days of old Princess Lousielle. This doughty trio still argued sharply against writing any of their songs down, persisting, they insisted, in the pure oral tradition of the Harper-god, Leander. Elisabeth was enough her mother's daughter to regard this as mere laziness, though their argument that words committed so to paper lost something critical to their power was a matter for which she could feel some hesitant respect.

Though Dame Julie had received a dispensation from the Prince *requiring* the bards to perform or share all their songs, the two oldest of the trio were not cooperating—or rather, their idea of cooperation was a dim one. Many of their songs had already been passed to their apprentices—but they querulously maintained seemingly infinite "lines of variation," as yet incompletely passed forward.

For a full summer week, Elisabeth had labored inside, scratching song summaries into wax tablets, and staring with yearning at the pleasant weather outside the windows, wondering when her mother would come to save her from Dame Julie. The old woman's life was not all music and play as Elisabeth had imagined it, observing Julie's rehearsals. She kept four of them working like demons. Julie herself, her daughter, granddaughter, and Elisabeth were roused every morning at first light and set to listening to the bards' recitals, teasing at them to remember variations. "What are we trying to find?" Elisabeth asked, as often as she dared. Many of the variants were repetitive in the extreme, yet Dame Julie insisted they listen to everything. "You will know it when you hear it," Dame Julie told her. "If not, Tamsanne is wrong about the talents she claims for you, and the three of us will have to repeat your work."

Elisabeth missed the tamarin. She missed the freedom she had not understood she possessed, to linger at court with few duties. She'd been assigned to Tyrannis of the magnificent beard, by a slim margin the least obstreperous of the three ancient bards. Listening for hours to his hollow croak, his voice long since lost to wine and age, made her head ache. She suspected Dame Julie had assigned her Tyrannis because she herself along with her kin, so keenly trained in music, could not bear his atonal cacophony.

With few exceptions, the old man's songs were not at all the stuff of rousing legend. So far, the interminable "Ballad of Briern-Bold" proved the worst. Instead of describing feats of boldness, its verses numbered the dukes and counts who fought beside Briern in his final confrontation with the Bissanties. Back then the Climenses had not yet taken possession of Vaux-Torres' ducal estates and the Climens ancestor who had fought in that battle had been an undistinguished horseman. Tyrannis's account detailed men and women so far down the ranks that Elisabeth had almost expected to hear of his deeds.

She had been free of the old man for one afternoon only. Dame Julie had taken over for his rendition of the "Love Story of Far Mountain," which described in ponderous detail the dowry accorded Briern's sister,

Briessine, whom Briern had given in marriage to the Lanai King of Far Mountain after the allied Tielmaran-Lanaya victory over the Bissanty. Some element of this pair's marriage had confirmed the petty chieftain of Far Mountain to his Kingly throne—but what, the song did not say. The description of the dowry was followed by a lengthy paean to Briessine's beauty, an endless roster of the Bissanty soldiers Algeorn Far-Mountain had smote in battle, and numerous verses describing the withdrawal of the Lanai troops from Llara's Kettle, the lakeside battlefield where the Lanai traditionally descended to Tielmark's plains. The song seemed no more interesting than any other of Tyrannis's stories, yet Dame Julie stayed with the old man for hours, meticulously quizzing him over every line and its variants.

The next morning Elisabeth got Tyrannis back. She hated the old man's stuttering delivery, his frequent breaks for water, the consequent breaks to relieve his bladder, his querulous complaints. She would have complained to her mother, but Argat was distant in the week leading up to her trial and always in ill temper.

Only on the eighth day of Elisabeth's servitude, two days before Andion's Ides and her mother's assizes-date, did Argat's spirits lift. On that day her mother greeted her return to chambers with the highest good humor.

"You'll never guess what has happened," Argat said.

Elisabeth looked at her warily. Her mother had been angry for so long, it was hard to credit this lightening of the clouds.

"Mother—tell me."

"Today I crossed paths with Gaultry Blas's assassin-boy. She's been keeping him tight within her own chambers. I used a most clumsy ruse to gain access, even for that moment."

Elisabeth's heart went into her mouth. "Is he all right?"

"It's the most astonishing thing. I had begun to suspect it was something unwholesome—the boy is too young to be kept so closely by her in such, shall we say, intimate circumstances." Argat had rattled on, blind to her daughter's apprehensions. Her mother had finally arranged the required abduction—

"Gods in me, the Blas sisters have played a merry game. It's not *Gaultry* and the boy who've been holed up in their rooms this past week. It's that errant young knight, the old Chancellor's past-champion, and Mervion, the sister. The Great Ones only know how long Gaultry and the boy have been away. The court toads, Ronsars among them, have spread a rumor that the pair of them accepted Lepulio's offer of safe haven." Argat snorted through her nose. "Myself, I don't see that of young Gaultry. I think she's gone west to put the boy under Benet's protection."

Elisabeth was speechless. Her pure relief made her mother smile.

"It's true, it's true," Argat said. Behind her composedly amused façade, Elisabeth could tell she was laughing uproariously. "I wish you could have been there. Dervla High Priestess butted her way in on my heels to determine the boy's true identity, and young Mervion was most delightfully cool in her greeting. Said it was no one's business if she and her man had chosen to keep *couvert*, and what business did Dervla have with her sister, in any case?"

"But what does this mean?"

For just a moment, her mother cooled. "It means that when Dervla stands witness at my assizes two days hence, there is nothing she'll be able to prove against me. She had intended to call some Bissanty witnesses, you know, but with the boy out of Princeport, my guess is they won't stand to testify. You really don't need to know all the details! What I say that day may prove hard for you, ma petite, but there should be nothing a Climens cannot weather."

Elisabeth returned to old Tyrannis the next morning in such a glaze of happiness that the old goat softened to her, offering her a series of variants without even requiring her begging. With her mother's news, the grind of the past week had been much leavened.

The footman, jittering at her side, brought her back to the present. Pretending not to notice that she had lost herself in thought, Elisabeth rapped again on the Princess's door.

Still no response. This was unprecedented. Elisabeth was not sure what she should do. Though early still, she did not have the time for this business to drag out. She'd told Dame Julie that she could not work on Andion's Ides, that she needed to be in court to stand at her mother's back. Dame Julie had agreed to grant her a few hours of freedom to fulfill this duty. Then, when she'd reported to the library this morning, Julie had sent Elisabeth with this missive for the Princess, rather than starting her up with old Tyrannis.

Elisabeth looked at the footman. "Go find one of the woman-servants," she said. "I cannot wait here all day."

With an agreeing nod, he disappeared through a low servant door to fetch someone with due authority to enter.

Elisabeth, left alone in the hallway, knocked again.

This time, a slight sound answered her. A chittering sound. She recognized it at once: the tamarin.

Somehow, Elisabeth's hand was on the latch. She pushed the door open. Afterward, she could not have said why or how, but in that moment, old Tamsanne's mocking words echoed in her ears: *Every door is open to you.*

Inside was the room for the Princess's formal levees, a chamber several out from that private room where Lily had given Elisabeth's service to Dame Julie. The huge princely bed dominated the chamber, its cover richly embroidered in blue and silver. On the bed—

Elisabeth stepped into the room, swept by a wave of horror and fear.

A young woman lay strewn across the great bed, her neck at an unnatural angle. That broken neck had not been what killed her. She had vomited copiously before she'd died: phlegm that was mostly blood. Two other women lay, unmoving, on the polished inlay of the floor, streams of blood and bile similarly poured from their mouths.

Princess Lily's slight figure was nowhere to be seen. Elisabeth advanced farther into the room, stunned.

Her first experience of violent death. She had never expected to meet it in these finely appointed chambers. "Princess?" she said in a quivering voice. "My lady?"

A scrabbling sound arose from under the side of the great bed, and the tamarin erupted into view. It bounded into Elisabeth's arms, chittering and furious, then fought free as Elisabeth reflexively clutched it, jumping back down. Skirting the corpses on the floor, it beelined for the painted wardrobe that stood at the side of the great bed. Keening in a concerned tone, it scratched at this cabinet's painted doors. When she did not respond quickly enough, it began to make despairing leaps up at the doors' latch, high over the height of its reach.

"Princess?" On shaking legs, Elisabeth approached the wardrobe's side. A scuffling sound and a frightened moan whispered from inside, almost too subdued to reach the ear. "Princess, is it you?"

Elisabeth unlatched the doors and hastily swung them open. There, pressed in among sheaves of gorgeous brocaded robes, almost suffocated in their material bounty, was Alyssa Hardee, Ranault's pregnant young duchess, Lily's closest assigned companion. The woman's face was contorted with pain. She had been crushed into the closet with her knees drawn into an unnatural position against her heavily pregnant stomach, and she tumbled out, belly-first, as Elisabeth swung open the doors.

"Oh!" Alyssa cried, clutching at the robes to brake her descent. "Help me!"

Elisabeth caught her reflexively, and almost fell beneath the woman's weight. "Where is the Princess?"

From behind her, a terrified shriek drowned Alyssa's weak answer. The red-headed footman, accompanied by a pair of serving women, burst in at the door. One of these women screamed again as Elisabeth turned around, and bolted back into the hall. The footman, with a little more regard to duty, stepped inside and yanked on the nearest bell-pull, summoning help.

Not knowing what else to do, Elisabeth helped the young duchess across to the corpse-soiled bed. Though she seemed otherwise uninjured, the stress of her imprisonment had prematurely started her labor. "Have mercy, Emiera," Alyssa whimpered, falling back on the bed scant inches from the corpse Elisabeth had spied on entering the room. "My babe is sworn to the Prince-heir's health. Have mercy, Elianté. Protect my child. For Tielmark's sake, if not for mine."

"Lady Hardee—Alyssa." Elisabeth tried to reassure her. "We'll send for a woman to help you." The young duchess's eyes were half-mad with terror. Her arms clutched with surprising strength over the bulge of her belly. "Tell me what happened." When the young woman did not or could not answer, Elisabeth glanced sharply over her shoulder at the footman. "Find someone to go for a midwife."

"The Princess—"

"You've called for help already. It will be coming soon." Taking in the man's hesitation, she abruptly changed her tone. "You. Go yourself and find someone who can succor this lady."

When he would have argued, she drew herself up, fierce and sharp as ever her mother might have proven. "Get out of here!" she snapped. "And don't come back until you find someone who can save this woman's child. The future of the realm lies on it!"

It surprised her, the satisfaction she felt as the man jumped in fear and ran to do her bidding. Maybe this was what her mother felt so often. If so—it felt surprisingly good.

The disappearance of the Princess was unprecedented. Servants came running, high and low together. Ronsars. Courtiers. Lesser serving-maids. No one seemed to know what to do, and no one assumed any chain of command or order. They shouted questions at Elisabeth, then at each other, as the levee chamber filled chaotically. The corpses were turned and mauled in a disorganized search for clues. Elisabeth did not know what she should do, other than stand by Alyssa. She pressed herself against the bed and tried to whisper encouragement. Ranault's young duchess had fallen into a whimpering haze of pain, incapable of answering questions and almost unaware of the mêlée. The tamarin, fearful of the crush, huddled on the bed's pillow, its eyes closed to frightened slits.

When relief came, it was not in any form Elisabeth had anticipated. Gaultry Blas's ancient grandmother, the terrifying Tamsanne, appeared as if out of the air, followed by a pair of matronly women. The red-headed footman trailed behind, looking nervous. Tamsanne, unlike the others in the room, was notably composed.

She took one look at poor Alyssa Hardee, writhing in agonies, and her strong, age-thickened claw of a hand fastened on the unfortunate red-haired footman's shoulder.

"There is no time to lose," the old woman said in a knifelike tone, quickly snapping the footman's wandering attention from the surrounding chaos. "Run quickly to the Singer's Court. There you will find Dame Julie of Basse-Demaine. You will bring her here in all due haste—or I will know the reason." She thrust him away. He disappeared into the throng at something approaching a run.

"Elisabeth," the old woman's eyes lit with something like satisfaction. "You did well to call me."

Nothing had been further from her mind, but Elisabeth sensed this was not a time to argue an explanation.

Tamsanne drew a twist of vine from her belt-pouch. "Hush," she said soothingly, tying it on Alyssa's wrist. "Forget. Close yourself, and hold your babe." Incredibly, Alyssa was able to take a deep breath, and also to relax her legs. Her pretty eyes lit with dawning hope—until another spasm hit. Tamsanne brushed a worried hand across the young woman's arched belly, as if feeling for the life within.

"What happened?" Her dark eyes bore into Elisabeth, her attention momentarily leaving Alyssa to regard the chaos of the room. Somehow, perhaps with a spell, the old woman had created a circle of calm around the great bed's edge. The hysteria beyond was a distant thing, even its noises fading.

Elisabeth quickly recounted the events that had led her to the Princess's chamber. "I have Dame Julie's missive here," she concluded, pulling it in wonder from her pocket, amazed that it was still there.

Tamsanne took it. Ignoring the seal, she tore it open.

"If my mother's trial were not scheduled for today, I don't think Dame Julie would have sent me," Elisabeth concluded, appalled by Tamsanne's nonchalant infringement of the privacy of Dame Julie's seal. Tamsanne shot her an amused look.

"So shocked." She flapped the opened letter in her hand. "Even when all this goes forward around us?"

"The one is not a license for the other," Elisabeth replied stiffly.

"Dame Julie and I have an understanding," Tamsanne answered, passingly amused. "My action is not as it may seem." She turned her attention downward. "Now," she said. "Do you feel an improvement, my lady?"

Alyssa nodded weakly. Tamsanne bent over, her voice gentle. "Your water has broken. It is too late to hold your child within. What I have done," the old witch touched the vine on the woman's wrist, "is set a spell that will quicken the birth. There will be great pain for you, but it gives your child a chance to survive. Will you take this chance? The child within your womb will never take a breath without my spell. But you are young. There can be others. You can spare yourself this pain."

Alyssa clamped her fingers over the vine, as fiercely protective of it now as earlier she had been of her belly. Tamsanne nodded, whether approving or no, Elisabeth could not guess. The old woman gestured to one of the matrons who had arrived with her. The woman, nodding, advanced and began to rub the young duchess's back. Alyssa groaned and turned her face against the bed.

Tamsanne bent over her one last time. "It was Dervla," she said roughly. "It was Dervla who took Lily, wasn't it?"

Alyssa glanced up from her pain, her eyes opened in startled assent.

"Do not believe anything the High Priestess told you," Tamsanne said. "Only a madwoman would think to sacrifice her Prince's heir. Does she imagine the gods will grant him another, having used the first like that?"

An invisible, indrawn dam of fear seemed to melt in Alyssa's body. Somehow, she found the strength to reach for Tamsanne's hand. She fought to speak. The old woman soothed her, closing her lips with a gentle finger. "Hush. Keep your strength for your own trial. That is your only business now." She turned to the matronly women. "Pull the bedcurtains. Attend her as best you can. The one woman who could control this rabble will not be appearing to do it."

She meant the High Priestess, of course. The Prince had left Prince-port without appointing a new chancellor. In the Princess's absence, Dervla was next in line to assume control, at least until the cabinet of Benet's ministers could agree upon an appointment.

"What are you suggesting?" Elisabeth asked. "What has happened?"

"Dervla will not come because she is already busy with the Princess," Tamsanne said grimly. "The question must be—where has she taken her? Thanks to my Gaultry, I think I know."

She looked at Elisabeth squarely then. "Come with me, if you would serve your Prince."

There was nothing for it. Elisabeth, bewildered but obedient, followed the old witch as she led the way from the room.

The light—it was indescribable. Elisabeth stumbled on the tight coil of steps, dazzled. Save for Dame Julie's quick reaction, she would have fallen. "What is it?" she gasped, falling into an awkward squat on one of the narrow steps. "What is it doing to me? I can't hardly see—" With every step she took downward, the green light intensified, thickened. It was almost a glowing green mist, unnatural, eerie, wet like morning fog against her skin.

Julie shot her a curious look. The light was not affecting her similarly, other than to show her the way on. "Tamsanne was right," the singer murmured. "Damn her eyes, I don't see why." In the delay while Elisabeth found her feet and once again stood up, the border-witch outpaced them, disappearing ahead down the stairs. "Go, keep moving. We've got to catch her now."

They rounded a last twist of the stairs, and fell out of a rocky notch into a broad chamber. Elisabeth had a sense of a high, sensuously curving dome rising over her head and of piles of cluttered paper stacked around the sides of the room, but there was no time to look further. The center of the room's stone floor, with papers pushed back on all sides, had been cleared and marked all over with signs painted in blood. One of Dervla's acolytes—the Brood-blood woman whose sister had been killed by Gaultry's assassin-boy—had just completed the last figure, using a brush dipped in a small clay cup. Dervla herself stood at the center of the room, rampant over the Princess's body.

Lily's dress had been cut open in front, revealing the pale, flat curve of her meager gut, the ridges of her ribs. Nothing showed of the Princess's pregnancy yet. A circle had been traced upon her skin with a knife, drawing an even line of blood; her thin arms and legs were pinned by strings and pegs wedged tightly between the floor's stone cobbles. For a moment Elisabeth thought the princess was already dead. Then the thin stomach gave a shuddering heave.

Elisabeth would have sobbed in relief, if at that moment a sickening sensation had not passed through her. The light emitted by the room—so pure, so strange, a green so perfect it merged almost into white—it was working on her strangely. Without being told, she knew that Palamar's vessel was filled with Lily's blood; the runes painted on the stones were Lily's blood also.

And the blade that she sensed, concealed within Dervla's robes, that was the *Ein Raku*, the blade that could kill a god's child without incurring a god's vengeance. Lily's blood was on that blade already—it was what Dervla had used to cut her.

"You have not done it yet," said Tamsanne, stepping forward. "Benet may yet forgive you."

"Forgive me?" Dervla shrieked. "For what I am about to do, he will kneel in worship!" Her pale eyes scanned the room angrily, settling on Dame Julie. "I see you have brought reinforcements. Singer—I bid you welcome. Have you come to cast your vote?"

Elisabeth she did not acknowledge. It was as though, for Dervla, she did not exist.

"What are you trying to do?" Dame Julie asked levelly.

"Protect Tielmark," said Dervla. "That one's arrogance . . ." She pointed at Tamsanne. "She sent the boy away, and there is no time left to go after him. Andion's Moon has touched its course in the sky. Because of what she did, this is the only chance left."

"Hold," Tamsanne called. "Hold your hand. You know I want to see Benet made King. I as much as anyone. Where do you think I sent Tullier? To Benet's side. They may be together, even now, and they will certainly be together before the month's close, when Andion's eyes swing closest to us, and there is another chance for the ceremony. If anyone has the power to make this sacrifice work, it is Benet, standing as Prince at the head of his army—not a passel of old women offering prayers in a hidden room. Leave the choice to Benet. Tullier will reach him soon. We could travel there, and arrive in time to bring the knife to Benet before the month's close. Let the choice be in the hands of the Prince."

"Benet?" Dervla's voice was ice. "Do you think I would have concealed that I had the *Ein Raku* if I believed he had the stomach to put the boy down? He would never do it. Not even for his own country."

Elisabeth turned to Dame Julie. "I thought we did not know how to make Benet King," she whispered. "Why have we been listening to the ballads, if we already know?"

Julie shook her head. "The Common Brood's charge is to make Benet King. Ultimately, our lives will be forfeit if we do not fulfill it. We have two chances this summer: today, with Andion Sun-King's moon half-triumphant, or at month's end, when the moon is full. Then not again, for fifty years." She grimaced. "But a human sacrifice   that price is too high. We have been trying to discover a way to do it without bloodshed. But you have heard the bards. So far they have been useless. I do not like our chances—"

"Our chances are nothing with the boy in Benet's hands!" Dervla shrieked. Elisabeth quavered, glad not to be the focus of that cry. "Benet will never be strong enough to strike the boy down with his own hands."

"That is so," Tamsanne said grimly. "He does not have the will for it. But do you really imagine I would betray my granddaughter's trust, and send her ward west to be killed? Great Twins above, give thanks Benet does not have the heart for such a betrayal! Flip the coin, High Priestess— and remember what Gaultry's boy has been trained to do. To protect this child's future," she pointed at Lily's naked belly, "Benet would willingly put the *Ein Raku* in the assassin-boy's hand, and offer his own throat. The Gods, I think, will accept that as a pledge worthy of Kingship."

Dervla gasped. "You would see the assassin-boy crowned our King? Treachery!"

"Only if you are a fool," Tamsanne said, "and you eliminate Benet's heir here today. If Benet dies, the King will be this unborn child, not Tullier. So you see, High Priestess. I am not opposing you. Truly our hearts are set to the same course: Benet and his line can be made Kings. We do not have to suffer another turning of the cycle without that change-of-rule."

For a moment, Elisabeth thought Tamsanne had convinced her. Dervla hung her head, confused, staring into the face of the helpless woman who lay beneath her. "Perhaps—" she said hesitantly.

Dervla's acolyte, unexpectedly, was not so easily swayed. "You would see the boy honored as Kingmaker?" the woman said, dangerously soft. She had a gentle-looking, meek sort of face, but the tone of her voice was iron.

"Honored?" Tamsanne said sharply, shifting her focus from Dervla. "Outcast forever, and stained with blood is more like."

"History always honors the Kingmakers." The softness of the acolyte's voice was fearful. "You would see that child-murderer raised to such eminence? That cannot be. I will not allow it."

"It is not for you to stop it," Tamsanne said bluntly, less careful with her words now that Dervla was seemingly won over.

The acolyte's round face lit with incandescent rage. "I surely can," she said. "Do you think I have no power? I am born to a warrior race. Marie Laconte, Countess of Tierce, is the greatest of my ancestors."

Elisabeth could not be sure, but at these words from Palamar, Tamsanne and Julie passed a quick look toward her, *Elisabeth*, as if they expected her to respond.

Tamsanne spoke again when she did not. "Marie was like us all: prophecy-bound to protect Tielmark's interests over those of her own family."

"It is not in Tielmark's interests to have that boy play Kingmaker!" Palamar screamed. "The sacrifice will not be in that boy's hands. Not while I live. I will see myself cursed and make the King myself, if that's what it takes to stop him." The acolyte flung down the clay pot. It shattered on the floor, the blood within spattering and overwriting the mystic figures.

"Palamar," Dervla said caustically, the girl's tone drawing her back from her confusion. "Be quiet. These are not matters for you."

Instead of backing down, as Dervla had obviously expected, Palamar answered with a unexpected pulse of dark power. The High Priestess was driven to her knees, almost atop the pinned-down Princess, a look of shock on her face.

"I am done with quiet!" Palamar shrieked. "My grandmother's power moves within me. I will see vengeance for my kin!"

The bloody runes on the floor blazed with green fire as she stepped into the circle with the High Priestess and the Princess, and began to emit a high-pitched singing noise.

"Treachery!" Dervla screamed. "Trespass! This circle is for the High Priestess alone!"

Palamar, ignoring her, lunged. The High Priestess parried the blow clumsily. For Dervla, this attack was like a thunderbolt. Her defense of the young Princess, a reflexive act, was all she had time for—self-protection, from this young woman whom she had so obviously trusted, so obviously mistaken for her obedient pawn, was beyond her, and Palamar, as she threw her former mistress down, was unreasonably, unexpectedly strong.

Within the dancing circle of green fire, there was a confused tussle. Then, with a triumphant cry, the young acolyte drew the *Ein Raku* clear from her mistress's robes. Elisabeth was surprised to see how old, how worn, how plain the blade's appearance. It was narrow, dull grey, inscribed with glistening runes.

"For my sister's lives!" Palamar cried. "For all my kin! Goddess-Twins! Andion above! Take this sacrifice, and make it yours!"

She drove the knife down. Dervla got in the way, taking the knife in the thick padding of her robes. Palamar, thwarted, struck again, and once again missed her mark. Seeing Dervla's determination, the acolyte's next strike was with her magic, an ugly, searing green-black blaze. It knocked Dervla back from Lily's body, throwing her outside the rune circle. When she attempted to recross the line of magical flame, it rejected her. Palamar, smiling weirdly, took a stance above Lily and raised the knife. "Tielmark will have its King," she said. "From sacrifice. From the sacrifice made by one who will freely accept the taint of cruelty, that Tielmark may be set free."

"Elisabeth." Tamsanne propelled her forward roughly. She almost fell over in her surprise, but the old woman, with startling strength, jerked her up. "Julie and I cannot breach that circle. This is your moment: You can do what we cannot. Lily needs you. Call the Twins, and step within the flames."

Elisabeth stumbled forward, more by the old witch's force than by her own will. She stumbled against the spell-shield. The singing of the green flames rose as she impacted against them. Then, to her surprise, she sank into them, passing through. The green fire sent up by the runes sheathed her body, cloaking her with cold green light, but it was not at all painful. Rather, it made the entire room seem clear and light, the focus more intense. Across and outside the circle, Dervla's eyes grew wide—as though she had been blind to Elisabeth until this very moment, and Elisabeth's ability to step into the circle had stripped that blindness away. "What is this I see?" Dervla cried. "New trespass? How is it that *she* can pass the shield, and I cannot?"

The domed curve overhead sang with power. Even Palamar looked up. Great arcs of green light lanced across the room, tumbling over piles of paper, collapsing the ancient stacks of books. Elisabeth, certain this apparent disaster was her fault, tried to withdraw.

"What is happening?" she screamed. "What is happening?"

Tamsanne was behind her, just outside the magic wall. "Forward!" she urged. "Forward still! Take the knife! Elisabeth—remember—for you *every door is open!*"

Right in front of Elisabeth's eyes, a shimmering halo of light opened, then expanded, broad enough for her to step through like a door. Through it, Elisabeth saw the figure of the pinned Princess, Palamar straddled atop her. That image was a frozen tableau, Palamar driving downward with the knife.

Elisabeth—she alone had the power to change that picture. She stepped forward through the halo of light, into the frozen picture, time-suspended as she made up her mind to move, and bent and twisted the grim blade from Palamar's hand. There was no strength in Palamar's fingers to resist her. With a savagery Elisabeth had not known she possessed, she picked up Palamar's body by the front of her dress, and bodily threw the young woman clear of the Princess. With a frozen, wrathful expression on her face, the acolyte flew backward and away, like a mannequin stuffed with straw, sparking as she breached the magic wall, then falling back into a tottering pile of paper.

"Princess," Elisabeth said, kneeling in fright to free the girlish, unmoving body. "Speak to me. Tell me you are not hurt."

The halo of light snapped shut, and the magic's effect dissipated. Lily turned and met Elisabeth's gaze. "I am alive," she said wonderingly, as Elisabeth pulled the pins of her bonds free to allow her up. There was an ugly bruise below her right eye, and her mouth was cut in two places. "What are you?"

A scuffling sound drew their attention. Dervla and Palamar, panting behind the invisible wall raised by the glyphs. "What have you done?" Dervla ranted, turning to Tamsanne, who stood, along with Dame Julie, also outside the green fire-wall. "What have you done? What have you done to me?"

Elisabeth, staring curiously at the High Priestess, realized that Dervla was trying to call forth a spell—and failing.

"Ask better, what have you done to yourself?" Tamsanne replied. "By your own acts of treason, you are no longer High Priestess." She glanced at Palamar, who was cowering back from the green flames of magic that marked the spell-shield, panic suffusing her features. "And you are no longer heir to Marie Laconte. You and your acolyte together—you no longer possess the gift of magic. Elisabeth has earned it of you both."

"I don't understand," Elisabeth said. She felt dizzy and weak, yet the grey blade was still clutched in her fist, and no one, it seemed, could come at her. She leaned against the tiny Princess, whether for support or to support her she could not have said.

"You are that woman's half-sister." Tamsanne pointed to Palamar. "For whatever purpose of her own, your mother got herself with child by Rivière Laconte, Countess Marie Laconte's son and heir. You are blood of the Common Brood—and now you are Tielmark's new High Priestess. The power has moved from Dervla and become vested within yourself, and with it has come all the power that was vested in your family.

"Sometimes the gods are ages slow, acknowledging the shift of human power—and sometimes they move like lightning to countenance change, as they have done here today."

Elisabeth could hardly take in all Tamsanne was telling her. "How do you know this?" she asked helplessly. "Why would you choose me for such an honor?"

Julie, with a touch of her earlier bossiness, pushed Tamsanne out of her way. "Tamsanne didn't choose you. The gods did." She glanced up to the apex of the dome. "Child, this room, from now, will be your personal sanctum. Listen to its voices, and you will know we speak the truth. Close your eyes, and listen for the music."

The stacks of paper, of junk, of vellum, seemed to loom in from all sides, encroaching on her powers of concentration. "What am I to hear?" Elisabeth whispered. But even as she spoke she heard it: her own voice, reverberated back to her, from the great vault. "Hear," came her own voice. "Hear."

After that, it was like a harmonized flood. Elisabeth did not know if it was images, or song, or the scent of past days. She saw the turning spiral of the seasons, saw her place in that dance. She lowered her head, humbled, as it almost overwhelmed her. Yes. This was her place. Fouled with paper and boxes though it might be, this was her place to stand and listen.

She looked down at the dull grey knife that she held in her hand, the *Ein Raku*, the knife that could kill a god's own child. Held in her hand, she could recognize it for what it was: a human soul. Trapped within the blade there was a human soul, bound with magics dark and fell. It was ancient and alive together, one emotion left to it: the desire for release, for the end that would come to it when it was ritually driven into a man or woman's heart. "The gods no longer give us the power to make such an evil thing," she whispered, staring at the foul weapon she held in her hand. "Elianté and Emiera, bless them for that."

She raised her head and looked into Tamsanne's eyes. The old woman did not have the power to frighten her. Not anymore.

"Did Gaultry know what you intended for the Prince when you sent her westward?" she said sharply.

"She would not have agreed to go if I had told her," Tamsanne admitted, her dark gaze unrepentant.

"Then we must go to her. All of us. Without us there to guide him, in desperation, I fear that Benet may try for the Kingship sacrifice as selflessly as you have described it—on a plain sword instead of the *Ein Raku*. We must prepare ourselves quickly. There is scarcely time to reach the border before Andion's moon is upon us."

"You want us to travel?" Dervla said angrily. "My place is here at court."

"You have no place at court," said Elisabeth coldly. "Injustice will not serve the Prince." She looked at Tamsanne. "Whatever the price."

"Benet must be made King," Tamsanne said.

Elisabeth shook her head. "The blood price is too high, even if Benet is willing. We will find another way."

"Twins in you, High Priestess, I believe you." Through the glaze of fire, Dame Julie was staring, a new look of respect on her face. "Your eyes are open now. We will find a way."

Elisabeth, closing her eyes, winced within, wondering at the certainty with which she had committed herself. "The Court Bards will travel with us," she said curtly. "I so order it, in my first act as High Priestess."

O Emiera, Elisabeth quailed, *O Huntress. Have I really just committed myself to two weeks in a horse cart, listening to Tyrannis witter?*

Steadying herself, she opened her eyes. Yes, that is exactly what she had done.

Now, all she had to hope was that Gaultry and Tullier would be waiting safely at the battle-front for her arrival, and that she would get there before anything terrible happened.

For that, she would have to pray to the Great Twins. Long and hard.

chapter **21**

▼

I t was the Ides of Andion, the center of the Sun-King's month. The
sun had reached its apex in the sky. Gaultry and Tullier had not seen
a human soul since morning, when they passed a tiny hamlet—six houses
and their outbuildings. Those houses had been deserted save for a pair of
young men who greeted them with unreserved hospitality, welcoming
them to a massive, and greatly appreciated, farmer's breakfast. The other
members of the little farming enclave were away, celebrating the Feast
Day at a slightly larger hamlet to the west, near where a priestess of the
Goddess-Twins tended a sacral grove.

Gaultry intermittently regretted her decision not to co-opt mounts
from the horse-children, but reflecting on their fragile innocence, she
could not help but be glad she had left them unburdened by such an
appropriation. Some great force had twisted their trail since they had
turned south from the high road. She did not want to see those young
innocents threatened by any connection to herself and Tullier, however
obscure.

Her experience at the preceding day's dawn had deeply shaken her.
She did not understand the impulse that had moved in her as the dawn's
light had moved into the sky. The image of the dryad's face flashed back
to her repeatedly. The unreadable expression on the creature's face. The
beauty of his hands, reaching to touch her brow, just once, so gently. She
had dared the border of the Changing Lands, and returned again.

The secret image of the creature's beautiful yet alien face was to be her punishment. Unless she crossed over, she would never see it again—and she would never live to forget it.

That dryad's face . . . its likeness to her own was no coincidence.

Fiery like the sun. That was how Tamsanne had described her lover, Gaultry and Mervion's grandsire. *He never left the woods.* Gaultry had known who the dryad must be the instant she'd seen his face, and she had finally understood Sieur Jumery's mistake. Tamsanne had not got her daughter on a dead man. She had got her daughter on a man whose soul had been taken from him by the trees.

Tamsanne must have loved him before he had crossed over, before he became a creature of moss and moonbeams.

But why had he chosen to show himself to her? Why now? Did his appearance explain the way their trail had shifted so inexplicably beneath their feet? Was it the magic of the Changing Lands that had called her this far south, finally revealing itself in that magic-charged moment of dawning, when time seemed almost to stand still, suspended between darkness and light?

He had come into the water to prevent the magic lands from taking her. Of that at least, she was certain. The instant when the dryad's eyes had held hers made her quiver still, the beautiful smile on his face—mocking, inscrutable. He had touched her brow so lightly, and turned her away. The moment of their encounter had been so ephemeral, yet the image of him burned behind her eyes: every flower in his moss-tangled hair, every line of his body and face, as clear as though he stood before her. Why had he chosen *this* moment to reveal himself? Why had he called her to him, if only to send her away?

Gaultry paused to drink from her waterskin. The sun blazed overhead, sending up shimmers of heat from the fields of unkempt wild oats that surrounded them. A few hours before, they had refilled their water supply from a marshy brook. Gaultry, washing her mouth from the skin, wished that they had not gone through the supply they'd taken from the breakfast farmers, but with neither horses nor an adequate stock of skins, they could not carry a good supply. As she swallowed, the faintly briny taste made her wonder if it might not have been fouled. That would not have surprised her. She did not like the heat or the smells of this place.

The track was marked with the hooves of herding beasts, spread out in places among broken oat-shoots, as though their herders had moved them quickly and without a care for the ground. This land was still too far east for these to be signs of Lanai raiders, and no one at the village they had passed in the early morning had reported any such thing. That *should* have been reassuring.

She glanced at Tullier. He was walking head down, cheeks flushed with twin roses of fever color, his skin beneath its sheen of sweat a little pale.

"Where do you think we are?" he asked, noticing her attention.

"I've no idea," Gaultry said. "I don't understand the ground here. We've been heading northwest all day. From what those farmingmen said this morning, we should have reached the road between Pontoeil and the north. But I'm not seeing anything like that, and this ground," she gestured at the low wooded hills that surrounded them, "it doesn't give any clues as to what lies ahead. We've reached Haute-Tielmark, I'm sure of that. But that's all I know, until we can find another farmer to set us to rights." Much of Haute-Tielmark's land was thinly populated. Not simply because of the Lanai raiders who threatened every summer, but because the soil was thin, discouraging a settled style of farming. Although the land had been herded successfully since ancient times, using the land more intensively would spoil it.

"We'll just have to keep going," Gaultry said. She smiled wanly. "At least we'll get plenty of warning before we reach the border. They say the mountains are tall enough there to keep their snow, even in high summer. That will be a signpost we won't be able to mistake."

"Snow." Tullier wiped the sweat from his eyes. "That's hard to believe with a sun like this beating down."

Gaultry took another swig from her waterskin, wondering again at its mossy taste. The waves of heat off the ripening oats made her feel headachy and weak. Or perhaps it was the image of her grandfather, so young-looking, so alien—

"It's Andion's Ides," Tullier said abruptly. "Do you suppose the Sun-King truly looks down on us today?"

"I do. It's his feast day. He has to be watching." Gaultry left unspoken her fervent prayer that if this were true, the Great God would have the will to keep them safe until the day had passed.

The hills around them deepened and began to open out, gradually taking on a grander, untamed aspect. Low ridges of grainy rock began to appear, splitting the land into a giant's playground. This was the Haute-Tielmark Gaultry remembered from her visit to Prince Clarin's tomb, in those confused days before Benet had renewed his God-pledge. It gave her hope that they might soon rejoin a road.

It was deep afternoon, the height of the day's heat, when they came to the lip of a lovely valley. Its bottom was lush grass. Natural terraces of the grainy rock formed its sides. Their track descended sinuously to the valley floor and wound off into the distance. Halfway along the valley, over several humps of land, was evidence of an extensive manor. Pens, low outbuildings, and a patchwork of irregular pastures. Perhaps the holding of one of Haute-Tielmark's knights. There was no obvious stronghold or manor-building, but the folds of the land could easily have concealed a small fortress or keep.

"Have we lost our way again?" Tullier asked. "Those men this morning didn't mention anything like this."

Gaultry stared down, frustrated. The buildings were clearly occupied. She could see the smoke of at least one fire. The empty paddocks were not so surprising. To escape the worst heat of the day, the stock would have been driven up the valley sides to cooler pasture. "I have no idea. I don't understand any of this. Elianté in me, I don't think I've understood anything since we came away from the High Road."

"It's like someone is leading us," Tullier said tentatively. He sounded embarrassed to be speaking such a thing aloud. "Maybe it is just too odd to me, to be traveling in a land where everyone we've met has been so pleasant and hospitable. The serfs I knew on Bissanty farms—back at Fructibus Arbis—they all seemed like they were keeping darker secrets."

"Fructibus Arbis was a special case." The estate where Tullier had summered away from the Sha Muira was secretly owned by Tullier's father, a part of the old Prince's festering schemes of vengeance.

"I know," Tullier said. "But in a way it was a comfort, the certainty that any of the serfs would have risen against you, had their slave-bond not been holding them back. Here, it's so much less clear what keeps the people we meet from knocking travelers on the head and stripping their bodies of their valuables."

"The truce of the traveler's sign is not lightly violated," Gaultry snapped, annoyed for the umpteenth time by Tullier's paranoid world view.

In her efforts to curb her temper, Tullier's suggestion that they were being led went by her without further comment.

·   ·   ·

As they neared the cluster of buildings, Gaultry became more puzzled by its layout. For a farming spread of this size, she would have expected to see an extravagant manor-house. Tullier, she could tell, was similarly nonplussed. If they had not passed the empty hamlet of the morning, the buildings' deserted air would have felt threatening—evidence of a plague, or a Lanai raid. But everything was neat and orderly: tools put away, windows tightly shuttered. Clearly, the folk who would be necessary to tend the beasts of these well-kept paddocks, pens, and low-eaved barns had traveled away to spend the Feast Day at some nearby village. All they could see was a skinny old rail of a woman, standing by the well on the bare square of ground that was the nexus of three of the larger buildings, watching their approach. Their path would take them right past her, in a matter of a few more minutes.

Afterward, Gaultry would wonder why she didn't see it. But really, there was nothing in the scene to give her warning.

Good day to you!" Gaultry called, when they were near enough for hailing. "Best wishes of the Feast Day!" A rail fence enclosed the yard where the well and the old woman stood: a rail fence with broad gaps left open at both ends of the yard, accommodating the path. As Gaultry stepped inside this pale, she made the traveler's sign.

The woman nodded curtly. Her hands were busy hauling up the bucket, and she could not offer the countersign. "Well met," she said loudly, half over her narrow shoulder. Her hands as she hauled on the rope were surprisingly quick and strong. From the woman's leathery, sun-darkened face and grimy yellow-white hair, tied in a long braid that straggled down past her hips, Gaultry would have taken her for a far older woman than that strong voice and her nimble strength with the bucket implied.

"Almost with you." Huffing from her effort, the old woman heaved the brimming bucket into view over the edge of the well. It was a large bucket. More than Gaultry would have liked to see her own grandmother lift.

"Can we help?" Gaultry asked, drawing nearer.

"Help? Oh yes." The woman swung the bucket onto the well's edge, and steadied it there with her hand. Her face was set like chiseled stone, her eyes fierce and dark, malevolent. "Great Twelve above. You've done all that, and more."

Almost the last thing Gaultry knew, the old witch upturned the bucket toward her. She understood fleetingly that the woman's failure to acknowledge the traveler's sign had been intentional, and she did not need her sudden glimpse of the ram's-head amulet at the woman's throat to know who she was. In the long, spindly lines of the woman's body, her grey robes, Gaultry saw suddenly the figure that had intruded into her dream back at Princeport palace. Not the unseen presence who had driven her deep within the palace labyrinth or the green-black enemy who had sheathed her with the vines, but the grey figure, the grim figure, who had spoken to her from the distant hill.

But realization, and with it her fear, arrived too late. The black circle of lead that bound the bucket's upper rim expanded toward her, encompassing her in darkness. Something that was not water drenched her skin. "Run, Tullier!" were her last conscious words.

Then there was only darkness.

Gaultry came to with water burning in her sinuses. Gasping with pain, she groggily comprehended that a bucket of water had been flung in her face to rouse her. Not the bespelled bucket from the well. Another, simpler bucket, full of older, dirtier water.

After the pain, the first thing to strike her senses was the thick musk of animal, pressed in on her from all sides.

With an effort of will, she overcame the pain, the startlement. From the rough rafters and beams overhead, the partial darkness, it was obvious that she had been taken into one of the larger barns and lashed by her hands to an overhead beam. Already, her raised arms and shoulders felt on fire. Only by straining up onto the balls of her feet could she somewhat relieve the pain.

Around her were the low slatted walls of a lambing pen. Beyond, the rest of the barn's floor had been emptied of similar separators. Crowded into that space was a milling, tightly packed flock of sheep.

All this she took in during the brief moment before she became aware of the figure who stood before her, blocking the lambing pen's gate.

The old woman leered at her with something like pleasure, a second bucket brimful at her feet, ready to douse her again if the first hadn't taken effect. Tullier, to her deep dismay, was nowhere in sight.

"What have you done with my friend?" Her voice came out weak and cracked.

"What have I done with you?" the woman cackled. "Better to ask that, Glamour-witch. You are powerful and bold, but I have hold of your measure."

Gaultry glared, and tried to kick out, but it did her little good. She was weak from the aftereffects of whatever magic the witch had used outside by the well. The shooting agony in her shoulders as her hands took her body's full weight made her cry out, and the awful moment of scrambling to regain her balance told her she would be a fool to attempt an attack that way again. "What have you done?" she said, panting and trying to catch her breath. Her arms were aching. As soon as she gathered herself, she would burn through her bond with the full angry power of her Glamour. There was no reason to suffer this: In rescuing Tamsanne from the syphon-spell, her power had finally broken free, and she no longer feared to use it. She would call her strength and crush this woman; she would fight—

The old woman, reading her expression, cackled maddeningly. "Save your strength. Do you imagine I would have woken you if there were any risk that you could fight me?" Flinging one skinny arm outward, she indicated the milling sheep. "You are one with the herd, pretty one. And sheep—alas for you, sheep are not greatly aggressive."

"What do you mean?" Gaultry glanced again, this time more suspiciously, at the sea of woolly white backs. They had unkempt coats in need of trimming, ugly skinny legs, and short, dished faces. A breed with which Gaultry was not familiar. But the silly, brainless way they milled and mobbed—there was nothing unusual there.

The light of triumph in the old woman's eyes was an ugly thing. "I am master," she hissed. She stepped into the pen, closing the little gate behind her to keep the sheep out. Her teeth were a grim yellow bridge in her face, more snarl than smile. "Learn that quickly, and your suffering will be less." She reached and drew an imaginary line down Gaultry's body, from her collar all the way down onto her gut, across the front of her filthy, water-soaked shirt. There was nothing Gaultry could do to shake that touch off. Then the witch brought her face close to Gaultry's, still smiling her grim yellow smile. She caressed the young woman's cheek. "Try using your powers within this space, and you will find that you have mightily enriched this herd, in return only for exhaustion. These animals are mine, born and bred. Their first dam—I bred her from the Changing Lands, fifty years back, when your own granddam played me clever, and slipped her head from my noose. I was not a fool like Delcora—I knew

Tamsanne's child was alive, and I made due provision. You cannot imagine the number of sheep I lost to those woods, before I managed to contrive a tether that would bring one which I sent over *back*. I have prepared for this day all those many years."

"Good pet," she said, withdrawing her hand. Her face was so close that Gaultry could smell the stink of grain and blood on her breath. "Young one, you are a woman with powers like unto a god, but you will not be able to use them here. All you can do is hang from your wrists and wait for the screaming to stop."

"I don't understand."

"All to the better." The woman smirked. "I have no intention of explaining." As she spoke, she reached inside her grey overrobes and pulled out a deck of cards.

There was no misunderstanding what it was: a deck so ancient and powerful the cards had turned rimy mahogany reddish-black, the design on their backs hardly distinguishable. A Rhasan deck.

"You are Richielle," Gaultry breathed. "You are the goat-herder."

"It is not just goats I drive before me." The woman chuckled. "It was a pretty thing, seeing you and your boy puzzle as the land waxed and waned beneath you. If the Changing Lands had not called you, I would have had you here last night." She shuffled the deck, those nimble, powerful hands Gaultry had noticed before moving quick and sure.

Gaultry's attention sharpened. It was *Richielle* who had drawn her and Tullier south, not her dryad grandfather. The knowledge touched her like a fresh feeling of abandonment. Or was that right? If what Richielle said was true, then he'd sent power to her and *interfered*—

"I know you," Gaultry said, cold certainty moving through her as the goat-herder cut the cards. "You are the witch from Bissanty. The one who read Rhasan cards for Columba. And Issachar Dan. And even for Lukas Soul-breaker." She said it more from terror than from any hope of understanding. "Why even pretend to shuffle those cards? You already know what you intend to pull for me."

"Is that how it works?" Richielle cocked her head, mocking. "If it were that simple, your grandmother would be dead these fifty years past, and Benet would reign now on Tielmark's throne as King." She shuffled a last time, with those clever card-sharp's hands, and held the cards, fanned, out to Gaultry. "I do not make the future, child." Her eyes glittered evilly. "Poor lambkin. You have no hand free to make your choice. How will you choose with your hands tied over your head?"

For one blazing moment of hope, Gaultry thought that Richielle would free her. Then the taunt of the old woman's expression revealed the truth. With a last spiteful smile, she touched the fanned deck to Gaultry's stomach and whispered a word of power, so quietly that Gaultry might not have felt it if its touch had not resounded upon her skin.

"Everyone has secret desires," Richielle said. "How difficult is it to see them, when it is only a matter of looking closely? The desire of the deepest soul: That is what the Rhasan brings to the surface."

Gaultry twisted against her bonds, not caring about the pain. Richielle was forced to take a half-step back. "Columba didn't want what she got," Gaultry said softly, accusing. A memory of Tullier's sad, treacherous sister, bound by Richielle to a slave's lot, rose before her. "You degraded her," she said, staring at the old woman with fresh loathing. "You robbed her of Imperial protection, as well as of Imperial power. Do you have any idea of the terrible things that happened, once that protection was stripped from her?"

"And that isn't what she wanted? Are you so sure she was unwilling?" Richielle tapped the top card of her deck. "This is your card. What lies at the secret heart of your soul?"

Gaultry closed her eyes and tested the line binding her hands. A cord of twisted leather and twine, bound together with a spell. Hating Richielle, determined not to let her read that card, she flung her power outward. It left her like a wave. a wave that parted around Richielle like water around a stone. Gathering power, it crashed outward and spread toward the sheep.

They baaed with confusion, some making animal cries of alarm. Gaultry's power, mysteriously, had dissipated among them.

She looked at the sheep with new understanding. Sponges. These animals were woolly hoofed sponges, bred specifically to absorb her Glamour.

"You chained my power to them." Panic rose in her like another wave. "What are they, that you could do that?"

Richielle laughed. The blaze of triumph in her eyes told the younger woman that she had not been entirely confident that her magical contrivance with the sheep would be a success. "Use your power again," she taunted. "Use it as many times over as you desire." She held up the Rhasan deck, and once again tapped the top card. "Now. What do you think I will read for you here?"

Gaultry drew a shuddering breath. Something the woman had said earlier came back to her. *I have no intention of explaining.* Nothing Richielle said was meant to help her understand—it was intended only to herd her in the direction where Richielle wanted her to go. She would not help Tullier—she would not help herself—by listening to the woman's patter, by answering her questions.

She closed her eyes again, shutting out the heaving backs of the sheep, the horrible light that shone in the old woman's eyes. Richielle had spoken of seeing people's hidden desires, had hinted at the strength that gave her to form their hidden futures. What were the things in herself that old Richielle couldn't see? What were the things she could not imagine?

The dryad's face rose before her like a cooling rain. His wildness, the twisted flowers in his ruddy hair. The alien velvety green of his skin. The glittering darker green of his eyes. Richielle had sent her and Tullier racketing down to the southern border, pushing them out of their path, but Gaultry didn't believe that she had controlled what had happened in the Changing Lands. She would not have known about the dryad.

Jarret never left the woods, Tamsanne had whispered. No one at court had ever shared her secret loss. Not even Sieur Jumery, who had come closest to it, had understood. Protecting that secret, keeping it safe, had been Tamsanne's hidden, unshared pain, making iron of her will. Richielle feared the Changing Lands. She would not have plumbed their secrets.

"You must have had a terrible time with those poor sheep." Gaultry opened her eyes, an eerie calm possessing her. "How did you ever manage to ferry them across the river? They are not very brave, poor things. The Changing Land must have been a terror, even as its powers entered their flesh."

The expression on Richielle's face hardened. It was frightening—her expression had not been overfriendly to start.

"Your own fears must have been terrible indeed," Gaultry said. "Tamsanne was so much braver than you—so much more dangerous. But of course you must have known that, or you wouldn't have persevered with your sheep."

"I have the power to kill you now," Richielle said coldly. "I could butcher you, right here and now, like one of my own animals. I could bury a knife in the flesh of your throat even before I finish my business with the boy."

"Would it make you feel braver to do it?" Gaultry closed her ears to the woman's threats. She would not allow herself to think on her own helplessness. "Tamsanne never had to kill to believe in her own power."

"Take your card!" Richielle flipped it toward her with an angry gesture. "I am through with talking!"

Grandfather, Gaultry prayed, *stay with me. Protect me.* But she glanced at the flimsy rectangle of paper before she could stop herself.

It was not what she expected: the Slaves' card, or the Chained man. It was the Orchid. The Glamour card. The drawing of the flower was ancient and crude, a line tipped with a bulblike shape and two leaves. Unlike the two representations of the symbol which she had seen previously, this flower was not grounded in earth. It was held in the upraised fingers of a man wearing a strange ragged cape that might have been made of raw sheepskin, save for the moss flowers that were twined into the flowing locks of the garment's hair. The ragged man brandished the flower skyward, as if making an offering to the brazen sun in the card's upper corner.

Her grandfather. Holding the gift of her Glamour-power on high to Andion Sun-King.

"Is that what you expected?" Gaultry sagged against her bonds, cold wonder filling her. She had been braced for the image to expand and take her—as it would have done, had it been dealt from Tamsanne's Rhasan deck, casting her into a wild vision world. Tamsanne had told her Richielle's deck was more powerful than her own. Was Tamsanne wrong?

The expression on Richielle's face was pure murder, and there Gaultry read the truth: Whether or not the image was what Richielle expected, something *had* intervened to block the card from spreading its power to control her. The deck was horribly strong, horribly dangerous. When the goat-herder had pulled cards for Columba and her dark lover, Issachar, they had been forced by Richielle's Rhasan to couple, right there on the temple floor before her. She could only wonder at her own escape.

"It does not matter," Richielle said coldly. "It will not affect the outcome. You will not be able to stop me from slitting the boy's throat. You will not prevent me from burning his heart in the sacral fire."

The old woman stepped back, still staring at the image. Gaultry could see now that the image had startled her, as well as its apparent lack of effect. The Rhasan card images—they were not stable. That was part of the danger inherent in their use.

"You will not be Kingmaker," Richielle said abruptly. "You are only the tool who has brought the boy to me." Saying that seemed to give her comfort. She thrust the Rhasan deck back into its hidden pocket inside her robes.

"Why are you doing this?" Gaultry shouted, desperate to stall her. "Why are you even alive to care? The *Ein Raku* is safe in Princeport. What would you gain if you killed Tullier now? A dead child, blood on your hands, and all for nothing. You can't make Tielmark a kingdom if you don't have the Kingmaker knife."

Richielle smiled, reveling in the note of hysteria that Gaultry was unable to purge, the setback with her Rhasan cards put from her. It was more horrible than her expression of murder—for there was no real joy in it. Then she spoke. "Do you really imagine I would have gone to all this trouble if I did not mean to see Tielmark free?"

Stepping back, she pushed her robes open, revealing a dirty, double-belted leather dress beneath. The first belt, narrow, low-slung against her hips, was weighted with a bulging purse.

But it was the second that caught and held her attention: a dagger belt, with the blade hanging in a simple leather scabbard, comfortably riding Richielle's right hip. "You are right. I no longer possess the *Ein Raku* with which I would have made Corinne queen. Delcora stole it." Richielle's voice was pure venom. "As High Priestess, she was not without power herself, and once she had it, there was no reclaiming it. The power that formed the *Ein Raku*—there is nothing like it on earth today. I had to wait more than forty years, almost despairing, before the stars aligned, and I could at last replace it. The gods have grown selfish of their powers. The days when they made light of raising a man to Kingship are long behind us."

As she spoke, she slipped the blade from the scabbard. It was a simple design, silver-colored with runes carved on the flat. Yet somehow, there could be no mistaking it for was it was.

"You have an *Ein Raku* blade?" Gaultry whispered. "There are two Kingmakers? How is that possible?" But Richielle had spoken of power like unto that which was no longer given to the world, so Gaultry knew. "Lukas Soul-breaker," she said, louder. "He gave you—he made you—the *Ein Raku*, in return for you raising him to the power of the triple-souled. That's why you helped him steal his sister's Blood-Imperial."

Richielle stepped forward and pressed the blade against Gaultry's throat, just shy of breaking her skin. "You will never understand the price I paid for it—and I, only I, Richielle goat-herder, had the power and foresight to see this weapon made and forged. Fifty years planning, and all has come to pass as I envisioned it. Perhaps my vengeance on your grandmother will never come about; but I will live at least to see Tielmark free, Clarin's heirs King, and Bissanty shattered." Turning on her heel, she made her way out through the herd of sheep, leaving Gaultry alone.

Gaultry stopped throwing herself against the line when her hands began to bleed. She had succeeded in moving the tether along the beam a little distance—far enough to chivy herself closer to one of the pen's slatted walls—but a vertical strut from beam to roof prevented her from getting close enough to the wall for her to try to scramble atop it. Maddeningly, the angled tension of the line was just enough to prevent her from balancing and clambering up.

She had attempted to use her magic to embrittle either the line or the beam, but to no effect. With each pulse of power she sought to send outward, the sheep bleated and milled in confusion—absorbing her power, muting her effectiveness.

Richielle would not be long about her business with Tullier. A moment to gloat, surely, a moment to enjoy her triumph, but she would not waste breath in explanations or arguing. She would cut out his heart, as she had promised—unless Tullier found some way to save himself, or unless Gaultry found some way to help him.

In sheer frustration, Gaultry kicked out the slats at the side of the pen closest to her. That weakened the low wall of the pen but did nothing to improve her situation, though it did make her feel less than completely useless for something like the space of four heartbeats.

The sheep outside were frightened by the noise, but Richielle had packed them into the barn so tightly that they soon came crowding back. There was hay in the pen under Gaultry's feet. An obese ram rolled a speculative eye up at Gaultry, gauging her degree of threat, then greed overcame the animal's caution and it forced its way through the broken slats to grab the fresh fodder. A pair of ewes, encouraged when Gaultry did not react offensively, soon followed. One brushed against Gaultry's legs, investigating the fallen bucket. Near enough for Gaultry to spirit-take from it, she realized with a jolting gleam of hope. She did not need her Glamour to do that.

But what would that accomplish? What could a sheep do, that she could not do better, even with her own miserable human strength? Bleat? Grow woolly? Panic like a fool?

Panic. Gaultry looked down at the heaving backs. The obese ram gazed up at her foolishly, hay straws at the corners of its mouth. If she took one of these sheep and panicked, perhaps she could spread that to the rest of the flock. Suitable for creating a diversion—though of course, with the sheep-spirit still in her, she would be no good for thinking, and that would be of little help to Tullier.

And of course, she would be no help to Tullier, even spreading panic, if she remained appended to this stupid beam. She drew a deep breath, and tried to think.

The barn was constructed with wide gated doors at each end. Late golden light filtered in via the western door frame. Twilight could not be far away. Andion's Ides would soon be over. Just as Tamsanne had used the power of dawn to heighten the spell that she had cast on Dervla's fetish-crown, Gaultry guessed Richielle intended to use the power of the sunset.

Where was Benet now? What would he experience when Richielle's blade entered Tullier's body? Would the gods greet him in a vision, announcing his new rank as King? Would the strength of the earth, of Tielmark, come coursing through him? What would the Lanai feel? Would they sense the change, the realignment of the Gods' loyalties, and know it was time to retreat? Victor Haute-Tielmark at least would be pleased by that.

A small side door shot open, and Richielle stuck her head inside. She glanced at the destruction Gaultry had wrought at the side of the pen, and then at the sheep, who had flooded the pen by now and were butting up against Gaultry's legs. Seeing Gaultry's situation effectively stable, she flashed her teeth in her gruesome smile, shut the door, and retreated. She could not have made a clearer statement of her confidence.

"Hag!" Gaultry spat angrily, shamed as well as frightened. There was nothing she could do but go down the path on which Richielle had set her. There was nothing she could do—nothing but make herself more like a sheep.

The angle of the sun moved ever lower in the doorway. Gaultry began to shake all over, imagining Tullier's fate. She had promised him her protection. In the beginning, she had even forced it on him.

Richielle would be concentrating her power now on preparing him for the sacrifice. Gaultry forced herself to think. Tullier would not be unconscious at the moment the knife descended. Richielle would want to look in his eyes as she killed him. But Tullier was not a helpless boy.

He was a trained Sha Muira. If she could distract Richielle even for a moment, maybe it would be enough.

There was only one thing to try, so she would try it. She would take from a sheep, become one with the flock, and see what happened next.

She looked down, dubious, at the milling animals.

Never before in her life had she spirit-taken from a sheep. What would have been the point? She tried at first to straddle the obese ram, but he skittered to one side, suspicious. She had to settle for a scrawny ewe that another sheep bumped against her. It was a feeble thing with a scraggly coat, not dexterous enough to escape. Gaultry clutched it gracelessly between her legs. It bleated hopelessly, and then subsided and lowered its head to pull at a wisp of straw.

Her infuriation at its stupidity almost ruined it. Her first attempt, using her Glamour, soaked into it like water through a sieve, to no effect other than riling it. It crunched one of its hard little hooves down on her instep, and kicked her leg. In the fresh shock of pain, she almost let it escape.

She had grown so accustomed to calling on her Glamour to power these small spirit-taking magics. Now she had to remember humility, and call for strength from the gods. "Huntress Elianté," she intoned. "Fair Lady Emiera. This is a little thing I ask of you. The spirit of this sheep. I call it to me. I need the strength of it—"

The scrawny ewe grunted a protest. Its spirit struggled weakly, sensing the unfamiliar corridor open before it, but only for a moment. Its shadowy spirit-substance made its way tremulously forward into her body, reluctant at the strangeness but not yet scared. Between her legs the animal's light body slumped, its skinny legs folding. Gaultry glanced down uneasily, and positioned her feet to protect it. Any injuries its body took while she possessed it would manifest as pain in her own flesh. Where it had fallen, it could easily be trampled. That might add to the panic Gaultry was feeling, and in turn transmit to the rest of the sheep, but Gaultry felt almost queasy, imagining that sympathetic pain.

With the befuddled ewe's spirit dumb and puzzled inside of her, it was time to start.

She cautiously gave the ewe's spirit the power to control her limbs, feeling its puzzlement as she did so. Then she made it aware of her bonds. The little sheep did not like how it had been tied—the upright position of Gaultry's body alone was enough to spook it. The animals crowded around Gaultry's legs drew away as she began to flail about, less purposefully than she had done earlier because the ewe-spirit in control of her body did not understand the use or the shape of her limbs.

It was not enough to spook the flock. Trying to turn back a rising tide would have been easier.

Gaultry, maddened, began to tease the stupid thing. The asinine creature kicked, but refused to panic. This was no good, she thought. She would have to be more brutal. She poked at it, prodded—the animal was so stupid that nothing had any effect.

Eventually she tried hitting it with a slap of her Glamour-power. The golden strength cracked down, hard as a whip. This time, the creature reacted, but not as Gaultry expected. It absorbed the power into itself— and then it projected it outward. Gaultry had tapped inadvertently into the part of it that dissipated her power throughout the flock.

But this time that power was suffused with her angry frustration. The flock moved uneasily. A few of the rams snapped at their fellows.

All right, Gaultry told them. *If I need to be a sheep to get this going, I will be a sheep.*

She began to struggle in earnest. She threw more lashes of Glamour at the sheep-spirit, then began to twist violently against her bonds. Gallingly, the little sheep remained disengaged, throwing the worst of the emotion out onto the others, and dumbly refusing to respond itself.

It was not until one of the other sheep in the pen stepped onto the ewe's body with a razor hoof that Gaultry at last managed to engage it.

Seething with that cut of reflected pain, Gaultry opened herself to let the sheep-spirit share. And that—rage and anger the sheep did not understand, but pain—that was the beginning of a panic in the ewe that was strong enough to reflect back even on Gaultry. She lashed out with a wave of Glamour—this time to protect herself. It manifested itself as fear, driving the animals inside the pen against the slatted walls, protecting for a brief moment her downed ewe. She lashed out again as they came surging back, and then again. Soon blood was slick on her body, evidence that she had pushed to her Glamour's limit. She was reaching the edge of her power, had put it all into the damned flock, and still the panic stayed below the level where she needed it.

"I am a sheep!" she screamed. "I am a sheep! I am a sheep!" Waves of power reverberated out from her; concurrently, a stabbing pain cut at her hands. Looking up, what she saw made her let out a shriek of true bloodcurdling terror.

Her hands—they were shrinking. Already her fingers were vestigial stubs, the nails thickened, broadening. A horrid, scouring feeling itched across her skin, as if a woolen jersey were creeping over her flesh.

Whatever emotion it was she felt next, it went directly to the flock, bypassing conscious intent. They were a mirror of her feelings, milling now in real terror. The gate across the east door of the barn had not been made very fast. The mass of terrified sheep surged against it, once, and then again, and it crashed open like a barrier breaking beneath a heavy tide. The panicked creatures began to stream away from the irrational screaming that was Gaultry, no clear direction to them, just wanting escape.

And Gaultry, as the last rays of sunlight slipped away from the barn door on the building's far side, slipped free of her bonds, and tumbled down onto the floor.

"Not!" she whimpered. "I am not an animal." Her heart was drumming in her chest. She was barely conscious—except for one thing. Her hands were soft and supple. Her fingers—they were as they should be. She jerked herself up to her feet, relief mingling with renewed determination.

She freed the little ewe's spirit, then, kicking sheep out of her path without compunction, strode for the western door.

Perhaps Richielle's magic had forced her to waste the strength of her Glamour-power, but that wasn't going to prevent her for one moment from trying to help Tullier.

chapter 22

T he sun showed scarcely a finger's width above the steep ridgeline
of the valley. Sunset would come early in Richielle's domain, followed
by a lingering twilight.

Gaultry emerged from the barn borne on a wave of panicked sheep.
Breaking free of that wave, she made for a clear space by the barn's wall,
needing to collect her wits.

Save for bleating animals, the yard around the well was deserted. This
was no reassurance. The sheep were making such an awful ruckus, she
had to believe that Richielle would know something was up.

The goat-herder's farm rambled in all directions along the valley
floor. Some of the barns were ancient, with thick rubble walls, heavily
mossed, and low pole roofs, piled high with slate. The sheep barn where
Richielle had tied her was one of the more recent constructs. The roof
was rough-hewn wooden shakes. The work she could see was more than
one woman could handle by herself, even swollen with power and magic.
What poor souls had helped Richielle cut those shingles?

Her eye fell on a miserable shed. For all its paucity, there was a fire
hole at one end of the roof's ridgepole. Not a place to keep animals. A
place to prepare magic? Gaultry ran to it, kicking sheep out of her way,
and threw open the door.

Five frightened, emaciated faces turned toward her. Gaultry, smeared
all over with her own blood from the Glamour she had expended, did
nothing to assure them with her startling entrance. There were three thin
men, one little more than Tullier's age, and a pair of tired-looking women.

All five were tall, sturdily built people, but their clothes were worn rags, and all were clearly near exhaustion from overwork. The women had been preparing a meal of grain and milk mashed together to make a sort of cold porridge.

"Who are you?" Gaultry demanded. Halting but obedient, they began to give their names. She cut them short. "No. I mean what are you doing here? Have you come here of your own free will?"

One of the men snorted. "The herder comes by our farms for new hands every spring. She is fair, in her own mind. She never takes those who can't be spared."

"She leaves restitution," a woman protested. "We'll all take stock home at the summer's end." Her weary face lighted with hope. "The herder's cattle are a special gift. They breed true, and never throw their get. It's worth the labor, to win that."

The others frowned but did not contradict her claim.

"Where has she taken my boy?" The silence that greeted this question was fearful. It would have been kinder to be polite, but she was in no mood to care. "You must know who I am. Your own Prince's Glamour-witch, Richielle, expected me. Her preparations to hold me while she took care of the boy were extensive. As you can see, I defeated those preparations. Imagine what I will do to you, if you won't help me now."

The aggrieved man who had spoken first started to answer. The others overrode him with concerned noises.

"Tell me," Gaultry insisted. She pushed into the room, thrusting aside the first person who opposed her. She could not tell if the feeling that possessed her was anger or fear. "On your honor for Benet and Tielmark, tell me."

"She's taken him to the riverbed." The man who had answered before kept his gaze focused her face, avoiding the worried eyes of his fellow laborers, their hushed whispers, urging him back to silence. "There's an old stone there where she makes sacrifice. Two stones. One upright, one fallen. Follow the old path to the river and you will find it easily. The water rises and cleans the flat stone, come spring flood. That's where she'll do it."

"Where are my weapons?" Her bow, her hunting knife. Tullier's short sword and daggers.

The man shook his head. Either he did not know or he was unwilling to risk himself so far as to tell her. Seeing he had nothing further, Gaultry snatched up a farm tool that had been laid against the near wall—a long pole with a curved metal blade, intended for cutting high branches. "Point me the way," she said. "And may the gods give the rest of you just reward, for valuing nothing beyond your own skins."

From the door, the man showed her the path. It led out past the barns, between some paddocks with woven branch fences, and down across a meadow to a line of low trees and scrub, obviously marking a river's banks.

The man put his hand on her arm. His pale grey eyes were intense. "Do not think of us so poorly. We are bound here by spells. Think on it. To die in the Herder's service—that is a sorry fate."

"The gods will judge, not I," Gaultry answered tiredly. But she let his hand slip into hers, and she briefly shook it.

The great ball of the sun had almost dropped to the ridgeline now. Was it sinking unnaturally fast, or was that her imagination?

The man nodded, understanding that her thoughts had already gone past him, that she would, perhaps, have spoken less harshly, had circumstances been less dire. "If you get a chance to flee, follow the river. The water is low, and the flats will afford an escape path. Ignore the trails you see. They twist—you will find yourselves back here before you know it."

"The Great Twins give you thanks," Gaultry said. She turned toward the river and started running.

From a distance the tall stone gave the appearance of a giant standing figure, its head bowed in contemplation. Gaultry, who had run like a madwoman across the fields to find this place, sank back into the scrub and tried to catch her breath.

Richielle was standing on the recumbent stone, within the upright stone's long shadow. She had just dispatched a goat—numerous goats, judging by the pile of fresh carcasses to the stone's side—and she was pulling another up onto the stone to kill it too.

The riverbed was flat and wide. Around the sacrifice stones, it had the appearance of an ancient fording place, with the stones erected to propitiate the Gods and allow safe passage over the floods. But whatever the place's history, as the man had promised, in this season the river ran only in a small channel at the center, leaving scoured sand and pebbled flats to either side. Come winter, both the recumbent stone and the upright stone would be surrounded by water, if not, in the case of the former, completely submerged.

The goat, a fat black-and-white nanny, struggled in the old witch's hands, diverting Richielle's attention. Around the stone, a large herd of the animals waded clumsily in the shallow water. They were nervous and angry, as goats can be, and clearly aware of the fate of their kindred upon the stone. Richielle apparently maintained some loose magical control, preventing them from bolting. Even from where she stood, Gaultry could smell the creatures' manure as they defecated their protest at being held.

Richielle finished with the black-and-white nanny and heaved it onto the pile of dead animals. She bent for a moment. When she rose, a flame had started. Gaultry could not make it out from her distance, but it appeared that the carcasses had been interlaced with wood and kindling. Whatever the case, it did not take long for the heap to catch, sending up greasy dark smoke.

The goat herd did not like it. The animals—there were more than a hundred of them, maybe more than two hundred—balked and skittered. Richielle, still up on the flat stone, did a slow pirouette, deepening the holding spell. The revolt subsided. Then she bent into the shadow of the upright stone and pulled Tullier into sight.

He was hog-tied, hands and feet bound together, his body bent in a bow. Richielle dragged him forward and pushed his head down against the flat stone. For a moment, it appeared that she had pushed it right into the stone, as the boy's head disappeared from sight. When it reemerged, his features were streaming with gore, and the boy himself spluttered, half drowned. There was a basin cut into the flat stone. Richielle had filled it with goat blood before ritually dunking him.

Laying the boy next to the heap of burning goat flesh, the old witch busied herself with erecting a simple pole tripod, wedging each of its legs in crevices in the stone. When she was done, she heaved Tullier up and lashed him to the main support, suspending him with his head hanging downward, his pale throat exposed.

Her hand fanned open against his chest, just over his heart, the goatherder faced the ridgeline, waiting. Her timing was unnervingly precise. The great round of the sun lowered, its bottom edge touching the purple-blue of the evening ridge. As she stood there, poised, it began to slip out of view.

On this cue, Richielle knelt, her manner reverent, and reached into the basin where she had doused Tullier's head. Her arm went in past her elbow. After a short pause, she stood, flourishing a short, narrow blade.

Gaultry caught her breath. The *Ein Raku*. When Richielle held it up to the fading sun, a single bright ray flashed down, connected it briefly to that bright ball on the horizon, linking sky to earth.

For that flashing moment, Gaultry stood riveted. Belief swept through her that Andion, the gods' High King, would honor the goat-herder's sacrifice; belief that there was nothing she could—or should—do to interfere. For that brief instant, as the fire of the sky was reflected in the goat-herder's blade, all Tielmark's proud history crowded before her. She saw Clarin, the first free Prince, and Briern-bold, laughing and wild. Benet, at the end of this glittering chain, flashed by, riding the Tielmaran lines in victory.

In that swirl of sunlight, Grey Llara Thunderbringer, Bissanty's cruel mother, relented, freeing Tielmark and Bissanty together as she ceded her god-claim to Tielmark's soil. Generations of Emperors breathed relief, Bissanty's three-hundred-year-old wound at long last mended, their empire reformed to hold the thrones of four princes only, complete. In that visionary moment as the sun touched the *Ein Raku*, the world, the lands, lay reformed and peaceful.

Then the wind shifted and the charred scent of burnt goat-hair hit her. Death, it struck Gaultry then, was also a kind of peace. But it was not a peace she would sacrifice Tullier to sustain.

Richielle's back was to her and the goats were making a worse ruckus than the earlier terrified sheep. Still, the open space of the pebble beach that led across to the stone seemed impossibly broad. Gaultry wanted to pass it at a run, but she did not quite dare. That quick movement would surely catch the old witch's attention.

Slowly, steadily, she walked forward. One step, and then another. The river-washed rubble shifted treacherously underfoot, stone-ground stone moving against stone, but she kept coming, silent, every stalking skill she had learned as a hunter strained to its limit. The goats sensed her, then saw her, and waded suspiciously out of reach. She was two-thirds through the watery shallows, almost at the recumbent stone, when Richielle turned finally and spied her.

"It is not time!" The old witch cast a flickering look at the horizon, dismay flashing on her leathery face. "It is not time!"

Gaultry closed on her at a run, swinging the bladed pole. The old woman ducked under it, nimble and quick as a cat, then slipped on the blood underfoot. Gaultry, screaming, scrambled up onto the stone and jabbed down. She nicked the old woman's side. Then Richielle got a hand on the pole, twisted, and it was Gaultry's turn to lose her footing. For one crazy moment, she was underneath, struggling, forced to release her grip on the wooden shaft as Richielle stabbed for her with the King-maker blade. Beyond the old witch's arm, she glimpsed the half round of the sun blazing down from the glowing backlit skyline of the ridge. In descent, it had the appearance of a great fiery eye, half-lidded.

"You cannot use your power!" Richielle hissed. "My flock at least has robbed you of that!"

"I can still fight and pray, you godless bitch!" Gaultry shot back. "Whose prayers do you think the gods would rather answer?"

Grunting, Richielle pushed her away and disengaged. Both women scrambled unsteadily to their feet, the farm tool clattering against the rock, unheeded. The flat of the rock beneath them was fluid with goat gore. Below them, in the shadow of the rocks, the herd bleated protest-ingly, riled up. Gaultry should have been the stronger of the pair, but the old woman possessed fearful strength, and undepleted magical power—and she was armed with the *Ein Raku*. Gaultry risked a closer look. It was a narrow blade, inscribed with runes, shiny clean, as though its metal had repelled the blood in which Richielle had bathed it. Indeed, Richielle was all over blood from the fall she'd taken, except for the hand holding the knife. That hand, her sleeve, the fold of robe that fell on that arm— all those were gore-clear, in a pattern that suggested this was the action of the knife.

Richielle closed again, biting downward with the *Ein Raku*. Gaultry ducked away, barely in time to save herself. The old woman screamed and bore down on her like a fury, hurling some sort of spell. The frission of magic knocked the younger woman off her balance, and Gaultry felt the kiss of the knife. If Richielle hadn't accidentally planted her foot in the pothole where she'd doused Tullier's head, spell and knife together would have found their mark. As it was, the goat-herder's strike trans-formed awkwardly into a close grapple. Gaultry, desperately afraid of that shining blade, planted her hands against Richielle's chest, trying to push her back.

Her hands touched something hard within the old witch's robes. Ri-chielle, too late aware of her groping hands, loosed an angry cry. Gaultry, losing her balance once more, found herself clutching at the old woman's clothes to save herself, tearing away a sizeable swath of the ancient ma-terial—and with it something else.

From the feel of the object in her hands, from the look on the old witch's face, Gaultry knew instantly what she had taken. Within the cloth's folds, she had Richielle's Rhasan deck.

"No!" The old witch made a darting move toward her.

"Don't try it!" Gaultry said sharply. "One more step, and these cards will go in the stream."

The old woman invoked a spell with a curt pass of her hand, and the mass of cloth and card deck blazed hotter than a red-burning ember. Gaultry did not care. She clutched the cursed thing against her chest. A burned smell touched her nostrils, along with the pain. She ignored it. "Put down the knife," she said.

Incredibly, Richielle obeyed.

The Rhasan deck was getting hotter. Gaultry, one-handed, grabbed up the knife. The angry passion on Richielle's face daunted her, but she could not stop this now. She backed over to Tullier, and began to cut him free. There was no time for niceties. Wielding the knife one-handed, behind her back, she made a poor job of it, sliced him in one or more places, and at the end when he finally fell free there was nothing she could to do prevent him from tumbling head-downward against the rock. She heard him swear, which at least meant that he had not knocked himself unconscious in the fall.

"Gaultry!" His fingers touched hers. She passed him the knife so he could cut his ankles free.

Twilight was on them. Only the tiniest sliver of the sun's ball remained in sight over the ridge. "Andion's Ides are over," Gaultry said, as level and calm as she was able. "You have missed your chance to play Kingmaker, old woman."

Richielle did not answer. The expression on her face was more than murder. It was a look of ancient, primitive evil. For this moment she was not thinking of the Kingmaking game. She was focused only on her deck. She wanted it back—oh, how she wanted it. The fire of that desire fueled the burning of the deck in Gaultry's hands.

Gaultry's strength was fading—what little she had left. Stripped of her power, worn down with fatigue, she was not sure how she maintained the will to hold on to those burning cards. She stared into Richielle's face, trying to understand what she saw there.

Richielle's mouth twisted, observing her fatigue. The fiery heat of the deck leapt higher. Gaultry's sleeves began to smolder. The goats began to move, dispersing, as the old woman's hold on them faded, and Gaultry understood then that to Richielle, Tullier and Kingmaking, at least for the moment, did not exist. All she cared was that she reclaimed the source of her deepest power. Behind her, the land, Richielle's land, seemed to shiver and move, as though some enchantment was draining from it—

"Take it then!" Gaultry fanned the deck—a movement that seared her fingers—and scattered it into the stream among the churning goats. "Take it!"

Richielle screamed and threw herself into the water after the strewn cards. Gaultry grabbed Tullier and dragged him down off the altar on the side of the stone away from her. "This is our only chance," she told him. "Follow the river! Even if you lose me, follow the river. It's the only way to safety—the bitch owns all the other land hereabouts with her magic."

They began to run—first flat out, and then, as the tall marker stone disappeared around a bend of the river, at a more sustainable jog.

"She'll come after us," Gaultry puffed. "After she gathers her cards."

"Why didn't we kill her?"

"Tullier, I don't think we could. Her magic—she's been twisting our path ever since we left the Tielmaran High Road, back on the other side of the Fingerland."

"Where are we going now?"

"I don't know. But a man Richielle was holding prisoner told me this was the only way out." She noticed the look he gave her. "Yes, I trusted him. I don't think we have a choice."

"How did you save me? How did you break free?"

Gaultry thought back to the chaos of the barn; the horrible thing she had had to do with the sheep; the ugly scrawny ewe she had been forced to allow inside her body; the desperate, empty sensation she had felt as she had thrown all her Glamour-power into those animals. Worst of all, the hallucinogenic moment when she had looked up at her hands and seen nothing but deformed stumps, something like a sheep's trotters. "I momentarily became one with the herd. And that," Gaultry wheezed, her voice hoarse from the running, "is really all the detail that you need to know."

How long they had been running, Gaultry could not have said, but twilight deepened quickly in these rolling hills. The streambed became coarser, narrowing, the gravelly flats roughening, becoming interspersed with larger chunks of stone. It was becoming hard to maintain anything like a running pace.

They pulled up by a small pool to take a breather. Tullier bent briefly and scrubbed the sweat and goat blood from his face and hair. "Will she follow us?" he asked, emerging with water streaming on him.

"Of course," Gaultry said. "Andion's Ides may be over, but the summer stars will align at the end of the month to give her another chance. Two weeks. We have two weeks to get you safely out of her reach." She hesitated. "Never let her take you, Tullier. I will do what I can to hold her back. Tielmark needs a King—but this isn't the way."

Tullier gave her a sober look. "She cut me before you came, you know." He touched his throat, revealing a shallow line Gaultry had not noticed. "My blood on that stone—I could feel the Gods watching. Andion, the Great Twins—all of them. The sacrifice would have proved acceptable."

"Not to me!" Gaultry said fiercely. "The gods accept many things, but it is up to us to choose which of them we will live by!"

At that moment they first heard the clattering. Looking back, they spotted the first goat. A long-haired, bearded billy, running toward them with a goat's awkward gait but easy balance.

"She's coming," Gaultry said.

"We can fight her," Tullier answered. "Look. I have her knife!" He flourished the *Ein Raku*. The look on Gaultry's face dampened his enthusiasm. "What? She took all of our weapons. And far better to keep this blade in our own control."

"It is an evil thing," Gaultry said.

"Then better in our hands than hers." His eyes glinted. She could tell he liked the idea of the knife's power in his hand. Liked the idea that he controlled it. "We'll have to stop running sometime. We can't keep this up through the night."

"Neither can she," Gaultry said roughly. Now was not the time to discourage anything that might make him stronger, might tip the balance of him surviving or falling prey to the old witch. But the killer in him—that she did not like. "We have to keep going. Even with her magic to help her, we are both of us more than fifty years her junior. Surely we can outrun her."

They began to move again, but the heart for running had gone from them both. They had lost the surge of triumphant energy that had first sent them sprinting from Richielle's sacrifice stones. Not knowing where they were heading made it harder to keep on. One goat came up on them, then another. Finally, eerily, they were surrounded by a bleating pack. A pack that butted against them, maneuvering them away from the riverbed. "If she's trying to turn our course," Gaultry gasped, "there must be some hope still that we can elude her."

Tullier, focused on the ground beneath his feet, did not answer.

Around them, the outlines of the rock slopes softened. Twilight deepened, increasing the difficulty of finding their footing. The river flats contracted as the stream moved into a deepening valley. Gaultry and Tullier were forced to slow and pick their ground more carefully. The goats took this as a chance to hem them in, aggressive.

Then, just as Gaultry was sure they could run no more, they reached the end of their road. The river took one last hairpin turn, and there the ground ended. It was not a long drop—no more than twenty feet, or thirty. The stream fell over in a cascade, dropping into a frothy pool. Gaultry craned and looked sideways at the sheer face of stone. To either side, the cliff face quickly steepened as it moved away from the low V carved by the river. The stone of the cliff—she recognized this stone. They had reached the edge of Haute-Tielmark's rocky plateau.

"Tullier," she said. "I recognize this place. This is the border. We've come to the western edge of the Fingerlands. That land down there belongs to Bissanty! I think—I think if we can get down there we'll be safe from Richielle. That must be why she sent the goats—to keep us from crossing over."

Tullier shook his head. "It won't work."

"Maybe so. But at least we have some idea where we are, and maybe down there in the Fingerlands she won't have the power to send the ground slipping under us."

Tullier glanced at the goats, milling around them now. "Llara mine, let's pray you're right."

Near the cascade there was a place where a steep ramp of rock hung partway down the drop, overhanging the pool. Tullier, who had the best balance, went first. He tentatively lowered his body over the edge, feet scrabbling to find purchase. Gaultry glanced up the streamway nervously, wishing he would hurry. For all her brave words, she could not really be sure that they would be safe once they had passed into Bissanty lands—

and if they had the bad luck of encountering a Bissanty patrol, they were in no position to fight their way clear of that, armed only with Richielle's *Ein Raku.*

"Hurry up!"

"If you're in such a hurry, why didn't you offer to go first?" Tullier snapped. "Faugh. If only my hands were not so slippery—"

As he said it, his eyes widened. Gaultry reached for him, a hair late. He slipped sickeningly downward, fingers scraping ineffectively as he scrabbled in vain to regain his grip.

"Jump out!" Gaultry screamed. "Try to hit the pool! Jump!"

"Oh Llara—!" With that cry, he peeled free, falling backward with his hands outstretched—the worst possible position. It happened so quickly, Gaultry could scarcely understand what she was seeing. Like a cat, the boy twisted in midair and got his feet underneath him—just as he plunged into the little cascade pool.

He spluttered to his feet, swearing. She was so relieved, she didn't care. In her concern for him, she scrambled downward, half panicked that he had broken bones—only to discover, on her arrival poolside, that the dangerous descent was already behind her.

"You idiot! You could have killed yourself!" She had to shout to be heard over the pounding cascade.

"I didn't fall on purpose. Trust me there." Tullier hobbled out of the shallows, shaking water out of his clothes. He managed a shaky grin. "You weren't too careful coming down yourself. But you're bloody enough, a quick dip might have been worth it."

Gaultry self-consciously cupped a handful of water to wipe clean her mouth and chin, still fouled from her fight with the goat-herder. They were down. That was the important thing. "Let's take cover. It won't be long before she's on us."

Tullier frowned. "It won't be any use. This wet will leave a trail that any fool could follow."

There was a clatter of hooves behind them, louder than the cascade of water. Two goats had risked the drop, somehow managing to find a path downward. The rest of the herd ranged themselves in an arc across the cascade's top, staring down at the exhausted pair with a fixed, un-goatlike intensity.

"There!"

Above the cascade, Richielle came into view. She was running full out, a dark fury, nothing tired or aged about her. The falling darkness did not even slow her as she ran nimbly along the stones where Gaultry and Tullier had slowed and stumbled.

"Llara's heart," Tullier said softly. "How can we fight that?" She was like a great dark omen of doom.

Even knowing that there would be no more running for them tonight, they backed away. Richielle reached the top of the cascade, shoving goats aside to glare down at them. "There is still the end of the month!" she screamed. "I will take you then!"

She made to climb the falls, then paused. With a gesture of her hands, she sent goats scrambling forward as her vanguard. One big billy came down, brown coat with a black head and spine, and then another, beige and white. Four more followed that pair, one falling and landing clumsily on its knees. It got up, bleating in pain, and then another followed it down—this one at a controlled pace, its nimble feet somehow finding stable holds for its hooves—showing Richielle the easiest route. The old witch cackled, triumphant, and stepped confidently to follow it.

A steel-blue flash of power threw her back, singeing her hair. Puzzlement came over the old witch's face, but she was not deterred. She stepped forward again. Once again, that blue-grey flash, repulsing her.

"What is it?" Tullier said. But the awe in his voice told that he already recognized the color of that magic.

Richielle, abandoning caution, hurled herself forward. If that flash of power had not come again, thrusting her back, she would have gone headlong over the cliff. Beginning to understand, she thrust herself forward in a frenzy, screaming, invoking spells, intoning the names of all the Great Twelve. The goats began to melt uneasily away into the darkness, frightened by those flashes of steely power.

"She cannot cross over," Gaultry said wonderingly. "The border is closed to her."

"It's Llara Thunderer's fire," Tullier whispered reverently. "She cannot truly hope to defeat the Mother Thunderer's will—can she?"

Richielle would not accept what was happening. Quieting for a moment, and beginning to approach the problem more methodically, she tested the barrier that lay before her, first by rolling a boulder over the edge, then by flinging another goat. This one landed, squealing, on its side, and did not get up. Then she tried again herself. Her fury, even pent up away from them, was a terrible thing.

"It must be that nothing like this has ever happened to her," Gaultry said, staring upward, awed. "Tamsanne told me that Richielle followed the old wanderers' ways. The borders are not something that she ever learned to respect." She glanced at Tullier. "You're Blood-Imperial. That must be protecting you. Sciuttarus made you a Prince, and now Llara has closed the border to the woman who would threaten you."

He looked at her blankly while she stared at him in wonder.

"Richielle did not understand that Great Llara would turn against her if she raised her hand against an Imperial Prince. What a horrible thing, to discover the gods' notice in such a way."

Richielle rained curses on their heads. Gaultry turned to look at Tullier. She realized dully that they'd have to kill the poor goats that had made it down the cascade. They could not risk having the animals follow them. It was peculiarly unpleasant, chasing the creatures down, all the while with Richielle threatening and ranting over their heads, and beginning even to pelt them with stones, but it was soon done. Gaultry's guess about the *Ein Raku* blade was shown correct—it repelled blood like oilskin shedding water. Tullier did not need even to wipe it clean when he pocketed it inside his shirt.

"We've not done with her," Tullier said, as they moved somberly toward the cover of the trees, the sound of Richielle's ranting fading behind them.

"I fear not." Gaultry scraped her hair tiredly back from her face. She was exhausted and hungry. They had no provisions, nor anything else to sustain them. Only the *Ein Raku* knife, and she would sooner starve than consume an animal that had been killed with that blade. "And how we're going to pass through Haute-Tielmark and reach Benet's side *now* is a pretty question."

▼

chapter 23

They were in the Fingerland swamps for three days, surviving off
thin foraging, heading always northward, away from Richielle and her
valley. In that time, they had brushes with two Bissanty patrols, but neither saw nor heard evidence of pursuit by Richielle or her animals. By
dint of combined good fortune and vigilance, they passed into Tielmaran
territory without incident and found their way to the High Road. Though
Gaultry had lost the Prince's sigil along with the rest of their meager
equipment at Richielle's farm, once they reached the Black Man Inn, the
first way station in Haute-Tielmark over the border, they were able to
reprovision. The owner of the Black Man knew Gaultry's face from her
visit earlier in the spring—on the occasion when she'd first seen, if not
met, Victor Haute-Tielmark—and he did not question her word that she
was on the Prince's duty.

Better still—the Black Man Inn, which was well fortified and busy
with couriers running to and from the western border, offered them a
place of safe haven and rest. It was now getting on for a fortnight since
their departure from Princeport. The days since their encounter with Richielle had passed under the strain of fear and uncertainty, and despite
the pressing need to reach the Prince at the border, neither Gaultry nor
Tullier had the strength to continue without a full day to recover. Gaultry,
still depleted by her efforts to free herself from Richielle's magic, slept
through a full night and day, waking fitfully to swallow a little water, and
rising only once, shortly before dinner, to eat a few bites of bland stew
before returning gratefully to her bed.

When she woke the next morning, empty-stomached, light-headed, but tremendously refreshed, Tullier was already up. She caught up with him outside the forge for which the inn was named, watching the soldiers with whom they had arranged to ride as they oversaw the farrier attend their horses' feet.

"They're good," he said, as she came to stand by him. "They wouldn't let the man start the work until they were there to see it." Gaultry was pleased to hear the boy's judgment. She and Tullier had been able to attach themselves to a courier and his men who were shuttling news from the Fingerland border to the battlefields on the shores of Llara's Kettle.

Gaultry had liked the look of the lean captain, Yveir, and the way he commanded his little detachment. His unit was composed of two short, sturdy-looking women, fast riders who worked as his scouts; a stocky, muscular man who rode with an ax at his stirrup; and three younger soldiers, still lean and adolescently gangly, but agile in the saddle, as though they had been riding since infancy. The little troop had the strength of numbers that would deter a casual attack, but also enough speed and flexibility to slip a single rider or more through, should any larger band of Lanai outriders come up on them.

Whether or not that would help them if Richielle attempted a frontal assault, Gaultry did not dare hazard.

Something about the way the farrier was manipulating the horses' hooves made Gaultry rub her still-bruised wrists, and shiver at the memory of the skinny sheep's trotters. The power of her Glamour, even controlled, was fearful. The idea of such a transformation—not a fetch-cover, but bones, skin, and hair, truly altered, truly animal—it frightened her. Certainly, the gods were capable of such transformations. Half their stories described them assuming such forms to appear, hidden, on raging battle-fields, within the beds of well-guarded maidens, or at other such decisive moments. But in all the stories that spoke of human beings transformed or so translated, the change was described as a curse, something cast down as divine punishment.

Would that be her fate? She was not certain, even now, if she had performed the transformation herself, or if it had been some trap, some syphon-like spell, that Richielle had deliberately set to snare her.

"Have you eaten?" she asked Tullier, putting these grim thoughts momentarily aside.

The boy shook his head. "I was waiting for you. We still have time. Yveir is waiting for a last runner from the border."

"Excellent," Gaultry said. "I am eager for us to be on our way."

. . .

They rode for two days on the High Road, keeping a decent pace, but cautious of foundering the horses on the increasingly rough road. The land felt barren and wild. It was subtly rising as it made its way toward the as-yet-unseen mountains, and that rise in the land also cooled the heat of the nights. Summer in Haute-Tielmark was not marked by the humid heat that gripped the lowlands to the east and south of the Fingerland. To Gaultry, the chill was ominous, like an early breath of fall, of the dying season that lay ahead.

They spent the first night at an old stone inn with fortresslike walls and tiny windows, then the second in a tiny manor drawn inside a wooden stockade. That manor marked the end of their travels on the High Road. From there the road turned north to Haute-Tielmark's stronghold at Arciers. Westward, the road toward Llara's Kettle dwindled to a narrow track. For obvious reasons, none of the routes from this point toward the border were maintained to encourage the swift movement of large numbers of riders.

The third day was long and hard. One of Captain Yveir's trio of young riders lamed his horse, and Gaultry, the worst equestrian of the company, was required to give over her mount and ride pillion behind him after the Captain had taken stock of the situation. Tullier rode close by her constantly after that, much to the young soldier's annoyance. The two of them exchanged words at a place where the track traversed the side of a rocky valley and the level ground dwindled. "You'll have both of us off the track, and our mounts broken in that rubble below," the soldier, a thin, dark-haired man named Elthois, snapped. After that Tullier, however unwillingly, ceded them more space.

Come evening, the riders spent an unrestful night in the grim manor holding of one of Haute-Tielmark's counts, strategically but uncomfortably set to guard a valley confluence among the first of the foothills. The count himself was away at the front, fighting with the best of his knights. In his absence, his lady's welcome was as cold as the drafty stronghold. She granted them a remount for Elthois with obvious reluctance. Gaultry was glad they would be sleeping there only the one night.

Rather than draw attention to herself and Tullier, she spoke with Yveir for places in his company's quarters. "Better we should be thought of as part of your troop than otherwise." So they were assigned to pallets in the damp, cell-like barracks along with the rest.

The Countess Ruelevy would not have any of them in her own kitchens. She sent in servitors with a cold kettle of stew and a pail of overcooked barley. It was eaten standing around the small table in front of the room's single, long-disused hearth.

"Tomorrow will be better," Yveir told them, catching Gaultry's expression as she picked at her dinner. It was burnt. Even after the hard rations she and Tullier had endured during their wretched cross-country journey through the Fingerlands, she had trouble chewing it down. "Tomorrow will be Sieur Denys and his lady. A smaller house, but a warmer keep."

Gaultry found herself looking forward to it.

Something ahead has been set to fire." Pulling his horse to an abrupt halt, Yveir stood up in the stirrups. "That is not good." Riding at the bottom of a wooded valley, they had come to a place where the track began a steep descent, giving them a broken view out over the treetops. Far down this new valley, a curl of smoke drifted, half-obscured by the trees and the turns of the land. The lean captain reached back into his saddlebags and pulled out a chart.

His woman—Gaultry had come to realize that one of the two women who rode with him was his partner, the other, her young sister—pulled up at Gaultry's side. "It has to be Sieur Denys's holding," she said worriedly. "I hope the good Sieur and his lady have not been harmed."

"Is it possible that the Lanai have penetrated this far East?" Gaultry asked.

The woman, Fredeconde, nodded. "This summer, after what the Bissanty did to them in their High Pastures, their raids have been a constant threat. This season, the Lanai have bowed to the command of a single man, and Ratté Gon is clever, bold, and dangerous all together."

Gaultry shook her head. Fredeconde, seeing her confusion, explained. Most of the Lanai forces were rallied at Llara's Kettle, but there were two other places where they had descended from the mountains. It was these secondary forces who were doing most of the raiding Gaultry had heard tale of, back in Princeport.

"The Ratté found a way to send his own tribesmen down the 'backdoor' pass behind Durreau Massif—a place where only the most skilled riders can take a horse." Fredeconde made an angle with her hand, demonstrating the pass's steepness. "It was an unwelcome surprise. Cutting those men from their retreat was an easy thing—but once they were down on the plateau, it was almost impossible to guess where their riders would next emerge. Eventually three of the seven ducal armies were diverted to contain them. 'Hunting rats in a haystack' was how one commander described it. It took almost a month to regain control."

Gaultry looked out at the billow of smoke up ahead. "If we regained control, then why are the Lanai still here, burning out people like your friend Sieur Denys?"

"The backdoor sortie was only a cover for the real raid." Fredeconde frowned. "That came farther north. They penetrated almost as far as Arciers—it was so bad they stole cattle from Victor Haute-Tielmark's personal stock. That attack's being called the 'Long Raid'—the Lanai scoured the manors around Arciers for almost three weeks. Even with the raid contained, they still have a camp in the foothills near there. It's been more than a hundred years since the Lanai maintained more than a single encampment on our lands." The scout loosed her reins while she adjusted her riding gloves, and then followed Gaultry's gaze out across the trees. They were too far away to smell the burn, but knowing it was there made the air seem heavier.

"We are lucky that Far Mountain is separated from our lands by four great massifs. Ratté Gon's mercenaries are excellent war-leaders, and they've kept better discipline among the tribesmen than ever I've seen. We have to hope the local raiders don't learn too much from them."

"Or that the Ratté doesn't come back here another year." The unfamiliar title felt clumsy on Gaultry's lips. The King, she wanted to say. Far Mountain's King.

Fredeconde nodded her head. "He wouldn't be here but for the sins of his son-in-law, letting the Bissanties slaughter the cattle he'd been left to safeguard in the High Pastures. The Ratté's made that clear, even to us." She sighed. "It's been a terrible season. Tielmark's armies can cut the Long Raid Lanai off from a retreat to the mountain passes, but neither side wants the full-scale engagement that move would provoke. It's the scattered Lanai who made the backdoor sortie who are the worst problem: They can't rejoin the main Lanai forces, either at the Kettle or at the Long Raid's encampment, and our supply lines have cut them off from going home the way they came.

"This land where we're riding now is in the space between the pincers of the divided forces of Tielmark's ducal armies. There's little enough to steal here, now that the locals have been alerted. My guess—the fire up ahead must have been started by whatever remains of the Ratté's men who risked the backdoor raid. Discipline among them is breaking down—quite sensibly. With young Neuvy Basse-Demaine's army blocking their retreat up into the mountains, they're peeling off in small units and making their way toward the Kettle, trying to find holes in the Tielmaran lines so they can rejoin their own people."

"So they're *between* us and the Prince's armies?" Gaultry asked, alarmed.

"I do not know. I think now I must speak with Yveir."

Gaultry followed her, seriously concerned.

Yveir confirmed Gaultry's greatest worries. "But it is not as bleak as you may think." He folded up his chart and carefully stowed it. "The Ratté's men are still somewhat organized, but not to the purpose that concerns you—preventing us from reaching Tielmark's main force. Most of them just want to get home. Their horses' heads are pointing the same direction as ours. If we are careful, and do not come upon them by mistake, we should be able to avoid trouble. The greater risk will be our own friends cutting us down before they understand who we are—but that's also avoidable if we follow proper protocols. So—from here we will split into two groups, the better to slip by the Lanai, and the better not to appear a threat as we ride into the Tielmaran lines. Fredeconde and Shostra will stay with you." Shostra was the big ax-man. "Elthois too, to fill out your number. I will ride with the others and head a little northward. Five and four. Better than nine. We'll camp together tonight—no fires, I'm afraid—and get a good start on the morning."

His manner was a little too cheerful for Gaultry to entirely believe his assurances, but he did prove that his map was good—they slept that night in a hidden hollow with a partially overhung roof. Gaultry did not sleep soundly. Her brain teased her with fears that this temporary sanctuary would prove false—should any of the Lanai have discovered them in the hollow, they would have been trapped like squirrels in a bottle. But beyond these nerves, nothing disturbed them.

When dawn came, Yveir would not allow anyone an early start, fearing an inadvertent overrun of some late-sleeping Lanai warriors. But finally they were underway. Fredeconde was to guide their fivesome on a slightly longer route, taking a roundabout, southerly advance to the Kettle, while Yveir would try the more direct approach, sending reinforcements to collect them if he succeeded in broaching the lines. Gaultry, who was once again tired of all the hard riding, almost wished she was going with his group, save that Yveir intended to investigate the source of the fire they had seen the night before, determining, as best he could, the fate of Sieur Denys and his family.

"Good riding!" Fredeconde would not touch her man before they parted—perhaps from some sense that it would bring bad luck. Yveir saluted her from his saddle. Followed closely by his abbreviated company, he kicked his horse into a trot and disappeared among the trees.

The route Fredeconde led them on was much overgrown. She stuck to the wooded ridgelines rather than the more open brush of the valley floors. Not entirely to Gaultry's dissatisfaction, they spent a good part of the first day leading their horses rather than riding, and they broke off their journey early in the day. While it was clear the scout knew her ground and was picking her route with care—she made no mystery of the landmarks for which she was searching, and there could be little doubt when they came upon them—Gaultry's impatience grew as her boredom mounted. Fredeconde was amused. "You would not like it so well if I chose an interesting route," she commented wryly. "Interesting would be Lanai warriors forcing open your knees."

Gaultry gave her a sharp look. In the wake of Richielle's attack, she had guided Tullier for three days through the Fingerland marshes before regaining the High Road. Guided him and fed him and kept both of them safe. Unburdened by horses, her woodcraft easily surpassed this woman's— even without small assists of magic. She could sense that every time they struggled up another briar-infested slope. There were ways, she knew, of doing this sort of climb more easily. Perhaps her poor horse skills had been a hindrance to their pace at times—but this was no good reason for the woman's amusement now. "The last man who tried to tangle with me that way died quickly," she said shortly. "The next one will fall faster still."

Beyond Fredeconde's shoulder, she caught Tullier's eye. She had the impression he wanted to add further words. She shook her head. They had almost reached their goal now. Better to keep the peace.

Late in the afternoon they reached the end of the wooded ground. The hills flattened and opened, giving the first views of the high mountain massif that lay ahead. These mountains shouldered aggressively up from the foothills, like nothing Gaultry had ever seen. They formed a barren shield of rock, filmy blue and grey colored at this distance, save for darker horizontal striations. With this first glimpse of the Lanaya high country, Gaultry finally understood why the places where the tribesmen could descend to attack Tielmark were so limited, and why this summer's campaigning under the Ratté Gon, Far Mountain's King, had taken Tielmark so much by surprise.

Fredeconde named the two peaks that were separate and distinct even from this distance. Ittanier and Hawkshead. The great lake and waterfall called Llara's Kettle lay south of Ittanier.

"It's scrub and bare rock from here forward," Fredeconde told Gaultry, as they lingered among the trees and finished off a waterskin. "With rolling limestone gullies. Easy to come upon a friend—or an enemy— when you least expect it. But we are not so far from the Kettle now. Those mountains are closer than they look. If anything should happen to separate us, ride due east. You'll bump into *somebody* friendly if you keep going east long enough." She smiled, and stared hungrily out at the mountains, drawing a deep lungful of air. Her round face lit with pleasure, revealing a surprising prettiness, usually kept soberly concealed. "They are beautiful, no? You feel the gods close, when you look upon such things."

What Gaultry felt was closer to awe than pleasure, but she did not say so aloud. Tullier, she noticed, was similarly subdued. "Llara in me," he said, as she came by him to adjust her saddle. His voice was for her ears alone. "Attacking down from these mountains, I can just barely fathom. The country here would be impossible to protect. All these rolling valleys—keeping track of a small group of riders just isn't practicable. They could descend on any outlying farm with no notice. But to successfully force an attack upward—no wonder my forefathers could never subdue the Lanai. And how our army managed a successful attack on the High Pastures this year—the gods must have been riding with them."

"Either that or they invoked powerful battle magic." Gaultry thought of Issachar Dan, Columba's lover, the dark Bissanty warrior who had been sent to Tielmark in the days of the Chancellor's rule. His battle mount was the fabulous eagle, Gyviere, a monstrous creature with feathers as sharp as steel. But she doubted even an army of Issachars would have an easy time of it, attacking upward into those treacherous gullies and slides.

The mood of the little party took on a seriousness that had not been there through all their stumbling about among the trees. As they made ready for the final leg of the journey, Fredeconde, Elthois, and Shostra knelt in prayer. Gaultry and Tullier, after casting each other a doubting look, joined them. A faintly nauseated feeling opened in Gaultry's stomach as she sensed the likelihood of upcoming bloodshed. Shostra shifted the scabbard of his ax to a position closer to his knee; Fredeconde readied her sword. Tullier, watching the scout's efficient movements, fiddled with his wrist sheath—a Sha Muira device, aiding the launch of a knife or dagger. The slim spring sheath, which he always wore on his wrist beneath his long sleeves, was the only piece of equipment he had rescued from Richielle's, other than the Kingmaker dagger. Unloaded and bound flat against his wrist, it was virtually invisible—which was probably why Richielle had neglected to strip it from his body. Now, Tullier was loading it with a knife he'd picked up at the Black Man Inn, where he had also been provided with the clumsy-looking sword he now wore at his waist. After meticulously checking the loading and the sheath's spring action, he unbuckled the sword in its scabbard, copying Fredeconde. The contrast between his smoothness with the first and awkwardness with the second was striking.

"If Elianté and Emiera watch us, we will miss the Lanai line completely," Fredeconde said, rising from her knees and whistling to her horse.

Gaultry could tell from her preparations that the scout did not think it would be so easy as that. "And if we meet them?"

"We'll have to fight. Whoever we meet will be a detachment of the Ratté's finest warriors. He planned the backdoor sortie to spread the broadest possible confusion, trusting only his most cunning and loyal men to the task. They went knowing that the longer they held out against our forces, the less likely it would be that they would safely regain the mountains—save in a hostage exchange at the summer's end—yet they were particularly charged with holding out in the lowlands until the Long Raid could be completed. To their honor, they achieved that goal. Now their aim is to regroup with their people—but they would be equally happy to ride into camp with a last trophy, freshly seized as proof of their valor."

She looked at Gaultry, taking in her travel-grimed face and simple traveling clothes. "Dressed as you are, they will not know that you are Gaultry Blas, the Prince's Glamour-witch, but they are rough men, with different means of assessing value. They won't notice your dirty cheeks. They'll see only that you are unarmed, that you have an escort—and they may try to seize you simply because of that." The words seemed an apology, or perhaps simply an explanation, for her earlier crude humor.

"I'll make them regret it if they do," Gaultry said. "I had hoped to reach the Prince without making my presence public, but if I must use my power to ensure that Tullier and I reach him, I won't hesitate. And to protect you too, of course," she added belatedly, glancing at the others.

Gaultry's horse, a rangy gelding, rolled her an inquiring look as she came to untie him. She patted his shoulder, feeling his nervous life-force. "Something's sure to go wrong," she told the quivering animal, trying to speak soothingly. "But I'll do what I can to see you through unscathed."

A snort from behind her announced that Tullier had overheard. "Gaultry." He put a restraining hand on her bridle. "I don't want you to be exposed to a mêlée for no good reason. Anything can happen. It's not worth the risk. Why can't we just wait here among the trees until we hear word from Yveir?"

"Because of Richielle. She knows this is where we've headed. If she hasn't been following us, it's a good guess that's because she came straight here instead." Gaultry shivered. In the days since Richielle's attack, she had regained her strength, but the thought that the old witch might meet them here—perhaps even herding the flock of her Changing Land sheep before her—was still daunting.

Tullier picked up a chunk of loose limestone and turned it over in his hands. "You can't fight her? Why not? If we fought together, surely . . ." His voice trailed off momentarily, then he found the words. "We defeated the Soul-breaker together. We can defeat this horrible crone too, if that's what you want."

Gaultry patted the gelding's side, trying to decide how to answer. She had fought Lukas's magic to a standstill—and then, while she held him engaged, Tullier had killed him. For her, that encounter had been full of terror, Lukas's death a horrible thing. For Tullier—perhaps that moment had held terror too, but defeating his powerful half-brother had also been an unhealthy moment of triumph.

"You're right," she said. "Together we are an unstoppable force."

The light in his face was a terrible thing. All his boyish love was suddenly revealed there openly, naked and hopeful. She tried to make her next words firm but gentle. "But I can't ask you to risk yourself going after Richielle, and it is your blood she seeks, not mine. I'm not ready to fight her on my own account. That is a decision for Benet to make. Let's just get through this next bit and join up with Martin and the Prince."

He turned rigidly to his own horse. "I don't want to join them. I want to go on traveling as we are. Just us, alone."

"While your gods and mine ride with us? That's not possible, Tullier, and you know it."

Shostra came to untie his big barrel-chested mount, and that ended their conversation.

Setting into her saddle, Gaultry pressed her hands against her breastbone and took a steadying breath. She could feel her power, coiled beneath her palms, potent and ready, filling her torso like a deeply drawn breath—impatient to be exhaled. Now—if only she could keep it in control, she would use it to break the Lanai lines. It was almost a more daunting thought than facing Richielle. She would have to remain cool, detached.

How she was to do that with trained warriors riding down on her was the real question.

For only the second time in her life she was riding deliberately toward a fight with armed men. The first time, Martin had been there with her, and his familiarity with this battle scenario had steadied her. Now Tullier would be her closest companion. The thought made her uneasy. The boy was trained in hand-to-hand combat, not in surviving a frontal assault, mounted like a knight. This time, she would be responsible for protecting Tullier as well as herself. She glanced over at him, and saw him staring at her, his expression troubled—probably imagining how he was going to protect her back. The thought was not reassuring.

Fredeconde, seeing everyone was ready, started her horse forward at a trot.

Out from under the trees, the sun glared unmercifully down on them. The limestone terrain, thin pastureland broken up by sculpted ridges of white, sun-bleached rock, reflected rather than absorbed the light. Fredeconde had picked a route that kept them down in the gullies, hidden for the most part below the horizon line. The stagnant air of these parched gullies was as stifling as a furnace fire. After days of coolness among the trees and on Haute-Tielmark's high plateau, this resurgence of full summer was an unexpected purgatory. Scant minutes into the ride, sweat was pouring beneath her clothes, and Gaultry fervently regretted not having doffed her tunic before they had left cover.

The heat made the ride seem endless, their jolting pace unendurable as their tension rose. On the few occasions they ascended to the horizon plain, the ground around them shimmered with heat. Gaultry began to think she would have to insist they take a brief respite. Then Fredeconde herself, just after they reached a pass up to the horizon line, held up her hand, motioning for a halt.

"Quiet," she snapped, as Gaultry's mount side-danced, hoofs clattering on rock.

Then Gaultry, even with her mount not quite under control, heard it. Horses. Moving toward them? Fredeconde paused for a further heartbeat, listening. "Half a dozen at least. Maybe more." She snapped her horse's reins. "Follow me!" Slapping her horse's rump, she took off at a canter.

It took Gaultry a moment to get her horse moving, but her travels at least had taught her how to encourage a horse to keep on the tail of a leader, so it was not quite the nightmare she had experienced previously, with a balking animal that she simply could not get to move. Tullier, a fine horseman, jockeyed his horse to her side, ensuring that her animal would match its pace as they all accelerated. Shostra, a heavier man on a heavier animal, was in the rear, Elthois with him.

They rode for a long time in that formation: Fredeconde in the lead, Gaultry and Tullier together, the two others tailed at their back. Gaultry found the rhythm of a canter easier to maintain than a trot. She crouched against her horse's neck, whispering encouragement. To her slight astonishment, the beast responded, relaxing and stretching out its legs. The sun blistered down on her bent back, but the movement of the air cooled her, and the heat began to center itself at the front of her body, taking on its own eagerness, its own urgency. She whispered a prayer as she rode, the words coming clumsily at first, then falling into a cadence with the movement of the horse's legs.

Despite the danger, she found she was shifting into a tranquil, almost suspended mental state. The sound of their pursuers' hoofbeats receded. The place where she had touched her breastbone earlier, feeling for her power, still felt warm. Like the caress of Martin's hands as he had touched her in the water. Like the summer warmth in Arleon Forest, lazy by some quiet pool. She focused, and the warmth languidly grew and spread. Soon her horse could feel it too. Its ears flickered backward, fear touching it, but she whispered the Huntress's name aloud, and immediately it soothed. Its gait picked up, enlivened. She extended her power outward, delicately feeling for the shape of its spirit, running through its body as its legs churned, and then, scarcely conscious of what she was doing, she began to lift herself away from it, lightening the animal's load, easing its run. She was still in the saddle, then, but somehow also above it. A sudden freeness and lightness rushed through her. The jolting movement of the horse, cantering across the rough ground, fell away.

She had expended so much strength, thrown so much power, into Richielle's sheep. Today, all that power had returned to her, and more. This lightness—this lightness as she rode above the horse—was only playing with the edge of her strength. This—she could easily control this.

From her floating place, she looked calmly outside of her trance, checking for Tullier at her side, the riders behind them. Ahead, Frede-conde's horse was ascending once again toward the plain. Gaultry set her animal to follow it. The ground was shimmering all around, but ahead two spots of more solid movement emerged amidst the waves of heat: a posse of riders to their left; and a singleton, ahead of them, riding back in their direction. Fredeconde's horse rose on its hind legs as she turned it, and the lithe scout stood up in the stirrups, just managing to keep her seat.

Gaultry, with a little more time to react, had time enough to turn her mount to follow. Fredeconde drove her animal on, glancing from side to side as she sought a safe place to descend. Then, before she could chose a new route, a mounted rider erupted right in front of her, seemingly from out of the ground. With astonishing agility, the scout retained her seat, swerved, and then fell from sight as her horse charged downward into a hidden gully, barely avoiding a collision with this new aggresser.

Gaultry, blocked along both of the obvious paths, pulled her horse to a halt. Ahead of her was a broken steepness of rock. Her horse would surely break a leg if she forced it on in that direction. "Which way?" she shouted at Tullier. He gestured ahead and down to the left—the steepness gentled there, opening a narrow route into another gully, if the rider who had challenged Fredeconde did not reach it first, cutting off their route.

"Go ahead of me." She did not think she could make her animal descend that narrow route without a leader. "I'll make my horse follow you. Or the others will keep me moving." Shostra and Elthois were still with them. He cast her an anxious glance, then obeyed, taking the lead.

It seemed for a time that they would be lucky. They reached the descent a heartbeat before the other rider, a rangy, flat-faced man, cheeks and arms blue with painted woad, riding a stocky dun-colored pony. Their horses were faster than his. Still, he managed to cut Shostra short. The big ax-man's horse refused the descent when the rider's pony challenged it, just short of the edge. Shostra was forced to continue along the high ridge, quickly dropping away from Gaultry's line of sight.

Glancing back, she saw that rather than chase Shostra or risk the descent following them, their pursuer had pulled up his horse and raised his thin lance. There was something red tied to that lance—a rag or a cluster of feathers.

"We're going to have company," Tullier called back. He too had seen the man's raised lance. "He's signaling ahead." Elthois, still with them and bringing up the rear, shouted confirmation from a little higher on the slope.

They slowed their horses almost to a walk, searching for a side route out of the gully. Atop them on the ridge, a rider appeared, tracking their progress, and then another. "Three at least," Gaultry said. "If we can avoid those other ones."

"Not if they're signaling each other," Tullier said dismally. They had already lost Fredeconde and Shostra. "They'll herd us into a blind valley, and disarm us at their leisure."

"That won't happen." Despite the interruptions, Gaultry had not lost the smooth building rhythm of her power. This time there was not a herd of sheep to sponge up her energy. This time there was no syphon-spell to counter her. There was no splitting of her power between separate forces. No dream confusion. The Glamour was in her, potent and pure. She could feel its substance, as solid as a weapon in her hand. "We've played that game once already—with Richielle. These men don't have the power to take us."

"What do you mean?"

Gaultry slowed her horse. "Tullier, come onto my saddle. We can't risk being separated in what comes next."

"We'll founder it. Your horse can't carry the weight. . . ."

"Don't argue." She ignored his hesitation, making a space for him in front of her on the saddle. "Just come."

Seeing she would not be dissuaded, he leapt smoothly across to her, his young body light and agile as an acrobat's. His horse snorted with disgust at the last violent kick he had made to launch himself, and swerved aside—Elthois, riding now at a short distance behind them, gave an admiring exclamation. There was a slight struggle as the two of them reorganized the reins and the stirrups.

"Do your best not to slip off," Tullier said tautly, toeing into the stirrups.

"Take us up that line there." Gaultry gestured to an unlikely rabbit track running up to the ridgeline on the far side from the riders.

"We'll founder the horse."

"Just do it." She wrapped her arms around his waist and pressed against him. It was awkward with the horse jostling beneath them, but necessary for the magic she intended to perform. The sudden contact made him shiver, and he sawed unintentionally on the reins. "Try to relax," she whispered, jolting against his ear by the break in the horse's stride. "I'm going to help the horse take our weight."

Tullier gasped as the first tendril of her power touched him. "Gaultry—"

She pressed her eyes shut and concentrated on the rhythm, feeling it build as the horse once more moved into its canter. That movement, driving them forward, was all that mattered. As her sense of her physical surroundings dropped away, ghostly shapes appeared to her: her own body, Tullier's, the horse's. She could tell from the placement of the horse's hooves that it had reached the approach to the treacherous rabbit-track, and she redoubled her concentration.

Vaguely, she sensed Tullier kicking the horse to force it up the steep track. She projected herself farther outward, feeling for the ground. As she reached out, a path opened before them through the darkness, veined with shifting, colored light like the aurora that would fill the night sky over her beloved southern forests come mid-winter. She kept her eyes pressed tightly closed, keeping herself in that spectral darkness where she was one with the horse, one with Tullier, herself a bright knot of power, her strength projected outward into them both. They rode upward, onward—

"Gaultry." Tullier's voice sounded far away, torn back into her ears by the rushing wind of their motion. "I need to pull up! Stop a minute!"

She opened her eyes. They had escaped the maze of gullies, and were thundering across a dry plain of yellow sod. The grass here was dense but thin, the limestone bedrock covered by a fragile layer of topsoil. She sensed they had come a fair distance, though the horse was still moving easily. It nickered with excited pleasure. Elthois, she glanced back and noted with a stab of concern, had not been able to keep pace with them.

The first cluster of their pursuers was lost somewhere behind them, but ahead—ahead was a fresh Lanai war party. A full dozen warriors, mounted low on stocky mountain ponies. One man, obviously the leader, directed the others with hand signals as they spread out to encircle them. They were an experienced raiding party, men who would not telegraph their intentions with noisy shouts.

"Doesn't Tielmark control any of its own territory around here?" Gaultry said bitterly, clinging to Tullier's waist as the boy pulled the horse up. It was not clear where their best chance lay in breaking the swift-tightening Lanai line.

Tullier's hands were tense on the reins. "This is just what Fredeconde was saying. These lot are trophy-hunters, trying to seize a last prize before running home to the pack. We must be close to the Tielmaran lines now if there are so many of them."

"We'll have to try to crash through."

Tullier nodded agreement. "If we wait for the Tielmarans to see us, we risk being taken. Those men behind us were signaling. It won't be long before every Lanai in the area converges on us. I don't know what you are doing to the horse—but it's fit to keep on running, even with our combined weight. We were doing well until this lot spread out in front of us."

Gaultry looked out beyond the Lanai line. They were closing on the mountains now. Ittanier, the mountain Fredeconde had pointed out, was large enough to still look far away, but despite how distant it appeared they had already begun to flank it. Surely they must reach the lake at Llara's Kettle soon, and the ground held by the Tielmaran armies.

Tullier flexed his wrist, engaging the knife in his sheath. Then he drew his sword. "Let them think we mean an honest attack. I'll take one in the throat with my knife as we close on them—from there, we will see how it goes."

Gaultry leaned into him. "We will take them," she whispered. Knowing that she and Tullier had the strength to destroy these men felt sad. "Too much is at stake, and we can't allow them to stop us—so we won't. This poor crew ahead does not have the strength to take us in an open contest of power."

"I know it." Disquietingly, he put a hand over hers where she had clasped his waist. "This—this is how I want it. Us together, unconquerable."

"Tullier—"

He kicked the horse into action rather than allow her to gainsay him. "For Llara!" he screamed. "For the blood of my god!"

Gaultry could only cling to his back and call once again on her magic. She matched his war cry, riding it deep through her body and down into the horse, urging its spirit forward as fiercely as Tullier urged its body.

Tullier drove the horse toward the largest rider. Perhaps he guessed the man would be clumsy on his small pony. Perhaps he wanted the best fight the Lanai could offer them. Their rangy gelding bore down on the man, even as the line of the other riders converged on them from the sides. Tullier held his sword out before him—trying as he did so not to slice off their horse's ears. The attackers on the sides began screaming, unnerving ululating screams that went on and on without any pause for breathing. If Gaultry had not been so focused on the internal pictures unfolding before her, she might have been frightened. As it was, the surging power on this plane absorbed all her capacity for emotion.

A focus of angry strength had leapt up in the boy's body. It sharpened to the point on his wrist where his knife waited, unsprung. Gaultry felt his eagerness, his unconscious gratification as he calculated the distance to the moment of his strike. The big man wheeled his pony to face them and came straight at them, presenting very little target around the front of his mount. He seemed set on ramming them—only at the last possible moment shearing aside, flicking his light lance for an unseating blow. That same moment, Tullier shifted his sword to his riding hand and raised his wrist. The dagger flashed from his sleeve, cutting a terrible furrow across the man's throat. With an awful, bubbling cry, the man dropped his reins and rode on past them, no longer in control of his mount.

The riders at their backs had not been close enough to see what had transpired, only knowing that their war comrade was sorely wounded. Their cries intensified. Tullier forced the gelding forward—pressing it now, as he had not done before, when he had been afraid it would be unable to carry their combined weight. But the direct attack had given their Lanai pursuers new purpose. They whipped their horses up, closing the gap.

One rider outpaced the rest, a light man on a fast pony. Gaultry tapped even more deeply into her strength, lightening herself and Tullier further, but it was not enough to beat the man's sheer speed. The narrow muzzle of his pony drew even with their horse's rump. Tullier fumbled by his hip, still driving the gelding on. "Get ready," he bit out. "This will hurt."

He yanked the reins sideways, pulling the gelding so the pony careened off its haunch. Stunning pain shot up through her leg as her foot was crunched between the two animals' bodies. Then she saw, with a flicker of horror, that Tullier had discarded his borrowed sword in favor of the Kingmaker blade.

"Don't!" she cried. The blade, a star of light, shimmered at the focused point of his spirit-shape. "Tullier, don't!"

As she screamed the words, he checked the horse and stabbed downward. Through the flash of the mêlée, she saw that they had drawn even with the swift rider. Even among the jostling of the cantering horses, Tullier's aim was sure. Killing, this close killing, was what he had been trained for. The blade slipped under the tribesman's guard, found his belly, twisted and touched something mortal, all in a flash that was quicker than the space between one heartbeat and the next.

A concussive burst of power billowed outward. Tullier screamed in surprised pain, then Gaultry felt it too—the Lanai's death agony reverberating outward through the *Ein Raku*, through Tullier, and into her own body. A rushing rainbow of color exploded within the spirit field, dazzling her, akin to pain. Their horse screamed, whether affected by the spirit-shock or by the physical explosion, Gaultry could not determine. It rolled away from the mortally injured tribesman and his frantic mount.

Gaultry, still blinded, was thrown backward over the horse's rump. Detached so unexpectedly from Tullier and the horse, it took her a burst of panicked will to maintain control. She landed inelegantly on her tailbone, the impact jarring but fortuitously mitigated by the lightening-magic. She sat, catching her breath, and set to reforming her spirit-self, bringing her weight back to earth, clearing the radiance from her eyes.

The horror that awaited her almost made her wish for the return of blindness. The corpse of the man killed by the *Ein Raku* blade lay twisted on the ground, his body split open by a wound that ran the entire length of his body, black and burned all through, as though he had been scoured by flame. Tullier, who had maintained his seat in the saddle through the clash of magic, was rounding the panicked and unwilling gelding back toward her, his face white, the shining *Ein Raku* blade brandished in his fist. His sleeve was covered with gore—the blade, and the hand that clutched it, shone unstained and clean, as before when they'd slaughtered the goats.

In a panicked moment it became clear that the gelding would die itself before agreeing to come any nearer the fallen corpse. Gaultry scrambled up and ran to meet them. Tullier slipped free from the saddle and released the reins, allowing the frenzied animal to bolt.

As he gained her side, he reached to seize her hand, managing a crooked, disturbing smile. "The tents of your army are not far over the next ridge. Even just a few paces on, I could see them from the horse's back. We can try to make it." He shoved the *Ein Raku* into his belt, guilt fleeting on his face. "I'm sorry. I didn't know."

The dead Lanai's war party had turned their horses and regrouped.

More men had come up to join them. A pair of riders paused over the corpse of the man killed by the *Ein Raku*. One let out a piercing, desolate cry, and would have run up on them, had he not been restrained. In a sharp, angry rush, these two regrouped with their fellows, then en masse they closed in. One of them threw a lance, fortunately with more strength than accuracy. It buried itself a good foot into the dirt, just missing Gaultry's hip. Tullier pulled the *Ein Raku* back out of his belt, and made a show of loading it back into his wrist launcher. "No," she hissed. "Not again."

"I won't—"

"Use it again and I'll kill you myself," she spat back. "That blade is not for combat."

"All right," he mouthed back. "But let's use the threat of it—"

The Lanai war-leader was a short man with a grizzled moustache. He made a signal for his men not to approach too closely, and sat back in his saddle to study them.

"Throw down your weapons," he said, in a strongly accented voice. "You will be hostages. Throw down your weapons."

Neither Tullier nor Gaultry moved.

"I think I am very lucky today." The war-leader looked at Gaultry. His eyes were cold. "A beautiful Tielmaran woman and her squire. More important than she might seem. She must be important, I think, or otherwise a fool, to risk herself to the Lanaya." He said something in a language Gaultry did not understand, and two of his remaining men moved to flank them. "Throw down your weapons, and you have my word for your safety. We would barter you for safe passage through the Tielmaran lines."

"I have not come here to play games with soldiers." Gaultry stared at him coolly, ignoring his shifting men. "My business is with Tielmark's Prince. Get out of my way, or I will not leave you the time to regret it."

The war-leader shot her a keen assessing look, and spoke sharply to one of his men. That soldier craned around in his saddle and freed a small crossbow, surprisingly advanced for a tribesman, from among the equipment tied to his saddle.

"Serjay is very good," the moustached man drawled, taunting her. "He can certainly kill your boy, who cares for you so much that he would abandon safe passage to come back and aid you. Your words are brave, but the choice—it is yours. Surrender to us on my word, or watch your boy die."

"I don't think so." Gaultry shook her head, trying to maintain her cool, even as the blood rushed through her body, so intense was her focus, her fear, her readiness. "If you don't yield us passage to the Tielmaran encampment, you will be the ones to die."

The crossbowman had not been instructed to hesitate. In one smoothly practiced movement, he raised the bow, sighted, and drew the trigger. Gaultry had time to react only in that swift second as he raised the bow to his shoulder, only time to take a single instinctive step toward him.

It was enough. Her power scorched the air like golden lightning. Bow and quarrel together exploded in a haze of golden light, the quarrel a mere flash of a handspan free of its cradle. The bowman's pony went wild, arrowed by slivers of bone and wood, and the crossbowman himself fell to the ground, wounded in many places by his shattered equipment, and screaming. Gaultry opened her palms, wailing with anger and sorrow together as she thrust her power outward. She had never before channeled her power in this way, but now—finally—was a time for no hesitations, no holding back.

In the past, she'd depended on physical contact to anchor her spells. Now, in her fury, she struck out without mercy. Who were these men to play at running her and Tullier through the valleys, when Tielmark's life and future lay in the balance? Tielmark's life, Tullier's, Benet's, and perhaps even her own. As her wrath rose, her power scorched free of her with a purity, a cleanness, that was entirely unfamiliar. The channels of her power burned, but not with pain. Unsuspected blockages vaporized, seared by the cleansing flame of her power, and were swept away in the blistering torrent that was her magic finally releasing itself in its full freedom, its full strength. For so long, she had feared that to allow her magic free rein would offer her only blood, self-immolation, loss of control. Now she stood, as if at the eye of a roiling hurricane, watching the storm of her power precipitate outward, obedient to her focus. The war-leader and his men—after the first flash of her power had destroyed the bow—were thrown violently backward against the ground, eyes blank with fear, mouths rounded in terror, helpless even to raise their hands in a vain gesture of protection.

She quelled the storm as abruptly as she had summoned it. The men who had stood in the front rank had fallen with twisted limbs and would not soon again be moving, but others, even as the magic died, struggled, if feebly, to regroup. Gaultry had had enough. She raised her hands and made a swift wiping motion, blinding them, to the last man, with a washing like gilt foil.

"You are right," she whispered, watching as one man, then another, cried out and raised their hands to their faces. "I am more important than I seem." She turned to Tullier, who had fallen a little aside, and was staring at her with an awed expression. "Let's go. I haven't blinded them permanently, and when their sight comes back who knows what they will do."

Tullier, in a rare moment of vulnerability, groped for her hand. "I don't think they'll come after us again," he said. "But better not risk it." Together, the two of them began to run in the direction of the Tielmaran lines, their uneven gaits soon jarring them from that contact, though Tullier kept close by her.

The boy had not been exaggerating about the closeness of the Prince's camp. When they gained one more ridge, they could see the points of the Tielmaran tents, rising over the curve of the land, closer even than Gaultry had hoped.

"Someone is coming for us!" Tullier gasped out. "Hear the hoofbeats?"

"Perhaps Yveir got someone through!"

Only one ridgeline away, a rider burst into sight. He was wearing half armor and mounted on a massive grey stallion. The horse was blowing and snorting, obviously being pushed harder than it liked, and angry for it. Recognizing the animal, Gaultry's heart sang with relief and joy. "It's Martin!"

There was barely time for her to wave before he thundered down on them.

"My heart!" he said, swinging down from his saddle. He did not mean it as an endearment. "It will most surely fail if you pull another stupid trick like this again! What do you think you are doing here?"

"We don't need your approval!" Tullier countered angrily. "We were doing perfectly fine without help from you!"

She ignored the anger on both sides and threw her arms around Martin's shoulders. "Elianté's eyes, it's good to see you. Did Yveir bring word we were coming?"

He stopped her words with a hasty kiss, a smile spreading through him. "Yes, he made it through hours back. I've been waiting all afternoon for any sign that you were near. But why have you come?" He cast a suspicious glance over her shoulder toward Tullier. "Yveir could tell us nothing, and Benet, even more than I, is hungry for an answer. The Brood were supposed to stay in Princeport, where you'd be safe." He grinned. "That order was meant for you too, you know."

Gaultry nodded. "It couldn't be helped. The Common Brood has been divided since its founding. I'm afraid it's divided still." She sighed, thinking of all that had transpired, at court and on the road, since she had last seen him. "It's a long story, and it got longer as we traveled. But Tamsanne thought it would be safest for Tullier to be with Benet—and now, from what's happened on the road, I'm certain she was right."

"Safest for whom?" Martin offered her a stirrup up onto his horse's back. "No, let's get you both back to camp. You can tell me then." He gave her a boost into the saddle.

His stallion was much taller than the brave gelding that had carried them across the limestone plain and through the gullies. Gaultry, from her high perch, craned around, wondering what had become of the animal, but it was nowhere to be seen. The Lanai warriors she could hear, still screaming and terrified, but out of sight beyond the stony ridge.

"What about Tullier?" she asked.

"I'll jog alongside," the boy said sullenly. He stood for a moment, alone, a closed look on his face as Martin shortened the stirrup strap on that side and seated Gaultry's foot. The contrast between them was suddenly intense: Martin's assured ease of strength and Tullier's skinny boyish frame, his promise yet unfulfilled.

"We should get moving," she said uneasily. "I exposed my magic back there, and Tullier killed two men."

Martin cast a quick look at Tullier before looping the reins over the horse's head to lead it. The huge animal shook its head, protesting, and Martin chucked it under its chin to quiet it. "I felt two bursts of magic," he said. "One I knew at once was you. The other—I thought it must be from the Lanai side. It was very dark."

Tullier made a sound that might have been a swear. "I already admitted I was wrong to Gaultry," he said angrily.

"Admitted what?" Martin asked.

Tullier flexed his wrist, and shot the Kingmaker blade into the turf at Martin's feet. It went straight in for a few inches, then touched rock and skittered sideways. "Admitted that." The boy was almost trembling with feeling. "I knew it was a mistake as soon as I used it!"

Martin looked down at the narrow blade, and then back at Tullier. "What is this?" he said softly. "No—I know what it is. The *Ein Raku.*"

He picked it up. Securely sheathing it among the weaponry tied to his saddle, he turned back to Gaultry. For one moment he reached out to her—then let his hand reluctantly drop away. "We need to get back to camp and find Benet. It's obvious you have a great deal to report."

chapter **24**

▼

They attended the Prince in his tent, for reasons that were immediately evident. Benet lay prone on a sumptuous camp bed, one leg elevated under wadded blankets. From the strained look of him, he had been wounded and then treated by an overzealous healer, causing the pain to rebound in his body. The only cure for that was rest, which, from the look of the fussing retainers around him, was just about the only thing he wasn't getting.

The Prince's tent emptied as Gaultry and Martin entered—Tullier had been left to wait in a covered, guarded area outside the main tent. A trio of knights wearing the household colors of the dukes of Haute-Tielmark, Ranault, and Arleon were among those being ushered out. Their aggrieved muttering as they departed bespoke an unsatisfactorily shortened meeting.

Benet's clerk cleared a table at the Prince's side. While the slight, serious-faced man returned scrolls to an iron rack in one of the tent's side alcoves and Benet gave him some last instructions, Gaultry had a chance to examine the prince covertly. Benet, never a fleshy man to begin with, had lost considerable weight in the three weeks since Gaultry had last seen him. He had the look of a man with a suppressed fever: His blue eyes were overbright, and even his simple directions to the clerk were spoken with discomfiting intensity. The carpeted interior of the tent was overheated and stuffy. Despite this Benet was dressed in a full-length riding coat, long enough to conceal his legs, along with whatever wound he might have taken. His tawny blond hair was slightly damp across his temples, and there was a slight tremor in his hands.

When the clerk gathered up some final papers, he finally turned to Gaultry. "Well?" His manner was somewhere between humored and disapproving. "I will waste neither my time nor yours asking why you have once again disobeyed my orders. We both know that you should not be here. Spare me the excuses and just tell me why you have come." He held out his hand, the Princely signet glinting in the tent's dim light.

Gaultry bent and kissed the Twins' double spiral. "The Great Twins are kind," she said, making the goddesses' sign as she looked up to him. From the floor, she could see the neatly wrapped bandages that bound nearly the entire length of his thigh.

She had suffered great hardships to reach this man. Now, looking upon him, she was suddenly uncertain. The Prince, in convalescence, did not look fit enough to oppose one such as Richielle, should she make her appearance at these battlegrounds. Yet Gaultry had to submit herself to his judgment, or her journey would be wasted. "If the Great Twins had not been with me these past weeks, I would not be here today," she told him.

"Doubtless true." Benet lapsed back on the couch, his expression still intense. "You have a tired look about you, lady. Tell me what has happened."

As she recounted her adventures, Gaultry soon discovered that the Prince had a better idea of many of courts' doings than she could give him, at least up until the fateful morning when Tullier had met with the Bissanty Envoy. But after that, much of what Gaultry had to tell him truly came as news. He sat up, freshly intent, when she described the fetish-crown that had been found in her bed and Tamsanne's near-death when she had spelled the fetish to determine its maker.

Then she came to the part of the story where Elisabeth Climens had told her of the High Priestess's plan to turn Tullier over to the Bissanties, along with the Kingmaker blade. At the mention of the *Ein Raku*, Benet exploded.

"Dervla possessed the blade all this time? Gods above, what can she be thinking? She lied to me directly. For that, I could revoke her Priestess's chain."

Gaultry shrugged unhappily. "My Prince, I cannot tell you with truth that I trust or admire your High Priestess, however strongly the power of the Great Twins runs in her. But Tullier and I left Princeport before anyone confronted her with Elisabeth's accusations. I cannot say with all certainty that she possessed a Kingmaker blade."

"Oh, she had it, I'm sure," Benet said grimly. "Hints she made—I can see now what she intended with her words. I have been a figure of fun for her, no doubt." His mouth thinned. "My own recent heroics," he rolled his eye ironically at Martin, "suddenly take on an embarrassing flavor. I have been a fool, imagining I could stand on my own for my country."

Gaultry stared blankly between the two men, not sure if it was safe to ask the Prince what action exactly it was that he was bemoaning. In the short time it had taken Martin to escort her to the Prince's tent, he had filled her in on little to nothing that had touched on Benet's recent activities.

"Don't say anything, Martin," Benet went on bitterly. "You gave me fair warning, and I would not listen." He turned to Gaultry. "Perhaps if my High Priestess had seen fit to share the Kingmaking tool, I would not have botched my chance for summoning the Gods."

"You did well, Sire," Martin said. "Few better."

Gaultry shook her head, not following their conversation. "With all due respect, my Prince—what are you talking about?"

"On the night of the Ides, the King of Far Mountain challenged me to a duel," Benet explained, taking pity on Gaultry's obvious confusion. "Three bloods before the setting of the sun. He wanted to take the Lanai home to their mountains—all of them—and he knows we are ready to end this season's fighting. It was a clever challenge—as the superior power, I would not stake my life on a Lanai withdrawal, but neither would I wish to reject an honorable chance to abbreviate this summer's campaign. I agreed to meet him."

Gaultry made an unconscious noise of dismay, and Benet looked at her sharply. "It was well worth the risk. A little blood shed from my body, or the Ratté's, to preserve the lives of my soldiers. A small price. The Lanai who remain trapped in Tielmark have become increasingly desperate, and the fighting has taken on a nasty tone. Just this past week they made a reckless attempt to muster their strength and break through our lines. Your man there," he gestured to Martin, "routed them. It was a sorrowful and expensive victory, but we could not show weakness and let them through. Many died on both sides before the Lanai disengaged. The Ratté was most affected by the display we made of the heads: On his side of the lines, with their backs protected by the mountains, they seldom suffer such losses. That was when he sent his heralds with the offer: If we would allow his men safe passage, he would declare the season of war ended, and retreat back up to the high plateau."

"You agreed?"

Benet nodded. "After much discussion among my war-leaders. After all the Ratté's men have perpetrated in my valleys, our soldiers were not eager simply to let them go." He closed his eyes, briefly, as though sudden pain had stabbed him, and shifted his injured leg among the blankets. "Though of course some were eager to see if I had courage enough to rise to the Ratté's challenge."

"The Lanai will be returning to the mountains soon enough," Martin interjected. "Whether or not the Ratté's men rejoin them. Once the Lanai go, the stragglers will make a separate peace, however little they like it. Andion's moon is almost done, and lovely Sennechrys's month is not a timely season for war. The Golden Lady is a harvester of fields, not men."

"That may well be true," Benet said. It was evident from his tone that he and Martin had argued this point many times over. "But this is not an ordinary season, nor is it an ordinary campaign. The Ratté didn't only retrieve his honor by seizing our cattle. He gave the rest of the Lanai tribes a taste of what they can accomplish, driven by a real leader. Whatever the turning of the Gods' moons, few of them are ready to ride back up into the mountains. Not, at least, until they have accomplished something that looks like a valiant victory. If only I could have bested the Ratté, they would have retreated in disorder. And perhaps they would have been less keen to descend on us in strength next season."

Benet's wandering gaze again found Gaultry. "Right or wrong, the Ratté and I fought to a most unsatisfying denouement. We will each go to our graves bearing the other's scars—but nothing more to show for our combat. The gods laughed at our pledges. We fought for almost an hour. I touched him twice, a scratch and a running wound to his side, before he hit me square across my leg. But between ceremony and the time lost between rounds to attend our wounds, the sun fell below the mountains before either of us made third blood." His hand unconsciously reached to rub his thigh, and Gaultry understood at last the rushed work of his healer, trying to patch him together so he could return to the duel and try for that third cut. "Damn Dervla to Achavell!" Benet swore. "If she had been honest, I might have faced the Ratté armed with the Kingmaker blade. Two God-sworn rulers battling, man to man, for victory. Surely Andion himself would have held his chariot to see that!"

He stared up into the ceiling of the tent, bleak disappointment on his face. "Twins in me, I was stronger than the Ratté. He had the experience, the years of combat, but I was stronger. Also fresh to the front. Had the stakes been higher, I could have found the power to beat him, I am sure. The Gods would honor the courage of a Prince who slew a King in single combat, driving to with the *Ein Raku*. Such things are spoken of in legend. By that act," his voice shook, "surely the mantle of Kingship would have fallen on me, and Tielmark would have been extracted, for once and always, from this web of Bissanty subversion."

"Either that, or the Ratté could have killed you, leaving your throne empty save for your unborn child, and the tribesmen overrunning our borders." Martin shook his head. "Those aren't odds on which a Prince can stake his life."

"Your Highness," Gaultry said hesitantly. "About the Kingmaker blade . . . There is more that I must tell you."

Martin looked at her sharply. "Don't encourage him. There won't be a second duel. You see the marks that the Ratté put on him? The Ratté received as good in return, and the Lanai healers are considerably less skilled than our own. For Benet to propose a second duel to a man in recovery from such wounds—there is no honor in that."

Gaultry shook her head. "That may be so." Could Martin really hope that she—that they—would be able to keep Richielle's Kingmaker dagger from the Prince? "But Benet must know the full truth. Show him the blade we brought from Richielle."

Reluctantly, Martin drew forth the *Ein Raku*. Benet's eyes lit avidly. "The sacred blade! But—you told me you did not know for certain if Dervla had this knife."

"This knife did not come from Dervla," Gaultry said slowly. The look in Benet's eyes—it had too much of the eagerness she had seen in Tullier before a fight. "It came from the missing member of the Common Brood. The goat-herder, Richielle."

"Richielle? I thought she was dead."

"Very much not so."

The Prince opened his hand. Martin reluctantly handed over the blade. "It is unclean," he said. "The boy used it today in battle."

Benet tilted the blade upward, turning the flat to the light. "So this is the blade that could kill an Emperor's son," he said softly. "A man born to Great Llara's blood burning his veins. I never thought to hold it in my own hand." Noticing Gaultry's expression, he grimaced. "Allay your fears, Lady Gaultry. I have made your boy a promise of my protection, and I am not one to break my pledges. I only wonder what can be the source of this blade's power. Why do the gods heed it? What is in this knife that they should care?"

"Richielle must know," Gaultry said. An uneasiness crossed her. "My Prince, I must tell you what happened when we met Richielle."

Tullier was waiting outside, seated on a narrow camp bench between a young knight and another ducal messenger. Gaultry went to him and lightly clasped his shoulders. "You are safe," she whispered. "Benet will honor his pledge." She released him, ruffled his hair, and turned once more to Martin. "Where would you have us stay, now we have reached you?" She was a little unsure how things would stand now between them. His manner all the while they had been with the Prince had been very formal.

"I'll requisition some tents." He beckoned to a young ensign, waiting beyond the shelter of the Prince's canvas. Gaultry recognized the man as one of Martin's grandmother's men. "Lebrantine here will soon see you comfortably settled."

"Aren't you going to show us the camp?"

Martin passed a weary hand across his face. "I have to go out again. The men may have managed to round up your companions. Your Captain Yveir got through this early this morning. Indeed, he was the one who told me to expect you, and where you were likely to try to come through. I hope he will soon be reunited with his wife."

Gaultry had not known that Yveir and Fredeconde were married. She had made no assumptions as to what those two had pledged. She found herself picturing a homey cot, a little run wild, and perhaps two or three children, waiting in the care of doting grandparents. A brief pang of envy pierced her. "I hope they're safe. We lost them only a little before you found us."

"A matter to be quickly determined." Martin bent and kissed Gaultry's hand. The wolfish grey eyes were warm, filled with a smile for her alone. "As you can see, with Benet off his feet, I've become something of an errand boy. But I'll return to you soon. I am very glad you have reached us safely."

"I hope Fredeconde escaped," Tullier interjected brusquely, interrupting their moment. "She at least was kind."

Gaultry rolled her eyes where the boy could not see her and pulled her fingers free of Martin's hand. "Elianté keep you safe," she said. "I hope at least we can sup together this evening."

"Gods and the Prince willing." He signaled a waiting soldier to bring his horse, and left them.

"Will he be fighting again today?" she asked Lebrantine, watching Martin ride out of sight between the clustered tents.

The young ensign shook his head. "He put in his hours this morning." He grinned. "That Yveir of yours didn't make it through without a fight."

Martin had mentioned nothing of that.

"Can you show us the camp?" she asked. "I'd prefer to do that before we get ourselves settled. Plenty of time to stake tents later tonight."

It was not an easy thing, concealing her disappointment that Martin had not asked her to join him in his quarters.

Gaultry and Tullier spent the last days before the Full Moon quietly, safe in the heart of the camp. They barely got to see Martin, which bothered Gaultry more than she had anticipated, but which obviously pleased Tullier. From what Gaultry observed, Martin, following his grandmother's last wish, had declined to accept the title of Prince's Champion. But despite this, every soldier she met in camp made it covertly clear to her that even without the title, everyone recognized that such was his stature. The big soldier was called constantly to the rear lines to run down yet another company of Lanai. It was obvious that the Prince had come to depend on him, particularly since his duel with the Ratté.

She saw Victor Haute-Tielmark once, from a distance. Victor was employed on the front lines, facing the bulk of the Lanai. Watching the men array themselves, her picture of the war was very much changed. The Tielmaran camp lay between the crests of two small hills, with a good water source and a view of the glorious lake, Llara's Kettle, and the immense mountain cascade which fed it. It was a surprisingly pleasant place, with permanent camp kitchens built into the turf, and many fine tents as well as the foot-soldiers' more spartan quarters. On a year when the Lanai aggression was light, she could imagine the battles and the smaller sorties were more like an extended, extra-dangerous tourney than a field of war. This year, of course, things were more serious than that—but still, the confines of the innermost camp remained comfortably civilized.

Between the Tielmaran camp, the lake, and the valley that ascended from behind Ittanier Peak up into the mountains, was a great gently rolling bowl of ground—the perfect field to stage a battle. Beyond, the Lanai camp was naturally well defended, on a little plateau partway up the Ittanier valley—invulnerable to heavy assault unless with dire cost to the attacker. Instead, both sides spent most of their time lining up their soldiers to attack, sallying forward to great effect—and then slipping away from each other before a true clash of the men, avoiding confrontation. It was clear to Gaultry after the first day that the Lanai had no intention of engaging the Tielmarans whatsoever, though they feinted forward with a great appearance of boldness and clashing of arms. The Tielmarans did their best to cut off these bravos' retreat back up into the valley, with mixed success. By the second day it was clear to Gaultry that the Tielmaran soldiers knew they had superiority of strength, but were reluctant to engage, save where they could annihilate their opponent utterly.

When she considered that every soldier ranked below sergeant was eagerly anticipating his fast-approaching return to the family farm once the Lanai aggression had faded, she hardly blamed them their lack of eagerness for the kill. There were crops to be brought in and a harvest to be attended. The Lanai had been successfully pent up in the field at Llara's Kettle—what more service could the Prince require of them?

Victor Haute-Tielmark's troops were the notable exception to this detachment. With the great golden bear of a Duke charging along his own lines, mounted on an equivalently enormously fat and muscular horse, that was quite understandable. Even from a distance, it was easy to be infected by the Duke's enthusiasm, and this land, after all, was his soldiers' home. But the Duke of Ranault's men, who hailed from the midlands, were noticeably less eager, as were the Arleon men—some of whom spoke with the familiar accents of Gaultry's home forest—who were serving under a professional war-leader. She found herself wondering about the army of Melaudiere, led by Martin's sister Mariette, and still away to the North. Melaudiere's army had got stuck with tidying up after the ugliness of the Long Raid, where the majority of the stock had been seized and farms unexpectedly ravaged. But if the ducal armies took their character from their war-leader, she suspected that Mariette's men would also keen. Gaultry herself had always found Mariette's bold yet insouciant character an inspiration.

As she learned the different characters of the respective ducal armies, she picked up some interesting gossip. Before the Prince's arrival in the West, quarreling between the Ducal war-leaders had cost Tielmark victory in two important battles. It was rumored that the Ratté's men had been able to run wild so long because the war-leaders of Longesse and Basse-Demaine were quarreling.

But mostly Gaultry worried. Tullier was avoiding her. She took supper with Martin in the evenings, at which time the boy would always disappear. She was grateful for the privacy this afforded her with Martin, but also concerned about the boy's feelings.

"He has been a part of me so many days," Gaultry told Martin, the evening before the day of the Full Moon. They were alone—a rarity. Martin's mess-man usually hovered over them. "And I will have to watch him like a hawk tomorrow. With Richielle still free . . . Even if we have stripped her of the Kingmaker blade, she is still strong enough to make me worry."

"You are right to be cautious," Martin said. "But the Prince knows your fears. He has posted extra guards tonight. No one is making light of the significance of this month's closing, Benet least of all. He promised you that the boy will be kept safe, and he'll keep that promise."

Having finished his meal, he had been lingering over his last glass of wine. Now he pushed it restlessly away. "I have bad news. Tomorrow Benet means to celebrate Andion's Full Moon by announcing Lily's pregnancy. Normally, that should be left to the High Priestess, but Dervla is not here, Lily has already announced it in Princeport, and already there are many who have heard the rumor of that news. There will be a push against the Lanai in the afternoon. Benet intends to dedicate the charge to his unborn child, and to lead it."

Gaultry felt her heart run cold. "You will ride with him?"

Martin nodded. "When a Prince 'leads' a charge, he is never really quite at its head. That would not be such a glorious sight. The realities of war would cut such a one down far too quickly. Someone must be there by him—or a little ahead—to clear his path."

That, of course, was how Martin's brother had died. And his father, and his uncle. Staining the Prince's path with the red of their blood. This sortie was fair begging for the Brood-curse to rise up and take him. Gaultry shook her head. "Tell Benet someone else must go."

"I have a reputation among the Lanaya," Martin said unhappily, unconsciously using the tribesmen's own term for themselves. "If we want to get Benet through this foolhardiness alive, I see no other way. It will not be so dangerous as it sounds." He reached, coming closer to her than he had done for days, and brushed her cheek. With that gesture, she realized at last that he was speaking more to reassure himself than her.

"The Lanaya will see us preparing all morning. They'll know what's coming. They won't be so eager to get in our way. Benet has promised me he will press to their first outposts, no farther. We won't go near the Widow-maker."

The Widow-maker, Gaultry had learned on one of her camp tours, was a ledgelike bridge of rock from which Lanai defenders could easily destroy anyone who rode beyond a certain point up into Ittanier valley. In her fear for him, she barely heard the rest of Martin's words.

"It's doubtful we'll even have to push to the first of the trenches." Clearly, Martin was playing through the most obvious variants of the attack, even as he was speaking. "Benet should get exactly what he wants. A bold show to remind the Lanai that they can't hope to accomplish anything more this year, and that it's time for them to go home, even if it means leaving the Ratté's men to a harsh fate."

"Will it work?" Her voice cracked.

Martin shrugged. "Maybe. The Ratté is greatly respected, but few among the tribal Lanaya really admire the man. He makes them work too hard. Besides, they know he came to help them out of an honor-bond, not of free choice, and they resent him for that."

He abruptly put aside his wine and stood up, pacing away from her. "I have asked Benet about Helena," he said curtly, abruptly changing the subject in a confused rush of feeling. "I wanted to tell you before now, but somehow . . ." his voice trailed away.

"What did he say?" Gaultry wondered if this explained Benet's more formal manners toward her.

"He said that he'd already discussed it with Dervla," Martin said bluntly, "and that she was adverse. I cannot have my divorce."

In her conflicted surprise, Gaultry did not know how to answer him. It was impossible not to react, angrily, to what could only be Dervla's vindictive pettiness, in this contemptible bid to deny them their desire, but the risks he would be facing tomorrow—surely that was the important thing here! She looked at the strong length of Martin's body, and pictured it riddled with arrows—or crossbow quarrels like the one thrown from the weapon that had threatened Tullier, back on the limestone plain. "Martin," she said helplessly, and made the mistake of touching him, of brushing her hand across his. No more than that, but already it was too much.

The physical compulsion that swept over her was unbearable. This was the impulse, the rational part of her mind screamed, that drove so many men and women together on the night before any battle. She did not have to fall to it. But—would these indeed be their last hours together, this side of the Great Goddess's table? Knowing that he must feel this passion in return, could she allow them to part this night without satisfying this impulse?

She glanced around the tent. Was it an ugly place, stark and bare, evidence of his busy killing days, nothing more than a place to sleep and eat? Or was it a place of beauty, the place where she and Martin might finally lie together as something like husband and wife?

She looked at him, lovingly, remembering all the dangers they had shared, the trust and steady respect that underlay their bickering, their love. Looking into Martin's eyes, her resolve hardened.

She was not willing to cede victory to Dervla's attempts to keep them apart.

Mervion had been wise. She had acknowledged Coyal as her lover early, and never allowed herself to become entangled in meaningless court questions of honor and place. Gaultry thought back to the simple warm comforts of the quarters her sister shared with Coyal in Princeport. Nothing in their love was a test. They merely were together, and took their happiness in that. By comparison, she and Martin had meekly played at the game that court expected of them, avoiding public acknowledgment of their feelings.

All that had got them was this awkward moment in this dirty tent, with both of them knowing what the other was feeling, both of them wanting the same thing, yet half-believing any indulgence of those feelings tempted the gods to punish them for stealing even a moment from duty.

"You are afraid for me," Martin said. His voice was husky. His body almost quivered as he restrained himself from reaching for her.

"I am afraid of everything." She turned and met his eyes, challenging.

"Except for Derlva High Priestess. I am *not* afraid of her. If she thinks she can keep us apart—that's pettiness, nothing more. It should not concern you."

"Let me hold you," he said. His eyes were intense on her face, but he did not reach for her—not yet. "I will drive away your other fears."

Gaultry opened her arms, and he came to her.

For a time, for them both, that was the only thing that mattered.

Gaultry lay on her back, listening to the sounds of the camp, the grey fabric of the tent ceiling above her. The spot where Martin had lain at her side was still warm. It was not quite dawn, but already there was movement. The experienced soldiers, like Martin, were already up and readying themselves for the day's push.

Her body felt utterly relaxed. With Martin gone, the fear was returning, but only gradually. The gods were kind. The love she had shared with Martin—it would never be enough to fill her, but at least the Great Twelve had allowed her a taste.

She had cried at first when Martin had rolled away from her. He had been distressed until he realized that her tears were for worry, for fear of what lay ahead—not for what they had just shared: the peace she felt with him, the rightness. "I am very afraid of what the Bissanty plan for Tielmark next," she had told him. "Yet every road that leads to Kingship is painted with ugly death. Must there be such a brutal compromise? One death to save many lives of pain?"

In the darkness, Martin had reached out and pulled her against him. "The gods admire more than death-mongering, though sometimes that is hard to see. Take heart. Tamsanne and Dame Julie may have discovered something in Princeport. Perhaps today, as Benet and I ride across that great field to the Lanai side, the skies will open, and we will see Andion riding on his chariot, acknowledging our Prince's ascendance to the King's rank." She'd felt him smile against the crown of her head. "Wouldn't that be a sight to behold?"

"Benet holds Tullier's life in his hands." She had sighed against Martin's shoulder as she slipped back toward sleep. "The gods should reward a man who constrains his ambitions, even where he sees a clear course to their achievement."

She woke again with a start, conscious that since Martin had left her, she had been drowsing. She rolled out of bed and fumbled for her clothes.

It was still not quite yet morning, but the place where Martin had lain had lost its heat. Stumbling over to Martin's basin, she splashed a little water on her neck and hands and tied her hair back from her face.

Outside, the great expanse of Llara's Kettle was a smooth mirror, reflecting the bruised purple of the predawn sky, its waters sheeted over with skeins of morning fog. The dark mountains, the great descending round of the moon—which would rise again tonight, completely full, marking the close of Andion's month—were all there in the water, as perfect as a mirror. There was some movement in the outskirts of the camp, but here in the inner precincts mostly it was quiet. Her small tent, and Tullier's, were staked nearby. Gaultry, lingering at the door of Martin's tent, stiffened with alarm. She did not see the promised guards— only one man, sitting hunched in a cloak, and obviously mostly asleep, drowsing by the embers of a small fire.

There was no aura to tell her that something was wrong. Martin, she knew, would have called her, had anything been untoward when he had risen—which could have been no more than a few moments before. Nevertheless, she walked over to the single remaining guard and roused him with a less than gentle kick.

"What's happened? Where is the guard for young Tullirius?"

The man glanced up at her, aggrieved, and rubbed the spot where her boot had hit him.

"They're with him," he said sulkily.

"Him? What do you mean? Tullirius is not here?" In her sudden panic, she could not help but restate the obvious.

"The Prince came for him."

"Why didn't you rouse me?"

The man smirked. "The boy wanted you—right up to the moment when he found you hadn't slept in your own tent. Then, not for nothing would he have searched for you in the Stalkingman's house."

Gaultry could not conceal her blush. She had given little thought to Tullier last night. "Where have they gone?"

"My orders—"

Gaultry seized the soldier by the front of his shirt. "If you don't tell me where they have gone, I will kill you, right here and now."

He was a strong man, and he put his big hands over hers, thinking he could force her back. Unthinking, she used her power to slap him down. His eyes went bright with fear. Gaultry, even realizing what she had done, did not back down. "Don't waste my time," she said. "Dawn is a time for power to blossom. Now tell me where Benet has taken young Tullirius."

chapter 25

A s she ran through the wet summer grass, cutting between the ghostly shapes of the soldiers' tents, obscured by rising trails of the predawn fog, she felt almost as though she was the only soul left living this morning, the only one alive with a sense of color and wonder and fear. Her night with Martin already seemed so far away, and yet she had brought great new strength away, great new confidence. She wondered if Martin too shared this feeling. Shared it, even as he purposefully moved, alone, among the lines of men who were armoring themselves for battle, assisting them in their preparations.

She recognized the place the soldier-guard had given as her destination: a circular, slightly raised field ringed by old, half-fallen earthwork walls. Tielmarans traditionally met there for duels of honor in any of the miscellaneous disputes that arose while the ducal armies waited in camp for call to action. There had been no such arguments since her arrival, but Gaultry had been shown the field's location. It lay a little outside the largest grouping of the soldiers' tents, below a guarded rise with a good view of the lake.

Leaving the main camp behind her, her approach to the field led her through a thin screen of scrub. The fog hung low on the ground here, casting mysterious, shifting shapes among the spindly trees. This area of the camp was sanctified ground—it abutted the land dedicated to the Goddess-Twins' sacred grove, and the pair of consecrated does that lived within the grove could forage here unthreatened. With its handful of broken trees and ragged overgrown bushes, the area had desolate aura. Gaultry, shivering from the coldness of the mist, had to remind herself that she was indeed safely within the Tielmaran lines, and there was no real chance of Lanai intruders.

She wished she knew what Benet intended with this early morning rendezvous. *Some* sort of ceremony, surely, with Andion's Moon in its final descent, and the dawn hour ripe for ritual. Benet's bond to the land was a mystery which Gaultry did not completely understand. Surely the Prince could not be planning to violate the pledge of protection he had made to Tullier? But what if the temptations of Kingship had proved too great, or if something in the land had risen and spoken to him? Perhaps he simply had decided his life was hostage to a deeper pledge than his word to a boy who could never really be anything other than his enemy. As she ran, Gaultry cursed herself, again and again, for ever thinking it could be the right thing to let Benet have Richielle's *Ein Raku*. She should have hidden it, or tried to destroy it—anything that would have kept it safely out of his and Tullier's way both, until after the passing of the moon.

The overgrown earthworks that surrounded the old dueling ground loomed up sooner than she expected. Gaultry, reaching the path that circumnavigated the field, almost stumbled over a young soldier who had been set to guard the perimeter. One of many, he was quick to inform her, his face a little white at her unexpected appearance out of the mist.

"Huntress in me, let me pass."

"Lady, you must have a permit—"

"Elianté's Spear!" Gaultry swore. "Don't you know me? I am young Tullirius Caviedo's guardian. Let me by, or the Prince and the boy together will hear my screams. By all the gods together, you will feel the fullness of their displeasure then."

"I can't let you through," the soldier said pleadingly, obviously recognizing that he was beyond his league, yet unwilling to disobey his orders. "Why not petition the Captain? He's around at the next guard post." He pointed along the track.

"The next post?" That sounded close enough not to make any odds. Gaultry relented. "Your captain better be there as you say." Not wasting time, she sprinted onward.

To her relief and surprise, the guard captain at the next post was Yveir. Unlike the first soldier, he recognized her, and though he frowned at her request to enter, he reluctantly acquiesced. "But only because the Prince would have allowed you to accompany us, had you been back there in your tent when we came for him."

Gaultry gritted her teeth. Both Benet and Tullier must have known exactly where she had spent the night. There was no good reason she could see that neither had sent a guard to retrieve her. "Benet *personally* appointed me the boy's guardian," she snapped. "That was not intended as merely an honor post."

Yveir nodded toward a crooked track that led through a wide breach in the earthwork wall. A beaten earthen path, bracketed by the spindly brush that had grown up over and onto the earthworks. "Go along in that way. That's where you'll find them."

Gaultry acknowledged Yveir with the goddesses' sign, and moved tentatively forward. The ground was soft underfoot as she approached the breach, and then packed and hard as she passed through the wall and down toward the field. The brush had grown up against the interior of the wall as well as the exterior, that, combined with the fog, shielded her from a clear view of the field. Then she turned a gentle bend in the path, and the grassy round field opened before her. She drew a startled breath.

Some force of magic had cleared the fog from the dueling ground's field. The outward-thrown mist swirled against the field's perimeter, re-buffed, like smoke outside a bulb of glass.

What she saw within defied her expectations. Benet and Tullier, un-accompanied, stood alone on the low, daislike hummock that marked the fields' center. Both were unfamiliarly dressed in matching grey field clothes: tunics, boots and trousers, the Prince set apart only by the silvery blue scarf he wore around his neck. Their voices were a little raised, but nothing between them was overtly aggressive. With waves of doubt as-sailing her, she dropped back into the masking fog.

Then Tullier turned, and she caught a glimpse of the weapon in his hand: the Kingmaker knife.

"This is a trick," the boy said hoarsely. "And not a kind one."

"No trick," Benet answered. "This is what you were raised to do. A moment of destiny for us both."

"My past is done. I seek a different future."

"What future? The Great Thunderer has claimed you. How can you escape that?"

"I will serve Llara always," Tullier said stoutly enough, though a boy-ish tremor in his voice betrayed the perplexity of his feelings. "But she does not deny her disciples love, and I will never have that if I slay you."

"Love?" Benet said, disbelieving. "You mean with Lady Gaultry? That cannot be. Martin Stalker has made me a formal petition for her troth. And as for the Lady—you know she has made her choice."

"She should have her joy," Tullier said suddenly, hotly. "I will not be your tool, to poison the things she holds dear!" Fidgeting, his fingers touched the edge of the blade. Something in the feel of the metal distracted him. "The metal," he said, leaving aside for a moment his personal passion. "It feels alive. There is something alive moving in it!"

"Do you know what it is?" Benet said. To Gaultry, in contrast to the boy's agitated manner, he seemed dangerously controlled, composed.

Tullier shook his head.

"Richielle's own soul. Stripped from her body and preserved for one single purpose within this metal. Can you imagine? Only one sorcerer in this generation earned the strength to wield such magic, and to such a vile end. That sorcerer was your brother Lukas. Putting her soul into the metal to make this *Ein Raku* blade was the price she demanded, in return for vesting him with the very strength that he needed to do it."

"Lukas Soul-breaker was only my half-brother," Tullier corrected him. "I killed him. I will kill the goat-herder too, and all her acts, if you will let me."

Benet, caught up in his own vision, did not heed him. "She used it to speak to me," he said softly. "I cut my finger against it to try its power, and in that moment she spoke to me."

Gaultry, standing at the field's side in the mist and fog, was suddenly uncomfortably conscious that she was most probably not the only person using the mist as cover. Richielle! When had she arrived at Llara's Kettle? More importantly—where was she now? At Gaultry's back? At Benet's?

At the circle's center Benet continued talking, unaware of Gaultry's presence. "But it would seem that Richielle's luck has broken as a herder of men. The old witch tried to coerce me into sinking this knife in your neck as the sun rose this morning—but I stood by my crown as Prince of Tielmark and called on the Goddess-Twins to stand witness, and her witcheries lost their power, even as I prayed. My faith gave me the strength to refuse her." Gaultry could hear the pride in his voice, even from this distance.

"Richielle is here?" Tullier glanced uneasily around, pierced by the same revelation that had just come to Gaultry. "Since when?"

"Days," said Benet. "More than a week. She approached my Priestesses and took over the battle-blessings the morning she arrived, but only revealed herself to me in person the night you made camp—when she attempted to suborn my pledge to protect you. Gods above, boy, hear what I am telling you! I faced her down alone, with the power of my faith!"

Something changed in the Prince as he spoke these words. There was a charge about him, an energy, that Gaultry had only before seen in him at those times when he had conducted ritual ceremonies as Tielmark's Prince. The hair went up at the back of her neck. At these times, she unavoidably felt a sense, however elusive, of the man's connection to Tielmark's soil.

"Elianté and Emiera claimed me," the Prince solemnly swore. "They gave me the strength to stand even against one so strong as Richielle. I will not be a pledge-breaker King, destroying my integrity and the land's together in a single corrupted oath." He paused, then reached out with a single finger for the point of the *Ein Raku*. Tullier stepped back, drawing the blade out of his reach, but not quite fast enough. The darkness that was the spot of Benet's blood seemed to absorb into the metal.

"But at last I see a way to give Tielmark a King without murdering a boy I have sworn to protect. I call upon you, Tullirius Caviedo, Bissanty Prince of Tielmark, to strike. Take my body for the earth, and free Bissanty for once and ever of Tielmark. History will call you Kingmaker, and you will live in ballads through the ages."

Tullier stepped backward, increasing the distance between them. He pressed the blade flat between his palms, covering its sharp edges. "Does Richielle want this?"

"This is not Richielle's choice." Benet pressed forward. "Why do you even hesitate? You need not fear reprisals. I have arranged to guarantee your safety."

"That may be," Tullier said harshly, once more backing away. "But I have passed words with your wife, and nothing is plainer than this: If I were to take your life, there would be no sanctuary for me in Tielmark. That, you wouldn't control from the tomb."

Gaultry did not like the steady way Benet was holding the boy with his eyes. He was waiting for something. This talk with Tullier was merely preliminaries. He had something in reserve. Something he thought would force the boy to act.

"My Prince." It was time to interrupt, time to try to disperse the rising aura of inevitability that Benet was invoking. She stepped forward out of the mist, revealing her presence. The air of the dueling field had an un-familiar dryness, a little shocking on her skin after the misty air where she had so long stood. "I apologize for not arriving sooner." She glanced at Tullier, offering the boy a wobbly smile of what she hoped was en-couragement. "I wish you had woken me."

"Lady Gaultry," Benet said easily. She did not deem it a good sign that he seemed to expect her. "It was good of you to come. A gathering of my witches indeed."

There was a movement among the mist directly opposite. Richielle, with her long white hair bound up in an elaborate headdress of braids and leather sheathing. Her body was even more attenuated and gaunt than Gaultry remembered, but her expression was no less fierce.

"Brood-member," she greeted Gaultry, bowing her head slightly. "You have come to vie with me to play Kingmaker after all. I won't say it's unexpected." Her teeth were a flash of brightness in her shadowed face. Her hands moved within her robes, gathering power.

"What is she doing here?" Gaultry demanded. "After all you know of her evil history, why have you welcomed her? You know she doesn't care what kind of a King rules Tielmark, what price we pay for our freedom "

"Richielle has learned many things in her years of travel," the Prince said in a hard tone. "Kingmaking among them. To discover the lore that produced her *Ein Raku*, she had to learn a great deal concerning weap-onry, and the craft that it takes to vest it with the gods' power. It may surprise you to learn that she has even made study of the Sha Muira cult."

At this Tullier turned his head, a little too sharply.

"As you may know," the Prince continued, beginning to unwind the blue scarf at his neck, "the Sha Muira sorceries do much to blur the line between the weapon, the one who wields it, and the one who falls to its attack." The cloth came free, revealing a silver chain formed of diamond-shaped, elongated links, looped four times around his throat. Benet drew it off in one smooth swift motion and ran the links through his fingers. He turned to Gaultry, coming down a little from the earthen dais. He did not quite hold out the chain to her, but the suggestion was there in his movements. "From Richielle, I have learned astonishing things about the Sha Muira training—"

"Don't!" Tullier begged abruptly, verging almost on panic.

Benet ignored him, implacable. "The rituals the young apprentices undertake are most appalling. Each draws the supplicants deeper inside the cult, binding them with a guilt so strong that only the blessing of their Goddess can relieve them. You know, of course, that the acolytes are all poisoned, and wear internal chains of pain. But that is the least of what they undergo to become Sha Muira. Your Tullier, of course, had completed the entire course—save for returning to Sha Muira island with proofs of his first kill."

"What is that chain?" Gaultry could not hold back the question.

"Gaultry," Tullier said softly. "Please. Don't touch it. Don't even look at it. I am not that. I am—everything that I am is what you made me."

She hesitated, torn between his plea and a terrible desire to know what knowledge, what act, could so fill him with remorse and dread. As she delayed, a ray of the new day's light daggered over the rim of the earthwork walls and pierced the mist. Benet swung around and opened his hands over his head, snapping the chain tight. He was just tall enough that the light caught the chain's links, preternaturally bright.

Beyond the Prince, Richielle had made the same motion. This light flashing on the chain was no act of the gods, but neither was it coincidence. Richielle's spells had wreathed the field with its barrier cover of fog, now she was playing tricks with the light she allowed to penetrate. No doubt she intended to hold the light of dawn in abeyance until the Prince and Tullier reached the moment of climax in her desired tableau.

"You know what this chain is." The Prince spoke directly to Tullier. "You know what it will reveal. Banish the hope that you will have her love, Tullirius. Banish the hope that you will keep even her respect."

Tullier cast Gaultry a forlorn look. All she could do back was shake her head, not understanding. Despite this, something he saw in her expression steadied him. His young face lit with sudden unexpected pride, with determination. "You have no understanding of my life," he told Benet. "No understanding of the threats by which you could move me. I never expected to live these past weeks. Every day has been a gift. I will not taint the beauty of that benefaction with my greed." He made as if to hand the dagger back to Benet. "I submit to you, Benet of Tielmark. As Llara is my god, I offer this to you freely: Keep my secrets, and take my life in their stead."

Benet could not conceal his surprise. "Boy—" he started.

Then Richielle took a step forward. Her head was bent, as if in submission, but her hands moved a binding gesture.

When Benet spoke again, his voice was cold. "That sounds almost noble, coming from a Sha Muira. But the price for keeping your secrets— it will not be *your* life. I vowed to protect you, and I will not be swayed from that. So if you would keep your secrets from Lady Gaultry—you know what you must do."

This lack of mercy was not like Benet. Clearly, Richielle was influencing him, even if that influence was not so strong that she could force him to break his protection pledge.

"My Prince," Gaultry said. "If Tullier does not wish me to learn what that chain has to tell me, I will honor his request. Goddess-Twins! Do not twist our friendship to such foul purpose."

"Lady Gaultry, it is not for you to choose what you will or will not know." Benet, shaking his head, coiled the chain around his hand. "I have already learned the Sha Muira secret of these links. As your liege, it is my right to share that grief with you."

He would have spoken further, but Tullier leapt. His hands were empty—the Kingmaker blade had been slipped away, hidden somewhere among his clothes. He grabbed for the diamond-linked chain. Benet made the error of sweeping it up, above the boy's reach, opening his stomach for a blow—which Tullier readily supplied. The two of them crumpled into a tangle of limbs and elbows. Benet was by far stronger, but Tullier was Sha Muira–trained, and he quickly took the advantage. If the chain had not tangled about Benet's wrist, the boy would have had it away in quick seconds.

The Prince was martially trained himself, and he fell into a defensive posture. Regrouping from his surprise, he closed on Tullier with all his angry strength, forcing the boy back. The two whirled in a circle like a big dog fighting a cat. The cat would do all the damage—until the moment the dog caught it in its jaws.

As Benet lunged, pushing Tullier backward off the dueling hummock, a sense of movement drew Gaultry's attention from the struggle. Richielle was almost at her sleeve. Gaultry took a swift pace back, maintaining a cautious distance.

"Your boy's weakness and strength both are in that chain." The goatherder smirked to see the younger women's retreat.

"Don't come near me!" It was terrible enough, watching the two men fight, without having to fend off Richielle.

The goat-herder's extended hand opened wide like a spider's legs. "As you love the boy," she said tauntingly, "wouldn't you like to know what he did to forge that chain's links?"

"You can never leave events to take their own course, can you?" Gaultry raged, her attention torn between her desire to separate the

Prince from Tullier and her fear of this old woman. "You impose a hidden influence; you force everything with magic. Do you trust yourself so little that you must distrust everyone else?"

Atop the earthen dais, the fighting was becoming uglier. Benet let out a cry of anger and pain combined as Tullier struck him, hard, across the side of his neck. In retaliation, he swung the chain at Tullier's face. If Tullier had not been standing on uneven ground, his reflexive step backward would not have been enough to save the ear on the side of his head where the chain struck him.

"Duty has finally laid its hands on Tielmark's Prince," Richielle jeered at Gaultry, once more reaching out. "Now all we need to do is call forth your boy's deepest instincts." Somehow, the herder touched her wrist. A crackle of power ran up Gaultry's arm, fleet as liquid wildfire. "Here, boy!" Richielle cried. "Look what you are fighting for!"

A sheath of yellow flame formed a flashing aureole around Gaultry's body, then faded. Tullier, casting over a flickering glance in the moment Richielle called, paled, then ducked a blow from Benet.

"What did he see?" Gaultry said furiously. The spell had faded as quickly as it had come.

Richielle smiled, and did not answer.

The two men closed, briefly grappling. When they spun apart, Tullier had somehow taken charge of the silver chain. He flung it, in a shining arc, so hard and far that it disappeared into the mist. But Benet—in the split second when everyone's eyes were on the chain's arc, Benet located the Kingmaker blade among Tullier's clothes. He pulled it free, and feinted with it at Tullier.

"You have sworn not to harm him!" Gaultry howled. She would have darted forward then, but a movement from Richielle at her side forestalled her. "You *are* maneuvering the Prince." Gaultry swung accusingly on the goat-herder. "He defied your sorcerous compulsion to kill, but he couldn't stop you from insinuating yourself into his plans."

Richielle's eyes were amused and malevolent. "I have only brought what he already wants to the surface. I told you: No future will grow from seeds that are not there from the start. Even a brave man has within a kernel of desperation. And your boy—" The old woman shot Gaultry a calculating look, its evil so strong that the young woman shuddered. "Your boy lived almost fifteen years for the pure joy of killing. It is not a desire two months have buried deep!"

Gaultry swung back to the grappling figures, appalled.

Whatever it was that Richielle was doing, *both* men were abetting it. Benet's attack on Tullier was calculated to fill him with the heat of a killing rage—but Tullier *wanted* to be angry enough to kill him now. The light Richielle had flared on Gaultry's skin—it had shown him something that made him want to fight.

In a sudden flurry of movement, the boy wrested the *Ein Raku* from his opponent's hand. Benet threw himself forward and grabbed a handful of Tullier's hair. As the boy fended him off, the blade flashed perilously close to Benet's jugular.

"Andion, God-King," Richielle intoned, sensing the approach of one man's victory. She made a wiping motion up to the sky, over in the direction where the sun was rising, and the fog began to burn away. "Stand witness: A King will be made today, and we beg your reverence for the blessing of it. I stand here today as Kingmaker, begging your acquiescence."

The sun's golden face burst suddenly through, transforming all it touched from ghostly grey to brilliant color. Gaultry shivered. *Andion God-King!* she prayed. *Don't listen to her. She is too bitter and angry to make a king.*

At her side, Richielle repeated her invocation.

"Shut your face." Gaultry struck Richielle in the mouth with a force that surprised them both. "Old woman, your time came and went fifty years past. I'm not going to stand here and let you do this."

For a moment, a quiver of doubt glistened in the goat-herder's eyes. Then the old woman reached for the breast of her robes, where she carried her Rhasan cards. "You cannot stop me!"

"Your cards are watered!" Gaultry told her, the wrath inside her building. "Your words have lost their strength to form the future! Fifty years of planning have made you weak, not strong!" She lashed out with a blow of golden power. "If you want to keep me out of this, you should have brought your magic sheep!"

The old woman staggered back.

The young woman struck again, with a queasy confidence that the old woman's bones could not withstand her, and drove Richielle to her knees. The golden power that surged through her was like an echo of the pleasure she had felt with Martin. Gaultry would have laughed, had Richielle's fear not been there to taint the moment. She had feared her Glamour power for so long—if only she had known how good it would feel to possess it!

A cry from behind her, either Benet or Tullier, returned her in a flash from this interlude of exhilaration. Gaultry glanced down at Richielle, on her knees but still mumbling: calling a spell that would part the fog and bring Andion's full light upon them. Even on her knees, the goat-herder was still trying to play Kingmaker.

Timing, Gaultry thought. This was about timing. Richielle—she was the distraction, not the focus. The important thing here was that Andion's light not shine down upon a violent death. Summoning her strength, she turned back to Benet and Tullier. "Stop it, both of you," she shrieked. As she touched Benet's cloak, a muffled sensation numbed her fingers. The Prince and Tullier were shielded by a powerful magic that bound them both to the *Ein Raku*: The power of Richielle's soul, pulsing outward from the metal.

For a moment Gaultry scrabbled ineffectively at the surface of the magic shield. Tullier's hand, with Benet's clasped over it, slashed by her face. She jerked away—almost not fast enough. A blaze of heat touched her cheek as the *Ein Raku* tagged her, miraculously not opening the skin.

Behind her, Richielle was laughing.

It was too much. She would not let the old hag win. Her magic flared outward, a searing golden ball of flame, and she thrust it toward the darkness that was Richielle's soul, that was the Kingmaker blade. Tullier and Benet cried together in pain—and then the blade spun clear of both men's hands. Richielle shrieked in rage, but could not regroup before Gaultry had fallen on the blade and seized it up.

Gaultry scrambled up the hummock to the center of the dueling ground. She held the Kingmaker up to the rising sun. "God-King! See! The goat-herder spoke what she could not deliver!"

"Achavell take you!" Richielle shrieked. "You will not stop me so easily!"

The old witch spread her hands wide, as if greeting a powerful presence. Gaultry felt a dangerous gathering of magic. "I acknowledge it for truth: My Kingmaker days are gone! But Tielmark must be freed of Bissanty chains, and another must rise to take my place." The goat-herder staggered and fell, the effort she was putting into this new spell overwhelming her. "The Kingmaker is *Gaultry Blas!*"

The compulsion that swept the young huntress-witch was more sadness than killing-rage. As she stood, sheathed in golden power, holding the ugly dark shard that was Richielle's soul, the presence of every man who had stood on this earthen dais before her rose through her. Brave men, cowards, braggarts, fools, all come west to Haute-Tielmark to fight for the land's integrity.

Now it was her turn.

Her Prince stood before her, unarmed and willing to offer his heart's blood to the earth. All that was needed was a loyal subject, a subject who could do what must be done to free Tielmark ever and always from the specter of Bissanty rule. The image was so strong, so real, she could not conceive that it could be a false sending. This was her moment. As if through a cloud, she saw the truth: *She must grant the Prince's wish. She could play Kingmaker; she would be the one to fulfill the old Brood-prophecy, freeing Tielmark, her family, everyone she loved.*

Benet, seeing her expression, extricated himself from Tullier and joined her on the hummock. The rising sun caught the rich wheat color of his hair, lighting it like flame. His eyes were serious and serene together.

"Do it," he said. He went on his knees before her, his chin rising as he knelt. "Break the God-chains, Kingmaker, and forge them anew with my blood."

"My Prince." She was shaking, not liking this feeling of unbalance, after all the euphoric joy of her power's full control. Yet all the same, as if from a distance, she saw herself drawing up the blade to strike. "I appeal to the Great Twelve to guide me here. Their command must be above your own—"

A terrified scream cut through the haze. Looking up, Gaultry thought for a moment that she was dreaming. On the path that led into the dueling ground, Princess Lily was running forward, her arms outstretched. Behind were others, equally unexpected. Tamsanne and Dame Julie and behind them were Julie's kin; also Mervion, Palamar, and Dervla. Martin too, wearing half his armor, a look on his face as though he had been summoned in haste from his expected morning of soldiering. The Common Brood, out in force.

Inexplicably, Elisabeth Climens accompanied them. She was wearing a black robe over a fluid green sheath of a dress that fell in supple flutes down to her ankles. It took Gaultry a moment to realize she had seen that dress before: It was the High Priestess of Tielmark's most formal robes, reserved for rituals of the highest importance.

All this flashed by Gaultry in the instant that Lily came screaming toward her, ahead of the Brood-members and Elisabeth by several lengths.

"Monster!" Lily cried out. It occurred to Gaultry distantly that the Princess meant Gaultry herself, damned as she stood over the Prince, the Kingmaker raised. "Take me," Lily implored, an expression of terrified sorrow contorting her features. "Don't hurt him!" The distance between them seemed wide at first, and then unbearably short. "Take me instead." The young Princess flung herself forward. Gaultry, holding the *Ein Raku*, stood frozen like a statue, still half-bedazzled by the vision Richielle had laid upon her. Lily, screaming, thrust herself at the blade, intending to take the blow intended for her husband.

Gaultry, by this time, had pulled herself just barely enough free of Richielle's thrall never to intend the blow. But at that moment, the blade itself came to life. It swept downward, outside of Gaultry's volition, plunging for the Princess's breast.

A fabulous, tearing crackle of magic interrupted the fatal blow. Pure green power, shot through with the colors of all things living and dead, spasmed outward, creating a halo that opened out like a frame, freezing the world like ice engendered on a winter pond. Even Lily was suspended in time and place, her mouth frozen in a wail of woe, her hands outstretched.

Gaultry, half-blinded by the shards of light, was the only thing still moving. Slowly, like an ant suspended in treacle, but still moving. The bitter magic of the Kingmaker blade had its own momentum. Gaultry fought to turn it, but she could not. All she could do was lash out with her Glamour, sheathing everything over with golden light, but succeeding in no other discernable effect.

But then something else moved within the frozen scene. Elisabeth Climens. Her determined young face appeared at the center of the glowing frame. Her crisp red lips were drawn in an intense frown, and she made awkward-looking motions with her hands—as though what she was doing was unfamiliar and demanded the greatest concentration. Picking her way in through the glittering shards of light, she brushed past Lily and reached up to take the *Ein Raku* from Gaultry's hand. There she hit a wall—she could not penetrate the shield of golden Glamour light that sheathed the huntress-witch and everything she was holding. Elisabeth paused, wrinkled her nose in concentration, trying to pierce the magic. Finally, stalled, she glanced into Gaultry's eyes. Her expression changed when she saw that Gaultry's consciousness was unfrozen. "Give me the blade," Elisabeth said urgently. "I cannot hold this spell much longer. Give it to me or Lily will surely be hurt."

"What are you?" Gaultry mouthed, even as she thinned the Glamour so she could cede the weapon.

"Tielmark's new High Priestess." Elisabeth grinned awkwardly, more nerves than humor. She shot Gaultry an anxious look. "I hardly believe it myself—but see? It cannot be other than true. Who else could command this power?" As she spoke, she plucked the blade from Gaultry's hand, covered it with the edge of her robe, and stepped back. The green halo of power vanished.

Lily collapsed against Gaultry's knees, the momentum of her rush fulfilling itself. She did not know for a moment that Elisabeth had plucked the knife safely away, and her hysterical determination to protect her husband was a terrible thing, until Elisabeth managed to calm her.

There was an unforgiving sullen look in the young Princess's eyes, even when she understood.

chapter 26

The blazing morning sun, its rays delayed so long by Richielle's enveloping fog, had risen entirely over the edge of the earthworks. Elisabeth's mouth thinned. "We must hurry," she said commandingly. "Form a circle around the table-field." Taking the Princess's hand in her own, she gestured for Gaultry to step down into that circle.

Richielle made a move as if to defy her, then stilled as Elisabeth shot her a steady look, laying her hand on her High Priestess's girdle. There was a measured firmness to her gesture, reminiscent of a lady-knight making ready for battle. "We can't fight Bissanty forever, goat-herder," Elisabeth told her coolly. "Tielmark must have its King. By old Lousielle's prophecy, Kingmaking must be shared among all the Brood, not just held to one person. Now take your place in the circle, or I will see you held there."

Richielle looked as though she were about to choke. "I recognize you," she said. "You are no more than blood of the blood of the Brood. That does not give you the right to order me."

"You have defied your own pledge to Lousielle long enough," Elisabeth said fiercely. "Besides, I am now risen to Tielmark's High Priestess, and that gives me the authority to command you. You *will* stand there." Elisabeth pointed. "There, with your face in shadow. Lady Gaultry." Elisabeth gestured to the point she had fixed. "I will thank you to move the goat-herder to her place. You will stand at her left hand when we form the circle." She glanced at the other Brood-members. "You know what to do. Go to your places and make ready." Only one other was unassigned. "The Stalkingman will take Richielle's right."

Gaultry, moving with Richielle into place, gave the old woman a wary glare, to which the goat-herder, her expression dull and closed, did not respond.

"What's happening?" she demanded, as Martin strode up to Richielle's other side.

He shook his head. "The gods only know. The Brood rode through the night to arrive for the dawn-hour. It seems Dervla has been deposed as High Priestess—and this young one has taken her place. I was just going forward to the lists when their runner called me back."

In a few quick moments the Brood-blood were ranged around the earthen dais as Elisabeth had directed—some of them, echoing Richielle, very unwilling indeed, but submissive. Gaultry was not sure how to interpret what she was seeing. Dervla, stripped of her rank, seemed half-insane with rage, half-broken with sorrow. Palamar, inexplicably, seemed utterly dead of emotion, emotionally collapsed. It was obvious that the many days riding from Princeport to the border had left her completely exhausted, but there was something wrong beyond that. Gaultry had never imagined that Palamar commanded much of her grandmother Marie Laconte's warrior magic, but the young acolyte's appearance was so depleted and wan, she found herself mentally revising this presumption. What had happened in Princeport to bring Dervla and Palamar into disgrace?

Dame Julie appeared at Gaultry's other shoulder. There was a faint reassurance to be found in the old singer's composure: Though she barely acknowledged Gaultry, her gaze rested on Elisabeth with an expression of possessive pride.

"What's happening?" Gaultry asked the singer.

Julie shushed her. "Follow Elisabeth," she said. "Great Twins! We will see a god today, if only you follow Elisabeth."

Gaultry looked helplessly over her shoulder, trying to spy Tullier. She had lost him since the moment her magic had swatted the *Ein Raku* from his hand. But the dueling ground was no longer empty—soldiers and servants and camp-followers of every description had followed the Brood-members in, eager to serve witness to their actions. She spotted Yveir, and near by him Fredeconde, and even young Elthois and the others of the courier's party.

But before her eye could find Tullier in all this mêlée, Elisabeth called her attention back.

The young High Priestess had stood Benet and Lily side-by-side and faced them into the sun. She put the *Ein Raku* she had taken from Gaultry in Benet's hand, and handed the knife that had once been Dervla's to Lily.

"Cross the blades," Elisabeth instructed, blinking as she too turned into the sun. "Commit yourselves to Andion's grace, and cross the blades. Do it sudden and hard." Richielle let out an angry sound, and made as if to break from the circle. Elisabeth glanced down at her coldly. "Hold her," she snapped to Martin and Gaultry.

"It is not my will to be so used!" Richielle shrieked in protest, as Gaultry and Martin laid hold of her. The goat-herder's skin felt clammy. She was frightened, but also for some reason desperate. Gaultry caught Martin's eye as they struggled to subdue her, to conform her to the dutiful figure in the stark tableau as Elisabeth required. There was an unexpected moment as power sang, and Gaultry and Martin together wove magic in cords to subdue her. Over the top of Richielle's struggling head, their eyes met again in pleased surprise, though her joy to be working with Martin in this way was much diminished by the sheer terror of the old woman they were binding.

"Free me!" Richielle pleaded.

"You have bound yourself," Elisabeth said, implacable. "It is the Brood-prophecy that includes you in the circle—not my will. If you fear it—that is only because you must reap what you have sown."

Richielle went deathly still. "This was not how I wanted it to be," was all she said.

Elisabeth turned back to the Prince. "Quickly, before the sun rises higher! Strike your partner's blade!"

"To what purpose?" Benet demanded. The spectacle of the old goat-herder's struggles was disturbing, and he had not gotten used to the idea of this slim young girl as his new High Priestess.

"Do you want to make a King?" Elisabeth charged him.

"I do," Benet said.

"Then you and your partner must cross these blades. As Elianté and Emiera Twins have always been your masters, show the Great Twelve Above the love you bear Tielmark. Breaking these blades will loose the magic within them, and then you can choose your own course."

"But the King's red—"

"Look there in the sky." Elisabeth threw her hands open toward the sun. "Andion's eye is on you. You alone can show him your faith. Your Brood—we will support you, meshing all our selves in magic to focus the god-call." She stepped backward down off the dais and took a place in the circle between Palamar and Dervla.

"Join hands," she commanded. Gaultry and Martin, with something of a struggle, took hold of Richielle's. Dame Julie took Gaultry's other hand, and the circle closed. Gaultry felt in a quick rush the powerful High-Priestess green of Elisabeth's magic, the gold of Mervion's, and then color after color of each of the other witches, unbroken in a conduit through their flesh.

For a dizzying moment Gaultry was lost in the earth as Tamsanne felt it: the secret spread of root and stem, the ancient dance beneath the earth's crust. Then a taint of angry black-green, shrunken to almost nothing, purged of its magical power, touched her—that was Palamar. Martin was flashing blue, the power of the sea.

Elisabeth sent the many-colored skein of their combined strength spiraling upward, reaching for the sun.

Above the circle of witches, Benet and Lily turned to stare at each other, a little apprehensive, at the center of the dueling ground's hummock. They had not seen each other for the best part of a month. Both saw changes that made the other a little strange. Lily: the pains her husband had suffered, fighting, and being himself wounded; Benet: his wife's quickening motherhood and her travails leading his court.

Lily raised her dagger first. The blade caught the clear rays of the sun's light. Her eyes were bright with hope. "Strike, my Love, for Tielmark's future."

Catching her mood, Benet too raised his blade. "For Tielmark!" he cried, and smashed it hard against hers.

As blade touched blade, Richielle let out a terrible cry. There was a fusion of power, a sparking. Lily stumbled back, overcome by the force of Benet's blow. Both blades lit up and pulsed with white immolating heat.

"Again!" Elisabeth called. As she spoke, the magic of the Brood-member's circle rose even higher, spinning upward, a tornado twisting, a vivid skein of power.

Benet struck again. This time Lily, expecting the blow, held steady. He raised his *Ein Raku* to strike a third time.

A shock of power, searing like flame, forestalled him. A lance of light slashed down from the sun, connecting ground to sky with a vivid train of fire.

—WHAT WOULD YOU HAVE OF ME?—

The very air trembled with power.

Andion was not a young god like the Twins of Tielmark. He was ancient, with his consort Llara and the Sea-god Allegrios, the deepest power that had formed the world. When the Goddess-Twins had come to earth, they had cloaked themselves with the human forms—terrible, awesome human forms, but human nonetheless. This morning, Andion's power shriveled the mist to nothing, the reverberations of his words echoing along the lance of his fire, but there was nothing human about him, save for the form of his voice. Gaultry, twisting around, realized with a quaking heart that the Great God-King had no intention of showing himself as anything other than this raw force.

"A King!" After the reverberations of the god's voice, Elisabeth's voice sounded thin and pale. "Strike, my Prince, and show the gods you will be King!"

At the center of the hummock, the royal couple's legs buckled, but they managed, by leaning into each other, not to fall upon their knees. Benet struck Lily's blade again. White light shone out from the metal, and the Brood's swirling power surrounded it, spiraling high to form a shape like a funnel, along the length of Andion's lance of light.

Andion's shaft of power momentarily intensified, but nothing beyond that happened.

Gaultry, holding Richielle's clawlike hand on one side and Julie's well-tended fingers on the other, sensed the doubt that assailed the circle. Something in this wasn't working. All their power, all the strength of their magical fire—it was not enough.

A murmur of dismay swept the circle of witnesses. In the wider dawning light, the fire of the God began to diffuse, the moment of cataclysmic power dissipating. Across the circle, Elisabeth's face twisted in frightened dismay. She had not expected her arrangements to fall short, to founder. In that moment, she looked to Gaultry, a question, a prayer in her eyes. "The circle needs more," she cried. "Gaultry, give it more!"

Gaultry reached out with her Glamour, further than she had ever reached before, trying to keep the power of the god's fiery lance concentrated. The whirling skein of the Brood-magic took on a golden hue—a hue which abruptly intensified, as Mervion, seeing what Gaultry was attempting, joined her, also reached out with her rare golden strength. Gaultry felt a flowing warmth, the familiarity, of her sister's love.

Andion's shaft of fire, still, barely, connected to the *Ein Raku* by a fine thread, gleamed freshly red within the whirling embrace of their twinned power, momentarily refocused.

—AH—said the god,—GLAMOUR'S HEAT. THAT PLEASES ME, BETTER THAN THIS BROKEN COIL.—

These words—from the Brood's lack of reaction, Gaultry understood that only she and Mervion had been privy to them. Looking across the circle, she found and met Mervion's eyes. Her sister nodded, a private acknowledgment of the burning pain, the pleasure they shared, touched and touching the great god's power.

"Put out more," Gaultry called to her sister, redoubling her own efforts.

Mervion shook her head. "I can't," she screamed, all the while attempting to retain the level of her magical engagement. "You can't. He is only toying with us. We do not have the power he wants. With the circle—the coil—broken, nothing we do will be enough."

As she spoke, Benet smashed his *Ein Raku* against Lily's again, growing desperate. The blades were streaming white heat now, the black of the souls within pulsing like pupating moths. But still—the transformation would not come.

Gaultry glanced around the Brood-circle, trying to understand what her sister—what the god—meant by the broken coil. There were no gaps in the circle that she could see. Every hand held another's; even Palamar and Dervla, who had lost their magic, were doing their part.

Then, in a strange moment of revelation as she met Dervla's angry eyes, and understood for the first time that her High Priestess's magic had been stripped from her, Gaultry saw the problem. Where were the Brood-members not born to the gift of magic? Dervla's niece; Martin's sister? Others, whose names she did not know.

"Elisabeth," Gaultry called out. "You needed to bring all the Brood, not just the sorcerers. Without the full Brood, the power will not be enough. Not everyone is here!"

The new High Priestess stared back, stunned. "But we have called Andion's eye upon us!" she cried, dismayed. "This will be our only chance!"

"We have to try something else!" Gaultry screamed back. Her Glamour—and Mervion's—it was enough to hold the god's interest, but not enough to push over and make the Kingship-change. "Elisabeth—we can try with both the Princes!" She twisted around to the crowd, trying to locate the boy's face. "Tullier!" she cried. "Tullier! Where are you? If ever you sought redemption, join Benet and call to the gods! Tullier—this moment is what you were made for—not for death!"

The ground shuddered as she spoke, and the lance of fire streaming through the sky and over her head drew back into itself, sharpening, expectant. Gaultry knew she must have guessed aright. Their Glamour-souls were not enough to move this change. But Tullier and his Blood-Imperial—

The boy was at her side, the pale green of his eyes unreadable. Gaultry made an attempt to drop the Brood's hands, but the circuit was so strong, she could not let go.

"Tullier," she breathed helplessly.

Glancing by her, he met Martin's eye with a grimace. Then he reached out to her, and gently touched her cheek. The power surging in her was so strong that the touch seared him, but Tullier, true to his training, did not flinch from her.

"There needs to be a sacrifice," he said. His narrow face was pale but resolute. "Willing, but still a sacrifice. Benet has too much to live for. So be it. You have taught me at least that."

He slipped under her arm and darted up onto the dueling dais. Gaultry screamed, frightened for him. "Tullier!" she cried. "Not that! You must not offer yourself! We don't want to pay a price in blood!"

Elisabeth's face, beyond, went paper-white, seeing her circle disrupted. She did not understand what was happening, and imagined some new Bissanty treachery. "Quickly!" she shrieked to Benet, her poise and confidence falling away, her girlishness re-emerging. "Strike again, before he can reach you!"

Benet drove downward. This time, Lily, fearful as ever of Bissanty interference, actively raised her blade to meet him. There was a slash of white fire, and the edges of the blades merged.

But Tullier was too quick. He seized the Kingmakers at their nexus. Their white flare shot out along his arms, and his body jerked, taking into itself the full force of the god's power as it finally surged down into those blades and broke them. "Andion!" he called. "Andion Sun-King! Take this! Take me. Break forever the chain! Tielmark free of Bissanty! Through me! Break that chain through me!"

As he spoke, the deep-purple of his Blood-Imperial flowed from between his fingers, sheeting the *Ein Raku* blades.

—BISSANTY'S ORPHAN PRINCE—Again, the words shook the sky.—LLARA'S SCION, BLOOD OF MY QUEEN, I ACCEPT YOUR OFFER—

The lance of light pulsed, enveloping the boy in fire, throwing Benet and Lily back. Tullier, clutching the melded Kingmakers, screamed, his clothes bursting into flame, the God-fire searing his skin. The flame was thickest at his hands, where it sparked and leapt, consuming the substance of his Blood-Imperial. Tullier screamed again. The entire Brood circle jerked outward. Some among them would perhaps have run or fallen, save that they could not release each other's hands. The skein of their magic tangled and rose, just barely restraining the destructive stream of God-fire contained within. Benet, throwing Lily off the dueling dais to protect her, ripped off his cloak.

Instead of retreating, he stepped toward the God-fire and threw his garment over Tullier, attempting to shield him. The fire incinerated the cloth in a fearful flashing instant, then started on Benet's sleeves. "Great Twelve above!" Benet shouted, refusing to draw back. "I will not claim my crown through this boy's blood! Tielmark will not make a King through Bissanty's claims!" He would have spoken more, but his words trailed away in a distressed cry.

Then—louder than Benet, there was a scream, a scream more shattering than anything Gaultry could have imagined possible. If the air had trembled before, now it seemed to shatter.

—NEVER NEVER NEVER! HE IS NOT FOR YOU! NEVER NEVER NEVER!—

A thousand dazzling bolts of lightning lit the sky, spearing down all around the earthen dais.

—NEVER NEVER NEVER! HE IS MINE! HE IS MINE!—The Grey Thundermother, Llara, had come to claim her own.

The light over the dueling dais, silver and red, was so intense Gaultry could no longer see—nor could anyone else. She had a dim perception of Tullier, screaming still, fenced round with silver light. Then all she could see was sheer white light. There was a terrible clash of power: Andion's fire, Llara's lightning bolts. Gaultry's magic, with the rest of the Brood's, was sucked into the maelstrom. For a moment it seemed it would be swept away, that her magic, already attenuated, would be torn from her completely.

Amidst the clashing, the violence, Dame Julie began singing. Her voice should have been drowned—by everything—yet it rose clear and high, its sound self-contained, beautiful, sealing out the awesome clash. After an uncertain moment, it established a rhythm, created an anchor. A sweet note joined it—Julie's granddaughter, across the circle, harmonizing. An excruciating interval passed, the white blindness still burgeoning, threatening to overwhelm everything. Then Tamsanne too began to sing, joining the anchor, broadening it, the old woman's crackling voice a not unpleasant counter to the beauty and purity of the others' sound.

After that, like a rush of streaming water, the Brood's magic reformed the skein, each of them cautiously retrieving their own thread, unraveling it, returning it to the skein in a new and stronger shape. Gaultry, along with Mervion the most extended of the Brood, took the longest to come to herself, but slowly, she too opened her cracked lips and joined her voice to the chorus. Her blindness endured, but the whiteness was no longer the terror of ancient gods descended. It was the blindness of eyes that had seen more than they should see, recovering. She sang earnestly, and loud, and was hardly even aware of the change when waves of comfort rolled back toward her, along with coils of her own magic. It was not until her Glamour returned to her that she realized how scared she had been to lose it, how frightened.

A greater fear, of course, had momentarily overwhelmed it. Tullier! Tears streamed down from her blinded eyes, dampening her chest.

Whatever stake Andion God-King had intended to take for raising Tielmark to a Kingship, it was quite clear that his Thunderer-consort Llara had intervened to argue the price.

Julie led the song to a tranquil close, and slipped her hand free of Gaultry's.

Around them, all was silence.

Gaultry's fears that everything around them had been annihilated were alleviated as the first sounds she heard came from the soldiers who had followed the Brood onto the dueling ground. Reassuring, normal sounds, of folk blinded like herself, and querulous and a little frightened as their neighbors moved and stepped on their toes, or bumped them.

"Can anyone else see anything?" Dame Julie's voice asked plaintively. "I've got spots, but nothing else yet."

On Gaultry's other side, Richielle, the old goat-herder, would not let go of her hand. Her fingers enclosed Gaultry's, viselike, her ragged nails cutting Gaultry's skin.

"Martin?" Gaultry asked tremulously, trying unsuccessfully to free herself.

"She's dead." Martin answered grimly. For an unpleasant moment, the two of them struggled blindly with the old woman's dead weight, then successfully managed to free themselves. Replacing the dead vise of Richielle's fingers with the warmth of Martin's hand was a terrific comfort, even as the white blindness began to break into black spots, followed by the sluggish return of her vision. Gaultry, blinking, turned toward the dais, relieved as she did so to see others rubbing their eyes and shaking their heads. At least she was not the last one to recover her sight.

At the center of the dueling dais, Benet was on his knees, protectively hunched, his arms clasped around Tullier's fallen body. The Prince's clothes were charred, his hair was dark with ash, and his skin was soot-covered and darkened, as if by the passage of flame. He raised his head just as her gaze touched him, his blue eyes strangely pale in the darkness of his skin. Those eyes searched the emptiness of the blue sky overhead—whether for god, goddess, or new omens, it was impossible to tell.

Atop Benet's head was a jagged, silver-colored circlet, the transformed remains of the Kingmaker knives.

A crown for the new King.

Benet, dropping his gaze, met Gaultry's eyes. She quailed before what she saw in them—a nakedness, a wildness, like nothing she had ever seen. Then, still holding the young huntress's gaze, he opened his arms, a gesture curiously like a benediction.

From within, Tullier feebly raised his head. Like Benet, he was braised by flame—but more fiercely. His clothes were completely burnt away, and his green eyes bore a stunned, bewildered look.

"Behold," Benet said. "Through my passage of flame, Tielmark sees its new King. But here in my arms lies something that one Goddess rules more precious still."

Gaultry felt she should say something, anything, to acknowledge the new King's words, but overwhelmed emotion choked her. It was Martin, touching her hand, who jogged her to movement. Together they stumbled forward, Martin shrugging out of his military cloak, then helping her to cover Tullier's burnt nakedness. The boy seemed numb as they first touched him, then started to shake and quiver as Gaultry put her arms around him. She and Martin half-carried him down from the earthen dais.

Behind her, Benet reached for Lily's hand, pulling her back up onto the dais next to him. The Princess looked frazzled but otherwise well—the shove Benet had given her before turning to protect Tullier had evidently preserved her from the worst of the God-fire. The new King placed his hand gently against Lily's midsection, still to the outward eye girlish and slim—but, as the gods knew, planted with fresh potential.

"By the great love that brought you and those who served you here in time to save me from myself," he said solemnly. "I pledge myself here to you once again. This crown is for the child that we have made together."

Tears overflowed from Lily's eyes. She bowed her head. "May all the gods grant our child a love of country equal to our own."

chapter **27**

▼

Gaultry was not sure why she ended up being assigned to oversee Richielle's burial, but she did know that standing over this grave-hole as the four soldiers dug was far down on the list of places where she wanted to be.

The news of Tielmark's triumph had passed from the dueling grounds like flame spreading in grass, lighting the ducal armies with a fresh fever to fight, to prove themselves before their new King. Benet, flush with energy from the transformation sent down by the gods, acceded to their cries to carry him away on their shoulders, to rally his armies into what would be perhaps the season's final battle against the Lanai. With a new flag raised before them, Tielmark's Princely blue-and-white hastily embellished with the brazen image of the sun, he had every hope of leading his warriors to victory.

Other members of the Brood, even the wretched Dervla and Palamar, were likewise seized and carried in his train. It seemed that only Gaultry and her four digging-men were going to be left out.

With the display of godly pyrotechnics that had lit the sky over the dueling ground, there was little doubt that the Lanai would have seen the omens against their winning victory today. Surely Tielmark, in its new flush of Kingship, would have a triumph today—and just as surely, she had earned a chance to see it.

Instead, Elisabeth High Priestess had insisted that Gaultry stay and oversee the old witch's burial beneath the dueling dais. "It cannot be trusted to anyone else," she had said. "It is an important completion, and must be carried through quickly." Gaultry could not find any arguments to raise against her. She had been obliged to entrust Tullier into her family's hands; and to kiss good-bye to Martin (who would ride alongside the new King into battle). Even as the crowd was dispersing, the soldiers cut up the sod and started to dig.

She had not overseen the work with the best of tempers.

At grave depth, they discovered signs that another burial had been made here, centuries gone by. Gaultry sent a runner to get Elisabeth and kept the men grimly working.

The foursome of soldiers assigned to her were little more happy than she. "Not a way to spend the last day of battle," the oldest complained, as he and his dig-partner climbed out of the deepening hole to give the other pair a turn.

"It's honorable service," Gaultry said dauntingly, in an insufficient effort to hide her fervent agreement. From the dueling ground, they could hear the clarion calls of battle, the distant shouts of men organizing for the charge. "Be happy you've drawn safe service."

The man grunted, and leaned to rest on the handle of his spade. "Elianté's Spear! That one needs to be in the ground all right. I just don't want to be the one to do it." He cast the goddesses' sign, and spat.

A movement by the earthwork wall caught her eye. Elisabeth, coming to inspect. Gaultry turned to the pair of men who had replaced the complainer in the hole. "It's the new High Priestess! Get a move on."

They applied themselves with an enthusiasm hitherto conspicuously absent.

"Lady Gaultry. How goes it?"

"Your Veneracy." The formal address came clumsily to Gaultry's lips. To Gaultry, Elisabeth was still the court-bewildered girl who had taken such an impulsive shine to the tamarin. "What do you think? Deep enough to lay the old hag to rest? With the mound atop it will be deeper still. Haven't these men done good work?"

Elisabeth looked tiredly at the heaps of loose earth around the grave hole. "The histories don't record it," she said. "But my belief is that this is the site where Algeorn of Far Mountain married Tielmark's Princess Briessine. I don't believe it's a grave that you've found—I think it's the markers of their pledge."

The diggers looked unconvinced. For some time now, they had been turning human bones out of the earth, along with coins gone black with age. It seemed unlikely these could signify anything other than a grave—

although Algeorn had been a barbarian war-leader, and the possibility that he might have lain the bodies of those he'd slain within a commemorative cairn, long since beaten flat by time, was not entirely improbable.

Elisabeth climbed, a little clumsily, over the piles of turf mounded around the hole, and then unexpectedly jumped down in, giving the two diggers in the hole a nervous moment. They cast Gaultry a beseeching look—she signaled to them simply to stay out of the young woman's way as best they could, and let Elisabeth get on with her business.

Tielmark's new High Priestess bent and kneeled, with a certainty owed to magic, and dug briefly in the soil with her soft fingers. When the dense soil defeated her, she had one of the diggers move in to help her with his spade. It obviously took more effort than Elisabeth had expected, but when she stood again, she was holding a fist-sized earthen clump.

"Help me out," she told the diggers. Abashed by such a casual address from one so distant to them in power, the men put aside their spades, wiped guiltily at their dirt-soiled hands, then, reluctantly, hefted her out, fair cringing as their hands made obvious marks on her skirts. Elisabeth took no notice. Bringing the clump of compacted earth over to Gaultry, she halted a few steps away, as if suddenly uncertain.

"I did not expect to need your powers this morning," she admitted shyly, speaking softly so the diggers would not hear her. "Great Twins together, after what I did to stop Dervla and become High Priestess, I thought all the answers would come so easily—in a rush, with each answer pulling along the answer to the next question in its wake! My blindness shames me—how could I have not included the Brood-members who lacked in magical powers? My own have been open to me for such a short time. How could I have not seen it? The price Benet might have paid for my slowness of mind!"

"You had most of the answers," Gaultry said uncomfortably. "And I can't claim I expected exactly what happened either. There were signs that Llara was protecting Tullier—I suppose beginning with the fact that Mervion and I were able to save him from the Sha Muira. But that was before the Bissanties made him Prince of Tielmark and gave him a throne, however empty its powers. I never imagined that Llara would interfere so directly."

Elisabeth nodded. "The Goddess-Queen is breaking her own rules. There is precedent for that in Bissanty—but in the past the Empire has always suffered grave upset for it."

As she spoke, she crumpled the clump of earth she'd retrieved from the grave-hole. Within was revealed a brooch of twisted gold, twined in a lover's knot. Pure gold, uncorroded by time or the earth. One of the diggers made a noise of astonishment. At the center of the knot a sun was boldly emblazoned: Andion God-King's sign.

"How did you know?" Gaultry asked.

Elisabeth, brightening the brooch with the edge of her sleeve, made a self-conscious half-shrug. "The land talks to me a little of its secrets. Nothing like Benet feels, or will come to feel, but it sufficed for this." She glanced over to where Richielle lay, her stiffening body stretched out on a winding cloth brought over from camp. "We will rebury it with her body, and rebuild the dueling dais. And so the Brood of Old Princess Lousielle ends."

Gaultry glanced nervously to the mountain skyline, toward the unseen battle lines. "I thought the Brood ended when Benet took the red of Kingship. I wouldn't want Martin to be fighting at Benet's side today unless the blood-bond is done."

"Martin is safe," Elisabeth said reassuringly. "Or as safe as any soldier can be this day. Richielle's blood and soul paid the final debt. That pledge is done."

They walked over to look at the corpse.

Richielle in life had been a terror. In death her body seemed a pitiable bundle of sticks. Her yellow-white hair had fallen free from its proud crown in her last struggle to evade the Brood-circle. Its long strands spread over her fallen body like stray weavings from a giant spiderweb. "Her last moments were bad," Gaultry said. It had not been pleasant to hold the woman's hand in the moment that life had left her. "She knew death was coming."

Elisabeth frowned. "Don't waste your pity. She was dead from the moment she vested her soul in the *Ein Raku*. She would have died if the blade had buried itself in Benet's heart. Or your boy Tullier's. She knew that. She knew that from the moment she made her soul into a weapon."

"Did all her hatred make the fuel that called the gods to listen?"

Elisabeth shook her head. "It was not Richielle. The gods were already listening. Ultimately even the Great Twelve must acknowledge the new configurations that arise within the lands they rule. Even an old god, like Llara, who has stubbornly given the Bissanty Emperor five princes for millennia, even as lands like Tielmark have slipped away from their grasp." She bent over Richielle's wizened body, straightening her limbs.

The golden marriage brooch, she clasped in the old woman's already skeletal hands. Then, methodically, she tied the winding sheet closed, all except the area over Richielle's stern face. "Would you like to say good-bye?"

"I said good-bye when I held her quiescent for death," Gaultry said grimly.

Elisabeth shrugged, and tied the last windings closed. In a final blessing, she traced the goddesses' spiral over the old woman's chest. "Then everything here is done. Commit her to the earth," she told the diggers.

"Wait," Gaultry said. She turned to Elisabeth. "There is a favor I must ask you."

"Tell me." The girl's pragmatic carefulness would not let her give an answer until she knew the question.

Gaultry showed her instead, taking her to the place in the grass where the mysterious diamond-linked chain with which Benet had threatened Tullier had fallen. "I want this to go in the earth with the goat-herder."

Elisabeth did not, of course, recognize it, so Gaultry had to tell her the story. The young High Priestess considered the matter very seriously, then agreed. They used one of the diggers' shovels to pick up the chain and drop it into the grave, where it would lie, Gaultry hoped for all time, beneath the goat-herder's corpse.

"What did you mean, the gods were already listening?" Gaultry asked, as they watched the men fill in the hole.

Elisabeth shrugged. "Bissanty has grown decadent and weak, and Tielmark—we have earned our freedom many, many times over, even without the gods' intervention. It has come to such a point: Even if we had broken our God-pledge and lost the protection of the Twins, the Empire would not have found it easy to retake our lands. To turn this tide of history would have taken godly intervention beyond anything that has been seen for centuries. The gods knew it was time for Tielmark to have a King."

"You make it sound too simple," Gaultry said. "For all I've suffered these past months—"

Elisabeth shook her head. "It's simple only in the sense of how clear the view seems when one has reached a mountain's summit. We've struggled for three hundred years to reach this height. When people—not just a Prince or King—have worked so hard and long to change the state of a nation, all the gods need is a point of power, and they find the excuse they need to acknowledge the change."

"Andion wanted more than an excuse," Gaultry said shortly.

"His inclination was to be greedy, and take the highest sacrifice on offer," Elisabeth agreed. "But his consort made him settle for rather less than that, didn't she?"

Gaultry smiled wanly at the memory of Llara's spears. "She applied more than a little pressure to that end."

"Of course," said Elisabeth, "the gods are not politicians, like my mother. They are eager to see a pattern set, and once settled, they are disinclined to vary it. Your grandmother was right. A tyrant king will always bear tyrants. A martyr, martyrs." She shuddered. "I am glad we arrived in time to prevent Benet from condemning Tielmark to that."

"How did you even discover that the sacrifice was unnecessary?" Gaultry asked. "How did you know?"

Elisabeth looked toward the morning sun, shading her eyes with her hand. "I was almost wrong. Andion would surely have taken your boy's life-sacrifice if Llara had let him." Then her face brightened, taking on the enthusiastic expression that Gaultry recognized from their meetings at court. "How did I know? Much of it I discovered as we traveled. We had packed up old Delcora's manuscripts, and the Prince's bards traveled with us, like troubadours of old. You should have heard those old sticks complaining! But after two days of traveling, we began to find the old rhythms of movement. The turning point came in one of Tyrannis's older songs. It described the powers of Tielmark's High Priestess. About how she had the power to hold time still—as I did this morning, when I stopped the blow that might have killed the Princess. But this power was something Dervla had never managed, despite having inherited all old Delcora's strength. Once I heard that, I recognized what Delcora had done, and I began to destroy Delcora's manuscripts as I read them."

"Tyrannis?" Gaultry was not familiar with the name.

"One of the Prince's older bards. He trained back under the Princess Lousielle."

"He told you to destroy the manuscripts?"

Elisabeth shook her head. "No, but something he said reminded me about the creating powers of the original Brood-members. Each had their specialty. My grandmother," there was pride in her eyes as she spoke, "was Marie Laconte, one of Tielmark's greatest warriors. Old Melaudiere was a sculptor. Dame Julie has her music. Delcora's power was to trap magic in words on paper. She did that even with the powers of the High Priestess. That robbed so much from her daughter—and would have kept so much from me, had I allowed it. So as I read Delcora's papers, I took that magic back."

Gaultry stared at the young woman's face, light dawning. It was little wonder that Tamsanne, who had known Marie Laconte in her prime, had little trouble recognizing her granddaughter. Looking at Elisabeth's features, she subtracted Argat Climens—and was left with something puzzlingly like Palamar, without the rabbity touches and plump neck. "That's why Richielle said you were Brood-blood," she said, in revelation.

Elisabeth nodded, a little sadness touching her. "My father was Rivière Laconte—Palamar's father, and Marie's sole heir. Julie tells me he was a comely man, both in character and in person. Perhaps there was some truth in my mother's claim that she lay with him for love."

Gaultry did not know what to say. An image of Argat's arrogant face rose before her. "Your mother gave you a gift," she said awkwardly. "If you had known you wore the Brood-blood chains, your life would have been very different. My own grandmother did the same for me—"

"That may be so," Elisabeth said, in a tone that begged Gaultry to speak no further. "Certainly it did Palamar no good to know she was power's heir. Did your grandmother tell you yet? Palamar has admitted to setting the syphon-spell which killed Gabrielle of Melaudiere."

"Palamar!" Gaultry was shocked.

"She held the Duchess responsible for her older sister's death, at the traitor-chancellor's hands."

Gaultry was stunned, then furious. "Will she be punished?"

"Oh yes. And Dervla too, for her many abuses of power. My mother was among the first of those let off her trial, but others were ill-prosecuted before her, and must receive restitution."

For a moment, the two women stood in silence. The diggers had all but filled the hole, and were starting on raising the flat-topped mound above it.

"Enough," Elisabeth said. "Our business here is completed."

Charging the diggers to complete the rebuilding of the earthwork dais alone, she gestured for Gaultry to follow her, and headed toward the passage out through the earthworks. Emerging through the wall, they came to a fork in the path. One road led to the overlook where the new King's command had gathered, the other, down among the tents. Elisabeth, preparing to leave her there, paused.

"You asked about the sacrifice. I can only tell you that I thought long and hard about Algeorn of Far Mountain. He married Tielmark's Briessine, and became Far Mountain's first King. But there was nothing in the songs or legends that told of him making blood-sacrifice to earn that title. So what was it that made the gods recognize him as King? It came to me that it could only have been because of power he had already earned, sending his men across four great massifs to aid the brother of the woman he had promised the gods he would wed. I learned from a variant of one of Tyrannis's songs that Briessine was not Algeorn's battle-prize—she was his beloved, and Algeorn's efforts on her brother's behalf were the lofty bridal-price he paid to make her his wife. Those heroics—they only confirmed a power he had already consolidated as his own.

"Think on it, Gaultry. This very morning Tielmark's armies face the King who was made the day that Briessine took Algeorn to husband. The Ratté Gon is Algeorn's heir, and the Ratté, above all, is an honorable man, where it comes to his family. He owes little allegiance to the other Lanai tribes—and yet he has treated Tielmark to this summer of hardship, and sacrificed many of his best men, all because his daughter's honor was threatened. The pattern remains as the gods set it, the day of Algeorn and Briessine's marriage. Algeorn, above all, honored the oaths he made to his family. That is the hallmark of Far Mountain's Kings.

"So: What did we want for Tielmark? In Far Mountain, they are honorable to their kin, but ruthless to outsiders. Tielmark, I hope, has a kinder future than that." Elisabeth shrugged. "The gods were ready to acknowledge our King, when we were ready to claim him. It was up to Benet himself what kind of choice that would be."

"So what did Benet choose?" Gaultry asked.

Elisabeth smiled. "I hope that he chose love, and to pass power forward optimistically to the future. Is that not what all expectant parents hope? To have a child who is greater than themselves? I am quite sure it was what my mother had in mind—whether or not any of us turned out the way she expected."

Argat Climens. Gaultry could only wonder what the woman made of her daughter's precipitous rise to power.

Still, one puzzlement remained. "Why was Richielle so certain a death was necessary? And not just Richielle—all the members of the Brood."

"Richielle's mistake lay in seeing only a single purpose for the King-maker knives. Perhaps it was because she has so long been a herder of animals—she didn't see that even the gods allow humans choices. The others—well, she was a herder, and they followed the force of her lead."

"So we have a King," Gaultry said. She looked out at the rolling bowl of the land that seemed to sweep open before them, promising infinite choice. She looked up to the beautiful clear morning sky, and then out at the great wall of mountains, leading away to the north.

"I wonder where that leaves Bissanty?"

Grandmother." Gaultry had left Elisabeth at the fork in the path, and returned to camp to find Tamsanne and Mervion, attending Tullier, safe in the cool of Martin's big tent.

Tullier was laid on the bed there, his braised skin raw but cleansed, his wounds carefully bound and tended, apparently asleep. When Gaultry came in, Mervion had just returned with a fresh bucket of water. Tamsanne was sitting by the boy's side, cleaning her own somewhat char-covered hands with an oily rag. She got up with uncommon alacrity as Gaultry entered and fervently embraced her.

"Is the goat-herder safely under?" When Gaultry nodded, she gave a relieved sigh. "It was right of Elisabeth to see that business concluded quickly. I should have warned you of her better."

"I was well protected," Gaultry said, portentously, squeezing her grandmother's shoulders. It was so seldom that Tamsanne expressed her feelings in this way. "Even against her Rhasan."

Tamsanne pushed out of the hug and looked up into her youngest granddaughter's face. "Tell me that Richielle did not read a card for you," she said, alarmed.

In answer, Gaultry reached into her tunic and brought forth the rimy cards she had taken from Richielle's body. "She did, but in the end, she did not pull the card either of us expected. These were too dangerous to commit to the earth, grandmother. I want you to have them, for everyone's safety—though from what Benet said to me, it would seem that their power has faded a little, since they were bathed in water on Andion's Ides." She drew a deep breath. "I want to give them to you, grandmother, but first I need to show you the card that Richielle played for me. The gods owe you that, at least."

Before Tamsanne could protest, Gaultry put her hand on the top card, feeling as she did the ancient power of the deck resist her. She battened it back with her Glamour, unrelenting. *I am not ambitious to rule you*, she told that power, *but I will be showing my grandmother this card*.

She turned the card, and held it out to Tamsanne, who flinched, then paled as the image opened to her. Bent to Gaultry's Glamour-will, it was only a little different than the card she had seen before: the ragged man, the orchid-flower. But the sun was now ascendant in the corner of the card.

"My Jarret!" Tamsanne whispered, ignoring the image's other elements.

"I saw him," Gaultry said, taking her grandmother's hand and pressing the card into it. "Over in the Changing Lands. I saw him." She paused, uncertain. "He protected me. Richielle was twisting the land beneath us, herding us, but somehow, he broke the chains of her spell for a time, ruining her timing. I don't really understand what it was he did."

"If you could understand the Changing Lands," Tamsanne said, a little shakily, "you would no longer have a human soul to rule you."

"He touched me," Gaultry said. "Just once, here on my brow." Her fingers went to the place, as once more she remembered the dryad's wild beauty. "I think he was curious to see what you had made of the gift that you shared with him."

Tamsanne looked again at the card. "He had that much of memory left?" she said. "Perhaps it is better that I never knew that." Then she reached and took the entire deck, and shuffled the Glamour-card in with the others.

Her eyes when she looked once more to Gaultry were bright with unshed tears. "For me, losing Jarret was the first link in the chain of history that led us all to this day." She tucked the cards out of sight, within the sleeves of her fusty dress, and wiped her face with the rag in her hand, forgetting that it was char-stained.

Reaching out, she took both Gaultry's and Mervion's hands. "Already, both of you have made better choices than I. You have won your Prince a crown, and you did not sacrifice your own heart's joy to do it."

She did not offer any other explanation, and Gaultry and Mervion, sharing a sisterly glance, did not press her. Soon after, Tamsanne quietly laid down the rag, and retreated from the tent.

"You can wake up now," Gaultry said, a little sourly, taking Tamsanne's seat by the bed. She took the boy's hand in her fingers, and was relieved to feel the steady pulse that beat within.

Tullier's eyes slitted painfully open, and she saw that he was less far from pretending to sleep than she'd imagined.

"Your chain is in the ground," she told him. "It shares Richielle's grave. I hope that was right."

"You know that the Sha Muira don't bury their dead?" Tullier asked sadly. "They just weight them down, and dump them into the sea."

"Well, the chain is buried," Gaultry said. "With all of its secrets."

"If Llara loves me, it will stay there."

Gaultry gently folded his hands beneath the blanket. "I don't think anyone can have any doubts about that, after today."

"She means me to go back to Bissanty, doesn't she?" Tullier said weakly. "That was why she wouldn't let Andion have me for Tielmark." There was no question who he meant by "she." Llara Thunderer.

"I think so," said Gaultry. "But the time has not come yet. Rest, and recover yourself." She had no idea how the thrones of Bissanty would realign, now that Tielmark was truly lost to the empire. Bissanty's Orphan Prince of Tielmark was no more. So what did that make Tullier? No less a Prince, that was clear, if the Grey Thunderer's response this morning was anything to go by. She stroked his cheek, and her hand came away ash-covered, despite all Tamsanne and Mervion had done to clean him. "Go to sleep, my Prince of Ashes," she told him. The words seemed fitting. That was how he had seemed, when Benet, newly crowned with the King's fire, had stood and revealed him, following the great blaze of Llara's wrath, and Andion's submission.

She and Mervion stayed by his side until he had completely fallen asleep.

It was a rout. The Lanai were not fools. They had seen the clash of godly magics, they had heard the surging victory cries that had followed. On such a day, they had known from the beginning of the Tielmaran's charge that they were not likely to prevail. A realignment of the ruling powers came but seldom and there was not a single ballad that told of the gods failing to reward it. The Lanai might come back to fight next year, but for this year, they knew they were finished.

Gaultry and Mervion had watched the turning point of the battle from the King's command overlook, straining to see the action in the valley. It had been thrilling, standing in safety and seeing the Tielmarans push the Lanai back, but also unpleasant. Witnessing the Lanai in retreat all the way into its heights had of course been exciting, but it had taken much longer to resolve the tangle of fighting men, about a third of the way up. Martin, Coyal, and Benet had all been in the Tielmaran vanguard.

The sisters had agreed that the only worse thing would have been not to watch.

This aside, the uncertainty was all worth it, for being able to stand witness to the moment the Lanai discipline at last completely broke and the mass of fighting Lanai shattered into scattered groups of men, some crushed by their opponents, some fleeing, some attempting to surrender, but at last, all of them, save for small knots of hold-outs—quickly suppressed or called to order by their captains—ending the fight.

Organizing the surrender took fewer men, and a shorter time, than Gaultry would have imagined. It was not long before the first of the ducal armies were sent back down the valley. They came, running, laughing and urging their horses at incautious, heedless speeds, plunging past the Tielmaran camp, and on into the shallow, balmy waters of the lake. The victory was truly the Sun-King's—the heat within the rocky limestone valley where the fighting had mostly taken place had been intense, and many of the men, despite their exhilaration, were close to heat stroke.

The second army to be withdrawn flew the yellow rose of the Vaux-Torres on its standards. Vaux-Torres' war-leader was Beaumorreau, the High Priestess's brother, and when the clarions finally called their retreat Elisabeth, who had been standing throughout at the center of the Prince's command, eagerly called for a horse, mounted up, and galloped out to meet him.

The new High Priestess made quite a picture, riding with her black and green robes furled out behind her like swallow's wings, and her curling, jet-black hair all tumbled over her shoulders. The withdrawing soldiers spontaneously cheered her on, even though half of them yet did not know who she was.

"I *was* surprised, if you are curious to know. She was a mistake, if you can believe that—not that it matters if you do. But accepting your own mistakes so often can make for the best outcome, don't you think?"

That fruity voice—it could be no one else but Argat Climens. Gaultry whirled round, not sure whether to be on her guard or pleased by the woman's appearance.

"Your Grace," she said politely. "I was pleased to hear that the charges against you had been dropped."

Argat looked more tired than Gaultry expected. The long ride west had taken its toll on the woman's pristine presentation, and the hints of age were more marked below her eyes than Gaultry remembered. There were also laugh lines around her mouth. Gaultry did not remember those either, but the humor revealed beneath the court polish somehow less surprised her.

"The charges dropped? The court-toads are all saying it's my new-found influence," Argat said, tossing her head. "More fools they, not to realize that my pretty darling would be the first to string me up, if there truly was a stitch of evidence against me. But better for Elisabeth—she'll catch them out, at least the first time they try to cross her."

Elisabeth had crossed the great bowl of the battlefield and met her brother at the valley entrance. Farther up, the stag-headed red standards of Haute-Tielmark were making their way down, and at last, above even them, Gaultry could see the blue-and-white checkered coats of the Prince's soldiers. Martin's grey and green could not, of course, be distinguished among them, but her heart pounded, hoping that soon he would hove into sight. Mervion, at her side, squeezed her hand, flush with a similar longing.

"Elisabeth will not, however, be entirely immune to my influence," Argat was saying. Gaultry swung back to her, not sure what the woman was talking about.

"I hope not," she said, resoundingly, and then had to flush as Argat smiled, feline. "I mean to say only, I believe, the High Priestess's judgment should remain independent."

"Oh, I would try to lead her on small matters only," the Duchess said. "She will have much to do, and I am sure her focus will not be very strong on her social responsibilities. I will certainly be able to lead her there, if only to remind her of her duties."

Gaultry cast the woman a suspicious look. Argat only smiled, archly. "You have performed many high services for Tielmark, Lady Gaultry. Yes," she turned to where Elisabeth was riding, her smile deepening as she watched her daughter ride, "I think I will have to remind Elisabeth that it is time for the High Priestess to reopen the marriage rolls. A few changes are in order there."

This aspect of the change in High Priestess—Gaultry stared across at the Duchess, longing churning through her. "I would not ask such a favor," she said stiffly.

"It's too late," Argat told her. "I've already done it, and Elisabeth has already agreed. You will simply have to be indebted to me, and that's the end of it." She signaled across the crowd atop the command overlook to a servant, standing patiently by, holding the reins a beautiful grey mare, saddled and ready to ride. "Now compound the debt. Take my horse here, and go ride over and tell him."

Gaultry could not move. She stared at the horse, then Argat, then back again. "You are speaking of a matter of property," she said primly, not quite willing to bend herself to Argat's cajoling. "It makes no odds to me, whether or not Martin and I can marry. We are already as one."

"So take the horse," Argat said, laughing, "and go to him."

That is what Gaultry did.

Coda

▼

Vidryas Lanaya-Killer stared out through the velvet curtains of the gently bobbing palanquin. He had never thought to visit Bassorah City. He had never thought to be carried through its marble-paved streets, splendidly recumbent on a swaying bed of silk, as the center attraction in a triumphal victory parade. Ranks of soldiers clad in shining uniforms cleared a path through the screaming, adoring mob; lines of heavily tranquilized Lanai cattle were dragged along in mooing, lowing misery, spewing manure in their nervousness, but docile beneath the drugs.

It should have been his uncle's victory, but the glory had fallen all to Vidryas, with his handsome Bissanty face.

He had argued with Ochsan, trying to convince him to claim his proper share of the victory, but his uncle had only smiled and shaken his head. "They want you, Viddy my lad. Enjoy the honors that have fallen to you."

Vidryas had grown enough in wisdom to recognize Ochsan's ironic gleam. "This is all a part of your planning, isn't it?" he had accused his uncle. "You must always have intended for me to have the credit for the victory in your place. This is all a part of your plan for Dramaya, even down to the Bissanty crowds, cheering me in the streets."

His uncle had not bothered to deny him. "Let them call you Lanai-Killer," was all he'd added. "Better not to insist on the 'Lanaya.' The crowds will shout Lanai-Killer in any case—why insist on 'Lanaya'? Your captains will be the only ones to notice, and do you think your pride will faze them? They'll report you up the ranks—that's all. But it could be enough that later you'll come to regret it. Let them call you Lanai-Killer, after their own manners. What is a little piece of language, to sully their celebration?"

"I can accept that I am a soldier beneath your command," Vidryas had told him, sighing. The impenetrable stolidity of his uncle's jowly face revealed nothing of his cunning, of his dauntless ability to lead men, but Vidryas was no longer a young fool—he knew what lay under his uncle's impassive surface. "My Uncle, as you saved my life in the mountains, as you showed me what it was to be a man and a soldier, I will honor your orders. Llara in me, for that I have agreed to this pretense that I was the man who led your soldiers to victory. But I will not deny my blood. You cannot have that, along with all the rest of my allegiance."

Despite what Ochsan had declared that he wanted, Vidryas knew that he had decided rightly. He had seen that in his uncle's eyes, even as Ochsan grumbled and hawed, and made his little pacing movements, exactly like the little black bull that the terrible goat-herder witch had called him.

"Have it your way then," Ochsan had said. "Now—go on. Enjoy your procession. You have earned it—whether for the reasons the crowds believe or not."

The impassioned cheering of the crowd surrounding him now almost had him believing his uncle's words. One day, surely, there would be a price for this pleasure: the rising crowds shouting his name, wealth of flowers and coins hurled into his lap. He had grown enough as a man to know that. The Emperor had rallied this triumphal parade for a reason, and the reason was surely not to celebrate Bissanty's victory over the Lanaya. Rebel Tielmark had raised a King. The throne of Bissanty's Tielmaran Prince, a sacral altar in Great Llara's Temple, had cracked and fallen, a dreadful portent of loss.

This parade—if to Vidryas, this parade was the epitome of his young life, to the Emperor it was only a distraction, while he decided his next move. Vidryas could count on none of today's popularity to remain with him—he could not even count on the Emperor wanting him to retain these garlands of victory.

The parade, passing along the grand avenue, reached Bassorah's ancient victory arch, and passed beneath its cooling shade. Beyond lay the square dedicated to all the Great Twelve, and across it, the rising dome of Llara's temple. As Vidryas's palanquin emerged from the arch, the cheering struck him with fresh strength.

"Lanai-Killer! Lanai-Killer! Vidryas, Llara-Blessed!"

The faces staring up at him were alive with a joy, with an energy to which it was impossible not to respond.

For today, for this hour, Vidryas could pretend that his boyhood dreams were true. He was the leader of a great parade, and at its finish, there would be the Emperor to honor him. The Emperor and his melancholy wives, surrounded by the four remaining princes of Bissanty and their children—the Pallidon heir with his two beautiful little boys, and the ancient Sea Prince with his strange white daughter. It was the fit conclusion to any soldier boy's fable.

Today—for this moment—his boy's dreams were true.

About the Author

KATYA REIMANN lived for six years in Oxford, England, where she wrote a Ph.D. dissertation about pirates. She put this knowledge to active use in founding the (now defunct) Kamikaze Punt Club.

She enjoys going down caves and up mountains, being out of doors and in boats.

Prince of Fire and Ashes concludes the Tielmaran Chronicles. Katya lives in Saint Paul, Minnesota, where she is currently at work on her new novel, assorted smaller writing projects, and raising her identical twin daughters, to whom this book is lovingly dedicated.

Katya's webpages can be found at www.katyareimann.com.